D1449487

Tor Books by Terry Goodkind

Soul
of the
Fire

TERRY GOODKIND

TOR®
fantasy

A TOM DOHERTY ASSOCIATES BOOK
NEW YORK

SOUL OF THE FIRE

Copyright © 1999 by Terry Goodkind

Edited by James Frenkel
Maps by Terry Goodkind

A Tor Book
Published by Tom Doherty Associates, LLC
175 Fifth Avenue
New York, NY 10010

www.tor.com

Tor® is a registered trademark of Tom Doherty Associates, LLC.

ISBN: 0-812-55149-4
Library of Congress Catalog Card Number: 98-55518

First edition: April 1999
First international mass market edition: October 1999
First mass market edition: March 2000

Printed in the United States of America

0 9 8 7 6 5 4 3

To James Frenkel, a man of great patience,
courage, integrity, and talent.

Beware when day meets dark. Beware crossroads, where they skulk. They can lurk in fire's crackle and easily travel on sparks. Beware gloomy places among rocks, under things, down holes and caves and shafts of every kind. Beware crags and edges and water's brink—the fey creatures slip along borders, where this meets that.

Some are of terrible icy beauty. Most are shaped by whim. They often crave attention. Pray not provoke them, for they revel in causing extravagant harm, and are dangerous in the extreme. They are tireless hunters, these thieves of magic, without empathy, without a soul.

Mark well my words: Beware the Chimes, and if need be great, draw for yourself thrice on the barren earth, in sand and salt and blood, a Fatal Grace.

—translated from Koloblicin's Journal

CHAPTER 1

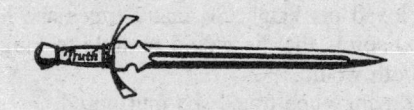

"I WONDER WHAT'S BOTHERING the chickens," Richard said.

Kahlan nuzzled tighter against his shoulder. "Maybe your grandfather is pestering them now, too." When he didn't reply, she tilted her head back to squint up at him in the dim firelight. He was watching the door. "Or maybe they're grouchy because we kept them awake most of the night."

Richard grinned and kissed her forehead. The brief squawking on the other side of the door had ceased. No doubt the village children, still reveling in the wedding celebration, had been chasing the chickens from a favorite roost on the squat wall outside the spirit house. She told him as much.

Faint sounds of distant laughter, conversation, and singing drifted into their quiet sanctuary. The scent of the balsam sticks that were always burned in the spirit-house hearth mingled with the tang of sweat earned in passion, and the spicy-sweet aroma of roasted peppers and onions. Kahlan watched the firelight reflecting in his gray eyes a moment before lying back in his arms to sway gently to the sounds of the drums and the boldas.

Paddles scraped up and down ridges carved on the hollow, bell-shaped boldas produced an eerie, haunting melody that seeped through the solitude of the spirit house on its

1

way out onto the grasslands, welcoming spirit ancestors to the celebration.

Richard stretched to the side and retrieved a round, flat piece of tava bread from the platter Zedd, his grandfather, had brought them. "It's still warm. Want some?"

"Bored with your new wife so soon, Lord Rahl?"

Richard's contented laugh brought a smile to her lips. "We really are married, aren't we? It wasn't just a dream, was it?"

Kahlan loved his laugh. So many times she had prayed to the good spirits that he would be able to laugh again— that they both would.

"Just a dream come true," she murmured.

She urged him from the tava bread for a long kiss. His breathing quickened as he clutched her in his powerful arms. She slid her hands across the sweat-slick muscles of his broad shoulders to run her fingers through the thick tangle of his hair as she moaned against his mouth.

It had been here in the Mud People's spirit house, on a night that now seemed lifetimes ago, that she had first realized she was hopelessly in love with him, but had to keep her forbidden feelings secret. It was during that visit, after battle, struggle, and sacrifice, that they had been accepted into the community of these remote people. On another visit, it was here in the spirit house, after Richard accomplished the impossible and broke the spell of prohibition, that he had asked her to be his wife. And now they had at last spent their wedding night in the spirit house of the Mud People.

Though it had been for love and love alone, their wedding was also a formal joining of the Midlands and D'Hara. Had they been wedded in any of the great cities of the Midlands, the event undoubtedly would have been a pageant of unparalleled splendor. Kahlan was experienced in pageantry. These guileless people understood their sincerity and simple reasons for wanting to be married. She preferred the joyous wedding they had celebrated among people bonded to them in their hearts, over one of cold pageant.

Among the Mud People, who led hard lives on the plains

of the wilds, such a celebration was a rare opportunity to gather in merriment, to feast, to dance, and to tell stories. Kahlan knew of no other instance of an outsider being accepted as Mud People, so such a wedding was unprecedented. She suspected it would become part of their lore, the story repeated in future gatherings by dancers dressed in elaborate grass-and-hide costumes, their faces painted with masks of black and white mud.

"I do believe you're plying an innocent girl with your magic touch," she teased, breathlessly. She was beginning to forget how weak and weary her legs were.

Richard rolled onto his back to catch his breath. "Do you suppose we ought to go out there and see what Zedd is up to?"

Kahlan playfully smacked the back of her hand against his ribs. "Why Lord Rahl, I think you really are bored with your new wife. First the chickens, then tava bread, and now your grandfather."

Richard was watching the door again. "I smell blood."

Kahlan sat up. "Probably just some game brought back by a hunting party. If there really was trouble, Richard, we would know about it. We have people guarding us. In fact, we have the whole village watching over us. No one could get past the Mud People hunters unseen. There would at least be an alarm and everyone would know about it."

She wasn't sure if he even heard her. He was stone still, his attention riveted on the door. When Kahlan's fingers glided up his arm and her hand rested lightly on his shoulder, his muscles finally slackened and he turned to her.

"You're right." His smile was apologetic. "I guess I can't seem to let myself relax."

Nearly her whole life, Kahlan had trod the halls of power and authority. From a young age she had been disciplined in responsibility and obligation, and schooled in the threats that always shadowed her. She was well steeled to it all by the time she had been called upon to lead the alliance of the Midlands.

Richard had grown up very differently, and had gone on

to fulfill his passion for his forested homeland by becoming a woods guide. Turmoil, trial, and destiny had thrust him into a new life as leader of the D'Haran Empire. Vigilance was his valuable ally and difficult to dismiss.

She saw his hand idly skim over his clothes. He was looking for his sword. He'd had to travel to the Mud People's village without it.

Countless times, she had seen him absently and without conscious thought reassure himself that it was at hand. It had been his companion for months, through a crucible of change—both his, and the world's. It was his protector, and he, in turn, was the protector of that singular sword and the post it represented.

In a way, the Sword of Truth was but a talisman. It was the hand wielding the sword that was the power; as the Seeker of Truth, he was the true weapon. In some ways, it was only a symbol of his post, much as the distinctive white dress was a symbol of hers.

Kahlan leaned forward and kissed him. His arms returned to her. She playfully pulled him back down on top of her.

"So, how does it feel being married to the Mother Confessor herself?"

He slipped onto an elbow beside her and gazed down into her eyes. "Wonderful," he murmured. "Wonderful and inspiring. And tiring." With a gentle finger he traced the line of her jaw. "And how does it feel being married to the Lord Rahl?"

A throaty laugh burbled up. "Sticky."

Richard chuckled and stuffed a piece of tava bread in her mouth. He sat up and set the brimming wooden platter down between them. Tava bread, made from tava roots, was a staple of the Mud People. Served with nearly every meal, it was eaten by itself, wrapped around other foods, and used as a scoop for porridge and stews. Dried into biscuits, it was carried on long hunts.

Kahlan yawned as she stretched, feeling relieved that he was no longer preoccupied by what was beyond the door. She kissed his cheek at seeing him once again at ease.

Under a layer of warm tava bread he found roasted peppers, onions, mushroom caps as broad as her hand, turnips, and boiled greens. There were even several rice cakes. Richard took a bite out of a turnip before rolling some of the greens, a mushroom, and a pepper in a piece of tava bread and handing it to her.

In a reflective tone, he said, "I wish we could stay in here forever."

Kahlan pulled the blanket over her lap. She knew what he meant. Outside, the world awaited them.

"Well . . ." she said, batting her eyelashes at him, "just because Zedd came and told us the elders want their spirit house back, that doesn't mean we have to surrender it until we're good and ready."

Richard took in her frolicsome offer with a mannered smile. "Zedd was just using the elders as an excuse. He wants me."

She bit into the roll he had given her as she watched him absently break a rice cake in half, his thoughts seeming to drift from what he was doing.

"He hasn't seen you for months." With a finger, she wiped away juice as it rolled down her chin. "He's eager to hear all you've been through, and about the things you've learned." He nodded absently as she sucked the juice from her finger. "He loves you, Richard. There are things he needs to teach you."

"That old man has been teaching me since I was born." He smiled distantly. "I love him, too."

Richard enfolded mushrooms, greens, pepper and onion in tava bread and took a big bite. Kahlan pulled strands of limp greens from her roll and nibbled them as she listened to the slow crackle of the fire and the distant music.

When he finished, Richard rooted under the stack of tava bread and came up with a dried plum. "All that time, and I never knew he was more than my beloved friend; I never suspected he was my grandfather, and more than a simple man."

He bit off half the plum and offered her the other half.

"He was protecting you, Richard. Being your friend was the most important thing for you to know." She took the proffered plum and popped it in her mouth. She studied his handsome features as she chewed.

With her fingertips, she turned his face to look up at her. She understood his larger concerns. "Zedd is back with us, now, Richard. He'll help us. His counsel will be a comfort as well as an aid."

"You're right. Who better to counsel us than the likes of Zedd?" Richard pulled his clothes close. "And he is no doubt impatient to hear everything."

As Richard drew his black pants on, Kahlan put a rice cake between her teeth and held it there as she tugged things from her pack. She halted and took the rice cake from her mouth.

"We've been separated from Zedd for months—you longer than I. Zedd and Ann will want to hear it all. We'll have to tell it a dozen times before they're satisfied.

"I'd really like to have a bath first. There are some warm springs not too far away."

Richard halted at buttoning his black shirt. "What was it that Zedd and Ann were in such a fret about, last night, before the wedding?"

"Last night?" She pulled her folded shirt from her pack and shook it out. "Something about the chimes. I told them I spoke the three chimes. But Zedd said they would take care of it, whatever it was."

Kahlan didn't like to think about that. It gave her gooseflesh to remember her fear and panic. It made her ache with a sick, weak feeling to contemplate what would have happened had she delayed even another moment in speaking those three words. Had she delayed, Richard would now be dead. She banished the memory.

"That's what I thought I remembered." Richard smiled as he winked. "Looking at you in your blue wedding dress . . . well, I do remember having more important things on my mind at the time.

"The three chimes are supposed to be a simple matter. I

6

guess he did say as much. Zedd, of all people, shouldn't have any trouble with that sort of thing."

"So, how about the bath?"

"What?" He was staring at the door again.

"Bath. Can we go to the springs and have a warm bath before we have to sit down with Zedd and Ann and start telling them long stories?"

He pulled his black tunic over his head. The broad gold band around its squared edges caught the firelight. He gave her a sidelong glance. "Will you wash my back?"

She watched his smile as he buckled on his wide leather over-belt with its gold-worked pouches to each side. Among other things, they held possessions both extraordinary and dangerous.

"Lord Rahl, I will wash anything you want."

He laughed as he put on his leather-padded silver wrist-bands. The ancient symbols worked onto them reflected with points of reddish firelight. "Sounds like my new wife may turn an ordinary bath into an event."

Kahlan tossed her cloak around her shoulders and then pulled the tangle of her long hair out from under the collar. "After we tell Zedd, we'll be on our way." She playfully poked his ribs with a finger. "Then you'll find out."

Giggling, he caught her finger to stop her from tickling him. "If you want a bath, we'd better not tell Zedd. He'll start in on us with just one question, then just one more, and then another." His cloak glimmered golden in the firelight as he fastened it at his throat. "Before you know it, the day will be done and he'll still be asking questions. How far are these warm springs?"

Kahlan gestured to the south. "An hour's walk. Maybe a bit more." She stuffed some tava bread, a brush, a cake of fragrant herb soap, and a few other small items into a leather satchel. "But if, as you say, Zedd wants to see us, don't you suppose he'll be nettled if we go off without telling him?"

Richard grunted a cynical laugh. "If you want a bath, it's best to apologize later for not telling him first. It isn't that far. We'll be back before he really misses us, anyway."

Kahlan caught his arm. She turned serious. "Richard, I know you're eager to see Zedd. We can go bathe later, if you're impatient to see him. I wouldn't really mind. . . . Mostly I just wanted to be alone with you a little longer."

He hugged her shoulders. "We'll see him when we get back in a few hours. He can wait. I'd rather be alone with you, too."

As he nudged open the door, Kahlan saw him once again absently reach to touch the sword that wasn't there. His cloak was a golden blaze as the sunlight fell across it. Stepping behind him into the cold morning light, Kahlan had to squint. Savory aromas of foods being prepared on village cook fires filled her lungs.

Richard leaned to the side, looking behind the short wall.

His raptorlike gaze briefly swept the sky. His scrutiny of the narrow passageways among the jumble of drab, square buildings all around was more meticulous.

The buildings on this side of the village, such as the spirit house, were used for various communal purposes. Some were used only by the elders as sanctuaries of sorts. Some were used by hunters in rites before a long hunt. No man ever crossed the threshold of the women's buildings.

Here, too, the dead were prepared for their funeral ceremony. The Mud People buried their dead.

Using wood for funeral pyres was impractical; wood of any quantity was distant, and therefore precious. Wood for cook fires was supplemented with dried dung but more often with billets of tightly wound dried grass. Bonfires, such as the ones the night before at their wedding ceremony, were a rare and wondrous treat.

With no one living in any of the surrounding buildings, this part of the village had an empty, otherworldly feel to it. The drums and boldas added their preternatural influence to the mood among the deep shadows. The drifting voices made the empty streets seem haunted. Bold slashes of sunlight slanting in rendered the deep shade beyond nearly impenetrable.

Still studying those shadows, Richard gestured behind. Kahlan glanced over the wall.

In the midst of scattered feathers fluttering in the cold breeze lay the bloody carcass of a chicken.

CHAPTER 2

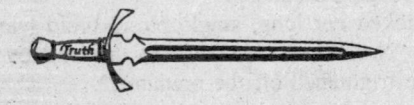

KAHLAN HAD BEEN WRONG. It hadn't been children bothering the chickens.

"Hawk?" she asked.

Richard checked the sky again. "Possibly. Maybe a weasel or a fox. Whatever it was, it was frightened off before it could devour its meal."

"Well, that should put your mind at ease. It was just some animal after a chicken."

Cara, in her skintight, red leather outfit, had immediately spotted them and was already striding their way. Her Agiel, appearing to be no more than a thin, bloodred leather rod at most a foot in length, dangled from her wrist on a fine chain. The gruesome weapon was never more than a flick of her wrist away from Cara's grasp.

Kahlan could read the relief in Cara's blue eyes at seeing that her wards had not been stolen away by invisible forces beyond the spirit-house door.

Kahlan knew Cara would rather have been closer to her

charges, but she had been considerate enough to give them the privacy of distance. The consideration extended to keeping others away, too. Knowing how deadly serious was Cara's commitment to their protection, Kahlan appreciated the true depth of the gift of that distance.

Distance.

Kahlan glanced up at Richard. That was why his suspicion had been aroused. He had known it wasn't children bothering the chickens. Cara wouldn't have allowed children to get that close to the spirit house, that close to a door without a lock.

Before Cara could speak, Richard asked her, "Did you see what killed the chicken?"

Cara flicked her long, single blond braid back over her shoulder. "No. When I ran over to the wall by the door I must have frightened off the predator."

All Mord-Siths wore a single braid; it was part of the uniform, lest anyone mistake who they were. Few, if any, ever made such a dangerous mistake.

"Has Zedd tried to come back to see us again?" Richard asked.

"No." Cara brushed back a stray wisp of blond hair. "After he brought you the food, he told me that he wishes to see you both when you are ready."

Richard nodded, still eyeing the shadows. "We're not ready. We're going first to some nearby warm springs for a bath."

A sly smile stole onto Cara's face. "How delightful. I will wash your back."

Richard leaned down, putting his face closer to hers. "No, you will not wash my back. You will watch it."

Cara's sly smile widened. "Mmm. That sounds fun, too."

Richard's face turned as red as Cara's leather.

Kahlan looked away, suppressing her own smile. She knew how much Cara enjoyed flustering Richard. Kahlan had never seen bodyguards as openly irreverent as Cara and her sister Mord-Sith. Nor better.

The Mord-Sith, an ancient sect of protectors to the Lord

10

Rahl of D'Hara, all shared the same ruthless confidence. From adolescence, their training was beyond savage. It was merciless. It twisted them into remorseless killers.

Kahlan grew up knowing little of the mysterious land of D'Hara to the east. Richard had been born in Westland, far from D'Hara, and had known even less than she. When D'Hara had attacked the Midlands, Richard had been swept up into the fight, and in the end had killed Darken Rahl, the tyrannical leader of D'Hara.

Richard never knew Darken Rahl had raped his mother and sired him; he had grown up thinking George Cypher, the gentle man who had raised him, was his father. Zedd had kept the secret in order to protect his daughter and then his grandson. Only after Richard killed Darken Rahl had he discovered the truth.

Richard knew little of the dominion he had inherited. He had assumed the mantle of rule only because of the imminent threat of a larger war. If not stopped, the Imperial Order would enslave the world.

As the new master of D'Hara, Richard had freed the Mord-Sith from the cruel discipline of their brutal profession, only to have them exercise that freedom by choosing to be his protectors. Richard wore two Agiel on a thong around his neck as a sign of respect for the two women who had given their lives while protecting him.

Richard was an object of reverence to these women, and yet with their new Lord Rahl they did the previously unthinkable: they joked with him. They teased him. They rarely missed a chance to bait him.

The former Lord Rahl, Richard's father, would have had them tortured to death for such a breach of discipline. Kahlan speculated that their irreverence was their way of reminding Richard that he had freed them and that they served only by choice. Perhaps their shattered childhoods simply left them with an odd sense of humor they were now free to express.

The Mord-Sith were fearless in protecting Richard—and by his orders, Kahlan—to the point of seeming to court death. They claimed to fear nothing more than dying in bed, old and toothless. Richard had vowed more than once to visit that fate upon them.

Partly because of his deep empathy with these women, for their torturous training at the hands of his ancestors, Richard could rarely bring himself to reprimand their antics, and usually remained above their jabs. His restraint only encouraged them.

The redness of this Lord Rahl's red face when Cara said she was going to watch him take a bath betrayed his upbringing.

Richard finally schooled his exasperation and rolled his eyes. "You're not watching, either. You can just wait here."

Kahlan knew there was no chance of that. Cara barked a dismissive laugh as she followed them. She never gave a second thought to disregarding his direct orders if she thought they interfered with the protection of his life. Cara and her sister Mord-Sith only followed his orders if they judged them important and if they didn't seem to put him at greater risk.

Before they had gone far, they were joined by a halfdozen hunters who materialized out of the shadows and passageways around the spirit house. Sinewy and well proportioned, the tallest of them was not as tall as Kahlan. Richard towered over them. Their bare chests and legs were cloaked with long streaks and patches of mud for better concealment. Each carried a bow hooked over his shoulder, a knife at his hip, and a handful of throwing spears.

Kahlan knew their quivers to be filled with arrows dipped in ten-step poison. These were Chandalen's men; among the Mud People, only they routinely carried poison arrows. Chandalen's men were not simply hunters, but protectors of the Mud People.

They all grinned when Kahlan gently slapped their faces—the customary greeting of the Mud People, a gesture of respect for their strength. She thanked them in their language for standing watch and then translated her words to Richard and Cara.

12

"Did you know they were scattered about, guarding us?" Kahlan whispered to Richard as they started out once more.

He stole a look back over his shoulder. "I only saw four of them. I have to admit I missed two."

There was no way he could have seen the two he missed—they had come from the far side of the spirit house. Kahlan hadn't seen even one. She shuddered. The hunters seemed able to become invisible at will, though they were even better at it out on the grasslands. She was grateful for all those who silently watched over their safety.

Cara told them Zedd and Ann were over on the southeast side of the village, so they stayed to the west as they walked south. With Cara and the hunters in tow, they skirted most of the open area where the villagers gathered, choosing instead the alleys between the mud-brick buildings plastered over with a tan clay.

People smiled and waved in greeting, or patted their backs, or gave them the traditional gentle slaps of respect.

Children ran among the legs of the adults, chasing small leather balls, each other, or invisible game. Occasionally, chickens were the not so invisible game. They scattered in fright before the laughing, leaping, grasping young hunters.

Kahlan, with her cloak wrapped tight, couldn't understand how the children, wearing so little, could stand the cold morning air. Almost all were at least bare-chested, the younger ones naked.

Children were watched over, but allowed to run about at will. They were rarely called to account for anything. Their later training would be intense, difficult, strict, and they would be accountable for everything.

The young children, still free to be children, were a constant, ever-present, and eager audience for anything out of the ordinary. To the Mud People children, like most children, a great many things seemed out of the ordinary. Even chickens.

As the small party cut across the southern edge of the open area in the center of the village, they were spotted by Chandalen, the leader of the fiercest hunters. He was dressed

13

in his best buckskin. His hair, as was the custom among the Mud People, was fastidiously slicked down with sticky mud.

The coyote hide across his shoulders was a new mark of authority. Recently he had been named one of the six elders of the village. In his case, "elder" was simply a term of respect and not reflective of age.

After the slaps were exchanged, Chandalen finally grinned as he clapped Richard's back. "You are a great friend to Chandalen," he announced. "The Mother Confessor would surely have chosen Chandalen for her husband had you not married her. You will forever have my thanks."

Before Kahlan had gone to Westland desperately seeking help and there met Richard, Darken Rahl had murdered all the other Confessors, leaving Kahlan the last of her kind. Until she and Richard had found a way, no Confessor ever married for love, because her touch would unintentionally destroy that love.

Before now, a Confessor chose her mate for the strength he would bring to her daughters, and then she took him with her power. Chandalen reasoned that put him at great risk of being chosen. No offense had been intended.

With a laugh, Richard said he was happy to take the job of being Kahlan's husband. He briefly looked back at Chandalen's men. His voice lowered as he turned more serious. "Did your men see what killed the chicken by the spirit house?"

Only Kahlan spoke the Mud People's language, and among the Mud People, only Chandalen spoke hers. He listened carefully as his men reported a quiet night after they had taken up their posts. They were the third watch.

One of their younger guards, Juni, then mimed nocking an arrow and drawing string to cheek, quickly pointing first one direction and then another, but said that he was unable to spot the animal that had attacked the chicken in their village. He demonstrated how he'd cursed the attacker with vile names and spat with contempt at its honor, to shame it into showing itself, but to no avail. Richard nodded at Chandalen's translation.

14

Chandalen hadn't translated all of Juni's words. He left out the man's apology. For a hunter—one of Chandalen's men especially—to miss such a thing right in their midst while on watch was a matter of shame. Kahlan knew Chandalen would later have more to say to Juni.

Just before they once again struck out, the Bird Man, over on one of the open pole structures, glanced their way. The leader of the six elders, and thus of the Mud People, the Bird Man had conducted the wedding ceremony.

It would be inconsiderate not to give their greetings and thanks before they left for the springs. Richard must have had the same thought, for he changed direction toward the grass-roofed platform where sat the Bird Man.

Children played nearby. Several women in red, blue, and brown dresses chatted among themselves as they strolled past. A couple of brown goats searched the ground for any food people might have dropped. They seemed to be having some limited success—when they were able to pull themselves away from the children. Some chickens pecked at the dirt, while others strutted and clucked.

Off in the clearing, the bonfires, most little more than glowing embers, still burned. People yet huddled about them, entranced by the glow or the warmth. Bonfires were a rare extravagance symbolizing a joyous celebration, or a gathering to call their spirit ancestors and make them welcome with warmth and light. Some of the people would have stayed up the whole night just to watch the spectacle of the fires. For the children, the bonfires were a source of wonder and delight.

Everyone had worn their best clothes for the celebration, and they were still dressed in their finery because the celebration officially continued until the sun set. Men wore fine hides and skins and proudly carried their prize weapons. Women wore brightly colored dresses and metal bracelets and broad smiles.

Young people were usually painfully shy, but the wedding brought their daring to the surface. The night before, giggling young women had jabbered bold questions at Kah-

15

lan. Young men had followed Richard about, satisfied to grin at him and simply be near the important goings-on.

The Bird Man was dressed in the buckskin pants and tunic he seemed always to wear, no matter the occasion. His long silver hair hung to his shoulders. A leather thong around his neck held his ever-present bone whistle, used to call birds. With his whistle he could, seemingly effortlessly, call any kind of bird desired. Most would alight on his outstretched arm and sit contentedly. Richard was always awed by such a display.

Kahlan knew the Bird Man understood and relied on signs from birds. She speculated that perhaps he called birds with his whistle to see if they would give forth some sign only he could fathom. The Bird Man was an astute reader of signs given off by people, as well. She sometimes thought he could read her mind.

Many people in the great cities of the Midlands thought of people in the wilds, like the Mud People, as savages who worshiped strange things and held ignorant beliefs. Kahlan understood the simple wisdom of these people and their ability to read subtle signs in the living things they knew so well in the world around them. Many times she had seen the Mud People foretell with a fair degree of accuracy the weather for the next few days by watching the way the grasses moved in the wind.

Two of the village elders, Hajanlet and Arbrin, sat at the back of the platform, their eyelids drooping, as they watched their people out in the open area. Arbrin's hand rested protectively on the shoulder of a little boy sleeping curled up beside him. In his sleep, the child rhythmically sucked a thumb.

Platters holding little more than scraps of food sat scattered about, along with mugs of various drinks shared at celebrations. While some of the drinks were intoxicating, Kahlan knew the Mud People weren't given to drunkenness.

"Good morning, honored elder," Kahlan said in his language.

His leathery face turned up to them, offering a wide smile. *"Welcome to the new day, child."*

His attention returned to something out among the people of his village. Kahlan caught sight of Chandalen eyeing the empty mugs before directing an affected smile back at his men.

"Honored elder," Kahlan said, *"Richard and I would like to thank you for the wonderful wedding ceremony. If you have no need of us just now, we would like to go out to the warm springs."*

He smiled and waved his dismissal. *"Do not stay too long, or the warmth you get from the springs will be washed away by the rain."*

Kahlan glanced at the clear sky. She looked back at Chandalen. He nodded his agreement.

"He says if we dally at the springs it will rain on us before we're back."

Mystified, Richard appraised the sky. "I guess we'd best take their advice and not dally."

"We'd better be off, then," she told the Bird Man.

He beckoned with a finger. Kahlan leaned closer. He was intently observing the chickens scratching at the ground not far away. Leaning toward him, Kahlan listened to his slow, even breathing as she waited. She thought he must have forgotten he was going to say something.

At last he pointed out into the open area and whispered to her.

Kahlan straightened. She looked out at the chickens.

"Well?" Richard asked. "What did he say?"

At first, she wasn't sure she had heard him right, but by the frowns on the faces of Chandalen and his hunters, she knew she had.

Kahlan didn't know if she should translate such a thing. She didn't want to cause the Bird Man embarrassment later on, if he had been doing too much celebrating with ritual drink.

Richard waited, the question still in his eyes.

Kahlan looked again at the Bird Man, his brown eyes staring out at the open area before him, his chin bobbing in time to the beat of the boldas and drums.

She finally leaned back until her shoulder touched Richard. "He says that that one there"—she pointed—"is not a chicken."

CHAPTER 3

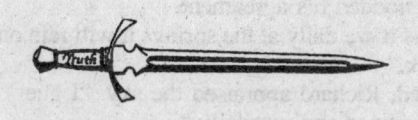

KAHLAN PUSHED WITH HER feet against the gravel and glided backward into Richard's embrace. Lying back as they were in the waist-deep water, they were covered to their necks. Kahlan was beginning to view water in a provocative new light.

They had found the perfect spot among the web of streams flowing through the singular area of gravel beds and rock outcroppings in the vast sea of grassland. Runnels meandering past the hot springs a little farther to the northwest cooled the nearly scalding water. There were not many places as deep as the one they had chosen, and they had tested several of those at various distances from the hot springs until they found a warm one to their liking.

Tall tender shoots of new grasses closed off the surrounding country, leaving them to a private pool capped with a huge dome of sunny sky, although clouds were beginning to steal across the edges of the bright blue. Cold breezes bowed the gossamer grass in waves and twisted it around in nodding whorls.

Out on the plains the weather could change quickly. What was warm spring the day before had turned frigid. Kahlan knew the cold wouldn't linger; spring had set in for good even if winter was blowing them a departing kiss. Their refuge of warm water rippled under the harsh touch of that forget-me-not.

Overhead, a harrier hawk wheeled on the sharp winds, searching for a meal. Kahlan felt a twinge of sorrow, knowing that while she and Richard were relaxing and enjoying themselves, talons would soon snatch a life. She knew something of what it was like to be the object of carnal hunger when death was on the hunt.

Distantly stationed, somewhere off in the expanse of grasslands, were the six hunters. Cara would be circling the perimeter like a mother hawk, checking on the men. Kahlan guessed that, being protectors, each would be able to understand the other's purpose, if not language. Protectors were charged with a serious duty, and Cara respected the hunters' sober attention to that duty.

Kahlan scooped warm water onto Richard's upper arms. "Even though we've had only a short time for ourselves, for our wedding, it was the best wedding I could have imagined. And I'm so glad I could show you this place, too."

Richard kissed the back of her head. "I'll never forget any of it—the ceremony last night, the spirit house, or here."

She stroked his thighs under the water. "You'd better not, Lord Rahl."

"I've always dreamed of showing you the special, beautiful places near where I grew up. I hope someday I can take you there."

He fell silent again. She suspected he was considering weighty matters, and that was why he seemed to be brooding. As much as they might sometimes like to, they couldn't forget their responsibilities. Armies awaited orders. Officials and diplomats back in Aydindril impatiently awaited an audience with the Mother Confessor or the Lord Rahl.

Kahlan knew that not all would be eager to join the cause of freedom. To some, tyranny had its appeal.

Emperor Jagang and his Imperial Order would not wait on them.

"Someday, Richard," she murmured as her finger stroked the dark stone on the delicate gold necklace at her throat.

Shota, the witch woman, had appeared unexpectedly at their wedding the night before and given Kahlan the necklace. Shota said it would prevent them from conceiving a child. The witch women had a talent for seeing the future, although what she saw often unfolded in unexpected ways. More than once Shota had warned them of the cataclysmic consequences of having a child and had vowed not to allow a male child of Kahlan and Richard's union to live.

In the struggle to find the Temple of the Winds, Kahlan had come to understand Shota a little better, and the two of them had reached an understanding of sorts. The necklace was a peace offering, an alternative to Shota trying to destroy their offspring. For now, a truce had been struck.

"Do you think the Bird Man knew what he was saying?"

Kahlan squinted up at the sky. "I guess so. It's starting to cloud up."

"I meant about the chicken."

Kahlan twisted around in his arms. "The chicken!" She frowned into his gray eyes. "Richard, he said it wasn't a chicken. What I think is that he's been celebrating a bit too much."

She could hardly believe that with all the things they had to worry about, he was puzzling over this.

He seemed to weigh her words, but remained silent. Deep shadows rolled over the waving grass as the sun fled behind the billowing edge of towering milky clouds with hearts of greenish slate gray. The bleak breeze smelled heavy and damp.

On the low rocks behind Richard, his golden cloak fluttered in the wind, catching her eye. His arm tightened around her. It was not a loving gesture.

Something moved in the water.

A quick twist of light.

Maybe a reflection off the scales of a fish. It was almost there, but wasn't—like something seen out of the corner of her eye. A direct look betrayed naught.

"What's the matter?" she asked as Richard pulled her farther back. "It was just a fish or something."

Richard rose up in one swift smooth movement, lifting her clear of the water. "Or something."

Water sluiced from her. Naked and exposed to the icy breeze, she shivered as she scanned the clear stream.

"Like what? What is it? What do you see?"

His eyes flicked back and forth, searching the water. "I don't know." He set her on the bank. "Maybe it was just a fish."

Kahlan's teeth chattered. "The fish in these streams aren't big enough to nibble a toe. Unless it's a snapping turtle, let me back in? I'm freezing."

To his chagrin, Richard admitted he didn't see anything. He put out a hand for support as she climbed back down into the water. "Maybe it was just the shadow moving across the water when the sun went behind the clouds."

Kahlan sank in up to her neck, moaning with relief as the sheltering warmth sheathed her. She peered about at the water as her tingling gooseflesh calmed. The water was clear, with no weeds. She could see the gravel bottom. There was no place for a snapping turtle to hide. Though he had said it was nothing, the way he was watching the water belied his words.

"Do you think it was a fish? Or are you just trying to frighten me?" She didn't know if he had actually seen something that left him worried, or if he was simply being overly protective. "This isn't the comforting bath I envisioned. Tell me what's wrong if you really think you saw something."

A new thought jolted her. "It wasn't a snake, was it?"

He took a purging breath as he wiped back his wet hair. "I don't see anything. I'm sorry."

"You sure? Should we go?"

He smiled sheepishly. "I guess I just get jumpy when I'm

swimming in strange places with naked women."

Kahlan poked at his ribs. "And do you often go bathing with naked women, Lord Rahl?"

She didn't really like his idea of a joke, but was just about to seek the shelter of his arms anyway when he shot to his feet.

Kahlan stood in a rush. "What is it? Is it a snake?"

Richard shoved her back into the pool. She coughed out water as he lunged at their things.

"Stay down!"

He snatched his knife from its sheath and crouched at the ready, peeking over the grass.

"It's Cara." He stood straight to get a better view.

Kahlan looked over the grass and saw a dab of red cutting a straight line across the brown and green landscape. The Mord-Sith was coming at a dead run, charging through the grass, splashing through shallow places in the streams.

Richard tossed Kahlan a small blanket as he watched Cara coming. Kahlan could see the Agiel in her fist.

The Agiel a Mord-Sith carried was a weapon of magic, and functioned only for her; it delivered inconceivable pain. If she wished it, its touch could even kill.

Because Mord-Sith carried the same Agiel used to torture them in their training, holding it caused profound pain—part of the paradox of being a giver of pain. The pain never showed on their faces.

Cara stumbled to a panting halt. "Did he come by here?"

Blood matted the left side of her blond hair and ran down the side of her face. Her knuckles were white around her Agiel.

"Who?" Richard asked. "We've seen no one."

Her expression twisted with scarlet rage. "Juni!"

Richard caught her arm. "What's going on?"

With the back of her other wrist, Cara swiped a bloody strand of hair away from her eyes as she scanned the vast grassland. "I don't know." She ground her teeth. "But I want him."

Cara tore away from Richard's grasp and bolted, calling back, "Get dressed!"

Richard grabbed Kahlan's wrist and hauled her out of the water. She pulled on her pants and then scooped up some of her things as she dashed after Cara. Richard, still tugging up his trousers over his wet legs, reached out with a long arm and snagged the waist of her pants, dragging her to a halt.

"What do you think you're doing?" he asked, still trying to pull on his trousers with his other hand. "Stay behind me."

Kahlan yanked her pants from his fingers. "You don't have your sword. I'm the Mother Confessor. You can just stay behind me, Lord Rahl."

There was little danger to a Confessor from a single man. There was no defense against the power of a Confessor. Without his sword, Richard was more vulnerable than she.

Barring a lucky arrow or spear, nothing was going to keep a committed Confessor's power from taking someone once she was close enough. That commitment bound them in magic that couldn't be recalled or reversed.

It was as final as death. In a way, it was death.

A person touched by a Confessor's power was forever lost to himself. He was hers.

Unlike Richard, Kahlan knew how to use her magic. Having been named Mother Confessor was testament to her mastery of it.

Richard growled his displeasure as he snatched up his big belt with its pouches before chasing after her. He caught up and held her shirt out as they ran so she could stuff her arm in the sleeve. He was bare-chested. He hooked his belt. The only other thing he had was his knife.

They splashed through a shallow network of streams and raced through the grass, chasing the flashes of red leather. Kahlan stumbled going through a stream, but kept her feet. Richard's hand on her back steadied her. She knew it wasn't a good idea to run breakneck and barefoot across unfamiliar ground, but having seen blood on Cara's face kept her from slowing.

Cara was more than their protector. She was their friend.

They crossed several ankle-deep rivulets, crashing through the grass between each. Too late to change course, she came upon a pool and jumped, scarcely making the far bank. Richard's hand once more steadied and reassured her with its touch.

As they plunged through grass and sprinted across open streams, Kahlan saw one of the hunters angling in from the left. It wasn't Juni.

At the same time as she realized Richard wasn't behind her, she heard him whistle. She slid to a stop on the slick grass, putting a hand to the ground to keep her balance. Richard, not far back, stood in a stream.

He put two fingers between his teeth and whistled again, longer, louder, a piercing sound, rising in pitch, cutting across the silence of the plains. Kahlan saw Cara and the other hunter turn to the sound, and then hasten toward them.

Gulping air, trying to get her breath, Kahlan trotted back to Richard. He knelt down on one knee in the shallow water, resting a forearm over the other bent knee as he leaned toward the water.

Juni lay facedown in the stream. The water wasn't even deep enough to cover his head.

Kahlan dropped to her knees beside Richard, pushing her wet hair back out of her eyes and catching her breath as Richard dragged the wiry hunter over onto his back. She hadn't seen him there in the water. The covering of sticky mud and grass the hunters tied to themselves had done its intended job of hiding him. From her, anyway.

Juni looked small and frail as Richard lifted the man's shoulders to pull him from the icy water. There was no urgency in Richard's movements. He gently laid Juni on the grass beside the stream. Kahlan didn't see any cuts or blood. His limbs seemed to be in place. Though she couldn't be sure, his neck didn't look to be broken.

Even in death, Juni had an odd, lingering look of lust in his glassy eyes.

Cara rushed up and lunged at the man, stopping short only when she saw those eyes staring up in death.

One of the hunters broke through the grass, breathing as hard as Cara. His fist gripped his bow. Fingers curled over an arrow shaft kept it in place and ready. In his other hand his thumb held a knife to his palm while his first two fingers kept the arrow nocked and tension on the string.

Juni had no weapons with him.

"What has happened to Juni?" the hunter demanded, his gaze sweeping the flat country for threat.

Kahlan shook her head. *"He must have fallen and struck his head."*

"And her?" he asked, tipping his head toward Cara.

"We don't know yet," Kahlan said as she watched Richard close Juni's eyes. *"We only just found him."*

"Looks like he's been here for a while," Cara said to Richard.

Kahlan tugged on red leather, and Cara slumped willingly to the bank, sitting back on her heels. Kahlan parted Cara's blond hair, inspecting the wound. It didn't look grievous.

"Cara, what happened? What's going on?"

"Are you hurt badly?" Richard asked atop Kahlan's words.

Cara lifted a dismissive hand toward Richard but didn't object when Kahlan scooped cold water in her hand and tried to pour it over the cut to the side of her temple. Richard wrapped his fingers around a fistful of grass and tore it off. He dunked it in the water and handed it to Kahlan.

"Use this."

Cara's face had turned from the rage of before to a chalky gray. "I'm all right."

Kahlan wasn't so sure. Cara looked unsteady. Kahlan patted the wet grass to the woman's forehead before wiping away at the blood. Cara sat passively.

"So what happened?" Kahlan asked.

25

"I don't know," Cara said. "I was going to check on him, and here he comes right up a stream. Walking hunched over, like he was watching something. I called to him. I asked him where his weapons were while I made motions, like he had done back in the village, pretending to use a bow to show him what I meant."

Cara shook her head in disbelief. "He ignored me. He went back to watching the water. I thought he had left his post to catch a stupid fish, but I didn't see anything in the water.

"He suddenly charged ahead, as if his fish was trying to flee." Color rushed into Cara's face. "I was looking to the side, checking the area. He caught me off balance, and my feet slipped out from under me. My head hit a rock. I don't know how long it took before I regained my senses. I was wrong to trust him."

"No you weren't," Richard said. "We don't know what he was chasing."

By now, the rest of the hunters had appeared. Kahlan held up a hand, halting their tumbling questions. When they fell silent, she translated Cara's description of what had happened. They listened dumbfounded. This was one of Chandalen's men. Chandalen's men didn't leave their duty of protecting people to chase a fish.

"I'm sorry, Lord Rahl," Cara whispered. "I can't believe he caught me off guard like that. Over a stupid fish!"

Richard put a concerned hand on her shoulder. "I'm just glad you're all right, Cara. Maybe you'd better lie down. You don't look so good."

"My stomach just feels upside down, that's all. I'll be fine after I've rested for a minute. How did Juni die?"

"He was running and must have tripped and fallen," Kahlan said. "I almost did that myself. He must have hit his head, like you did, and blacked out. Unfortunately, he blacked out facedown in the water, and drowned."

Kahlan started to translate as much to the other hunters when Richard spoke. "I don't think so."

Kahlan paused. "It had to be."

"Look at his knees. They're not skinned. Nor his elbows or the heels of his hands." Richard turned Juni's head. "No blood, no mark. If he fell and was knocked unconscious, then why doesn't he at least have a bump on his head? The only place his mud paint is scraped off is on his nose and chin, from his face resting on the gravel of the stream bottom."

"You mean you don't think he drowned?" Kahlan asked.

"I didn't say that. But I don't see any sign that he fell." Richard studied the body for a moment. "It looks like he drowned. That would be my guess, anyway. The question is, why?"

Kahlan shifted to the side, giving the hunters room to squat beside their fallen comrade, to touch him in compassion and sorrow.

The open plains suddenly seemed a very lonely place.

Cara pressed the wad of wet grass to the side of her head. "And even if he was disregarding his guard duty to chase a fish—hard to believe—why would he leave all his weapons? And how could he drown in inches of water, if he didn't fall and hit his head?"

The hunters wept silently as their hands caressed Juni's young face. Tenderly, Richard's hand joined theirs. "What I'd like to know is what he was chasing. What put that look in his eyes."

CHAPTER 4

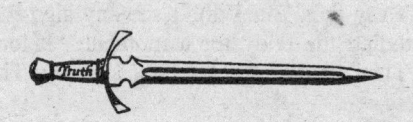

THUNDER RUMBLED IN FROM the grassland, echoing through the narrow passageways as Richard, Cara, and Kahlan left the building where Juni's body had been laid out to be prepared for burial.

The building was no different from the other buildings in the Mud People's village: thick walls of mud brick plastered over with clay, and a roof of grass thatch. Only the spirit house had a tile roof. All the windows in the village were glassless, some covered with heavy coarse cloth to keep out the weather.

With the buildings being all the same drab color, it wasn't hard to imagine the village as lifeless ruins. Tall herbs, raised as offerings for evil spirits, grew in three pots on a short wall but lent little life to the passageway frequented mostly by the amorphous wind.

As two chickens scattered out of their way, Kahlan gathered her hair in one hand to keep the gusts from whipping it against her face. People, some in tears, rushed past, going to see the fallen hunter. It somehow made Kahlan feel worse to have to leave Juni in a place smelling of sour, wet, rotting hay.

The three of them had waited until Nissel, the old healer,

had shuffled in and inspected the body. She said she didn't think the neck was broken, nor did she see any other kind of injury from a fall. She had pronounced that Juni had drowned.

When Richard asked how that could have happened, she seemed surprised by the question, apparently believing it to be obvious.

She had declared it a death caused by evil spirits.

The Mud People believed that in addition to the ancestors' spirits they called in a gathering, evil spirits also came from time to time to claim a life in recompense for a wrong. Death might be inflicted through sickness, an accident, or in some otherworldly manner. An uninjured man drowning in six inches of water seemed a self-evident otherworldly cause of death as far as Nissel was concerned. Chandalen and his hunters believed Nissel.

Nissel hadn't had the time to speculate on what transgression might have angered the evil spirits. She had to rush off to a more gratifying job; her help was needed in delivering a baby.

In her official capacity as a Confessor, Kahlan had visited the Mud People a number of times, as she had visited other peoples of the Midlands. Though some lands closed their borders to everyone else, no land of the Midlands, regardless of how insular, secluded, distrustful, or powerful, dared close its borders to a Confessor. Among other things, Confessors kept justice honest—whether or not rulers wished it so.

The Confessors were advocates before the council for all those who had no other voice. Some, like the Mud People, were distrustful of outsiders and sought no voice; they simply wanted to be left alone. Kahlan saw that their wishes were respected. The Mother Confessor's word before the council was law, and final.

Of course, that had all changed.

As with other peoples of the Midlands, Kahlan had studied not only the Mud People's language, but their beliefs.

In the Wizard's Keep in Aydindril, there were books on the languages, governance, faiths, foods, arts, and habits of every people of the Midlands.

She knew that the Mud People often left offerings of rice cakes and nosegays of fragrant herbs before small clay figures in several of the empty buildings at the north end of the village. The buildings were left for the exclusive use of the evil spirits, which the clay figures represented.

The Mud People believed that when the evil spirits occasionally became angered and took a life, the soul of the slain went to the underworld to join the good spirits who watched over the Mud People, and thus helped keep the malevolent spirits in check. Balance between worlds was thus only enhanced, and so they believed that evil was self-limiting.

Though it was early afternoon, it felt like dusk as Kahlan, Richard, and Cara made their way across the village. Low dark clouds seemed to boil just above the roofs. Lightning struck closer, the flash illuminating the high walls of buildings. A painfully sharp crack of thunder followed almost immediately, jarring the ground.

Gusty wind smacked fat drops of rain against the back of Kahlan's head. In a way she was glad for the rain. It would douse the fires. It wasn't right to have celebration fires burning when a man had died. The rain would spare someone the disconcerting task of having to put out what was left of the joyful fires.

Out of respect, Richard had carried Juni the entire way back. The hunters understood; Juni had died while on guard protecting Richard and Kahlan.

Cara, however, had quickly come to a different conclusion: Juni had turned from protector to threat. The how or why wasn't important—just that he had. She intended to be prepared the next time one of them suddenly transformed into a menace.

Richard had had a brief argument with her about it. The hunters hadn't understood their words, but recognized the heat in them and hadn't asked for a translation.

In the end, Richard let the issue drop. Cara was probably just feeling guilty about letting Juni get past her. Kahlan took Richard's hand as they walked behind, letting Cara have her way and walk point, checking for danger in a village of friends, as she turned them down first one passageway and then another, leading the way to Zedd and Ann.

Despite her conviction that Cara was wrong, Kahlan did feel inexplicably uneasy. She saw Richard glance over his shoulder with that searching look that told her he was feeling anxious, too.

"What's wrong?" she whispered.

Richard's gaze swept the empty passageway. He shook his head in frustration. "The hair at the back of my neck is prickling like someone is watching me, but no one is there."

While she did feel unsettled, she didn't know if she really felt malevolent eyes watching, or it was just his suggestion that kept her glancing over her shoulder. Hurrying along the gloomy alleys between hulking buildings, she rubbed the icy gooseflesh nettling up her arms.

The rain was just starting to come down in earnest as Cara reached the place she was seeking. Agiel at the ready, she checked to each side of the narrow passageway before opening the simple wooden door and slipping inside first.

Wind whipped Kahlan's hair across her face. Lightning flashed and thunder boomed. One of the chickens roaming the passageway, frightened by the thunder and lightning, darted between her legs and ran in ahead of them.

A low fire burned in the small hearth in the corner of the humble room. Several fat tallow candles sat on a wooden shelf plastered into the wall beside the domed hearth. Small pieces of firewood and bundled grass were stored beneath the shelf. A buckskin hide on the dirt floor before the hearth provided the only formal seating. A cloth hanging over a glassless window flapped open in the stronger gusts, fluttering the candle flames.

Richard shouldered the door shut and latched it against the weather. The room smelled of the candles, the sweet aroma of the bundled grass burning in the hearth, and pungent smoke that failed to escape through the vent in the roof above the hearth.

"They must be in the back rooms," Cara said, indicating with her Agiel a heavy hide hanging over a doorway.

The chicken, its head twitching from side to side as it clucked contentedly, strutted around the room, circling the symbol drawn with a finger or maybe stick in the dirt floor.

From a young age, Kahlan had seen wizards and sorceresses draw the ancient emblem representing the Creator, life, death, the gift, and the underworld. They drew it in idle daydreaming, and in times of anxiety. They drew it merely to comfort themselves—to remind themselves of their connection to everyone and everything.

And they drew it to conjure magic.

To Kahlan, it was a comforting talisman of her childhood, of a time when the wizards played games with her, or tickled her and chased her through the halls of the Wizard's Keep as she squealed with laughter. Sometimes they told her stories that made her gasp in wonder as she sat in their laps, protected and safe.

There was a time, before the discipline began, when she was allowed to be a child.

Those wizards were all dead, now. All but one had given their lives to help her in her struggle to cross the boundary and find help to stop Darken Rahl. The one had betrayed her. But there was a time when they were her friends, her playmates, her uncles, her teachers, the objects of her reverence and love.

"I've seen this before," Cara said, briefly considering the drawing on the floor. "Darken Rahl would sometimes draw it."

"It's called a Grace," Kahlan said.

Wind lifted the square of coarse cloth covering the window, allowing the harsh glare of lightning to cascade across the Grace drawn on the floor.

Richard's mouth opened, but he hesitated, his question unasked. He was eyeing the chicken pecking at the floor near the hide curtain to the back rooms.

He gestured. "Cara, open the door, please."

As she pulled it open, Richard waved his arms to coax the chicken out. The chicken, feathers flying as it flapped its wings in fright, darted this way and that, trying to avoid him. It wouldn't cross the room to the open door and safety.

Richard paused, hands on hips, puzzling down at the chicken. Black markings in the white and brown feathers gave it a striated, dizzying effect. The chicken squawked in complaint as Richard began moving forward, using his legs to shepherd the confused bird across the room.

Before it reached the drawing on the floor, it let out a squall, flapped its wings in renewed panic, and broke to the side, sprinting around the wall of the room and finally out the door. It was an astonishing display of an animal so terrified it was unable to flee in a straight line to a wide-open door and safety.

Cara shut the door behind it. "If there is an animal dumber than a chicken," she griped, "I've yet to see it."

"What's all the racket?" came a familiar voice.

It was Zedd, coming through the doorway to the back rooms. He was taller than Kahlan but not as tall as Richard—about Cara's height, although his mass of wavy white hair sticking out in disarray lent an illusion of more height than was there. Heavy maroon robes with black sleeves and cowled shoulders fostered the impression that his sticklike frame was bulkier than it really was. Three rows of silver brocade circled the cuffs of his sleeves. Thicker gold brocade ran around the neck and down the front. A red satin belt set with a gold buckle gathered the outfit at his waist.

Zedd had always worn unassuming robes. For a wizard of his rank and authority, the fancy outfit was bizarre in the extreme. Flamboyant clothes marked one with the gift as an initiate. For one without the gift, such clothes befit nobility in some places, or a wealthy merchant just about anywhere, so although Zedd disliked the flashy accoutrements, they had been a valuable disguise.

Richard and his grandfather embraced joyously, both

chortling with the pleasure of being together. It had been a long time.

"Zedd," Richard said, holding the other at arm's length, apparently even more disoriented by his grandfather's outfit than was Kahlan, "where did you ever get such clothes?"

With a thumb, Zedd tilted the gold buckle up to his scrutiny. His hazel eyes sparkled. "It's the gold buckle, isn't it. A bit too much?"

Ann lifted aside the heavy hide hanging over the doorway as she ducked under it. Short and broad, she wore an unadorned dark wool dress that marked her authority as the leader of the Sisters of the Light—sorceresses from the Old World, although she had created the illusion among them that she had been killed so as to have the freedom to pursue important matters. She looked as old as Zedd, though Kahlan knew her to be a great deal older.

"Zedd, quit preening," Ann said. "We have business."

Zedd shot her a scowl. Having seen such a scowl going in both directions, Kahlan wondered how the two of them had managed to travel together without more than verbal sparks. Kahlan had met Ann only the day before, but Richard held her in great regard, despite the circumstances under which he had come to know her.

Zedd took in Richard's outfit. "I must say, my boy, you're quite the sight, yourself."

Richard had been a woods guide, and had always worn simple clothes, so Zedd had never seen him in his new attire. He'd found most of his distant predecessor's outfit in the Wizard's Keep. Apparently, some wizards once wore more than simple robes, perhaps in forewarning.

The tops of Richard's black boots were wrapped with leather thongs pinned with silver emblems embossed with geometric designs, and covered black wool trousers. Over a black shirt was a black, open-sided tunic, decorated with symbols twisting along a wide gold band running all the way around its squared edges. His wide, multilayered leather belt cinched the magnificent tunic at his waist. The belt bore more of the silver emblems and carried a gold-worked pouch to each side. Hooked on the belt was a small, leather purse. At each wrist he wore a wide, leather-padded silver band bearing linked rings encompassing more of the strange symbols. His broad shoulders held the resplendent cape that appeared like nothing so much as spun gold.

Even without his sword, he looked at once noble and sinister. Regal, and deadly. He looked like a commander of kings. And like the embodiment of what the prophecies had named him: the bringer of death.

Under all that, Kahlan knew him to still possess the kind and generous heart he had as a woods guide. Rather than diminish all the rest, his simple sincerity only reinforced the veracity of it.

His sinister appearance was both warranted and in many ways an illusion. While single-minded and fierce in opposition to their foes, Kahlan knew him to be profoundly gentle, understanding, and kind. She had never known a man more fair, or patient. She thought him the most rare person she had ever met.

Ann smiled broadly at Kahlan, touching her face much as a kindly grandmother might do with a beloved child. Kahlan felt heartwarming honesty in the gesture. Her eyes sparkling, Ann did the same to Richard.

Fingering gray hair into the loose bun at the back of her head, she turned to feed a small stick of bundled grass into the fire. "I hope your first day married is going well?"

Kahlan briefly met Richard's gaze. "A little earlier today we went to the warm springs for a bath." Kahlan's smile, along with Richard's, faded. "One of the hunters guarding us died."

Her words brought the full attention of both Zedd and Ann.

"How?" Ann asked.

"Drowned." Richard held out a hand in invitation for everyone to sit. "The stream was shallow, but near as we can tell, he didn't stumble or fall." He waggled a thumb over his shoulder as the four of them settled around the Grace drawn in the dirt in the center of the room. "We took him to a building back there."

Zedd glanced over Richard's shoulder, almost as if he might be able to see through the wall and view Juni's body. "I'll have a look." He peered up at Cara, standing guard with her back against the door. "What do you think happened?"

Without hesitation, Cara said, "I think Juni became a danger. While looking for Lord Rahl in order to harm him, Juni fell and drowned."

Zedd's eyebrows arched. He turned to Richard. "A danger! Why would the man turn belligerent toward you?"

Richard scowled over his shoulder at the Mord-Sith. "Cara's wrong. He wasn't trying to harm us." Satisfied when she didn't argue, he returned his attention to his grandfather. "When we found him—dead—he had an odd look in his eyes. He saw something before he died that left a mask of . . . I don't know . . . longing, or something, on his face.

"Nissel, the healer, came and inspected his body. She said he had no injuries, but that he drowned."

Richard braced a forearm on his knee as he leaned in. "Drowned, Zedd, in six inches of water. Nissel said evil spirits killed him."

Zedd's eyebrows rose even higher. "Evil spirits?"

"The Mud People believe evil spirits sometimes come and take the life of a villager," Kahlan explained. "The villagers leave offerings before clay figures in a couple of the buildings over there." She lifted her chin toward the north. "Apparently, they believe that leaving rice cakes will appease these evil spirits. As if 'evil spirits' could eat, or could be easily bribed."

Outside, the rain lashed at the buildings. Water ran in a dark stain below the window and dripped here and there through the grass roof. Thunder rumbled almost constantly, taking the place of the now silent drums.

"Ah, I see," Ann said. She looked up with a smile Kahlan

found curious. "So, you think the Mud People gave you a paltry wedding, compared to the grand affair you would have had back in Aydindril. Hmm?"

Perplexed, Kahlan's brow tightened. "Of course not. It was the most beautiful wedding we could have wished for."

"Really?" Ann swept her arm out, indicating the surrounding village. "People in gaudy dress and animal skins? Their hair slicked down with mud? Naked children running about, laughing, playing, during such a solemn ceremony? Men painted in frightening mud masks dancing and telling stories of animals, hunts, and wars? This is what makes a good wedding to your mind?"

"No . . . those things aren't what I meant, or material," Kahlan stammered. "It's what was in their hearts that made it so special. It was that they sincerely shared our joy that made it meaningful to us. And what does that have to do with offering rice cakes to imagined evil spirits?"

With the side of a finger, Ann ordered one of the lines on the Grace—the line representing the underworld. "When you say, 'Dear spirits, watch over my departed mother's soul,' do you expect the dear spirits to rush all of a sudden to do so because you've put words to the wish?"

Kahlan could feel her face flush. She often asked the dear spirits to watch over her mother's soul. She was beginning to see why Zedd found the woman so vexing.

Richard came to Kahlan's rescue. "The prayers are not actually meant as a direct request, since we know the spirits don't work in such simple ways, but are meant to convey heartfelt feelings of love and hope for her mother's peace in the next world." He stroked his finger along the opposite side of the same line Ann had ordered. "The same as my prayers for my mother," he added in a whisper.

Ann's cheeks plumped as she smiled. "So they are, Richard. The Mud People must know better than to try to bribe with rice cakes the powerful forces they believe in and fear, don't you suppose?"

"It's the act of making the offering that's important,"

Richard said. By his unruffled attitude toward the woman it was apparent to Kahlan that Richard had learned to pick the berries out of the nettles.

Too, Kahlan understood what he meant. "It's the supplication to forces they fear that is really meant to appease the unknown."

Ann's finger rose along with her brow. "Yes. The nature of the offering is really only symbolic, meant to show homage, and by such an obeisance to this power they hope to placate it." Ann's finger wilted. "Sometimes, the act of courteous yielding is enough to stay an angry foe, yes?"

Kahlan and Richard both agreed it was.

"Better to kill the foe and be done with it," Cara sniped from back at the door.

Ann chuckled, leaning back to look over at Cara. "Well, sometimes, my dear, there is merit to such an alternative."

"And how would you 'kill' evil spirits," Zedd asked in a thin voice that cut through the drumming of the rain.

Cara didn't have an answer and so she glared instead.

Richard wasn't listening to them. He seemed to be transfixed by the Grace as he spoke. "By the same token, evil spirits . . . and such could be angered by a gesture of disrespect."

Kahlan was just opening her mouth to ask Richard why he was suddenly taking the Mud People's evil spirits so seriously when Zedd's fingers touched the side of her leg. His sidelong glance told her that he wanted her to be quiet.

"Some think it so, Richard," Zedd offered quietly.

"Why did you draw this symbol, this Grace?" Richard asked.

"Ann and I were using it to evaluate a few matters. At times, a Grace can be invaluable.

"A Grace is a simple thing, and yet it is infinitely complex. Learning about the Grace is a lifetime's journey, but like a child learning to walk, it begins with a first step. Since you were born with the gift, we also thought this would be a good time to introduce you to it."

Richard's gift was largely an enigma to him. Now that

they were back with his grandfather, Richard needed to delve the mysteries of that birthright and at last begin to chart the foreign landscape of his power. Kahlan wished they had the time Richard needed, but they didn't.

"Zedd, I'd really like you take a look at Juni's body."

"The rain will let up in a while," Zedd soothed, "and then we will go have a look."

Richard dragged a finger down the end of a line representing the gift—representing magic. "If it's a first step, and so important," Richard pointedly asked Ann, "then why didn't the Sisters of the Light try to teach me about the Grace when they took me to the Palace of the Prophets in the Old World? When they had the chance?"

Kahlan knew how quickly Richard become wary and distrustful when he thought he felt the tickling of a halter being slipped over his ears, no matter how kindly done, or how innocent its intent. Ann's Sisters had once put a collar around his throat.

Ann stole a glance at Zedd. "The Sisters of the Light had never before attempted to instruct one such as yourself—one born with the gift for Subtractive Magic in addition to the usual Additive." She chose her words carefully. "Prudence was required."

Richard's voice had made the subtle shift from questioned to questioner.

"Yet now you think I should be taught this Grace business?"

"Ignorance, too, is dangerous," Ann said in a cryptic murmur.

CHAPTER 5

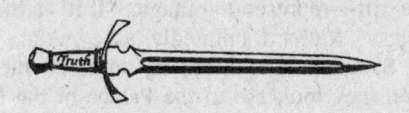

ZEDD SCOOPED UP A handful of dry dirt from the ground to the side. "Ann is given to histrionics," he griped. "I would have taught you about the Grace long ago, Richard, but we've been separated, that's all."

His apprehension alleviated by his grandfather's words, if not Ann's, the sharply defined muscles in Richard's shoulders and thick neck relaxed as Zedd went on.

"Though a Grace appears simple, it represents the whole of everything. It is drawn thus."

Zedd leaned forward on his knees. With practiced precision, he let the dirt drizzle from the side of his fist to quickly trace in demonstration the symbol already drawn on the ground.

"This outer circle represents the beginning of the underworld—the infinite world of the dead. Out beyond this circle, in the underworld, there is nothing else; there is only forever. This is why the Grace is begun here: out of nothing, where there was nothing, Creation begins."

A square sat inside the outer circle, its corners touching the circle. The square contained another circle just large enough to touch the insides of the square. The center circle held an eight-pointed star. Straight lines drawn last radiated out from the points of the star, piercing all the way through both circles, every other line bisecting a corner of the square.

The square represented the veil separating the outer circle of the spirit world—the underworld, the world of the dead—from the inner circle, which depicted the limits of the world of life. In the center of it all, the star expressed the Light—the Creator—with the rays of His gift of magic coming from that Light passing through all the boundaries.

"I've seen it before." Richard turned his wrists over and rested them across his knees.

The silver wristbands he wore were girded with strange symbols, but on the center of each, at the insides of his wrists, there was a small Grace on each band. As they were on the undersides of the wrists, Kahlan had never before noticed them.

"The Grace is a depiction of the continuum of the gift," Richard said, "represented by the rays: from the Creator, through life, and at death crossing the veil to eternity with the spirits in the Keeper's realm of the underworld." He burnished a thumb across the designs on one wristband. "It is also a symbol of hope to remain in the Creator's Light from birth, through life, and beyond, in the afterlife of the underworld."

Zedd blinked in surprise. "Very good, Richard. But how do you know this?"

"I've learned to understand the jargon of emblems, and I've read a few things about the Grace."

"The jargon of emblems . . . ?" Kahlan could see that Zedd was making a great effort at restraining himself. "You need to know, my boy, that a Grace can invoke alchemy of consequence. A Grace, if drawn with dangerous substances such as sorcerer's sand, or used in some other ways, can have profound effects—"

"Such as altering the way the worlds interact so as to accomplish an end," Richard finished. He looked up. "I've read a little about it."

Zedd sat back on his heels. "More than a little, it would seem. I want you to tell us everything you've been doing

41

since I was with you last." He shook a finger. "Every bit of it."

"What's a fatal Grace?" Richard asked, instead.

Zedd leaned in, this time clearly astounded. "A what?"

"Fatal Grace," Richard murmured as his gaze roamed the drawing on the floor.

Kahlan didn't have any more idea what Richard was talking about than did Zedd, but she was familiar with his behavior. Now and again she had seen Richard like this, almost as if he were in another place, asking curious questions while he considered some dim, dark dilemma. It was the way of a Seeker.

It was also a red flag that told her he believed there was something seriously amiss. She felt goose bumps tingling up her forearms.

Kahlan caught the grave twitch of Ann's brow. Zedd was straining near to bursting with a thousand questions, but Kahlan knew that he, too, was familiar with the way Richard sometimes lost himself for inexplicable reasons and asked unexpected questions. Zedd was doing his best to oblige them.

Zedd rubbed his fingertips along the furrows of his forehead, taking a breath to gather his patience. "Bags, Richard, I've never heard of such a thing as a fatal Grace. Where did you?"

"Just something I read somewhere," Richard murmured. "Zedd, can you put up another boundary? Call forth a boundary like you did before I was born?"

Zedd's face scrunched up in sputtering frustration. "Why would I—"

"To wall off the Old World and stop the war."

Caught off guard, Zedd paused with his mouth hanging open, but then a grin spread, stretching his wrinkled hide tight across the bones of his face.

"Very good, Richard. You are going to make a fine wizard, always thinking of how to make magic work for you to prevent harm and suffering." The smile faded. "Very good thinking, indeed, but no, I can't do it again."

42

"Why not?"

"It was a spell of threes. That means it was bound up in three of this and three of that. Powerful spells are usually well protected—a prescript of threes being only one means of keeping dangerous magic from being easily loosed. The boundary spell was one of those. I found it in an ancient text from the great war.

"Seems you take after your grandfather, taking an interest in reading old books full of odd things." His brow drew down. "The difference is, I had studied my whole life, and I knew what I was doing. Knew the dangers and how to avoid or minimize them. Knew my own abilities and limitations. Big difference, my boy."

"There were only two boundaries," Richard pressed.

"Ah well, the Midlands were embroiled in a horrific war with D'Hara." Zedd folded his legs under himself as he told the story.

"I used the first of the three to learn how to work the spell, how it functioned, and how to unleash it. The second I used to separate the Midlands and D'Hara—to stop the war. The last of the three I used to partition off Westland, for those who wanted a place to live free of magic, thereby preventing an uprising against the gifted."

Kahlan had a hard time imagining what a world without magic would be like. The whole concept seemed grim and dark to her, but she knew there were those who wanted nothing more than to live their lives free from magic. Westland, though not vast, provided such a place. At least it had for a time, but no longer.

"No more boundaries." Zedd threw his hands up. "That's that."

It had been almost a year since the boundaries were brought down by Darken Rahl, fading away to rejoin the three lands again. It was unfortunate that Richard's idea wouldn't work, that they couldn't cordon off the Old World and prevent the war from enveloping the New World. It would have saved countless lives yet to be lost in a struggle only just beginning.

"Do either of you," Ann asked into the silence, "have any idea of the whereabouts of the prophet? Nathan?"

"I saw him last," Kahlan said. "He helped me save Richard's life by giving me the book stolen from the Temple of the Winds, and telling me the words of magic I needed to use to destroy the book and keep Richard alive until he could recover from the plague."

Ann was looking like a wolf about to have dinner. "And where might he be?"

"It was somewhere in the Old World. Sister Verna was there. Someone Nathan cared deeply for had just been murdered before his eyes. He said that sometimes prophecy overwhelms our attempts to outwit it, and that sometimes we think we are more clever than we are, believing we can stay the hand of fate, if we wish it hard enough."

Kahlan dragged a finger through the dirt. "He left with two of his men, Walsh and Bollesdun, saying he was giving Richard back his title of Lord Rahl. He told Verna to save herself the trouble of trying to follow. He said she wouldn't succeed."

Kahlan looked up into Ann's suddenly sorrowful eyes. "I think Nathan was going off to try to forget whatever it was that ended that night. To forget the person who had helped him, and lost her life for it. I don't think you'll find him until he wishes it."

Zedd slapped the palms of his hands against his knees, breaking the spell of silence. "I want to know everything that's happened since I've last seen you, Richard. Since the beginning of last winter. The whole story. Don't leave anything out—the details are important. You may not understand that, but details can be critical. I must know it all."

Richard looked up long enough to catch his grandfather's expression of intent expectation. "I wish we had time to tell you about it, Zedd, but we don't. Kahlan, Cara, and I need to get back to Aydindril."

Ann's fingers fussed with a button on her collar; Kahlan thought the garden facade of her forbearance looked to be growing weeds. "We can begin now, and talk more on the journey."

"You can't imagine how much I wish we could stay with you, but there's no time for such a journey," Richard said. "We must hurry back. We'll have to go in the sliph. I'm sorry, I really am, but you can't come with us through the sliph; you'll have to travel to Aydindril on your own. When you get there, we can talk."

"Sliph?" Zedd's nose wrinkled with the word. "What are you talking about?"

Richard didn't answer, or even seem to hear. He was watching the cloth-covered window. Kahlan answered for him.

"The sliph is a . . ." She paused. How did one explain such a thing? "Well, she's sort of like living quicksilver. She can communicate with us. Talk, I mean."

"Talk," Zedd repeated in a flat voice. "What does she talk about?"

"It's not the talking that's important." With a thumbnail, Kahlan picked at the seam in her pant leg as she stared into Zedd's hazel eyes. "The sliph was created by those wizards, in the great war. They created weapons out of people; they created the sliph in much the same way. She was once a woman. They used her life to create the sliph, a being that can use magic to do what is called traveling. She was used to quickly travel great distances. Really great distances. Like from here all the way to Aydindril in less than a day, or many other places."

Zedd considered her words, as startling as she knew they must be to him. It had been so for her at first. Such a journey would ordinarily take many days, even on horseback. It could take weeks.

Kahlan put a hand on his arm. "I'm sorry, Zedd, but you and Ann can't go. The sliph's magic, as you were explaining, has dictates protecting it. That's why Richard had to leave his sword behind; its magic is incompatible with the magic of the sliph.

45

"To travel in the sliph, you must have at least some small amount of Subtractive Magic as well as the Additive. You don't have any Subtractive Magic. You and Ann would die in the sliph. I have an element of it bound into my Confessor's power, and Cara used her ability as a Mord-Sith to capture the gift of an Andolian, who has an element of it, so she can travel, too, and of course, Richard has the gift for Subtractive Magic."

"You've been using Subtractive Magic! But, but, how ... what do ... where ..." Zedd sputtered, losing track of which question he wanted to ask first.

"The sliph exists in these stone wells. Richard called the sliph, and now we can travel in her. But we have to be careful, or Jagang can send his minions through." Kahlan tapped the insides of her wrists together. "When we're not traveling, Richard sends her into her sleep by touching his wristbands together—on the Graces they have—and she rejoins her soul in the underworld."

Ann's face had gone ashen. "Zedd, I've warned you about this. We can't let him run around by himself. He's too important. He's going to get himself killed."

Zedd looked ready to explode. "You used the Graces on the wristbands? Bags, Richard, you have no idea what you're doing! You are messing about with the veil when you do such a thing!"

Richard, his attention elsewhere, snapped his fingers and gestured toward the fat sticks under the bench. He waggled his fingers urgently. Frowning, Zedd passed him one of the stout branches. Richard broke it in two over his knee while he watched the window.

With the next flash of lightning, Kahlan saw the silhouette of a chicken perched on the sill of the window, on the other side of the cloth. As the lightning flashed and thunder boomed, the chicken's shadow sidled to the other corner of the window.

Richard hurled the stick.

It caught the bird square on the breast. With a flapping

of wings and a startled squawk, it tumbled backward out the window.

"Richard!" Kahlan snatched his sleeve. "Why would you do such a thing? The chicken wasn't bothering anyone. The poor thing was just trying to stay out of the rain."

This, too, he seemed not to hear. He turned toward Ann. "You lived in the Old World with him. How much do you know about the dream walker?"

"Well, I, I, guess I know a bit," she stammered in surprise.

"You know about how Jagang can invade a person's mind, slip in between their thoughts, and entrench himself there, even without their knowledge?"

"Of course." She almost looked indignant at such a basic question about the enemy they were fighting. "But you and those bonded to you are protected. The dream walker can't invade the mind of one devoted to the Lord Rahl. We don't know the reason, only that it works."

Richard nodded. "Alric. He's the reason."

Zedd blinked in confusion. "Who?"

"Alric Rahl. An ancestor of mine. I read that the dream walkers were a weapon devised three thousand years ago in the great war. Alric Rahl created a spell—the bond—to protect his people, or anyone sworn to him, from the dream walkers. The bond's power to protect passes down to every gifted Rahl."

Zedd opened his mouth to ask a question, but Richard turned instead to Ann. "Jagang entered the mind of a wizard and sent him to kill Kahlan and me—tried to use him as an assassin."

"Wizard?" Ann frowned. "Who? Which wizard?"

"Marlin Pickard," Kahlan said.

"Marlin!" Ann sighed with a shake of her head. "The poor boy. What happened to him?"

"The Mother Confessor killed him," Cara said without hesitation. "She is a true sister of the Agiel."

Ann folded her hands in her lap and leaned toward Kahlan. "But how did you ever find out—"

"We would expect him to try such a thing again," Richard interrupted, drawing Ann's attention back. "But can a dream walker invade the mind of . . . of something other than a person?"

Ann considered the question with more patience than Kahlan thought it merited. "No. I don't believe so."

"You 'don't believe so.' " Richard cocked his head. "Are you guessing, or are you certain? It's important. Please don't guess."

She shared a long look with Richard before finally shaking her head. "No. He can't do such a thing."

"She's right," Zedd insisted. "I know enough about what he can do to know what he can't do. A soul is needed. A soul like his own. Otherwise, it just won't work. Same as he couldn't project his mind into a rock to see what it was thinking."

With his first finger, Richard stroked his lower lip. "Then it's not Jagang," he muttered to himself.

Zedd rolled his eyes in exasperation. "What's not Jagang?"

Kahlan sighed. Sometimes attempting to follow Richard's reasoning was like trying to spoon ants.

CHAPTER 6

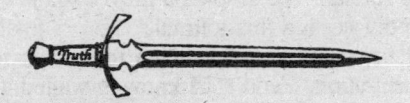

RATHER THAN ANSWER ZEDD'S question, Richard seemed
to once again already be half a mile down a different road.

"The chimes. Did you take care of them? It's supposed
to be a simple matter. Did you take care of it?"

"A simple matter?" Zedd's face stood out red against his
shock of unruly white hair. "Who told you that!"

Richard looked surprised at the question. "I read it. So,
did you take care of it?"

"We determined there was nothing to 'take care of,' "
Ann said, her voice taking on an undertone of annoyance.

"That's right," Zedd grumbled. "What do you mean it's
a simple matter?"

"Kolo said they were quite alarmed at first, but after investigating they discovered the chimes were a simple
weapon and easily overcome." Richard threw up his hands.
"How do you know it's not a problem? Are you certain?"

"Kolo? Bags, Richard, what are you talking about! Who's
Kolo?"

Richard waggled a hand as if begging forbearance before
he rose up and strode to the window. He lifted the curtain.
The chicken wasn't there. While he stretched up on his toes
to peer out into the driving rain, Kahlan answered for him.

"Richard found a journal in the Keep. It's written in High

D'Haran. He and one of the Mord-Sith, Berdine, who knows a little of the dead language of High D'Haran, have worked very hard to translate some of it.

"The man who wrote the journal was a wizard at the Keep during the great war, but they don't know his name, so they call him Kolo, from a High D'Haran word meaning 'strong advisor.' The journal has proved invaluable."

Zedd turned to peer suspiciously at Richard. His gaze returned to Kahlan. The suspicion moved to his voice. "And just where did he find this journal?"

Richard began pacing, his fingertips to his forehead in deep concentration. Zedd's hazel eyes waited for her answer.

"It was in the sliph's room. Down in the big tower."

"The big tower." The way Zedd repeated her words sounded like an accusation. He again glanced briefly at Richard. "Don't tell me you mean the room that's sealed."

"That's the one. When Richard destroyed the towers between the New and Old Worlds so he could get back here, the seal was blasted off that room, too. That's where he found the journal, Kolo's bones, and the sliph."

Richard halted over his grandfather. "Zedd, we'll tell you about all this later. Right now, I'd like to know why you don't think the chimes are here."

Kahlan frowned up at Richard. "Here? What does that mean, here?"

"Here in this world. Zedd, how do you know?"

Zedd straightened a finger toward the empty spot in their circle on the floor around the Grace. "Sit down, Richard. You're making me jumpy, pacing back and forth like a hound wanting to be let out."

As Richard checked the window one last time before returning to sit, Kahlan asked Zedd, "What are the chimes?"

"Oh," Zedd said with a shrug, "they're just some vexatious creatures. But—"

"Vexatious!" Ann slapped her forehead. "Try catastrophic!"

"And I called them forth?" Kahlan asked, anxiety rising

in her voice. She had spoken the names of the three chimes to complete magic that saved Richard's life. She hadn't know what the words meant, but she had known that without them Richard would have died within a breath or two at most.

Zedd waggled a hand to allay her fears. "No, no. As Ann says, they have the potential to be troublesome, but—"

Richard hiked up his trousers at the knees as he folded his legs. "Zedd, please answer the question. How do you know they aren't here?"

"Because, the chimes are a work of threes. That's partly why there are three: Reechani, Sentrosi, Vasi."

Kahlan nearly leaped to her feet. "I thought you weren't supposed to say them aloud!"

"You are not. An ordinary person could say them with no ill effect. I can speak them aloud without calling them. Ann can, and Richard, too. But not those exceedingly rare people such as yourself."

"Why me?"

"Because you have magic powerful enough to summon their aid on behalf of another. But without the gift, which protects the veil, the chimes could also ride your magic across into this world. The names of the three chimes are supposed to be a secret."

"Then I might have called them into this world."

"Dear spirits," Richard whispered. His face had gone bloodless. "They could be here."

"No, no. There are countless safeguards, and numerous requirements that are exacting and extraordinary." Zedd held up a finger to silence Richard's question before it could come out his open mouth. "Among many other things, Kahlan, for example, would have to be your third wife."

Zedd flashed Richard a patronizing smirk. "Satisfied, Mister Read-it-in-a-book?"

Richard let out a breath. "Good." He sighed aloud again as the color returned to his face. "Good. She's only my second wife."

"What!" Zedd threw up his arms, nearly toppling backward. He huffed and hauled his sleeves back down. "What do you mean, she is your second wife? I've known you your whole life, Richard, and I know you've never loved anyone but Kahlan. Why in Creation would you marry someone else!"

Richard cleared his throat as he shared a pained expression with Kahlan. "Look, it's a long story, but the end of it is that in order to get into the Temple of the Winds to stop the plague, I had to marry Nadine. That would make Kahlan my second wife."

"Nadine." Zedd let his jaw hang as he scratched the hollow of his cheek. "Nadine Brighton? That Nadine?"

"Yes." Richard poked at the dirt. "Nadine . . . died shortly after the ceremony."

Zedd let out a low whistle. "Nadine was a nice girl—going to be a healer. The poor thing. Her parents will be devastated."

"Yes, the poor thing," Kahlan muttered under her breath.

Nadine's dogged ambition had been to have Richard, and there had been few bounds to that ambition. Any number of times, Richard had told Nadine in explicit terms there was nothing between the two of them, never would be, and he wanted her gone as soon as possible. To Kahlan's exasperation, Nadine would simply smile and say, "Whatever you wish, Richard," as she continued to scheme.

Though she would never have wished Nadine any real harm, especially the horrible death she suffered, Kahlan could not pretend pity for the conniving strumpet, as Cara called her.

"Why is your face all red?" Zedd asked.

Kahlan looked up. Zedd and Ann were watching her.

"Um, well . . ." Kahlan changed the subject. "Wait a minute. When I spoke the three chimes I wasn't married to Richard. We weren't married until we came here, to the Mud People. So, you see, I wasn't even his wife at the time."

"That's even better," Ann said. "Removes another stepping-stone from the chimes' path."

Richard's hand found Kahlan's. "Well, that may not be exactly true. When we had to say the words to fulfill the requirements for me to get into the temple, in our hearts we said the words to each other, so it could be said that we were married because of that vow of commitment.

"Sometimes magic, the spirit world's magic, anyway, works by such ambiguous rules."

Ann shifted her weight uncomfortably. "True enough."

"But no matter how you reason it out, that would still only make her your second wife." Zedd eyed them both suspiciously. "This story gets more complicated every time one of you opens your mouth. I need to hear the whole thing."

"Before we leave, we can tell you a bit of it. When you get to Aydindril, then we'll have the time to tell it all to you. But we need to return through the sliph right away."

"What's the hurry, my boy?"

"Jagang would like nothing better than to get his hands on the dangerous magic stored in the Wizard's Keep. If he did, it would be disastrous. Zedd, you would be the best one to protect the Keep, but in the meantime don't you think Kahlan and I would be better than nothing?

"At least we were there when Jagang sent Marlin and Sister Amelia to Aydindril."

"Amelia!" Ann closed her eyes as she squeezed her temples. "She's a Sister of the Dark. Do you know where she is, now?"

"The Mother Confessor killed her, too," Cara said from back at the door.

Kahlan scowled at the Mord-Sith. Cara grinned back like a proud sister.

Ann opened one eye to peer at Kahlan. "No small task. A wizard being directed by the dream walker, and now a woman wielding the Keeper's own dark talent."

"An act of desperation," Kahlan said. "Nothing more."

Zedd grunted a brief agreeable chuckle. "There can be powerful magic in acts of desperation."

"Much like the business of speaking the three chimes,"

she said. "An act of desperation to save Richard's life. What are the chimes? Why were you so concerned?"

Zedd squirmed to get more comfortable on his bony bottom.

"The wrong person speaking their names to summon their assistance in keeping a person from crossing the line"—he tapped the line of the Grace representing the world of the dead—"can by misfortune of design call them into the world of life, where they can accomplish the purpose for which they were created: to end magic."

"They soak it up," Ann said, "like the parched ground soaks up a summer shower. They are beings of sorts, but not alive. They have no soul."

The lines in Zedd's face took a grim set as he nodded his agreement. "The chimes are creatures conjured of the other side, of the underworld. They would annul the magic in this world."

"You mean they hunt down and kill those with magic?" Kahlan asked. "Like the shadow people used to? Their touch is deadly?"

"No," Ann said. "They can and do kill, but just their being in this world, in time, is all it would take to extinguish magic. Eventually, any who derived their survival from magic would die. The weakest first. Eventually, even the strongest."

"Understand," Zedd cautioned, "that we don't know much about them. They were weapons of the great war, created by wizards with more power than I can fathom. The gift is no longer as it was."

"If the chimes were to somehow get to this world, and they ended magic," Richard asked, "would all those with the gift just not have it anymore? Would the Mud People, for instance, simply not be able to contact their spirit ancestors anymore? Would creatures of magic die out and that would be that? Just regular people and animals and trees and such left? Like where I grew up in Westland, where there was no magic?"

Kahlan could feel the faint rumble of thunder in the

ground under her. The rain drummed on. The fire in the hearth hissed its ill will for its liquid antagonist.

"We can't answer that, my boy. It's not like there is precedent to which we can point. The world is complex beyond our comprehension. Only the Creator understands how it all works together."

The firelight cast Zedd's face in harsh angular shadows as he spoke with grim conviction. "But I fear it would be much worse than you paint it."

"Worse? Worse how?"

Fastidiously smoothing his robes along his thighs, Zedd took his time in responding.

"West of here, in the highlands above the Nareef Valley, the headwaters of the Dammar River gather, eventually to flow into the Drun River. These headwaters leach poisons from the ground of the highlands.

"The highlands are a bleak wasteland, with the occasional bleached bones of an animal that stayed too long and drank too much from the poison waters. It's a windy, desolate, deadly place."

Zedd opened his arms to gesture, suggesting the grand scale. "The thousand tiny runnels and runoff brooks from all the surrounding mountain slopes collect into a broad, shallow, swampy lake before continuing on to the valley below. The paka plant grows there in great abundance, especially at the broad south end, from where the waters descend. The paka is able to not only tolerate the poison, but thrive on it. Only the caterpillar of a moth eats some of the leaves of the paka and spins its cocoon among the fleshy stems.

"Warfer birds nest at the head of the Nareef Valley, on the cliffs just below this poison highland lake. One of their favorite foods is the berries of the paka plant that grows not far above, and so they are one of the few animals to frequent the highlands. They don't drink the water."

"The berries aren't poison, then?" Richard asked.

"No. In a wonder of Creation, the paka grows strong on the contaminates from the water, but the berries it produces don't contain the poison, and the water that flows on down the mountain, filtered by all the paka, is pure and healthy.

"Also living in the highlands is the gambit moth. The way it flits about makes it irresistible to warfer birds, which otherwise eat mostly seeds and berries. Living where it does, it is preyed on by few animals other than warfer birds.

"Now, the paka plant, you see, can't reproduce by itself. Perhaps because of the poisons in the water, its outer seed casing is hard as steel and will not open, so the plant inside can't sprout.

"Only magic can accomplish the task."

Zedd's eyes narrowed, his arms spread wide, and his fingers splayed with the spinning of the tale. Kahlan recalled her wide-eyed child wonder at hearing the story of the gambit moth for the first time while sitting on the knee of a wizard up in the Keep.

"The gambit moth has such magic, in the dust on its wings. When the warfer birds eat the moth, along with the berries of the paka, the magic dust from the moth works inside the birds to breach the husk of the tiny seeds. In their droppings, the warfer birds thus sow the paka seeds, and because of the singular magic of the gambit moth, the paka's seeds can sprout.

"It is upon the paka, thus brought to leaf, that the gambit moth lays it eggs and where the new-hatched caterpillars eat and grow strong before they spin their cocoon to become gambit moths."

"So," Richard said, "if magic is ended, then . . . what are you saying? That even creatures such as a moth with magic would no longer have it, and so the paka plant would die out, and then the warfer bird would starve, and the gambit moth would in turn have no paka plant for its caterpillars to eat, so it would perish?"

"Think," the old wizard whispered, "what else would happen."

"Well, for one thing, as the old paka plants died and no new ones grew, it would only seem logical that the water going into the Nareef Valley would become poisonous."

"That's right, my boy. The water would poison the animals below. The deer would die. The raccoons, the porcupines, the voles, the owls, the songbirds. And any animal that ate their carcasses: wolves, coyotes, vultures. All would die." Zedd leaned forward, raising a finger. "Even the worms."

Richard nodded. "Much of the livestock raised in the valley could eventually be poisoned. Much of the cropland could become tainted by the waters of the Dammar. It would be a disaster for the people and animals living in the Nareef Valley."

"Think of what would happen when the meat from that livestock was sold," Ann coached, "before anyone knew it was poison."

"Or the crops," Kahlan added.

Zedd leaned in. "And think of what more it would mean."

Richard looked from Ann to Kahlan to Zedd. "The Dammar River flows into the Drun. If the Dammar was poison, then too would be the Drun. Everything downstream would be tainted as well."

Zedd nodded. "And downstream is the land of Toscla. The Nareef is to Toscla as a flea is to a dog. Toscla grows great quantities of grain and other crops that feed many people of the Midlands. They send long trains of cargo wagons north to trade."

It had been a long time since Zedd had lived in the Midlands. Toscla was an old name. It lay far to the southwest; the wilds, like a vast sea, isolated it from the rest of the Midlands. The dominant people there, now calling themselves Anders, repeatedly changed their name, and so the name of their land. What Zedd knew as Toscla was changed to Vengren, then Vendice, then Turslan, and was presently Anderith.

"Either poison grain would be sold before it was known to be such, thus poisoning countless unknowing souls," Zedd was saying, "or the people of Toscla would find out in time, and then couldn't sell their crops. Their livestock might soon die. The fish they harvest from the coastal waters could likely be poisoned by the waters of the Drun flowing into it. The taint could find its way to the fields, killing new crops and hope for the future.

"With their livestock and fishing industries poisoned, and without crops to trade for other food, the people of Toscla could starve. People in other lands who relied on purchasing those crops in trade would fall on hard times, too, because they, in turn, then couldn't sell their goods. With trade disrupted, and with shortages driving prices up, people everywhere in the Midlands would begin to have have trouble feeding their families.

"Civil unrest would swell on the shortages. Hunger would spread. Panic could set in. Unrest could turn to fighting as people flee to untainted land, which others already occupy. Desperation could fan the flames. All order could break down."

"You're just speculating," Richard said. "You aren't predicting such a widespread calamity, are you? If magic were to fail, might it not be that bad?"

Zedd shrugged. "Such a thing has never happened, so it's hard to predict. It could be that the poison would be diluted by the water of the Dammar and the Drun, and it would cause no harm, or at most only a few localized problems. When the Drun flows into the sea, that much water might render the poison harmless, so fishing might not be affected. It could end up being nothing more than a minor inconvenience."

In the dim light, Zedd's hair reminded Kahlan of white flames. He peered with one eye at his grandson. "But," he whispered, "were the magic of the gambit moth to fail, for all we know it could very well begin a cascade of events that would result in the end of life as we know it."

Richard wiped a hand over his face as he contemplated how such a disaster might ripple through the Midlands.

Zedd lifted an eyebrow. "Do you begin to get the idea?" He let the uncomfortable silence drag before he added, "And that is but one small thing of magic. I could give you countless others."

"The chimes are from the world of the dead. That would certainly fit their purpose," Richard muttered as he raked his fingers back through his hair. "Would that mean that if magic were to fail, with the weakest dying out first, the magic of the gambit moth would be among the first to fail?"

"And how strong is the gambit moth's magic?" Zedd spread his hands. "There is no telling. Could be among the first, or the last."

"What about Kahlan? Would she lose her power? It's her protection. She needs it."

Richard was the first person to accept her as she was, to love her as she was, power and all. That, in fact, had been the undiscovered secret to her magic and the reason he had been rendered safe from its deadly nature. It was the reason they were able to share the physical essence of their love without her magic destroying him.

Zedd's brow bunched up. "Bags, Richard, aren't you listening? Of course she would lose her power. It's magic. All magic would end. Hers, mine, yours. But while you and Kahlan would simply lose your magic, the world might die around you."

Richard dragged a finger through the dirt. "I don't know how to use my gift, so it wouldn't mean so much to me. But it matters a great deal for others. We can't let it happen."

"Fortunately, it can't happen." Zedd tugged his sleeves straight in an emphatic gesture. "This is just a rainy-day game of 'what if.' "

Richard drew up his knees and clasped his arms around them as he seemed to sink back into his distant silent world.

"Zedd is right," Ann said. "This is all just speculation. The chimes are not loose. What is important, now, is Jagang."

"If magic ended," Kahlan asked, "wouldn't Jagang lose his ability as a dream walker?"

"Of course," Ann said. "But there is no reason to believe—"

"If the chimes were loosed on this world," Richard interrupted, "how would you stop them? It's supposed to be simple. How would you do it?"

Ann and Zedd shared a look.

Before either could answer, Richard's head turned toward the window. He rose up and in three strides had crossed the room. He pulled aside the curtain to peer out. Gusts blew the pelting rain in against his face as he leaned out to look both ways. Lightning crackled through the murky afternoon air, and thunder stuttered after it.

Zedd leaned close to Kahlan. "Do you have any idea what's going on in that boy's head?"

Kahlan wet her lips. "I think I have an inkling, but you wouldn't believe me if I told you."

Richard cocked his head, listening. Kahlan, in the silence, strained to hear anything out of the ordinary.

In the distance, she heard the terrified wail of a child.

Richard bolted for the door. "Everyone wait here."

As one, they all rushed after him.

CHAPTER 7

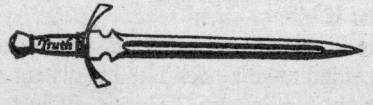

SPLASHING THROUGH THE MUD, Zedd, Ann, Cara, and Kahlan chased after Richard as he raced out into the passageways between the stuccoed walls of buildings. Kahlan had to squint to see through the downpour. The deluge was so cold it made her gasp.

Hunters, their ever-present protectors, appeared from the sweeping sheets of rain to run along beside them. The buildings flashing by were mostly single-room homes sharing at least one common wall, but sometimes as many as three. Together, they clustered into a complex maze seemingly without design.

Following right behind Richard, Ann surprised Kahlan with her swift gait. Ann didn't look a woman designed to run, but she kept up with ease. Zedd's bony arms pumped a swift and steady cadence. Cara, with her long legs, loped along beside Kahlan. The sprinting hunters ran with effortless grace. At the lead, Richard, his golden cape billowing out behind, was an intimidating sight; compared with the wiry hunters, he was a mountain of a man avalanching through the narrow streets.

Richard followed the meandering passageway a short distance before darting to the right at the first corner. A black and two brown goats thought the rushing procession a curiosity, as did several children in tiny courtyards planted with rapeseed for the chickens. Women gaped from doorways flanked by pots of herbs.

Richard rounded the next corner to the left. At the sight of the charging troop of people, a young woman beneath a small roof swept a crying child into her arms. Holding the little boy's head to her shoulder, she pressed her back against the door, to be out of the way of the trouble racing her way. The boy wailed as she tried to hush him.

Richard slid to a fluid but abrupt stop, with everyone behind doing their best not to crash into him. The woman's frightened, wide-eyed gaze flitted among the people suddenly surrounding her as she stood in her doorway.

"What is it?" she asked. *"Why do you want us?"*

Richard wanted to know what she was saying before she had finished saying it. Kahlan squeezed her way through to the fore of the group. Blood beaded along scratches and ran from cuts on the boy the woman clutched in her arms.

"We heard your son cry out." With tender fingers, Kahlan stroked the bawling child's hair. *"We thought there was*

61

trouble. We were concerned for your boy. We came to help."

Relieved, the woman let the weight of the boy slip from her hip to the ground. She squatted and pressed a blood-stained wad of cloth to his cuts as she briefly cooed comfort to calm his panic.

She looked up at the crowd around her. *"Ungi is fine. Thank you for your concern, but he was just being a boy. Boys get themselves in trouble."*

Kahlan told the others what the woman had said.

"How did he get all clawed up?" Richard wanted to know.

"Ka chenota," the woman answered when Kahlan asked Richard's question.

"A chicken," Richard said before Kahlan could tell him. Apparently, he had learned that *chenota* meant chicken in the Mud People's language. "A chicken attacked your boy? *Ka chenota?"*

She blinked when Kahlan translated Richard's question. The woman's cynical laughter rang out through the drumbeat of the rain. *"Attacked by a chicken?"* Flipping her hand, she scoffed, as if she had thought for a moment they were serious. *"Ungi thinks he is a great hunter. He chases chickens. This time he cornered one, frightening it, and it scratched him trying to get away."*

Richard squatted down before Ungi, giving the boy's dark fall of wet hair a friendly tousle. "You've been chasing chickens? *Ka chenota?* Teasing them? That isn't what really happened, is it?"

Instead of interpreting Richard's questions, Kahlan crouched down on the balls of her feet. "Richard, what's this about?"

Richard put a comforting hand on the child's back as his mother wiped at blood running down his chest. "Look at the claw marks," Richard whispered. "Most are around his neck."

Kahlan heaved a chafed sigh. "He no doubt tried to pick it up and hold it to himself. The panicked chicken was simply trying to get away."

Reluctantly, Richard admitted that it could be so.

"This is no great misadventure," Zedd announced from above. "Let me do a little healing on the boy and then we can get in out of this confounded rain and have something to eat. And I have a lot of questions yet to ask."

Richard, still squatted down before the boy, held up a finger, stalling Zedd. He looked into Kahlan's eyes. "Ask him. Please?"

"Tell me why," Kahlan insisted. "Is this about what the Bird Man said? Is that really what this is about? Richard, the man had been drinking."

"Look over my shoulder."

Kahlan peered through the writhing ribbons of rain. Across the narrow passageway, under the dripping grass eaves at the corner of a building, a chicken ruffled its feathers. It was another of the striated Barred Rock breed, as were most of the Mud People's chickens.

Kahlan was cold and miserable and soaking wet. She was beginning to lose her patience as she once again met Richard's waiting gaze.

"A chicken trying to stay out of the rain? Is that what you want me to see?"

"I know you think—"

"Richard!" she growled under her breath. "Listen to me."

She paused, not wanting to be cross with Richard, of all people. She told herself he was simply concerned for their safety. But it was misbegotten concern. Kahlan made herself take a breath. She clasped his shoulder, rubbing with her thumb.

"Richard, you're just feeling bad because Juni died today. I feel bad, too. But that doesn't make it sinister. Maybe he just died from the exertion of running; I've heard of it happening to young people. You have to recognize that sometimes people die, and we never know the reason."

Richard glanced up at the others. Zedd and Ann were busying themselves with admiring Ungi's young muscles in order to avoid what was beginning to sound suspiciously like a lover's spat at their feet. Cara stood near by, scruti-

63

nizing the passageways. One of the hunters offered to let Ungi finger his spear shaft to distract the boy from his mother as she ministered to his wounds.

Looking reluctant to quarrel, Richard wiped back his wet hair. "I think it's the same chicken I chased out," he whispered at last. "The one in the window I hit with the stick."

Kahlan sighed aloud in exasperation. "Richard, most of the Mud People's chickens look like that one." She again peered across to the underside of the roof. "Besides, it's gone."

Richard looked over his shoulder to see for himself. His gaze swept the empty passageway.

"Ask the boy if he was teasing the chicken, chasing it?"

Under the small roof over the door, as Ungi's mother soothed his wounds, she had also been warily watching the conversation she didn't understand going on at her feet. Kahlan licked the rain from her lips. If it meant this much to Richard, Kahlan decided, she could do no less than ask for him. She touched the boy's arm.

"Ungi, is it true that you chased the chicken? Did you try to grab it?"

The boy, still sniffling back tears, shook his head. He pointed up at the roof. *"It came down on me."* He clawed the air. *"It attacked me."*

The mother leaned down and swatted his bottom. *"Tell these people the truth. You and your friends chase the chickens all the time."*

His big black eyes blinked at Richard and Kahlan, both down at his level, down in his world. *"I am going to be a great hunter, just like my father. He is a brave hunter, with scars from the beasts he hunts."*

Richard smiled at the translation. He gently touched one of the claw cuts. "Here you will have the scar of a hunter, like your brave father. So, you were hunting the chicken, as your mother says? Is that really the truth?"

"I was hungry. I was coming home. The chicken was hunting me," he insisted. His mother spoke his name in admonition. *"Well . . . they perch on the roof there."* He

64

again pointed up at the roof over the door. *"Maybe I scared it when I came running home, and it slipped on the wet roof and fell on me."*

The mother opened the door and shoved the boy inside. *"Forgive my son. He is young and makes up stories all the time. He chases chickens all the time. This is not the first time he has been scratched by one. Once, a cock's spur gashed his shoulder. He imagines they are eagles.*

"Ungi is a good boy, but he is a boy, and full of stories. When he finds a salamander under a rock, he runs home to show me, to tell me that he found a nest of dragons. He wants his father to come slay them before they can eat us."

Everyone but Richard chuckled. As she bowed her head and turned to go into her home, Richard gently took ahold of her elbow to halt her while he spoke to Kahlan.

"Tell her I'm sorry her boy was hurt. It wasn't Ungi's fault. Tell her that. Tell her I'm sorry."

Kahlan frowned at Richard's words. She changed them a little when she translated, lest they be misconstrued.

"We are sorry Ungi was hurt. We hope he is soon well. If not, or if any of the cuts are deep, come tell us and Zedd will use magic to heal your boy."

The mother nodded and smiled her gratitude before bidding them a good day and ducking through her doorway. Kahlan didn't think she looked very eager to have magic plied on her son.

After watching the door close, Kahlan gave Richard's hand a squeeze. "All right? Are you satisfied it wasn't what you thought? That it was nothing?

He stared off down the empty passageway a moment. "I just thought . . ." He finally conceded with contrite smile. "I just worry about your safety, that's all."

"As long as we're all wet," Zedd grumbled, "we might as well go over and see Juni's body. I'm certainly not going to stand here in the rain if you two are going to start kissing."

Zedd motioned Richard to lead the way and let him know he meant him to be quick about it. As Richard started out,

Zedd hooked Kahlan's arm and let everyone else pass. He held her back as they slogged on through the mud, allowing the others to gain a little distance on them.

Zedd put an arm around her shoulders and leaned close, even though Kahlan was sure his words wouldn't be heard over the roar of the rain. "Now, dear one, I want to know what it is you think I wouldn't believe."

From the corner of her eye, Kahlan marked his intent expression. He was serious about this. She decided it would be better to put his concern to rest.

"It's nothing. He had a passing wild idea, but I got him to see reason. He's over it."

Zedd narrowed his eyes at her, a disconcerting sight, coming from a wizard. "I know you're not stupid enough to believe that, so why should you think I am? Hmm? He's not buried this bone. He's still got it between his teeth."

Kahlan checked the others. They were still several strides ahead. Even though Richard was supposed to be leading, Cara, ever protective, had put herself ahead of him.

Although she couldn't understand the words, Kahlan could tell that Ann was making cheery small talk with Richard. As much as they seemed to nettle each other, when it suited them Zedd and Ann worked together as effortlessly as teeth and tongue.

Zedd's sticklike fingers tightened on her arm. Richard wasn't the only one with a bone between his teeth.

Kahlan heaved a sigh and told him. "I suspect that Richard believes there is a chicken monster on the loose."

Kahlan had covered her nose and mouth against the stench, but dropped her hands to her sides when the two women looked up from their work. Both smiled to the small troop shuffling in the door, shaking off water, looking like they'd fallen in a river.

The two women were working on Juni's body, decorating it with black-and-white mud designs. They had already woven decorative grass bands around his wrists and ankles and had fixed a leather fillet around his head with grass positioned under it in the manner of hunters going out on a hunt.

Juni was laid out on a mud-brick platform, one of four such raised work areas. Dark stains drooled down the sides of each. A layer of fetid straw covered the floor. When a body was brought in, the straw was kicked up against the base of the platform to absorb draining fluids.

The straw was alive with vermin. When there were no bodies, the door was left open so the chickens could feast on the bugs and keep them down.

Off to the right of the door was the only window. When no one was attending a body, supple deerskin shut out light so the deceased might have peace. The women had pulled the deerskin to the side and hooked it behind a peg in the wall to let the gloomy light seep into the cramped room.

Bodies were not prepared at night, so as not to strain the peace of the soul going over to the other side. Reverence for the departing soul was fundamental to the Mud People; these new spirits might someday be called upon to help their people still living.

Both women were older and smiling as if their sunny nature could not be masked with a somber façade even for such grim work. Kahlan assumed them to be specialists in the task of insuring that the dead were properly adorned before they were laid in the ground.

Kahlan could see the fragrant oils that were rubbed over the body still glistening where the mud was yet to be applied. The oils failed to shroud the gagging stink of the tainted straw and platforms. She didn't understand why the straw wasn't changed more often. But then, for all she knew, perhaps it was; there was no escaping the consequence of the process of death and decay.

Probably for that reason the dead were buried quickly—either the day they died or at the latest the next. Juni would

67

not be made to wait long before he was put in the ground. Then his spirit, seeing that all was as it should be, could turn to those of his kind in the spirit world.

Kahlan bent close to the two women. Out of reverence for the dead, she whispered. *"Zedd and Ann, here"*—she lifted a hand, indicating the two—*"would like to look at Juni."*

The women bowed from the waist and stepped back, with a finger hooking their pots of black and white mud off the platform and out of the way. Richard watched as his grandfather and Ann put their hands lightly to Juni, inspecting him, no doubt with magic. While Zedd and Ann conferred in hushed tones as they conducted their examination, Kahlan turned to the two women and told them what a fine job they were doing, and how sorry she was about the young hunter's death.

Having had enough of looking at his dead guardian, Richard joined her. He slipped an arm around her waist and asked her to relate his sentiments. Kahlan added his words to hers.

It wasn't long before Zedd and Ann nudged Richard and Kahlan to the side. Smiling, they gestured the women back to their chore.

"As you suspected," Zedd whispered, "his neck is not broken. I could find no injury to his head. I'd say he drowned."

"And how do you suppose that could have happened?" A scintilla of sarcasm laced Richard's voice.

Zedd squeezed Richard's shoulder. "You were sick once, and you passed out. Remember? There was nothing sinister to it. Did you crack your skull? No. You slumped to the floor, where I found you. Remember? It could be something as simple as that."

"But Juni showed no signs—"

Everyone turned as the old healer, Nissel, shambled in the door cradling a small bundle in her arms. She paused for an instant at seeing everyone in the small room, before she turned to another of the platforms for the dead. She laid the bundle tenderly on the cold brick. Kahlan put a hand over her heart as she saw Nissel unwrap a newborn baby.

"What happened?" Kahlan asked.

"Not the joyous event I expected it would be." Nissel's sorrowful eyes met Kahlan's gaze. *"The child was born dead."*

"Dear spirits," Kahlan whispered, *"I'm so sorry."*

Richard brushed a shiny green bug off Kahlan's shoulder. "What happened to the baby?"

Nissel shrugged when Kahlan spoke his question. *"I have watched the mother for months. Everything had seemed to point to a joyous event. I foresaw no problem, but the child was stillborn."*

"How is the mother?"

Nissel's gaze sank to the floor. *"For now she weeps her heart out, but the mother will soon be well."* She forced a smile. *"It happens. Not all children are strong enough to live. The woman will have others."*

Richard leaned close after the exchange appeared to be finished. "What did she say?"

Kahlan stamped twice to dislodge a centipede wriggling up her leg. "The baby just wasn't strong enough, and was stillborn."

Frowning, he looked over at the heartbreaking death. "Wasn't strong enough . . ."

Kahlan watched him stare at the small form, still, bloodless, unreal-looking. A new child was a uniquely beautiful entity, but this, lacking the soul its mother had given it so that it might stay in this world, was naked ugliness.

Kahlan asked when Juni would be buried. One of the two women glanced at the small death. *"We will need to prepare another. Tomorrow, they will both be put to their eternal rest."*

As they went out the door, Richard turned and looked up into the waterfall of rain. A chicken perched in the low eaves overhead fluffed its feathers. Richard's gaze lingered a moment.

The reasoning that had been so clearly evident on his face turned to resolution.

Richard peered up the passageway. He whistled as he beckoned with an arm. Their guardian hunters started toward them.

As the hunters were jogging to a halt, Richard grasped Kahlan's upper arm in his big hand. "Tell them I want them to go get more men. I want them to gather up all the chickens—"

"What!" Kahlan wrenched her arm from his grip. "Richard, I'm not going to ask them that. They'll think you've gone crazy!"

Zedd stuck his head between them. "What's going on?"

"He wants the men to gather up all the chickens just because one of them is perched above the door."

"It wasn't there when we arrived. I looked."

Zedd turned and squinted up in the rain. "What chicken?" Kahlan and Richard both looked for themselves. The chicken was gone.

"It probably went searching for a drier roost," Kahlan growled. "Or one more peaceful."

Zedd wiped rain from his eyes. "Richard, I want to know what this is about."

"A chicken was killed outside the spirit house. Juni spat at the honor of whatever killed that chicken. Not long after, Juni died. I threw a stick at the chicken in the window, and not long after, it attacked that little boy. It was my fault Ungi got clawed. I don't want to make the same mistake again."

Zedd, to Kahlan's surprise, spoke calmly. "Richard, you're bridging some yawning chasms with gossamer reasoning."

"The Bird Man said one of the chickens wasn't a chicken."

Zedd frowned. "Really?"

"He'd been drinking," Kahlan pointed out.

"Zedd, you named me the Seeker. If you wish to reconsider your choice, then do it now. If not, then let me do my job. If I'm wrong you can all lecture me later."

Richard took Zedd's silence for acquiescence and again grasped Kahlan's arm, if a little more gently than the first time. Conviction ignited his gray eyes.

"Please, Kahlan, do as I ask. If I'm wrong, I'll look a fool, but I'd rather look a fool than be right and fail to act."

Whatever had killed the chicken had done it right outside the spirit house, where she had been. That was the skein from which Richard had woven this tapestry of threat. Kahlan believed in Richard, but suspected he was merely getting carried away with concern over protecting her.

"What is it you would have me say to the men?"

"I want the men to gather up the chickens. Take them to the buildings they keep empty for the evil spirits. I want every last chicken herded in there. Then, we can have the Bird Man look at them and tell us which one is not a chicken.

"I want the men to be gentle and courteous as they gather the chickens. Under no circumstances do I want anyone to show disrespect to any of the chickens."

"Disrespect," Kahlan repeated. "To a chicken."

"That's right." Richard checked the waiting hunters before locking his gaze on her. "Tell the men I fear one of the chickens is possessed by the evil spirit that killed Juni."

Kahlan didn't know if that was what Richard believed, but she knew without doubt that the Mud People would believe it.

She looked to Zedd's eyes for counsel, but found none. Ann's visage had no more to offer. Cara was sworn to Richard; although she routinely disregarded orders she thought trifling, were Richard to insist, she would walk off a cliff for him.

Richard would not give up. If Kahlan didn't translate for him, he would go find Chandalen to do it. Failing that, he would gather up the chickens by himself, if necessary.

The only thing to be accomplished by not doing as he

asked would be to display a lack of faith in him. That alone persuaded her.

Shivering in the icy rain, Kahlan took in Richard's resolute gray eyes one last time before she turned to the waiting hunters.

CHAPTER 8

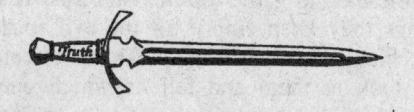

"HAVE YOU FOUND THE evil spirit, yet?"

Kahlan looked back over her shoulder to see that it was Chandalen, carefully shuffling his way through the squawking throng of chickens. The muted light helped calm the flock in their confinement, if they did still raise quite the clamor. There were a few Reds and a sprinkling of other types, but most of the Mud People's chickens were the striated Barred Rocks, a breed more docile than most. It was a good thing, too, or the simple pandemonium would be feathered chaos.

Kahlan nearly rolled her eyes to hear Chandalen muttering ludicrous apologies to the birds he urged out of his way with a foot. She might have quipped about his risible behavior were it not for the disquieting way he was dressed, with a long knife at his left hip, a short knife at the right, a full quiver over one shoulder, and a strung bow over the other.

More troubling, a coiled *troga* hung from a hook at his

belt. A *troga* was a simple wire long enough to loop and drop over a man's head. It was applied from behind, and then the wooden handles yanked apart. A man of Chandalen's skill could easily and accurately place his *troga* at the joints in a man's neck and silence him before he could make a sound.

When they had fought together against the Imperial Order army that had attacked the city of Ebinissia and butchered the innocent women and children there, Kahlan had more than once seen Chandalen decapitate enemy sentries and soldiers with his *troga*. He wouldn't be carrying his *troga* to battle evil-spirit-chicken-monsters.

His fist held five spears. She guessed the razor-sharp spear points, with their gummy, dark varnished look, were freshly coated with poison. Once so charged, they had to be handled with care.

In the buckskin pouch at his waist, he carried a carved bone box filled with dark paste made by chewing and then cooking *bandu* leaves to render it into ten-step poison. He also carried a few leaves of *quassin doe*, the antidote for ten-step poison, but as the poison's name implied, haste with the *quassin doe* was essential.

"No," Kahlan said, "the Bird Man has not yet found the chicken that is not a chicken. Why are you painted with mud, and so heavily armed? What's going on?"

Chandalen lifted a foot over a chicken that didn't seem to want to move. "My men, the ones on far patrol, have some trouble. I must go see to it."

"Trouble?" Kahlan's arms unfolded. "What sort of trouble?"

Chandalen shrugged. "I am not sure. The man who came for me said there are men with swords—"

"The Order? From the battle fought to the north? It could be some stragglers who got away, or combat scouts. Maybe we can get word to General Reibisch. His army might still be within striking distance, if we can get them to turn back in time."

Chandalen lifted a hand to allay the alarm in her voice.

"No. You and I together fought the men of the Imperial Order. These are not Order troops, or scouts.

"My man does not think they are hostile, but they are reported to be heavily armed and they had a calm about them when approached, which says much. Since I can speak your language, as they do, my men would like my direction with such dangerous-looking people."

Kahlan began to lift her arm to get Richard's attention. "Richard and I had better go with you."

"No. Many people wish to travel our land. We often meet strangers out on the plains. This is my duty. I will take care of it and keep them away from the village. Besides, you two should stay and enjoy your first day as a newly wedded couple."

Without comment, Kahlan glowered at Richard, who was still sorting through the chickens.

Chandalen leaned past her and spoke to the Bird Man, standing a few steps away. *"Honored elder, I must go see to my men. Outsiders approach."*

The Bird Man looked over at the man who was, in effect, his general charged with the defense of the Mud People. *"Be careful. There are wicked spirits about."*

Chandalen nodded. Before he turned away, Kahlan caught his arm. "I don't know about evil spirits, but there are other dangers about. Be careful? Richard is concerned about trouble. If I don't understand his reasons, I trust his instincts."

"You and I have fought together, Mother Confessor." Chandalen winked. "You know I am too strong and too smart for trouble to catch me."

As she watched Chandalen work his way through the milling mass of the chickens, Kahlan asked the Bird Man, *"Have you seen anything . . . suspicious?"*

"I do not yet see the chicken that is not a chicken," the Bird Man said, *"but I will keep looking until I find it."*

Kahlan tried to think of a polite way to ask if he was sober. She decided to ask another question, instead.

"How can you tell the chicken is not a chicken?"

His sun-browned face creased with thought. *"It is something I can sense."*

She decided there was no avoiding it. *"Perhaps, since you were celebrating with drink, you only thought you sensed something?"*

The creases in his face bent with a smile. *"Perhaps the drink relaxed me so that I could see more clearly."*

"And are you still . . . relaxed?"

He folded his arms as he watched the teeming flock.

"I know what I saw."

"How could you tell it was not a chicken?"

He stroked a finger down his nose as he considered her question. Kahlan waited, watching Richard urgently searching through the chickens as if looking for a lost pet.

"At celebrations, such as your wedding," the Bird Man said after a time, *"our men act out stories of our people. Women do not dance the stories, only men. But many stories have women in them. You have seen these stories?"*

"Yes. I watched yesterday as the dancers told the story of the first Mud People: our ancestor mother and father."

He smiled, as if the mention of that particular story touched his heart. It was a smile of private pride in his people.

"If you had arrived during that dance, and did not know anything of our people, would you have known the dancer dressed as the mother of our people was not a woman?"

Kahlan thought it over. The Mud People made elaborate costumes expressly for the dances; they were brought out for no other reason. For Mud People, seeing dancers in the special costumes was awe-inspiring. The men who dressed as women in the stories went to great lengths to make themselves look the part.

"I am not certain, but I think I would recognize they were not women."

"How? What would give them away to you? Are you sure?"

"I don't think I can explain it. Just something not quite

right. I think, looking at them, I would know it was not a woman."

His intent brown-eyed gaze turned to her for the first time. *"And I know it is not a chicken."*

Kahlan entwined her fingers. *"Maybe in the morning, after you have had a good sleep, you will see only a chicken when you look at a chicken?"*

He merely smiled at her suspicion of his impaired judgment. *"You should go eat. Take your new husband. I will send someone for you when I find the chicken that is not a chicken."*

It did sound like a good idea, and she saw Richard heading in their direction. Kahlan clasped the Bird Man's arm in mute appreciation.

It had taken the whole afternoon to gather the chickens. Both structures reserved for evil spirits and a third empty building were needed to house all the birds. Nearly the entire village had joined in the grave cause. It had been a lot of work.

The children had proven invaluable. Fired by responsibility in such an important village-wide effort, they had revealed all the places the chickens hid and roosted. The hunters gently gathered all the chickens, even though it was a Barred Rock the Bird Man had at first pointed out, the same striated breed Richard chased out when they went to see Zedd, the same breed Richard said had waited above the door while they'd been in to see Juni.

An extensive search had been conducted. They were confident every chicken was housed in one of the three buildings.

As he cut a straight line through the chickens, Richard smiled briefly in greeting to the Bird Man, but his eyes never joined in. As Richard's gaze met hers, Kahlan slipped her fingers up his arm to snug around the bulge of muscle, glad to touch him, despite her exasperation.

"The Bird Man says he hasn't yet found the chicken you want, but he will keep searching. And there are still the two other buildings full of them. He suggested we go get something to eat, and he will send someone when he sees your chicken."

Richard started for the door. "He won't find it here."

"What do you mean? How do you know?"

"I have to go check the other two places."

If she was only annoyed, Richard looked frantic at not finding what he wanted. Kahlan imagined that he must feel his word was at stake. Back near the door, Ann and Zedd waited, silently observing the search, letting Richard have the leeway to look all he wanted, to do as he thought necessary.

Richard paused, combing his fingers back through his thick hair. "Do either of you know of a book called *Mountain's Twin*?"

Zedd held his chin as he peered up at the underside of the grass roof in earnest recollection. "Can't say as I do, my boy."

Ann, too, seemed to consider her mental inventory for a time. "No. I've not heard of it."

Richard took a last look at the dusty room packed with chickens and muttered a curse under his breath.

Zedd scratched his ear. "What's in this book, my boy?"

If Richard heard the question over the background of bird babel, he didn't let on, and he didn't answer. "I have to go look at the rest of the chickens."

"I could ask Verna and Warren for you, if it's important." Ann drew a small black book from a pocket, drawing, too, Richard's gaze. "Warren might know of it."

Richard had told Kahlan that the book Ann carried and was now flashing at him, called a journey book, retained ancient magic. Journey books were paired; any message written in it appeared simultaneously in its twin. The Sisters of the Light used the little books to communicate when they went on long journeys, such as when they had come to the New World to take Richard back to the Palace of the Prophets.

Richard brightened at her suggestion. "Please, yes. It's important." He started for the door again. "I've got to go."

"I'm going to check on the woman who lost the baby," Zedd told Ann. "Help her get some rest."

"Richard," Kahlan called, "don't you want to eat?"

As she was speaking, Richard gestured for her to come along, but was through the door and gone before she finished the question. Zedd followed his grandson out, shrugging his perplexity back at the two women. Kahlan growled and started after Richard.

"It must be like a fanciful children's story come to life for you, for a Confessor, to marry for love," Ann commented while remaining rooted to the spot where she had been for the last hour.

Kahlan turned back to the woman. "Well, yes, it is."

Ann smiled up with sincere warmth. "I'm so happy for you, child, being able to have such a wonderful thing as a husband you dearly love come into your life."

Kahlan's fingers lingered on the lever of the closed door. "It still leaves me utterly astonished, at times."

"It must be disappointing when your new husband seems to have more important things to attend to than his new wife, when he seems to be ignoring you." Ann pursed her lips. "Especially on your very first day being his wife."

"Ah." Kahlan released the lever and clasped both hands loosely behind her back. "So that's why Zedd left. We are to have a woman-to-woman talk, are we?"

Ann chuckled. "Oh, but how I do love it when men I respect marry smart women. Nothing marks a man's character better than his attraction to intelligence."

Kahlan sighed as she leaned a shoulder against the wall. "I know Richard, and I know he's not trying my patience deliberately . . . but, this is our first day married. I somehow thought it would be different than this . . . this chasing imaginary chicken monsters. I think he's so worried about protecting me he's inventing trouble."

Ann's tone turned sympathetic. "Richard loves you dearly. I know he is worried, though I don't understand his reasoning. Richard bears great responsibility."

The sympathy evaporated from her voice. "We all are called upon to make sacrifices where Richard is concerned."

The woman pretended to watch the chickens.

"In this very village, before the snow came," Kahlan said in a careful, level tone, "I gave Richard over to your Sisters of the Light in the hope you could save his life, even though I knew doing so could very well end my future with him. I had to make him think I had betrayed him in order to get him to go with the Sisters. Do you even have any idea . . ."

Kahlan made herself stop, lest she needlessly dredge up painful memories. Everything had turned out well. She and Richard were together at last. That was what mattered.

"I know," Ann whispered. "You do not have to prove yourself to me, but since it was I who ordered him brought to us, perhaps I must prove myself to you."

The woman had surely picked the peg Kahlan wanted pounded, but she kept her response civil, anyway. "What do you mean?"

"Those wizards of so very long ago created the Palace of the Prophets. I lived at the palace, under its unique spell, for over nine hundred years. There, five hundred years before it was to happen, Nathan the prophet foretold the birth of a war wizard.

"There, together, we worked on the books of prophecy down in the palace vaults, trying to understand this pebble yet to be dropped into the pond, trying to foresee the ripples this event might cause."

Kahlan folded her arms. "From my experience, I would say prophecy may be far more occluding than revealing."

Ann chortled. "I am acquainted with Sisters hundreds of years your senior who have yet to understand that much about prophecy."

Her voice turned wistful as she went on. "I traveled to see Richard when he was newborn life, newborn soul, glimmering into the world. His mother was so astonished, so grateful, for the balance of such a magnificent gift come of such brutality as had been inflicted upon her by Darken

Rahl. She was a remarkable woman, not to pass bitterness and resentment on to her child. She was so proud of Richard, so filled with dreams and hope for him.

"When Richard was that newborn life, suckling at his mother's breast, Nathan and I took Richard's stepfather to recover the Book of Counted Shadows so when Richard was grown he might have the knowledge to save himself from the beast who had raped his mother and given him life."

Ann glanced up with a wry smile. "Prophecy, you see."

"Richard told me." Kahlan looked back at the Bird Man concentrating on the chickens pecking at the ground.

"Richard is the one come at last: a war wizard. The prophecies do not say if he will succeed, but he is the one born to the battle—the battle to keep the Grace intact, as it were. Such faith, though, sometimes requires great spiritual effort."

"Why? If he is the one for whom you waited—the one you wanted?"

Ann cleared her throat and seemed to gather her thoughts. Kahlan thought she saw tears in the woman's eyes.

"He destroyed the Palace of the Prophets. Because of Richard, Nathan escaped. Nathan is dangerous. He is the one, after all, who told you the names of the chimes. That perilously rash act could have brought us all to ruin."

"It saved Richard's life," Kahlan pointed out. "If Nathan hadn't told me the names of the chimes, Richard would be dead. Then your pebble would be at the bottom of the pond—out of your reach and no help to anyone."

"True enough," Ann admitted—reluctantly, thought Kahlan.

Kahlan fussed with a button as she began to imagine Ann's side of it. "It must have been hard to bear, seeing Richard destroying the palace. Destroying your home."

"Along with the palace, he also destroyed its spell; the Sisters of the Light will now age as does everyone else. At the palace I would have lived perhaps another hundred years. The Sisters there would have lived many hundreds of years more. Now, I am but an old woman near the end of my time. Richard took those hundreds of years from me. From all the Sisters."

Kahlan remained silent, not knowing what to say.

"The future of everyone may one day depend on him," Ann finally said. "We must put that ahead of ourselves. That is why I helped him destroy the palace. That is why I follow the man who has seemingly destroyed my life's work: because my life's true work *is* that man's fight, not my own narrow interests."

Kahlan hooked a strand of damp hair behind her ear. "You talk about Richard as if he's a tool newly forged for your use. He is a man who wants to do what's right, but he has his own wants and needs, too. His life is his to live, not yours or anyone else's to plan for him according to what you found in dusty old books."

"You misunderstand. That is precisely his value: his instincts, his curiosity, his heart." Ann tapped her temple. "His mind. Our aim is not to direct, but to follow, even if it is painful to tread the path down which he takes us."

Kahlan knew the truth of that. Richard had destroyed the alliance that had joined the lands of the Midlands for thousands of years. As Mother Confessor, Kahlan presided over the council, and thus the Midlands. Under her watch as Mother Confessor, the Midlands had fallen to Richard, as Lord Rahl of D'Hara. At least the lands which had so far surrendered to him. She knew the benevolence of his actions, and the need for them, but it certainly had been a painful path to follow.

Richard's bold action, though, was the only way of truly uniting all the lands into one force that had any hope of standing against the tyranny of the Imperial Order. Now, they trod that new path together, hand in hand, united in purpose and resolve.

Kahlan folded her arms again and leaned back against the wall, watching the stupid chickens. "If it is your intent, then, to make me feel guilty for my selfish wishes about my first day with my new husband, you have succeeded. But I can't help it."

Ann gently gripped Kahlan's arm. "No, child, that is not my intent. I understand how Richard's actions can sometimes be exasperating. I ask only that you be patient and allow him to do as he thinks he must. He is not ignoring you to be contrary, but doing as his nature demands.

"However, his love for you has the power to distract him from what he must do. You must not interfere by asking that he abandon his task when he otherwise would not."

"I know," Kahlan sighed. "But chickens—"

"There is something wrong with the magic."

Kahlan frowned down at the old sorceress. "What do you mean?"

Ann shrugged. "I am not sure. Zedd and I believe we have detected a change in our magic. It is a subtle thing to endeavor to discern. Have you noticed any change in your ability?"

In a cold flash of panic, Kahlan wheeled her thoughts inward. It was hard to imagine a subtle difference in her Confessor's magic—it simply was. The core of the power within, and her restraint on it, seemed comfortingly familiar. Although . . .

Kahlan recoiled from that dark curtain of conjecture.

Magic was ethereal enough as it was. Through artifice, a wizard had once gulled her into thinking her power gone, when in fact it had never left her. Believing him had nearly cost Kahlan her life. She survived only because she realized in time that she still had her power and could use it to save herself.

"No. It's the same," Kahlan said. "I've learned it's easy to mislead yourself into believing your magic is waning. It's probably nothing—you're just worried, that's all."

"True enough, but Zedd thinks it would be wise to let Richard do as Richard does. That Richard believes, on his own, without our knowledge of magic, that there is grave trouble of some sort, lends credence to our suspicions. If true, then he is already farther in this than are we. We can but follow."

Ann returned the gnarled hand to Kahlan's arm. "I would

ask you not to badger him with your understandable desire to have him pay court to you. I ask that you allow him to do what he must do."

Pay court indeed. Kahlan simply wanted to hold his hand, to hug him, to kiss him, to smile at him and have him smile back.

The next day they needed to return to Aydindril. Soon the thorn of mystery over Juni's death would be shed for more important concerns. They had Emperor Jagang and the war to worry about. She simply wished she and Richard could have one day to themselves.

"I understand." Kahlan stared out at the clucking, churning, throng of stupid chickens. "I'll try not to meddle."

Ann nodded without joy at having gotten what she wanted.

Outside, in the gloom of nightfall, Cara paced. By her chafed expression, Kahlan guessed Richard had ordered the Mord-Sith to remain behind and guard his new wife. That was the one order inviolate for Cara, the one order even Kahlan could not invalidate for the woman.

"Come on," Kahlan said as she tramped past Cara. "Let's go see how Richard is doing in his search."

Kahlan was discontent to find the miserable rain still coming down. If it wasn't falling as hard as before, it was just as cold, and it wouldn't be long before she was just as wet.

"He didn't go that way," Cara called out.

Kahlan turned along with Ann to see Cara still standing where she had been pacing.

Kahlan lifted a thumb over her shoulder in the direction of the other house for evil spirits. "I thought he wanted to go see the rest of the chickens."

"He started toward the other two buildings, but changed his mind." Cara pointed. "He went off in that direction."

"Why?"

"He didn't say. He told me to remain here and wait for you." Cara started out through the rain. "Come. I will take you to him."

"You know where to find him?" Kahlan realized it was a foolish question before she had finished it.

"Of course. I am bonded to Lord Rahl. I always know where he is."

Kahlan found it disquieting the way the Mord-Sith could sense Richard's proximity, like mother hens with a chick. Kahlan was envious, too. She pressed a hand to Ann's back, urging her along, lest they be left behind in the dark.

"How long have you and Zedd had this suspicion about something being wrong," Kahlan whispered to the squat sorceress, only implying that she meant what Ann had told her about there being something wrong with the magic.

Ann kept her head bowed, watching where she was walking in the near darkness. "We noticed it first last night. Though it is a difficult thing to quantify, or confirm, we did a few simple tests. They did not conclusively verify our impression. It's a bit like trying to say if you can see as far as you could yesterday."

"You telling her about our speculation that our magic might be weakening?"

Kahlan started at the familiar voice suddenly coming from behind.

"Yes," Ann said over her shoulder as they followed Cara around a corner, sounding as if she wasn't at all surprised that Zedd had come up behind them. "How was the woman?"

Zedd sighed. "Despondent. I tried to calm and comfort her, but I didn't seem to have as much luck as I thought I might."

"Zedd," Kahlan interrupted, "are you saying you're sure there is trouble? That's a serious assertion."

"Well, no, I'm not asserting anything—"

The three of them bumped into Cara when she halted unexpectedly in the dark. Cara stood stock-still, staring off into rainy nothingness. At last, she growled under her breath and pushed at their shoulders, turning them around.

"Wrong way," she grumbled. "Back this way."

Cara pushed and prodded them back to the corner and then led them the other way. It was nearly impossible to see where they were going. Kahlan wiped wet hair from her face. She didn't see anyone else out in the foul weather. In the whispering rain, with Cara out in front and Zedd and Ann carrying on a hushed conversation several paces behind, Kahlan felt alone and forlorn.

The rain and darkness must have confused Cara perceiving Richard's location by her bond to him; she had to backtrack several times.

"How much farther?" Kahlan asked.

"Not far" was all Cara had to offer.

As she slogged through the passageways-turned-quagmire, mud had found its way into Kahlan's boots. She grimaced at the feel of the cold slime squeezing between her toes with each step. She dearly wished she could wash out her boots. She was cold, wet, tired, and muddy—all because Richard feared there was some stupid evil-spirit-chicken-monster on the loose.

She recalled with longing the warm bath of that morning, and wished she were there again.

Remembering Juni's death, she reconsidered. There were worse problems than her selfish wish for warmth. If Zedd and Ann were right about the magic . . .

They reached the open area in the center of the village. The living shadow that was Cara halted. Rain drummed on roofs to run in rills from eaves, spattered mud, and splashed in puddles made of every footstep.

The Mord-Sith lifted an arm and pointed. "There."

Kahlan squinted, trying to see through the drizzle of rain. She felt Zedd press close at her right and Ann at her left. Cara, off to the side just a bit, with the manifest vision of her bond, watched Richard, while the rest of them scanned the darkness trying to spot what she saw.

It was the diminutive fire that suddenly caught Kahlan's attention. Petite languid flames licked up into the wet air.

That it burned at all was astonishing. It appeared to be a remnant of their wedding bonfire. Impossibly, in the daylong downpour, this tiny refuge of their sacred ceremony survived.

Richard stood before the fire, watching it. Kahlan could just make out his towering contour. The knife edge of his golden cloak lifted in the wind, reflecting sparkles of the miraculous firelight.

She could see raindrops splattering on the toe of his boot as he used it to nudge the fire. The flames grew as high as his knee as he stirred whatever was still burning in all the rain. The wind whipped the flames around in a fiery gambol, red and yellow arms swaying and waving, prancing and fluttering, undulating in a spellbinding dance of hot light amid the cold dark rain.

Richard snuffed the fire.

Kahlan almost cursed him.

"Sentrosi," he murmured, grinding his boot to smother the embers.

The chill wind lifted a glowing spark upward. Richard tried to snatch it in his fist, but the kernel of radiance, on the wings of a gust, evaded him to disappear into the murky night.

"Bags," Zedd muttered in a surly voice, "that boy finds a pocket of rock pitch still burning in an old log, and he's ready to believe the impossible."

Civility fled Ann's voice. "We have more important things to do than to entertain the cockamamy conjecture of the uneducated."

Aggravated and in agreement, Zedd wiped a hand across his face. "It could be a thousand and one things, and he's settled on the one, because he's never heard of the other thousand."

Ann shook a finger up at Zedd. "That boy's ignorance is—"

"That's one of the three chimes," Kahlan said, cutting Ann off. "What does it mean?"

Both Zedd and Ann turned and stared at her, as if they had forgotten she was still there with them.

"It's not important," Ann insisted. "The point is we have consequential matters which require attention, and the boy is wasting time worrying about the chimes."

"What is the meaning of the word—"

Zedd cleared his throat, warning Kahlan not to speak aloud the name of the second chime.

Kahlan's brow drew down as she leaned toward the old wizard.

"What does it mean?"

"Fire," he said at last.

CHAPTER 9

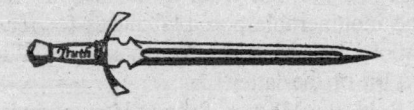

KAHLAN SAT UP AND rubbed her eyes as thunder boomed outside. The storm sounded rekindled. She squinted, trying to see in the dim light. Richard wasn't beside her. She didn't know what time of night it was, but they'd gotten to bed late. She sensed it was the middle of darkness, nowhere near morning. She decided Richard must have gone outside to relieve himself.

Heavy rain against the roof made it sound as if she were under a waterfall. On their first visit, Richard had used the spirit house to teach the Mud People how to make tile roofs that wouldn't leak in the rain as did their grass roofs, so this was probably the driest structure in the entire village.

People had been enthralled by the idea of roofs that didn't leak. She imagined it wouldn't be too many years before the entire village was converted from grass roofs to tile. She, for one, was grateful for the dry sanctuary.

Kahlan hoped Richard was starting to simmer down now that they knew there was nothing sinister in Juni's death. He'd had his look at every chicken in the village, as had the Bird Man, and neither man had found a chicken that wasn't a chicken. Or a feathered monster of any sort, for that matter. The issue was settled. In the morning, the men would turn the flocks loose.

Zedd and Ann were not at all happy with Richard. If Richard really believed the burning pitch pocket was a chime—a thing from the underworld—then just what in Creation did he suppose he was going to do with it if he caught it in his fist? Richard hadn't thought of that, or else kept silent for fear of giving Zedd more reason to think him lacking in good sense.

At least Zedd was not cruel in his lengthy lecturing on some of the innumerable possible causes for recent events. It leaned more toward educating than castigating, though there was a bit of the latter.

Richard Rahl, the Master of the D'Haran empire, the man to whom kings and queens bowed, the man to whom nations had surrendered, stood mute as his grandfather paced back and forth admonishing, preaching, and teaching, at times speaking as First Wizard, at times as Richard's grandfather, and at times as his friend.

Kahlan knew Richard respected Zedd too much to say anything; if Zedd was disappointed, then so be it.

Before they'd retired for the night, Ann told them she'd received a reply in her journey book. Verna and Warren knew the book Richard had asked about, *Mountain's Twin*. Verna wrote that it was a book of prophecy, mostly, but had been in Jagang's possession. At Nathan's instructions, she and Warren had destroyed it along with all the other books

Nathan named, except *The Book of Inversion and Duplex*, which Jagang didn't have.

When they had finally gotten to bed, Richard seemed sullen, or at least distracted with inner thoughts. He was in no mood to make love to her. The truth be known, after the day they'd had, she wasn't unhappy about it.

Kahlan sighed. Their second night together, and they were in no mood to be intimate. How many times had she ached for the chance to be with him?

Kahlan flopped back down, pressing a hand over her weary eyes. She wished Richard would hurry and come back to bed before she fell asleep. She wanted to kiss him, at least, and tell him she knew he was only doing as he thought best, doing what he thought right, and to tell him she didn't think him foolish for it. She hadn't been angry, really— she'd simply wanted to be with him, not out in the rain all day collecting chickens.

She wanted to tell him she loved him.

She turned on her side, toward his missing form, to wait. Her eyelids drooped, and she had to force them open. When she went to put a hand over the blanket where he belonged, she realized he'd put his half of the blanket over her. Why would he do that, if he would be right back?

Kahlan sat up. She rubbed her eyes again. In the dim light from the small fire she saw that his clothes were gone.

It had been a long day. They hadn't gotten much sleep the night before. Why would he be out in the rain in the middle of the night? They needed sleep. In the morning they had to leave. They had to get back to Aydindril.

Morning. They were leaving in the morning. He had until then.

Kahlan growled as she scurried across the floor to their things. He was out looking for proof of some sort. She knew he was. Something to show them he wasn't being foolish.

She groped through her pack until her fingers found her little candle holder. It had a conical roof so it would stay dry and burn in the rain. She retrieved a long splinter from beside the hearth, lit it in the fire, and then lit the candle.

She closed the little glass door to keep the wind from blowing out the flame. The holder and candle were diminutive and didn't provide much light, but it was the best she had and better than nothing on a pitch black night in the rain.

Kahlan yanked her damp shirt from the pole Richard had set up beside the fire. The touch of cold wet cloth against her flesh as she poked her arms through the sleeves sent a shuddering ache through her shoulders. She was going to give her new husband a lecture of her own. She would insist he come back to bed and put his arms dutifully around her until she was once again warm. It was his fault she was already shivering. Grimacing, she drew her frigid soggy pants up her bare legs.

What proof could he be going to look for? The chicken?

Drying her hair by the fire, before bed, Kahlan had asked him why he believed he had seen the very same chicken several times. Richard said the dead chicken outside the spirit house that morning had a dark mark on the right side of its upper beak, just below its comb. He said the chicken the Bird Man had pointed out had the same mark.

Richard hadn't made the connection until later. He said the chicken waiting above the door to where Juni's body lay had the same mark on the side of its beak. He said none of the chickens in the three buildings had such a mark.

Kahlan pointed out that chickens pecked at the ground all the time and it was raining and muddy, so it was probably dirt. Moreover, dirt and such was probably on the beaks of more than one bird. It simply washed off as they were being carried through the rain to the buildings.

The Mud People were positive they had collected every chicken in the village, so the chicken for which he was searching had to be one of the chickens in the three buildings. Richard had no answer for that.

She asked why this one chicken—risen from the dead—would have been following them around all day. To what purpose? Richard had no answer for that, either.

Kahlan realized she hadn't been very supportive. She knew Richard was not given to flights of fancy. His persistence wasn't really bullheaded, nor was it meant to rile her.

She should have listened more receptively, more tenderly. She was his wife. If he couldn't count on her, then who? No wonder he hadn't been in the mood to make love to her. But a chicken . . .

Kahlan pushed open the door to be greeted by a sodden gust. Cara had gone to bed. The hunters protecting the spirit house spotted her and rushed over to gather around. All their eyes stared up at her candlelit face floating in the rainy darkness. Their glistening bodies materialized like apparitions whenever lightning crackled.

"Which way did Richard go?" she asked.

The men blinked dumbly.

"Richard," she repeated. *"He is not inside. He left a while ago. Which way did he go?"*

One of the men looked at all his fellows, checking, before he spoke. All had given him a shake of their heads.

"We saw no one. It is dark, but still, we would see him if he came out."

Kahlan sighed. *"Maybe not. Richard was a woods guide. The night is his element. He can make himself disappear in the dark the same way you can disappear in the grass."*

The men nodded with this news, not the least bit dubious. *"Then he is out here, somewhere, but we do not know where. Sometimes, Richard with the Temper can be like a spirit. He is like no man we have ever seen before."*

Kahlan smiled to herself. Richard was a rare person—the mark of a wizard.

The hunters one time had taken him to shoot arrows, and he had astonished them by ruining all the arrows he shot. He put them in the center of the target, one on top of the other, each splitting apart the one before.

Richard's gift guided his arrows, though he didn't believe it; he thought it simply a matter of practice and concentration. "Calling the target" was how he termed it. He said he called the target to him, letting everything else vanish, and when he felt the arrow find that singular spot in the air, he loosed it. He could do it in a blink.

Kahlan had to admit that when he taught her to shoot, she could sometimes feel what he meant. What he had taught her had even once saved her life. Even so, she knew magic was involved.

The hunters had great respect for Richard. Shooting arrows was only part of it. It was hard not to have respect for Richard. If she said he could be invisible, they had no reason to doubt it.

It had almost started out very badly. At the first meeting out on the plains, when Kahlan had brought him to the Mud People, Richard had misunderstood the greeting of a slap, and had clouted Savidlin, one of their leaders. By doing so he had inadvertently honored their strength and made a valuable friend, but had also earned him the name "Richard with the Temper."

Kahlan wiped rain water from her face. *"All right. I want to find him."* She signaled off into the darkness. *"Each of you, go a different way. If you find him, tell him I want him. If you don't see him, meet back here after you have looked in your direction, and we will go off in new places, until we find him."*

They started to object, but she told them she was tired and wanted to get back to bed, and she wanted her new husband with her. She pleaded with them to just please help her, or she would search alone.

It occurred to her that Richard was doing that very thing: searching alone, because no one believed him.

Reluctantly, the men agreed and scattered in different directions, vanishing into the darkness. Without cumbersome boots, they didn't have the time she did navigating the mud.

Kahlan pulled off her boots and tossed them back by the door to the spirit house. She smiled to herself at having outwitted that much of the mud.

There were any number of women back in Aydindril, from nobility, to officials, to wives of officials, who, if they could have seen the Mother Confessor at that moment, bare-foot, ankle-deep in mud, and soaked to the skin, would have fainted.

Kahlan slopped out into the mud, trying to imagine if Richard would have any method to his search. Richard rarely did anything without reason. How would he go about searching the entire village by himself in the dark?

Kahlan reconsidered her first thought, that he was searching for the chicken. Maybe he realized that the things she, Zedd, and Ann said made sense. Maybe he wasn't looking for a chicken. But then what was he doing out in the middle of the night?

Rain pelted her scalp, running down her neck and back, making her shiver. Her long hair, which she had so laboriously dried and brushed, was now again loaded with water. Her shirt clung to her like a second skin. A miserably cold one.

Where would Richard have gone?

Kahlan paused and held up the candle.

Juni.

Maybe he went to see Juni. She felt a stab of heartache; maybe he had gone to look at the dead baby. He might have wanted to go grieve for both.

That would be something Richard would do. He might have wanted to pray to the good spirits on behalf of the two souls new to the spirit world. Richard would do that.

Kahlan walked under an unseen streamlet of icy cold run-off from a roof, gasping as it caught her in her face, dousing the front of her. She pulled back wet strands of hair and spat some out of her mouth as she moved on. Having to hold up the candle in the frigid rain was numbing her fingers.

She searched carefully in the dark, trying to tell exactly where she was, to confirm she was going the right way. She found a familiar low wall with three herb pots. No one lived anywhere near; they were the herbs grown for the evil spirits housed not far away. She knew the way from there.

A little farther and then around a corner she found the

door to the house for the dead. Fumbling with unfeeling fingers, she located the latch. The door, swollen in the rain, stuck enough to squeak. She stepped through the doorway and eased closed the door behind her.

"Richard? Richard, are you in here?"

No answer. She held up the candle. With her other hand she covered her nose against the smell. She could taste the stink on her tongue.

Light from her candle's little window fell across the platform with the tiny body. She stepped closer, wincing when she felt a hard bug pop under her bare foot, but the tragedy lying there on the platform before her immediately deadened her care.

The sight held her immobilized. Little arms were frozen in space. Legs were stiff, with just an inch of air under the heels. Tiny hands cupped open. Such wee little fingers seemed impossible.

Kahlan felt a lump swell in her throat. She covered her mouth to stifle the unexpected cry for the might-have-been. The poor thing. The poor mother.

Behind, she heard an odd repetitious sound. As she stared at the little lifeless form, she idly tried to make sense of the soft staccato smacking. It paused. It started. It paused again. She absently dismissed it as the drip of water.

Unable to resist, Kahlan reached out. She tenderly settled her finger into the cup of the tiny hand. Her single finger was all the palm would hold. She almost expected the fingers to close around hers. But they didn't.

She stifled another sob, feeling a tear roll down her cheek. She felt so sorry for the mother. Kahlan had seen so much death, so many bodies, she didn't know why this one should affect her so, but it did.

She broke down and wept over the unnamed child. In the lonely house for the dead, her heart poured out for this life unlived, this vessel delivered into the world without a soul.

The sound behind at last intruded sufficiently that she

turned to see what disturbed her prayer to the good spirits.

Kahlan gasped in her sob with a backward cry.

There, standing on Juni's chest, was a chicken.

It was pecking out Juni's eyes.

CHAPTER 10

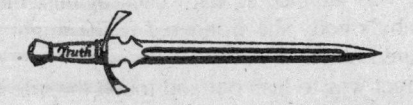

KAHLAN WANTED TO CHASE the chicken away from the body, but she couldn't seem to make herself do so. The chicken's eye rolled to watch her as it pecked.

Thwack thwack thwack. Thwack. Thwack. That was the sound she had heard.

"Shoo!" She flicked a hand out toward the bird. "Shoo!"

It must have come for the bugs. That was why it was in there. For the bugs.

Somehow, she couldn't make herself believe it.

"Shoo! Leave him alone!"

Hissing, hackles lifting, the chicken's head rose.

Kahlan pulled back.

Its claws digging into stiff dead flesh, the chicken slowly turned to face her. It cocked its head, making its comb flop, its wattles sway.

"Shoo," Kahlan heard herself whisper.

There wasn't enough light, and besides, the side of its

beak was covered with gore, so she couldn't tell if it had the dark spot. But she didn't need to see it.

"Dear spirits, help me," she prayed under her breath.

The bird let out a slow chicken cackle. It sounded like a chicken, but in her heart she knew it wasn't.

In that instant, she completely understood the concept of a chicken that was not a chicken. This looked like a chicken, like most of the Mud People's chickens. But this was no chicken.

This was evil manifest.

She could feel it with visceral certitude. This was something as obscene as death's own grin.

With one hand, Kahlan wrung her shirt closed at her throat. She was jammed so hard back against the platform with the baby's body she wondered if she might topple the solid mortared mass.

Her instinct was to lash out and touch the vile thing with her Confessor's power. Her magic destroyed forever the essence of a person, creating in the void a total and unqualified devotion to the Confessor. In that way, those condemned to death truthfully confessed their heinous crimes—or their innocence. It was an ultimate means of witnessing the veracity of justice.

There was no immunity to the touch of a Confessor. It was as absolute as it was final. Even the most maniacal murderer had a soul and so was vulnerable.

Her power, her magic, was also a weapon of defense. But it would only work on people. It would not work on a chicken. And it would not work on wickedness incarnate.

Her gaze flicked toward the door, checking the distance. The chicken took a single hop toward her. Claws gripping Juni's upper arm, it leaned her way. Her leg muscles tightened till they trembled.

The chicken backed a step, tensed, and spurted feces onto Juni's face.

It let out the cackle that sounded like a laugh.

She dearly wished she could tell herself she was being silly. Imagining things.

96

But she knew better.

Much as her power would not work to destroy this thing, she sensed, too, that her ostensible size and strength were meaningless against it. Far better, she thought, just to get out.

More than anything, that was what she wanted: out.

A fat brown bug scurried up her arm. She let out a clipped cry as she smacked it off. She shuffled a step toward the door.

The chicken leaped off Juni, landing before the door.

Kahlan frantically tried to think as the chicken bawk-bawk-bawked. It pecked up the bug she had flicked off her arm. After downing the bug, it turned to look up at her, its head cocking this way, then that, its wattles swinging.

Kahlan eyed the door. She tried to reason how best to get out. Kick the chicken out of the way? Try to frighten it away from the door? Ignore it and try to walk past it?

She remembered what Richard said. *"Juni spat at the honor of whatever killed that chicken. Not long after, Juni died. I threw a stick at the chicken in the window, and not long after, it attacked that little boy. It was my fault Ungi got clawed. I don't want to make the same mistake again."*

She didn't want to make that mistake. This thing could fly at her face. Scratch her eyes out. Use its spur to tear open the carotid artery at the side of her neck. Bleed her to death. Who knew how strong it really was, what it might be able to do.

Richard had been adamant about everyone being courteous to the chickens. Suddenly Kahlan's life or death hung on Richard's words. Only a short time before she had thought them foolish. Now, she was weighing her chances, marking her choices, by what Richard had said.

"Oh, Richard," she implored in a whisper, "forgive me."

She felt something on her toes. A quick glance was not enough in the dim light to see for sure, but she thought she saw bugs crawling over her feet. She felt one scurry up her ankle, up under her pant leg. She stamped her foot. The bug clung tight.

She bent to swat at the thing under her pant leg. She wanted it off. She smacked too hard, squashing it against her shin.

She straightened in a rush to swipe at things crawling in her hair. She yelped when a centipede bit the back of her hand. She shook it off. As it hit the floor, the chicken plucked it up and ate it.

With a flap of wings, the chicken suddenly sprang back up on top of Juni. Claws working with luxuriant excess, it turned slowly atop the body to peer at her. One black eye watched with icy interest. Kahlan slipped one foot toward the door.

"Mother," the chicken croaked.

Kahlan flinched with a cry.

She tried to slow her breathing. Her heart hammered so hard it felt like her neck must be bulging. Flesh scraped from her fingers as they gripped at the rough platform behind.

It must have made a sound that sounded like the word "Mother." She was the Mother Confessor, and was used to hearing the word "Mother." She was simply frightened and had imagined it.

She yelped again when something bit her ankle. Flailing at a bug running under her shirtsleeve, she accidentally swatted the candle off the platform behind her. It hit the dirt floor with a clink.

In an instant, the room fell pitch black.

She spun around, scraping madly at something wriggling up between her shoulder blades, under her hair. By the weight, and the squeak, it had to be a mouse. Mercifully, as she twisted and whirled about, it was flung off.

Kahlan froze. She tried to hear if the chicken had moved, if it had jumped to the floor. The room was dead silent except for the rapid whooshing of her heart in her ears.

She began shuffling toward the door. As she scuffed through the fetid straw, she dearly wished she had worn her boots. The stench was gagging. She didn't think she would ever feel clean again. She didn't care, though, if she could just get out alive.

In the dark, the chicken thing let out a low chicken cackle laugh.

It hadn't come from where she expected the chicken to be. It was behind her.

"Please, I mean no harm," she called into the darkness. "I mean no disrespect. I will leave you to your business now, if that's all right with you."

She took another shuffling step toward the door. She moved carefully, slowly, in case the chicken thing was in the way. She didn't want to bump into it and make it angry. She mustn't underestimate it.

Kahlan had on any number of occasions thrown herself with ferocity against seemingly invincible foes. She knew well the value of a resolute violent attack. But she also somehow knew beyond doubt that this adversary could, if it wanted, kill her as easily as she could wring a real chicken's neck. If she forced a fight, this was one she would lose.

Her shoulder touched the wall. She slid a hand along the plastered mud brick, groping blindly for the door. It wasn't there. She felt along the wall in each direction. There was no door.

That was crazy. She had come in through the door. There had to be a door. The chicken thing let out a whispering cackle.

Sniffling back tears of fright, Kahlan turned and pressed her back to the wall. She must have gotten confused when she turned around, getting the mouse off her back. She was turned around, that was all. The door hadn't moved. She was just turned around.

Then, in which direction was the door?

Her eyes were open as wide as they would go, trying to see in the inky darkness. A new terror stabbed into her thoughts: What if the chicken-thing pecked her eyes out? What if that was what it liked to do? Peck out eyes.

She heard herself sobbing in panic. Rain leaked through the grass roof. When it dripped on her head she flinched. Lightning struck again. Kahlan saw the light come through the wall to the left. No, it was the door. Light was coming in around the edge of the door. Thunder boomed.

Frantic, she raced for the door. In the dark, she caught the edge of a platform with a hip. Her toes slammed into the brick corner. Reflexively, she grabbed at the stunning pain. Hopping on her other foot to keep her balance, she came down on something hard. Burning pain seared her foot. She grasped for a handhold, recoiling when she felt the hard little body under her hand. She went down with a crash.

Cursing under her breath, she realized she had stepped on the hot candle holder. She comforted her foot. It hadn't really burned her; her frantic fear only made her envision the hot metal burning her. Her other foot, though, bled from smacking the brick.

Kahlan took a deep breath. She must not panic, she admonished herself, or she would not be able to help herself. No one else was going to get her out of here. She had to gather her senses and stay calm enough to escape the house of the dead.

She took another breath. All she had to do was reach the door, and then she would be able to leave. She would be safe.

She felt the floor ahead as she inched forward on her belly. The straw was damp, whether from the rain or from the foul things draining from the platforms, she didn't know. She told herself the Mud People respected the dead. They would not leave filthy straw in there. It must be clean. Then why did it stink so?

With great effort, Kahlan ignored the bugs skittering over her. When her concentration on remaining silent wandered, she could hear little pules escape her throat. With her face right at the floor, she saw the next lightning flash under the door. It wasn't far.

She didn't know where the chicken had gone. She prayed it would go back to pecking at Juni's eyes.

With the next flash of lightning, she saw chicken feet standing between her and the crack under the door. The thing wasn't more than a foot from her face.

Kahlan slowly moved a trembling hand to her brow to cup it over her eyes. She knew that any instant, the chicken-monster-thing was going to peck her eyes, just like it pecked Juni's eyes. She panted in terror at the mental image of having her eyes pecked out. Of blood running from ragged, hollow sockets.

She would be blind. She would be helpless. She would never again see Richard's gray eyes smiling at her.

A bug wriggled in her hair, trying to free itself from a tangle. Kahlan brushed at it, failing to get it off.

Suddenly, something hit her head. She cried out. The bug was gone. The chicken had pecked it off her head. Her scalp stung from the sharp hit.

"Thank you," she forced herself to say to the chicken. "Thank you very much. I appreciate it."

She shrieked when the beak struck out, hitting her arm. It was a bug. The chicken hadn't pecked at her arm, but had gobbled up a bug.

"Sorry I screamed," she said. Her voice shook. "You startled me, that's all. Thank you again."

The beak struck hard on the top of her head. This time, there was no bug. Kahlan didn't know if the chicken-thing thought there was, or if it meant to peck her head. It stung fiercely.

She moved her hand back to her eyes. "Please, don't do that. It hurts. Please don't peck me."

The beak pinched the vein on the back of her hand over her eyes. The chicken tugged, as if trying to pull a worm from the ground.

It was a command. It wanted her hand away from her eyes.

The beak gave a sharp tug on her skin. There was no

mistaking the meaning in that insistent yank. Move the hand, now, it was saying, or you'll be sorry.

If she made it angry, there was no telling what it was capable of doing to her. Juni lay dead above her as a reminder of the possibilities.

She told herself that if it pecked at her eyes, she would have to grab it and try to wring its neck. If she was quick, it could only get in one peck. She would have one eye left. She would have to fight it then. But only if it went for her eyes.

Her instincts screamed that such action would be the most foolish, dangerous thing she could do. Both the Bird Man and Richard said this was not a chicken. She no longer doubted them. But she might have no choice.

If she started, it would be a fight to the death. She held no illusion as to her chances. Nonetheless, she might be forced to fight it. With her last breath, if need be, as her father had taught her.

The chicken snatched a bigger beakful of her skin along with the vein and twisted. Last warning.

Kahlan carefully moved her trembling hand away. The chicken-thing cackled softly with satisfaction.

Lightning flashed again. She didn't need the light, though. It was only inches away. Close enough to feel its breath.

"Please, don't hurt me?"

Thunder crashed so loud it hurt. The chicken squawked and spun around.

She realized it wasn't thunder, but the door bursting open.

"Kahlan!" It was Richard. "Where are you!"

She sprang to her feet. "Richard! Look out! It's the chicken! It's the chicken!"

Richard grabbed for it. The chicken shot between his legs and out the door.

Kahlan went to throw her arms around him, but he blocked her way as he snatched the bow off the shoulder of one of the hunters standing outside. Before the hunter could shy from the sudden lunge, Richard had plucked an arrow from the quiver over the man's shoulder. In the next instant the arrow was nocked and the string drawn to cheek.

The chicken dashed madly across the mud, down the passageway. The halting flickers of lightning seemed to freeze the chicken in midstride, each flash revealing it with arresting light, and each flash showing it yet farther away.

With a twang of the bowstring, the arrow zipped away into the night.

Kahlan heard the steel tipped arrow hit with a solid thunk.

In the lightning, she saw the chicken turn to look back at them. The arrow had caught it square in the back of the head. The front half of the arrow protruded from between its parted beak. Blood ran down the shaft, dripping off the arrow's point. It dripped in puddles and matted the bird's hackles.

The hunter let out a low whistle of admiration for the shot.

The night went dark as thunder rolled and boomed. The next flash of lightning showed the chicken sprinting around a corner.

Kahlan followed Richard as he bolted after the fleeing bird. The hunter handed Richard another arrow as they ran. Richard nocked it and put tension on the string, holding it at the ready as they charged around the corner.

All three slowed to a halt. There, in the mud, in the middle of the passageway, lay the bloody arrow. The chicken was nowhere to be seen.

"Richard," Kahlan panted, "I believe you now."

"I figured as much," he said.

From behind, they heard a great "whoosh."

Poking their heads back around the corner, they saw the roof of the place where the dead were prepared for burial go up in flames. Through the open door, she saw the floor of straw afire.

"I had a candle. It fell into the straw. But the flame went out," Kahlan said. "I'm sure it was out."

"Maybe it was lightning," Richard said as he watched the flames claw at the sky.

The harsh light made the buildings all around seem to

waver and dance in synchrony with the flames. Despite the distance, Kahlan could feel the angry heat against her face. Burning grass and sparks swirled up into the night.

Their hunter guardians appeared out of the rain to gather around. The arrow's owner passed it to his fellows, whispering to them that Richard with the Temper had shot the evil spirit, chasing it away.

Two more people emerged from the shadow around the corner of a building, taking in the leaping flames before joining them. Zedd, his unruly white hair dyed a reddish orange by the wash of firelight, held out his hand. A hunter laid the bloody arrow across his palm. Zedd inspected the arrow briefly before passing it to Ann. She rolled it in her fingers, sighing as if it confessed its story and confirmed her fears.

"It's the chimes," Richard said. "They're here. Now do you believe me?"

"Zedd, I saw it," Kahlan said. "Richard's right. It was no chicken. It was in there pecking out Juni's eyes. It spoke. It addressed me—by title—'Mother Confessor.' "

Reflections of the flames danced in his solemn eyes. He finally nodded.

"You are in a way right, my boy. It is indeed trouble of the gravest sort, but it is not the chimes."

"Zedd," Kahlan insisted, pointing back toward the burning building, "I'm telling you, it was—"

She fell silent as Zedd reached out and plucked a striated feather from her hair. He held up the feather, spinning it slowly between a finger and thumb. Before their eyes it turned to smoke, evaporating into the night air.

"It was a Lurk," the wizard murmured.

"A Lurk?" Richard frowned. "What's a Lurk? And how do you know?"

"Ann and I have been casting verification spells," the old wizard said. "You've given us the piece of evidence we needed to be sure. The trace of magic on this arrow confirms our suspicion. We have grave trouble."

"It was conjured by those committed to the Keeper," Ann said. "Those who can use Subtractive Magic: Sisters of the Dark."

"Jagang," Richard whispered. "He has Sisters of the Dark."

Ann nodded. "The last time Jagang sent an assassin wizard, but you survived it. He now sends something more deadly."

Zedd put a hand on Richard's shoulder. "You were right in your persistence, but wrong in your conclusion. Ann and I are confident we can disassemble the spell that brought it here. Try not to worry; we'll work on it, and come up with a solution."

"You still haven't said what this Lurk thing is. What's its purpose? What is it sent to do?"

Ann glanced at Zedd before she spoke. "It's conjured from the underworld," she said. "With Subtractive Magic. It is meant to disrupt magic in this world."

"Just like the chimes," Kahlan breathed with alarm.

"It is serious," Zedd confirmed, "but nothing like the chimes. Ann and I are hardly novices and not without resources of our own.

"The Lurk is gone for now, thanks to Richard. Unmasked for what it is, it will not soon return. Go get some sleep. Fortunately, Jagang was clumsy, and his Lurk betrayed itself before it could cause any more harm."

Richard looked back over his shoulder at the crackling fire, as if reasoning through something. "But how would Jagang—"

"Ann and I need to get some rest so we can work out precisely what Jagang has done and know how to counter it. It's complex. Let us do what we know we must."

At last, Richard slipped a comforting arm around Kahlan's waist and drew her close as he nodded to his grandfather. Richard clasped Zedd's shoulder in an affable gesture on the way by as he walked Kahlan toward the spirit house.

CHAPTER 11

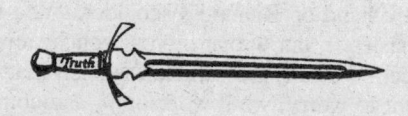

WHEN RICHARD STARTED, IT woke her. Kahlan, her back
pressed up against him, wiped her hair from her eyes, hastily
trying to gather her senses. Richard sat up, leaving a cold
breach where he had been a warm presence. Someone
knocked insistently.

"Lord Rahl," came a muffled voice. "Lord Rahl."

It hadn't been a dream; Cara was banging on the door.
Richard danced into his pants as he rushed to answer her
knock.

Daylight barged in. "What is it, Cara?"

"The healer woman sent me to get you. Zedd and Ann
are sick. I couldn't understand her words, but I knew she
wanted me to go for you."

Richard snatched up his boots. "How sick?"

"By the healer woman's behavior, I don't think it's serious, but I don't know about such things. I thought you
would want to see for yourself."

"Of course. Yes. We'll be right out."

Kahlan was already pulling on her clothes. They were still
damp, but at least they weren't dripping wet.

"What do you think it could be?"

Richard drew down his black sleeveless undershirt. "I've
no idea."

Disregarding the rest of his outfit, he buckled on his broad belt with the gold-worked pouches and started for the door. He never left the things inside it unguarded. They were too dangerous. He glanced back to see if she was with him. Hopping to keep her balance, Kahlan tugged on her stiff boots.

"I meant, do you think it could be the magic? Something wrong with it? Because of the Lurk business?"

"Let's not give our fears a head start. We'll know soon enough."

As they charged through the door, Cara took up and matched their stride. The morning was blustery and wet, with a thick drizzle. Leaden clouds promised a miserable day. At least it wasn't pouring rain.

Cara's long blond braid looked as if she'd left it done up wet all night. It hung heavy and limp, but Kahlan knew it looked better than her own matted locks.

In contrast, Cara's red leather outfit looked to have been freshly cleaned. Their red leather was a point of pride for Mord-Sith. Like a red flag, it announced to all the presence of a Mord-Sith; few words could convey the menace as effectively.

The supple leather must have been treated with oils or wool fat, by the way water beaded and ran from it. Kahlan always imagined that, as tight as it was, Mord-Sith didn't undress so much as they shed their skin of leather.

As they hurried down a passageway, Cara gave them an accusing glare. "You two had an adventure last night."

By the way her jaw muscles flexed, it was easy enough to tell that Cara wasn't pleased to have been left to sleep while they struck out alone like helpless fawns to see if they could put themselves in grave danger of some sort for no good reason whatsoever.

"I found the chicken that wasn't a chicken," Kahlan said.

She and Richard had been exhausted as they had trudged back to the spirit house through the dark, the mud, and the rain, and had spoken only briefly about it. When she asked, he told her he was looking for the chicken thing when he

107

heard her voice coming from the place where Juni's body lay. She expected him to say something about her lack of faith in him, but he didn't.

She told him she was sorry for giving him a rough day, inasmuch as she hadn't believed him. He said only that he thanked the good spirits for watching over her. He hugged her and kissed the top of her head. Somehow, she thought she would have felt better had he instead reproved her.

Dead tired, they crawled beneath their blankets. Weary as she was, Kahlan was sure she would be awake the remainder of the night with the frightful memories of the incarnate evil she felt from the chicken-thing, but with Richard's warm and reassuring hand on her shoulder, she had fallen asleep in mere moments.

"No one has yet explained to me how you can tell this chicken is not a chicken," Cara complained as they rounded a corner.

"I can't explain it," Richard said. "There was just something about it that wasn't right. A feeling. It made the hairs at the back of my neck stand on end when it was near."

"If you'd been there," Kahlan said, "you'd understand. When it looked at me, I could see the evil in its eyes."

Cara grunted her skepticism. "Maybe it needed to lay an egg."

"It addressed me by my title."

"Ah. Now that would tip me off, too." Cara's voice turned more serious, if not troubled. "It really called you 'Mother Confessor'?"

Kahlan nodded to the genuine anxiety creeping onto Cara's face. "Well, actually, it started to, but only spoke the Mother part. I didn't wait politely to hear it finish the rest."

As the three of them filed in the door, Nissel rose from the buckskin hide on the floor before the small hearth. She was heating a pot of aromatic herbs above the small fire. A stack of tava bread sat close beside the hearth on the shelf, where it would stay warm. She smiled that odd little something-only-she-knew smile of hers.

"Mother Confessor. Good morning. Have you slept well?"

"Yes, thank you. Nissel, what's wrong with Zedd and Ann?"

Nissel's smile vanished as she glanced at the heavy hide hanging over the doorway to the room in the rear. *"I am not sure."*

"Well then what's ailing them?" Richard demanded when Kahlan translated. "How are they sick? Fever? Stomach? Head? What?" He threw up his arms. "Have their heads come off their shoulders?"

Nissel held Richard's gaze as Kahlan asked his questions. Her odd little smile returned. *"He is impatient, your new husband."*

"He is worried for his grandfather. He has great love for his elder. So, do you know what could be wrong with them?"

Nissel turned briefly to give the pot a stir. The old healer had curious, even puzzling ways about her, like the way she mumbled to herself while she worked, or had a person balance stones on their stomach to distract them while she stitched a wound, but Kahlan also knew she possessed a sharp mind and was nearly peerless at what she did. There was a long lifetime of experience and vast knowledge in the hunched old woman.

With one hand, Nissel drew closed her simple shawl and at last squatted down before the Grace still drawn in the dirt in the center of the floor. She reached out and slowly traced a crooked finger along one of the straight lines radiating out from the center—the line representing magic.

"This, I think."

Kahlan and Richard shared a troubled look.

"You could probably find out a lot quicker," Cara said, "if you would just go in there and have a look for yourself."

Richard shot Cara a glower. "We wanted to know what to expect, if that's all right with you."

Kahlan relaxed a bit. Cara would never be irreverent

109

about something this important to them if she really believed it might be life or death battling beyond the hide curtain. Still, Cara knew little about magic, except that she didn't like it.

Cara, like the fierce D'Haran soldiers, feared magic. They were forever repeating the invocation that they were the steel against steel, while Lord Rahl was meant to be the magic against magic. It was part of the D'Haran people's bond to their Lord Rahl: they protected him, he protected them. It was almost as if they believed their duty was to protect his body so that in return he could protect their souls.

The paradox was that the unique bond between Mord-Sith and their Lord Rahl was a symbiotic relationship giving power to the Agiel—the staggering instrument of torture a Mord-Sith wore at her wrist—and, more important, that because of the ancient link to their Lord Rahl, Mord-Sith were able to usurp the magic of one gifted. Until Richard freed them, the purpose of Mord-Sith was not just to protect their Lord Rahl, but to torture to death his enemies who possessed magic, and in the process extract any information they had.

Other than the magic of a Confessor, there was no magic able to withstand the ability of a Mord-Sith to appropriate it. As much as Mord-Sith feared magic, those with magic had more to fear from Mord-Sith. But then, people always told Kahlan that snakes were more afraid of her than she was of them.

Clasping her hands behind her back and planting her feet, Cara took up her station. Kahlan ducked through the doorway as Richard held the hide curtain aside for her.

Candles lit the windowless room beyond. Magical designs dappled the dirt floor. Kahlan knew they were not practice symbols, as the Grace in the outer room had been. These were drawn in blood.

Kahlan caught the crook of Richard's arm. "Careful. Don't step on any of these." She held out her other hand to the symbols on the floor. "They're meant to lure and snare the unwary."

Richard nodded as he moved deeper into the room, weaving his way through the maze of ethereal devices. Zedd and Ann lay head to head on narrow grass-stuffed pallets against the far wall. Both were covered up to their chins with coarse woolen blankets.

"Zedd," Richard whispered as he sank to a knee, "are you awake?"

Kahlan knelt beside Richard, taking his hand as they sat back on their heels. As Ann's eyes blinked open and she looked up, Kahlan took her hand, too. Zedd frowned, as if exposing his eyes to even the mellow candlelight hurt.

"There you are, Richard. Good. We need to have a talk."

"What's the matter? Are you sick? What can we do to help?"

Zedd's wavy white hair looked more disheveled than usual. In the dim light his wrinkles weren't so distinct, but he somehow still looked a very old man at that moment.

"Ann and I . . . are just feeling a little tired out, that's all. We've been . . ."

He brought a hand out from under the blanket and gestured at the garden of designs sown across the floor. Cara's leather was tighter than the skin stretched over his bones.

"Tell him," Ann said into the dragging silence, "or I will."

"Tell me what? What's going on?"

Zedd rested his bony hand on Richard's muscular thigh and took a few labored breaths.

"You know that talk we had? Our 'what if' talk . . . about magic going away?"

"Of course."

"It's begun."

Richard's eyes widened. "It is the chimes, then."

"No," Ann said. "The Sisters of the Dark." She wiped sweat from her eyes. "In conjuring a spell to bring the . . . the chicken-thing . . ."

"The Lurk," Zedd said, helping her. "In conjuring the Lurk, they have either intentionally or accidentally begun a runaway degeneration of magic."

"It wouldn't be accidental," Richard said. "They would intend this. At least Jagang would, and the Sisters of the Dark do his bidding."

Zedd nodded, letting his eyes close. "I'm sure you're right, my boy."

"You weren't able to stop it, then?" Kahlan asked. "You made it sound as if you would be able to counter it."

"The verification webs we cast have cost us dearly." Ann sounded as bitter as Kahlan would have been in her place. "Used up our strength."

Zedd lifted his arm, and then let it flop back down to rest again on Richard's thigh. "Because of who we are, because we have more power and ability than others, the taint of this atrophy is affecting us first."

Kahlan frowned. "You said it would start with the weakest."

Ann simply rolled her head from side to side.

"Why isn't it affecting us?" Richard asked. "Kahlan has a lot of magic—with her Confessor power. And I have the gift."

Zedd lifted his hand to give a sickly wave. "No, no. Not the way it works. It starts with us. With me, more than Ann."

"Don't mislead them," Ann said. "This is too important." Her voice gathered a little strength as she went on. "Richard, Kahlan's power will soon fail. So will yours, though you don't depend on it as do we, or she, so it won't matter so much to you."

"Kahlan will lose her Confessor's power," Zedd confirmed, "as will everyone of magic. Every thing of magic. She will be defenseless and must be protected."

"I'm hardly defenseless," Kahlan objected.

"But there has to be a way for you to counter it. You said last night that you were not without resources of your own." Richard's fists tightened. "You said you could counter it. You must be able to do something!"

Ann lifted an arm to weakly whack at the top of Zedd's head. "Would you please tell him, old man? Before you give the boy apoplexy and he is of no help to us?"

Richard leaned forward. "I can help? What can I do? Tell me and I'll do it."

Zedd managed a feeble smile. "I always could count on you, Richard. Always could."

"What can we do?" Kahlan asked. "You can count on us both."

"You see, we know what to do, but we can't manage it alone."

"Then we'll help you," Richard insisted. "What do you need?"

Zedd struggled to take a breath. "In the Keep."

Kahlan felt a surge of hope. The sliph would spare them weeks of travel over land. In the sliph she and Richard could get to the Keep in less than a day.

Seeming nearly insensate, Zedd's breath wheezed out. In frustration, Richard pressed his own temples between thumb and second finger of one hand. He took a deep breath. He dropped the hand to Zedd's shoulder and jostled gently.

"Zedd? What is it we can do to help? What about the Wizard's Keep? What's in the Keep?"

The old wizard swallowed lethargically. "In the Keep. Yes."

Richard took another shaky breath, trying to preserve calm and reassurance in his own voice. "All right. In the Keep. I understand that much. What is it you need to tell me about the Keep, Zedd?"

Zedd's tongue worked at wetting the roof of his mouth. "Water."

Kahlan put a hand on Richard's shoulder, almost as if to keep him from springing up and bouncing off the ceiling. "I'll get it."

Nissel met her at the doorway but instead of the water Kahlan requested, handed her a warm cup. *"Give him this. I have just finished making it. It is better than water. It will give him strength."*

"Thank you, Nissel."

Kahlan hurried the cup to Zedd's lips. He gulped a few

swallows. Kahlan offered the cup to Ann, and she finished it. Nissel leaned over Kahlan's shoulder to hand her a piece of tava bread spread with something that looked like honey and carried a faint smell of mint, as if laced with a curative. Nissel whispered to Kahlan to get them to eat some.

"Here, Zedd," Kahlan said, "have a bite of tava with honey."

Holding up his hand, Zedd blocked the proffered food from his mouth. "Maybe later."

Kahlan and Richard glanced at each other out of the corner of their eyes. It was nearly unheard of for Zedd to refuse food. Cara must have taken her belief that it wasn't serious from the calm Nissel. While the old healer seemed unruffled by the condition of the two on the floor, Richard and Kahlan's concern was mounting by the moment.

"Zedd," Richard prompted, now that his grandfather had had a drink, "what about the Keep?"

Zedd opened his eyes. Kahlan thought them a bit brighter, the hazel color more limpid, less cloudy. He sluggishly grasped Richard's wrist.

"I think the tea is helping. More."

Kahlan twisted to the old woman. *"He says the tea is helping. He would like more."*

Pulling her head back, Nissel made a face. *"Of course it helps. Why does he think I make it?"*

She shook her head at such foolishness and shuffled off to the outer room to retrieve more tea. Kahlan was sure it wasn't her imagination that Zedd seemed just the tiniest bit more alert.

"Listen closely, my boy." He lifted a finger for emphasis. "In the Keep, there is a spell of great power. A sort of bottled antidote to the taint wafting through the world of life."

"And you need it?" Richard guessed.

Ann, too, looked to have been helped by the tea. "We tried to cast the counterspells, but our power has already deteriorated too much. We did not discover what was happening soon enough."

114

"But the vaporous spell in that bottle will do to the taint as the taint does to us," Zedd drawled.

"And thereby equalize the power so you can cast the counterspell and eliminate it," Richard impatiently finished in a rush.

"Yes," Zedd and Ann said as one.

Kahlan smiled eagerly. "It's not a problem, then. We can get the bottle for you."

Richard grinned his zeal. "We can get to the Keep through the sliph. We can retrieve this bottled spell of yours and be back with it in no time, almost."

Ann covered her eyes with a hand as she muttered a curse. "Zedd, did you never teach this boy anything?"

Richard's grin gave out. "Why? What's wrong with that?"

Nissel shuffled in carrying two clay cups of tea. She handed one to Kahlan and one to Richard. *Make them drink it all.*

"Nissel says you must drink this down," Kahlan told them.

Ann sipped when Kahlan held the cup to her lips. Zedd wrinkled his nose, but then had to start swallowing as Richard poured the tea down his grandfather's gullet. Balking and coughing, he was forced to gulp it all or drown.

"Now, what's the problem with us getting this spell thing from the Keep?" Richard asked as his grandfather caught his breath.

"First of all," Zedd managed between gasps, "you don't need to bring it here. You must only break the bottle. The spell will be released. It doesn't need direction—it's already created."

Richard was nodding. "I can break a bottle. I'll break it."

"Listen. It's in a bottle designed to protect the magic. It will only be released if it's broken properly—with an object possessing the correct magic. Otherwise, it will simply evaporate without helping."

"What object? How do I break the bottle correctly?"

"The Sword of Truth," Zedd said. "It has the proper magic to release the spell intact as it breaches the container."

"That's not a problem. I left the sword in your private enclave in the Keep. But won't the sword's magic fail, too?"

"No. The Sword of Truth was created by wizards with the knowledge to ward its power from assaults against its magic."

"So you think the Sword of Truth will stop a Lurk?"

Zedd nodded. "Much of this matter is unknown to me, but I strongly believe this: The Sword of Truth may be the only thing with the power to protect you." Zedd's fingers gripped Richard's undershirt, pulling him close. "You must retrieve the sword."

His eyes brightened when Richard nodded earnestly. Zedd tried to push himself up on an elbow, but Richard pressed a big hand to the old man's chest, forcing him to lie down.

"Rest. You can get up after you rest. Now, where is this bottle with the spell."

Zedd frowned at something and pointed behind Richard and Kahlan. They both turned to look. When they didn't see anything but Cara watching from the doorway, they turned back to see Zedd up on the elbow. He smiled at his little triumph. Richard scowled.

"Now, listen carefully, my boy. You said you got into the First Wizard's private enclave?" Richard's head bobbed as Zedd talked. "And you remember the place?" Richard was still nodding. "Good. There is an entrance. A long walk between things."

"Yes, I remember. The long entryway has a red carpet down the middle. To each side are white marble columns about as tall as me. There are different things atop each. At the end—"

"Yes," Zedd held up a hand, as if to stop him. "The white marble columns. You remember them? The things atop them?"

"Some. Not every one. There were gems in brooches, gold chains, a silver chalice, finely wrought knives, bowls, boxes." Richard paused with a frown of effort at recollection. He snapped his fingers. "Fifth column on the left has a bottle atop it. I remember because I thought it was pretty.

An inky black bottle with a gold filigree stopper."

A sly smile stole onto the Zedd's face. "Quite right, my boy. That's the bottle."

"What do I do? Just break it with the Sword of Truth?"

"Just break it."

"Nothing fancy? No incantations? No placing it some certain place some certain way? No waiting for the right moon? No special time of day or night? No turning round first? Nothing fancy?"

"Nothing fancy. Just break it with the sword. If it were me, I'd carefully set it on the floor, just in case my aim was bad and I knocked it off without breaking the glass and it fell to the marble to break there. But that's me."

"The floor it is, then. I'll set it on the floor and smash it with the sword." Richard started to rise. "It will be done before dawn breaks tomorrow."

Zedd caught Richard's hand and urged him back down. "No, Richard, you can't." He flopped back, sighing unhappily.

"Can't what?" Richard asked as he leaned close once more.

Zedd took a few breaths. "Can't go in that sliph thing of yours."

"But we have to," Richard insisted. "It will get us there in less than a day. Over land would take . . . I don't know. Weeks."

The old wizard lifted a grim finger toward Richard's face. "The sliph uses magic. If you go in the sliph, you will die before you reach Aydindril. You will be in the dark recesses of that quicksilver creature, breathing her magic, when that magic fails. You will drown. No one will ever find your body."

Richard licked his lips. He raked his fingers back through his hair. "Are you sure? Might I be able to make it before the magic fails? Zedd, this is important. If there is some risk, then we must take it. I'll go alone. I'll leave Kahlan and Cara."

Alarm swelled in Kahlan's chest at the idea of Richard

being in the sliph, and having its magic fail. Of him drowning in the dark forever of the sliph. She clutched at his arm to protest, but Zedd spoke first.

"Richard, listen to me. I am First Wizard. I am telling you: Magic is failing. If you go in the sliph, you will die. Not maybe. Will. All magic is failing. You must go without magic."

Richard pressed his lips tight and nodded. "All right, then. If we must, then we must. It will take longer, though. How long can you and Ann . . . ?"

Zedd smiled. "Richard, we are too weak to travel or we would go with you now, but we will be fine. We would only slow you for no good reason. You can accomplish what must be done. As soon as you break the bottle and release the spell, then these things here"—he gestured to the spells drawn all over the floor—"will let us know. Once they do, I can cast the counterspells.

"Until then, the Wizard's Keep will be vulnerable. Extraordinarily powerful and dangerous things could be stolen when the Keep's shields of magic fail. After I restore magic's power, anything stolen could then be used against us."

"Do you know how much of the Keep's magic will fail?"

Zedd shook his head in frustration. "This is without precedent. I can't predict the exact sequences, but I'm sure all will fail. We need you to stay at the Keep and protect it as you planned. Ann and I will follow after this business is finished. We're counting on you. Can you do that for me, my boy?"

Richard, his eyes glistening, nodded. He took up his grandfather's hand. "Of course. You can count on me."

"Promise me, Richard. Promise me you will go to the Keep."

"I promise."

"If you don't," Ann warned in a low voice, "Zedd's optimism about his being fine may prove . . . flawed."

Zedd's brow tightened. "Ann, you are making it sound—"

"If I am not telling the truth, then call me a liar."

Zedd rested the back of his wrist over his eyes and remained silent. Ann tilted her head back enough to meet Richard's gaze.

"Am I making myself clear?"

He swallowed. "Yes, ma'am."

Zedd reached out for the comfort of Richard's hand. "This is important, Richard, but don't break your neck getting there?"

Richard smiled. "I understand. A swift journey, not impetuous reckless haste, is more likely to get you to your destination."

Zedd managed a low chuckle. "So you did listen when you were younger."

"Always."

"Then listen now." The sticklike finger once more lifted from his slack fist. "You must not use fire, if you can avoid it at all. The Lurk could find you by fire."

"How?"

"We believe the spell can seek by fire's light. It was sent for you, so it can search for you with fire. Keep away from fire.

"Water, too. If you must ford a river, use a bridge if at all possible, even if you must go days out of your way. Cross streams on a log, or swing over on a rope, or jump, if you can."

"You mean to say we risk ending up like Juni, if we go near water?"

Zedd nodded. "I'm sorry to make it more difficult for you, but this is perilous business. The Lurk is trying to get you. You will only be safe—all of us will only be safe—if you can get to the Keep and break that bottle before the Lurk finds you."

Undaunted, Richard smiled. "We'll save time—not having to gather firewood or bathe."

Zedd again let out the breathy little chuckle. "Safe journey, Richard. And you, too, Cara. Watch over Richard." His sticklike fingers gripped Kahlan's hand. "And you too, my new granddaughter. I love you dearly. Keep each other safe and well. I will see you when we reach Aydindril, and we will have the joy of each other's company again. Wait at the Keep for us."

Kahlan gathered up his bony hand in both of hers as she sniffled back the tears. "We will. We'll be there waiting for you. We'll be a family together again, when you get there."

"Safe journey, all," Ann said. "May the good spirits be with you always. Our faith and prayers will be with you, too."

Richard nodded his thanks and started to rise, but then paused. He seemed to consider something for a moment. He spoke at last in a soft voice.

"Zedd, all the time I was growing up, I never knew you were my grandfather. I know you did that to protect me, but . . . I never knew." He fidgeted with a piece of grass sticking out of the pallet. "I never got a chance to hear about my mother's mother. She almost never spoke of her mother— just a word here and there. I never learned about my grandmother. Your wife."

Zedd turned his face away as a tear rolled down his cheek. He cleared his throat. "Erilyn was . . . a wonderful woman. Like you have a wonderful wife now, so I once did, too.

"Erilyn was captured by the enemy, by a quad sent by your other grandfather, Panis Rahl, when your mother was very young. Your mother saw it all—what they did to her mother. . . . Erilyn only lived long enough for me to find her. She was already at the brink of death, but I tried to heal her. My magic activated a sinister spell the enemy had hidden in her. My healing touch was what killed her. Because of what she saw, your mother found it painful to speak of Erilyn."

After an uncomfortable moment, Zedd turned back to them and smiled with a memory of genuine joy. "She was beautiful, with gray eyes, like your mother. Like you. She was as smart as you, and she liked to laugh. You should know that. She liked to laugh."

Richard smiled. He cleared his throat to find his voice.

"Then she surely married the right person."

Zedd nodded. "She did. Now, gather your things and be on your way to Aydindril so we can get our magic back to right.

"When we finally join you in Aydindril, I will tell you all the things about Erilyn—your grandmother—that I never could before." He smiled a grandfather's smile. "We will talk of family."

CHAPTER 12

"FETCH! HERE, BOY! FETCH!"

The men laughed. The women giggled. Fitch wished his face wouldn't always go as red as his hair when Master Drummond mocked him with that epithet. He left the scrub brush in the crusty cauldron and scurried to see what the kitchen master wanted.

Dashing around one of the long tables, his elbow whacked a flagon someone had set near the edge. He caught the heavy, cobalt blue glass vessel just before it toppled to the floor. Exhaling in relief, he pushed it back near the stack of braided bread. He heard his name yelled again.

Fitch jigged to a halt before Master Drummond, keeping his eyes to the floor—he didn't want a lump on his head for appearing to protest being the butt of jokes.

"Yes, Master Drummond?"

The portly kitchen master wiped his hands on a white towel he always kept tucked behind his belt. "Fitch, you have to be the clumsiest scullion I've ever seen."

"Yes, sir."

Master Drummond stretched up on his toes, peering out the back window. Someone in the distance behind Fitch cursed as they burned themselves on a hot pan and in recoiling knocked metalware clattering across the brick floor near the baking hearth. There was no angry shouting, so Fitch knew it wasn't one of the other Haken scullions.

Master Drummond gestured toward the service door of the sprawling kitchen. "Fetch in some wood. We need the oak, and also a bit of apple to flavor the ribs."

"Oak and apple. Yes, sir."

"And get a four-hand cauldron up on a racking crook first. Hurry up with the oak."

Fitch sagged with a "Yes, sir." The big split slabs of oak for the roasting hearth were heavy and always gave him splinters. Oak splinters were the worst kind, and would plague him for days after. The apple wasn't so bad, at least. It was going to be a big affair; he knew to bring enough of it.

"And keep your eye out for the butcher's cart. It's due here any minute. I'll wring Inger's neck if he sends it late."

Fitch perked up. "Butcher's cart?" He dared not ask what he wanted to ask. "Would you like me to unload it, then, sir?"

Master Drummond planted his fists on his wide hips. "Don't tell me, Fitch, that you're starting to think ahead?" Nearby, several women working at sauces snorted a laugh. "Of course I want you to unload it! And if you drop any, like the last time, I'll roast your scrawny rump instead."

Fitch bowed twice. "Yes, Master Drummond."

As he withdrew, he moved aside to make way for the dairymaid bringing a sample of cheese for Master Drummond's approval. One of the women saucers snagged Fitch's sleeve before he could be off.

"Where are those skimmers I asked for?"

"Coming, Gillie, as soon as I see to—"

She snatched him by an ear. "Don't patronize me," Gillie growled. She twisted the ear. "Your kind always fall to that, in the end, don't they?"

"No, Gillie—I wasn't—I swear. I have nothing but respect for the Ander people. I daily school my vile nature so there may be no room in my heart or mind for hate or spite, and I pray the Creator gives me strength to transform my flawed soul, and that he burns me for eternity should I fail," he prated by rote. "I'll get the skimmers for you, Gillie. Please, let me get them?"

She shoved his head. "Go on then, and be quick."

Comforting his throbbing ear, Fitch raced to the rack where he'd left the skimmers to dry. He snatched a handful and bore them to Gillie with as much respect as he could muster, considering that Master Drummond was watching out of the corner of his eye, no doubt thinking about beating him for not having the skimmers to Gillie sooner so he could be doing as ordered and have the cauldron hung and the firewood on its way in.

He bowed as he held out the skimmers.

"I hope you see fit to take yourself to an extra penance assembly this week." Gillie snatched up the skimmers. "The humiliations from your kind we Anders must endure," she muttered with a rueful shake of her head.

"Yes, Gillie, I need the reassurance of an extra penance. Thank you for reminding me."

When she snorted her contempt and turned to her work, Fitch, feeling the shame of having thoughtlessly let his wicked nature demean an Ander, hurried off to get one of the other scullions to help him lift the heavy cauldron onto the racking crook. He found Morley up to his elbows in scalding water and only too happy for any excuse to pull them free, even for heavy lifting.

Morley checked over his shoulder as he helped lift the iron cauldron. It wasn't as hard for him as it was for Fitch.

Fitch was gangly; Morley had a muscular build.

Morley smiled conspiratorially. "Big affair tonight. You know what that means."

Fitch smiled that he did. With all the guests, there would be the noise of laughter, shouting, singing, eating, and drinking. With all that, and people running hither and yon, wine and ale would be in endless supply, and whether in half-full glasses or half-full bottles, it would be little missed.

"It means one of the only advantages of working for the Minister of Culture," Fitch said.

Morley, the cords in his muscular neck straining from the weight, leaned closer over the cauldron as they lugged it across the floor. "Then you'd better be more respectful of the Ander people or you'll not have that advantage. Nor the one of a roof over your head and meals to fill your belly."

Fitch nodded. He hadn't meant to be disrespectful—that was the last thing he would want to do; he owed everything to the Anders. But every now and then, he felt the Anders took offense too easily, though he knew it was his insensitivity and ignorance that lead to such misunderstandings, so he guessed he had no one to blame but himself.

As soon as the cauldron was hung, Fitch rolled his eyes and hung his tongue out the side of his mouth, intimating to Morley that they would drink themselves sick that night. Morley swiped his red Haken hair back from his face and simulated a drunken, if silent, hiccup before plunging his arms back into the soapy water.

Smiling, Fitch trotted out the postern to retrieve the firewood. The recent drenching rains had moved east, leaving behind the sweet aroma of fresh, damp earth. The new spring day promised to be warm. In the distance, the lush fields of verdant new wheat shimmered in the sun. On some days, when the wind was from the south, the smell of the sea drifted in to wash over the fields, but not today, though a few gulls wheeled in the sky.

Fitch checked the avenue each time he trotted back out for another armload, but didn't see the butcher's cart. His tunic was damp with sweat by the time he'd finished with the oak. He'd managed to hustle it in with only one splinter, a long one, in the web of his thumb.

As he plucked billets from the mound of apple wood, he caught the rhythmic creaking of an approaching cart. Sucking at the painful oak splinter, trying unsuccessfully to catch hold of the buried end with his teeth, he surreptitiously glanced to the shade of the great oaks lining the long avenue into the estate and saw the plodding gait of Brownie, the butcher's swayback horse. Whoever was bringing the load was on the other side of the cart. With that, and the distance, he couldn't tell who it was.

Besides the butcher's cart, a number of other people were also arriving at the sprawling estate; everyone from scholars visiting the Anderith Library, to servants bringing messages and reports, to workers bringing wagons with deliveries. There were also a number of well-dressed people coming with some other purpose.

When first Fitch had come to work in the kitchen, he had found it, and the whole estate, a huge and baffling place. He had been intimidated by everyone and everything, knowing it would be his new home and he had to learn to fit into the work if he was to have a sleeping pallet and food.

His mother had told him to work hard and with luck he would always have both. She had warned him to mind his betters, do as he was told, and even if he thought the rules harsh, follow them. She said that if the behests were onerous, he should still do them without comment, and especially without complaint.

Fitch didn't have a father, one he knew anyway, though at times there had been men he'd thought might marry his mother. She had a room provided by her employer, a merchant named Ibson. It was in the city, beside Mr. Ibson's home, in a building that housed other of his workers. His mother worked in the kitchen, cooking meals. She could cook anything.

She was always hard-pressed to feed Fitch, though, and wasn't able to watch over him much of the time. When he wasn't at penance assembly, she often took him to work with her, where she could keep an eye on him. There, he turned spits, carried this and that, washed smaller items, swept the courtyard, and often had to clean out the stables where some of Mr. Ibson's wagon horses were kept.

His mother had been good to him, whenever she saw him, anyway. He knew she cared about him and about what would become of him. Not like some of the men she occasionally saw. They viewed Fitch as little more than an annoyance. Some, wanting to be alone with his mother, opened the door to his mother's single room and heaved him out for the night.

Fitch's mother would wring her hands, but she was too timid to stop the men from putting him out.

When the men put him out, he'd have to sleep on the doorstep to the street, under a stairway, or at a neighbor's, if they were of a mind to let him in. Sometimes, if it was raining, the night stablehands at Mr. Ibson's place next door would let him sleep in the stables. He liked being with the horses, but he didn't like having to endure the flies.

But enduring the flies was better than being caught alone at night by Ander boys.

Early the next day his mother would go off to work, usually with her man friend who worked in the household, too, and Fitch would get to go back inside. When she'd come home on the days after he'd been shoved out for the night, she'd usually bring him some treat she'd filched from the kitchen where she worked.

His mother had wanted him to learn a trade, but she didn't know anyone who would take him on as a helper, much less as an apprentice, so, about four years before, when he was old enough to earn his own meals, Mr. Ibson helped her place him for work in the kitchen at the Minister of Culture's estate, not far outside the capital city of Fairfield.

Upon his arrival, one of the household clerks had sat Fitch down along with a few other new people and explained the rules of the house, where he would sleep with the other scullions and such, and what his duties were to be. The clerk explained in grave tones the importance of the place where they labored; from the estate, the Minister of Culture directed the affairs of his high office, overseeing nearly every aspect of life in Anderith. The estate was also his home. The post of Minister of Culture was second only to that of the Sovereign himself.

Fitch had simply thought he'd been sent to some merchant's kitchen to work; he'd had no idea his mother had managed to get him placed in such a high household. He'd been immensely proud. Later, he found that it was hard work, like any other work, in any other place. There was nothing glamorous about it. But still, he was proud that he, a Haken, worked in the Minister's estate.

Other than what Fitch had been taught about the Minister making laws and such to insure that Anderith culture remained exemplary and the rights of all were protected, Fitch didn't really understand what the Minister of Culture did that required so many people coming and going all the time. He didn't even understand why there needed to be new laws all the time. After all, right was right, and wrong was wrong. He'd asked an Ander once, and had been told that new wrongs were continually being uncovered, and needed to be addressed. Fitch didn't understand that, either, but hadn't said so. Just asking the first question had brought a scowl to the Ander's face.

Unable to pull out the oak splinter, he bent to pick up a stick of apple wood while keeping an eye to the avenue and the butcher's cart. One of the approaching strangers, a brawny man in unfamiliar military attire, wore an odd cloak that almost looked to Fitch like it was covered in patches of hair.

Each of the man's fingers was ringed, with a leather strap from each of those rings going over a knuckle to a studded black leather bracer around his wrists and forearms. Silver studs girded his boots, too. Fitch was stunned to see the glint of metal studs in the man's ear and nose.

The man's leather belts held weapons the likes of which Fitch had never even conjured in his nightmares. Riding in a hanger at his right hip was an axe with the great horns of its blade curling back around until they almost touched. A wooden handle, dark with age and use, had a spiked ball attached to its top via a chain. A long spike, like a single talon, capped the bottom of the handle.

The man's thatch of thick dark hair made him look as if he were possibly an Ander, but his thick brow spoke that he wasn't. The tangle of dark hair fell around a bull neck that must have been nearly as big around as Fitch's waist. Even at a distance, the sight of the man made Fitch's stomach go queasy.

As the stranger passed the slow butcher's cart, the man drank in a long look at the person on the other side of Brownie. He finally moved on, turning his attention back to the windows of the estate, searching them, too, with dark intent.

CHAPTER 13

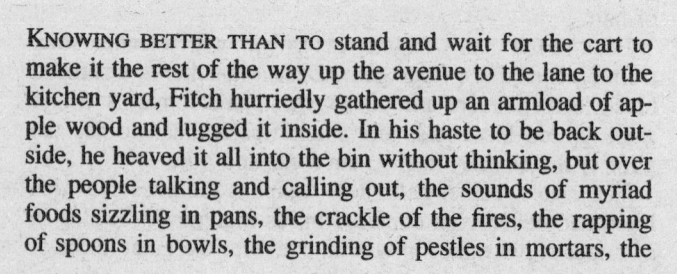

KNOWING BETTER THAN TO stand and wait for the cart to make it the rest of the way up the avenue to the lane to the kitchen yard, Fitch hurriedly gathered up an armload of apple wood and lugged it inside. In his haste to be back outside, he heaved it all into the bin without thinking, but over the people talking and calling out, the sounds of myriad foods sizzling in pans, the crackle of the fires, the rapping of spoons in bowls, the grinding of pestles in mortars, the rasp of brushes, and the general clatter of everyone working, no one heard his wood carelessly thunking home. Some spilled out, and he was going to leave it, but when he spied Master Drummond not far off, he dropped to his knees and quickly stacked the wood in the bin.

When he rushed back out, his heart hammering, his breath caught up short when he saw who'd brought the butcher's cart.

It was her.

Fitch wrung his hands as he watched her leading Brownie into the turn round. His hand-wringing twisted the splinter lying under his flesh, making him grimace. He cursed under his breath, then snapped his mouth shut, hoping she hadn't heard. He trotted over to the cart, shaking the stinging hand to dispel the pain.

"Good day, Beata."

She only glanced up. "Fitch."

He groped for something to say, but couldn't think of anything meaningful. He stood mute as she clucked her tongue, urging Brownie to back up. One hand held the trace chain as her other hand stroked the horse's chest, guiding, reassuring, as he clopped backward. What Fitch wouldn't give to have that hand touch him in such a gentle manner.

Her short red hair, so soft, so lustrous, so fetching the way its fullness tapered to turn in and caress the nape of her neck, ruffled in the warm spring breeze.

Fitch waited beside the cart, fearing to say something stupid and have Beata think him a fool. Even though he thought about her often, he figured thoughts about him probably never passed through her mind. That was one thing, but to have her think him a fool would be unbearable. He wished he knew some interesting bit of news, or *something* to make her have pleasant thoughts about him.

Expressionless, Beata gestured as she walked back to the cart where he stood. "What's wrong with your hand?"

The shape of her, so close, paralyzed him. The dusky blue dress swept up from the top of the flare of the long skirt, hugging her ribs, swelling over her bosom in a way that made him have to swallow to get his breath. Worn wooden buttons marched up the front. A pin with a simple spiral head held the collar closed at her throat.

It was an old dress; she was, after all, a Haken, like him, and not deserving of better. Edges of the blue fabric were frayed here and there, and it faded a little at the shoulders, but Beata made it look somehow majestic.

With an impatient sigh, she snatched up his hand to look for herself.

"It's nothing . . . it's a splinter," he stammered.

She turned his hand over, laying it palm up in her other as she pinched up the skin to inspect the splinter's depth. He was stunned by the unexpected warm touch of her hand holding his. He was horrified to see that his hands, from being in the hot soapy water cleaning pots and cauldrons, were cleaner than her hands. He feared she would think he did no work.

"I was washing pots," he explained. "Then I had to bring in oak. Lots of heavy oak. That's why I'm sweating."

Without a word, Beata pulled the pin from the top of her dress. The neckline fell open a few inches, revealing the hollow at the base of her neck. His jaw went slack at seeing so much of her, so much she ordinarily kept hidden. He wasn't worthy of her help, much less to look upon the flesh at her throat she meant to be kept hidden. He made himself look away.

Fitch yelped when he felt the sharp pin probe. Frowning in concentration, she absently muttered an apology as she dug at the splinter. Trying not to contort his face with pain, he instead curled his toes against the dirt as he waited.

He felt a deep, sharp, painful tug. She briefly inspected the long, needle-like oak splinter she'd pulled out, and then tossed it aside. She closed her collar and secured it once again with the pin.

"There you go," she said, turning to the cart.

"Thank you, Beata." She nodded. "That was very kind." He followed in her steps. "Uh, I'm to help you take in the load."

He dragged a huge hind section of beef to the end of the cart and ducked under to hoist it onto his shoulder. The weight nearly buckled his knees. When he managed to get it wheeled around, he saw Beata already going up the path with a fat net full of pullets in one hand, and a section of mutton ribs balanced on the other shoulder, so she didn't see his mighty effort.

Inside, Judith, the pantler, told him to get a list of everything the butcher had sent. He bowed and promised he would, but inwardly, he cringed.

When they returned to the cart, Beata ticked off the cargo for him, slapping a hand to each item as she called it out. She knew he couldn't read and so had to commit the list to memory. She took care to make each item clear. There was pork, mutton, ox, beaver, and beef, three crocks of marrow, eight fat skins of fresh blood, a half-barrel of pig stomachs for stuffing, two dozen geese, a basket of doves, and three nets of pullets, counting the one she had already taken in.

"I know I put . . ." Beata pulled over a net of the pullets, looking for something. "Here it is," she said. "I feared for a moment I didn't have them." She dragged it free. "And a sack of sparrows. The Minister of Culture always wants sparrows for his feasts."

Fitch could feel the heat of his face going red. Everyone knew sparrows, and sparrow eggs, were consumed to stimulate lust—although he couldn't fathom why; lust hardly seemed to him in need of any more stirring. When Beata looked up into his eyes to see if he'd added it to his mental list, he felt the overwhelming need to say something—anything—to change the subject.

"Beata, do you think we'll ever be absolved of our ancestral crimes, and be as pure of heart as the Ander people?"

Her smooth brow twitched. "We are Haken. We can never be as good as the Ander; our souls are corrupt and unable to be pure; their souls are pure, and unable to be corrupt. We cannot ever be completely cleansed; we can only hope to control our vile nature."

Fitch knew the answer as well as she. Asking probably

made her think him hopelessly ignorant. He was never any good at explaining his thoughts in a way that spoke what he really meant.

He wanted to pay his debt—gain absolution—and earn a sir name. Not many Hakens ever achieved that privilege. He could never do as he wished until he could do that much. He hung his head as he sought to amend his question.

"But, I mean . . . after all this time, haven't we learned the errors of our ancestors' ways? Don't you want to have more of a say in your own life?"

"I am Haken. I am not worthy of deciding my destiny. You should know that down that path lies wickedness."

He picked at the torn flesh where she'd taken out the splinter. "But some Hakens serve in ways that go toward absolution. You said once that you might join the army. I'd like to join, too."

"You are male Haken. You are not allowed to touch weapons. You should know that, too, Fitch."

"I didn't mean to say . . . I know I can't. I just meant—I don't know." He shoved his hands in his back pockets. "I just meant that I wish I could, that's all, so that I could do good—prove myself. Help those who we've made to suffer."

"I understand." She gestured to the windows on the upper floors. "It is the Minister of Culture himself who passed the law allowing Haken women to serve in the army, along with the Ander women. That law also says all must show respect to those Haken women. The Minister is compassionate to all people. The Haken women owe him a great debt."

Fitch knew he wasn't getting across what he really meant. "But don't you want to marry and—"

"He also passed the law that Haken women must be given work so that we might feed ourselves without having to marry and be slaves to the Haken men, for it is their nature to enslave, and given the chance through marriage, they will even do it with their own kind. Minister Chanboor is a hero to all Haken women.

"He should be a hero to Haken men, too, because he

brings culture to you, so that you may give over your warlike ways and come into the community of peaceful people. I may decide to join because serving in the army is a means by which Haken women may earn respect. It is the law. Minister Chanboor's law."

Fitch felt as if he were at penance. "I respect you, Beata, even though you aren't in the army. I know you will do good for people whether or not you join the army. You are a good person."

Beata's heat faltered. She lifted one shoulder in a little shrug. The edge in her voice softened. "The main reason I might one day join the army is like you say—to help people and do good. I, too, want to do good."

Fitch envied her. In the army she would be able to help communities facing difficulties with everything from floods to famine. The army helped needy people. People in the army were respected.

And, it wasn't like the past, when being in the army could be dangerous. Not with the Dominie Dirtch. If the Dominie Dirtch were ever unleashed, it could school any opponent into submission without those in the army having to do battle. Thankfully, the Anders were in charge of the Dominie Dirtch, now, and they would only use such a weapon to keep peace—never to intentionally bring harm.

The Dominie Dirtch was the one thing Haken that the Anders used. The Ander people could never have conceived such a thing themselves—they were not capable of even thinking the vile thoughts that must have been required to conceive such a weapon. Only Hakens could have created a weapon of such outright evil.

"Or I might hope to be sent here to work, like you were," Beata added.

Fitch looked up. She was staring at the windows on the third floor. He almost said something, but instead closed his mouth. She stared up at the windows as she went on.

"He walked into Inger's place once, and I actually saw him. Bertrand—I mean Minister Chanboor—is much more attractive to look upon than Inger the butcher."

Fitch didn't know how to judge such things in a man, not with the way women fussed over men Fitch thought unattractive. Minister Chanboor was tall and perhaps had once been good-looking, but he was starting to get wisps of gray in his dark Ander hair. Women in the kitchen all giggled to each other over the man. When he came into the room, some reddened and had to fan their faces as they sighed. He seemed repulsively old to Fitch.

"Everyone says the Minister is a very charming man. Do you ever see him? Or talk with him? I heard that he even speaks with Hakens, just like regular folks. Everyone speaks so highly of him.

"I've heard Ander people say that one day he will likely be the Sovereign."

Fitch sank back against the cart. "I've seen him a couple of times." He didn't bother to tell her that Minister Chanboor had once cuffed him when he'd dropped a dull butter knife right near the Minister's foot. He'd deserved the smack.

He glanced back at her. She was still looking up at the windows. Fitch gazed down at the ruts in the damp dirt. "Everyone likes and respects the Minister of Culture. I am joyous to be able to work for such a fine man, even though I am unworthy. It is a mark of his noble heart that he would give Hakens work so that we won't starve."

Beata suddenly glanced around self-consciously as she brushed her hands clean on her skirts. He sought once more to try to make her see his worthwhile intentions.

"I hope someday to do good. To contribute to the community. To help people."

Beata nodded approvingly. He felt emboldened by that approval. Fitch lifted his chin.

"I hope one day to have my debt paid and earn my sir name, and then to travel to Aydindril, to the Wizard's Keep, to ask the wizards to name me the Seeker of Truth, and present me with the Sword of Truth so that I might return to protect the Ander people and do good."

Beata blinked at him. And then she laughed.

"You don't even know where Aydindril is, or how far it is." She shook her head between her fits of laughter.

He did too know where Aydindril was. "North and east," he mumbled.

"The Sword of Truth is said to be a thing of magic. Magic is vile and dirty and evil. What do you know about magic?"

"Well . . . nothing, I guess—"

"You don't know the first thing about magic. Or swords. You'd probably cut off your foot." She bent to the cart, hoisted the basket of doves and another net of pullets as she chuckled, and then headed for the kitchens.

Fitch wanted to die. He'd told her his secret dream, and she'd laughed. His chin sunk to his chest. She was right. He was Haken. He could never hope to prove his worth.

He kept his eyes down and didn't say anything else as they unloaded the cart. He felt a fool. With every step, he silently rebuked himself. He wished he'd kept his dreams to himself. He wished he could take back the words.

Before they pulled the last of it from the cart, Beata caught his arm and cleared her throat, as if she intended to say more. Fitch again cast his gaze down, resigned to hear what else she would have to say about his foolishness.

"I'm sorry, Fitch. My corrupt Haken nature caused me to slip and be cruel. It was wrong of me to say such cruel things."

He shook his head. "You were right to laugh."

"Look, Fitch . . . we all have impossible dreams. That too is just part of our corrupt nature. We must learn to be better than our base dreams."

He wiped hair off his forehead as he peered up at her gray-green eyes. "You have dreams, too, Beata? Real dreams? Something you wish?"

"You mean like your foolish dream to be the Seeker of Truth?" He nodded. She at last looked away from his eyes. "I suppose it's only fair, so that you can laugh at me in turn."

"I wouldn't laugh," he whispered, but she was staring off at small puffs of white clouds drifting across the bright blue sky and didn't seem to hear him.

"I wish I could learn to read."

She stole a look to see if he was going to laugh. He didn't.

"I've dreamed that, too." He checked to see if anyone was watching. No one was about. He hunched over the back of the cart and with a finger made marks in the dirt there.

Her curiosity overcame her disapproval. "Is that writing?"

"It's a word. I learned it. It's the only one I know, but it's a word and I can read it. I heard a man at a feast say it's on the hilt of the Sword of Truth." Fitch drew a line under the word in the dirt. "The man cut it into the top of the butter, to show a woman there at the feast. It's the word 'Truth.'

"He told her it used to be that the one named Seeker was a person of great repute, meant to do good, but now Seekers were no more than common criminals at best and cutthroats at worst. Like our ancestors."

"Like all Hakens," she corrected. "Like us."

He didn't argue, because he knew she was right. "That's another reason I'd like to be Seeker: I would restore the good name to the post of Seeker, the way it used to be, so people could trust in truth again. I'd like to show people that a Haken could serve honorably. That would be doing good, wouldn't it? Wouldn't that help balance our crimes?"

She rubbed her upper arms briskly as she glanced about, checking. "Dreaming of being the Seeker is childish and silly." Her voice lowered with import. "Learning to read would be a crime. You had better not try to learn any more."

He sighed. "I know, but don't you ever—"

"And magic is vile. To touch a thing of magic would be as bad as a crime."

She stole a glance at the brick façade over her shoulder. With a quick swipe, Beata wiped the word from the floor of the cart. He opened his mouth to protest, but she spoke first, cutting him off.

"We'd better get finished."

With a flick of her eyes, she indicated the upper windows. Fitch looked up and felt icy tingling terror skitter up his spine. The Minister of Culture himself was at a window watching them.

Fitch hefted a rack of mutton and made for the kitchen larder. Beata followed with a noose of geese in one hand and the sack of sparrows in the other. Both finished lugging in the load in silence. Fitch wished he hadn't said so much, and that she had said more.

When they'd finished, he intended to walk with her back out to the cart, to pretend to check to see if they'd gotten everything, but Master Drummond asked and Beata told him they had it all in. With a stiff finger, he jabbed Fitch's chest, ordering him back to his scrubbing. Fitch rubbed at the stinging poke as he scuffed his feet along the smooth, unfinished wooden floor on his way to the tubs of soapy water. He glanced back over his shoulder to watch Beata leave, hoping she would look back at him so he could give her a departing smile, at least.

Minister Chanboor's aide, Dalton Campbell, was in the kitchen. Fitch had never met Dalton Campbell—he would have no occasion to—but he thought favorably about the man because he never seemed to cause anyone any trouble, as far as Fitch had heard, anyway.

New to the post of aide to the Minister, Dalton Campbell was an agreeable-enough-looking Ander, with the typical Ander straight nose, dark eyes and hair, and strong chin. Women, especially Haken women, seemed to find that sort of thing appealing. Dalton Campbell did look noble in his dark blue quilted jerkin over a like-colored doublet, both offset with pewter buttons.

A silver-wrought scabbard hung from a finely detailed double-wrapped belt. Dark reddish brown leather covered the hilt of the handsome weapon. Fitch dearly wished he could carry such a fine sword. He was sure girls were drawn to men carrying swords.

Before Beata had a chance to look over at Fitch, or to leave, Dalton Campbell quickly closed the distance to her and grabbed her under an arm. Her face paled. Fitch, too, felt sudden terror grip his gut. He knew instinctively that this was potentially big trouble. He feared he knew the cause. If the Minister, when he'd been looking down, saw Fitch writing the word in the dirt . . .

Dalton Campbell smiled, speaking soft assurance. As her shoulders slowly relaxed, so did the knot in Fitch's belly. Fitch couldn't hear most of the words, but he heard Dalton Campbell say something about Minister Chanboor as he tilted his head toward the stairway on the far side of the kitchen. Her eyes widened. Rosy color bloomed on her cheeks.

Beata beamed incandescently.

Dalton Campbell in turn smiled his invitation at her all the way to the stairwell, pulling her along by the arm, although she looked not to need the encouragement—she looked as if she was nearly floating through the air. She never looked back as she disappeared through the doorway and up the stairs.

Master Drummond suddenly swatted the back of Fitch's head.

"Why are you standing there like a stump? Get to those fry pans."

CHAPTER 14

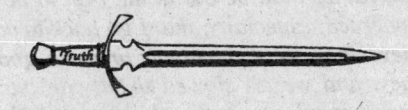

ZEDD WOKE AT THE sound of the door in the other room closing. He opened one eye just enough to peer toward the doorway as the hide was lifted to the side.

He relaxed a bit at seeing it was Nissel. The stooped healer took her time shuffling across the room.

"*They are gone,*" she said.

"What did she say?" Ann whispered, she, too, slitting one eye enough to peek through.

"*Are you sure?*" Zedd whispered to Nissel.

"*They packed everything they brought. They gathered food for the journey. Some of the women helped by putting together supplies they might take to sustain them. I gave them herbs that may be of use for little ills. Our hunters gave them waterskins and weapons. They said quick farewells to their friends, to those they have come to love. They made me promise to do my best to keep you well.*"

Nissel scratched her chin. "*Not much of a promise, the way I see it.*"

"*And you saw them leave?*" Zedd pressed. "*You are sure they are gone?*"

Nissel turned a little, skimming a hand through the air out toward the northeast. "*They started out. All three. I watched them go, just as you asked of me. I had walked with everyone else to the edge of the village, but most of our people wanted to walk a ways out into the grassland to be that much longer with them, and to watch our new Mud People go. These people urged me to come with them, so I, too, went out onto the grassland, even though my legs are not as swift as they used to be, but I decided they would be swift enough for a short walk.*

"When we had all gone a goodly distance, Richard urged us to return, rather than be out in the rain to no good end. He was concerned, especially, that I go back to care for you two. I believe they were impatient to make good time on their journey, and we all slowed them with our pace, but they were too considerate to speak those thoughts to us.

"Richard and Kahlan hugged me and wished me well. The woman in red leather did not hug me, but she did give me a bow of her head to show her respect and Kahlan told me the woman's words. She wished me to know she would protect Richard and Kahlan. She is a good woman, that strange one in red, even if she is not Mud People. I wished them well.

"All of us who had walked out into the grassland stood in the drizzle and waved as the three of them journeyed to the northeast, until they became spots too small to see anymore. The Bird Man then asked us all to bow our heads. Together, with his words leading us, we beseeched our ancestors' spirits to watch over our new people and keep them safe on their journey. He then called a hawk and sent it to travel with them for a ways, as a sign that our hearts were with them. We waited until we could no longer see even the hawk circling in the sky over the three of them.

"Then we returned straight away."

Tilting her head toward him, Nissel lifted an eyebrow. *"Does that satisfy you better than my simple word that they are gone?"*

Zedd cleared his throat, thinking the woman must practice sarcasm when there was no healing to be done.

"What did she say?" Ann asked again.

"She says they're gone."

"Is she sure?" Ann asked.

Zedd threw off his blanket. "How should I know? The woman gabs a lot. But I believe they're gone on their way."

Ann, too, threw aside her woolen blanket. "Thought I'd sweat to death under this scratchy thing."

They had remained under the blankets the whole time, silent and patient, fearing Richard might pop back in with some forgotten question or new idea. The boy frequently did such unexpected things. Zedd dared not precipitately betray himself, dared not let incautious action spoil their plans.

While they had waited, Ann had fretted and sweated. Zedd had taken a nap.

Pleased that Zedd had asked for her help, Nissel had promised to watch and let them know when the three were gone. She said those with age must stick together and that the only defense against youth was cunning. Zedd couldn't agree more. She had that twinkle in her eye that made Ann scowl in confused annoyance.

Zedd brushed his hands clean of the straw and straightened his robes. His back ached. At last he embraced the healer. *"Thank you, Nissel, for all your help. It is deeply appreciated."*

She giggled softly against his shoulder. *"For you, anything."* Upon parting, she pinched his bottom.

Zedd gave her a wink. *"How about some of that tava with honey, honey?"*

Nissel blushed. Ann's gaze shifted from one to the other. "What are you telling her?"

"Oh, just told her I appreciated her help and asked if we might have something to eat."

"Those are the itchiest blankets I've ever seen," Ann grumbled as she scratched furiously at her arms. "Tell Nissel she has my appreciation, too, but if you don't mind, I'll skip having my bottom pinched for it."

"Ann adds her sincere appreciation to mine. And she is much older than I." Among the Mud People, age lent weight to words.

Nissel's face wrinkled with a grin as she reached up and gave his cheek a doting pinch. *"I will get you both some tea and tava."*

"She seems to have grown quite fond of you." Ann smoothed back her hair as she watched the healer duck under the hide covering the door.

"And why not?"

Ann rolled her eyes and then brushed straw from her dark dress. "When did you learn the Mud People's language? You never mentioned to Richard or Kahlan that you knew their language."

"Oh, I learned it a very long time ago. I know a lot of things; I don't mention them all. Besides, I always think it best to leave yourself a little wiggle room, should it come in useful, such as now. I never really lied."

She conceded the point with a sound deep in her throat. "While it might not be a lie, it is still a deception."

Zedd smiled at her. "By the way, speaking of deceptions, I thought your performance was brilliant. Very convincing."

Ann was taken aback. "Well, I . . . well, thank you, Zedd. I guess I was pretty convincing."

He patted her shoulder. "That you were."

Her smile turned to a suspicious scowl. "Don't you try to sweet-talk me, old man. I'm a lot older than you and I've seen it all." She shook her finger up at him. "You know good and well I'm cross with you!"

Zedd put his fingertips to his chest. "Cross? With me? What have I done?"

"What have you done? Need I remind you of the word *Lurk*?" She stalked around in a little circle, arms raised, wrists bent over, fingers clawed, mimicking a fiend. "Oh, how frightening. Here comes a Lurk. Oh, how terrifying. Oh, how very scary."

She stamped to a halt before him. "What was going through your witless head! What possessed you to spout such a nonsensical word as *Lurk*! Are you crazy?"

Zedd pouted indignantly. "What's wrong with the name Lurk?"

Ann planted her fists on her wide hips. "What's wrong with it? What kind of a word is *Lurk* for an imaginary monster!"

"Well, quite a good one, actually."

"A good one! I nearly had heart failure when you first said it. I thought for sure Richard was going to realize we were making up a story and suddenly burst out laughing. It was all I could do to keep from laughing myself!"

"Laugh? Why would he laugh at the word *Lurk*? It's a perfectly good word. Has all the elements of a frightening creature."

"Have you gone loony? I've had ten-year-old boys I've caught at mischief come up with stories of pretend monsters plaguing them. They could, on the spot, when I snatched them by the ear, think up better names for those monsters than a 'Lurk.'

"Do you know the time I had keeping a straight face? Had it not been for the seriousness of our problem, I'd not have been able to do so. When you then again today insisted on repeating it I feared our ruse would be unmasked for sure."

Zedd folded his arms. "I didn't see them laughing. The three of them thought it was frightening. I think it had Richard's knees knocking there for a moment when I first revealed the name."

Muttering, Ann slapped her forehead. "Only luck preserved our artifice. You could have ruined it with such foolishness." She shook her head. "A Lurk. A *Lurk*!"

Zedd surmised it was probably her frustration and genuine fear bubbling to the surface, so he let her rant as she paced. Finally, she came to a halt, peering up with sputtering ire.

"Just where in Creation did you ever get such an asinine name for a monster? Lurk indeed," she added in a mutter.

Zedd scratched his neck as he cleared his throat. "Well, actually, in my youth when I was first married, I brought home a kitten for my new bride. She loved the little thing, and laughed endlessly at its antics. It pleased me to my toes to see the tears of joy in Erilyn's eyes as she laughed at that little ball of fur.

"I asked her what she wished to name the kitten, and she said that she enjoyed so much watching the way it incessantly lurked about, pouncing on things, that she would call it Lurk. That was where I got the name. I always like it, because of that."

Ann rolled her eyes. She sighed as she considered his words. She opened her mouth to say something, but closed it again and, with another sigh, instead gave his arm a consoling pat.

"Well, no harm done," she conceded. "No harm done." She bent and with a finger hooked the blanket. As she stood folding it, she asked, "What about the bottle? The one you told Richard was in the First Wizard's enclave at the Keep? What trouble is it likely to cause when he breaks it?"

"Oh, it was just a bottle I picked up in a market when I was traveling one time. When I saw it, I was immediately taken with the mastery it must have taken to make such a beautiful, graceful piece. After a long negotiation with the peddler, I finally wore him down and purchased it for a exceptionally good price.

"I liked the bottle so well that when I returned, I set it up on that pedestal. It was also a reminder of how, because of my skill at bargaining, I had obtained it at a remarkably good price. I thought it looked nice, there, and it made me proud of myself."

"Well, aren't you the clever one," Ann sniped.

"Yes, very. Not long after, I found a bottle exactly like it for half the price, and that was without haggling. I kept the bottle there on that pedestal to remind myself not to get cocky, just because I was First Wizard. It's just an old bottle kept as a lesson; no harm will come when Richard breaks it."

Ann chuckled as she shook her head. "If not for the gift, I fear to think what would have become of you."

"What I fear is that we are about to find out."

Already, as his magic was failing, he felt aches in his

bones, and lassitude in his muscles. It would get worse.

Ann's smile faded at the grim reality of his words.

"I don't understand it. What you told Richard was true: Kahlan would have to be his third wife to have called the chimes into this world. We know the chimes are here, yet it's impossible.

"Even given the convoluted ways magic can interpret incidents to constitute the fulfillment of requirements and conditions to trigger an event, she can be counted as no more than his second wife. There was that other one, that Nadine girl, and Kahlan. One and one equals two; Kahlan can be no more than number two."

Zedd shrugged. "We know the chimes have been unleashed. That is the problem we must address, not the how of it."

Ann grudgingly nodded her assent. "Do you think that grandson of yours will do as he says and go straight to the Keep?"

"He promised he would."

Ann's eyes turned up to him. "We are talking about Richard, here."

Zedd opened his hands in a helpless gesture. "I don't know what else we could have done to insure he goes to the Keep. We gave him every motivation, from noble to selfish, to rush there. He has no wiggle room. We made the consequences, should he fail to do as we told him he must, frighteningly clear to him."

"Yes," Ann said, smoothing the blanket folded over her arm, "we did everything except tell him the truth."

"We mostly told him the truth of what would happen if he doesn't go to the Keep. That was no lie, except that the truth is even more grim than we painted it for him.

"I know Richard. Kahlan loosed the chimes to save his life; he would be bound and determined to set it right, to help. He could only make what is bleak worse. We can't allow him to play with this fire. We gave him what he needs most: a way to help.

"His only safety is the Keep. The chimes can't get him

where they were called forth, and the Sword of Truth is the only magic likely to still work. We will see to this. Who knows, without him in their grasp, the threat could even die out on its own."

"Slim thread to hang the world on. However, I suppose you're right," Ann said. "He is one resolute man—like his grandfather."

She tossed the blanket on the pallet. "But at all costs, he must be protected. He leads D'Hara and is pulling the lands together under that banner to resist the scourge of the Imperial Order. In Aydindril, besides being safe, he can continue the task of forging unity. He has already proven his leadership ability. The prophecies warn that only he has a chance to successfully lead us in this struggle. Without him, we are lost for sure."

Nissel shuffled in carrying a tray of tava bread spread with honey and mint. She smiled at Zedd as she let Ann unload the three steaming cups of tea she was also holding. Nissel set the tray of tava on the floor before the pallets and sat down where Zedd had been lying. Ann handed her one of the cups and sat on the folded blanket at the head of the other pallet.

Nissel patted the bedding beside her. *"Come, sit, and have tava and tea before you must leave on your journey."*

Zedd, considering weighty matters, offered her a weak smile as he sat beside her. She sensed his somber mood and silently lifted the platter to offer him tava. Zedd, seeing she understood his worry if not its cause, slipped a thankful arm around her shoulders. With his other hand, he took a piece of sticky tava.

Zedd licked honey from the crusty edge. "I wish we knew something about that book Richard mentioned, *Mountain's Twin*. I wish I knew if he knew anything about it."

"He didn't seem to. All Verna told me at the time was that *Mountain's Twin* was destroyed."

Ann had already known that much when Richard asked. She had offered to inquire through her journey book, even

146

though its magic had already faded, so they might conceal from Richard the spreading extent of the trouble.

"I wish I'd had a look at it before it was destroyed."

Ann ate a few bites of her tava bread before she asked, "Zedd, what if we can't stop them? Our magic is already beginning to dwindle. It won't be long until it fails completely. How are we going to stop the chimes without magic?"

Zedd licked honey from his lips. "I'm still hoping answers can be found at the place they were entombed, somewhere in the land of Toscla. Or whatever they call it now. Perhaps I can find books there, books of the history or culture of the land. They might give me the clue I need."

Zedd was growing weaker by the day. His departing power sapped vitality as it bled away. His journey would be slow and difficult. Ann had the same trouble.

Nissel cuddled close to him, happy to simply be with someone who liked her as a woman, and didn't want healing from her. Her healing would not help him. He genuinely did like her. He felt sympathy for her, too, for a woman most people didn't understand. It was hard to be unlike those around you.

"Do you have any theories at all of how to banish the chimes from this world?" Ann asked between bites.

Zedd tore his tava bread in half. "Only what we discussed; if Richard stays at the Keep, then without him the chimes very well may be pulled back to the underworld even without our help. I know it's a slim hope, but I will just have to find a way to fight them back into the underworld if need be. How about you? Any ideas?"

"None."

"And do you still have your mind set on trying to rescue your Sisters of the Light from Jagang?"

She swished away a gnat. "Jagang's magic will fail just the same as all other magic. The dream walker will lose his grip on my Sisters. In danger there is opportunity. I must use the opportunity while it is available."

"Jagang still has a huge army. For one who often criticizes my plans, you prove no more ingenious at the task of scheming."

"The reward is well worth the risk." Ann lowered the hand with her tava. "I shouldn't admit it . . . but, since we are to part ways, I will say it. You are a clever man, Zeddicus Zu'l Zorander. I will miss your vexing company. Your trickster ways have saved our hides more than once. I admire your perseverance—and see where Richard gets his."

"Really? Well, I still don't like your plan. Flattery will not change that."

Ann simply smiled to herself.

Her plan was too artless, but he understood her commitment. Rescuing the Sisters of the Light was essential, and not simply because they were captives being brutalized. If the chimes could be banished, Jagang would again control those sorceresses, and so their power.

"Ann, fear can be a powerful master. If some of the Sisters don't believe you that they can escape, you can't allow them to remain a menace, albeit an unwilling one, to our cause."

Ann looked over out of the corner of her eye. "I understand."

He was asking her to either rescue them or assassinate them.

"Zedd," she said in soft compassion, "I don't like mentioning it, but if what Kahlan has done . . ."

"I know."

In calling forth the chimes, Kahlan had invoked their aid to save Richard's life. There was a price.

In return for keeping Richard in the world of life until he recovered, she had unwittingly pledged the chimes the one thing they needed in order to also remain in the world of life.

A soul. Richard's soul.

But he would be safe at the Keep; the place where they had been called was a safe haven for the one pledged.

Zedd put half his tava bread to Nissel's lips. She smiled

and chomped a big bite. She fed him a bite of her tava bread, after touching it to the end of his nose first. The foolishness of this old healer putting a dot of honey on his nose, like some mischievous little girl, made him chuckle.

Finally, Ann asked, "What ever happened to your cat, Lurk?"

Zedd frowned as he puzzled, trying to recollect. "To tell you the truth, I don't recall. So much was happening back then. The war with D'Hara—led by Richard's other grandfather, Panis Rahl—was just igniting. The lives of thousands hung under threat. I was yet to be named First Wizard. Erilyn was pregnant with our daughter.

"I guess with all that was going on, we just lost track of the cat. There are countless places in the Keep with mice; it probably found lurking about more appealing than two busy people."

Zedd swallowed at the painful memories. "After I moved to Westland, and Richard was born, I always kept a cat as a reminder of Erilyn and home."

Ann smiled in kind, sincere sympathy.

"I hope you never named one 'Lurk,' so that Richard would have cause to suddenly recall the name."

"No," Zedd whispered. "I never did."

CHAPTER 15

"FETCH!" MASTER DRUMMOND CALLED out.

Fitch pressed his lips tight trying unsuccessfully, he knew, to keep his face from going red. His smiled politely as he trotted past the snickering women.

"Yes, sir?"

Master Drummond wagged a hand toward the rear of the kitchen. "Fetch in some more of the apple wood."

Fitch bowed with a "Yes, sir," and headed toward the door out to the wood. Even though the kitchen was a fog of marvelous aromas, from sizzling butter and onions and spices to the mouthwatering savor of roasting meats, he was glad for the chance to get away from the crusty cauldrons. His fingers ached from scraping and scrubbing. He was glad, too, that Master Drummond didn't ask for any oak. Fitch was relieved to have done one thing right by having brought in enough of the oak.

Trotting through the patches of warm sunlight on his way down to the heap of apple wood, he wondered again why Minister Chanboor had wanted to see Beata. She had certainly looked happy enough about it. Women seemed to go all giddy whenever they got a chance to meet the Minister.

Fitch didn't see what was so special about the man. After all, he was starting to get gray in his hair; he was old. Fitch couldn't imagine himself ever getting old enough to have gray hairs. Just thinking about it made his nose wrinkle with disgust.

When he reached the woodpile, something caught his eye. He put a hand to his brow, shielding his eyes from the sunlight as he peered over to the shade of the turn round. He'd assumed it was just another delivery, but it was Brownie, still standing there with the butcher's cart.

He'd been busy in the kitchen and had thought Beata would have left long ago. There were any number of doors out, and he would have no way of knowing when she'd left. He'd just assumed she had.

It must have been an hour since she'd gone upstairs. Minister Chanboor probably wanted to give her a message for the butcher—some special request for his guests. Surely, he would have finished with her long ago.

So why was the cart still there?

Fitch bent and plucked a stick of apple wood. He shook his head in frustration; Minister Chanboor was probably telling her stories. Fitch hefted another billet from the woodpile. For some reason, women liked listening to the Minister's stories, and he liked telling them. He was always talking to women, telling them stories. Sometimes, at dinners and feasts, they gathered around him in giggling groups. Maybe they were just being polite—he was an important man, after all.

No girls worried about being polite to him, and they never much liked listening to his stories, either. Fitch gathered up the armload of apple wood and headed for the kitchen. He thought his stories about getting drunk were pretty funny, but girls weren't much interested in listening to them.

Morley liked his stories, at least. Morley, and the others who had pallets in the room where Fitch slept. They all liked telling each other stories, and they all liked to get drunk. There was nothing else to do on their rare time off from work and penance assembly.

At least at penance assembly they could sometimes talk to girls afterward, if their work was done and they didn't have to get back to it. But Fitch, like the others, found assembly a depressing experience, hearing all those terrible things. Sometimes, when they got back, if they could filch some wine or ale, they would get drunk.

After Fitch had brought in a dozen armloads, Master Drummond snagged his sleeve and shoved a piece of paper into his hand.

"Take this down to the brewer."

Fitch bowed and said his "Yes, sir" before starting out. He couldn't read the paper, but since there was going to be a feast and he'd carried such papers in the past, he guessed the columns of writing were probably orders for what the kitchen wanted brought up. He was glad for the errand because it didn't involve any real work, and it gave him a chance to get away from the heat and noise of the kitchen for a time, even if he did enjoy the aromas and could occasionally snatch a delicious scrap—all that tempting food was for guests, not the help. Sometimes, though, he just wanted away from the noise and confusion.

The old brewer, his dark Ander hair mostly gone and what was left mostly turned white, grunted as he read the paper Fitch handed him. Rather than sending Fitch on his way, the brewer wanted him to lug in some heavy sacks of trial hops. It was a common behest; Fitch was just a scullion, and so everyone had the right to order him to do work for them. He sighed, figuring it was the price for the slow walk he'd had, and the one he'd have on the way back.

When he went out to the service doors where much of the estate goods were delivered, he noticed that across the way Brownie was still standing there with the butcher's cart. He was relieved to see, stacked to the side of the loading dock, that there were only ten sacks to be lugged down to the brewery. When he'd finished with the sacks he was sent on his way.

Still catching his breath, he sauntered back through the service halls toward the kitchen, seeing few people, and all but one of them Haken servants so he had only to pause to bow that once. Echoing footsteps swished back to him as he climbed the flight of stairs up to the main floor and the kitchen. Just before going through the door, he paused.

He looked up at the stairwell's square ascent all the way to the third floor. No one was on the stairs. No one was in the halls. Master Drummond would believe him when he explained that the brewer wanted sacks brought in. Master Drummond was busy with preparations for that night's feast; he wouldn't bother asking how many sacks, and even if he did, he wasn't going to take the time to double-check.

Fitch was taking the steps two at a time almost before he'd realized that he'd decided to go have himself a quick look. At what, or for what, he wasn't sure.

He'd been on the second floor only a few times, and the third floor only once, just the week before to take the Minister's new aide, Dalton Campbell, an evening meal he'd ordered down to the kitchen. Fitch had been told by an Ander underling to leave the tray of sliced meats on the table in the empty outer office. The upper floors, in the west wing with the kitchen where Fitch worked, was where a number of officials' offices were located.

The Minister's offices were supposed to be on the third floor. From the stories Fitch had heard, the Minister had a number of offices. Why he would need more than one, Fitch couldn't guess. No one had ever explained it.

The first and second floors of the west wing, Fitch had heard it said, were where the vast Anderith Library was located. The library was a store of the land's rich and exemplary culture, drawing scholars and other important people to the estate. Anderith culture was a source of pride and the envy of all, Fitch had been taught.

The third floor of the east wing was the Minister's family quarters. His daughter, younger than Fitch by a maybe two or three years and dirt plain as Fitch heard it told, had gone off to an academy of some sort. He had only seen her from a distance, but he'd judged the description fair. Older servants sometimes whispered about an Ander guard who was put in chains because the Minister's daughter, Marcy or Marcia, depending on who was telling the story, accused him of something. Fitch had heard versions running from he was doing nothing but standing quietly guarding in a hall, to eavesdropping on her, to rape.

Voices echoed up the stairwell. Fitch paused with a foot on the next step, listening, every muscle stiff and still. As he remained motionless, it turned out to be someone passing along the first-floor hall, below. They weren't coming upstairs.

Thankfully, the Minister's wife, Lady Hildemara Chanboor, rarely came into the west wing where Fitch worked. Lady Chanboor was one Ander who made even other Anders tremble. She had a foul temper and was never pleased with anyone or anything. She had dismissed staff just because they'd glanced up at her as they passed her in a hall.

People who knew had told Fitch that Lady Chanboor had a face to match her temper: ugly. The unfortunate staff who had looked up at Lady Chanboor as they passed her in the hall were put out on the spot. Fitch learned they'd become beggars.

Fitch had heard the women in the kitchen say that Lady Chanboor would go unseen for weeks because the Minister would have enough of one thing or another from his wife and give her a black eye. Others said that she was just on a drunken binge. One old maid whispered that she went off with a lover from time to time.

Fitch reached the top step. There was no one in the halls of the third floor. Sunlight streamed in windows trimmed with gauzy lace to fall across bare wooden floors. Fitch paused on the landing at the top of the stairs. It had doors on three sides and the stairs on the other to his back. He looked down empty halls running left and right, not knowing if he dared walk down them.

He could be stopped by any number of people, from messengers to guards, and asked to explain what he was doing there. What could he say? Fitch didn't think he wanted to be a beggar.

As much as he didn't like to work, he did like to eat. He

seemed to always be hungry. The food wasn't as good as what was served to the important people of the household or to the guests, but it was decent, and he got enough. And when no one was watching, he and his friends did get to drink wine and ale. No, he didn't want to be put out to be a beggar.

He took a careful step into the center of the landing. His knee almost buckled and he nearly cried out as he felt something sharp stick him. There, under his bare foot, was a pin with a spiral end. The pin Beata used to close the collar of her dress.

Fitch picked it up, not knowing what it could mean. He could take it and give it to her later, possibly to her joy to have it returned. But maybe not. Maybe he should leave it where he'd found it, rather than have to explain to anyone, Beata especially, how he'd come to have it. Maybe she'd want to know what he was doing going up there; she'd been invited, he hadn't. Maybe she'd think he'd been spying on her.

He was bending to put the pin back when he saw movement—shadows—in the light coming from under one of the tall doors ahead. He cocked his head. He thought he heard Beata's voice, but he wasn't sure. He did hear muffled laughter.

Fitch checked right and left again. He saw no one. It wouldn't be like he was going down a hall. He would just be stepping across the landing at the top of the stairs. If anyone asked, he could say he was only intending to step into a hall to get a look at the view of the beautiful grounds from the third floor—to look out over the wheat fields that surrounded the capital city of Fairfield, the pride of Anderith.

That seemed plausible to him. They might yell but, surely, they wouldn't put him out. Not for looking out a window. Surely.

His heart pounded. His knees trembled. Before he could consider if it was a foolish risk, he tiptoed across to the heavy, four-panel door. He heard what sounded like a woman's whimpers. But he also heard chuckling, and a man panting.

Hundreds of little bubbles were preserved forever in the glass doorknob. There was no lock and so no keyhole beneath the ornate brass collar around the base of the glass knob. Putting his weight on his fingers, Fitch silently lowered himself to the floor until he was on his belly.

The closer he got to the floor, and the gap under the door, the better he could hear. It sounded like a man exerting himself somehow. The occasional chuckle was from a second man. Fitch heard a woman's choppy plaintive sob, like she couldn't get a breath before it was gone. Beata, he thought.

Fitch put his right cheek to the cold, varnished oak floor. He moved his face closer to the inch-tall opening under the door, seeing, as he did so, off a little to the left, chair legs, and before them, resting on the floor, one black boot ringed with silver studs. It moved just a little. Since there was only one, the man must have had his other foot crossed over the leg.

Fitch's hair felt as if it stood on end. He clearly recalled seeing the owner of that boot. It was the man with the strange cape, with the rings, with all the weapons. The man who'd taken a long look at Beata as he'd passed her cart.

Fitch couldn't see the source of the sounds. He silently snaked his body around and turned his face over to use his left eye to look under the door off to the right. He slid closer until his nose touched the door.

He blinked in disbelief and then again in horror.

Beata was on her back on the floor. Her blue dress was bunched up around her waist. There was a man, his backside naked, between her bare, open legs, going at her fast and furious.

Fitch sprang to his feet, jolted by what he'd seen. He retreated several steps. He panted, his eyes wide, his gut twisting with the shock of it. With the shock of having seen

Beata's bare, open legs. With the Minister between them. He turned to run down the stairs, tears stinging his eyes, his mouth hanging open, pulling for air like a carp out of water.

Footsteps echoed. Someone was coming up. He froze in the middle of the room, ten feet from the door, ten feet from the steps, not knowing what to do. He heard the footsteps shuffling up the stairs. He heard two voices. He looked to the halls on each side, trying to decide if one might offer escape, if one or both might offer a dead end where he would be trapped, or guards who might throw him in chains.

The two stopped on the landing below. It was two women. Ander women. They were gossiping about the feast that night. Who was going to be there. Who wasn't invited. Who was. Though their words were hardly more than whispered, in his stiff state of wide-eyed alarm he could make them out clear enough. Fitch's heart pounded in his ears as he panted in frozen panic, praying they wouldn't come up the stairs all the way to the third floor.

The two fell to discussing what they were going to wear to catch Minister Chanboor's eye. Fitch could hardly believe he was hearing a conversation about how close above their nipples they dared wear their neckline. The image it put in Fitch's head would have been blindingly pleasant had he not been trapped and about to be caught where he shouldn't be, seeing something he shouldn't have seen, and maybe get himself put out on the street, or worse. Much worse.

One woman seemed bolder than the second. The second said she intended to be noticed, too, but didn't want more than that. The first chuckled and said she wanted more than to be noticed by the Minister, and that the other shouldn't worry because either of their husbands would be lauded to have their wife catch the full attention of the Minister.

Fitch turned around to keep an eye on the Minister's door. Someone had already caught the attention of the Minister. Beata.

Fitch took a careful step to the left. The floor creaked. He stilled, alert, his ears feeling like they were stretching big. The two below were giggling about their husbands. Fitch pulled back the foot. Sweat trickled down the back of his neck.

The two below started moving as they talked. He held his breath. He heard a door squeak open. Fitch wanted to scream over his shoulder at them to hurry it up and go somewhere else to gossip. One of the women mentioned the other's husband—Dalton.

The door closed behind them. Fitch exhaled.

Right in front of him, the Minister's door burst open.

The big stranger had Beata by the upper arm. Her back was to Fitch as she was put out of the room. The man shoved her, as if she weighed no more than a feather pillow. She landed on her bottom with a thud. She didn't know Fitch was standing right behind her.

The stranger's unconcerned gaze met Fitch's wide eyes. The man's thick mat of dark hair, in tangled stringy strands, hung to his shoulders. His clothes were dark, covered in leather plates and straps and belts. Most of his weapons were lying on the floor in the room. He looked a man who didn't need them, though, a man who could, with his big calloused hands, crush the throat of nearly anyone.

When he turned back to the room, Fitch realized to his horror that the odd cape was made from scalps. That was why it looked like it was covered with patches of hair. Because it *was* covered with patches of hair, human hair. Every color from blond to black.

From beyond the doorframe, the Minister called the stranger by name, "Stein," and pitched him a small white handful of cloth. Stein caught it and then stretched Beata's underpants between two meaty fingers for a look. He tossed them into her lap as she sat on the floor struggling for breath, trying mightily not to cry.

Stein looked up into Fitch's eyes, completely unconcerned, and smiled. His smile wrinkled aside his heavy mat of stubble.

He gave Fitch a larking wink.

Fitch was stunned by the man's disregard for someone

being there, seeing what was happening. The Minister peered out as he buttoned his trousers. He, too, smiled, and then pulled the door shut behind himself as he stepped out into the hall.

"Shall we visit the library now?"

Stein held out a hand in invitation. "Lead the way, Minister."

Beata sat hanging her head as the two men, chatting amicably, strode off down the hall to the left. She seemed crushed by the ordeal, too disillusioned to be able to muster the will to stand, to leave, to go back to her life the way it had been.

Stock-still, Fitch waited, hoping that, somehow, the impossible would happen—that maybe she wouldn't turn, that maybe she would be confused and wander off down the other hall, and she wouldn't notice him there behind her, unblinking, holding his breath.

Sucking back her sobs, Beata staggered to her feet. When she turned and saw Fitch, she stiffened with a gasp. He stood paralyzed, wishing more than anything that he had never gone up the stairs for a look. He'd gotten considerably more of a look than he wanted.

"Beata . . ." He wanted to ask if she was hurt, but of course she was hurt. He wanted to comfort her, but didn't know how, didn't know the right words to use. He wanted to take her in his arms and shelter her, but he feared she might misconstrue his aching concern.

Beata's face warped from misery to blind rage. Her hand unexpectedly whipped around, striking his face with such fury that it made his head ring inside like a bell.

The wallop wrenched his head to the side. The room swam in his vision. He thought he saw someone in the distance down a hall, but he wasn't sure. As he tried to get his bearings, to grope for a railing as he staggered back, his hand found the floor instead. One knee joined his hand on the floor. He saw a blur of her blue dress as Beata raced down the stairs, the staccato sounds of her footfalls hammering an echo up the stairwell.

Dazing pain, sharp and hot, drove into his upper jaw just in front of his ringing ear. His eyes hurt. He was stupefied by how hard she had hit him. Nausea bloated in the pit of his stomach. He blinked, trying to force his vision to clear.

A hand under his arm startled him. It helped lift him back to his feet. Dalton Campbell's face loomed close to his.

Unlike the other two men, he did not smile but, rather, studied Fitch's eyes the way Master Drummond scrutinized a halibut brought in by the fishmonger. Just before he gutted it.

"What is your name?"

"Fitch, sir. I work in the kitchen, sir." Between the punch and his dread, Fitch's legs felt like boiled noodles.

The man glanced toward the stairs. "You seem to have wandered from the kitchen, don't you think?"

"I took a paper to the brewer." Fitch paused to gulp air, trying to make his voice stop trembling. "I was just on my way back to the kitchen, sir."

The hand tightened on Fitch's arm, drawing him closer. "Since you were rushing to the brewer, down on the lower level, and then right back to the kitchen, on the first floor, you must be a hardworking young man. I would have no reason to recall seeing you up here on the third floor." He released Fitch's arm. "I suppose I recall seeing you downstairs, rushing back to the kitchen from the brewer? Without wandering off anywhere along the way?"

Fitch's concern for Beata turned to a focused hope to keep himself from being thrown out of the house, or worse.

"Yes, sir. I'm on my way right back to the kitchen."

Dalton Campbell draped his hand over the hilt of his sword. "You've been working, and haven't seen a thing, have you?"

Fitch swallowed his terror. "No, sir. Nothing. I swear. Just that Minister Chanboor smiled at me. He's a great man, the Minister. I'm thankful that a man so great as he would give work to a worthless Haken such as myself."

The corners of Dalton Campbell's mouth turned up just enough that Fitch thought the aide might be pleased by what he'd heard. His fingers drummed along the length of the brass crossguard of his sword. Fitch stared at the lordly weapon. He felt driven to speak into the silence.

"I want to be good and be a worthy member of the household. To work hard. To earn my keep."

The smile widened. "That is indeed good to know. You seem a fine young man. Perhaps, since you are so earnest in your desire, I could count on you?"

Fitch wasn't sure exactly what he was to be counted on for, but he gave a "Yes, sir" anyway, and without hesitation.

"Since you swear you didn't see anything on your way back to the kitchen, you are proving to me that you are a lad of potential. Perhaps one who could be entrusted with more responsibility."

"Responsibility, sir?"

Dalton Campbell's dark eyes gleamed with a terrifying, incomprehensible intelligence, the kind Fitch imagined the mice must see in the eyes of the house cats.

"We sometimes have need of people desiring to move up in the household. We will see. Keep yourself vigilant against the lies of people wishing to bring disrepute to the Minister, and we will see."

"Yes, sir. I'd not like to hear anyone say anything against the Minister. He's a good man, the Minister. I hope the rumors I've heard are true, that one day we might be blessed enough by the Creator that Minister Chanboor would become Sovereign."

Now the aide's smile truly did take hold. "Yes, I do believe you have potential. Should you hear any . . . lies, about the Minister, I would appreciate knowing about it." He gestured toward the stairs. "Now, you had best get back to the kitchen."

"Yes, sir, if I hear any such thing, I'll bring it to you." Fitch made for the stairs. "I'd not want anyone lying about the Minister. That would be wrong."

"Young man—Fitch, was it?"

Fitch turned back from the top step. "Yes, sir. Fitch."

Dalton Campbell crossed his arms and turned his head to

peer with one questioning eye. "What have you learned at penance about protecting the Sovereign?"

"The Sovereign?" Fitch rubbed his palms on his trousers. "Well . . . um . . . that anything done to protect our Sovereign is a virtue?"

"Very good." Arms still folded, he leaned toward Fitch. "And, since you have heard that Minister Chanboor is likely to be named Sovereign, then . . . ?"

The man expected an answer. Fitch groped wildly for it. He cleared his throat, at last. "Well . . . I guess . . . that if he's to be named Sovereign, then maybe he ought to be protected the same?"

By the way Dalton Campbell smiled as he straightened his back, Fitch knew he'd hit upon the right answer. "You may indeed have potential to move up in the household."

"Thank you, sir. I would do anything to protect the Minister, seeing as how he'll be Sovereign one day. It's my duty to protect him in any way I can."

"Yes . . ." Dalton Campbell drawled in an odd way. He cocked his head, catlike, as he considered Fitch. "If you prove to be helpful in . . . whatever way we might need in order to protect the Minister, it would go a long way toward clearing your debt."

Fitch's ears perked up. "My debt, sir?"

"Like I told Morley, if he proves to be of use to the Minister, it might be that he could even earn himself a sir name, and a certificate signed by the Sovereign to go with it. You seem a bright lad. I would expect no less might be in your future."

Fitch's jaw hung open. Earning a sir name was one of his dreams. A certificate signed by the Sovereign proved to all that a Haken had paid his debt and was to be recognized with a sir name, and respected. His mind tumbled backward to what he'd just heard.

"Morley? Scullion Morley?"

"Yes, didn't he tell you I talked to him?"

Fitch scratched behind an ear, trying to imagine that Morley would have kept such astonishing news from him.

"Well, no, sir. He never said nothing. He's about my best friend; I'd recall if he'd said such a thing. I'm sorry, but he never did."

Dalton Campbell stroked a finger against the silver of the scabbard at his hip as he watched Fitch's eyes. "I told him not to mention it to anyone." He arched an eyebrow. "That kind of loyalty pays plums. I expect no less from you. Do you understand, Fitch?"

Fitch surely did. "Not a soul. Just like Morley. I got it, Master Campbell."

Dalton Campbell nodded as he smiled to himself. "Good." He again rested a hand on the hilt of his magnificent sword. "You know, Fitch, when a Haken has his debt paid, and earns his sir name, that signed certificate entitles him to carry a sword."

Fitch's eyes widened. "It does? I never knew."

The tall Ander smiled a stately farewell and with a noble flourish turned and started off down the hall. "Back to work, then, Fitch. Glad to have made your acquaintance. Perhaps we will speak again one day."

Before anyone else caught him up there, Fitch raced down the stairs. Confounding thoughts swirled through his head. Thinking again about Beata, and what had happened, he just wanted the day to end so he could get himself good and drunk.

He ached with sorrow for Beata, but it was the Minister, the Minister she admired, the Minister who would someday be Sovereign, that Fitch had seen on her. Besides, she struck him, a terrible thing for a Haken to do, even to another Haken, although he wasn't certain the prohibition extended to women. But even if it didn't, that wouldn't make him feel any less miserable about it.

For some unfathomable reason, she hated him, now.

He ached to get drunk.

CHAPTER 16

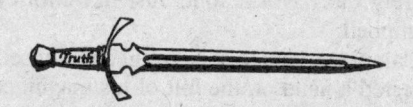

"FETCH! HERE, BOY! FETCH!"

Usually, when Master Drummond called him by that name, Fitch knew he blushed with humiliation, but this time he was in such anguish over what he had seen upstairs earlier that he hardly felt any shame over so petty a thing. Master Drummond's talking down to him as if he were dirt could not match Beata's hating him, and hitting him.

It had been a couple of hours, but his face still throbbed where she'd clouted him, so he was clear on that much of it: she hated him. It confused and confounded him, but he was sure she hated him. It seemed to him she should be angry at someone, anyone, besides him.

Angry at herself, maybe, for going up there in the first place. But he guessed she couldn't very well have refused to go see the Minister if he asked for her. Then Inger the butcher would have thrown her out when the Minister told him that his Haken girl refused to go up to take his special request. No, she couldn't very well have done that.

Besides, she wanted to meet the man. She'd told him she did. Fitch knew, though, that she never expected he would have his way with her. Maybe it wasn't the Minister she was so distraught about. Fitch remembered that man, Stein, winking at him. She was up there a long time.

That was still no reason for her to hate Fitch. Or to hit him.

Fitch came to a halt. His fingers throbbed from having them in scalding water for so long, scrubbing and scraping. The rest of him felt sick and numb. Except, of course, his face.

"Yes, sir?"

Master Drummond opened his mouth to speak, but then closed it and instead leaned down. He frowned.

"What happened to your face?"

"One of the billets of apple slipped and hit me as I picked up an armload, sir."

Master Drummond shook his head as he wiped his hands on his white towel. "Idiot," he muttered. "Only an idiot," he said, in a voice loud enough so others could hear, "would hit himself in the face with a stick of wood as he picked it up."

"Yes, sir."

Master Drummond was just about to speak when Dalton Campbell, studying a well-used piece of paper covered with messy lines of writing, glided up beside Fitch. He had a whole stack of disheveled papers, their curled and crumpled edges protruding every which way. He followed down the writing with one finger as he nested the papers in the crook of his other arm.

"Drummond, I came to make sure of a few items," he said without looking up.

Master Drummond quickly finished at wiping his hands and then straightened his broad back. "Yes sir, Mr. Campbell. Whatever I can do for you."

The Minister's aide lifted the paper to peer at a second sheet beneath.

"Have you seen to putting the best platters and ewers in the ambry?"

"Yes, Mr. Campbell."

Dalton muttered absently to himself about how they must have been changed after he'd looked. He scanned the paper and then flipped to a third piece. "You will need to make two additional places at the high table." He flipped back to the second page.

Master Drummond's mouth twisted in agitation. "Two more. Yes, Mr. Campbell. If you could, in the future, would you kindly let me know such as this a little earlier in the day?"

Dalton Campbell's finger flicked at the air, but his eyes never left his papers. "Yes, yes. Only too happy to do so. If the Minister informs me of it sooner, that is." He tapped a place in his papers and looked up. "Lady Chanboor objects to the musicians' stomachs grumbling along with their music. Please see to it that they are fed something first, this time? Especially the harpist. She will be closest to Lady Chanboor."

Master Drummond dipped his head in acknowledgment. "Yes, Mr. Campbell. I will see to it."

Fitch, ever so slowly so as not to be obvious, slipped backward several paces, keeping his head down, trying not to appear as if he were listening to the Minister's aide giving the kitchen master instructions. He wished he could leave, rather than risk being thought a snoop, but he knew he'd be yelled at if he left without being sent off, so he compromised at trying to be inconspicuous but at hand.

"And the spiced wine, there needs to be more of a variety this time. Some people thought last time's selection skimpy. Hot and cold, both, please."

Master Drummond pressed his lips together. "Short notice, Mr. Campbell. If you could, in the future—"

"Yes, yes, if I am informed, so will you be." He flipped over another page. "Dainties. They are to be served at the head table only, until they have had their fill. Last time the Minister was embarrassed to discover them gone and some guests at his table left wanting more. Let the other tables go wanting, first, if for some reason you have been unable to acquire a proper supply."

Fitch remembered that incident, too, and he knew that this time Master Drummond had ordered more of the deer testicles fried up. Fitch had pilfered one of the treats as he took the fry pan to be washed, although he had to eat it without the sweet-and-sour sauce. It was still good.

As Dalton Campbell checked his papers, he asked questions about different salts, butters, and breads, and gave Master Drummond a few more corrections to the dinner. Fitch, as he waited, trying not to watch the two men, watched instead the woman at a nearby table make the pig's stomachs, stuffed with ground meats, cheeses, eggs, and spices, into hedgehogs by covering them with almond "spines."

At another table, two women were re-feathering roasted peacocks with feathers colored by saffron and yellow turnsole. Even the beaks and claws were colored, so that the newly plumed birds looked like spectacular creatures of gold—like gold statues—only more lifelike.

Dalton Campbell, at last seeming to finish with his list of questions and instructions, lowered his arms, one hand loosely holding the hand holding the papers.

"Is there anything you would like to report, Drummond?"

The kitchen master licked his lips, seeming not to know what the aide was talking about. "No, Mr. Campbell."

"And everyone in your kitchen, then, is doing their job to your satisfaction?" His face was blank of emotion.

Fitch saw eyes in the room cautiously turn up for a quick peek. The work going on all about seemed to grow quieter. He could almost see ears getting bigger.

It seemed to Fitch like maybe Dalton Campbell was working around the edges of accusing Master Drummond of not running a good kitchen by allowing lazy people to avoid their duties and then failing to punish them. The kitchen master seemed to suspect the same accusation.

"Well, yes sir, they are doing their job to my satisfaction. I keep them in line, Mr. Campbell. I'll not have slackers ruining the workings of my kitchen. I couldn't have that; this is too important a household to allow any sluggard to spoil things. I don't allow it, no sir, I don't."

Dalton Campbell nodded his pleasure at hearing this. "Very good, Drummond. I, too, would not like to have slackers in the household." He scanned the room of silent, quietly hardworking people. "Very well. Thank you, Drummond. I will check back later, before it's time to begin serving."

Master Drummond bowed his head. "Thank you, Mr. Campbell."

The Minister's aide turned and started to leave, and as he did so, he caught sight of Fitch standing there. As he frowned, Fitch lowered his head on his shoulders even more, wishing he could melt into the cracks in the wood floor. Dalton Campbell glanced back over his shoulder at the kitchen master.

"What is this scullion's name?"

"Fitch, Mr. Campbell."

"Fitch. Ah, I get it, then. And how long has he worked in the household?"

"Some four years, Mr. Campbell."

"Four years. That long." He turned fully around to face Master Drummond. "And is he a slacker, then, who ruins the workings of your fine kitchen? One who should have been put out of the household long ago, but has not been for some mysterious reason? You haven't been overlooking your responsibility as kitchen master, allowing a slacker to be under the Minister's roof, have you? Are you truly guilty of such dereliction?"

Fitch stood in frozen terror, wondering if he would be beaten before they threw him out, or if they would simply show him the door and send him away without so much as a morsel of food. Master Drummond's gaze flicked back and forth between Fitch and the aide.

"Well, uh, no sir. No, Mr. Campbell. I see to it that Fitch pulls his share of the load. I'd not let him be a slacker under the Minister's roof. No sir."

Dalton Campbell peered back at Fitch with a puzzling expression. He looked once again to the kitchen master. "Well, then, if he does as you ask, and does his work, I see no reason to demean the young man by calling him Fetch, do you? Don't you think that reflects badly on you, Drummond, as kitchen master?"

"Well, I—"

"Very good, then. I'm glad you agree. We'll have no more of that kind of thing in the household."

Either with stealth or bold intent, nearly every eye in the kitchen was on the exchange between the two men. That fact was not lost on the kitchen master.

"Well, now, just a minute, if you don't mind. No real harm is meant, and the boy doesn't mind, do you now, Fitch—"

Dalton Campbell's posture changed in a way that halted the words in Master Drummond's mouth before they could finish coming out. The noble-looking aide's dark Ander eyes took on a dangerous gleam. He seemed suddenly taller, his shoulders broader, his muscles more evident under his fine, dark blue doublet and quilted jerkin.

His offhanded, distracted, casual, and at times stuffy official tone was suddenly gone. He'd transformed into a threat as deadly-looking as the weapon at his hip.

"Let me put it another way for you, Drummond. We'll not have that sort of thing under this roof. I expect you to comply with my wishes. If I ever again hear you demean any of our staff by calling them by names intended to be humiliating, I will have a new kitchen master and you put out. Is that clear?"

"Yes, sir. Very clear, thank you, sir."

Campbell started to leave, but turned back, his whole person conveying the image of menace. "One other thing. Minister Chanboor gives me orders, and I carry them out without fail. That is my job. I give you orders, and you carry them out without fail. That is your job.

"I expect the boy to do his work or be put out, but you put him out and you had better be prepared to provide proof of why, and moreover, if you make it hard on him because of my orders, then I will not put you out, but instead I will gut you and have you roasted on that spit over there. Now, is all that absolutely clear, Mr. Drummond?"

Fitch hadn't known Master Drummond's eyes could go so wide. Sweat beaded all over his forehead. He swallowed before he spoke.

"Yes sir, absolutely clear. It will be as you say. You have my word."

Dalton Campbell seemed to shrink back to his normal size, which was not small to begin with. The pleasant expression returned to his face, including the polite smile.

"Thank you, Drummond. Carry on."

Not once during the exchange had Dalton Campbell looked at Fitch, nor did he as he turned and strode out of the kitchen. Along with Master Drummond and half the people in the kitchen, Fitch let out his breath.

When he thought again about what had just happened, and he realized, for the first time, really, that Master Drummond would no longer be calling him "Fetch," he was overcome with weak-kneed astonishment. He suddenly thought very highly of Dalton Campbell.

Pulling his white towel from behind his belt and blotting his forehead, Master Drummond noticed people watching. "Back to work, all of you." He replaced the towel. "Fitch," he called in a normal voice, just like when he called the other people in his kitchen.

Fitch took two quick steps forward. "Yes, sir?"

He gestured. "We need some more oak. Not as much as the last time. About half that much. Be quick about it, now."

"Yes, sir."

Fitch ran for the door, eager to get the wood, not even caring about the splinters he might get.

He would never again have to be humiliated by that hated name. People would not laugh at him over it. All because of Dalton Campbell.

At that moment, Fitch would have carried hot coals in his bare hands if Dalton Campbell asked it, and smiled all the way.

CHAPTER 17

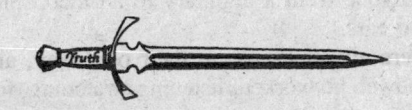

UNBUTTONING THE TOP BUTTON of his doublet, Dalton Campbell, with his other hand, nudged the tall mahogany door to their quarters until he felt the latch click home. At once, the balm of quiet began to soothe him. It had been a long day, and it was far from over; there was still the feast to attend.

"Teresa," he called across the sitting room back toward the bedroom, "it's me."

He wished they could stay in. Stay in and make love. His nerves needed the diversion. Later, perhaps. If business didn't interfere.

He unfastened another button and tugged open the collar as he yawned. The fragrance of lilacs filled his lungs. Heavy blue moire drapes at the far windows were drawn against the darkening sky, leaving the room to perfumed mellow lamplight, scented candles, and the flickering glow of a low fire in the hearth, burning for the cheer it brought, rather than the need of heat.

He noted the dark violet carpet and its wheat-colored fringe looked freshly brushed. The gilded chairs were angled to show off the tawny leather seats and backs as they posed beside elegant tables set with lush sprays of fresh flowers. The plush throws and pillows on the couches were set just so, the deliberate precision meant to convey a casual intimacy with luxury.

Dalton expected his wife to oversee the staff and insure that the quarters were kept presentable for business as well as entertaining, which were, although approached differently, one and the same. Teresa would know that with a feast that night, it was even more likely he would ask someone back to their apartments—someone important. That could be anyone from a dignitary to an inconspicuous pair of eyes and ears.

They were all important, in their own way, all meshing into the cobweb he worked, listening, watching, for any tiny little tug. Crowded feasts were concentrated confusion, alive with drinking, conversation, commotion, and emotion. They often provided opportunities to forge alliances, reinforce loyalties, or enforce fealties—to tend his cobweb.

Teresa stuck her head past the doorframe, grinning her joy upon seeing him. "There's my sweetheart."

Despite the weary mood enveloping him as he had closed the door behind, shutting out the day's troubles if only for the moment, he smiled helplessly at her dark, sparkling eyes.

"Tess, my darling. Your hair looks grand."

A gold comb decorated the front lift of the full top. The wealth of dangling dark tresses were tied with an abundance of sequined gold ribbons that added to her hair's length, almost forming a collar. Parting as she leaned forward, the sparkling strips teasingly revealed her graceful neck.

In her mid-twenties, she was younger than he by nearly ten years. Dalton thought her a ravishing creature beyond compare—a bonus to her allure of trenchant commitment to objectives. He could scarcely believe that a short six months ago she had finally and at long last become his wife. Others had been in contention, some of greater standing, but none with more ambition.

Dalton Campbell was not a man to be denied. Anyone who took him lightly came to a day of reckoning, when they learned better than to underestimate him, or came to regret the mistake.

Nearly a year ago, when he had asked her to be his wife, she had quizzed him, asking, in that velvet bantering manner of hers that often cloaked the steel of her aims, if he was really a man who intending on going places, as she certainly meant to rise up in the world. At the time, he had been an assistant to the magistrate in Fairfield, not an unimportant job, but only a convenient port as far as he was concerned, a place to gather his resources and cultivate connections.

He had not played into her chaffing questions, but instead assured her in all sobriety that he was a man on the way up, and no other man she was seeing, despite his present station, had any chance of approaching Dalton Campbell's future stature. She had been taken aback by his solemn declaration. It wiped the smile off her face. On the spot, in the spell of his conviction, the truth of his purpose, she consented to marry him.

She had been pleased to learn the reliability of his predictions. As plans proceeded for their wedding, he was awarded a better appointment. In their first few months of marriage, they had moved three times, always to improved quarters, and as a result of advanced positions.

The public who had cause to know of him, either because of his reputation or because of their dealings with Anderith government, valued his keen understanding of Anderith law. Dalton Campbell was widely recognized for his brilliant insight into the complexities of the law, the fortress bedrock it was built upon, the intricate structure of its wisdom and precedent, and the scope of its protective walls.

The men for whom Dalton worked appreciated his vast understanding of the law, but valued most his knowledge of the law's arcane passages, burrows, and obscure openings out of dark traps and corners. They also valued his ability to swiftly abandon the law when the situation required a different solution, one the law couldn't provide. In such cases, he was just as inventive, and just as effective.

In no more time than a snap of the fingers, it seemed, Teresa easily adjusted to the meliorated circumstances in which she regularly found herself, taking up the novel task

173

of directing household staff with the aplomb of one who had been doing it for the whole of her life.

Only weeks before, he had won the top post at the Minister's estate. Teresa had been jubilant to learn they would be taking on luxurious quarters in such a prestigious place. She now found herself a woman of standing among women of rank and privilege.

She might have been overjoyed, nearly tearing off his clothes to have him on the spot when he told her the news, but the truth be known, she had expected no less.

If there was one person who shared his ruthless ambition, it was Teresa.

"Oh, Dalton, will you tell me what dignitaries will be at the feast? I can't stand the suspense a moment longer."

He yawned again as he stretched. He knew she had her own cobwebs to tend.

"Boring dignitaries."

"But the Minister will be there."

"Yes."

"Well, silly, he's not boring. And I've gotten to know some of the women, the wives, of the estate. They're all grand people. Good as I could have hoped. Their husbands are all important."

She touched the tip of her tongue to her upper lip in a sly, teasing gesture. "Just not as important as my husband."

"Tess, my darling," he said with a smile, "you could inspire a dead man to become important for you."

She winked and then disappeared. "There were several messages slipped under the door for you," she called back from the other room. "They're in the desk."

The elegant desk in the corner glowed like a dark gem. Made of polished elm burl, each panel of quartered, book-matched veneer was outlined with diamond-patterned banding of alternating plain and dyed maple. Each dark diamond was inset with a dot of gold. The legs were varnished to a deep luster, rather than gilded, as were the legs of most of the other furniture in the room.

In the secret compartment behind an upper drawer, there

were several sealed messages. He broke the seals and scanned each message, assessing its importance. Some were of interest, but none were urgent. They mostly meant to pass along information—little vibrations from every corner of his cobweb.

One reported an odd and apparently accidental drowning in a public fountain. It had happened in early afternoon as crowds regularly passed the landmark in the Square of the Martyrs. Even though it had been daylight and in full view of everyone, no one noticed until it was too late. Having seen similar messages of unexplained deaths of late, Dalton knew the unspoken implication of the message was a admonition, that it might have been some sort of a vendetta involving magic, but made to look like an unfortunate accident.

One mentioned only a "perturbed lady," reporting that she was restless and that she had written a missive to a Director, asking for a moment of his time in private at the feast, and asking him to keep her letter confidential. Dalton knew the woman to whom the message referred, and, because of that, he knew also it would be Director Linscott to whom she had written—the person writing the message for him knew better than to write down names.

He suspected the reason for the restless part. It was the desire for the private meeting that concerned him. The message said the woman's letter was somehow lost, and never delivered.

Dalton slipped the messages back into the compartment for later review and replaced the drawer. He was going to have to do something about the woman. What, he didn't yet know.

Overreacting could sometimes cause as much trouble as doing nothing. It might be he need only give the woman an ear, let her vent her pique, as perhaps she meant to do with Director Linscott. Dalton could just as easily hear her grievance. Someone, somewhere in his intricate cobweb of contacts, would give him the bit of information he needed to make the right decision, and if not, talking to the woman in a reassuring manner might smooth things enough to give him the direction he needed.

Dalton had only had his new post a short time, but he'd wasted none of it in establishing himself in nearly every aspect of life at the estate. He became a useful colleague to many, a confidant to others, and shield to a few. Each method, in its own way, earned him loyalty. Along with the gifted people he knew, his evergrowing cobweb of connections virtually hummed like a harp.

From the first day, though, Dalton's primary objective had been to make himself indispensable to the Minister. During his second week on the job, a "researcher" had been sent out to the estate libraries by one of the Directors from the Office of Cultural Amity. Minister Chanboor had not been pleased. The truth be known, he had flown into a resentful rage, not an uncommon response from Bertrand Chanboor when presented with worrisome, even ominous, news.

Two days after the researcher arrived, Dalton was able to inform Minister Chanboor that the man had ended up getting himself arrested, drunk and in the bed of a harlot back in Fairfield. None of that was a crime of any consequence, of course, even though it would have looked bad enough to some of the Directors, but the man was found to have had an extremely rare and valuable book in the pocket of his coat.

An extremely rare and valuable book written by none other than Joseph Ander himself. The ancient text, valuable beyond price, had been reported missing from the Minister of Culture's estate right after the researcher went off drinking.

At Dalton's instructions, the Directors' office was immediately informed of the book's disappearance—hours before the culprit was apprehended. With the report, Dalton had sent his personal assurance to the Directors that he would not rest until the malefactor was found, and that he intended to launch an immediate public investigation to discover if such a cultural crime was the precursor to a treasonous plot. The stunned silence from the Office of the Directors had been thunderous.

The magistrate in Fairfield, the one for whom Dalton had once worked, was an admirer of the Minister of Culture, serving as he did at the Minister's pleasure, and of course did not take lightly the theft from the Anderith Library of Culture. He recognized the theft for what it was: sedition. The researcher who had been caught with the book was swiftly put to death for cultural crimes against the Anderith people.

Far from quelling the scandal, this caused the air to become rampant with ugly rumors of a confession, taken before the man was put to death—a confession, it was said, that implicated others. The Director who had sent the man to the estate to do "research," rather than be associated with a cultural crime, as a point of honor and in order to end speculation and innuendo, had resigned. Dalton, as the Minister's official representative looking into the whole affair, after reluctantly taking the Director's resignation, issued a statement discrediting the rumors of a confession, and officially closed the entire matter.

An old friend of Dalton's had been fortunate enough to earn the appointment to the suddenly vacant seat for which he had been working nearly his whole life. Dalton had been the first to shake his hand, the hand of a new Director. A more grateful and joyous man Dalton had never met. Dalton was pleased by that, by seeing deserving people, people he loved and trusted, happy.

After the incident, Bertrand Chanboor decided his responsibilities required a closer working relationship with his aide, and designated Dalton as chief of staff, as well as aide to the Minister, thus giving him authority over the entire household. Dalton now reported only to the Minister. The position had also accorded them their latest quarters—the finest on the estate other than those of the Minister himself.

Dalton thought Teresa had been even more pleased about it than he—if that was possible. She was in love with the apartment that came with the elevated authority. She was captivated by the people of noble standing among whom she now mingled. She was intoxicated with meeting important and powerful people who came to the estate.

Those guests, as well as people of the estate, treated Teresa with the deference due one of her high standing, despite the fact that most of them were nobly born and she, like Dalton, was well born but not noble. Dalton had always found matters of birth to be petty, and less consequential than some people thought, once they understood how auspicious allegiances could be considerably more significant to a providential life.

Across the room, Teresa cleared her throat. When Dalton turned from the desk, she lifted her nose and with noble grace stepped out into the sitting room to display herself in her new dress.

His eyes widened. Displaying herself was exactly what she was doing.

The fabric glimmered dreamlike in the light from lamps, candles, and the low fire. Golden patterns of leafy designs swirled across a dark background. Goldcolored piping trimmed seams and edges, drawing attention to her narrow waist and voluptuous curves. The silk fabric of the skirt, like new wheat hugging every nuance of the rolling lowland hills, betrayed the shape of her curvaceous legs beneath.

But it was the neckline that had him speechless. Sweeping down from the ends of her shoulders, it plunged to an outrageous depth. The sight of her sensuous breasts so exposed had a profound effect on him, as arousing as it was unsettling.

Teresa twirled around, showing off the dress, the deeply cut back, the way it sparkled in the light. With long strides Dalton crossed the room to catch her in his arms as she came back around the second time. She giggled to find herself trapped in his embrace. He bent to kiss her, but she pushed his face away.

"Careful. I've spent hours painting my face. Don't muss it, Dalton."

She moaned helplessly against his mouth as he kissed her anyway. She seemed pleased with the effect she was having on him. He was pleased with the effect she was having on him.

Teresa pulled back. She reached up and tugged the sequined gold ribbons tied to her hair.

"Sweetheart, does it look any longer yet?" she asked in a pleading voice. "It's pure misery waiting for it to grow."

With his new post and attendant new apartments, he was moving up in the world, becoming a man of power. With that new authority came the privileges of rank: his wife was allowed to wear longer hair to reflect her status.

Other wives in the household wore hair nearly to their shoulders; his wife would be no different, except perhaps that her hair would be just a little longer than all but a few other women in the house, or in the whole land of Anderith—for that matter, in the whole of the Midlands. She was married to an important man.

The thought washed through him with icy excitement, as it did from time to time when it really sank in just how far he had risen, and what he had attained.

Dalton Campbell intended this to be only the beginning. He intended to go further. He had plans. And he had the ear of a man with a lust for plans.

Among other things. But, no matter; Dalton could handle such petty matters. The Minister was simply taking the perks of his position.

"Tess, darling, your hair is growing beautifully. If any woman looks down her nose at you for it not yet being longer, you just remember her name, for your hair in the end will be longer than any of theirs. When it finally grows, you can then revisit that name for recompense."

Teresa bounced on the balls of her feet as she threw her arms around his neck. She squealed in giddy delight.

Intertwining her fingers behind his back, she peeked up at him with a coquettish look. "Do you like my dress?" To make her point, she pressed up against him while gazing into his eyes, watching deliberately as his gaze roamed lower.

In answer, he bent to her, and in one swift motion slipped his hand up under her silky skirt, along the inside of her leg, up to the bare flesh above her stockings. She gasped in mock surprise as his hand reached her private places.

Dalton kissed her again as he groped her. He was no longer thinking about taking her to the feast. He wanted to take her to the bed.

As he pushed her toward the bedroom, she squirmed out of his lustful grip. "Dalton! Don't muss me, sweetheart. Everyone will see the wrinkles in my dress."

"I don't think anyone will be looking at the wrinkles in the dress. I think they will be looking at what is spilling out of it.

"Teresa, I don't want you to wear such a thing anywhere but to greet your husband at the door upon his return home to you."

She playfully swatted his shoulder. "Dalton, stop."

"I mean it." He looked down her cleavage again. "Teresa, this dress is . . . it shows too much."

She turned away. "Oh, Dalton, stop. You're being silly. All the women are wearing such dresses nowadays." She twirled to him, the flirt back on her face. "You aren't jealous, are you? Having other men admire your wife?"

She was the one thing he had wanted more than power. Unlike everything else in his life, he entertained no invitations for understandings where Teresa was concerned. The spirits knew there were enough men at the estate who were admired, even envied, because they gained for themselves the courtesy of influence, inasmuch as their wives made themselves available to Minister Chanboor. Dalton Campbell was not one of them. He used his talent and wits to get where he was, not his wife's body. That, too, gave him an edge over the others.

His forbearance was rapidly evaporating, leaving his tone less than indulgent. "And how will they know it to be my wife? Their eyes will never make it up to your face."

"Dalton, stop. You're being insufferably stodgy. All the other women will be wearing dresses similar to this. It's the style. You're always so busy with your new job you don't know anything about prevailing custom. I do.

"Believe it or not, this dress is conservative compared to what others will be wearing. I wouldn't wear a dress as revealing as theirs—I know how you get—but I don't want to look out of place, either. No one will think anything of it, except that perhaps the wife of the Minister's right-hand man is a tad prissy."

No one was going to think her "prissy." They were going to think she was proclaiming herself available to invitation.

"Teresa, you can wear another. The red one with the V neck. You can still see . . . see enough of your cleavage. The red one is hardly prissy."

She showed him her back, folding her arms in a pout. "I suppose you will be happy to have me wear a homely dress, and have every other woman there whispering behind my back at how I dress like the wife of a lowly assistant to a magistrate. The red dress was what I wore when you were a nobody. I thought you would be happy to see me in my new dress, to see how your wife can fit in with the fashion of the important women here.

"But now I'll never fit in around here. I'll be the stuffy wife of the Minister's aide. No one will even want to talk to me. I'll never have any friends."

Dalton drew a deep breath, letting it out slowly. He watched her dab a knuckle at her nose. "Tess, is this really what the other women will be wearing at the feast?"

She spun around, beaming up at him. It occurred to him that it was not so unlike the way the Haken girl, down in the kitchen, had beamed at his invitation to meet the Minister of Culture.

"Of course it's like what the other women are wearing. Except that I'm not as bold as they, so it shows less. Oh, Dalton, you'll see. You'll be proud of me. I want to be a proper wife of the Minister's aide. I want you to be proud. I'm proud of you. Only you, Dalton.

"A wife is crucial to a man as important as you. I protect your station when you aren't there. You don't know what women can be like—petty, jealous, ambitious, scheming, treacherous, traitorous. One clever nasty word to their husband, and soon it's on every tongue. I make sure that if there is a nasty word, it dies quickly, that none dare repeat it."

He nodded; he knew full well that women brought their husbands information and gossip. "I suppose."

"You always said we were partners. You know how I protect you. You know how hard I work to make sure you fit in at each new place we go. You know I would never do anything to jeopardize what you've worked so hard to gain for us. You always told me how you would take me to the best places, and I would be accepted as the equal of any woman.

"You've done as you promised, my husband. I always knew you would; that was why I agreed to marry you. Even though I always loved you, I would never have married you had I not believed in your future. We have only each other, Dalton.

"Have I ever made a misstep when we went to a new place?"

"No, Tess, you never have."

"Do you think I would recklessly do so, now, at a place as important as this? When you stand on the brink of true greatness?"

Teresa was the only one in whom he confided his audacious ambitions, his boldest plans. She knew what he intended, and she never derided him for it. She believed him.

"No, Tess, you wouldn't jeopardize all that. I know you wouldn't." He wiped a hand over his face as he sighed. "Wear the dress, if you think it proper. I will trust your judgment."

The matter settled, she shoved him toward the dressing room. "Come on, now, change your clothes. Get ready. You will be the most handsome one there, I just know it. If there is any cause for jealously, it is I who will have it, for all

182

the other wives will be green with envy that I have the prize of the household, and it is you who will get the whispered invitations."

He turned her around and grasped her by the shoulders, waiting until she looked up into his eyes. "You just stay away from a man named Stein—Bertrand's guest of honor. Keep your . . . your new dress out of his face. Understand?"

She nodded. "How will I know him?"

He released her shoulders and straightened. "It won't be hard. He wears a cape of human scalps."

Teresa gasped. "No." She leaned closer. "The one you told me about, come from beyond the wilds to the south? From the Old World? Come to discuss our future allegiance?"

"Yes. Stay away from him."

She blinked again at such startling news. "How stimulating. I don't know that anyone here has ever met such an interesting foreigner. He must be very important."

"He is an important man, a man with whom we will be discussing business, so I'd like not to have to slice him into little pieces for trying to force you to his bed. It would waste valuable time, waiting for the emperor to send another representative from the Old World."

It was no idle boast, and she knew it. He studied the sword as intently as he studied the law. Dalton could behead a flea on a peach without disturbing the fuzz.

Teresa smirked. "He need not look my way, and he'll not sleep alone tonight, either. There will be women fighting over the chance to be with so outrageous a man. Human scalps . . ." She shook her head at so astounding a notion. "The woman who wins his bed will be at the head of every invitation for months to come."

"Maybe they would like to invite a Haken girl to tell them how exciting and grand it was," Dalton snapped.

"Haken girl?" Teresa grunted dismissively at such whimsy. "I think not. Haken girls don't count to those women."

She turned once more to the important part of his news.

"So, no decision has yet been made? We still don't know if Anderith will stick with the Midlands, or if we will break and join with Emperor Jagang from the Old World?"

"No, we don't yet know how it will go. The Directors are divided. Stein only just arrived to speak his piece."

She stretched up on her toes to give him a peck. "I will stay away from the man. While you help decide the fate of Anderith, I will watch your back, as always, and keep my ears open."

She took a step toward the bedroom, but spun back to him. "If the man has come to speak his side of matters . . ." Sudden realization stole into her dark eyes. "Dalton, the Sovereign is going to be here tonight, isn't he? The Sovereign himself will be at the feast."

Dalton took her chin in his fingertips. "A smart wife is the best ally a man can have."

Smiling, he let her seize him by his little fingers and tug, pulling him into the dressing room. "I've only seen the man from afar. Oh, Dalton, you are a marvel, bringing me to such a place as I would get to break bread with the Sovereign himself."

"You just remember what I said and stay away from Stein, unless I'm with you. For that matter, the same goes for Bertrand, though I doubt he'd dare to cross me. If you're good, I'll introduce you to the Sovereign."

She was struck speechless for only a moment. "When we retire to bed tonight, you will find out just how good I can be. The spirits preserve me," she added in a whisper, "I hope I can wait that long. The Sovereign. Oh, Dalton, you are a marvel."

While she sat before a mirror on her dressing table, checking her face to see what damage he had wrought with his kisses, Dalton pulled open the tall wardrobe. "So, Tess, what gossip have you heard?"

He peered into the wardrobe, looking through his shirts, looking for the one with the collar he liked best. Since her dress was a golden color, he changed his plans and decided to wear his red coat. Best, anyway, if he was to put forth an assured appearance.

As Teresa leaned toward the mirror, dabbing her cheeks with a small sponge she had dragged across a silver container of rose-colored powder, she rambled on about the gossip of the house. None of it sounded important to Dalton. His thoughts wandered to the real concerns with which he had to deal, to the Directors he had yet to convince, and about how to handle Bertrand Chanboor.

The Minister was a cunning man, a man Dalton understood. The Minister shared Dalton's ambition, if in a larger, more public sense. Bertrand Chanboor was a man who wanted everything—everything from a Haken girl who caught his eye to the seat of the sovereign. If Dalton had any say, and he did, Bertrand Chanboor would get what Bertrand Chanboor wanted.

And Dalton would have the power and authority he wanted. He didn't need to be Sovereign. Minister of Culture would do.

The Minister of Culture was the true power in the land of Anderith, making most laws and appointing magistrates to see them carried through. The Minister of Culture's influence and authority touched every business, every person in the land. He held sway over commerce, arts, institutions, and beliefs. He oversaw the army and all public projects. He was the embodiment of religion, as well. The Sovereign was all ceremony and pomp, jewels and exquisite dress, parties and affairs.

No, Dalton would "settle" for Minister of Culture. With a Sovereign who danced on the cobweb Dalton thrummed.

"I had your good boots polished," Teresa said. She pointed to the other side of the wardrobe. He bent to retrieve them.

"Dalton, what news is there from Aydindril? You said Stein is to speak his peace of the Old World, and the

Imperial Order. What about Aydindril? What has the Midlands to say?"

If there was one thing that could spoil Dalton's ambitions and plans, it was the events in Aydindril.

"The ambassadors returning from Aydindril reported that the Mother Confessor has not only thrown her lot, and that of the Midlands, in with Lord Rahl, the new leader of the D'Haran Empire, but she was to marry the man. By now, she must be wedded to him."

"Married! The Mother Confessor herself, married." Teresa returned her attention to the mirror. "That must have been a grand affair. I can imagine such a wedding would put anything in Anderith to shame." Teresa paused at her mirror. "But a Confessor's power takes a man when she marries him. This Lord Rahl will be nothing but a puppet of the Mother Confessor."

Dalton shook his head. "Apparently, he is gifted, and not subject to being destroyed by her power. She's a clever one, marrying a gifted Lord Rahl of D'Hara; it shows cunning, conviction, and deft strategic planning. Joining the Midlands with D'Hara has created an empire to be feared, an empire to be reckoned with. It will be a difficult decision."

The ambassadors had further reported Lord Rahl a man of seeming integrity, a man of great conviction, a man committed to peace and the freedom of those who joined with him.

He was also a man who demanded their surrender into the growing D'Haran Empire, and demanded it immediately.

Men like that tended to be unreasonable. A man like that could be no end of trouble.

Dalton brought out a shirt and held it up to show Teresa. She nodded her approval. He stripped to the waist and slipped his arms into the crisp, clean shirt, savoring the fresh aroma.

"Stein brings Emperor Jagang's offer of a place for us in his new world order. We will hear what he has to say."

If Stein was any indication, the Imperial Order understood the nuances of power. Unlike all indications from Aydindril, they were willing to negotiate a number of points important to Dalton and the Minister.

"And the Directors? What have they to say about our fate?"

Dalton grunted his discontent. "The Directors committed to the old ways, to the so-called freedom of the people of the Midlands, dwindle in number all the time. The Directors insisting we stay with the rest of the Midlands—join with Lord Rahl—are becoming isolated voices. People are tired of hearing their outdated notions and uninspired morals."

Teresa set down her brush. Worry creased her brow. "Will we have war, Dalton? With whom will we side? Will we be thrown into war, then?"

Dalton laid a reassuring hand on her shoulder. "The war is going to be a long, bloody struggle. I have no interest in being dragged into it, or having our people dragged into it. I'll do what I must to protect Anderith."

Much hinged on which side held the upper hand. There was no point in joining the losing side.

"If need be, we can unleash the Dominie Dirtch. No army, not Lord Rahl's, not Emperor Jagang's, can stand against such a weapon. But, it would be best, before the fact, to join the side offering the best terms and prospects."

She clasped his hand. "But this Lord Rahl is a wizard. You said he was gifted. There is no telling what a wizard might do."

"That might be a reason to join with him. But the Imperial Order has vowed to eliminate magic. Perhaps they have ways of countering his ability."

"But if Lord Rahl is a wizard, that would be fearsome magic—like the Dominie Dirtch. He might unleash his power against us if we fail to surrender to him."

He patted her hand before going back to his dressing. "Don't worry, Tess. I'll not let Anderith fall to ashes. And as I said, the Order claims they will end magic. If true, then a wizard wouldn't hold any threat over us. We will just have to see what Stein has to say."

He didn't know how the Imperial Order could end magic.

Magic, after all, had been around as long as the world. Maybe what the Order really meant was that they intended to eliminate those who were gifted. That would not be a novel idea and to Dalton's mind had a chance of success.

There were those who already advocated putting to the torch all the gifted. Anderith held several of the more radical leaders in chains, Serin Rajak among them. Charismatic, fanatical, and rabid, Serin Rajak was ungovernable and dangerous. If he was even still alive; they'd had him in chains for months.

Rajak believed "witches," as he called those with magic, to be evil. He had a number of followers he had incited into wild and destructive mobs before they'd arrested him.

Men like that were dangerous. Dalton had lobbied against his execution, though. Men like that could also be useful.

"Oh, and you just won't believe it," Teresa was saying. She had started back on the gossip she'd heard. As he pondered Serin Rajak, he only half listened. "This woman, the one I mentioned, the one who thinks so much of herself, Claudine Winthrop, well, she told us that the Minister forced himself on her."

Dalton was still only half listening. He knew the gossip to be true. Claudine Winthrop was the "perturbed lady" in the message in the secret compartment of his desk, the one for whom he needed to find a plum. She was also the one who had sent the letter to Director Linscott—the letter that never arrived.

Claudine Winthrop hovered around the Minister whenever she had the chance, flirting with him, smiling, batting her eyelashes. What did she think was going to happen? She'd gotten what she had to know she was going to get. Now she complains?

"And so, she's so angry to be treated in such a coarse manner by the Minister, that after the dinner she intends to announce to Lady Chanboor and all the guests that the Minister forced himself on her in the crudest fashion."

Dalton's ears perked up.

"Rape it is, she called it, and rape she intends to report it to the Minister's wife." Teresa turned in her seat to shake a small squirrel-hair eye-color brush up at him. "And to the Directors of Cultural Amity, if any are there. And Dalton, if the Sovereign is there, it could be an ugly row. The Sovereign is liable to hold up a hand, commanding silence, so she may speak."

Dalton was at full attention, now. The twelve Directors would be at the feast. Now, he knew what Claudine Winthrop was about.

"She said this, did she? You heard her say it?"

Teresa put one hand on a hip. "Yes. Isn't that something? She should know what Minister Chanboor is like, how he beds half the women at the estate. And now she plans to make trouble? It should create quite the sensation, I'd say. I tell you, Dalton, she's up to something."

When Teresa started prattling onto another subject, he broke in and asked, "What had the other women to say about her? About Claudine's plans?"

Teresa set down the squirrel-hair brush. "Well, we all think it's just terrible. I mean, the Minister of Culture is an important man. Why, he could be Sovereign one day—the Sovereign is not a young man anymore. The Minister could be called upon to step into the Seat of Sovereign at any moment. That's a terrible responsibility."

She looked back to the mirror as she worked with a hair pick. She turned once more and shook it at him. "The Minister is terribly overworked, and has the right to seek harmless diversion now and again. The women are willing. It's nobody's business. It's their private lives—it has no bearing on public business. And it's not like the little tramp didn't ask for it."

Dalton couldn't dispute that much of it. For the life of him, he couldn't understand how women, whether a noble or a Haken girl, could bat their lashes at the letch and then be surprised when he rose, so to speak, to the bait.

Of course, the Haken girl, Beata, hadn't been old enough, or experienced enough, to truly understand such mature games. Nor, he supposed, had she foreseen Stein in the bargain. Dalton felt a bit sorry for the girl, even if she was Haken. No, she hadn't seen Stein lurking in the tall wheat when she smiled in awe at the Minister.

But the other women, the women of the household, and mature women come from the city out to the estate for feasts and parties, they knew what the Minister was about, and had no grounds to call foul after the fact.

Dalton knew some only became unhappy when they didn't get some unspecified, but significant, recompense. Some plum. That was when it became Dalton's problem. He found them a plum, and did his best to convince them they would love to have it. Most, wisely, accepted such generosity—it was all many had wanted in the first place.

He didn't doubt that the women of the estate were agitated that Claudine was scheming to bring trouble. Many of those wives had been with the Minister, seduced by the heady air of power around the man. Dalton had reason to suspect many who had not been to the Minister's bed wanted to end there. Bertrand either simply hadn't gotten to them yet, or didn't wish to. Most likely the former; he tended to appoint men to the estate only after he'd met their wives, too. Dalton had already had to turn down a perfectly good man as regent because Bertrand thought his wife too plain.

Not only was there no end to the women swooning to fall under the man, but he was a glutton about it. Even so, he had certain standards. Like many men as they got older, he savored youth.

He was able to indulge his wont for voluptuous young women without needing, as most men passing fifty, to go to prostitutes in the city. In fact, Bertrand Chanboor avoided such women like the plague, fearing their virulent diseases.

Other men his age who could have young women no other way, and could not resist, did not get a chance to grow much older. Nor did the young women. Disease swiftly claimed many.

Bertrand Chanboor, though, had his pick of a steady supply of healthy young women of limited experience, and standards. They flew, of their own accord, into that candle flame of high rank and nearly limitless authority.

Dalton ran the side of his finger gently along Teresa's cheek. He was fortunate to have a woman who shared his ambition but, unlike many others, was discerning in how to go about it.

"I love you, Tess."

Surprised by his sudden tender gesture, she took his hand in both of hers and planted kisses all along it.

He didn't know what he could possibly have done in his life to deserve her. There had been nothing about him that would augur well for his ever having a woman as good as Teresa. She was the one thing in his life he had not earned by sheer force of will, by cutting down any opposition, eliminating any threat to his goal. With her, he had simply been helplessly in love.

Why the good spirits chose to ignore the rest of his life and reward him with this plum, he couldn't begin to guess, but he would take it and hold on for dear life.

Business intruded on his lustful wanderings as he stared into her adoring eyes.

Claudine would require attention. She needed to be silenced, and before she could cause trouble. Dalton ticked off favors he might have to offer her in return for seeing the sense in silence. No one, not even Lady Chanboor, gave much thought to the Minister's dalliances, but an accusation of rape by a woman of standing would be troublesome.

There were Directors who adhered to ideals of rectitude. The Directors of the Office of Cultural Amity held sway over who would be Sovereign. Some wanted the next Sovereign to be a man of moral character. They could deny an initiate the Seat.

After Bertrand Chanboor was named Sovereign, it would not matter what they thought, but it certainly mattered before.

Claudine would have to be silenced.

"Dalton, where are you going?"

He turned back from the door. "I just have to write a message and then send it on its way. I won't be long."

CHAPTER 18

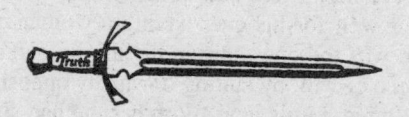

NORA STIRRED WITH A groan, thinking it must be light already. Her thoughts fumbled woodenly in the numb blur between asleep and awake. She wanted nothing so much as to sleep on. The straw beneath her was bunched just right. It always bunched just right in perfect, comfortable, cuddling lumps, right as it was time to be up and out of bed.

She expected her husband to slap her rump any moment. Julian always woke just before first light. The chores had to be done. Maybe if she lay still, he would leave her be for just a few moments longer, let her sleep for a few dreamy minutes more.

She hated him at that moment, for always waking just before first light and slapping her rump and telling her to get up and to the day's work. The man had to whistle first thing, too, when her head was still a daze in the morning, rickety with sleep still trying to get out of her head.

She flopped over on her back, lifting her eyebrows in an effort to wake by forcing her eyes open. Julian wasn't there beside her.

A feeling skittered up her insides, bringing her wide awake in an ice cold instant. She sat up in the bed. For some reason, something about him not being there gave her a feeling of queasy dismay.

Was it morning? Just about to be light? Was it still somewhere in the night? Her mind snatched wildly to get her bearings.

She leaned over, seeing the glow from the embers she'd banked in the hearth before she went to bed. A few on the top still glowed, hardly diminished at all from the way she'd left them. In that weak light, she saw Bruce peering at her from his pallet.

"Mama? What's wrong?" his older sister, Bethany, asked.

"What are you two doing awake?"

"Mama, we just gone to bed," Bruce whined.

She realized it was true. She was so tired, so dead tired from pulling rocks from the spring field all day, that she'd been asleep before she closed her eyes. They'd come home when it got too dark to work any more, ate down their porridge, and got right to bed. She could still taste the squirrel meat from the porridge, and she was still burping new radishes. Bruce was right; they'd only just gone to bed.

Trepidation trembled through her. "Where's your pa?"

Bethany lifted a hand to point. "Went to the privy, I guess. Mama, what's wrong?"

"Mama?" Bruce puled.

"Hush, now, it be nothin'. Lay back down, the both of you."

Both children stared at her, wide-eyed. She couldn't stick a pin in the alarm she felt. The children saw it in her face, she knew they did, but she couldn't hide it no matter how she tried.

She didn't know what was wrong, what the trouble was, but she felt it sure, crawling on her skin.

Evil.

Evil was in the air, like smoke from a woods fire, wrinkling her nose, sucking her breath. Evil. Somewhere, out in the night, evil, lurking about.

She glanced again to the empty bed beside her. Gone to the privy. Julian was in the privy house. Had to be.

Nora recalled him going to the privy house just after they ate, before they went to their bed. That didn't mean he couldn't go again. But he never did say he was having no problem.

Consternation clawed at her insides, like the fear of the Keeper himself.

"Dear Creator, preserve us," she whispered in prayer. "Preserve us, this house of humble people. Send evil away. Please, dear spirits, watch over us and keep us safe."

She opened her eyes from the prayer. The children were still staring at her. Bethany must feel it, too. She never let nothing go without asking why. Nora called her the "why child" in jest. Bruce just trembled.

Nora threw the wool blanket aside. It scared the chickens in the corner, making them flap with a start and let out a surprised squawk.

"You children go back to sleep."

They lay back down, but they watched as she squirmed a shift down over her nightdress. Shaking without knowing why, she knelt on the bricks before the hearth and stacked birch logs on the embers. It wasn't that cold—she'd thought to let the embers do for the night—but she felt the sudden need for the comfort of a fire, the assurance of its light.

From beside the hearth, she retrieved their only oil lamp. With a curl of flaming birch bark, she quickly lit the lamp wick and then replaced the chimney. The children were still watching.

Nora bent and kissed little Bruce on the cheek. She smoothed back Bethany's hair and kissed her daughter's forehead. It tasted like the dirt she'd been in all day trying to help carry rocks from the field before they plowed and planted it. She could only carry little ones, but it was a help.

"Back to sleep, my babies," she said in a soothing voice. "Pa just went to the privy. I'm only taking him a light to see his way back. You know how your pa stubs his toes in the night and then curses us for it. Back to sleep, the both of you. Everything is all right. Just takin' your pa a lamp."

Nora stuck her bare feet into her cold, wet, muddy boots, which had been set by the door. She didn't want to stub her toes and then have to work with a lame foot. She fussed with a shawl, settling it around her shoulders, fixing it good and right before she tied it. She feared to open the door. She was in near tears with not wanting to open that door to the night.

Evil was out there. She knew it. She felt it.

"Burn you, Julian," she muttered under her breath. "Burn you crisp for making me go outside tonight."

She wondered, if she found Julian sitting in the privy, if he'd curse her foolish woman ways. He cursed her ways, sometimes. Said she worried over nothing for no good end. Said nothing ever came of her worrying so why'd she do it? She didn't do it to get herself cursed at by him, that sure was the truth of it.

As she lifted the latch, she told herself how she wanted very much for him to be out in the privy and to curse her tonight, and then to put his arm around her shoulders and tell her to hush her tears and come back to bed with him. She shushed the chickens when they complained at her as she opened the door.

There was no moon. The overcast sky was as black as the Keeper's shadow. Nora shuffled quickly along the packed dirt path to the privy house. With a shaking hand, she rapped on the door.

"Julian? Julian, you in there? Please, Julian, if you're in there, say so. Julian, I'm begging you, don't trick with me, not tonight."

Silence throbbed in her ears. There were no bugs making noise. No crickets. No frogs. No birds. It was just plain dead quiet, like the ground in the lamp's little glow around her was all there was to the world and beyond that there was nothing, like if she left the lamp and stepped out there into the darkness she might fall through that black beyond till she was an old lady and then still fall some more. She knew that was foolish, but right then the idea seemed very real and scared her something fierce.

The privy door squeaked when she pulled it open. She hadn't even been hoping as she done it, because she knew Julian wasn't in there. Before she got out of the bed, she knew he wasn't in the privy house. She didn't know how she knew, but she did.

And she was right.

She was sometimes right about such feelings. Julian said she was daft to think she had some mind power to know things, like the old woman what lived back in the hills and came down when she knew something and thought she ought to tell folks of it.

But sometimes, Nora did know things. She'd known Julian wasn't in the privy.

Worse, she knew where he was.

She didn't know how she knew, no more than she knew how she knew he wasn't in the privy. But she knew, and the knowing had her shaking something fierce. She only looked in the privy because she hoped she was wrong, and because she didn't want to look where she knew he was.

But now she had to go look.

Nora held the lamp out, trying to see down the path. She couldn't see far. She turned as she tramped along, looking back at the house. She could make out the window, because the fire was going good. The birch logs had caught, and the fire was throwing off good light.

The feeling of terrible wickedness felt like it was grinning at her from the black night between her and the house. Clutching her shawl tight, Nora held the lamp out to the path again. She didn't like leaving the children. Not when she had her feelings.

Something, though, was pulling her onward, down the path.

"Please, dear spirits, let me be a foolish woman, with foolish woman ways. Please, dear spirits, let Julian be safe. We all needs him. Dear spirits, we needs him."

She was sobbing as she made her way down the hill, sobbing because she feared so much to find out. Her hand holding the lamp shook, making the flame jitter.

At last, she heard the sound of the creek, and was glad for it because then the night wasn't so dead quiet and frightfully empty. With the sound of the water, she felt better, because there was something out there, something familiar. She began to feel foolish for thinking there was no world beyond the lamplight, like she was on the brink of the underworld. She was just as likely wrong about the rest of it, too. Julian would roll his eyes, in that way of his, when she told him she was afraid because she thought the world was empty beyond the light.

She tried to whistle, like her Julian whistled, so as to make herself feel better, but her lips were as dry as stale toast. She wished she could whistle, so Julian could hear her, but no good whistling sound would come out. She could just call out to him, but she feared to do it. Feared to get no answer. She'd rather just come on him and find him there, and then get cursed for her foolish crying over nothing.

A gentle breeze lapped the water against the edge of the lake, so she could hear it before she could see it. She hoped to see Julian sitting there on his stump, tending a line, waiting to catch them a carp. She hoped to see him look up and curse her for scaring his fish.

The stump was empty. The line was slack.

Nora, her whole arm trembling, held up the lamp, to see what she came to see. Tears stung at her eyes so she had to blink to see better. She had to sniffle to get her breath.

She held the lamp higher as she walked out into the water till it poured over the tops of her boots. She took another step, till the water soaked the bottom of her nightdress and shift and dragged the dead weight back and forth with the movement of her steps and the waves.

When the water was up to her knees, she saw him.

He was floating there, facedown in the water, his arms limp out to his sides, his legs parted slightly. The little breeze-borne waves slopped over the back of his head, making his hair move as if it were some of the lake weed. He bobbed gently there in the water, like a dead fish floating on the surface.

Nora had feared to find him there, like that. It was just what she feared, and because she feared it so, she wasn't even shocked when she saw it. She stood there, water to her knees, Julian floating like a dead bloated carp twenty feet out in the lake. The water was too deep to wade out to get him. Out where he was it would be over her head.

She didn't know what to do. Julian always did the stuff she couldn't do. How was she going to get her husband in to shore?

How was she going to live? How was she going to feed herself and her children without Julian? Julian did the hard stuff. He knew the things she didn't know. He provided for them.

She felt numb, dead, stunned, like she did when she'd just come awake. It didn't seem possible.

Julian couldn't be dead. He was Julian. He couldn't die. Not Julian.

A sound made her spin around. A thump to the air. A howl, like wind on a blizzard night. A wail and a whoosh lifted into the night air.

From their house up on the hill, Nora could see sparks shooting up out the chimney. Sparks flew up in wild swirls, spiraling high up into the darkness. Thunderstruck, Nora stood in frozen terror.

A scream ripped the quiet night. The awful sound rose, like the sparks, screeching into the night air with horror such as she had never heard. It was such a brutal cry she didn't think it could be human.

But she knew it was. She knew it was Bruce's scream.

With a wail of wild terror of her own, she suddenly dropped the lamp in the water and ran for the house. Her screams answered his, feeding on his, shattering the silence with his.

Her babies were in the house.

Evil was in the house.

And she had left them to it.

She wailed in feral fright at what she had done, leaving her babies alone. She screamed to the good spirits to help her. She squalled for her children. She choked on her sobbing panic as she stumbled through the brush in the dark.

Huckleberry bushes snagged and tore her clothes. Branches slashed her arms as she ran with wild abandon. A hole in the ground caught and twisted her foot, but she stayed up and kept running toward her house, toward her babies.

Bruce's piercing scream went on without end, lifting the hair at the back of her neck. She didn't hear Bethany, just Bruce, little Bruce, screaming his lungs out, like he was having his eyes stabbed out.

Nora stumbled. Her face slammed the ground. She scrambled to her feet. Blood gushed from her nose. Stunning pain staggered her. She gagged on blood and dirt as she gasped for breath, crying, screaming, praying, panting, choking all at the same time. With desperate effort, Nora raced to the house, to the screams.

She crashed through the door. Chickens flew out around her. Bruce had his back plastered to the wall beside the door. He was in the grip of savage terror, out of his mind, shrieking like the Keeper had him by the toes.

Bruce saw her, and made to throw his arm around her, but flung himself back against the wall when he saw her bloody face, saw strings of blood dripping from her chin.

She seized his shoulder. "It's Mama! I just fell and hit my nose, that's all!"

He threw himself at her, his arms clutching her hips, his fingers snatching at her clothes. Nora twisted around, but even with the bright firelight, she didn't see her daughter.

"Bruce! Where's Bethany?"

His arm lifted, shaking so much she feared it would come undone. She wheeled to see where he pointed.

Nora screeched. She threw her hands up to cover her face, but couldn't, her fingers quaking violently before her mouth as she screamed with Bruce.

Bethany was standing in the hearth, engulfed in flames.

The fire roared around her, swirling in tumbling eddies as it consumed her little body. Her arms were lifted out into the angry white heat, the way you lifted your arms into the warm spring afternoon sunlight after a swim.

The stink of bubbling burning flesh suddenly wormed into Nora's bleeding nose, gagging her until she choked on the smell and taste and couldn't get another breath. She couldn't seem to look away from Bethany, look away from her daughter being burned up alive. It didn't seem real. She couldn't make her mind understand it.

Nora lunged a step toward the flames, to snatch her daughter out of the fire. Something inside, some last scrap of sense, told her it was far too late. Told her to get away with Bruce before it had them, too.

The tips of Bethany's fingers were all gone. Her face was nothing but yellow-orange whorls of flame. The fire burned with wild, roused, determined fury. The heat sucked Nora's breath from her lungs.

A shrill scream suddenly rose from the girl, as if her soul itself had finally caught fire. It made the very marrow in Nora's bones ache.

Bethany collapsed in a heap. Flames shot up around the crumbled form, tumbling out around the stone, licking briefly up over the mantel. Sparks splashed out into the room, bouncing and rolling across the floor. Several hissed out against the wet hem of Nora's dress.

Nora snatched at Bruce, clutching his nightshirt in a death grip, and ran with him from the house as evil consumed what was left of her daughter.

CHAPTER 19

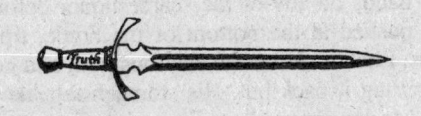

FITCH FOLDED HIS LEGS as he sat on the grass. The cool brick felt good against his sweaty back. He took a deep breath of the sweet-smelling night, the aromas of roasting meat wafting out through open windows, and the clean smell of the apple-wood pile. Since they would be working late cleaning up the mess after the feast, they'd been given a welcome respite.

Morley handed him the bottle. It would be late before they could get good and drunk, but at least they could have a sample. Fitch took a big swig. Instantly, he coughed violently, before he could get it down, losing most of the mouthful of liquor.

Morley laughed. "Told you it was strong."

Fitch wiped the back of his sleeve across his dripping chin. "You're right about that. Where'd you get it? This is good stuff."

Fitch had never had anything so strong that it burned that much going down. From what he'd heard, if it burned, that meant it was good stuff. He'd been told that if he ever had a chance, he'd be a fool to turn down good stuff. He coughed again. The back of his nose, back in his throat, burned something awful.

Morley leaned closer. "Someone important ordered it sent

back. Said it was swill. They were trying to be pompous in front of everyone. Pete, the cupbearer, he ran it back and set it down. When he grabbed another and ran out, I snatched it up and slipped it under my tunic before anyone noticed."

Fitch was used to drinking the wine they'd managed to scavenge. He'd drain almost empty small casks and bottles, collecting the dregs and what was left behind. He'd never gotten his hands on any of the scarce liquor before.

Morley pushed at the bottom of the bottle, tipping it to Fitch's lips. Fitch took a more cautious pull, and got it down without spitting it back out. His stomach felt like a boiling cauldron. Morley nodded approvingly. Fitch smiled with smug pride.

Through distant open windows, he could hear people talking and laughing in the gathering hall, waiting for the feast to begin. Fitch could already feel the effects of the liquor. Later, after they cleaned up, they could finish getting drunk.

Fitch rubbed the gooseflesh on his arms. The music drifting out from the windows put him in a mood. Music always did that, made him feel like he could rise up and do something. He didn't know what, but something. Something powerful.

When Morley held out his hand Fitch handed over the bottle. He watched the knob in Morley's throat move up and down with every swallow. The music built with emotion, quickened with excitement. On top of the effects of the drink, it gave him chills.

Off past Morley, Fitch saw someone tall coming down the path toward them. The person was walking deliberately, not just out for a stroll, but going someplace. In the yellow lamplight coming from all the windows, Fitch saw the glint off the silver scabbard. He saw the noble features and bearing.

It was Dalton Campbell. He was coming right for them.

Fitch elbowed his friend and then stood. He steadied himself on his feet before straightening his tunic. The front of it was wet with liquor he'd coughed out. He quickly swiped back his hair. With the side of his foot, he kicked Morley and signaled with a thumb for him to get up.

Dalton Campbell walked around the woodpile, headed straight toward them. The tall Ander seemed to know right where he was going. Fitch and Morley, when it was just the two of them lifting drink and sneaking off, never told anyone where they went.

"Fitch. Morley," Dalton Campbell called out as he approached.

"Good evening, Master Campbell," Fitch said, lifting a hand in greeting.

Fitch guessed, what with the light from the windows, it wasn't really that hard to see. He could see Morley good enough, see him holding the bottle behind his back. It must be that the Minister's aide saw them from a window as they were going out to the woodpile.

"Good evening, Master Campbell," Morley said.

Dalton Campbell looked them over, like he was inspecting soldiers. He held out his hand.

"May I?"

Morley winced as he pulled the bottle from behind his back and handed it over. "We was . . . that is . . ."

Dalton Campbell took a good swig.

"Ahh," he said, as he handed the bottle back to Morley. "You two are fortunate to have such a good, and full, bottle of liquor." He clasped his hand behind his back. "I hope I'm not interrupting anything."

Both Fitch and Morley, stunned at Dalton Campbell taking a swig of their bottle, and more so that he handed it back, both shook their heads vigorously.

"No, sir, Master Campbell," Morley said.

"Good, then," Campbell said. "I was looking for the two of you. I have a bit of trouble."

Fitch leaned a little closer, lowering his voice. "Trouble, Master Campbell? Is there anything we can do to help?"

Campbell watched Fitch's eyes, and then Morley's. "Well, yes, as a matter of fact, that's why I was looking for you. You see, I thought you two might like a chance to prove yourselves—to begin showing me you have the potential I hope you have. I could take care of it myself, but I thought you two might like to have a chance to do something worthwhile."

Fitch felt like the good spirits themselves had just asked if he'd like a chance to do good.

Morley set the bottle down and straightened his shoulders like a soldier going to attention. "Yes sir, Master Campbell, I surely would like a chance."

Fitch straightened himself up. "Me, too, Master Campbell. You just name it, and we'd both like a chance to prove to you we're men ready to take responsibility."

"Good . . . very good," he said as he studied them. He let the silence go on a bit before he spoke again. "This is important. This is very important. I thought about taking it to someone else, someone more experienced, but I decided to give you two a chance to show me you can be trusted."

"Anything, Master Campbell," Fitch said, and he meant it. "You just name it."

Fitch trembled with the excitement of having the chance to prove himself to Dalton Campbell. The music seemed to pump him full of need to do something important.

"The Sovereign is not well," Campbell said.

"That's terrible," Morley said.

"We're sorry," Fitch added.

"Yes, it's a shame, but he is old. Minister Chanboor is still young and vigorous. He's undoubtedly going to be named Sovereign, and it isn't likely to be long. Most of the Directors are here to discuss business with us—Seat of the Sovereign business. Making inquiries, as it were, while they have the leisure to do so. They want to determine certain facts about the Minister. They are looking into his character to see what kind of man he is. To see if he's a man they could support, when the times comes."

Fitch snatched a quick glance and saw Morley's wide eyes fixed on Dalton Campbell. Fitch could hardly believe he was hearing such important news from a man as important as this—they were just Hakens, after all. This was the

Minister's aide, an Ander, an important Ander, telling them about matters of the highest substance.

"Thank the Creator," Fitch whispered. "Our Minister is finally getting the recognition he deserves."

"Yes," Campbell drawled in an odd way. "Well, the thing is, there are people who would like to prevent the Minister from being named Sovereign. These people mean to harm the Minister."

"Harm him?" Morley asked, clearly astonished.

"That's right. You both recall learning how the Sovereign is to be protected, that anything done to protect our Sovereign is a virtue?"

"Yes, sir," Morley said.

"Yes, sir," Fitch echoed. "And since the Minister is to be Sovereign, then he should be protected just the same."

"Very good, Fitch."

Fitch beamed with pride. He wished the drink didn't make it so hard to focus his eyes.

"Master Campbell," Morley said, "we'd like to help. We'd like to prove ourselves to you. We're ready."

"Yes sir, we surely are," Fitch added.

"I shall give you both your chance, then. If you can do right, and keep silent about it no matter what—and that means to your graves—I will be pleased my faith in you was well placed."

"To our graves," Fitch said. "Yes sir, we can do that."

Fitch heard an odd metallic sound. He realized with horror that there was a sword point under his chin.

"But if either of you fails to live up to my faith, I would be very disappointed, because the Minister would then be in danger. Do you understand? I won't have people I trust let me down. Let the future Sovereign down. Do you both understand?"

"Yes, sir!" Fitch nearly shouted.

The sword point flashed to Morley's throat, poised before the prominent bump in his gullet. "Yes, sir!" he said.

"Did either of you tell anyone where you would be tonight having your drink?"

"No, sir," Morley and Fitch said as one.

"Yet I knew where to find you." The tall Ander lifted an eyebrow. "You just remember that, if you ever think to get it in your head that you could hide from me. If you ever cause me trouble, I will find you, no matter where you go to ground."

"Master Campbell," Fitch said, after he swallowed, "you just tell us what it is we can do to help, and we'll do it. We can be trusted. We'll not let you down—I swear."

Morley was nodding. "That's right. Fitch is right."

Dalton Campbell slid his sword back into its scabbard and smiled. "I'm already proud of you both. You two are going to advance around here. I just know you will prove my faith in you."

"Yes sir," Fitch said, "you can count on us both."

Dalton Campbell put one hand on Fitch's shoulder and the other on Morley's. "All right, then. You listen close, now."

"Here she comes," Morley whispered in Fitch's ear.

Fitch nodded after looking where his friend pointed. Morley moved off to the black maw of the open service doors while Fitch squatted down behind some barrels stacked to the side of the loading dock. Fitch recalled earlier in the day seeing Brownie standing with the butcher's cart across the way. Fitch wiped the palms of his hands on his trousers. It had been a day of important events.

They'd talked about it on the way over, and Morley felt the same way; as much as the idea of it had Fitch's heart hammering against his ribs, there was no way he was going to let Dalton Campbell's faith in him be spoiled. Morley thought the same.

The music coming from the open windows across the lawn—strings and horns and a harp—was filling his head with purpose, swelling his chest with pride to be chosen by Dalton Campbell.

The Minister—the future Sovereign—had to be protected.

Quietly, with light steps, she climbed the four steps up onto the dock. In the dim light, she looked around at the deep shadows, stretching her neck to peer about. Fitch swallowed at how good-looking she was. She was older, but she was a looker. He'd never looked so long and hard at an Ander lady as he did at her.

Morley made his voice come out deep in order to sound older.

"Claudine Winthrop?"

She wheeled expectantly toward Fitch's friend, standing in the dark doorway. "I'm Claudine Winthrop," she whispered. "You received my message, then?"

"Yes," Morley said.

"Thank the Creator. Director Linscott, it's important I speak with you about Minister Chanboor. He pretends to uphold Anderith culture, but he is the worst example we could have in his post, or any other. Before you consider his name for a future Sovereign, you must hear of his corruption. The pig forced himself on me—raped me. But that is only the beginning of it. It gets worse. For the sake of our people, you must hear my words."

Fitch watched as she stood with the soft yellow light from the windows falling across her pretty face. Dalton Campbell hadn't said she was going to be so pretty. She was older, of course, and so not someone he ordinarily thought of as pretty. It surprised him to realize he was thinking of someone so old—she looked almost thirty—as attractive. He took a slow, silent breath, trying to tighten his resolve. But he couldn't help staring at what she wore, or more accurately, at where she wasn't wearing anything.

Fitch recalled the two women in the stairwell talking about such dresses as the one Claudine Winthrop wore now. Fitch had never seen so much of a woman's breasts. The way they heaved as she wrung her hands had his eyes popping.

"Won't you come out?" she asked in a whisper toward the darkness where Morley waited. "Please? I'm frightened."

Fitch suddenly realized he was supposed to be doing his part. He sneaked out from behind the barrels, taking careful steps so she wouldn't hear him coming.

His stomach felt like it was in a knot. He had to wipe the sweat out of his eyes in order to see. He tried to breathe calmly, but his heart seemed to have a mind of its own. He had to do this. But, dear spirits, he was more than afraid.

"Director Linscott?" she whispered toward Morley.

Fitch snatched her elbows and wrenched her arms behind her back. She gasped. He was surprised at how easy it was for him to keep her arms pinned behind her as she struggled with all her might. She was confused and startled. Morley shot out from the dark, once he saw that Fitch had her.

Before she could get much of a scream out, Morley slugged her in the gut as hard as he could. The powerful blow nearly knocked both her and Fitch from their feet.

Claudine Winthrop doubled over, vomit spewing all over the dock. Fitch let go of her arms. She crossed them over her middle as she went to her knees, heaving violently. Both he and Morley stepped back as it splashed the dock and her dress, but they weren't about to get more than an arm's length away from her.

After a few long convulsions, she straightened, seeming to have finished, and tried to get to her feet as she struggled and gasped for breath. Morley lifted her and spun her around. With his powerful grip, he locked her arms behind her back.

Fitch knew this was his chance to prove himself. This was his chance to protect the Minister. This was his chance to make Dalton Campbell proud.

Fitch punched her in the stomach as hard as he dared.

He'd never punched anyone before, except his friends, and that was only in fun. Never like this, not for real, not deliberately to hurt someone. Her middle was small, and soft. He could see how much his fist had hurt her.

It made him feel sick. Made him feel like throwing up, too. This was the violent way his Haken ancestors behaved. This was what was so terrible about them. About him.

Her eyes were wide with terror as she tried over and over to suck in a breath, but couldn't seem to. She fought desperately to get her wind as her eyes fixed on him, like a hog watching the butcher. Like her Ander ancestors used to watch his.

"We're here to give you a message," Fitch said.

They'd agreed Fitch would do the talking. Morley didn't remember so well what they were to tell Claudine Winthrop; Fitch had always been better at remembering.

She finally got her breath back. Fitch hunched forward and landed three blows. Quick. Hard. Angry.

"Are you listening?" he growled.

"You little Haken bastard—"

Fitch let go with all his strength. The wallop hurt his fist. It staggered even Morley back a step. She hung forward in Morley's grip as she vomited in dry heaves. Fitch had wanted to hit her face—punch her in the mouth—but Dalton Campbell had given them clear instructions to only hit her where it wouldn't show.

"I'd not call him that again, were I you." Morley grabbed a fistful of her hair and savagely yanked her up straight.

Arching her up so forcefully made her breasts pop out the top of her dress. Fitch froze. He wondered if he should pull the front of her dress back up for her. His jaw hung as he stared at her. Morley leaned over her shoulder for a look. He grinned at Fitch.

She glanced down to see herself spilled out of her dress. Seeing it, she put her head back and closed her eyes in resignation.

"Please," she said, panting for breath toward the sky, "don't hurt me anymore?"

"Are you ready to listen?"

She nodded. "Yes, sir."

That surprised Fitch even more than seeing her naked breasts. No one in his whole life had ever called him "sir."

209

Those two meek words felt so strange to his ears that he just stood there staring at her. For a moment, he wondered if she was mocking him. As she looked him in the eye, her expression told him she wasn't.

The music was filling him with such feelings as he'd never had before. He'd never been important before, never been called "sir" before. That morning he'd been called "Fetch." Now, an Ander women called him "sir." All thanks to Dalton Campbell.

Fitch punched her in the gut again. Just because he felt like it.

"Please, sir!" she cried. "Please, no more! Tell me what you want. I'll do it. If you wish to have me, I'll submit— just don't hurt me anymore. Please, sir?"

Although Fitch's stomach still felt heavy with queasy disgust at what he was doing, he also felt more important than he'd ever felt before. Her, an Ander woman with her breasts exposed to him like that, and her calling him "sir."

"Now, you listen to me you filthy little bitch."

His own words surprised him as much as they surprised her. Fitch hadn't planned them. They just came out. He liked the sound of it, though.

"Yes sir," she wept, "I will. I'll listen. Whatever you say."

She looked so pitiful, so helpless. Not an hour ago, if an Ander woman, even this Claudine Winthrop, would have told him to get down on his knees and clean the floor with his tongue, he'd have done it and been trembling at the same time. He'd never imagined how easy this would be. A few punches, and she was begging to do as he said. He never imagined how easy it would be to be important, to have people do as he said.

Fitch remembered what it was Dalton Campbell told him to say.

"You were strutting yourself before the Minister, weren't you? You were offering yourself to him, weren't you?"

He'd made it clear it wasn't really a question. "Yes, sir."

"If you ever again think of telling anyone the Minister raped you, you'll be sorry. Saying such a lie is treason. Got that? Treason. The penalty for treason is death. When they find your body, no one will even be able to recognize you. Do you understand, bitch? They'll find your tongue nailed to a tree.

"It's a lie that the Minister raped you. A filthy treasonous lie. You ever say such a thing again, and you'll be made to suffer before you die."

"Yes sir," she sobbed. "I'll never lie again. I'm sorry. Please, forgive me? I'll never lie again, I swear."

"You were putting it out there for the Minister, offering yourself. But the Minister is a better man than to have an affair with you—or anyone. He turned you down. He refused you."

"Yes, sir."

"Nothing improper happened. Got that? The Minister never did nothing improper with you, or anyone."

"Yes, sir." She whined in a long sob, her head hanging.

Fitch pulled her handkerchief from her sleeve. He dabbed it at her eyes. He could tell in the dim light that her face paint, what with the throwing up and crying, was a shambles.

"Stop crying, now. You're making a mess of your face. You better go back to your room and fix yourself up before you go back to the feast."

She sniffled, trying to stop the tears. "I can't go back to the feast, now. My dress is spoiled. I can't go back."

"You can, and you will. Fix your face and put on another dress. You're going to go back. There will be someone watching, to see if you go back, to see if you got the message. If you ever slip again, you'll be swallowing the steel of his sword."

Her eyes widened with fright. "Who—"

"That's not important. It don't matter none to you. The only thing that matters is that you got the message and understand what will happen if you ever again tell your filthy lies."

She nodded. "I understand."

"Sir," Fitch said. Her brow twitched. "I understand, sir!"

She pressed back against Morley. "I understand, sir. Yes, sir, I truly understand."

"Good," Fitch said.

She glanced down at herself. Her lower lip trembled. Tears ran down her cheeks.

"Please, sir, may I fix my dress?"

"When I'm done talking."

"Yes, sir."

"You've been out for a walk. You didn't talk to no one. Do you understand? No one. From now on, you just keep your mouth shut about the Minister, or when you open it the next time, you'll find a sword going down your throat. Got all that?"

"Yes, sir."

"All right, then." Fitch gestured. "Go ahead and pull up your dress."

Morley leered over her shoulder as she stuffed herself back in the dress. Fitch didn't think covering herself with the dress, as low as it was, showed much less, but he surely enjoyed standing there watching her do it. He never thought he'd see such a thing. Especially an Ander woman doing such a thing.

The way she straightened with a gasp, Morley must have done something behind her, up under her dress. Fitch surely wanted to do something, too, but remembered Dalton Campbell.

Fitch grabbed Claudine Winthrop's arm and pulled her ahead a couple of steps. "You be on your way, now."

She snatched a quick glance at Morley, then looked back at Fitch. "Yes, sir. Thank you." She dipped a hasty curtsy. "Thank you, sir."

Without further word, she clutched her skirts in her fists, rushed down the steps, and ran off across the lawn into the night.

"Why'd you send her off?" Morley asked. He put a hand on his hip. "We could have had a time with her. She'd of had to do anything we wanted. And after a look at what she had, I wanted."

Fitch leaned toward his disgruntled friend. "Because Master Campbell never told us we could do anything like that, that's why. We was helping Master Campbell, that's all. No more."

Morley made a sour face. "I guess." He looked off toward the woodpile. "We still got a lot of drinking to do."

Fitch thought about the look of fear on Claudine Winthrop's face. He thought about her crying and sobbing. He knew Haken women cried, of course, but Fitch had never before even imagined an Ander woman crying. He didn't know why not, but he never had.

The Minister was Ander, so Fitch guessed he couldn't really do wrong. She must have asked for it with her low-cut dress and the way she acted toward him. Fitch had seen the way a lot of women acted toward him. Like they would rejoice if he had them.

He remembered Beata sitting on the floor crying. He thought about the look of misery on Beata's face, up there, when the Minister threw her out after he'd finished with her.

Fitch thought about the way she'd clouted him.

It was all too much for him to figure out. Fitch wanted nothing more right then than to drink himself into a stupor.

"You're right. Let's go have ourselves a drink. We've a lot to celebrate. Tonight, we became important men."

With an arm over each other's shoulders, they headed for their bottle.

CHAPTER 20

"WELL, ISN'T THAT SOMETHING," Teresa whispered.

Dalton followed her gaze to see Claudine Winthrop haltingly work her way among the roomful of milling people. She was wearing a dress he had seen before when he worked in the city, an older dress of modest design. It was not the dress she had worn earlier in the evening. He suspected that beneath the mask of rosy powder, her face was ashen. Mistrust would now color her vision.

People from the city of Fairfield, their eyes filled with wonder, gazed at their surroundings, trying to drink it all in so they might tell their friends every detail of their grand evening at the Minister of Culture's estate. It was a high honor to be invited to the estate, and they wished to overlook no detail. Details were important when vaunting one's self.

Patches of intricate marquetry flooring showed between each of the richly colored rare carpets placed at even intervals the length of the room. There was no missing the luxuriously thick feel underfoot. Dalton guessed that thousands of yards of the finest material had to have gone into the draperies swagged before the file of tall windows on each side of the room, all constructed with complex ornamental tracery to hold colored glass. Here and there a woman would, between thumb and finger, test the cloth's high-count weave. The edges of the azure and golden-wheat-colored fabric were embellished with multicolored tassels as big as his fist. Men marveled at the fluted stone columns rising to hold the massive, cut-stone corbel along the length of the side walls at the base of the gathering hall's barrel ceiling. A panoply of curved mahogany frames and panels, looking like the ends of elaborately cut voussoirs, overspread the arched barrel ceiling.

Dalton lifted his pewter cup to his lips and took a sip of the finest Nareef Valley wine as he watched. At night, with all the candles and lamps lit, the place had a glow about it. It had taken discipline, when he first arrived, not to gape as did these people come out from the city.

He watched Claudine Winthrop move among the well-dressed guests, clasping a hand here, touching an elbow there, greeting people, smiling woodenly, answering questions with words Dalton couldn't hear. As distressed as he knew she had to be, she had the resourcefulness to conduct herself with propriety. The wife of a wealthy businessman who had been elected burgess by merchants and grain dealers to represent them, she was not an unimportant member of the household in her own right. When at first people saw that her husband was old enough to be her grandfather, they usually expected she was no more than his entertainment; they were wrong.

Her husband, Edwin Winthrop, had started out as a farmer, raising sorgo—sweet sorghum grown widely in southern Anderith. Every penny he earned through the sale of the sorghum molasses he pressed was spent frugally and wisely. He went without, putting in abeyance everything from proper shelter and clothes, to the simple comforts of life, to a wife and family.

What money he saved eventually purchased livestock he foraged on sorghum left from pressing his molasses. Sale of fattened livestock bought more feeder stock, and equipment for stills so he could produce rum himself, rather than sell his molasses to distilleries. Profits from the rum he distilled from his molasses earned him enough to rent more farmland and purchase cattle, equipment and buildings for producing more rum, and eventually warehouses and wagons for transporting the goods he produced. Rum distilled by the Winthrop farms was sold from Renwold to Nicobarese, from just down the road in Fairfield all the way to Aydindril. By doing everything himself—or, more accurately, having his own hired workers do everything—from growing sorgo to pressing it to distilling it to delivering the rum, to raising cattle on the fodder of his leftover stocks of pressed sorghum to slaughtering the cattle and delivering the carcasses to butchers, Edwin Winthrop kept his costs low and made for himself a fortune.

Edwin Winthrop was a frugal man, honest, and well liked. Only after he was successful had he taken a wife. Claudine, the well-educated daughter of a grain dealer, had been in her mid-teens when she wed Edwin, well over a decade before.

Talented at overseeing her husband's accounts and records, Claudine watched every penny as carefully as would her husband. She was his valuable right hand—much as Dalton served the Minister. With her help, his personal empire had doubled. Even in marriage, Edwin had chosen carefully and wisely. A man who never seemed to seek personal pleasure perhaps had at last allowed himself this much; Claudine was as attractive as she was diligent.

After Edwin's fellow merchants had elected him burgess, Claudine became useful to him in legal matters, helping, behind the scenes, to write the trade laws he proposed. Dalton suspected she had a great deal to do with proposing them to her husband in the first place. When he was not available, Claudine discreetly argued those proposed laws on on his behalf. No one in the household thought of her as "entertainment."

Except, perhaps, Bertrand Chanboor. But then, he viewed all women in that light. The attractive ones, anyway.

Dalton had in the past seen Claudine blushing, batting her eyelashes, and flashing Bertrand Chanboor her shy smile.

The Minister believed demure women coquettish. Perhaps she innocently flirted with an important man, or perhaps she had wanted attention her husband couldn't provide; she hadn't, after all, any children. Perhaps she had cunningly thought to gain some favor from the Minister, and afterward discovered it wasn't to be forthcoming.

Claudine Winthrop was nobody's fool; she was intelligent and resourceful. How it had started—Dalton was not sure, Bertrand Chanboor denied touching her as he denied everything out of hand—had become irrelevant. With her seeking secret meetings with Director Linscott, matters had moved past polite negotiation of favors. Brute force was the only safe way to control her now.

Dalton gestured with his cup of wine toward Claudine. "Looks like you were wrong, Tess. Not everyone is going along with the fashion of wearing suggestive dresses. Or maybe Claudine is modest."

"No, it must be something else." Teresa looked truly puzzled. "Sweetheart, I don't think she was wearing that dress earlier. But why would she now be wearing something different? And an old dress it is."

Dalton shrugged. "Let's go find out, shall we? You do the asking. I don't think it would be right coming from me."

Teresa looked askance at him. She knew him well enough to know by his subtle reply that a scheme was afoot. She also knew enough to take his lead and play the part he had just assigned her. She smiled and hooked a hand over his offered arm. Claudine was not the only intelligent and resourceful woman in the household.

Claudine flinched when Teresa touched the back of her shoulder. She twitched a smile as she glanced up briefly.

"Good evening, Teresa." She dropped a half-curtsy to Dalton. "Mr. Campbell."

Teresa, concern creasing her brow, leaned toward the woman. "Claudine, what's wrong? You don't look well. And your dress, why, I don't recall you coming in wearing this."

Claudine pulled at a lock of hair over her ear. "I'm fine.

217

I . . . was just nervous about all the guests. Sometimes crowds get my stomach worked up. I went for a walk to get some air. In the dark, I guess I put my foot in a hole, or something. I fell."

"Dear spirits. Would you like to sit?" Dalton asked as he took the woman's elbow, as if to hold her up. "Here, let me help you to a chair."

She dug in her heels. "No. I'm fine. But thank you. I soiled my dress, and had to go change, that's all. That's why it's not the same one. But I'm fine."

She glanced at his sword as he pulled back. He had seen her looking at a lot of swords since she returned to the gathering hall.

"You look as if something is—"

"No," she insisted. "I hit my head, that's why I look so shaken. I'm fine. Really. It simply shook my confidence."

"I understand," Dalton said sympathetically. "Things like that make one realize how short life can be. Make you realize how"—he snapped his fingers—"you could go at any time."

Her lip trembled. She had to swallow before she could speak. "Yes. I see what you mean. But I feel much better, now. My balance is back."

"Is it now? I'm not so sure."

Teresa pushed at him. "Dalton, can't you see the poor woman is shaken?" She gave him another push. "Go on and talk your business while I see to poor Claudine."

Dalton bowed and moved off to allow Teresa some privacy to find out what she would. He was pleased with the two Haken boys. It looked as if they had put the fear of the Keeper into her. By the unsteady way she walked, they had obviously delivered the message in the way he had wanted it delivered. Violence always helped people understand instructions.

He was gratified to know he had judged Fitch correctly. The way the boy stared at Dalton's sword, he knew. Claudine's eyes reflected fear when she looked at his sword; Fitch's eyes held lust. The boy had ambition. Morley was ıseful, too, but mostly as muscle. His head, too, was not much more than muscle. Fitch understood instructions better and, as eager as he was, would be of more use. At that age they had no clue how much they didn't know.

Dalton shook hands with a man who rushed up to pay him a compliment about his new position. He presented a civil face, but didn't remember the man's name, or really hear the effusive praise; Dalton's attention was elsewhere.

Director Linscott was just finishing speaking with a stocky man about taxes on the wheat stored in the man's warehouses. No trifling matter, considering the vast stores of grain Anderith held. Dalton politely, distantly, extracted himself from the nameless man and sidled closer to Linscott.

When the Director turned, Dalton smiled warmly at him and clasped his hand before he had a chance to withdraw it. He had a powerful grip. His hands still bore the calluses of his life's work.

"I am so glad you could make it to the feast, Director Linscott. I pray you are enjoying the evening, so far. We yet have much the Minister would like to discuss."

Director Linscott, a tall wiry fellow with a sun-rumpled face invariably looking as if he were plagued by an everlasting toothache, didn't return the smile. The four oldest Directors were guild masters. One was from the important clothmaking guild, one from the associated papermaking guild, another a master armorer, and Linscott. Linscott was a master mason. Most of the remaining Directors were respected moneylenders or merchants, along with a solicitor and several barristers.

Director Linscott's surcoat was an outdated cut, but finely kept nonetheless, and the warm brown went well with the the man's thin gray hair. His sword, too, was old, but the leather scabbard's exquisite brassware at the throat and tip was in gleaming condition. The silver emblem—the mason's dividers—stood out in bright silhouette against the dark leather. The sword's blade, undoubtedly, would be just as well maintained as everything else about the man.

Linscott didn't deliberately try to intimidate people, it just seemed to come naturally to him, the way a surly disposition came naturally to a mother brown bear with cubs. Linscott considered the Anderith people, those working fields, or hauling nets, or at employment in a trade through a guild-hall, his cubs.

"Yes," Linscott said, "I hear rumors the Minister has grand plans. I hear he has thoughts of disregarding the strong advice of the Mother Confessor, and breaking with the Midlands."

Dalton spread his hands. "I'm sure I don't speak out of turn when I tell you from my knowledge of the situation that Minister Chanboor intends to seek the best terms for our people. Nothing more, nothing less.

"You, for instance. What if we were to surrender to the new Lord Rahl and join the D'Haran Empire? This Lord Rahl has decreed all lands must surrender their sovereignty—unlike our alliance with the Midlands. That would mean, I suppose, he would no longer have need for Directors of Cultural Amity."

Linscott's tanned face turned ruddy with heat. "This isn't about me, Campbell. It's about the freedom of the people of the Midlands. About their future. About not being swallowed up and having our land brutalized by a rampaging Imperial Order army bent on the conquest of the Midlands.

"The Anderith ambassador has relayed Lord Rahl's word that while all lands must surrender to him and be brought under one rule and one command, each land will be allowed to retain its culture, so long as we do not break laws common to all. He has promised that if we accept his entreaty while the invitation is still open to all, we will be party to creating those common laws. The Mother Confessor has put her word to his."

Dalton respectfully bowed his head to the man. "You misunderstand Minister Chanboor's position, I'm afraid. He will propose to the Sovereign we go with the Mother Confessor's advice, if he sincerely believes it to be in the best interest of our people. Our very culture is at stake, after all. He has no wish to choose sides prematurely. The Imperial Order may offer our best prospects for peace. The Minister wants only peace."

The Director's dark scowl seemed to chill the air. "Slaves have peace."

Dalton affected an innocent, helpless look. "I am no match for your quick wit, Director."

"You seem ready to sell your own culture, Campbell, for the empty promises of an invading horde obsessed with conquest. Ask yourself, why else have they come, uninvited? How can you so smoothly proclaim you are considering thrusting a knife into the heart of the Midlands? What kind of man are you, Campbell, after all they have done for us, to turn your back on the advice and urging of our Mother Confessor?"

"Director, I think you—"

Linscott shook his fist. "Our ancestors who fought so futilely against the Haken horde no doubt shiver in their eternal rest to hear you so smoothly consider bargaining away their sacrifice and our heritage."

Dalton paused, letting Linscott hear his own words fill the silence and echo between the two of them. It was for this harvest Dalton had sowed his seeds of words.

"I know you are sincere, Director, in your fierce love of our people, and in your unflinching desire to protect them. I am sorry you find my wish for the same insincere." Dalton bowed politely. "I pray you enjoy the rest of the evening."

To graciously accept such an insult was the pinnacle of courtesy. But more than that, it revealed the one who would inflict such wounds as beneath the ancient ideals of Ander honor.

Only Hakens were said to be so cruelly demeaning to Anders.

With the utmost respect for the one who had insulted him, Dalton turned away as if he had been asked to leave, as if he had been driven off. As if he had been humiliated by a Haken overlord.

The Director called his name. Dalton paused and looked back over a shoulder.

Director Linscott screwed up his mouth, as if loosening it to test rarely used courtesy. "You know, Dalton, I remember you when you were with the magistrate in Fairfield. I always believed you were a moral man. I don't now believe differently."

Dalton cautiously turned around, presenting himself, as if he were prepared to accept another insult should the man wish to deliver one.

"Thank you, Director Linscott. Coming from a man as respected as you, that is quite gratifying."

Linscott gestured in a casual manner, as if still brushing at cobwebs in dark corners in his search for polite words. "So, I'm at a loss to understand how a moral man could allow his wife to parade around showing off her teats like that."

Dalton smiled; the tone, if not the words themselves, had been conciliatory. Casually, as he stepped closer, he caught a full cup of wine from a passing tray and offered it to the Director. Linscott took the cup with a nod.

Dalton dropped his official tone and spoke as if he had been boyhood chums with the man. "Actually, I couldn't agree more. In fact, my wife and I had an argument about it before we came down tonight. She insisted the dress was the fashion. I put my foot down, as the man of the marriage, and unconditionally forbade her from wearing the dress."

"Then why is she wearing it?"

Dalton sighed wearily. "Because I don't cheat on her."

Linscott cocked his head. "While I am glad to hear you don't ascribe to the seeming new moral attitudes where indulgences are concerned, what has that to do with the price of wheat in Kelton?"

Dalton took a sip of his wine. Linscott followed his lead.

"Well, since I don't cheat on her, I'd have no play in bed if I won every argument."

For the first time, the Director's face took on a small smile. "I see what you mean."

"The younger women around here dress in an appalling

fashion. I was shocked when I came here to work. My wife is younger, though, and wishes to fit in with them, to have friends. She fears being shunned by the other women of the household.

"I have spoken with the Minister about it, and he agrees the women should not flaunt themselves in such a manner, but our culture grants to women prerogative over their own dress. The Minister and I believe that, together, we might think of a way to influence fashion to the better."

Linscott nodded approvingly. "Well, I've a wife, too, and I don't cheat, either. I am glad to hear you are one of the few today who adheres to the old ideals that an oath is sacred, and commitment to your mate is sacrosanct. Good man."

Anderith culture revolved a great deal around honor and word given in solemn oath—about holding to your pledge. But Anderith was changing. It was a matter of great concern to many that moral bounds had, over the last few decades, fallen to scorn by many. Debauchery was not only accepted, but expected, among the fashionable elite.

Dalton glanced over at Teresa, back at the Director, and to Teresa again. He held out a hand.

"Director, could I introduce you to my lovely wife? Please? I would consider it a personal favor if you lent your considerable influence to the issue of decency. You are a greatly respected man, and could speak with moral authority I could never begin to command. She thinks I speak only as a jealous husband."

Linscott considered only briefly. "I would, if it would please you."

Teresa was encouraging Claudine to drink some wine and was offering comforting words as Dalton shepherded the Director up beside the two women.

"Teresa, Claudine, may I introduce Director Linscott."

Teresa smiled into his eyes as he lightly kissed her hand. Claudine stared at the floor as the procedure was repeated on her hand. She looked as if she wanted nothing more than to either jump into the man's arms for protection or run away as fast as she could. Dalton's reassuring hand on her shoulder prevented either.

"Teresa, darling, the Director and I were just discussing the issue of the women's dresses and fashion versus decorum."

Teresa canted a shoulder toward the Director, as if taking him into her confidence. "My husband is so stuffy about what I wear. And what do you think, Director Linscott? Do you approve of my dress?" Teresa beamed proudly. "Do you like it?"

Linscott glanced down from Teresa's eyes only briefly. "Quite lovely, my dear. Quite lovely."

"You see, Dalton? I told you. My dress is much more conservative than the others. I'm delighted one so widely respected as yourself approves, Director Linscott."

While Teresa turned to a passing cupbearer for a refill, Dalton gave Linscott a why-didn't-you-help-me? look. Linscott shrugged and bent to Dalton's ear.

"Your wife is a lovely, endearing woman," he whispered. "I couldn't very well humiliate and disappoint her."

Dalton made a show of sighing. "My problem, exactly."

Linscott straightened, smiling all the way.

"Director," Dalton said, more seriously, "Claudine, here, had a terrible accident earlier. While taking a walk outside she caught her foot and took a nasty tumble."

"Dear spirits." Linscott took up her hand. "Are you badly hurt, my dear?"

"It was nothing," Claudine mumbled.

"I've known Edwin a good many years. I'm sure your husband would be understanding if I helped you to your rooms. Here, take my arm, and I will see you safely to your bed."

As he took a sip, Dalton watched over the top of his cup. Her eyes swept the room. Those eyes held a world of longing to accept his offer. She might be safe if she did. He was a powerful man, and would have her under his wing.

This test would tell Dalton what he needed to know. It

wasn't really a huge risk to play out such an experiment. People did disappear, after all, without ever being found. Still, there were risks in it. He waited for Claudine to tell him which way it would go. At last, she did.

"Thank you for your concern, Director Linscott, but I'm fine. I have so looked forward to the feast, and seeing the guests come to the estate. I would forever regret missing it, and seeing our Minister of Culture speak."

Linscott took a sip of wine. "You and Edwin have labored vigorously on new laws since he was elected burgess. You have worked with the Minister. What think you of the man?" He gestured with his cup for emphasis. "Your honest opinion, now."

Claudine took a gulp of wine. She had to catch her breath. She stared at nothing as she spoke.

"Minister Chanboor is a man of honor. His policies have been good for Anderith. He has been respectful of the laws Edwin has proposed." She took another gulp of wine. "We are fortunate to have Bertrand Chanboor as the Minister of Culture. I have a hard time imagining another man who could do everything he does."

Linscott lifted an eyebrow. "Quite a ringing endorsement, from a woman of your renown. We all know that you, Claudine, are as important to those laws as Edwin."

"You are too kind," she mumbled, staring into her cup. "I am just the wife of an important man. I would be little missed and quickly forgotten were I to have broken my neck out there tonight. Edwin will be honored long and well."

Linscott puzzled at the top of her head.

"Claudine thinks far too little of herself," Dalton said. He caught sight of the seneschal, impeccably dressed in a long-tailed red coat crossed with a sash of many colors, opening the double doors. Beyond the doors, the lavers, with rose petals floating in them, awaited the guests.

Dalton turned to the Director. "I suppose you know who will be the guest of honor tonight?"

Linscott frowned. "Guest of honor?"

"A representative from the Imperial Order. A high-ranking man by the name of Stein. Come to tell us Emperor Jagang's words." Dalton took another sip. "The Sovereign has come, too, to hear those words."

Linscott sighed with the weight of this news. Now the man knew why he had been summoned, along with the other Directors, to what they had thought was no more than an ordinary feast at the estate. The Sovereign, for his own safety, rarely announced his appearances in advance. He had arrived with his own special guards and a large contingent of servants.

Teresa's face glowed as she smiled up at Dalton, eager for the evening's events. Claudine stared at the floor.

"Ladies and gentleman," the seneschal announced, "if it would please you, dinner is served."

CHAPTER 21

SHE SPREAD HER WINGS, and her rich voice sang out with the somber strains of a tale more ancient than myth.

Came the visions of icy beauty,
from the land of death where they dwell.
Pursuing their prize and grisly duty,
came the thieves of the charm and spell.
The bells chimed thrice, and death came a-calling.

Alluring of shape though seldom seen,
they traveled the breeze on a spark.
Some fed twigs to their newborn queen,
while others invaded the dark.
The bells chimed thrice, and death came a-calling.

Some they called and others they kissed
as they traveled on river and wave.
With resolve they came and did insist:
every one touched to a grave.
The bells chimed thrice, and death came a-calling.

Roving to hunt and gathering to dance,
they practiced their dark desires
by casting a hex and a beautiful trance,
before feeding the queen's new fires.
The bells chimed thrice, and death came a-calling.

Till he parted the falls
and the bells chimed thrice,
till he issued the calls
and demanded the price.
the bells chimed thrice and death met the
*   Mountain.*

They charmed and embraced
and they tried to extoll
but he bade them in grace
and demanded a soul.
The bells fell silent and the Mountain slew them
*   all.*
And the Mountain entombed them all.

With an impossibly long note, the young woman concluded her bewitching song. The guests broke into applause.

It was an archaic lyric of Joseph Ander and for that reason
alone was cherished. Dalton had once leafed through old

texts to see what he could learn of the song's meaning, but found nothing to shed light on the intent of the words, which, there being a number of versions, weren't always the same. It was one of those songs which no one really understood but everyone treasured because it was obviously a triumph of some sort for one of their land's beloved venerable founders. For the sake of tradition the haunting melody was sung on special occasions.

For some reason, Dalton had the odd feeling that the words now meant more to him than ever before. They seemed somehow nearly to make sense. As quickly as the sensation came, his mind was on to other things and the feeling passed.

The woman's long sleeves skimmed the floor as she held her arms wide while bowing to the Sovereign, and then once again to the applauding people at the head table beside the Sovereign's table. A baldachin of silk and gold brocade ran up the wall behind and then in billowing folds out over the two head tables. The baldachin's corners were held up with outsized Anderith lances. The effect was to make the head tables appear as if they were on a stage—which, in many ways, Dalton supposed they were.

The songstress bowed to the diners at the long rows of tables running down each side of the dining hall. Her sleeves were overlaid with spotted white owl feathers, so that when she spread her arms in song she appeared to be a winged woman, like something out of the ancient stories she sang.

Stein, on the other side of the applauding Minister and his wife, applauded apathetically, no doubt envisioning the young woman without her feathers. On Dalton's right, Teresa added enthusiastic calls of admiration to her clapping. Dalton stifled a yawn as he applauded.

As the songstress strode away, her arms lifted to wave in winged acknowledgment of the whistles trailing after her. After she'd vanished, four squires entered from the opposite side of the room carrying a platform atop which sat a marzipan ship floating in a sea of marzipan waves. The ship's billowing sails looked to be made of spun sugar.

The purpose, of course, was to announce that the next course would be fish, just as the pastry deer, pursued by pastry hounds leaping a hedge of holly in which hid aspic boar, had announced one of the meat courses, and the stuffed eagle with its huge wings spread over a scene of the capital city of Fairfield made of paper board buildings had announced a course of fowl. Up in the gallery, a fanfare trumpeted and drums rolled to add a musical testament to the arrival of the next course.

There had been five courses, each with at least a dozen specialties. That meant there were seven courses yet to come, each with at least a dozen distinctive dishes of its own. Music from flute and fife and drum, jugglers, troubadours, and acrobats entertained the guests between courses as a tree with candied fruits toured the tables. Gifts of mechanical horses with opposing legs that moved in unison were passed out to the delight of all.

Meat dishes had included everything from Teresa's all-time favorite of suckers—she had eaten three of the infant rabbits—to fawn, to pig, to cow, to a bear standing on its hind legs. The bear was wheeled from table to table; at each table its hide, draped around the roasted carcass, was pulled back to allow carvers to slice off pieces for the guests. Fowl ranged from the sparrows the Minister favored for their stimulation of lust, to pigeons, to swan's neck pudding, to eagles, to baked heron that had been re-feathered and held by wires in a display depicting them as a flock in flight.

It was not expected that everyone would eat such a plenitude of food; the variety was meant to offer an abundance of choice, not only to please honored guests, but to astonish them with opulence. A visit to the Minister of Culture's estate was an occasion long remembered, and for many became a legendary event talked about for years.

As they sampled the dishes, most people kept an eye to the head table, where the Minister sat with two wealthy backers he had invited to dine at his table, and the other object of great interest: the representative from the Imperial Order. Stein had arrived earlier, to the whispered oohing and aahing of all at his man-of-war outfit and cape of human scalps. He was a sensation, drawing the inviting looks of a number of women weak in the knees at the prospect of winning such a man to their bed.

In vivid outward contrast to the warrior from the Old World, Bertrand Chanboor wore a close-fitting, sleeveless, padded purple doublet embellished with elaborate embroidery, gold trim, and silver braiding over a simple sleeved short jacket. Together, they gave his soft rounded shape the illusion of a more manly frame. A frill of white stood above the doublet's low, erect collar. A similar ruff stood out at wrists and waist.

Slung over the shoulders of the doublet and short jacket was a magnificent dress coat of a deeper purple with fur trim running around the collar and all the way down the front. Below the padded rolls standing at the ends of the shoulders, the baggy sleeves had slashes lined with red silk. Between the spiral slashes, galloon braiding separated rows of pearls.

With his intent eyes, his easy smile—which, along with those eyes, always seemed directed at no other than the person with whom he had eye contact at the moment—and his shock of thick, graying hair, he struck an impressive figure. That, and Bertrand Chanboor's presence, or rather the presence of the power he wielded as the Minister of Culture, left many a man in awed admiration and many a woman in breathless yearning.

If not watching the Minister's table, guests cast stealthy glances at the table beside it, where sat the Sovereign, his wife, and their three grown sons and two grown daughters. No one wanted to stare openly at the Sovereign. The Sovereign was, after all, the Creator's deputy in the world of life—a holy religious leader as well as the ruler of their land. Many in Anderith, Anders and Haken alike, idolized the Sovereign to the point of falling to the ground, wailing, and confessing sins when his carriage passed.

The Sovereign, alert and perceptive despite deteriorating health, was dressed in a glittering golden garment. A red vest emphasized the outfit's bulbous sleeves. A long, richly colored, embroidered silk stole was draped over his shoulders. Bright yellow stockings laced at midthigh to the bottom of teardrop-shaped puffed and padded breeches with colored slashes. Jewels weighed each finger. The Sovereign's head hovered low between his rounded shoulders, as if the gold medallion displaying a diamond-encrusted mountain had, over time, weighed so heavily on his neck that it bowed his back. Liver spots as large as the jewels mottled his hands.

The Sovereign had outlived four wives. With loving care, the man's latest wife dabbed at the food on his chin. Dalton doubted she was yet out of her teens.

Thankfully, even though the sons and daughters brought their spouses, they had left their children home; the Sovereign's grandchildren were insufferable brats. No one dared do anything more than chuckle approvingly at the little darlings as they rampaged unchecked. Several of them were considerably older than their latest stepgrandmother.

On the other side of the Minister from Dalton, Lady Hildemara Chanboor, in an elegant silvery pleated gown cut as low as any in the room, gestured with one finger, and the harpist, stationed before but below the head table's raised platform, gently trailed her soft music to silence. The Minister's wife directed the feast.

It actually needed no directing from her, but she insisted she be acknowledged as the regal hostess of the majestic and stately event, and therefore from time to time contributed to the proceedings by lifting her finger to silence the harpist at the appropriate time so that all might know and respect her social position. People were spellbound, believing the entire feast turned on Lady Chanboor's finger.

The harpist certainly knew when she was to let her music end for an impending slated event, but nonetheless waited and watched for that noble finger before daring to still her own. Sweat dotted her brow as she watched for Lady Chanboor's finger to rise, daring not to miss it.

Though universally proclaimed radiant and beautiful, Hil-

231

demara was rather thick of limb and feature, and had always put Dalton in mind of a sculpture of a woman chiseled by an artisan of greater ardor than talent. It was not a piece of work one wished to consider for long stretches.

The harpist took the chance of the break to reach for a cup on the floor beside her golden harp. As she bent forward for the cup, the Minister ogled her cleavage, at the same time giving Dalton an elbow in the ribs lest he miss the sight.

Lady Chanboor noticed her husband's roving eye, but showed no reaction. She never did. She relished the power she wielded, and willingly paid the requisite price.

In private, though, Hildemara occasionally clouted Bertrand with any handy object, more likely for a social slight to her than a marital indiscretion. She had no real cause to raise objections to his philandering; she was not exactly faithful, enjoying at times the discreet company of lovers. Dalton kept a mental list of their names.

Dalton suspected that, like many of her husband's dalliances, her partners were attracted to her power, and hoped they might earn a favor. Most people had no clue as to what went on at the estate, and could imagine her as nothing other than a faithful loving wife, an image she cultivated with care. The Anderith people loved her as the people of other lands loved a queen.

In many ways, she was the power behind the office of Minister; she was adept, knowledgeable, focused. While Bertrand was often at play, Hildemara, behind closed doors, issued orders. He relied on his wife's expertise, often deferring to her in material matters, disinterested in what patronage she doled out to miscreants, or the cultural carnage she left in her wake.

No matter what she might think of her husband in private, Hildemara worked zealously to preserve his dominion. If he fell, she would surely crash down with him. Unlike her husband, Hildemara was rarely drunk and discreetly confined whatever couplings she had to the middle of the night.

Dalton knew better than to underestimate her. She tended cobwebs of her own.

The company gasped with delighted surprise when a "sailor" sprang from behind the marzipan ship, piping a merry fisher's tune on his fife while accompanying himself on a tabor hung from his belt. Teresa giggled and clapped, as did many others.

She squeezed her husband's leg under the table. "Oh, Dalton, did you ever think we would live at such a splendid place, come to know such splendid people, and see such splendid things?"

"Of course."

She giggled again and gently bumped his shoulder with hers. Dalton watched Claudine applaud from a table to the right. To his left Stein stabbed a chunk of meat and with shameless manners pulled it from the knife with his teeth. He chewed with his mouth open as he viewed the entertainment. This didn't look to be the sort of entertainment Stein favored.

Servers had already begun carrying in silver chargers of the fish course, taking them to the dresser table for saucing and dressing before service. The Sovereign had his own servants at a sideboard to taste and prepare his food. They used knives they had brought with them to slice off for the Sovereign and his family the choice upper crust of rolls and breads. They had other knives just to prepare the trenchers upon which the Sovereign's food was placed, which, unlike everyone else's plates, were changed after each course. They had one knife to slice, one to trim, and one just to smooth the trenchers.

The Minister leaned close, his fingers holding a slice of pork he had dipped in mustard. "I heard a rumor that there is a woman who might be inclined to spread unpleasant lies. Perhaps you should inquire after the matter."

From the platter he shared with Teresa, Dalton plucked up with his second finger and thumb a slice of pear in almond milk. "Yes, Minister, I already have. She intends no

233

disrespect." He popped the pear in his mouth.

The Minister lifted an eyebrow. "Well and good, then."

He grinned and winked past Dalton. Smiling, Teresa bowed her head in acknowledgment of his greeting.

"Ah, my dear Teresa, have I yet told you that you look especially divine this evening. And your hair is wondrous—it makes you look as if you are a good spirit come to grace my table. If you weren't married to my right-hand man, I'd invite you to a dance, later."

The Minister rarely danced with anyone but his wife and, as a matter of protocol, visiting dignitaries.

"Minister, I would be honored," Teresa said, stumbling over the words, "as would my husband—I'm sure. I could be in no better hands on the dance floor—or anywhere."

Despite Teresa's usual ability to maintain a state of social equanimity, she blushed at the high honor Bertrand had almost extended. She fussed with the glittering sequins tied in her hair, aware of envious eyes watching her speak with the Minister of Culture himself.

Dalton knew by the scowl behind the Minister that there was no need to fret that such a dance—with the man doubtlessly pressing up against Teresa's half-exposed bosom—would take place. Lady Chanboor would not have Bertrand formally showing such a lack of complete devotion to her.

Dalton returned to business, steering the conversation in the direction of his intentions. "One of the officials from the city is very concerned about the situation we spoke of."

"What did he say?" Bertrand knew which Director they were discussing and wisely refrained from using names aloud, but his eyes flashed anger.

"Nothing," Dalton assured him. "But the man is persistent. He might inquire after matters—press for explanations. There are those who conspire against us, and would be eager to stir the cry of impropriety. It would be a bothersome waste of time and take us away from our duty to the Anderith people, were we forced to acquit ourselves of groundless accusations of misconduct."

"The whole idea is absurd," the Minister said, as he followed in the form of their cover conversation. "You don't really believe, do you, that people really plot to oppose our good works?"

His words sounded by rote, he used them so often. Simple prudence required that public discussion be circumspect. There might be gifted people slipped in among the guests, hoping to use their skill to overhear something not meant to be heard.

Dalton himself employed a gifted woman with such talent.

"We devote our lives to doing the work of the Anderith people," Dalton said, "and yet there are those greedy few who would wish to stall the progress we make on behalf of the working people."

From the trencher he shared with his wife, Bertrand picked up a roasted swan wing and dragged it through a small bowl of frumenty sauce. "You think fomenters might be intending to cause trouble, then?"

Lady Chanboor, closely following the conversation, leaned close to her husband. "Agitators would jump at the chance to destroy Bertrand's good work. They would willingly aid any troublemaker." She glanced pointedly to the Sovereign being fed from the fingers of his young wife. "We have important work before us and don't need antagonists meddling in our efforts."

Bertrand Chanboor was the most likely candidate to be named Sovereign, but there were those who opposed him. Once named, a Sovereign served for life. Any slip at such a critical time could remove the Minister from consideration. There were any number of people wishing he would make such a slip, and they would be watching and listening for it.

After Bertrand Chanboor was named Sovereign, they would be free of worry, but until then, nothing was certain or safe.

Dalton bowed his head in acknowledgment. "You see the situation well, Lady Chanboor."

235

Bertrand let out a little grunt. "I take it you have a suggestion."

"I do," Dalton said, lowering his voice to little more than a whisper. It was impolite to be seen whispering, but it was unavoidable; he needed to act, and whispers would not be heard. "I think it would be best if we upset the balance of things. What I have in mind will not only pull the weed from the wheat, but it will discourage other weeds from springing up."

Keeping an eye to the Sovereign's table, Dalton explained his proposal. Lady Chanboor straightened with a sly smile; Dalton's advice pleased her disposition. Without emotion, Bertrand, as he watched Claudine picking at her food, agreed.

Stein dragged his knife blade across the table, making a show of slicing through the fine white linen overcloth.

"Why don't I just slit their throats."

The Minister glanced about, checking to see if he could tell if anyone had overheard Stein's offer. Hildemara's face flushed with anger. Teresa's went white to hear such talk, especially from a man who wore a cape of human scalps.

Stein had been warned before. If overheard and reported, such words could open the floodgates of investigation, which would undoubtedly bring the Mother Confessor herself down on them. She would not rest until she discovered the truth of it, and if that happened, she very well might be inclined to use her magic to remove the Minister from office. For good.

With a deadly look, Dalton delivered a silent threat to Stein. Stein grinned out through yellow teeth. "Just a friendly joke."

"I don't care how large the Imperial Order's force is," the Minister growled for the ears of any who might have heard Stein. "Unless they are invited through—which is yet to be decided—they will all perish before the Dominie Dirtch. The emperor knows the truth of it, or he wouldn't ask us to consider the generous offers of peace he has made. I am sure he would be displeased to know how one of his men insults our culture and the laws by which we live.

"You are here as a delegate from Emperor Jagang to explain to our people the emperor's position and liberal offers—no more. If need be, we can get another to do such explaining."

Stein smirked at all the agitation directed his way. "I was joking, of course. Such empty talk is the custom among my people. Where I come from, such words are common and harmless. I assure you all, it was only meant for the sake of amusement."

"I hope you intend to exercise better judgment when you speak to our people," the Minister said. "This is a serious matter you have come to discuss. The Directors would not appreciate hearing such offensive humor."

Stein let out a coarse laugh. "Master Campbell did explain your culture's intolerance for such crude banter, but my unpolished nature caused me to forget his wise words. Please excuse my poor choice of a joke. No harm was intended."

"Well and good, then." Bertrand leaned back, his wary gaze sweeping over the guests. "All Anderith people take a dim view of brutality, and are not used to such talk, much less such action."

Stein bowed his head. "I have yet to learn the exemplary customs of your great culture. I look forward to being given the opportunity to learn your better ways."

With those precisely disarming words, Dalton raised his estimate of the man. Stein's unkempt hair was misleading; what was under it was not nearly so disordered.

If Lady Chanboor caught the mordant satire in Stein's repartee, she did not show it as her face relaxed back to its usual sweet-and-sour set. "We understand, and admire your sincere effort to learn what must be . . . strange customs to you." Her fingertips slid Stein's goblet toward him. "Please, have some of our fine Nareef Valley wine. We are all very fond of it."

If Lady Chanboor failed to grasp the subtle sarcasm in Stein's words, Teresa did not. Unlike Hildemara, Teresa had skirmished much of her adult life among the cut-and-thrust

237

front lines of female social structure, where words were wielded as weapons meant to draw blood. The higher the level of engagement, the more refined the edge. There, you had to be adept to know you had been cut and were bleeding, or the wound was all that much greater for others seeing it and you missing it.

Hildemara didn't need the blade of wit; raw power alone shielded her. Anderith generals rarely swung swords.

As she watched with practical fascination, Teresa took a sip when Stein swept up his goblet for a long swig.

"It is good. In fact, I would declare it to be the best I've ever tasted."

"We are pleased to hear such a widely traveled man's opinion," the Minister said.

Stein thunked his goblet down on the table. "I've had my fill of food. When do I get to speak my piece?"

The Minister lifted an eyebrow. "When the guests have finished."

Grinning again, Stein stabbed a chunk of meat and leaned back to gnaw it off the knifepoint. As he chewed, his eyes boldly met the sultry looks he was getting from some of the women.

CHAPTER 22

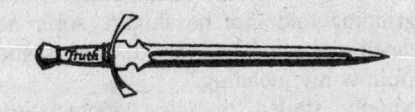

MUSICIANS UP IN THE gallery piped a nautical tune while ushers unfurled lengthy blue banners down into the dining hall. The pairs of men holding the banners flapped them in time with the music, giving the effect of ocean waves as the fishing boats painted on the banners bobbed upon the blue-cloth waters.

While the Sovereign's own servants catered to his table, squires in estate livery eddied around the Minister's head table, bearing silver platters arrayed with the colorfully prepared fish course. The Minister selected crab legs, salmon belly, fried minnows, bream, and eels in saffron sauce, the squire placing each item between the Minister and his wife for them to transfer as they would to their shared trencher.

Minister Chanboor swirled a long piece of eel in the saffron sauce and offered it, draped over a finger, to his wife. She smiled affectionately and with the tips of long nails plucked it from his finger, but before putting it to her lips, she instead set it down and turned to Stein to ask, as if suddenly taken with curiosity, about the food of his homeland. In the short time he had been at the estate, Dalton had learned that Lady Chanboor disliked eel above all else.

When one of the squires held out a platter of crayfish, Teresa told Dalton, by the hopeful lift of her eyebrows, that she would like one. The squire deftly split the shell, removed the vein, fluffed the meat, and stuffed the shell beneath with crackers and butter, as Dalton requested. He used his knife to lift a slice of porpoise from a platter held out by a squire with his head bowed low between his outstretched arms. The squire genuflected, as did they all, before moving on with a dancelike step.

Teresa's wrinkled nose told him she didn't want any eel. He took one for himself, only because the Minister's nodding and grinning told him he should. After he did, the Minister leaned close and whispered, "Eel is good for the eel, if you follow my meaning."

Dalton simply smiled, feigning appreciation for the pointer. His mind was on his job and the task at hand, and besides, he wasn't preoccupied with concern about his "eel."

As Teresa sampled the gingered carp, Dalton idly tasted the baked herring with sugar as he watched the Haken squires, like an invading army, sweep down on the tables of guests. They brought platters of fried pike, bass, millet, and trout; baked lamprey herring, haddock, and hake; roast perch, salmon, seal, and sturgeon; crabs, shrimp, and whelk on beds of glazed roe, along with tureens of spiced scallop bisque and almond fish stew, in addition to colorful sauces of every kind. Other dishes were served in inventive presentations of sauces and florid concoctions of combined ingredients, from porpoise and peas in onion wine sauce, to sturgeon roe and gurnard flanks, to great plaice and codling pie in sauce vert.

The abundance of food presented in such elaborate profusion was intended not only to be political spectacle wherein the Minister of Culture manifested his power and wealth, but also to convey—to protect the Minister from accusations of ostentatious excess—a profound religious connotation. The plenty was ultimately an exhibition of the Creator's splendor and, despite the seeming opulence, but an infinitesimal sampling of His endless bounty.

The feast was not convened to oblige a gathering of people, but a gathering of people had been called to attend the feast—a subtle but significant difference. That the feast wasn't held for a social reason—say, a wedding, or to celebrate an anniversary of a military victory—underlined its religious substance. The Sovereign's attendance, his being the Creator's deputy in the world of life, only consecrated the sacred aspects of the feast.

If guests were impressed with the wealth, power, and nobility of the Minister and his wife, that was incidental and unavoidable. Dalton incidentally, noticed a great many people being unavoidably impressed.

The room droned with conversation sprinkled with the chime of laughter as the guests sipped wine, nibbled food of every sort, and sampled with different fingers the variety of sauces. The harpist had started in again to entertain the guests while they dined. The Minister ate eel as he spoke with his wife, Stein, and the two wealthy backers at the far end of the table.

Dalton wiped his lips, deciding to make use of the opening offered by the relaxed mood. He took a last sip of wine before leaning toward his wife. "Did you find out anything from your talk earlier?"

Teresa used her knife to part a piece of fried pike, then picked up her half with her fingers and dipped it in red sauce. She knew he meant Claudine. "Nothing specific. But I suspect the lamb is not locked in her pen."

Teresa didn't know what the whole matter was about, or that Dalton had enlisted the two Haken boys to deliver a warning to Claudine, but she knew enough to understand that Claudine was probably making trouble over her tryst with the Minister. While they never discussed specifics, Teresa knew she wasn't sitting at the head table simply because Dalton knew the law forward and backward.

Teresa lowered her voice. "While I talked with her, she paid a lot of attention to Director Linscott—you know, watching him while trying to act as if she wasn't; watching, too, to see if anyone saw her looking."

Her word was always trustworthy, never embellished with supposition without being tagged as such.

241

"Why do you think she was so brazen before about telling the other women that the Minister forced himself on her?"

"I think she told others about the Minister as protection. I believe she reasoned that if people already knew about it, then she was safe from being silenced before anyone could find out.

"For some reason, though, she has suddenly become closemouthed. But, like I said, she was watching the Director a lot and pretending as if she wasn't."

Teresa left it to him to draw his own conclusions. Dalton leaned toward her as he rose. "Thank you, darling. If you will excuse me briefly, I must see to some business."

She caught his hand. "Don't forget you promised to introduce me to the Sovereign."

Dalton lightly kissed her cheek before meeting the Minister's eye. What Teresa had said only confirmed his belief in the prudence of his plan. Much was at stake. Director Linscott could be inquisitorial. Dalton was reasonably sure the message delivered by the two boys had silenced Claudine, but if it didn't, this would end her ability to sow her seeds. He gave Bertrand a slight nod.

As he moved around the room, Dalton stopped at a number of tables, leaning over, greeting people he knew, hearing a joke here, a rumor there, a proposal or two, and promised to get together with some. Everyone thought him a representative of the Minister, come from the head table to make the rounds of the tables, seeing to everyone's pleasure.

Arriving at last at his true destination, Dalton presented a warm smile. "Claudine, I pray you are feeling better. Teresa suggested I inquire—see if you need anything—seeing as how Edwin is not able to be here."

She flashed him a reasonably good imitation of a sincere smile. "Your wife is a dear, Master Campbell. I'm fine, thank you. The food and company has put me right. Please tell her I'm feeling much better."

"I am glad to hear it." Dalton leaned close to her ear. "I was going to relay an offer for Edwin—and you—but I'm reluctant to ask this of you not only with Edwin out of the city, but with your unfortunate tumble. I don't wish to force work on you when you aren't up to it, so please come to see me when you are fit."

She turned to frown at him. "Thank you for your concern, but I'm fine. If you have business that involves Edwin, he wishes me to hear it. We work closely and have no secrets where business is concerned. You know that, Master Campbell."

Dalton not only knew it, but was counting on it. He squatted down on the balls of his feet as she scooted her chair back to be out of the table's circle of conversation.

"Please forgive my presumption? Well, you see," he began, "the Minister feels profound sympathy for men unable to feed their families any other way but to beg food. Even if they can beg food, their families still go for want of clothes, proper shelter, and other necessities. Despite the charity of good Anderith people, many children go to bed with the ache of hunger in their bellies. Hakens as well as Anders suffer this fate, and the Minister feels compassion for both, for they are all his responsibility.

"The Minister has labored feverishly, and has at last worked out the final details of a new law to at last put a number of people to work who otherwise would have no hope."

"That's, that's very good of him," she stammered. "Bertrand Chanboor is a good man. We are lucky to have him as our Minister of Culture."

Dalton wiped a hand across his mouth as she looked away from his eyes. "Well, the thing of it is, the Minister often mentions his respect for Edwin—for all the unsung work Edwin has done—so I suggested to the Minister that it would be appropriate to somehow show our respect for Edwin's hard work and dedication.

"The Minister fervently agreed and instantly sprang to the idea of having the new law headed as proposed and sponsored by Burgess Edwin Winthrop. The Minister even wishes it to be called the Winthrop Fair Employment Law in honor of your husband—and you, too, of course, for all your work. Everyone knows the input you have in the laws Edwin drafts."

Claudine's gaze had already returned to meet his. She put a hand to her breast.

"Why, Master Campbell, that is very generous of you and the Minister. I am completely taken by surprise, as I'm sure Edwin will be. We will certainly review the law as soon as possible, so as to allow its most expeditious implementation."

Dalton grimaced. "Well, the thing is, the Minister just now informed me he is impatient to announce it tonight. I had originally planned to bring you a draft of the law, for you and Edwin to review before it was announced, but with all the Directors here the Minister decided that in good conscience he must act—that he couldn't bear to have those men out of work another day. They need to feed their families."

She licked her lips. "Well, yes, I understand . . . I guess, but I really—"

"Good. Oh, good. That is so very kind of you."

"But I really should have a look at it. I really must see it. Edwin would want—"

"Yes, of course. I understand completely, and I assure you that you will get a copy straightaway—first thing tomorrow."

"But I meant before—"

"With everyone here, now, the Minister was set on announcing it this evening. The Minister really doesn't want to have to delay the implementation, nor does he want to abandon his desire to have the Winthrop name on such a landmark law. And the Minister was so hoping that the Sovereign, since he is here tonight—and we all know how rare his visits are—would hear of the Winthrop Fair Employment Law designed to help people who otherwise have no hope. The Sovereign knows Edwin, and would be so pleased."

Claudine stole a glance at the Sovereign. She wet her lips. "But—"

"Do you wish me to ask the Minister to postpone the law? More than the Sovereign missing it, the Minister would be very disappointed to let the opportunity pass, and to let down those starving children who depend on him to better their lives. You can understand, can't you, that it's really for the sake of the children?"

"Yes, but in order to—"

"Claudine," Dalton said as he took up one of her hands in both of his, "you don't have any children, so I realize it must be particularly difficult for you to empathize with parents desperate to feed their young ones, desperate to find work when there is none, but try to understand how frightened they must be."

She opened her mouth, but no words came. He went on, not allowing her the time to form those words.

"Try to understand what it would be like to be a mother and father waiting day after day, waiting for a reason to hope, waiting for something to happen so that you could find work and be able to feed your children. Can't you help? Can you try to understand what it must be like for a young mother?"

Her face had gone ashen.

"Of course," she finally whispered. "I understand. I really do. I want to help. I'm sure Edwin will be pleased when he learns he was named as the law's sponsor—"

Before she could say anything else, Dalton stood. "Thank you, Claudine." He took up her hand again and gave it a kiss. "The Minister will be very pleased to hear of your support—and so will those men who will now find work. You have done a good thing for the children. The good spirits must be smiling on you right now."

By the time Dalton had returned to the head table, the squires were making the rounds again, quickly placing a turtle pie in the center of each table. Guests puzzled at the pies, their crusts quartered but not cut all the way through. Frowning, Teresa was leaning in staring at the pie placed before the Minister and his wife at the center of the head table.

"Dalton," she whispered, "that pie moved of its own accord."

Dalton kept the smile from his face. "You must be mistaken, Tess. A pie can't move."

"But I'm sure—"

With that, the crust broke, and a section of it lifted. A turtle poked its head up to peer at the Minister. A claw grasped the edge, and the turtle hauled itself out, to be followed by another. All around the room surprised guests laughed, applauded, and murmured in astonishment as turtles began climbing out of the pies.

The turtles, of course, had not been baked alive in the pies; the pies had been baked with dried beans inside. After the crust was baked, a hole was cut in the bottom to allow the beans to be drained out and the turtles put in. The crusts had been cut partly through so it would break easily and allow the animals to make good their escape.

The turtle pies, as one of the amusements of the feast, were a grand success. Everyone was delighted by the spectacle. Sometimes it was turtles, sometimes it was birds, both specially raised for the purpose of popping out of pies at a feast to delight and astonish guests.

While squires with wooden buckets began making the rounds of the tables to collect the liberated turtles, Lady Chanboor summoned the chamberlain and asked him to cancel the entertainment due to perform before the next course. A hush fell over the room as she rose.

"Good people, if I may have your attention, please." Hildemara looked to both sides of the room, making sure every eye was upon her. Her pleated dress seemed to glow with cold silver light. "It is the highest calling and duty to help your fellow citizens when they are in need. Tonight, at last, we hope to take a step to help the children of Anderith. It is a bold step, one requiring courage. Fortunately, we have a leader of such courage.

"It is my high honor to introduce to you the greatest man I have ever had the privilege to know, a man of integrity, a man who works tirelessly for the people, a man who never forgets the needs of those who need us most, a man who holds our better future above all else, my husband, the Minister of Culture, Bertrand Chanboor."

Hildemara pulled a smile across her face and, clapping, turned to her husband. The room erupted with applause and a great groan of cheering. Beaming, Bertrand stood and slipped an arm around his wife's waist. She stared adoringly up into his eyes. He gazed lovingly down into hers. People cheered louder yet, joyful to have such a high-minded couple boldly leading Anderith.

Dalton rose as he applauded with his hands over his head, bringing everyone to their feet. He put on his widest smile so the farthest guest would be able to see it and then, continuing to applaud loudly, turned to watch the Minister and his wife.

Dalton had worked for a number of men. Some he could not trust to announce a round of drinks. Some were good at following the plan as Dalton outlined it, but didn't grasp it fully until they saw it unfold. None were in Bertrand Chanboor's league.

The Minister had immediately grasped the concept and goal as Dalton had quickly explained it to him. He would be able to embellish it and make it his own; Dalton had never seen anyone as smooth as Bertrand Chanboor.

Smiling, holding a hand in the air, Bertrand both acknowledged the cheering crowd and finally silenced them.

"My good people of Anderith," he began in a deep, sincere-sounding voice that boomed into the farthest reaches of the room, "tonight I ask you to consider the future. The time is overdue for us to have the courage to leave our past favoritism where it belongs—in the past. We must, instead, think of our future and the future of our children and grandchildren."

He had to pause and nod and smile while the room again roared with applause. Once more, he began, bringing the audience to silence.

"Our future is doomed if we allow naysayers to rule our imagination, instead of allowing the spirit of potential, given us by the Creator, room to soar."

He again waited until the wild clapping died down. Dalton marveled at the sauce Bertrand could whip up on the spot to pour over the meat.

"We in this room have had thrust upon us the responsibility for all the people of Anderith, not just the fortunate. It is time our culture included all the people of Anderith, not just the fortunate. It is time our laws served all the people of Anderith, not just the few."

Dalton shot to his feet to applaud and whistle. Immediately following his lead, everyone else stood as they clapped and cheered. Hildemara, still beaming with the loving grin of wifely devotion and fawning, stood to clap for her husband.

"When I was young," Bertrand went on in a soft voice after the crowd quieted, "I knew the pang of hunger. It was a difficult time in Anderith. My father was without work. I watched my sister cry herself to sleep as hunger gnawed in her belly.

"I watched my father weep in silence, because he felt the shame of having no work, because he had no skills." He paused to clear his throat. "He was a proud man, but that nearly broke his spirit."

Dalton idly wondered if Bertrand even had a sister.

"Today, we have proud men, men willing to work, and at the same time plenty of work that needs to be done. We have several government buildings under construction and more planned. We have roads being built in order to allow for the expansion of trade. We have bridges yet to be built up in the passes over the mountains. Rivers await workers to come build piers to support bridges to those roads and passes.

"But none of those proud men who are willing to work and who need the work can be employed at any of these jobs or the many other jobs available, because they are unskilled. As was my father."

Bertrand Chanboor looked out at people waiting in rapt attention to hear his solution.

"We can provide these proud men with work. As the Minister of Culture, it is my duty to our people to see to it that these men have work so they can provide for their children, who are our future. I asked our brightest minds to come up with a solution, and they have not let me, nor the people of Anderith, down. I wish I could take credit for this brilliant new statute, but I cannot.

"These scholarly new proposals were brought to me by people who make me proud to be in office so that I might help them guide this new law into the light of day. There were those in the past who would use their influence to see such fair ideas die in the dark recesses of hidden rooms. I won't allow such selfish interests to kill the hope for our children's future."

Bertrand let a dark scowl descend upon his face, and his scowls could make people pale and tingle with dread.

"There were those in the past who held the best for their own kind, and would allow no others the chance to prove themselves."

There was no mistaking the allusion. Time meant nothing in healing the wounds inflicted by the Haken overlords—those wounds would always be open and raw; it served to keep them so.

Bertrand's face relaxed into his familiar easy smile, by contrast all the more pleasant after the scowl. "This new hope is the Winthrop Fair Employment Law." He held out a hand toward Claudine. "Lady Winthrop, would you please stand?"

Blushing, she looked about as people smiled her way. Applause started in, urging her to stand. She looked like a deer caught inside the garden fence at dawn. Hesitantly, she rose to her feet.

"Good people, it is Lady Winthrop's husband, Edwin, who is the sponsor of the new law, and, as many of you know, Lady Winthrop is his able assistant in his job as burgess. I have no doubt that Lady Winthrop played a critical role in her husband's new law. Edwin is away on business, but I would like to applaud her fine work in this, and hope she relays our appreciation to Edwin when he returns."

Along with Bertrand, the room applauded and cheered her and her absent husband. Claudine, her face red, smiled cautiously to the adoration. Dalton noticed that the Directors, not knowing what the law was about, were polite but reserved in their congratulations. With people leaning toward her, touching her to get her attention, and offering words of appreciation, it was a time before everyone returned to their seats to hear the nature of the law.

"The Winthrop Fair Employment Law is what its name implies," Bertrand finally explained, "fair and open, rather than privileged and closed, employment. With all the construction of indispensable public projects, we have much work to do in order to serve the needs of the people."

The Minister swept a look of resolve across the crowd.

"But one brotherhood holds itself to outmoded prerogative, thus delaying progress. Don't get me wrong, these men are of high ideals and are hard workers, but the time has come to throw open the doors of this archaic order designed to protect the special few.

"Henceforth, under the new law, employment shall go to anyone willing to put their back to the work, not just to the closed brotherhood of the Masons Guild!"

The crowd took a collective gasp. Bertrand gave them no pause.

"Worse, because of this shrouded guild, where only a few meet their obscure and needlessly strict requirements, the cost to the people of Anderith for public projects they construct is far and away above what would be the cost were willing workers allowed to work." The Minister shook his fist. "We all pay the outrageous cost!"

Director Linscott was near to purple with contained rage.

Bertrand uncurled a finger from his fist and pointed out at the crowd. "The masons' vast knowledge should be employed, by all means it should, but with this new law, the common man will be employed, too, under the supervision of masons, and the children will not go hungry for their fathers' want of work."

The Minister struck a fist to the palm of his other hand to emphasize each point he added.

"I call upon the Directors of Cultural Amity to show us, now, by their raised hands, their support of putting starving people to work, their support of the government finally being able to complete projects at a fair price by using those willing to work and not just the members of a secret society of masons who set their own exorbitant rates we all must bear! Their support for the children! Their support of the Winthrop Fair Employment Law!"

Director Linscott shot to his feet. "I protest such a show of hands! We have not yet had time to—"

He fell silent when he saw the Sovereign lift his hand.

"If the other Directors would like to show their support," the Sovereign said in a clear voice into the hush, "then the people gathered here should know of it, so that none may bear false witness to the truth of each man's will. There can be no harm in judging the sentiment of the Directors while they are all here. A show of hands is not the final word, and so does not close the matter to debate before it becomes law."

The Sovereign's impatience had just unwittingly saved the Minister the task of forcing a vote. Though it was true that a show of hands here would not make the law final, in this case such a schism among the guilds and professions would insure it did.

Dalton did not have to wait for the other Directors to show their hands; there was no doubt in his mind. The law the Minister had announced was a death sentence to a guild, and the Minister had just let them all see the glint off the executioner's axe.

Though they would not know why, the Directors would know one of their number had been singled out. While only four of the Directors were guild masters, the others were no less assailable. The moneylenders might have their allowed interest lowered or even outlawed, the merchants their trade

251

preferences and routes changed; the solicitors and barristers could have their charges set by law at a rate even a beggar could afford. No profession was safe from some new law, should they displease the Minister.

If the other Directors did not support the Minister in this, that blade might be turned on their guild or profession. The Minister had called for a public showing of their hands rather than a closed-door vote, the implication being that the axe would not swing in their direction if they went along.

Claudine sank into her chair. She, too, knew what this meant. Men were formerly forbidden work at the trade of mason unless they were members of the Masons Guild. The guild set training, standards, and rates, governed disputes, assigned workers to various jobs as needed, looked after members injured or sick, and helped widows of men killed on the job. With unskilled workers allowed to work as masons, guild members would lose their skilled wages. It would destroy the Masons Guild.

For Linscott, it would mean the end of his career. For the loss of the protection of guild law while under his watch as a Director, the masons would doubtless expel him within a day. The unskilled would now work; Linscott would be an outcast.

Of course, the land's projects would, in the end, cost more. Unskilled workers were, after all, unskilled. A man who was expensive, but knew his job, in the end cost less, and the finished job was sound.

A Director lifted his hand, showing his informal, but for all practical purposes final, support for the new law. The others watched that hand go up, as if seeing an arrow fly to a man's chest to pierce his heart. Linscott was that man. None wanted to join his fate. One by one, the other Directors' hands began going up, until there were eleven.

Linscott gave Claudine a murderous look before he stalked out of the feast. Claudine's ashen face lowered.

Dalton started applauding the Directors. It jolted everyone out of the somber drama, and people began joining in. All those around Claudine began congratulating her, telling her what a wonderful thing she and her husband had done for the children of Anderith. Tongues began indignantly scolding the masons' selfish ways. Soon a line of people wanting to thank her formed to file past and add their names to those on the side of the Minister of Culture and the courage of his fairness.

Claudine shook their hands but managed only a pallid smile.

Director Linscott was not likely to ever again wish to listen to anything Claudine Winthrop had to say.

Stein glanced over, giving Dalton a cunning smile. Hildemara directed a self-satisfied smirk his way, and her husband clapped Dalton on the back.

When everyone had returned to their seats, the harpist poised her hands with fingers spread to pluck a cord, but the Sovereign again raised his hand. All eyes went to him as he began to speak.

"I believe we should take this opportunity, before the next course, to hear what the gentleman from afar has to say to us."

No doubt the Sovereign was having trouble staying awake and, before he fell asleep, wanted to hear Stein speak. The Minister stood to once again address the room.

"Good people, as you may know, a war is spreading. Each side has arguments as to why we should join with them. Anderith wants only peace. We have no desire to see our young men and women bleed in a foreign struggle. Our land is unique in being protected by the Dominie Dirtch, so we have no need to fear violence visiting us, but there are other considerations, not the least of which is trade with the world beyond our borders.

"We intend to hear what the Lord Rahl of D'Hara and Mother Confessor have to say. They are pledged to wed, as you have all no doubt heard from the diplomats returning from Aydindril. This will join D'Hara with the Midlands to create a formidable force. We await listening respectfully to their words.

"But tonight we are going to hear what the Imperial Order

wishes us to know. The Emperor Jagang has sent a representative from the Old World beyond the Valley of the Lost, which has now for the first time in thousands of years been opened for passage." Bertrand held out a hand. "May I introduce the emperor's spokesman, Master Stein."

People applauded politely, but it trailed off as Stein rose up. He was an imposing, fearsome, and fascinating figure. He hooked his thumbs behind his empty weapon belt.

"We are engaged in a struggle for our future, much the same as the struggle you have just witnessed, only on a larger scale."

Stein picked up a small loaf of hard bread. His big hands squeezed until it broke apart. "We, the race of mankind, and that includes the good people of Anderith, are slowly being crushed. We are being held back. We are being suffocated. We are being denied our destiny, denied our future, denied life itself.

"Just as you have men without work because a self-interested guild held sway over the lives of others, denying them work and thus food for their children, magic holds sway over all of us."

A hum rose in the room as whispering spread. People were confused, and just a little worried. Magic was loathed by some, but respected by many.

"Magic decides for you your destiny," Stein went on. "Those with magic rule you, though you have not willingly consented to it. They have the power, and they keep you in their grip.

"Those with magic cast spells to harm those they resent. Those with magic bring harm to innocent people they fear, they dislike, they envy, and simply to keep the masses in check. Those with magic rule you, whether you like it or not. The mind of man could flourish, were it not for magic.

"It is time regular folks decided what will be, without magic holding its shadow over those decisions, and your future."

Stein lifted his cape out to the side. "These are the scalps of the gifted. I killed each myself. I have prevented each of these witches from twisting the lives of normal people.

"People should fear the Creator, not some sorceress or wizard or witch. We should worship the Creator, none other."

Low murmurs of agreement began to stir.

"The Imperial Order will end magic in this world just as we ended the magic that kept the people of the New and Old World separated for thousands of years. The Order will prevail. Man will decide his own destiny.

"Even without our help, fewer and fewer gifted are born all the time as even the Creator, with his nearly infinite patience, tires of their vile ways. The old religion of magic is dying out. The Creator Himself has thus given us a sign that the time has come for man to cast magic aside."

More rustles of agreement swept through the room.

"We do not wish to fight the people of Anderith. Nor do we wish to force you, against your will, to take up arms to join us. But we intend to destroy the forces of magic led by the bastard son of D'Hara. Any who join him will fall under our blade, just as those with magic"—he held out the cape— "fell under mine."

He slowly swept a finger before the crowd as he held his cape out with his other hand. "Just as I killed these gifted witches who came up against me, we will kill any who stand against us.

"We also have other means beyond the blade to end magic. Just as we brought down the magic separating us, we will bring an end to all magic. The time of man is upon us."

The Minister casually lifted a hand. "And what is it, then, if not the swords of our powerful army, the Order wishes from us?"

"Emperor Jagang gives his word that if you do not join with the forces fighting for those with magic, we will not attack you. All we wish is to trade with you, just as you trade with others."

"Well," the Minister said, playing the part of the skeptic for the benefit of the crowd, "we already have arrangements that commit a great deal of our commodities to the Midlands."

Stein smiled. "We offer double the highest price anyone else offers to pay."

The Sovereign lifted his hand, bringing even the whispering to a halt. "How much of the output of Anderith would you be interested in purchasing?"

Stein looked out over the crowd. "All of it. We are a huge force. You need not lift a blade to fight in the war, we will do the fighting, but if you sell us your goods, you will be safe and your land will become wealthy beyond your hopes and dreams."

The Sovereign stood, surveying the room. "Thank you for the emperor's words, Master Stein. We will want to hear more.

"For now, your words have given us much to consider." He swept a hand before the people. "Let the feast resume."

CHAPTER 23

FITCH'S HEAD HURT SOMETHING awful. The dawn light hurt his eyes. Despite sucking on a small piece of ginger, he couldn't get the foul sour taste in the back of his throat to go away. He figured the headache and awful taste was probably from too much of the fine wine and rum he and Morley had treated themselves to. Even so, he was in good spirits and smiled as he scrubbed the crusty pots.

Slow as he was moving, trying not to make his head feel any worse, Master Drummond wasn't yelling at him. The big man seemed relieved that the feast was over and they could go back to their regular cooking chores. The kitchen master had sent him after a number of things, not once calling him "Fetch."

Fitch heard someone coming his way, and looked up to see that it was Master Drummond.

"Fitch, dry your hands."

Fitch pulled up his arms and shook off some of the soapy water. "Yes, sir."

He snatched up a nearby towel as he recalled with acute pleasure the title of "sir" being directed to him the night before.

Master Drummond wiped his forehead with his own white towel. With the way his head was sweating, he looked like he might have had some drink the night before, too, and might not be feeling his best, either. It had been a tremendous amount of work getting ready for the feast, so Fitch grudgingly guessed that Master Drummond deserved to get drunk, too. At least the man got to be called "sir" all the time.

"Get yourself up to Master Campbell's office."

"Sir?"

Master Drummond tucked the white towel behind his belt. The nearby women were watching. Gillie was scowling, no doubt waiting for an opportunity to twist Fitch's ear and scold him for his wicked Haken ways.

"Dalton Campbell just sent word that he wants to see you. I'd guess he means right now, Fitch, so get to it and see what he needs."

Fitch bowed. "Yes, sir, right away."

Before she could give him much of a thought, he cut a wide path around Gillie, keeping out of her reach and disappearing as quickly as possible. This was one task Fitch was only too happy to rush to do, and he didn't want to be snagged by the sour-faced saucer woman.

As he took the stairs two at a time, his throbbing head seemed to be only a minor annoyance. By the time he'd reached the third floor, he suddenly felt pretty good. He rushed past the spot where Beata had clouted him and down the hall just a short ways to the right, to where only a week before he'd taken a plate of sliced meat late one evening, to Dalton Campbell's office.

The door to the outer office stood open. Fitch caught his breath and shuffled in, keeping his head low in a respectful sort of way; he'd only been there that once before, and he wasn't exactly sure how he was supposed to act in the offices of the Minister's aide.

There were two tables in the room. One had disorderly stacks of papers all over it, along with messenger pouches and sealing wax. The other dark shiny table was nearly clean except for a few books and an unlit lamp. The morning sun streaming in the tall windows provided light aplenty.

Along the far wall to the left, opposite the wall with the windows, four young men lounged and chatted on a long padded bench. They were talking about road conditions to outlying towns and cities. They were messengers, a coveted job in the household, so Fitch guessed it seemed a logical enough thing for them to discuss, but he always thought messengers would talk more of the grand things they saw in their job.

The four were well dressed, all the same, in the Minister's aide's exclusive livery of heavy black boots, dark brown trousers, white shirts with ruffled collars, and sleeved doublets quilted with an interlocking cornucopia design. The edges of the doublets were trimmed with distinctive brown and black braided wheat banding. To Fitch's way of thinking, the outfits made any of the messengers look almost noble, but especially so those messengers belonging to the Minister's aide.

There were a number of different kinds of messengers in the household, each with its own individual uniform, each working for a specific person or office. Fitch knew of messengers working for the Minister, Lady Chanboor, the chamberlain's office, the marshal's office; the sergeant-at-arms had several; there were a number of army messengers working out of the estate and those who brought messages to the estate but lived elsewhere—even the kitchen had a messenger. From time to time he saw others he didn't recognize.

Fitch couldn't understand why they were all needed. He couldn't understand how much messaging a person could possibly need to do.

Far and away the largest contingent of messengers—nearly an army's worth, it seemed—belonged to the office of the Minister's chief aide: Dalton Campbell.

The four men sitting on the padded bench watched him with friendly enough smiles. Two nodded in greeting, something messengers had done before when he came across them. Fitch always thought it odd when they did because, even though they too were Haken, he always figured messengers were better than he, as if, while not Ander, they were some indefinable step above a mere Haken.

Fitch nodded in kind to return the greeting. One of the men who had nodded, perhaps a year or two older than Fitch, lifted a thumb toward the room beyond.

"Master Campbell is waiting on you, Fitch. You're to go on in."

Fitch was surprised to be called by name. "Thank you."

He shambled over to the tall doorway to the inner room and waited at the threshold. He'd been in the outer waiting room before—the interior door had always been closed—and he expected Master Campbell's inner office to be more or less the same, but it was larger and much more grand, with rich-looking blue and gold drapes on the three windows, a wall of fancy oak shelves holding a colorful array of thick books, and, in the other corner, several magnificent Ander battle standards. Each long banner was of a yellow background with red markings along with a bit of blue. The standards were arranged in a display flanked by formidable-looking pole weapons.

Dalton Campbell looked up from behind a massive desk of shiny mahogany with curved legs and a scalloped skirt. The top had three inset leather squares, smaller ones to each side of a large one in the middle, each with a curly design painted in gold around its edges.

"Fitch, there you are. Good. Come in and shut the door, please."

Fitch crossed the big room and stood before the desk when he had done as bidden. "Yes, sir? You needed something?"

Campbell leaned back in his brown leather chair. His princely scabbard and sword stood beside a tufted bench, in their own special holder of hammered silver made to look like a scroll. Lines of writing were engraved on the scroll, but Fitch couldn't read, so he didn't know if they were real words.

Tipping his chair back on the two rear legs while he sucked on the end of a glass dipping pen, the Minister's aide studied Fitch's face.

"You did a good job with Claudine Winthrop."

"Thank you, sir. I tried my best to remember everything you told me you wanted me to do and say."

"And you did that quite well. Some men would have turned squeamish and failed to do as I instructed. I can always use men who follow orders and remember what I tell them I want done. In fact, I would like to offer you a new position with my office, as a messenger."

Fitch stared dumbly. He'd heard the words, but they didn't seem to make any sense to him. Dalton Campbell had plenty of messengers—a whole army of them, it seemed.

"Sir?"

"You did well. I'd like you to be one of my messengers."

"Me, sir?"

"The work is easier than kitchen work, and the job, unlike kitchen work, pays a wage in addition to food and living quarters. Earning a wage, you could begin to set money aside for your future. Perhaps one day when you earn your sir name, you might be able to buy yourself something. Perhaps a sword."

Fitch stood frozen, his mind focused intently on Dalton Campbell's words, running them through his head again. He never even dreamed such dreams as working as a messenger. He'd not considered the possibility of work that would give him more than a roof and food, the opportunity to lift some good liquor, and perhaps a penny bonus now and again.

Of course he dreamed of having a sword and reading and other things, but those were silly dreams and he knew it—they were just for fun dreaming. Daydreaming. He hadn't dared dream close to real things such as this, such as actually being a messenger.

"Well, what do you say, Fitch? Would you like to be one of my messengers? Naturally, you couldn't wear those ... clothes. You would have to wear messenger livery." Dalton Campbell leaned forward to look over the desk and down. "That includes boots. You would have to wear boots to be a messenger.

"You would have to move to new quarters, too. The messengers have quarters together. Beds, not pallets. The beds have sheets. You have to make up your bed, of course, and keep your own trunk in order, but the staff washes the messenger's clothes and bedding.

"What do you say, Fitch? Would you like to join my staff of messengers?"

Fitch swallowed. "What about Morley, Master Campbell? Morley did just as you said, too. Would he become a messenger with me?"

The leather squeaked when Dalton Campbell again tipped back onto the two rear legs of his chair. He sucked on the end of the spiraled-blue and clear-glass pen for a time as he studied Fitch's eyes. At last he took the pen away from his mouth.

"I only need one messenger right now. It's time you started thinking about yourself, Fitch, about your future. Do you want to be a kitchen boy the rest of your life?

"The time has come for you to do what's right for you, Fitch, if you ever want to get places in life. This is your chance to rise up out of that kitchen. It may be the only chance you get.

"I'm offering the position to you, not Morley. Take it or leave it. What's it going to be, then?"

Fitch licked his lips. "Well, sir, I like Morley—he's my friend. But I don't think there's anything I'd rather do in the whole world than be your messenger, Master Campbell. I'll take the job, if you'll have me."

"Good. Welcome to the staff, then, Fitch." He smiled in a friendly way. "Your loyalty to your friend is admirable. I hope you feel the same of this office. I will have a . . . part-time position for Morley for now, and I suspect that at some point in the future a position may open up and he could then join you on the messenger staff."

Fitch felt relief at that news. He'd hate to lose his friend, but he would do anything to get out of Master Drummond's kitchen and to be a messenger.

"That's awfully kind of you, sir. I know Morley will do right by you, too. I swear I will."

Dalton Campbell leaned forward again, letting the front legs of the chair thunk down. "All right, then." He slid a folded paper across the desk. "Take this down to Master Drummond. It informs him that I have engaged your services as a messenger, and you are no longer responsible to him. I thought you might like to deliver it yourself, as your first official message."

Fitch wanted to jump up and hoot a cheer, but he instead remained emotionless, as he thought a messenger would. "Yes, sir, I would." He realized he was standing up straighter, too.

"Right after, then, one of my other messengers, Rowley, will take you down to estate supply. They will provide you with livery that fits close enough for the time being. When you're down there, the seamstress will measure you up so your new clothes can be fitted to you.

"While in my service, I expect all my messengers to be smartly dressed in tailored livery. I expect my messengers to reflect well on my office. That means you and your clothes are to be clean. Your boots polished. Your hair brushed. You will conduct yourself properly at all times. Rowley will explain the details to you. Can you do all that, Fitch?"

Fitch's knees trembled. "Yes, sir, I surely can, sir."

Thinking about the new clothes he would be wearing, he suddenly felt very ashamed of what had to be his filthy scruffy look. An hour ago he thought he looked just fine as he was, but no longer. He couldn't wait to get out of his scullion rags.

He wondered what Beata would think when she saw him in his handsome new messenger's livery.

Dalton Campbell slid a leather pouch across the desk. The flap was secured with a large dribbling of amber wax impressed with a sheaf-of-wheat seal design.

"After you clean up and get on your new outfit, I want you to deliver this pouch to the Office of Cultural Amity, in Fairfield. Do you know where it is?"

"Yes, sir, Master Campbell. I grew up in Fairfield, and I know just about any place there."

"So I was told. We have messengers from all over Anderith, and they mostly cover the places they know—the places where they grew up. Since you know Fairfield, you will be assigned to that area for most of your work."

Dalton Campbell leaned back to fish something from a pocket. "This is for you." He flipped it through the air.

Fitch caught it and stared dumbly at the silver sovereign in his palm. He expected that most rich folk didn't even carry such a huge sum about.

"But, sir, I haven't worked the month, yet."

"This is not your messenger's wage. You get your wage at the end of every month." Dalton Campbell lifted an eyebrow. "This is to show my appreciation for the job you did last night."

Claudine Winthrop. That was what he meant—scaring Claudine Winthrop into keeping quiet.

She had called Fitch "sir."

Fitch laid the silver coin on the desk. With a finger, he reluctantly slid the coin a few inches toward Dalton Campbell.

"Master Campbell, you owe me nothing for that. You never promised me anything for it. I did it because I wanted to help you, and to protect the future Sovereign, not for a reward. I can't take money I'm not owed."

The aide smiled to himself. "Take the coin, Fitch. That's an order. After you deliver that pouch in Fairfield, I don't have anything else for you today, so I want you to spend some of that—all of it if you wish—on yourself. Have some fun. Buy candy. Or buy yourself a drink. It's your money; spend it as you wish."

Fitch swallowed back his excitement. "Yes, sir. Thank you, sir. I'll do as you say, then."

"Good. Just one thing, though." Campbell put an elbow on the desk and leaned forward. "Don't spend it on prostitutes in the city. There are some very nasty diseases going through the whores in Fairfield this spring. It's an unpleasant way to die. If you go to the wrong prostitute, you will not live long enough to be a good messenger."

While the idea of being with a woman was achingly tantalizing, Fitch didn't see how he would ever work up the nerve to go through with it and get naked in front of one. He liked looking at women, the way he liked looking at Claudine Winthrop and he liked looking at Beata, and he liked imagining them naked, but he never imagined them seeing him naked, in an aroused state. He had enough trouble hiding his aroused condition from women when he had his clothes on. He ached to be with a woman, but couldn't figure how the embarrassment of the situation wouldn't ruin the lust of it. Maybe if it was a girl he knew, and liked, and he kissed and cuddled and courted her for a period of time—came to know her well—he might see how he could get to the point of the procedure, but he couldn't imagine how anyone ever worked up the nerve to go to a woman he didn't even know and just strip naked right in front of her.

Maybe if it was dark. Maybe that was it. Maybe it was dark in the prostitutes' rooms, so the two people wouldn't actually see each other. But he still—

"Fitch?"

Fitch cleared his throat. "No, sir. I swear an oath not to go to any of the prostitutes in Fairfield. No, sir, I won't."

CHAPTER 24

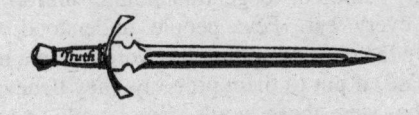

AFTER THE BOY LEFT, Dalton yawned. He had been up long before dawn, calling in staff, meeting with trusted assistants to hear their reports of any relevant discussions at the feast, and then seeing about the preparation of all the messages. The staff employed in the copying and preparation of messages, among other things, took up the next six rooms down the hall, but they had needed his outer offices to complete the task in such short order.

By first light Dalton had his messengers off to the criers in every corner of Anderith. Later, when the Minister was up and had finished with whoever had ended up as his bed partner, Dalton would let the man know the wording of the statement so he might not be taken by surprise, seeing as how he was the signatory to the announcement.

The criers would read the messages in meeting halls,

guild halls, merchant and trade halls, town and city council halls, taverns, inns, every army post, every university, every worship service, every penance assembly, every fulling, paper, and grain mill, every market square—anywhere people gathered—from one end of Anderith to the other. Within a matter of days, the message, the exact message as Dalton had written it, would be in every ear.

Criers who didn't read the messages exactly as written were sooner or later reported and replaced with men more interested in keeping their source of extra income. Besides sending the messages to the criers, Dalton, on a rotating basis, sent identical messages to people about the land who earned a bit of extra money by listening to the crier and reporting if the message was altered. All part of tending his cobweb.

Few people understood, as did Dalton, the importance of a precisely tailored, cogent-sounding, uniform message reaching every ear. Few people understood the power wielded by the one controlling the words people heard; what people heard, if put to them properly, they believed, regardless of what were those words. Few people understood the weapon that was a properly fashioned twist of information.

Now there was a new law in the land. Law forbidding partial hiring practices in the mason profession, and ordering the hiring of willing workers who presented themselves for work. The day before, such action against a powerful guild would have been unthinkable. His messages chided people to act by the highest Ander cultural ideals, and not to take understandably belligerent action against masons for their past despicable practices of being a party to children starving. Instead, his message insisted that they follow the new, higher standards of the Winthrop Fair Employment Law. And the startled masons, rather than attacking the new law, would be busily and vigorously trying to prove that they were not intentionally starving the children of their neighbors.

Before long, masons across the land would not only comply, but embrace the new law as if they themselves had all

266

along been urging its passage. It was either that, or be stoned by angry mobs.

Dalton liked to consider every eventuality and have the road laid before the cart arrived. By the time Rowley got Fitch cleaned up and into messenger livery, and the boy off on his way with the law pouch, it would be too late for the Office of Cultural Amity, if for some reason the eleven Directors changed their minds, to do anything about it. The criers would already be proclaiming the new law all over Fairfield, and soon it would be known far and wide. None of the eleven Directors would now be able to alter their show of hands at the feast.

Fitch would fit right in with the rest of Dalton's messengers. They were all men he had collected over the previous ten years, young men pulled from obscure places, otherwise doomed to a life of hard labor, degradation, few options, and little hope. They were the dirt under the heels of Anderith culture. Now, through the delivery of messages to criers, they helped shape and control Anderith culture.

The messengers did more than merely deliver messages; in some ways they were almost a private army, paid for by the public, and one of the means by which Dalton had risen to his present post. All his messengers were unshakably loyal to no one but Dalton. Most would willingly go to their death if he requested it. There had been occasions when he had.

Dalton smiled as his thoughts wandered to more pleasant things—wandered to Teresa. She was floating on air from having been introduced to the Sovereign. When they had returned to their apartments after the feast and retired to bed, as she had promised, she had soundly rewarded him with just how good she could be. And Teresa could be extraordinarily good.

She had been so inspired by the experience of meeting the Sovereign that she was spending the morning in prayer. He doubted she could have been more moved had she met the Creator Himself. Dalton was pleased that he could provide Teresa such an exalting experience.

267

At least she had not fainted, as had several women and one man when they were presented to the Sovereign. Were it not a common occurrence, it would have been embarrassing for those people. As it was, everyone understood and readily accepted their reaction. In some ways, it was a mark of distinction, a talisman of faith, proving one's devotion to the Creator. No one considered it anything but sincere faith laid bare.

Dalton, however, recognized the Sovereign as the man he was, a man in a high office, but a man nonetheless. For some people, though, he transcended such worldly notions. When Bertrand Chanboor, a man already widely respected and admired as the most outstanding Minister of Culture ever to serve, became Sovereign, he, too, would become the object of mindless adoration.

Dalton suspected, though, that a great many of the swooning women would be endeavoring to fall under him, rather than faint before him. To many, it would be a religious experience beyond the mere coupling with a man of power such as the Minister of Culture. Even husbands would be ennobled by their wives' holy acceptance into such congress with the Sovereign.

When he heard a knock at the door, Dalton looked up and began to say "Enter," but the woman was already barging in. It was Franca Gowenlock.

Dalton rose. "Ah, Franca, how good to see you. Did you enjoy the feast?"

For some reason, the woman had a dark look. Added to her dark eyes and hair, and the general aspect which made her seem as if she were somehow always standing in a shadow even when she wasn't, that made the look very dark indeed. The air always seemed still and cool whenever Franca was about.

She snatched the top rail of a chair on her way past, dragging it along to his desk. She set the chair before the desk, plopped herself down in front of him, and folded her arms. Somewhat taken aback, Dalton sank back into his chair.

Fine lines splayed out from her squinted eyes. "I don't like that one from the Order. Stein. I don't like him one bit."

Dalton relaxed back into his chair. Franca wore her black, nearly shoulder length hair loose, yet it swept back somewhat from her face, as if it had been frozen stiff by an icy wind. A bit of gray streaked her temples, but, rather than adding years to her looks, it added only to her serious mien.

Her simple sienna dress buttoned to her neck. A little higher up, a band of black velvet hugged her throat. It was usually black velvet, but not always. Whatever it was made from, it was always at least two fingers wide.

Because she always wore a throat band, Dalton wondered all the more why, and what, if anything, might be under it. Franca being Franca, he never asked.

He had known Franca Gowenlock for nearly fifteen years, and had employed her talents for well over half that time. He had sometimes mused to himself that she must have once been beheaded and sewn her own head back on.

"I'm sorry, Franca. Did he do something to you? Insult you? He didn't lay a hand to you, did he? I will have him dealt with, if that's the case—you have my word."

Franca knew his word to her was beyond reproach. She twined her long graceful fingers together in her lap. "He had enough women willing and eager; he didn't need me for that."

Dalton, truly at a loss, but cautious nonetheless, spread his hands. "Then what is it?"

Franca put her forearms on the desk and tipped her head in. She lowered her voice.

"He did something with my gift. He scrambled it all up, or something."

Dalton blinked, true concern roiling through him. "You mean you think the man has some kind of magical power? That he cast a spell, or something?"

"I don't know," Franca growled, "but he did something."

"How do you know?"

"I tried to listen to conversations at the feast, just like I

269

always do. I tell you, Dalton, I wouldn't know I had the gift if I didn't know I did. Nothing. I got nothing from no one. Not a thing."

Dalton's frown now mimicked hers. "You mean that your gift didn't help you overhear anything?"

"Don't you hear anything? Isn't that what I just said?"

Dalton drummed his fingers on the table. He turned and peered out the window. He got up and lifted the sash, letting in the warm breeze. He motioned to Franca, and she came around the desk.

Dalton pointed to two men engaged in conversation under a tree across the lawn. "Down there, those two. Tell me what they're saying."

Franca put her hands on the sill and leaned out a little, staring at the two men. The sun on her face showed how time truly was beginning to wrinkle, stretch, and sag what he had always thought was one of the most beautiful, if not the strangest, women he had ever known. Even so, despite the advance of time, her beauty was still haunting.

Dalton watched the men's hands move, gesturing as they spoke, but he could hear none of their words. With her gift, she should be able to easily hear them.

Franca's face went blank. She stood so still she looked like one of the wax figures from the traveling exhibition that came through Fairfield twice a year. Dalton couldn't even tell if the woman was breathing.

She finally pulled an annoyed breath. "Can't hear a word. They're too far away to see their lips, so I can't get any help by that, but still, I don't hear a thing, and I should."

Dalton looked down, close to the building, three stories below. "What about those two."

Franca leaned out for a look. Dalton could almost hear them himself; a chuckle rose up, and an exclamation, but no more. Franca again went still.

This time, the breath she pulled bordered on rage. "Nothing, and I can almost hear them without the gift."

Dalton closed the window. The anger went out of her face

in a rush, and he saw something he had never before seen from her: fear.

"Dalton, you have to get rid of that man. He must be a wizard, or something. He's got me all tied up in knots."

"How do you know it's him?"

She blinked twice at the question. "Well . . . what else could it be? He claims to be able to eliminate magic. He's only been here a few days, and I've only had this problem a few days."

"Have you had trouble with other things? Other aspects of your gift?"

She turned away, wringing her hands. "A few days ago I made up a little spell for a woman who came to me, a little spell so she would have her moon flow back, and not be pregnant. This morning she returned and said it didn't work."

"Well, it must be a complex kind of conjuring. There must be a lot involved. I expect such things don't always work."

She shook her head. "It always worked before."

"Perhaps you're ill. Have you felt different of late?"

"I feel exactly the same. I feel like my power is as strong as ever. It should be, but it's not. Other charms have failed, too—I'd not let this go without testing it, thorough like."

Troubled, Dalton leaned closer. "Franca, I don't know a lot about it, but maybe some of it is just confidence in yourself. Maybe you just have to believe you can do it for it to work again."

She glared back over her shoulder. "Where'd you ever get such a daft notion about the gift?"

"I don't know." Dalton shrugged. "I admit I don't know a great deal about magic, but I really don't believe Stein has the gift—or any magic about him. He's just not the sort.

"Besides, he's not even here today. He couldn't be interrupting your ability hearing those people down there; he went out to tour the countryside. He's been gone for hours."

She slowly rounded on him, looking fearsome and at the

271

same time frightened. Such opposing aspects at the same time gave him gooseflesh.

"Then I fear," she whispered, "that I've simply lost my power. I'm helpless."

"Franca, I'm sure—"

She licked her lips. "You have Serin Rajak locked away in chains, don't you? I'd not like to think him or his lunatic followers . . ."

"I told you before, we have him in chains. I'm not even sure he's still alive. After all this time, I doubt it, but either way there is no need to worry about Serin Rajak."

Staring off, she nodded.

He touched her arm. "Franca, I'm certain your power will return. Try not to be overly concerned."

Tears welled in her eyes. "Dalton, I'm terrified."

Cautiously, he took the weeping woman in his consoling arms. She was, after all, besides being a dangerous gifted woman, a friend.

The words from the song at the feast came to mind.
Came the thieves of the charm and spell.

CHAPTER 25

ROBERTA LIFTED HER CHIN high in the air, stretching her neck, to guardedly peer off past the brink of the cliff not far away and look out over the fertile fields of her beloved Nareef Valley far below. Freshly plowed fields were a deep rich brown among breathtakingly bright green carpets of new crops and the darker verdant pastures where livestock, looking like tiny slow ants, cropped at tender new grass. The Dammar River meandered through it all, sparkling in the early-morning sunshine, escorted along its route by a gathering of dark green trees, as if they'd come to watch the river's showy parade.

Whenever she went up in the woods near Nesting Cliff, she had herself a look from afar, just to see the pretty valley below. After allowing herself that brief look, she always lowered her eyes to the shaded forest floor at her feet, the leaf litter, and mossy stretches among dappled sunlight, where the ground was firm and comforting.

Roberta shifted the sack slung over her shoulder, and moved on. As she maneuvered through the clear patches among the huckleberry and hawthorn, stepped on stones set like islands among dark crevices and holes, and ducked under low pine boughs and alder limbs, she flipped aside with her walking stick a fern here or a low spreading balsam branch there, looking, always looking, as she moved along.

She spied a vase-shaped yellow cap and stooped for a look. Chanterelle, she was pleased to see, and not the poisonous jack-o'-lantern. Most folk favored the smooth yellow chanterelle mushroom for its nutlike flavor. She hooked the stem with a finger and plucked it up. Before sticking the prize in her sack, she ran her thumb over the featherlike gills just for the pleasure of the soft feel.

The mountain she searched for her mushrooms was only a small mountain, compared to the others jutting up all around, and but for Nesting Cliff, reassuringly round, with trails, a few made by man but most made by animal, criss-crossing the gentle wooded slopes. It was the kind of woods her aging muscles and increasingly aching bones favored.

It was said a person could see the ocean far off to the south from many of the taller mountains. She'd often heard it to be an inspiring sight. Many people went up there once every year or two just to view the splendor of the Creator by what He'd wrought.

Some of those trails took a person along the scruffy edges of cliffs and scree and such. Some folk even tended herds of goats up on those steep and rocky slopes. But for a journey when she was a small child, when her pa, rest his soul, took them off to Fairfield, for what she could no longer remember, she had never even been up there. Roberta was content to remain near the alluvial land. Unlike a lot of other folk, Roberta never climbed the higher mountains; she was afraid of high places.

Up higher yet, in the highlands above, were far worse places, like the wasteland up above where the warfer birds nested.

There was nothing in that desolate place, not a blade of grass nor a sprig of scrub brush, except those paka plants growing in that poison swampy water. Nothing else up there but the vast stretches of dark, rocky, sandy soil, and a few bleached bones, as she heard tell. Like another world, those who'd seen it said. Silent but for the wind that dragged the dark sandy dirt into mounds that shifted over time, always moving on, as if they were looking for something, but never finding it.

The lower mountains, like the ones she hunted for mushrooms, were beautiful, lush places, rounder and softer, mostly, and except for Nesting Cliff, not so steep and rocky. She liked it where it was full of trees and critters and growing things of all sorts. The deer trails she searched stayed away from the edges she didn't like, and never went very close to Nesting Cliff, as it was called because the falcons liked to nest there. She liked the deep woods, where her mushrooms grew.

Roberta collected mushrooms to sell at market; some fresh, some dried, some pickled, and others fixed in various ways. Most folk called her the mushroom lady, and knew her by no other name. Sold at market, the mushrooms helped earn her family some trading money for the things that made life easier: needles and thread, some ready-made cloth, buckles and buttons, a lamp, oil, salt, sugar, cinnamon, nuts—things to help a body have an easier time of it. Easier for her family, and especially for her four grandchildren still living. Roberta's mushrooms provided all those things to supplement what they grew or raised themselves.

Of course, they made good eating, too. She did like best the mushrooms that grew in the forests up on the mountain, rather than those down in the valley. Touched as they were up there by clouds so much of the time, the mushrooms grew well in the damp conditions. She always thought there were none better than those from up on the mountain, and many folk sought her out just for her mountain mushrooms. Roberta had her secret places, too, where she found the best ones every year. The big pockets in her apron were plump and full with them, as was the sack over her shoulder.

Because it was still early in the year, she'd mostly found heavy clusters of the tawny-colored oyster mushrooms. Their fleshy, tender caps were best for dipping in egg and frying, so she'd sell them fresh. But she'd been lucky, and would be setting out chanterelles to dry as well as offering fresh. She found a goodly number of pheasant's-backs, too, and they'd be best pickled, if she wanted to get the highest price.

It was too early for woolly velvet in most places, even though it would be common enough later on in the summer, but she'd gone to one of her special spots where there were a lot of pine stumps and she'd found some of the ocher-colored woolly velvet used to make dye. Roberta had even found a rotting birch with a cluster of smoky brown poly-pores. The kidney-shaped mushrooms were favored by cooks to keep a fire blazing and by men to strop their razors.

Leaning on her walking stick, Roberta bent over a harmless-looking brownish mushroom. It had a ring on the off-white stalk. She saw that the yellowish gills were just starting to turn a rust color. It was that time of year for this mushroom, too. Grunting her displeasure, she let the deadly galerina be and moved on.

Back under the spreading limbs of an oak, as big around as her two oxen shoulder-to-shoulder when they were yoked up, she plucked up three good sized spicy chanterelles. The spicy variety grew almost exclusively under oak wood. They had already turned from yellow to orange, so they'd be choice eating.

Roberta knew where she was, but was off her usual path, so she'd never seen the huge oak before. When she'd seen the tree's crown, she knew that with all the shade it provided it would be a good spot for mushrooms. She was not disappointed.

At the base of the oak, around part of the trunk where it came up from the ground, she was delighted to see a bunch of small pipes, or beef vein as some folk called them because the standing tubes were sometimes a vivid red like a whole passel of veins bunched together and cut off even like. These, though, were pinkish, streaked with just a bit of red. Roberta preferred the name small pipes, but she still didn't hold much favor with them. Some folk, though, bought them for their tart taste and they were on the rare side, so they brought a decent price.

Under the tree, in the deep shade, was a ring of spirit-bells, so called because of their bell-like tops. They weren't poisonous, but because of the bitter taste and woody texture, no one liked them. Worse, though, people thought that any-one stepping inside the ring would be bewitched, so folks generally didn't even want to see the lovely little spirit bells. Roberta had been walking through spirit-bell rings since she was a toddler when her mother would take her along mushrooming.

Since she held no favor with such superstition about her beloved mushrooms, she stepped through the ring of spirit bells, imagining she heard their delicate chimes, and gathered up the small pipes.

One of the spreading branches of the oak grew down low enough to make a seat. Big around as her ample waist, it was comfortable enough, and dry enough, for a good sit.

Roberta slipped her sack to the ground. She sighed with relief as she laid her weary bones back against another branch, which turned up at just the right angle to rest her shoulders and head against. The tree seemed to cup her in its sheltering hand.

Daydreaming as she was, she thought it was part of the dream when she heard a whisper that sounded like her name. It was a pleasing, low, warm sound, more a feeling of good things and pleasant thoughts than a word.

The second time, she knew it wasn't part of her daydream, and she was sure it was her name being spoken, but in a fashion somehow more intimate than a mere spoken word.

The thing was, the way it was spoken strummed the strings of her heart. Like the spirit's own music, it was. All lovely with kindness, compassion, and warmth. It made her sigh. It made her happy. It fell across her like warm sunlight on a chill day.

The third time, she sat up to look, longing to see the source of such a touching voice. Even as she moved, she felt like she was in one of her daydreams, all peaceful and content. The forest all about seemed to sparkle in the morning sun, seemed to glow.

Roberta let out a small gasp when she saw him not far away.

She'd never seen him before, but she'd always known him, it seemed. She realized he was a familiar friend, a comfort, a partner from her mind since youth, though she never really gave it much thought before. He was the one who had always been there with her, it seemed. The one she always thought about when she was daydreaming. The face without definition, yet one she knew well.

Now she realized he was as real as she had always imagined when she kissed him in her fancies, which she had done ever since she was young enough to know that a kiss was something more than your mother gave you before bed. His were kisses given in bed. All warm and ardent.

She'd never thought he was real, but now she was sure she'd always known he was. As he stood there, gazing into her eyes, how could he not be real? His tumble of hair swept back from his glorious face, showing his warm smile, though she thought it puzzling that she couldn't say just what he looked like. Yet at the same time, she knew his face as well as she knew hers.

And, she knew his every thought, just as he knew every thought and longing of hers. He was her soul's true mate.

She knew his thoughts; she didn't need his name. That she didn't know his name was only proof to her that they were connected on a spiritual level that transcended words.

And now he had stepped out of the mist of that spiritual world, needing to be with her, just as she needed to be with him. His hand opened to her, as if avowing his need. Roberta reached for the hand. She seemed almost to float above the ground. Her feet touched like dandelion fluff drifting on a breath. Her body floated like weed in water as she stretched out to him. Stretched out for his embrace.

The closer she got, the warmer she felt. Not warm as if from the sun on her face, but warmed as if from a lover's arms, a lover's smile, a lover's sweet kiss.

Her whole life came down to this, to needing to be in his arms feeling his tender embrace, needing to whisper her yearning because she knew he would understand, needing the breath from his lips on her ear, telling her he understood.

She burned to whisper her love, to have him whisper his.

She needed nothing in life so much as she needed to be in those arms she knew so well.

Her muscles were no longer weary; her bones no longer ached. She was no longer old. The years had slipped away from her like clothes slipping from lovers shedding encumbrances in order to get down to the bare essence of their being.

Because of him, because of him alone, she was again in the winsome bloom of youth, where everything was possible.

His arm floated out to her, his need for her as great as hers for him. She stretched for his hand, but it seemed farther away, and she stretched more, but it was more distant still.

Panic raced through her as she feared he would be gone

before she could at last touch him. She felt as if she were swimming in honey and could make no progress. Her whole life she had longed to touch him. Her whole life she had longed to tell him. Her whole life she had longed to have her soul join with his.

But now he was drifting from her.

Roberta, her legs leaden, leaped through the spring sunshine, through the sweet air, racing to her lover's arms.

And yet he was farther still.

Both his arms lifted to her. She could feel his need. She ached to comfort him. To shelter him from hurt. To sooth his strife.

He could feel those longings in her, and cried out her name that she might be strengthened in her effort to reach him. The sound of her name on his lips made her heart lift with joy, lift with a terrible pang of need to return such passion as he put into her name.

She wept to know his name, now, that she might put it to her undying love.

With all her might, she stretched out to him. She put her entire being into her reckless lunge for him, forsaking all care but her fierce need to reach him.

Roberta cried her nameless love, cried her need, as she reached for his fingers. His arms spread to take her into his loving embrace. As she rushed into those arms, the sun sparkled all about, the warm wind lifted her hair, ruffled her dress.

As he cried her name with such beauty it made her ache, her arms spread wide to take him at last into her embrace. She felt as if she were floating endlessly through the air toward him, the sun on her face, the breeze in her hair, but it was all right because now she was where she wanted to be—with him.

At that moment, there was no more perfect time in the whole of her life. No more perfect feeling in the whole of her existence. No more perfect love in the whole of the world.

She heard the perfect chimes of those feelings ring out with the glory of it all.

Her heart nearly burst as she at last plunged into his embrace in one wild rush, screaming out her need, her love, her completion, wanting only to know his name so she might give everything of herself to him.

His glowing smile was for her and her alone. His lips were for her and her alone. She closed that last bit of space toward him, longing to at last kiss the love of her life, the mate to her soul, the one and the only true passion in all of life.

His lips were there, at last, as she fell into his outstretched arms, into his embrace, into his perfect kiss.

In that flawless instant when her lips were just touching his, she saw through him, just beyond him, the merciless unyielding valley floor hurtling up toward her, and she knew at last his name.

Death.

CHAPTER 26

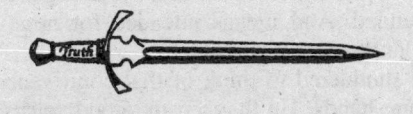

"THERE," RICHARD SAID, LEANING close so Kahlan could sight down his arm as he pointed off toward the horizon. "See that really dark fleck of cloud in front of the lighter part?" He waited for her nod. "Under that, and just a bit to the right."

Standing amid a seemingly endless sea of nearly waist-high grass, Kahlan straightened and held a hand to her brow to shield her eyes from the morning light.

"I still can't see him." Her frustration came out as a sigh. "But I've never been able to see distant things as well as you."

"I don't see him, either," Cara said.

Richard again checked over his shoulder, scanning the empty grassland all around to make sure they weren't about to be surprised by someone sneaking up while they watched the approach of this one man. He saw no other threat.

"You will, soon enough."

He reached over to check that his sword was clear in its scabbard, only realizing he was doing so when he found the sword absent from his left hip. He instead pulled his bow from his shoulder and nocked an arrow.

There had been countless times he had wished to be rid of the Sword of Truth and its attendant magic, inasmuch as it brought forth from within himself things he abhorred. The sword's magic could fuse with those feelings into a lethal wrath. Zedd, when he first gave Richard the sword, told him it was only a tool. Over time, he had come to comprehend Zedd's advice.

Still, it was a horrifying tool to have to use.

It was up to the one wielding the sword to govern not simply the weapon, but himself. Understanding that part of it, among other things, was essential to using the weapon as it was intended. And it was intended for none but a true Seeker of Truth.

Richard shuddered to think of that contrivance of magic in the wrong hands. He thanked the good spirits that, if he couldn't have it with him, it was at least safe.

Below distant billowing clouds, their interiors glowing in the morning light colors from a deep yellow to an unsettling violet that marked the violence of the storms contained within, the man continued to approach. Lightning, silent at this distance, flashed and flickered inside the colossal clouds, illuminating hidden canyons, valley walls, and seething peaks.

Compared with other places he had been, the sky and clouds above the flat plains somehow appeared impossibly grand. He guessed it was because from horizon to horizon there was nothing—no mountains, no trees, nothing—to interrupt the drama of the vast vault of stage overhead.

The departing storm clouds had only finally moved on eastward before dawn, taking with them the rain that had so vexed them when with the Mud People, their first day of traveling, and their first miserable cold night without a fire. Traveling in the rain was unpleasant. In its wake the rain had left the three of them irritable.

Like him, Kahlan was worried about Zedd and Ann and troubled by what the Lurk might bring next. It was also frustrating to have to undertake a long journey, when they were in such a rush and it was so vitally important, rather than return to Aydindril in short order through the sliph.

Richard was almost willing to take the risk. Almost.

With Cara, though, it seemed something more was disturbing her. She was as disagreeable as a cat in a sack. He wasn't eager to reach in and get scratched. He figured that if it was truly important, she would tell them.

Added to all that, Richard was unsettled by not having his sword with him when there was trouble about. He feared the Lurk trying to harm Kahlan, while he was unable to protect her. Even without the trouble caused by the Sisters of the Dark, there were any number of ordinary dangers for a Confessor, any number of people who would, were she defenseless, like to settle what they viewed as injustices.

With the spell eroding magic, sooner or later her Confessor's power would be gone, and she would be without its ability to protect her. He needed to be able to protect her, but without the sword he feared being inadequate to the task.

Every time he reached for his sword and it wasn't there, he felt an emptiness he couldn't express in words. It was as if part of him was missing.

Even so, Richard was for some reason uneasy about going to Aydindril. Something about it felt wrong. He rationalized it as worry about leaving Zedd when he was so weak and vulnerable. But Zedd had made it clear there was no choice.

Up until he had spotted the approaching stranger, their second day had been looking sunny, dry, and more agreeable. Richard put some tension to the bowstring. After their encounter with the chicken-thing, or rather the Lurk, and with so much at stake, he didn't intend to let anyone get close unless he knew them to be a friend.

Richard frowned over at Kahlan. "You know, I think my mother once told me a story or something about a cat named 'Lurk.' "

Holding a fistful of hair to keep the breeze from blowing it across her face, Kahlan frowned back. "That's odd. Are you sure?"

"No. She died when I was young. It's hard to remember if I'm really remembering, or just fooling myself into thinking I am."

"What do you think you remember?" Kahlan asked.

Richard stretched the bowstring to test it, and then relaxed it partway. "I think I fell down and skinned a knee, or something, and she was trying to make me laugh—you know, to make me forget my hurt. I think she just that one time told me how when she was little, her mother told her a story of a cat that lurked about pouncing on things, and so earned the name Lurk. I'd swear I remember her laughing and asking if I didn't think that was a funny name."

"Yes, very funny," Cara said, making clear she thought it wasn't.

With a finger, she lifted the point of his arrow, and thus his bow, in the direction of the danger she seemed to think he was ignoring.

"What made you think of that, now?" Kahlan asked.

Richard pointed with his chin toward the approaching man. "I was considering a man being out here—you know, thinking of what other dangers might be lurking about."

"And when you thought of all these dangers lurking about," Cara said, "did you also decide to just stand around and let them all come to attack you as they wish?"

Ignoring Cara, Richard tilted his head toward the man. "You must see him now."

"No, I still don't see where it is you . . . wait . . ." Hand to her brow, Kahlan rose up onto her tiptoes, as if that would help her see better. "There he is. I see him now."

"I think we should conceal ourselves in the grass, and then pounce on him," Cara said.

"He saw us at the same time I saw him," Richard said. "He knows we're here. We couldn't surprise him."

"At least there is only one." Cara yawned. "We will have no trouble."

Cara, standing the middle watch, hadn't wakened him as early as she was supposed to for his turn at watch. She had left him sleeping an extra hour, at least. Middle watch, too, usually got less sleep.

Richard checked over his shoulder again. "You may see only one, but there are a number more. A dozen, at least."

Kahlan put her hand back to her forehead to shield her

eyes. "I don't see any more." She looked to the sides and behind. "I only see the one. Are you sure?"

"Yes. When I first saw him, and he saw me, he left the others and came alone toward us. They still wait."

Cara snatched up a pack. She shoved Kahlan's shoulder, then Richard's. "Let's go. We can outdistance them until we're out of sight and then hide. If they follow we will take them by surprise and put a quick end to the pursuit."

Richard returned the shove. "Would you just settle down? He's coming alone so as not to draw any arrows. If it was an attack he would have brought all his men at once. We will wait."

Cara folded her arms and pressed her lips together in a bit of ire. She seemed to be beyond her usual protective self. Whether or not she was ready to tell him, they were going to have to talk to her and find out what her problem was. Maybe Kahlan would have some luck.

The man lifted his arms, waving at them in a friendly gesture.

Suddenly recognizing the man, Richard took his hand from the bowstring and returned the greeting.

"It's Chandalen."

It wasn't long until Kahlan waved her arm, too. "You're right, it is Chandalen."

Richard returned his arrow to the quiver hung on his belt. "I wonder what he's doing out here."

"When you were still searching the chickens gathered together in the buildings," Kahlan said, "he went to check on some of his men on far patrol. He said they had encountered some heavily armed people. His men were worried about the behavior of the strangers."

"They were hostile?"

"No." Kahlan pushed her damp hair back over her shoulder. "But Chandalen's men said they had a calm about them when approached. That troubled him."

Richard nodded as he watched Chandalen's approach, seeing that he brought no weapons except a belt knife. As was the custom, he didn't smile as he trotted up to them.

Until proper greetings were exchanged, Mud People didn't usually smile when they encountered even friends on the plains.

With a grim expression, Chandalen quickly slapped Richard, Kahlan, and Cara. Though he had run most of the way, he seemed hardly winded as he greeted them by their titles.

"Strength to the Mother Confessor. Strength to Richard with the Temper." He added a nod to his spoken greeting of Cara; she was a protector, the same as he.

All three returned the slap and wished him their strength.

"Where are you going?" Chandalen asked.

"There's trouble," Richard said as he offered his waterskin. "We have to get back to Aydindril."

Chandalen accepted the waterskin as he let out a grumble of worry. "The chicken that is not a chicken?"

"In a way, yes," Kahlan told him. "It turns out it was magic conjured by the Sisters of the Dark Jagang is holding prisoner."

"Lord Rahl used his magic to destroy the chicken that was not a chicken," Cara put in.

Chandalen, looking relieved to hear her news, took a swig of water. "Then why must you go to Aydindril?"

Richard rested the end of his bow on the ground and gripped the other end. "The spell the Sisters cast endangers everyone and everything of magic. It's making Zedd and Ann weak. They're waiting back at your village. In Aydindril we hope to unleash magic to counter the Sisters of the Dark, and then Zedd will be strong enough to put everything right again.

"The Sisters' magic made the chicken-thing that killed Juni. Until we can get to Aydindril, no one is safe."

Having listened carefully, Chandalen finally replaced the stopper and handed back the waterskin.

"Then you must soon be on your way to do what only you can." He checked over his shoulder. Now that Chandalen had identified himself, the others were approaching. "But my men have met strangers who must see you, first."

Richard hooked his bow back over his shoulder as he

peered off into the distance. He couldn't make out the people.

"So, who are they?"

Chandalen stole a glance at Kahlan before directing his answer to Richard. "We have an old saying. It is best to hold your tongue around the cook, or you may end up in the pot with the chicken that ate her dinner greens."

It seemed to Richard that Chandalen was trying very hard to keep from looking at Kahlan's puzzled expression. Although Richard couldn't fathom the reason, he thought he understood the figure of speech—odd as it was. He thought maybe it was a bad translation.

The approaching people weren't far off. Chandalen, having had one of his trusted hunters killed by the Lurk, would want Richard and Kahlan to do what they could to stop the enemy; he would not insist they delay their journey unless he had a good reason.

"If it's important for them to see us, then let's go."

Chandalen caught Richard's arm. "They only asked to see you. Perhaps you wish to go alone? Then you could be on your way."

"Why would Richard want to go alone," Kahlan asked, suspicion bubbling up in her voice. She then added something in the Mud People's language which Richard didn't understand.

Chandalen lifted his hands, showing her his empty palms, as if to say he held no weapon and wished no fight. For some reason, he seemed to want no part of whatever was going on.

"Maybe I should—" Richard closed his mouth when Kahlan's suspicious glower shifted to him. He cleared his throat.

"I was going to say we have no secrets." Richard hefted his gear. "Kahlan is always welcome at my side. We have no time to waste. Let's go."

Chandalen nodded and turned to lead them to their fate. Richard thought he saw the man roll his eyes in a don't-say-I-didn't-warn-you fashion.

Richard could see ten of Chandalen's hunters following

behind the seven oncoming travelers, with another three hunters winged out distantly to each side, hemming in the strangers without being overtly threatening. The Mud People hunters seemed merely to accompany and guide the strangers, but Richard knew they were ready to strike at any sign of hostility. Armed outsiders on Mud People land were like tinder before a lightning storm.

Richard hoped this storm, too, would move away and leave sunny skies to follow. Kahlan, Cara, and Richard hurried behind Chandalen through the wet new grass.

Chandalen's men were the first line of defense for the Mud People. That the Mud People's land was given a wide berth by almost everyone spoke to their fighting ferocity.

Yet Chandalen's skilled and deadly hunters, now turned escorts, elicited no more than detached indifference from the six men in loose flaxen clothes. Something about that indifference at being surrounded tickled at Richard's memory.

As the approaching group got close enough for Richard to suddenly recognize them, he missed a step.

It took a few moments of scrutiny before he could believe what he was seeing. He at last understood the strangers' fearless indifference to Chandalen's men. He couldn't imagine what these people were doing away from their own homeland.

Each man was dressed the same and carried the same weapons. Richard knew only one by name, but knew them all. These people were dedicated to a purpose laid down by their lawgivers thousands of years before—those wizards in the great war who had taken their homeland and created the Valley of the Lost to separate the New World from the Old.

Their black-handled swords, with their distinctive curved blades that widened toward clipped points, remained in their scabbards. One end of a cord was tied to a ring on the pommel of each man's sword; the other end of the cord looped around the swordsman's neck as a precaution against losing the weapon in battle. Additionally, each of the six carried spears and a small, round, unadorned shield. Richard had seen women clothed and armed the same, and committed to the same purpose, but this time they were all men.

For these men, practice with their swords was an art form. They practiced that art by moonlight, after the day did not provide them all the time they wished. Using their swords was near to a religious devotion, and they went about their bladework with pious commitment. These men were blade masters.

The seventh, the woman, was dressed differently, and not armed—at least not in the conventional sense.

Richard wasn't good at judging such things by sight, but a quick calculation told him she had to be at least six months pregnant.

A thick mass of long black hair framed a lovely face, her presence giving her features, especially her dark eyes, a certain edginess. Unlike the men's loose outfits of simple cloth, she wore a knee-length dress of finely woven flax dyed a rich earth color and gathered at the waist with a buckskin belt. The ends of the belt were decorated with roughly cut gemstones.

Up the outside of each arm and across the shoulders of the dress was a row of little strips of different-colored cloth. Each was knotted on through a small hole beneath a corded band and each, Richard knew, would have been tied on by a supplicant.

It was a prayer dress. Each of the little colored strips, when they fluttered in the breeze, meant to send a prayer to the good spirits. The dress was worn only by their spirit woman.

Richard's mind raced with possibilities as to why these people would have traveled so far from their homeland. He could come up with nothing good, and a lot that was unpleasant.

Richard had halted. Kahlan waited to his left, Cara to his right, and Chandalen to the right of her.

Ignoring everyone else, the men in the loose clothes all laid their spears on the ground beside themselves as they went to their knees before Richard. They bowed forward, touching their foreheads to the ground, and stayed there.

The woman stood silently regarding him. Her dark eyes bore the timeless look Richard had often seen in others; Sister Verna, Shota the witch woman, Ann, and Kahlan, among others. That timeless look was the mark of the gift.

As she gazed into Richard's eyes with a look that seemed to hint at wisdom he would never grasp, a ghost of a smile touched her lips. Without a word, she went to her knees at the head of the six men accompanying her. She touched her forehead to the ground and then kissed the toe of his boot.

"*Caharin,*" she whispered reverently.

Richard reached down and tugged on the shoulder of her dress, urging her up.

"Du Chaillu, it pleases my heart to see you are well, but what are you doing here?"

She rose up before him, a heartening handsome smile widening across her face. She bent forward and kissed his cheek.

"I have come to see you, of course, Richard, Seeker, *Caharin*, husband."

CHAPTER 27

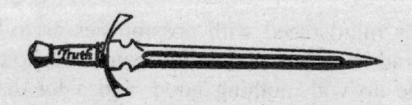

"HUSBAND?" RICHARD HEARD KAHLAN say in a rising tone of concern.

With a jolt of astonished shock that nearly took him from his feet, and did take his breath, Richard abruptly recalled

Du Chaillu's account of her people's old law. The dire implications staggered him.

At the time, he had dismissed her adamant assertions as either irrational conviction or perhaps misconceptions about their history. Now, this old ghost had unexpectedly returned to haunt him.

"Husband?" Kahlan repeated, a little louder, a little more insistently.

Her dark eyes turned to Kahlan, as if annoyed she had to take them from Richard. "Yes. Husband. I am Du Chaillu, wife of the *Caharin*, Richard, the Seeker." Du Chaillu rubbed her hand over her pronounced belly. Her look of annoyance passed and she beamed with pride. "I bear his child."

"Leave it to me, Mother Confessor," Cara said. There was no mistaking the resolute menace in her voice. "This time, I will take care of it."

Cara yanked the knife from Chandalen's belt and lunged for the woman.

Richard was quicker. He spun to Cara and shoved the tips of his stiffened fingers against her upper chest. It not only halted her forward progress, but drove her back three paces. He had enough problems without her causing more. He shoved her again and drove her back another three, and then another three, away from the group of people.

Richard twisted the knife from her grip. "Now, you listen to me. You don't know the first thing about this woman."

"I know—"

"You know nothing! Listen to me! You are fighting the last war. This is not Nadine. This is nothing like Nadine!"

His quiescent fury had at last erupted. With a cry of unleashed rage, Richard heaved the knife at the ground. The force drove it beneath the grass mat, burying it completely into the soil of the plains.

Kahlan laid her hand on the back of his shoulder.

"Richard, calm down. What's this about? What's going on?"

Richard raked his fingers back through his hair. Clenching

his jaw, he glanced about and saw the men still on their knees.

"Jiaan—the rest of you—get off your knees! Get up!"

The men rose up at once. Du Chaillu waited passively, patiently. Chandalen and his men backed off. The Mud People had named him Richard with the Temper and, while not surprised, looked to think it best to give ground.

Chandalen and his men had no idea his anger was for what had killed one of them—had most likely, he realized, killed two of them—and would surely kill more.

Kahlan regarded him with a look of concern. "Richard, calm down and get ahold of yourself. Who are these people?"

He couldn't seem to slow his breathing. Or his heart. Or unclench his fists. Or stop his racing thoughts. Everything seemed to be reeling out of control. Fears laid to rest seemed to have unshackled themselves and suddenly sprung up to snare him. He should have seen it before. He cursed himself for missing it.

But there had to be a way to stop it. He had to think. He had to stop fearing things that had not yet happened, and think of a way to prevent them from coming to be.

He realized it had already happened. He now had to think of the solution.

Kahlan lifted his chin to look into his eyes. "Richard, answer me. Who are these people?"

He pressed a hand to his forehead in frustrated rage. "The Baka Ban Mana. It means 'those without masters.' "

"We now have a *Caharin*; we are no longer the Baka Ban Mana," Du Chaillu said from not far away. "We are now the Baka Tau Mana."

Not really comprehending Du Chaillu's explanation, Kahlan turned her attention once more to Richard. This time her voice had a razor's edge to it. "Why is she saying you are her husband?"

His mind had already galloped so far off down another road he had to concentrate for a moment to understand what Kahlan was asking. She didn't realize the implications. To

Richard, Kahlan's question seemed insignificant past history in the face of the future looming before them.

He impatiently tried to wave away her concern. "Kahlan, it's not what you think."

She licked her lips and took a breath. "Fine." Her green eyes fixed on him. "So, why don't you just explain it to me, then."

It was not a question. Richard instead asked his own. "Don't you see?" Overwhelmed by impatience, he pointed at Du Chaillu. "It's the old law! By the old law, she is my wife. At least she thinks she is."

Richard pressed his fingertips to his temples. His head was throbbing.

"We are in a great deal of trouble," he muttered.

"You are, anyway," Cara said.

"Cara," Kahlan said through her teeth, "that's enough." She turned back to him. "Richard, what are you talking about? What's going on?"

Accounts from Kolo's journal echoed through his mind.

He couldn't seem to order his thoughts enough to put all the tumbling elements into words. The world was shredding apart, and she was asking him yesterday's questions. Since he saw it so clearly looming before them, he couldn't comprehend why Kahlan wouldn't comprehend the danger, too.

"Don't you see?"

Richard's mind picked madly through the shadowy possibilities as he tried to decide what to do next. Time was slipping away. He didn't even know how much they had.

"I see you got her pregnant," Cara said.

Richard turned a glare on the Mord-Sith. "After all we have been through, Cara, do you think no more of me?"

Looking galled, Cara folded her arms and didn't answer.

"Do the math," Kahlan told Cara. "Richard would have been a prisoner of the Mord-Sith, far off at the People's Palace in D'Hara, back when this woman got pregnant."

Unlike the Agiel Richard wore out of respect for the two women who had died protecting them, Kahlan wore the Agiel of Denna, the Mord-Sith who had, at the behest of

Darken Rahl, captured Richard and tortured him nearly to death. Denna had decided to take Richard as her mate, but she had never once implied it was marriage. To Denna, it was just another way to torture and humiliate him.

In the end, Richard forgave Denna for what she had done to him. Denna, knowing he was going to kill her in order to escape, gave him her Agiel and asked him to remember her as having been more in life than simply Mord-Sith. She had asked him to share her last breath of life. It had been through Denna that Richard had come to understand and empathize with these women, and by so doing he had been the only one ever to have escaped a Mord-Sith.

Richard was surprised at Kahlan already having done "the math." He would not have expected her to doubt him. He was wrong. She seemed to read his thoughts in his eyes.

"It's just something you do without thinking," she whispered. "All right? Richard, please, tell me what's going on?"

"You're a Confessor. You know how different arrangements can constitute marriage to different peoples. Except for you, Confessors always picked their mates for reasons of their own, reasons other than love, and then took them with their power before wedding them. The man had no say."

The man a Confessor singled out to be her husband was selected for little more reason than his value as breeding stock. Since her power would destroy the man she picked, love, despite what she might wish, had never been an option for a Confessor. A Confessor chose a man for the qualities he would contribute to her daughter.

"Where I came from," Richard went on, "parents often chose who their children would wed. A father would one day tell his child, 'This will be your husband' or 'This will be your wife.' Different people have different ways and different laws."

Kahlan cast a furtive glance at Du Chaillu. Her gaze pausing twice, once on Du Chaillu's face, and once on her belly.

When Kahlan's gaze returned to him, her eyes had turned brutally cold. "So tell me about her laws."

Richard didn't think Kahlan was aware that she was stroking the dark stone on the delicate gold necklace Shota had given her. The witch woman had appeared unexpectedly at their wedding, and Richard remembered well her words to them.

"This is my gift to you both. I do this out of love for you both, and for everyone else. As long as you wear it, you will bear no children. Celebrate your union and your love. You have each other, now, as you always wanted.

"Mark my words well—never take this off when you are together. I will not allow a male child of this union to live. I do not make a threat. I deliver you a promise. Disregard my request, and suffer the consequences of my vow."

The witch woman had then looked into Richard's eyes, and said, *"Better you battle the Keeper of the underworld himself, than me."*

Shota's elaborate throne was covered with the hide of an experienced wizard who had crossed her. Richard knew little of his birthright of the gift. He didn't necessarily believe Shota's claim that their child would be a fiend unleashed upon the world, but for now he and Kahlan had decided to heed the witch woman's warning. They had little choice.

Kahlan's fingers on his cheek drew his gaze to hers and reminded him she wanted an answer.

Richard made an effort to slow his words. "Du Chaillu is from the Old World, on the other side of the Valley of the Lost. I helped her when Sister Verna took me across to the Old World.

"These other people, the Majendie, had captured Du Chaillu and were going to sacrifice her. They held her prisoner for months. The men used her for their amusement.

"The Majendie expected me, being gifted, to help them sacrifice her in return for passage through their land. A gifted man helping with the sacrifice was part of their religious beliefs. Instead, I freed Du Chaillu, hoping she would see us through her trackless swamps, since we could no longer cross the Majendie's land."

"I provided men to guide Richard and the witch safely

through the swamps to the big stone witch house," Du Chaillu said, as if that would clarify matters.

Kahlan blinked at the explanation. "Witch? Witch house?"

"She means Sister Verna and the Palace of the Prophets," Richard said. "They led Sister Verna and me there not because I freed Du Chaillu, but because I fulfilled an ancient prophecy."

Du Chaillu stepped to Richard's side, as if by right. "According to the old law, Richard came to us and danced with the spirits, proving he is the *Caharin*, and my husband."

Richard could almost see Kahlan's hackles lifting. "What does that mean?"

Richard opened his mouth as he searched for the words. Du Chaillu lifted her chin and spoke instead.

"I am the spirit woman of the Baka Tau Mana. I am also the keeper of our laws. It is proclaimed that the *Caharin* will announce his arrival by dancing with the spirits, and spilling the blood of thirty Baka Ban Mana, a feat none but the chosen one could accomplish and only then with the aid of the spirits.

"It is said that when this happens, we are no longer a free people, but bound to his wishes. We are his to rule.

"It was for this our blade masters trained their entire lives. They had the honor of teaching the *Caharin* so that he might fight the Dark Spirit. This proved Richard was the *Caharin* come to return us to our land, as the old ones promised."

A light breeze ruffled Du Chaillu's thick hair. Her dark eyes revealed no emotion, but the slightest break in her voice betrayed it. "He killed the thirty, as set down in the old law. The thirty are now legend to our people."

"I didn't have any choice." Richard could manage little more than a whisper. "They would have killed me, otherwise. I begged them to stop. I begged Du Chaillu to stop them. I didn't save her life just to end up killing those people. In the end, I defended myself."

Kahlan gave Du Chaillu a long hard look before turning to Richard. "She was held prisoner, and you saved her life and then returned her to her people." Richard nodded. "And she then had her people try to kill you? That was her thanks?"

"There was more to it." Richard felt uncomfortable defending those people's actions—actions that had resulted in so much bloodshed. He could still remember the sickening stench of it.

Kahlan stole another icy sidelong glance at Du Chaillu. "But you saved her life?"

"Yes."

"So tell me what more there is to it, then."

Through the pain of the memories, Richard sought to explain, in words Kahlan would understand. "What they did was a kind of test. A live-or-die test. It forced me to learn to use the magic of the sword in a way I never before realized was possible. In order to survive, I had to draw on the experience of the people who had used the sword before me."

"What do you mean? How could you draw on their experience?"

"The magic of the Sword of Truth retains the essence of the fighting knowledge of all those who've used the sword before—both the good and the wicked. I figured out how to tap that skill by letting the spirits of the sword speak to me, in my mind. But in the heat of combat there isn't always time for me to comprehend it in words.

"So, sometimes the information I need comes to me in images—symbols—that relate it. That was a pivotal connection in understanding why I was named in prophecy *fuer grissa ost drauka*: the bringer of death."

Richard touched the amulet on his chest. The ruby represented a drop of blood. The lines around it were a symbolic portrayal of the dance. It held meaning for a war wizard.

"This," Richard whispered. "This is the dance with death. But back then, with Du Chaillu and her thirty, that was when I first understood.

"Prophecy said I would someday come to them. Prophecy

and their old laws said they had to teach me this—to dance with the spirits of those who had used the sword before. I doubt they fully understood how their test would do this, just that they were to uphold their duty and if they did and I was the one, I would survive.

"I needed that knowledge to stand against Darken Rahl and send him back to the underworld. Remember how I called him in the gathering with the Mud People, and how he escaped into this world, and then the Sisters took me?"

"Of course," Kahlan said. "So they forced you into a life-or-death fight against impossible odds in order to make you call upon your inner strength—your gift. And as a result you killed her thirty blade masters?"

"Yes, exactly. They were fulfilling prophecy." He shared a long look with his only true wife—in his heart, anyway. "You know how terrible prophecy can be."

Kahlan looked away at last and nodded, caught in her own painful memories. Prophecies had caused them many hardships and subjected them to many trials. His second wife, Nadine, forced upon him by prophecy, had been one of those trials.

Du Chaillu's chin lifted. "Five of those the *Caharin* killed were my husbands and the fathers to my children."

"Her five husbands . . . Dear spirits."

Richard shot Du Chaillu a look. "You're not helping."

"You mean, by her law, killing her husbands compels you to become her husband?"

"No. It's not because I killed her husbands, but because defeating the thirty proved I was their *Caharin*. Du Chaillu is their spirit woman; by their old laws the spirit woman is meant to be the wife of the *Caharin*. I should have thought of it before."

"That's obvious," Kahlan snapped.

"Look, I know how it must sound—I know it doesn't seem to make any sense—"

"No, it's all right. I understand." Her chill expression heated to simmering hurt. "So you did the noble thing, and married her. Of course. Makes perfect sense to me." She leaned close. "And you just got so busy and all, you forgot to mention it before you married me. Of course. I understand. Who wouldn't? A man can't be expected to recall all the wives he leaves lying about." She folded her arms and turned away. "Richard, how could you—"

"No! It wasn't like that. I never agreed. Never. There was no ceremony. No one said any words. I never stood and swore an oath. Don't you understand? We weren't married. It never happened!

"So much has been going on. I'm sorry I forgot to tell you, but it never entered my mind because at the time I dismissed it as an irrational belief of an isolated people. I didn't put any stock in it. She simply thinks that since I killed those men to defend myself, that makes me her husband."

"It does," Du Chaillu said.

Kahlan glanced briefly at Du Chaillu as she coolly considered his words. "So then you never, in any sense, really agreed to marry her?"

Richard threw up his hands. "That's what I've been trying to tell you. It's just the Baka Ban Mana's beliefs."

"Baka Tau Mana," Du Chaillu corrected.

Richard ignored her and leaned close to Kahlan. "I'm sorry, but can we talk about it later? We may have a serious problem." She lifted an eyebrow. He amended to, "Another serious problem."

She gave him an indulgent scowl. He turned away, pulling a stalk of grass as he considered the plausibility of worse trouble than Kahlan's ire.

"You know a lot about magic. I mean, you grew up in Aydindril with wizards who instructed you, and you've studied books at the Wizard's Keep. You're the Mother Confessor."

"I'm not gifted in the conventional sense," Kahlan said, "not like a wizard or a sorceress—my power is different— but, yes, I know about magic. Being a Confessor, I had to be taught about magic in many of its various forms."

"Then answer me this. If there's a requirement for magic,

can the requirement be fulfilled by some ambiguous rule without the actual required ritual taking place?"

"Yes, of course. It's called the reflective effect."

"Reflective effect. How does that work?"

Kahlan wound a long lock of damp hair on a finger as she turned her mind to the question. "Say you have a room with only one window and therefore the sun never reaches the corner. Can you get the sunlight to shine into a corner it never touches?"

"Since it's called the reflective effect, I'd guess you'd use a mirror to reflect the sunlight into the corner."

"Right." Kahlan let the hair go and held up the finger. "Even though the sunlight could never itself reach the corner, by using a mirror you can get the sunlight to fall where it ordinarily wouldn't. Magic can sometimes work like that. Magic is much more complex, of course, but that's the easiest way I can explain it.

"Even if only by some ancient law that completes a long-forgotten condition, the spell might reflect the condition to fulfill the arcane requirements of the magic involved. Like water seeking its own level, a spell will often seek its own solution—within the laws of its nature."

"That's what I was afraid of," Richard murmured.

He tapped the end of the stalk of grass flat between his teeth as he stared out at the lightning flickering ominously in the distant clouds.

"The magic involved dates from the time of that ancient mandate about the *Caharin*," he said at last. "Therein lies the problem."

Kahlan gripped his arm, turning him back to face her. "But Zedd said—"

"He lied to us. I fell for it." Exasperated, Richard flung the stalk of grass aside. Zedd had used the Wizard's First Rule—people will believe a lie either because they want to believe it's true, or because they fear it is—to mislead them.

"I wanted to believe him," Richard muttered. "He tricked me."

"What are you talking about?" Cara asked.

Richard heaved a crestfallen sigh. He had been careless in more ways than one. "Zedd. He made all that up about the Lurk."

Cara made a face. "Why would he do that?"

"Because for some reason he didn't want us to know the chimes are loose."

He couldn't believe how stupid he'd been, forgetting about Du Chaillu. Kahlan was right to be angry. When it came down to it, his excuse was pathetically inadequate. And he was supposed to be the Lord Rahl? People were supposed to believe in and follow him?

Kahlan rubbed her fingertips across the furrows of her brow. "Richard, let's think this through. It can't be—"

"Zedd said you would have to be my third wife in order to have called the chimes forth into this world."

"Among other things," Kahlan insisted. "He said, among other things."

Wearily, Richard lifted a finger. "Du Chaillu." He lifted a second finger. "Nadine." He lifted a third finger. "You. You are my third wife. In principle, anyway.

"I may not look at it that way, but the wizards who cast the spell wouldn't care how I may wish to look at it. They cast magic that would be set into motion by keying off a prescribed set of conditions."

Kahlan heaved a long-suffering sort of sigh. "You're forgetting one important element. When I spoke aloud the names of the three chimes, we weren't yet married. I wasn't yet your second wife, much less your third."

"When I was forced to wed Nadine in order to gain entrance to the Temple of the Winds, and you were likewise forced to wed Drefan, in our hearts we said the words to each other. We were married then and there because of that vow—as far as the spirits were concerned, anyway. Ann herself agreed it was so.

"As you have just explained, magic sometimes works by such ambiguous rules. No matter our feelings about it, the formal requirements—the requirements of some ancient magic conjured by wizards during the great war when the

prophecy about the *Caharin* and the old law were set
down—have been met."

"But—"

Richard gestured emphatically. "Kahlan, I'm sorry I fool-
ishly didn't think, but we have to face it—the chimes are
loose."

CHAPTER 28

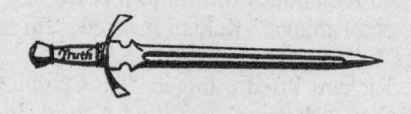

DESPITE HOW VALID HE thought his reasoning, it didn't at
all look to Richard that Kahlan was convinced. She didn't
even look amenable to reason. What she looked was angry.

"Did you tell Zedd about . . . her?" Kahlan gestured heatedly at Du Chaillu. "Did you? You had to have said something to him."

He could understand her feelings. He wouldn't like to
discover she had another husband she had neglected to mention—no matter how innocent she might have been—even
if it was as tenuous as was his connection with Du Chaillu.

Still, this was about something considerably more important than some convoluted condition that contrived to make
Du Chaillu his first wife. It was about something dangerous
in the extreme. Kahlan had to understand that. She had to
see that they were in a great deal of trouble.

They had already wasted valuable time. He prayed to the
good spirits that he could make her see the truth of what he

was telling her without having to reveal to her the full extent of why he knew it to be true.

"I told you, Kahlan, I didn't even remember it until now because at the time I didn't consider it authentic and so I didn't realize it could have any bearing on this. Besides, when would I have had time to tell him? Juni died before we had a chance to really talk to him, and then he made up that story about the Lurk and sent us on this fool task."

"Then how did he know? In order to be tricking us, he would have had to know about it first. How did Zedd know I am in fact your third wife—even if only by some . . ." Her fists tightened. ". . . some stupid old law you artfully forgot?"

Richard threw up his hands. "If it's raining at night, you don't have to be able to see the clouds in the dark to know the rain has to be falling from the sky. If Zedd knew the fact of something and knew it was trouble, he wouldn't worry about the how of it, he would worry about fixing the leak in the roof."

She pinched the bridge of her nose as she took a breath. "Richard, maybe he really believes what he told us about the Lurk." Kahlan cast a cool glance at his first wife. "Maybe he believes it because it's true."

Richard shook his head. "Kahlan, we have to face it. We make it worse if we ignore the truth and invest hope in a lie. People are already dying."

"Juni's death doesn't prove the chimes are really loose."

"It's not just Juni. The chimes' presence in this world caused that stillborn baby."

"What!"

In frustration, Kahlan ran her fingers back into her hair. Richard could understand her wishing it to be the Lurk, and not the chimes, because unlike the chimes they had a solution for the Lurk. But wishing didn't make it so.

"First you forget you already have another wife, now you rush off down some road of fancy. Richard, how could you come to such a conclusion?"

"Because the chimes being in this world somehow destroys magic. The Mud People have magic."

Though the Mud People were a remote people living a simple life, they were unlike any others; only they had the ability to call their ancestors' spirits in a gathering and talk to the dead. While they didn't think of themselves as having magic, only the Mud People could call an ancestor from beyond that outer circle of the Grace, bringing them across the boundary of the veil and into the inner circle of life, if only for a brief time.

If the Imperial Order won the war, the Mud People, among many others, would eventually all be slaughtered for possessing magic. With the chimes loose, they might not live long enough to face that possibility.

Richard noticed Chandalen, not far off, listening intently. "The Mud People have the unique magical ability of the gathering. Each is born with this ability, this magic. That makes them all vulnerable to the chimes.

"Zedd told us, and I also read it in Kolo's journal, that the weak are affected first." Richard's voice softened with sorrow. "What could be weaker than an unborn child?"

Kahlan, touching the stone of her necklace, looked away from his eyes. She dropped her hand to her side, and looked to be trying to veneer her ire with patient logic.

"I can still feel my power—just as always. As you said, if the chimes were loose, they would be causing the failure of magic. We have no proof that's happening. If it were true, don't you think I would know? Do you think me woefully inexperienced in knowing my own power?

"Richard, we can't leap to conclusions. Newborns die all the time. That is no proof magic is failing."

Richard turned to Cara. She was standing not far off, listening as she watched the grasslands, the Mud People hunters, and in particular, the Baka Tau Mana.

"Cara, how long has your Agiel been useless?" he asked.

Cara quailed. She could hardly have looked more startled had he unexpectedly slapped her. She opened her mouth, but no words came.

She lifted her chin, thinking better of admitting such defeat. "Lord Rahl, what makes you think—"

"You pulled Chandalen's knife. I have never before seen you forsake your Agiel in favor of another weapon. No Mord-Sith would. How long, Cara?"

She wet her lips. Her eyes closed in defeat as she turned away.

"In the last few days I have begun to have trouble sensing you. I don't feel any difference, except I have increasing difficulty sensing your location. At first, I thought it was nothing, but apparently the bond grows weaker by the day. The Agiel is powered by the bond to our Lord Rahl."

When the Mord-Sith were within a reasonable distance, they always knew precisely where he was by that bond. He imagined it had to be disorienting to suddenly lose that sense.

Cara cleared her throat as she stared off at the distant storm clouds. Tears glistened in her blue eyes.

"The Agiel is dead in my fingers."

Only a Mord-Sith would anguish over the failure of magic that gave her pain every time she touched it. Such was the nature of these women and their unqualified commitment to duty.

Cara looked back at him, the fire returning to her expression. "But I am still sworn to you and will do what I must to protect you. This changes nothing for the Mord-Sith."

"And the D'Haran army?" Richard whispered as he considered the spreading extent of their troubles. The D'Haran people were charged to purpose through their bond. "Jagang is coming. Without the army . . ."

The bond was ancient magic he had inherited because he was a gifted Rahl. That bond was created to be protection from the dream walkers. Without it . . .

Even if Kahlan believed it was the Lurk, and not the chimes, Zedd had told them that, too, would cause magic to fail. Richard knew Zedd would have had to make whatever story he invented relate closely to reality in order to fool them.

Either way, Kahlan would understand the rotting fruits of the dying tree of magic. Her reassuring fingers found his arm.

"The army may not feel their bond like before, Richard, but they are bonded to you in other ways. Most in the Midlands follow the Mother Confessor, and they are not bonded to her by any magic. In the same way, soldiers follow you because they believe in you. You have proven yourself to them, and they to you."

"The Mother Confessor is right," Cara said. "The army will remain loyal because you are their leader. Their true leader. They believe in you—the same as I."

Richard let out a long breath. "I appreciate that, Cara, I really do, but—"

"You are the Lord Rahl. You are the magic against magic. We are the steel against steel. It will remain so."

"That's just it. I can't be the magic against magic. Even if it were the Lurk instead of the chimes, magic won't work."

Cara shrugged. "Then you will figure a way for it to work. You are the Lord Rahl; that is what you do."

"Richard," Kahlan said, "Zedd told us the Sisters of the Dark conjured the Lurk and that's what's causing magic to fail. You have no proof it's really the chimes instead. We have but to do as Zedd has asked of us, and then he will be able to counter the Sisters' magic. As soon as we get to Aydindril, everything will be back to right."

Still, Richard could not bring himself to tell her. "Kahlan, I wish it were as you say, but it isn't," he said simply.

Her veneer of patience began cracking. "Why do you insist it's the chimes when Zedd told us it was the Lurk?"

Richard leaned closer to her. "Think about it. My grandmother—Zedd's wife—apparently told her little girl, my mother, a story about a cat named Lurk. Just that one time she told me about a cat named Lurk, but Zedd wouldn't know she did. It was a small thing my mother told me once when I was little, like a hundred other little words of comfort, or phrases, or stories to bring a smile. I never mentioned it to Zedd.

"For some reason Zedd wanted to hide the truth. 'Lurk,' because he once had a cat by that name, was probably just the first thing that came into his head. Admit it, doesn't the name 'Lurk' strike you as a bit . . . whimsical, once you think about it?"

Kahlan folded her arms across her breasts. She made a reluctant grimace.

"I thought I was the only one who thought so." She mustered her resolve. "But that doesn't really prove it. It could be coincidence."

Richard knew it was the chimes. In much the same way he could sense the chicken that wasn't a chicken, and had wished Kahlan would believe him, he dearly wished she would trust him in this.

"What are these things, these chimes?" Cara asked.

Richard turned away from the others and stared off toward the horizon. He didn't know a lot about them, but what he did know made his hair want to stand on end.

"Those in the Old World wanted to end magic, much as Jagang does today, and probably for the same reason—so they could more easily rule by the sword. Those in the New World wanted magic to live on. In order to prevail, the wizards on both sides created weapons of inconceivable horror, desperately hoping they would bring the war to an end.

"Many of those weapons—the mriswith, for example—were created from people by using Subtractive Magic to remove certain attributes from a person, and Additive Magic to put in some other desired ability or quality. Still others, they simply added some ability they wanted.

"I think dream walkers were such people, people who had a capability added, people who the wizards obviously intended as weapons. Jagang is a descendant of those dream walkers from the great war. Now the weapon is in charge of making war.

"Unlike Jagang, who only wants to end our magic so he

can use his against us, during the great war the people in the Old World truly were trying to end magic. All magic. The chimes were intended to do just that—to steal magic away from the world of life. They were conjured forth from the underworld—the Keeper's world of the dead.

"As Zedd explained, such a thing conjured from the underworld, once unleashed, not only may end magic but, in so doing, could very well extinguish life itself."

"He also said he and Ann could take care of it," Kahlan said.

Richard looked back over his shoulder. "Then why did he lie to us? Why didn't he trust us? If he really can take care of it, why not simply tell us the truth?" He shook his head. "Something more is going on."

Du Chaillu, long silent, impatiently folded her arms. "Our blade masters will easily cut down these filthy—"

"Hush!" Richard crossed his finger over her lips. "Don't say another word, Du Chaillu. You don't understand this. You don't know what trouble you might cause."

When Richard was sure Du Chaillu would remain silent, he turned away from everyone again to stare off toward the clearing skies to the northeast, toward Aydindril. He was tired of arguing; he knew the truth of the chimes being loose. He needed to think what to do about them. There were things he needed to know.

He remembered that while frantically searching Kolo's journal for other information, he had come across places where Kolo talked about the chimes, among a great many other things. Wizards were continually sending messages and reports back to the Wizard's Keep in Aydindril, not only relaying information concerning the chimes, but also reporting on any number of other frightening and potentially catastrophic events that were taking place.

Kolo wrote about those communications, at least the ones he found interesting, significant, or curious, but he didn't give complete accounts of them; he would have had no reason to reproduce them in his private journal. Richard doubted Kolo ever intended anyone to read the journals.

Kolo's habit was to briefly mention the pertinent information from a message, and then remark on the matter at hand, so the information Richard read on the reports had been frustratingly sketchy—and opinionated.

Kolo set down more information when he was frightened, seeming almost to use his journal as a way to think through a problem in an effort to find a solution. There was a period of time when he had been very frightened by what the reports were saying in regard to the chimes. In several places Kolo wrote down what he had read in reports, almost as if to justify his fear, to underscore for himself his grounds for concern.

Richard recalled Kolo mentioning the wizard who had been sent to deal with the chimes: Ander. Somebody Ander—Richard couldn't remember the whole name.

Wizard Ander proudly bore the cognomen "the Mountain." Apparently, he was big. Kolo didn't like the man, though, and in his private journal often derisively referred to him as "the Moral Molehill." Richard gathered from Kolo's journal that Ander thought a lot of himself.

Richard clearly remembered at one point Kolo expressing indignation that people were failing to properly apply the Wizard's Fifth Rule: Mind what people do, not only what they say, for deeds will betray a lie.

Kolo had seemed incensed when he scrawled that by not minding the totality of the actions people were failing to properly apply the Fifth Rule to Wizard Ander. He complained that if they had, they would have easily discovered that the man's true allegiance lay solely with himself, and not with the good of his people.

"You still have not said what the chimes are," Cara said.

Richard felt the insistent breeze tug at his hair and his golden cloak, as if urging him onward. To where, he didn't know. Here and there bugs lifted out of the wet spring grass to loop through the air. Far off to the east, backlit by the billowing honeyed storm clouds, the dark dots of geese in an undulating V formation were winging their way north.

Richard had never given any serious thought to the

309

chimes when the subject came up at the wedding. Zedd had dismissed their concern, and besides, Richard's mind was on other things.

But later, after the chicken had been killed outside the spirit house, after Juni had been murdered, after the chicken-thing gave him gooseflesh every time it was anywhere near, and after Zedd had filled in some of the details, Richard's rising sense of alarm had caused him to give himself over to recalling everything he could about the chimes. At the time, he had been searching Kolo's journal for solutions to other problems, and hadn't been paying particular attention to the information on the chimes, but nearly constant concentration and occasional trancelike effort had brought back a great deal.

"The chimes are ancient beings spawned in the underworld. The Grace must be breached to bring them into the world of life. Being from the underworld, they were conjured from the Subtractive side alone, and so create an imbalance once in this world. Magic needs balance. Being totally Subtractive, their mere presence here requires Additive Magic for them to exist in this state, since existence is a form of Additive power, and so the chimes drain magic away from this world as long as they're here."

Cara, never being one with any outward appearance of an aptitude for magic, appeared only more confused than ever by his answer. Richard understood her confusion. He didn't know much about magic, either, and barely had a grasp of what he had just told her. He wasn't even convinced it was accurate.

"But how do they do that?" she asked.

"You might think of the world of life as like a barrel of water. The chimes are a hole in that barrel that has just been uncorked, letting the water drain away. Once the water all drains off, the barrel will dry out, the staves will shrink, and it will no longer be the container it once was. You might say it is then a dead shell, only resembling what it once was.

"The chimes' mere existence here drains magic away from the world of life, like that hole in the barrel, but also, as a way to bring them into this world, they were conjured as creatures. They have a nature of their own. They can kill.

"Being creatures of magic they have the ability, if they wish, to take on the appearance of the creature they kill—such as a chicken—but they retain all the power of what they truly are. When I shot the chicken with an arrow, the chime fled its phantom form. From the beginning, the real chicken had been lying dead behind the wall; the chime only borrowed its form as a pattern—as a disguise—to taunt us."

Cara took on the unfamiliar countenance of worry. "You mean to tell me"—she glanced at the people around her—"that anyone here could really be a chime?"

"From what I gather, they're conjured creatures and have no soul, so they can't take on the appearance of a person—just animals. According to Zedd, the converse is true; Jagang has a soul and so can only enter the mind of a person because a soul is needed.

"When the wizards created weapons out of people, those things they created still had souls. That was how they could be controlled, at least to some extent. The chimes, once here, could not be governed. That was one of the things that made them so dangerous. It's like trying to reason with lightning."

"All right"—Cara held up a finger as if making a mental note for herself—"so it couldn't be a person. That's good." She gestured to the sky. "But could it be that one of those meadowlarks is a chime?"

Richard glanced up at the yellow-breasted birds flitting past. "I guess so. If it could be a chicken, it surely could kill any animal and take its form. It wouldn't need to, though." Richard pointed at the wet ground. "It could just as easily be hiding in that puddle at your feet. Some apparently have an affinity for water."

Cara looked down at the puddle and then took a step back.

"You mean the chime that killed Juni was hiding in the water? Stalking him?"

Richard glanced briefly at Chandalen and then with a single nod acknowledged his belief that it was so.

311

"Chimes hide, or wait, in dark places," he went on. "They somehow travel along the edges of things, such as cracks in rock, or along the water's edge. I'm assuming so, anyway; the way Kolo put it was that they slip along borders, where this meets that. Some hide in fire, and they can travel on sparks."

He glanced at Kahlan out of the corner of his eye as he recalled the way the house of the dead—where Juni's body lay—had burst into flame. "When annoyed or angered, they will sometimes burn a place down, just for spite.

"It was said that some are of such beauty that to see them is to take your breath away—forever. They are only vaguely visible, unless you catch their attention. Kolo's journal made it sound like once the victim sees them, they're partially shaped by the victim's own desire, and that desire is irresistible. That must be how they were able to seduce people to their death.

"Maybe that's what happened to Juni. Maybe he saw something so beautiful that he abandoned his weapons, his judgment, even his common sense and followed it down into the water where he drowned.

"Yet others crave attention and like to be worshiped. I guess, because they came from the underworld, they share the Keeper's hunger for veneration. It was said that some even protected those who uncritically revered them, but it's a dangerous balancing act. It lulls them, according to what Kolo said. But if you stop worshiping them, they will turn on you.

"They enjoy most the hunt, never tiring of it. They hunt people. They are without mercy. They enjoy especially killing with fire.

"The full translation of their name from High D'Haran roughly means 'the chimes of doom,' or 'the chimes of death.' "

Du Chaillu was scowlingly silent. The Baka Tau Mana blade masters for the most part managed to continue to look indifferent, aloof, and relaxed, but they had a new restiveness in their posture that to Richard was inescapable.

"Either way," Cara said with a sigh, "I think we can grasp the idea."

Chandalen, listening attentively, finally spoke up. "But you do not believe this, Mother Confessor? You believe what Zedd had to say, that it is not these chimes of death?"

Kahlan met Richard's gaze before addressing Chandalen. Her tone wasn't harsh.

"Zedd's explanation of the problem is in many ways similar, and so could just as easily account for what's happened, but being similar, it would be no less dangerous. The important difference, from what he told us, is that when we get to Aydindril we will be able to halt the trouble. I reluctantly hold Zedd was right. I don't believe it's the chimes."

"I wish that were the case, I really do, because as you said when we get to Aydindril we could counter it," Richard said. "But it's the chimes. I would guess Zedd simply wanted to get us out of harm's way while he saw to trying to solve the problem of sending the chimes back to the underworld."

"Lord Rahl is the magic against magic," Cara said to Kahlan. "He would know best about this. He believes it is the chimes, so it must be the chimes."

Sighing in frustration, Kahlan pushed her long hair back over her shoulder.

"Richard, you're talking yourself into believing this is the chimes. By talking about it as being true, you're starting to convince Cara, just as you've convinced yourself. Just because you're afraid of it being true, you're giving it more credence than it deserves."

She was obviously reminding him of the Wizard's First Rule, suggesting that he was believing a lie.

Richard weighed the fiery determination so evident in her green eyes. He needed her to help him. He couldn't face this alone.

He finally decided he had no choice. Asking everyone to wait, he put an arm around her shoulders and walked her away so he could be sure the others wouldn't hear.

He needed her to believe in him. He no longer had any choice.

He had to tell her.

CHAPTER 29

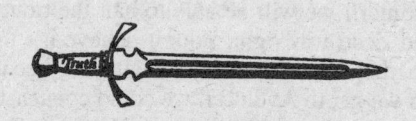

KAHLAN WENT WILLINGLY AS he walked her off through the wet grass, more content to argue with him alone than in front of everyone else. For Richard's part, he didn't want to tell her what he had to say in front of others.

Over his shoulder, Richard saw Chandalen's hunters leaning casually on their spears, spears dipped in poison. They looked to lazily wait for Richard and Kahlan to finish their talk and return. He knew there was nothing lazy about them. He could see they were strategically positioned to keep the Baka Tau Mana under guard. This was their land, after all, and despite them knowing Richard, the Baka Tau Mana were outsiders.

The Baka Tau Mana, for their part, looked completely indifferent to the Mud People hunters. The blade masters spoke a few nonchalant words to one another, looked out at the storm clouds on the horizon, or stretched and yawned.

Richard had fought Baka Ban Mana blade masters; he knew they were anything but indifferent. They were poised to kill. Having lived a tenuous existence surrounded by enemies bent on destroying them, their nature, by training, was to be prepared to kill at any moment.

When Richard had been with Sister Verna and they had first encountered the blade masters, he had asked her if they were dangerous. Sister Verna told him that when she was young, she had seen a Baka Ban Mana blade master who had gotten into the garrison in Tanimura kill nearly fifty well-armed soldiers before he was taken down. She said they fought as if they were invincible spirits, and that some people believed they were.

Richard wouldn't like some small lapse in judgment or misstep in understanding to bring the Mud People and the Baka Tau Mana to a fight. They were all too good at fighting.

Cara, looking anything but dispassionate, painted them all with her glares.

Like the three sides of a triangle, the Mud People, the Baka Tau Mana, and Cara were all part of the same struggle. They were all allied to Richard and Kahlan, and to their cause, even though each looked at the world differently. They all valued most of the same things in life. Family, friends, hard work, honesty, duty, loyalty, freedom.

Kahlan placed her hand gently but insistently on his chest.

"Richard, despite anything else I'm feeling at the moment, I know your heart is in the right place, but you simply aren't being reasonable. You're the Seeker of Truth; you have to stop insisting you're right and see the truth of this. We can stop the Sisters' magic and their Lurk. Zedd and Ann will counter the spell. Why are you being so obstinate?"

"Kahlan," he said, keeping his voice low, "the chicken-thing was a chime."

She absently, unconsciously, fingered the dark stone on the delicate gold chain around her neck. "Richard, you know I love you and you know I believe in you, but in this case I've just about—"

"Kahlan," he said, cutting her off. He knew what she thought and what she had to say. Now he wanted her only to listen. He waited until her eyes told him she would.

"You called the chimes into this world.

"You didn't do it intentionally, or to cause harm—no one would believe otherwise. You did it to save me. I was near death and needed your help, so I'm part of this, too. Without my actions, yours would not have been necessary."

"Don't forget our ancestors. Had they not borne children, we wouldn't have been born to commit our crimes. I suppose you'll want to hold them to account, too?"

He wet his lips as he gently gripped her shoulders. "I'm just saying that giving help is the thing that started this. That does not, however, in any sense, make you guilty of malicious intent. You must understand that. But because you spoke the words completing the spell, that makes you inadvertently responsible. You brought the chimes into this world.

"For some reason, Zedd didn't want us to know. I wish he would have trusted us with the truth, but he didn't. I'm sure he had reasons that to him seemed important enough to make him lie to us. For all I know, maybe they were."

Kahlan put her fingertips to her forehead, closed her eyes, and sighed with forbearance. "Richard, I agree there are puzzling aspects to what Zedd did, and there are matters yet to be answered, but that doesn't mean we have to leap to a different answer just for the sake of having one. Zedd is First Wizard; we must trust in what he's asked us to do."

Richard touched her cheek. He wished he could be alone with her, really alone, and he could try to make up for his foolish forgetfulness. He dearly didn't want to be telling her these things, but he had to.

"Please, Kahlan, listen to what I have to say, and then you decide? I want to be wrong, I really do. You decide.

"When the Mud People hunters were guarding us in the spirit house, the chimes were outside. One of them killed a chicken just because they like to kill.

"When Juni heard the noise, the same as I heard it, he investigated but found nothing. He then insulted the spirit of the killer in order to bring it out in the open. It came out in the open, and killed him for insulting them."

"I insulted the chicken-thing, so why didn't it kill me?" Kahlan wearily wiped a hand across her eyes. "Answer me that, Richard. Why didn't it kill me?"

He gazed into her beautiful green eyes for a moment as he gathered his courage.

"The chime told you why, Kahlan."

"*What?*" she said with a squint. "What are you talking about?"

"That chicken-thing wasn't a Lurk. It was a chime, and it wasn't calling you by your title of Mother Confessor. It was a chime. It said what it meant.

"It called you 'Mother.' "

Kahlan stared at him in startled wide-eyed shock.

"They respect you," he said, "to some limited extent, anyway, because you brought them into the world of life. You gave them life. They consider you their life-giver, their mother. You only assumed the chicken-thing was going to add the word 'Confessor' after it called you 'Mother' because you are so used to hearing yourself called by that title.

"But the chime wasn't calling you by title, Kahlan. It was calling you by the name it meant: Mother."

He could almost see the truth of his words inundating her carefully constructed fortress of rationale. Some truths, after a certain point, could be felt viscerally, and at that point everything clicked with the finality of a dead bolt on a prison of truth.

Kahlan's eyes filled with tears.

She pressed closer to him, into the comfort and understanding of his arms. She gasped a sob against his chest and then angrily wiped her cheek as a tear rolled down.

"I think that was the only thing that saved you," he said softly as he hugged her. "I wouldn't want to again trust your life to their charity."

"We have to stop them." She stifled another sob. "Dear spirits, we have to stop them."

"I know."

"Do you know what to do?" she asked. "Do you have

any idea how to send them back to the world of the dead?"

"Not yet. To find a solution, the first thing to be done is to recognize the true problem. I guess we've done that, now?"

Kahlan nodded as she wiped at her eyes. As quickly as understanding had brought tears, resolve banished them.

"Why would the chimes have been outside the spirit house?"

While they had been together after being married, exulting in their love, something had been outside the door exulting in death. It made him feel sick at his stomach just to think about it.

"I don't know. Maybe the chimes wanted to be near you." Kahlan simply nodded. She understood. Near their mother.

Richard remembered the stricken look on Kahlan's face when Nissel brought the stillborn baby into the house of the dead. The chimes had caused that, too. It was only the beginning.

"What's a fatal Grace? You mentioned it before, yesterday, when we went to see Zedd and Ann."

"Most of the stories about the chimes that I recounted came from an early report. Because Kolo was frightened, he wrote at greater length than usual. The report he quoted said at the end, 'Mark well my words: Beware the chimes, and if need be great, draw for yourself thrice on the barren earth, in sand and salt and blood, a fatal Grace.'

"And what does that mean?"

"I don't know. I was hoping maybe Zedd or Ann might know. He knows all about the Grace. I thought he might know about this."

"But do you think this fatal Grace would stop the chimes?"

"I just don't know, Kahlan. It occurred to me that it might be desperate advice on suicide."

Kahlan nodded absently as she mulled over the words from Kolo's journal.

"I could understand if it was advice on suicide. I could

feel its evil," she said as she stared off into her visions. "When I was in the house where the Mud People prepared bodies for burial, and the chicken-thing—the chime—was in there with me, I could feel its evil. Dear spirits, it was awful.

"It was pecking out Juni's eyes. Even though he was dead, it still wanted to peck out his eyes."

He pulled her into his arms again. "I know."

She pushed away with rekindled hope. "Yesterday, with Zedd and Ann, you told us Kolo said they were quite alarmed at first, but after investigating they discovered the chimes were a simple weapon and easily overcome."

"Yes, but Kolo only reported the relief at the Wizard's Keep when they discovered it wasn't the problem to counter they at first thought it would be. He didn't write down the solution. They sent a wizard they called the Mountain to see to it. Obviously, he did."

"Do you have any idea if there are any weapons that would be effective against them? Juni was heavily armed, and it didn't do him any good, but might there be others?"

"Kolo never gave any indication. Arrows didn't kill the chicken-thing, and fire certainly isn't going to harm them.

"However, Zedd was emphatic that I retrieve the Sword of Truth. If he lied about it being a Lurk, that may have been to keep us away from harm. I don't believe he would lie about the sword. He wanted me to get it, and he said it might be the only magic that would still work to protect us. I believe him in that much of it."

"Why do you suppose the chicken-thing fled from you? I mean, if they consider me their mother, I could understand them maybe having some kind of . . . reverence, for me, and being reluctant to harm me, but if they're so powerful, why would they run from you? You only shot at them with an arrow. You said arrows couldn't hurt them. Why would it run from you?"

Richard raked back his hair. "I've wondered about that myself. The only answer I've been able to come up with is that they're creatures of Subtractive Magic, and I'm the only

319

one in thousands of years born with that side of magic. Maybe they fear my Subtractive Magic can harm them—maybe it can. It's a hope, anyway."

"And the fire? That one lone bit of our wedding bonfires that was still burning that you snuffed out? That was one of them, wasn't it?"

Richard hated that they had been in their wedding bonfire. It was a defilement.

"Yes. Sentrosi—the second chime. It means 'fire.' Reechani, the first, means 'water.' The third, Vasi, means 'air.' "

"But you put out the fire. The chime didn't do anything to stop you. If they would kill Juni for insulting them, it certainly seems they would be angered by what you did. The chicken thing, too, ran from you."

"I don't know, Kahlan. I don't have an answer."

Peering into his eyes, she hesitated for a moment. "Maybe they didn't harm you for the same reason they didn't harm me."

"They think I, too, am their mother?"

"Father," she said, unconsciously stroking the dark stone at her throat. "I used the spell to keep you alive, to keep you from crossing over into the world of the dead. The spell called the chimes because they were from the other side and had the power to do that. Maybe, since we were both involved, they think of us as father and mother—as their parents."

Richard let out a long breath. "That's possible, I'm not saying it isn't, but when I felt them near, I just got the sense of something more to it—something that made my hair stand on end."

"More? More like what?"

"It was an overwhelming sense of their lust whenever they were near me, and at the same time monstrous loathing."

Kahlan rubbed her arms, chilled by such obscene wickedness among them. A humorless smile, bitter with irony, crossed her face.

"Shota always said we would together conceive a monstrous offspring."

Richard cupped her cheek. "Someday, Kahlan. Someday."

On the verge of tears, she turned from his hand, his gaze, to stare off at the horizon. She cleared her throat and gathered her voice.

"If magic is failing, at least Jagang will lose his help. He controls those with magic to help his army. At least if he could no longer do that, there would be that much good in all this.

"He used one of those wizards to try to kill us. He was able to use one of the Sisters of the Light to bring the plague from the Temple of the Winds. If magic fails because of the chimes, at least it will fail for Jagang, too."

Richard pulled his lower lip through his teeth. "I've been thinking about that. If the chicken-thing was afraid of me because I have Subtractive Magic, Jagang's control over those with magic might very well no longer work, but—"

"Dear spirits," she whispered, turning back to look up at him. "The Sisters of the Dark. They may not have been born with it, but they know how to use Subtractive Magic."

Richard nodded reluctantly. "I fear that Jagang, if nothing else, might still have the Sisters of the Dark. Their magic will work."

"Our only hope, then, is with Zedd and Ann. Let's hope they will be able to stop the chimes."

Richard couldn't force a smile for her. "How? Neither of them is able to use Subtractive Magic. The magic they do have is failing along with all other magic. They will be just as helpless as that unborn child that died. I'm sure they've gone, but where?"

She gave him a look, very much a Mother Confessor look. "Had you remembered your first wife when you should have, Richard, we could have told Zedd. It might have made a difference. Now that chance is lost to us. You picked a very bad time to become negligent."

He wanted to argue with her, tell her it wouldn't have

made any difference, tell her she was wrong, but he couldn't. She wasn't wrong. Zedd would have gone off alone to battle the chimes. Richard wondered if they might go back and track his grandfather.

She at last took his hand in hers, gave it a brave pat with her other, and then marched them back to where the others waited. She held her head erect. Her face was a Confessor's face, devoid of emotion, full of authority.

"We don't yet know what to do about them," Kahlan announced, "but I'm convinced beyond doubt: the chimes are loose upon the world."

CHAPTER 30

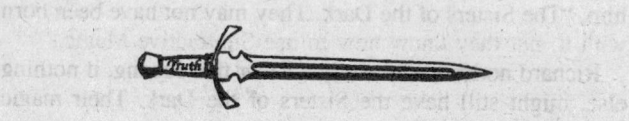

FOR THE BENEFIT OF the hunters, Kahlan repeated her announcement in the Mud People's language. Richard wished she had been right that it was the Lurk and not the chimes. They would have had a solution for the Lurk.

Everyone looked understandably disquieted to hear Kahlan, after having been so steadfast in her arguments it was the Lurk, now tell them she accepted beyond doubt the fact that they were confronted with nothing less than the full threat of the chimes.

It didn't look to Richard, once she had said she agreed with him, that anyone still harbored doubts of their own.

With Kahlan's words, it seemed the world had for everyone just changed.

Uneasy silence enveloped the plains.

Richard needed to get on with trying to figure out what to do next, but didn't really have any idea how to do that. He didn't even know where to start. He now realized what he should have done, when he had the chance. He had been so intent on the danger he had ignored everything else.

He was a long way from the woods he knew. He wished he were back in those woods. At least when he had been a guide, he never forgot what path he was on, or led anyone over a cliff.

He turned his attention to the Baka Tau Mana's dark-haired spirit woman.

"Du Chaillu, why have you came all this way? What are you doing here?"

"Ahh," Du Chaillu said as she folded her hands before herself with deliberate care. "Now the *Caharin* wishes me to speak?"

The woman was bottled ire. Richard didn't really see why, and he didn't really care.

"Yes, why have you come?"

"We have traveled many days. We have suffered hardship. We have buried some of those who started with us. We have had to fight our way through hostile places. We have shed the blood of many to reach you.

"We left our families and loved ones to bear warning to our *Caharin*. We have gone without food, without sleep, and without the comfort of a safe place. We have faced nights where we all wept for we felt afraid and sick at heart away from our homeland.

"I have traveled with the child the *Caharin* asked me to bear when I would have gone to an herb woman and shed it—shed the dreadful memories I carry with it. Yet he does not even acknowledge that I chose to honor his words and accept the responsibility of this child thrust upon me.

"The *Caharin* does not even recognize that I must every

day be reminded, by the child he asked me to bear, of the time I spent chained naked to a wall in the stinking place of the Majendie. Reminded of where I came to be with this child. Reminded of how those men used me for their pleasure and then laughed at me. Reminded of where I daily endured the fear that would be the day I was to be butchered and sacrificed. Reminded of where I wept my heart out for my own babies who would be left without their mother, and wept that I would never again see their little smiles or have the joy of watching them grow.

"But I honored the *Caharin*'s words and carry the child of dogs, because the *Caharin* asked it of me.

"The *Caharin* pays his own people, who have journeyed all this way, little more than passing notice, as if we were no more than fleas at which he must scratch. He asks not how we do in our homeland. He does not invite us to at long last sit with him that we might rejoice to be together. He asks not if we are at peace. He inquires not if we are fed, or if we are thirsty.

"He only shouts and argues that we are not his people because he is ignorant of the sacred laws by which we have lived for countless centuries, and dismisses those same laws solely because he was not taught their words, as if that alone makes them unimportant. Many have died by those laws so that he might learn by them and live another day.

"He gives his people no more thought than the dung beneath his boots. He turns his wife by our law away from his mind without a second thought. He treats his wife by law as a pest, to be put aside until he has want of her.

"The old laws promised us a *Caharin*. I admit they did not promise us one who would honor his people and their ways and laws that have joined us in purpose, although I thought any man would honor those who have suffered so much for him.

"I have suffered the loss of my husbands by your hand and grieved out of your sight so that you might not suffer for it. My children have endured with brave sorrow the loss of their fathers by your hand. They weep at bed for the man

324

who kissed their brow and wished them good dreams of their homeland. Yet you do not bother to ask how I fare without those husbands who I and my children loved dearly, nor do you even ask how my children fare in their heartache.

"You do not even ask how I fare without my new husband by our law while he is off acquiring other wives. You think so little of me that you bother not to mention my existence to your new wife."

Du Chaillu's chin rose with indignation.

"So, now I am permitted to speak? So, now you wish at last to hear my words after my long and difficult journey? So, now you wish to hear if I have anything worthy of your lofty ears?"

Du Chaillu spat at his feet. "You shame me."

She folded her arms and turned her back to him.

Richard stared at the back of her head. The blade masters were peering off as if deaf and wishing for little more than to spot a bird in the sky.

"Du Chaillu," Richard said, growing a bit heated himself, "don't lay the death of those people on me. I tried everything I knew to keep from having to fight them, from harming them. You know I did. I begged you to stop it. It was within your power, yet you would not halt it. I was loath to do as I did. You know I had no choice."

She glared over her shoulder. "You had choice. You could have chosen to die rather than to kill. In honor of what you had done for me, saving me from the Majendie's sacrifice, I promised you that if you did not resist, your death would be quick. It would have been your one life lost instead of thirty; if you are so noble and so concerned for preserving life, then you would have let it be so."

Richard ground his teeth and shook his finger at her. "You have your men attack me, and you expect me to simply let myself be murdered rather than defend myself? After I saved you? Had I died instead of those men, the killing would have then started in earnest! You know I brought a peace that saved many more lives. And you don't understand the first thing about the rest of it."

She huffed. "You are wrong, my husband." She turned her back again. "I understand more than you wish I did."

Cara rolled her eyes. "Lord Rahl, you really need to learn to respect your wives better, or you will never have a moment of domestic tranquillity." She spoke out of the side of her mouth as she stepped past him. "Let me speak with her—woman to woman. See if I can't smooth things over for you."

Cara hooked a hand under Du Chaillu's arm to walk her off for a private talk. Six swords cleared their scabbards. In the blink of an eye, steel was spinning in the morning light as the blade masters advanced, passing the whirling weapons back and forth from left hand to right and back again.

The Mud People hunters moved to block them. Within the space of a heartbeat, the plains had gone from uneasy peace to the brink of a bloody battle.

Richard threw up his hands. "Everyone stop!"

He moved in front of Cara and Du Chaillu, blocking the men's advance.

"Cara, let go of her. She is their spirit woman. You are not permitted to touch her. The Baka Ban Mana were persecuted and sacrificed by the Majendie for millennia. They are understandably fractious when it comes to strangers laying hands on them."

Cara released Du Chaillu's arm, but both groups of men were unwilling to be the first to back down. The Mud People had suddenly hostile strangers on their hands. The Baka Tau Mana suddenly had men about to attack them for defending their spirit woman. With all the heated blood, the risk was that someone would go for the advantage of striking first and later worry about counting the dead.

Richard held one hand up. "Listen to me! All of you!"

With his other hand, he reached out and tugged on the leather thong around Du Chaillu's neck, hoping it held under the neckline of her dress what he thought it did.

The hunters' eyes widened when Richard pulled it free and they saw the Bird Man's whistle on the end of that thong.

"This is the whistle the Bird Man gave to me." He glanced out of the corner of his eye at Kahlan and whispered for her to translate. She began talking to the hunters in the Mud People's language as Richard went on.

"You remember the Bird Man, in a gesture of peace, giving me this whistle. This woman, Du Chaillu, is a protector of her people. In the Bird Man's honor, and in his hope for peace, I gave her the whistle so she could call birds to eat the seeds her enemies planted. When her enemies feared they would have no crops and starve, they finally agreed to peace. It was the first time these two peoples ever had peace, and they all owe that peace to the great gift of the Bird Man's whistle.

"The Baka Tau Mana owe the Mud People a great debt. The Mud People also owe a debt to the Baka Tau Mana for honoring that gift as the Mud People intended it by using it to bring peace, rather than harm. The Mud People should be proud that the Baka Tau Mana would trust in the Mud People's gift to bring their families safety.

"Your two peoples are friends."

No one moved as they considered Richard's words. Finally, Jiaan put his sword over his shoulder, letting it hang behind his back by the cord around his neck. He pulled open his outfit, exposing his chest to Chandalen.

"We thank you and your people for the safety and peace brought to our people by your gift of powerful magic. We will not fight you. If you wish to take back the peace you have given us, you may strike at our hearts. We will not defend ourselves against such great peace-givers as the Mud People."

Chandalen withdrew his spear, planting the butt in the soil of his homeland. "Richard with the Temper speaks the truth. We are pleased your people used our gift as it was meant to be used—to bring peace. You will be welcomed and safe while in our homeland."

Accompanied by a lot of arm waving, Chandalen gave orders to his hunters. As all the men began standing down,

Richard at last let out his breath and thanked the good spirits for their help.

Kahlan took Du Chaillu's arm and spoke with finality. "I am going to have a talk with Du Chaillu."

The Baka Tau Mana clearly didn't like it, but were now unsure what to do about it. Richard wasn't sure if he liked the idea either. It might be the start of another war.

Reluctantly, though, he decided he had better let Kahlan have her way and talk to Du Chaillu. He could tell by the look on Kahlan's face that it wasn't his decision to make, anyway. He turned to the blade masters.

"Kahlan, my wife, is the Mother Confessor and the leader of all the people of the New World. She is to be respected as is our spirit woman, Du Chaillu. You have my word as *Caharin* that the Mother Confessor will not harm Du Chaillu. If I lie to you, you may consider my life forfeit."

The men nodded their agreement. Richard didn't know if he or Du Chaillu ranked higher in their eyes, but his calm and reassuring tone, if nothing else, helped to disarm their objections. He knew, too, that, if nothing else, these men respected him, not just because he had killed thirty of their number, but because he had done something much more difficult. He had returned them to their ancestral homeland.

Richard stood shoulder to shoulder with Cara watching Kahlan walk Du Chaillu off into the tall grass. It still glistened with droplets of water from the night's rain that had here and there left behind puddles.

"Lord Rahl," Cara asked under her breath, "do you think that is wise?"

"I trust Kahlan's judgment. We have a great deal of trouble on our hands. We don't have any time to waste."

Cara rolled her Agiel in her fingers, considering it for a long, silent moment. "Lord Rahl, if magic is failing, has yours failed yet?"

"Let's hope not."

Cara stayed close by his side as he approached the blade masters. Though he recognized several, he only knew one by name.

"Jiaan, Du Chaillu said some of your people died on your journey here."

Jiaan sheathed his sword. "Three."

"In battle?"

Looking uncomfortable, the man swiped his dark hair back off his forehead. "One. The other two . . . had accidents."

"Involving fire or water?"

Jiaan let out a heavyhearted breath. "Not water, but while standing watch one fell into the fire. He burned to death before we knew what had happened. At the time we thought he must have fallen and hit his head. From what you say, maybe this was not true. Maybe these chimes killed him?"

Richard nodded. He whispered in sorrow the name of one of the chimes of death—Sentrosi, the chime of fire. "And the third?"

Jiaan shifted his weight to his other foot. "Coming across a high trail, he suddenly thought he could fly."

"Fly?"

Jiaan nodded. "But he could fly no better than a rock."

"Maybe he lost his footing and fell."

"I saw his face just before he tried to fly. He was smiling as he did when he saw our homeland for the first time."

Again in sorrow, Richard whispered the name of the third chime. The three chimes, Reechani, Sentrosi, Vasi—water, fire, air—had claimed more lives.

"The chimes have killed Mud People, too. I had been hoping they were only here, where Kahlan and I are, but it seems the chimes are other places, too."

Over the shoulders of the six blade masters, Richard saw that the Mud People had flattened an area of grass and were preparing to start a fire in order to share a meal with their new friends.

"Chandalen!" The man looked up. "Don't start a fire."

Richard trotted over to where Chandalen and his hunters waited.

"What is the trouble?" Chandalen asked. "Why do you wish us not to have fire? As long as we are to stop here for a time, we wish to cook meat and share our food."

Richard scratched his brow. "The evil spirit that killed Juni can find people through water and fire. I'm sorry, but you need to keep your people from using fire for the time being. If you use fire you may have more evil spirits killing your people."

"Are you sure?"

Richard put a hand on Jiaan's shoulder. "These people are strong like the Mud People. On their way here, one of them was killed by an evil spirit from a fire."

Chandalen took in Jiaan's nod that it was true.

"Before we knew what was happening, he was burned alive by the fire," Jiaan said. "He was a strong man, and brave. He was not a man to be taken easily by an enemy, but we did not hear a word before he died."

Frustration tightened Chandalen's jaw as he looked out over the plains before returning his attention to Richard. "But if we cannot have fire, how are we to eat? We must bake tava bread and cook our food. We cannot eat raw dough and raw meat. The women use fire to make pottery. The men use it to make weapons. How are we to live?"

Richard let out a frustrated sigh. "I don't know, Chandalen. I only know that fire may bring the evil spirit—the chimes—again. I'm simply telling you the only thing I know to do to help keep our people safe.

"I guess you will be forced to use fire, but keep in mind the danger it may bring. If everyone knows of the danger, maybe it will be safe to use fire when you must."

"And are we not to drink for fear of going near water?"

"Chandalen, I wish I knew the answers." Richard wiped a weary hand across his face. "I only know that water, fire, and high places are dangerous. The chimes are able to use those things to harm people. The more we can stay away from them, the safer we will be."

"But even if we do this, from what you said before the chimes will still kill."

"I don't have nearly enough answers, Chandalen. I'm trying to tell you everything I can think of in order that you might help keep our people safe. There very well may be yet more dangers I don't even know about."

Chandalen put his hands on his hips as he looked out over his people's grasslands. His jaw muscles flexed as he thought on matters Richard could only guess. Richard waited silently until Chandalen spoke.

"Is it true, as you said, that a child yet to be born in our village died because of these chimes of death that are loose in the world?"

"I'm sorry, Chandalen, but I believe it is so."

His intent dark eyes met Richard's gaze. "How did these evil spirits come to be in this world?"

Richard licked the corners of his mouth. "I believe Kahlan, without realizing it or intending it, may have called them with magic in order to save my life. Because they were used to save my life, it is my fault they are here."

Chandalen considered Richard's admission. "The Mother Confessor would not intend harm. You would not intend harm. Yet it is because of you the chimes of death are here?"

Chandalen's tone had changed from confusion and alarm to authority. He was, after all, now an elder. He had a responsibility to the safety of his people that went beyond that of hunter.

In much the way the Mud People and the Baka Tau Mana shared many of the same values yet had nearly come to blows, Chandalen and Richard had at one time a fractious relationship. Fortunately, they both now understood that they shared much more in common than they disagreed about.

Richard looked out at the distant clouds and the sheets of rain lashing the dark and distant horizon. "I'm afraid that's the truth of it. Added to that, I neglected to remember valuable information to tell Zedd, when I had the chance. Now he will be gone in search of the chimes."

Chandalen again considered Richard's words before speaking.

"You are Mud People and have both struggled to protect us. We know you both did not mean to bring the chimes and cause harm."

Chandalen drew himself up tall—he didn't come up to Richard's shoulder—and delivered his pronouncement.

"We know you and the Mother Confessor both will do what you must to set this right."

Richard understood only too well the code of responsibility, obligation, and duty by which this man lived. Though he and Chandalen came from very different peoples, with very different cultures, Richard had grown up by many of the same standards. Perhaps, he thought, they weren't really that different. Maybe they wore different clothes, but they had much the same heart, the same longings, and the same desires. They shared, too, many of the same fears.

Not only Richard's stepfather but also Zedd had taught him many of the very things Chandalen's people had taught him. If you brought harm, no matter the reason, you had to set it right as best you could.

While it was understandable to be afraid, and no one would expect you not to be, the worst thing you could do was to run from the trouble you had caused. No matter how accidental it was, you didn't try to deny it. You didn't run. You did what you must to right it.

If not for Richard, the chimes would not be free. Kahlan's actions to save his life had already cost others theirs. She, too, would not waver for an instant from their duty to do whatever they could to stop the chimes. It wasn't even a question open to debate.

"You have my solemn word, Elder Chandalen. I will not rest until the Mud People and everyone else are safe from the chimes. I will not rest until the chimes are back in the underworld where they belong. Or I will die trying."

A small smile, warm with pride, crept onto Chandalen's face.

"I knew I did not need to remind you of your promise to always protect our people, but it is good to hear from your own lips that you have not forgotten your vow."

Chandalen surprised Richard with a hard slap.

"Strength to Richard with the Temper. May his anger burn hot and swift against our enemies."

Richard comforted his stinging jaw and had turned from Chandalen when he noticed Kahlan returning with Du Chaillu.

"For a woods guide," Cara said, "you manage to get yourself in a lot of trouble. Do you think you will have any wives left, now that they are finished?"

He knew Cara was only nettling him, in her odd way trying to buoy his spirits. "One, I hope."

"Well, if not," Cara said with a smirk, "we will always have each other."

Richard made for the other two women. "The position of wife is filled, thank you."

Kahlan and Du Chaillu walked side by side through the grass, their faces showing no emotion. At least he didn't see any blood.

"Your other wife has convinced me to talk to you," Du Chaillu said when Richard met them.

"You are fortunate to have us both," she added.

Richard thought better of opening his mouth, lest he allow to leap off his tongue the flip remark dancing impatiently there.

CHAPTER 31

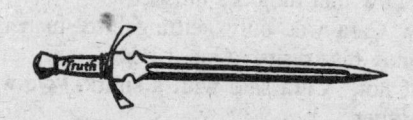

Du Chaillu walked off to her blade masters, apparently telling the men to sit and rest themselves while she spoke with the *Caharin*. While she was seeing to that, Kahlan, with the end of her finger in his ribs, prodded Richard in the direction of their gear.

"Get Du Chaillu a blanket to sit on," Kahlan murmured.

"Why does she need ours? They have their own blankets with them. Besides, she doesn't need a blanket to sit on to tell me why she's here."

Kahlan poked his ribs again. "Just get it," she said under her breath so the others wouldn't hear. "In case you hadn't noticed, the woman is pregnant and could use a rest off her feet."

"Well that doesn't—"

"Richard," Kahlan snapped, hushing him. "When you insist someone submit to your will, it is accomplished most easily if you give them a small victory so they can retain their dignity while they do as you insist. If you wish, I will carry it over to her."

"Well," Richard said, "all right, then. I guess—"

"See? You just proved it. And you will carry the blanket."

"So Du Chaillu gets a small victory, but I don't?"

"You're a big boy. Du Chaillu's price is a blanket to sit on while she tells you why she's here. The price is minuscule. Don't continue a war we have already won just to make the opponent's humiliation crushing and complete."

"But she—"

"I know. Du Chaillu was out of line in what she said to you. You know it, I know it, she knows it. But her feelings were hurt and not entirely without cause. We all make mistakes.

"She didn't understand the dimensions of the danger we have only just discovered we face. She has agreed to peace for the price of our blanket to sit upon. She only wants you to pay her a courtesy. It won't hurt you to indulge her sensibilities."

Richard glanced over his shoulder when they reached their things. Du Chaillu was speaking to the blade masters.

"You threaten her?" Richard whispered as he pulled his blanket from his pack.

"Oh yes," Kahlan whispered back. She put a hand on his arm. "Be gentle. Her ears are liable to be a bit tender after our little talk."

Richard marched over and made a show of flattening the grass and spreading his blanket on the ground before Du Chaillu. With the flat of his hand, he smoothed out the bigger wrinkles. He set a waterskin in the middle. When finished, he held out a hand in invitation.

"Please, Du Chaillu"—he couldn't make himself address her as his wife, but he didn't think that mattered—"sit and speak with me? Your words are important, and time is precious."

She inspected the way he had matted down the grass, all in one direction, and scrutinized the blanket. Satisfied with the arrangement, she sat at one end and crossed her legs under herself. With her back straight, her chin held high, and her hands clasped in her lap, she looked somehow noble. He guessed she was.

Richard flipped his golden cape back over his shoulders

and sat cross-legged at the other end of the blanket. It wasn't very big, so their knees almost touched. He smiled politely and offered her the waterskin.

As she graciously accepted the waterskin, he recalled the first time he had seen her. She had been in a collar and chained to a wall. She had been naked and filthy, and smelled as if she had been there for months, which she had, yet her bearing was such that she had somehow seemed to him just as noble as she did now, clean and dressed in her spirit-woman prayer dress.

He remembered, too, how when he had been trying to free her, she feared he was going to kill her and she had bitten him. Just recalling it, he could almost feel her teeth marks.

The troubling thought occurred to him that this woman had the gift. He wasn't sure the extent of her powers, but he could see it in her eyes. Somehow, his ability allowed him to see that timeless look in the eyes of others who were at least brushed with a dusting of the gift of magic.

Sister Verna had told Richard that she had tried little things on Du Chaillu, to test her. Verna said the spells she sent at Du Chaillu disappeared like pebbles dropped down a well, and they did not go unnoticed. Du Chaillu, Verna had said, knew what was being tried, and was somehow able to annul it.

From other things, Richard had long ago come to the realization that Du Chaillu's gift involved some primitive form of prophecy. Since she had been held in chains for months, he doubted she was able to affect the world around her with her magical ability. People whose magic could affect others in an overt manner didn't need to bite, he imagined, nor would they allow themselves to be held captive to await being sacrificed. But she was able to prevent others from using magic against her, not an uncommon form of mystical protection against the weapon of magic, Richard had learned.

With the chimes in the world of life, Du Chaillu's magic, whatever its extent, would fail, if it hadn't already. He waited until she had her drink and had handed back the waterskin before he began.

"Du Chaillu, I need—"

"Ask how are our people."

Richard glanced up at Kahlan. Kahlan rolled her eyes and gave him a nod.

Richard set down the waterskin and cleared his throat.

"Du Chaillu, I rejoice to see you are well. Thank you for considering my words of advice to keep your child. I know it is a great responsibility to raise a child. I am sure you will be rewarded with a lifetime of joy at your decision, and the child will be rewarded by your teachings. I also know my words were not as important in your decision as was your own heart."

Richard didn't have to try to sound sincere, because he truly was. "I'm sorry you had to leave your other babies to make this long and difficult journey to bring me your words of wisdom. I know you would not have undertaken such a long and arduous journey were it not important."

She waited, clearly not yet content. Richard, patiently trying to play her game, let out a breath and went on.

"Please, Du Chaillu, tell me how the Baka Tau Mana fare, now that they are returned at last to their ancestral homeland?"

Du Chaillu smiled at last with satisfaction. "Our people are well and happy in their homeland, thanks to you, *Caharin*, but we will talk of them later. I must now tell you of why I have come."

Richard made an effort to school his scowl. "I am eager to hear your words."

She opened her mouth, but then scowled herself. "Where is your sword?"

"I don't have it with me."

"Why not?"

"I had to leave it back in Aydindril. It's a long story and it isn't—"

"But how can you be the Seeker if you do not have your sword?"

337

Richard drew a breath. "The Seeker of Truth is a person. The Sword of Truth is a tool the Seeker uses, much like you used the whistle to bring peace. I can still be the Seeker without the sword, just as you can be the spirit woman without the gift of the whistle."

"It doesn't seem right." She looked dismayed. "I liked your sword. It cut the iron collar off my neck and left my head where it was. It announced you to us as the *Caharin*. You should have your sword."

Deciding that he had played her game long enough, and considering the vital matters on his mind, he leaned forward and let his scowl have its way.

"I will recover my sword as soon as I return to Aydindril. We were on our way there when we met you here. The less time I spend sitting around on a good traveling day, the sooner I will arrive in Aydindril and be able to recover my sword.

"I'm sorry, Du Chaillu, if I seemed in a rush. I mean no disrespect, but I fear for innocent lives and the lives of ones I love. It is for the safety of the Baka Tau Mana, too, that I am in a hurry.

"I would be thankful if you would tell me what you're doing here. People are dying. Some of your own people have lost their lives. I must see if there is anything I can do to stop the chimes. The Sword of Truth may help me. I need to get to Aydindril to get it. May we please get on with this?"

Du Chaillu smiled to herself, now that he had given her the proper respect. Slowly, she seemed to lose her ability to hold the smile, losing with it her bluster. For the first time, she seemed unsure, looking suddenly small and frightened.

"My husband, I had a troubling vision of you. As the spirit woman, I sometimes have such visions."

"Good for you, but I don't want to hear it."

She looked up at him. "What?"

"You said it was a vision."

"Yes."

"I don't want to hear about any visions."

338

"But—but—you must. It was a vision."

"Visions are a form of prophecy. Prophecy has yet to help me, and almost always causes me grief. I don't want to hear it."

"But visions help."

"No, they do not help."

"They reveal the truth."

"They are no more true than dreams."

"Dreams can be true, also."

"No, dreams are not true. They are simply dreams. Visions are not true, either. They are simply visions."

"But I saw you in a vision."

"I don't care. I don't want to hear it."

"You were on fire."

Richard heaved a breath. "I've had dreams where I can fly, too. That doesn't make it true."

Du Chaillu leaned toward him. "You dream you can fly? Really? You mean like a bird?" She straightened. "I have never heard of such a thing."

"It's just a dream, Du Chaillu. Like your vision."

"But I had a vision of this. That means it is true."

"Just because I can fly in my dreams, that doesn't make it true. I don't go jumping off high places and flapping my arms. It's just a dream, like your vision.

"I can't fly, Du Chaillu."

"But you can burn."

Richard put his hands on his knees and leaned back a little as he took a deep and patient breath.

"All right, fine. What else was there to this vision?"

"Nothing. That was all."

"Nothing? That was it? Me on fire? Just a little dream of me on fire?"

"Not a dream." She held up a finger to make her point. "A vision."

"And you journeyed all this way to tell me that? Well, thank you very much for coming such a distance to tell me, but we really must be on our way, now. Tell your people the *Caharin* wishes them well. Good journey home."

Richard made to look like he was going to get up.

"Unless you have something more to say?" he added.

Du Chaillu melted a little at the rebuff. "It frightened me to see my husband on fire."

"As well as it would frighten me to be on fire."

"I would not like it if the *Caharin* was on fire."

"Nor would the *Caharin* like to be on fire. So, did your vision tell you how I might avoid being on fire?"

She looked down and picked at the blanket. "No."

"You see? What good is it, then?"

"It is good to know such things," she said as she rolled a little fuzz ball across the blanket. "It might help."

Richard scratched his forehead. She was working up her courage to tell him something more important, more troubling. The vision was a pretext, he reasoned. He softened his tone, hoping to ease it out of her.

"Du Chaillu, thank you for your warning. I will keep it in mind that it might somehow help me."

She met his eyes and nodded.

"How did you find me?" he asked.

"You are the *Caharin*." She was looking noble again. "I am the Baka Tau Mana spirit woman, the keeper of the old laws. Your wife."

Richard understood. She was bonded to him, much like the D'Harans—like Cara. And like Cara, Du Chaillu could sense where he was.

"I was a day south of here. You nearly missed finding me. Have you begun to have difficulty telling where I am?"

She looked away from his eyes as she nodded. "I could always go and stand looking out at the horizon, with the breeze in my hair and the sun or stars upon my face, and I could point, and say, 'The *Caharin* is that way.' "

She took a moment to again find her voice. "It has become harder and harder to know where to point."

"We were in Aydindril until just a few days ago," Richard said. "You would have had to start on your journey long before I came to this place."

"Yes. You were not in this place when I first knew I must

come to you." She gestured over her shoulder. "You were much, much farther to the northeast."

"Why would you come here to find me if you could sense me to the northeast, in Aydindril?"

"When I began to feel you less and less, I knew that meant there was trouble. My visions told me I needed to come to you before you were lost to me. If I had traveled to where I knew you were when I started, you would not be there when I arrived. I consulted my visions, instead, while I still had them, and journeyed to where they told me you would be.

"Toward the end of our journey, I could feel you were now in this place. Soon after, I could no longer feel you. We were still a goodly distance away, so all we could do was to continue on in this direction. The good spirits answered my prayers, and allowed our paths to cross."

"I am pleased the good spirits helped you, Du Chaillu. You are a good person, and deserve their help."

She picked at the blanket again. "But my husband does not believe in my visions."

Richard wet his lips. "My father used to tell me not to eat mushrooms I found in the forest. He would say he could see me eating a poison mushroom and then getting sick and dying. He didn't really mean he could see it was going to happen, but that he feared for me. He was warning me what might happen if I ate mushrooms I didn't know."

"I understand," she said with a small smile.

"Was yours a true vision? Maybe it was a vision of something that's only possible—a vision of a danger—but not a certainty?"

"It is true some visions are of things that are possible, but not yet settled in the fates. It could be that yours was that kind."

Richard took up her hand in both of his. "Du Chaillu," he asked in a gentle voice, "please tell me now why you have come to me?"

She reverently smoothed the little colored strips running down her arm, as if reminding herself of the prayers her people sent with her. This was a woman who bore the mantle of responsibility with spirit, courage, and dignity.

"The Baka Tau Mana are joyous to be in their homeland after all these generations separated from the place of our hearts. Our homeland is all the old words passed down said it was. The land is fertile. The weather favorable. It is a good place to raise our children. A place where we can be free. Our hearts sing to be there.

"Every people should have what you have given to us, *Caharin*. Every people should be safe to live as they would."

A terrible sorrow settled through her expression. "You are not. You and your people of this land of the New World you told me about are not safe. A great army comes."

"Jagang," Richard breathed. "You had a vision of this?"

"No, my husband. We have seen it with our own eyes. I was ashamed to tell you of this, ashamed because we were so frightened by them, and I did not want to admit our fear.

"When I was chained to the wall, and I knew the Majendie would come any day to sacrifice me, I was not this frightened because it was only me, not all my people, who would die. My people were strong and they would get a new spirit woman to take my place. They would fight off the Majendie, if they came into the swamp. I could die knowing the Baka Ban Mana would live on.

"We practice every day with our weapons, so none may come and destroy us. We stand ready, as the old laws say, to do battle for our lives against any who come against us. There is no man but the *Caharin* who could face one of our blade masters.

"But no matter how good our blade masters, they could not fight an army like this. When they at last put their eye toward us, we will not be able to fight off this foe."

"I understand, Du Chaillu. Tell me what you saw?"

"What I have seen I have no way of telling you. I do not know how to tell you that you might understand how many men we have seen. How many horses. How many wagons. How many weapons.

"This army stretches from horizon to horizon for days as

they pass. They are beyond count. I could no more tell you how many blades of grass are on these plains. I have no word that can express such a vast number."

"I think you just have," Richard murmured. "They didn't attack your people, then?"

"No. They did not come through our homeland. Our fear for ourselves is but for the future, when these men decide to swallow us. Men like this will not forever leave us to ourselves. Men like these take everything; there is never enough for them.

"Our men will all die. Our children will all be murdered. Our women will all be taken. We have no hope against this foe.

"You are the *Caharin*, so you must be told these things. That is the old law.

"As spirit woman to the Baka Tau Mana, I am ashamed that I must show you my fear and tell you our people are frightened we will all perish in the teeth of this beast. I wish I could tell you we look with bravery to the jaws of death, but we do not. We look with trembling hearts.

"You are *Caharin*, you would not know. You have no fear."

"Du Chaillu," Richard said with a startled guffaw, "I'm often afraid."

"You? Never." Her gaze withdrew to the blanket. "You are just saying so that I might not be shamed. You have faced the thirty without fear and defeated them. Only the *Caharin* could do such a thing. The *Caharin* is fearless."

Richard lifted her chin. "I faced the thirty, but not without fear. I was terrified, as I am right now of the chimes, and the war facing us. Admitting your fear is not a weakness, Du Chaillu."

She smiled at his kindness. "Thank you, *Caharin*."

"The Imperial Order didn't try to attack you, then?"

"For now, we are safe. I came to warn you, because they come into the New World. They passed us by. They come for you, first."

343

Richard nodded. They were headed north, into the Midlands.

General Reibisch's army of nearly a hundred thousand men was marching east to guard the southern reaches of the Midlands. The general had asked Richard's permission not to return to Aydindril, his plan being to watch the southern passes into the Midlands, and especially the back routes into D'Hara. It made sense to Richard.

Fortune now put the man and his D'Haran army in Jagang's path.

Reibisch's force might not be large enough to take on the Imperial Order, but D'Harans were fierce fighters and would be well placed to guard the passes north. Once they knew where Jagang's forces were going, more men could be sent to join Reibisch's army.

Jagang had gifted wizards and Sisters in his army. General Reibisch had a number of the Sisters of the Light with him, too. Sister Verna—Prelate Verna, now—had given Richard her word that the Sisters would fight against the Order and the magic they used. Magic was now failing, but so would the magic of those aiding Jagang, except, perhaps, the Sisters of the Dark and the wizards with them who knew how to conjure Subtractive Magic.

General Reibisch, as well as Richard and the other generals back in Aydindril and D'Hara, had been counting on the Sisters to use their abilities to keep track of Jagang's army when it advanced into the New World, and with that knowledge, aid the D'Haran forces in selecting an advantageous place to take a stand. Now, magic was failing, leaving them blind.

Luckily, Du Chaillu and the Baka Tau Mana had kept the Order from surprising them.

"This is a great help, Du Chaillu." Richard smiled at her. "It is important news you bring. Now we know what Jagang is doing. They didn't try to come through your land, then? They simply passed you by?"

"They would have had to go out of their way to attack us now. Because of their numbers, the edges of their army

344

came near but, like a porcupine in the belly of a dog, our blade masters made it painful for them to brush against us.

"We captured some of the leaders of these dogs on two legs. They told us that for now their army was not interested in our small homeland and people, and they were content to pass us by. They hunt bigger game. But they will one day return, and wipe the Baka Tau Mana from the land."

"They told you their plans?"

"Everyone will talk, if asked properly." She smiled. "The chimes are not the only ones to use fire. We—"

Richard held up his hand. "I get the idea."

"They told us their army was going to a place that could provide them with supplies."

Richard idly stroked his lower lip as he considered that important bit of news.

"That makes sense. They've been gathering their forces in the Old World for some time. They can't stay put forever, not an army like that. An army has to be fed. An army that size would need to move, and would need supplies. A lot of supplies. The New World would offer them a tempting meal along with their conquests."

He looked up at Kahlan, standing behind his left shoulder. "Where would they likely go to find supplies?"

"There are any number of places," Kahlan said. "They could pillage from each place as they invade, getting what they need as they strike deeper into the Midlands. As long as they pick their route with that in mind, they could feed the army as they go, like a bat scooping up bugs.

"Or, they might strike at a place with larger stocks. Lifany, for example, could net them a lot of grain, Sanderia has vast sheep herds and would get them meat. If they picked targets with enough food, they could supply their army for a long time to come, allowing them the freedom to pick their targets at will, for strategic reasons alone. We would have a difficult time of it.

"If I were them, that would be my plan. Without their urgent need for food, we would be at their mercy as far as picking a place to stand against them."

"We could use General Reibisch," Richard said, thinking aloud. "Maybe he could block the Order, or at least slow them, while we evacuate people and supplies before Jagang can get to them."

"That would be a huge task, moving so many supplies. If Reibisch surprises Jagang's troops," Kahlan said, also thinking aloud, "engages him to stall their advance, and we could move enough other forces in from the sides . . ."

Du Chaillu was shaking her head. "When we were banished from our homeland by the law-givers," she said, "we were made to live in the wet place. When it rained to the north for many days, great floods came. The river overflowed its banks and spread wide.

"In its rush, churning with mud and big uprooted trees, it swept everything before it. We could not stand against the weight and fury of so much water—no one could. You think you can, until you see it coming. You find higher ground, or die.

"This army is like that. You cannot imagine how big it is."

Seeing the burden of dread in her eyes and hearing the weight of her words made gooseflesh rise on Richard's arms. Though she couldn't express the number, it was unimportant. He understood the concept as if she were somehow pouring her image and impressions of the Imperial Order directly into his mind.

"Du Chaillu, thank you for bringing us this information. You may have saved a great many lives with your words. At least, now, we won't be caught unawares—as we might well have been. Thank you."

"General Reibisch is already headed east, so we have that much in our favor," Kahlan said. "We must now get word to him."

Richard nodded. "We can take a roundabout way to Aydindril so we can meet up with him and decide what to do next. Also, we can get horses from him. That would save us time in the long run. I only wish he wasn't so far away. Time is vital."

346

After the battle in which the D'Haran army had defeated Jagang's huge expeditionary force, Reibisch had turned his army and was racing east. The D'Harans were returning to guard the routes north from the Old World, where Jagang had gathered his forces in preparation for marching into the Midlands or possibly D'Hara.

"If we can get to the general and warn him Jagang's army is coming," Cara offered, "then we could get his messengers sent off to D'Hara to call reinforcements."

"And to Kelton, Jara, and Grennidon, among others," Kahlan said. "We have a number of lands with standing armies already on our side."

Richard nodded. "That makes sense. We'll know where they're needed, at least. I just wish we could get to Aydindril faster."

"Are we sure it really even makes any difference, now?" Kahlan asked. "Remember, it's the chimes, not the Lurk."

"What Zedd asked us to do may not help," Richard said, "but then again, we don't know that for sure, do we? He might have been telling us the truth about the urgency of what we need to do, but simply cloaked it with the name Lurk instead of chimes."

"We could lose to Jagang before the chimes can get us. Dead is dead." Kahlan let out a frustrated sigh. "I don't know Zedd's game, but the truth would have served us in better stead."

"We must get to Aydindril," Richard said with finality. "That's all there is to it."

His sword was in Aydindril.

In much the same way Cara could sense him by her bond, and Du Chaillu could tell where he was, Richard had been named Seeker and was connected to the Sword of Truth. He was bonded to the blade. He felt as if something inside him was missing without it.

"Du Chaillu," Richard asked, "when this great army went past you on its way north—"

"I never said they went north."

Richard blinked. "But . . . that's where they would have

to be going. They're coming up into the Midlands—or else D'Hara. They have to come north for either."

Du Chaillu shook her head emphatically. "No. They are not going north. They went past our land on our south side, staying near the shore—turning with it, and now go west."

Richard stared dumbfounded. "West?"

Kahlan sank to her knees beside him. "Du Chaillu, are you sure?"

"Yes. We shadowed them. We had men scout in all directions, because my visions warned me these men were a great danger to the *Caharin*. Some of the men of rank we captured knew the name 'Richard Rahl.' That is why I had to come to warn you. This army knows you by name.

"You have dealt them blows and frustrated their plans. They have great hate for you. Their men told us these things."

"Could your visions of me and fire really be the fire of hatred these men have in their hearts for me?"

Du Chaillu mulled over his question. "You understand visions, my husband. It could be as you say. A vision does not always mean what it shows. It sometimes means only this thing is possible and a danger that must be watched, and it sometimes is as you say, a vision of an impression of an idea, not an event."

Kahlan reached out and snatched Du Chaillu's sleeve. "But where are they going? Somewhere they will turn north into the Midlands. Lives are at stake. Did you find out where? We must know where they will turn to the north."

"No," Du Chaillu said, looking befuddled by their surprise. "They plan on following the shoreline with the great water."

"The ocean?" Kahlan asked.

"Yes, that was their name for it. They intend to follow the great water and go to the west. The men did not know what the place they go is called, only that they are to go far to the west, to a land that has, as you said, vast supplies of food."

Kahlan let go of the woman's sleeve. "Dear spirits," she whispered, "we are in trouble."

"I'd say so," Richard said as he clenched a fist. "General Reibisch is far off to the east, and running in the wrong direction."

"Worse," Kahlan said as she turned to look southwest, as if she could see where the Order was headed.

"Of course," Richard breathed. "That's the land Zedd was talking about, near that Nareef Valley place, the isolated land to the southwest of here that grows so much grain. Right?"

"Yes," Kahlan said, still staring off to the horizon. "Jagang is headed for the breadbasket of the Midlands."

"Toscla," Richard said, remembering what Zedd had called it.

Kahlan turned back to him, nodding in resigned frustration.

"It looks that way," she said. "I never thought Jagang would go that far out of the way. I would have expected him to strike quickly into the New World, so as not to allow us time to gather our forces."

"That's what I was expecting. General Reibisch thought so, too; he's racing to guard a gate Jagang isn't going to use."

Richard tapped a finger against his knee as he considered their options. "At least it may buy us time—and now we know where the Imperial Order is going. Toscla."

Kahlan shook her head, she, too, seeming to be considering the options. "Zedd knew the place by an old name. The name of that land has changed over time. It's been known as Vengren, Vendice, and Turslan, among others. It hasn't been known as Toscla for quite some time."

"Oh," Richard said, not really listening as he started making a mental list of things they had to weigh. "So, what's it called, now?"

"Now, it's Anderith," she said.

Richard's head came up. He felt a tingling icy wave ripple

up through his thighs. "Anderith? Why? Why is it called Anderith?"

Kahlan's brow twitched at the look on his face. "It was named after one of their ancient founders. His name was Ander."

The tingling sensation raced the rest of the way up Richard's arms and back.

"Ander." He blinked at her. "Joseph Ander?"

"How do you know that?"

"The wizard called 'the Mountain'? The one Kolo said they sent to deal with the chimes?" Kahlan nodded. "That was his cognomen—what everyone called him. His real name was Joseph Ander."

CHAPTER 32

RICHARD FELT AS IF his thoughts were going to war in his head. At the same time that he groped for solutions to the spectral threat, he was assailed by the image of endless enemy soldiers pouring up from the Old World.

"All right," he said, holding his hand out to stop everyone from talking at once. "All right. Slow down. Let's just reason this out."

"The whole world might be dead from the chimes before Jagang can conquer the Midlands," Kahlan said. "We need to address the chimes above all else—you're the one who convinced me of that. It's not just that the world of life might very well need magic to survive, but we need magic to counter Jagang. He would like nothing better than for us to have to battle him by sword alone.

"We must get to Aydindril. As you yourself said, what if Zedd was telling the truth about what we need to do at the Wizard's Keep—with that bottle? If we fail to carry out our charge, we may aid the chimes in taking over the world of life. If we don't act soon enough, it may forever be too late."

"And I need my Agiel to work again," Cara said with painful impatience, "or I can't protect you both as I need to. I say we must go to Aydindril and stop the chimes."

Richard looked from one woman to the other. "Fine. But how are we going to stop the chimes if Zedd's task is only a fool's journey to keep us out of his way? What if he's just worried and wants us out of harm's way while he tries to deal with the problem himself?

"You know, like a father, when he sees a suspicious stranger approaching, might tell his children to run into the house because he needs them to count the sticks of firewood in the bin."

Richard watched both their faces sour with frustration. "I mean, it's a good piece of information that Joseph Ander was the one sent to stop the chimes, and he's the same one who founded this land of Anderith. Maybe it means something, and maybe Zedd wasn't aware of it.

"I'm not saying we should go to Anderith. The spirits know I want to get to Aydindril, too. I just want not to overlook something important." Richard pressed his fingers to his temples. "I don't know what to do."

"Then we should go to Aydindril," Kahlan said. "We know that at least has a chance."

Richard reasoned it through aloud. "That might be best. After all, what if the Mountain, Joseph Ander, stopped the chimes way in the opposite direction—at the other end of the Midlands—and afterwards, later in life, after the war or something, went on to help establish this land now called Anderith?"

"Right. Then we must get to Aydindril as soon as possible," Kahlan insisted. "And hope it will stop the chimes."

"Look," Richard said, holding up a finger to ask for patience, "I agree, but what are we going to do to stop the chimes if it's all for naught? If it's part of Zedd's trick? Then we have done nothing to stop either threat. We must consider that, too."

"Lord Rahl," Cara weighed in, "going to Aydindril would still be of value. Not only could you get your sword and try what Zedd asked of you, but you would also have Kolo's journal.

"Berdine is there. She can help you with translating it. She would be working on it while we have been gone; she may have already translated more about the chimes. She may have answers sitting there waiting for you to see them. If not, you will have the book and you know what to search for."

"That's true," Richard said. "There are other books at the Keep, too. Kolo said the chimes turned out to be much simpler to counter than they all thought."

"But they all had Subtractive Magic," Kahlan pointed out.

Richard did, too, but he knew precious little about using it. The sword was the only thing he really understood.

"Perhaps one of the books in the Wizard's Keep has the solution to dealing with the chimes," Cara said, "and maybe it isn't complicated. Maybe it doesn't take Subtractive Magic."

The Mord-Sith folded her arms with obvious distaste at the thought of magic. "Maybe you can stir your finger in the air and proclaim them gone."

"Yes, you are a magic man," Du Chaillu offered, not realizing Cara had been exercising her sarcastic wit. "You could do that."

"You give me more credit than I deserve," he said to Du Chaillu.

"It still sounds like our only real option is to go to Aydindril," Kahlan said.

Unsure, Richard shook his head. He wished it weren't so

hard to decide the right thing to do. He was balanced on a divide, leaning first one way, and then the other. He wished he had some other bit of information that would tip the balance.

Sometimes he just wished he could scream that he was only a woods guide, and didn't know what to do, and have someone who did step in and make everything look simple.

Sometimes he felt like an impostor in his role as Lord Rahl, and felt like simply giving up and going home to Westand. Now was one of those times.

He wished Zedd hadn't lied to him. Lives now hung in the balance because they didn't know the truth. And because Richard had not used Zedd's wisdom when he had the chance. If only he had used his head and remembered Du Chaillu.

"Why are you against going to Aydindril?" Kahlan asked.

"I wish I knew," Richard said. "But we do know where Jagang is going. We need to do something about it. If he conquers the Midlands, we'll be dead, beyond doing anything about the chimes."

He started pacing. "What if the chimes aren't as big a threat as we fear? I mean, in the long run, yes, of course, but what if they take years to bring about the erosion of magic that would cause any real harm? Irreversible harm? For all we know, it could take centuries."

"Richard, what's wrong with you? They're killing people now." Kahlan gestured back across the grasslands toward the Mud People's village. "They killed Juni. They killed some of the Baka Tau Mana. We have to do whatever we can to stop them. You're the one who convinced me of this."

"Lord Rahl," Cara said, "I agree with the Mother Confessor. We must go to Aydindril."

Du Chaillu stood. "May I speak, *Caharin*?"

Richard looked up from his thoughts. "Yes, of course."

She was about to do so when she paused with her mouth open. A puzzled expression came over her face. "This man who leads them, this Jagang, he is a magic man?"

"Yes. Well, in a way. He has the ability to enter the minds

of people and in that way control them. He's called a dream walker. He has no other magic, though."

Du Chaillu considered his words a moment. "An army cannot long persevere without the support of the people of their land. He controls all the people of his land, then, in this way—everyone on his side?"

"No. He can't do this with everyone at once. He must pick who he will take. Much like a blade master, in a battle, would first pick the most important targets. He picks those with magic and controls them in order to use their magic to his advantage."

"So, the witches, then, are forced to do his evil. With their magic, they hold his people by their throat?"

"No," Kahlan said from behind Richard. "The people submit willingly."

Du Chaillu looked dubious. "You believe people would choose to allow such a man to be their leader?"

"Tyrants can only rule by the consent of their people."

"Then they are bad people, too, not just him?"

"They are people like any other," Kahlan said. "Like hounds at a feast, people gather round the table of tyranny, eager for tasty scraps tossed on the floor. Not everyone will wag their tail for a tyrant, but most will, if he first makes them salivate with hate and gives license to their covetous impulses by making them feel it is only their due. Many would rather take than earn.

"Tyrants make the envious comfortable with their greed."

"Jackals," Du Chaillu said.

"Jackals," Kahlan agreed.

Disturbed at hearing such a thing, Du Chaillu's eyes turned down. "That makes it more horrible, then. I would rather think these people possessed by this man's magic, or the Keeper himself, than to think they would follow such a beast of their own will."

"You were going to say something?" Richard asked. "You said you wanted to say something. I'd like to hear it."

Du Chaillu clasped her hands before herself. Her look of

dismay was overcome by a yet graver expression.

"On our way here, we shadowed the army to see where they went. We also captured some of their men to be sure. This army travels very slowly.

"Their leader, each night, has his tents put up for him and his women. The tents are big enough to hold many people, and have many accommodations for his comfort. They also put up other tents for other important men. Each night is a feast. Their leader, Jagang, is like a great and wealthy king on a journey.

"They have wagons of women, some willing, some not. At night, all are passed around among the soldiers. This army is driven by lust for pleasure as well as conquest. They tend well to their pleasures as they go in search of conquest.

"They have much equipment. They have many extra horses. They have herds of meat on the hoof. Long trains of wagons carry food and other supplies of every kind. They have wagons with everything from flower mills to black-smith forges. They bring tables and chairs, carpets, fine plates and glassware they pack in shavings in wooden boxes. Each night they unpack it all and make Jagang's tents like a palace, surrounded by the houses of his important men.

"With their big tents and all the comforts they carry with them, it is almost like a city that travels."

Du Chaillu glided the flat of her hand through the air. "This army moves like a slow river. It takes its time, but nothing stops it. It keeps coming. Every day a little more. A city, sliding across the land. They are many, and they are slow, but they come.

"I knew I must warn the *Caharin*, so we did not want to shadow these men any longer." She turned the hand in the air, like dust stirring before a high wind. "We returned to our swift travel. The Baka Tau Mana can travel as swiftly on foot as men on running horses."

Richard had traveled with her. It was a false boast, but not by much. He had once made her ride a horse; she thought it an evil beast.

355

"As we made swift journey northwest across this vast and open land, to come here, we arrived unexpectedly at a great city with high walls."

"That would be Renwold," Kahlan said. "It's the only big city in the wilds anywhere near your route here. It has the walls you describe."

Du Chaillu nodded. "Renwold. We did not know its name." Her intense gaze, like that of a queen with grave news, moved from Kahlan to Richard. "They had been visited by the army of this man, Jagang."

Du Chaillu stared off, as if seeing it again. "I have never thought people could be that cruel to others. The Majendie, as much as we hated them, would not do such things as these men did to the people there."

Tears welled in Du Chaillu's eyes, finally overflowing to run down her cheeks. "They butchered the people there. The old, the young, the babies. But not before they spent days—"

Du Chaillu's sob broke loose. Kahlan put an understanding arm around the woman's shoulder. Du Chaillu seemed suddenly a child in Kahlan's embrace. A child who had seen too much.

"I know," Kahlan soothed, near tears along with Du Chaillu. "I know. I, too, have been to a great walled city where men who follow Jagang had been. I know the things you've seen.

"I have walked among the dead inside the walls of Ebinissia. I have seen the slaughter at the hands of the Order. I have seen what these beasts first did to the living."

Du Chaillu, the woman who led her people with grit and guts, who had faced with defiance and courage months of capture and the prospect of her imminent sacrifice, who watched her husbands die to fulfill the laws she kept, who willingly confronted death to help Richard destroy the Towers of Perdition in the hope of returning her people to their land, buried her face in Kahlan's shoulder and wept like a child at recalling what she had seen in Renwold.

The blade masters turned away rather than see their spirit

woman so heartsick. Chandalen and his hunters, waiting not far off for everyone to finish with their deliberations, also turned away.

Richard wouldn't have thought anything could bring Du Chaillu to tears in front of others.

"There was a man there," Du Chaillu said between sobs. "The only one we could find still alive."

"How did he survive?" It sounded pretty far-fetched to Richard. "Did he say?"

"He was crazy. He wailed to the good spirits for his family. He cried endlessly for what he said was his folly, and asked the spirits to forgive him and return his loved ones.

"He carried the rotting head of a child. He talked to it, as if it were alive, begging its forgiveness."

Kahlan's face took on a saddened aspect. Slowly, with apparent reluctance, she said, "Did he have long white hair? A red coat, with gold braiding at the shoulders?"

"You know him?" Du Chaillu asked.

"Ambassador Seldon. He didn't live through the attack—he wasn't there when it came. He was in Aydindril."

Kahlan looked up at Richard. "I asked him to join us. He refused, saying he believed the same as the assembly of seven, that his land of Mardovia would be vulnerable if they joined with one side or the other. He refused to join us or the Order, saying they believed neutrality was their safety."

"What did you tell him?" Richard asked.

"Your words—your decree that there are no bystanders in this war. I told him that as Mother Confessor, I have decreed no mercy against the Order. I told Ambassador Seldon we were of one mind in this, you and I, and that his land was either with us, or stood against us, and that the Imperial Order would view it the same way.

"I tried to tell him what would happen. He wouldn't listen. I begged him to consider the lives of his family. He said they were safe behind the walls of Renwold."

"I wouldn't wish that lesson on anyone," Richard whispered.

Du Chaillu sobbed anew. "I pray the head was not his

own child. I wish I did not see it in my dreams."

Richard's touch was gentle on Du Chaillu's arm. "We understand, Du Chaillu. The Order's terror is a calculated means of demoralizing future victims, of intimidating them into surrender. This is why we fight these people."

Du Chaillu looked up at him, wiping her cheek with the back of her hand as she sniffed back the tears.

"Then I ask you to go to this place the Order goes to. Or at least send someone to warn them. Have the people there flee before they are tortured and butchered like those we saw in this place, Renwold. These Ander people must be warned. They must flee."

Her tears returned, accompanied by racking sobs. Richard watched as she wandered off into the grass to weep in private.

Richard felt Kahlan's hand settle on his shoulder, and turned back. "This land, Anderith, hasn't surrendered to us yet. They had representatives in Aydindril to hear our side of it, didn't they? They know our position?"

"Yes," Kahlan said. "Their representatives were warned the same as those of other lands. They were told of the threat and that we mean to stand against it.

"Anderith knows the alliance of the Midlands is a thing of the past, and we expect the surrender of their sovereignty to the D'Haran Empire."

"D'Haran Empire." The words seemed so harsh, so cold. Here he was, a woods guide, feeling like an impostor on some throne he wasn't even sure existed except in title, responsible for an empire. "Not that long ago I was terrified of D'Hara. I feared they would have all the lands. Now that's our only hope."

Kahlan smiled at the irony. "Its name, D'Hara, is the only thing the same, Richard. Most people know you fight for people's freedom, not their enslavement. Tyranny now wears the iron cloak of the Imperial Order.

"Anderith knows the terms, the same as we've given every land, that if they join us willingly they will be one people with us, entitled to the same equal and honest treatment as everyone and governed by fair and just laws we all obey. They know there are no exceptions. And they know the sanctions and consequences should they fail to join us."

"Renwold was told the same," he reminded her. "They didn't believe us."

"Not all are willing to face the truth. We can't expect it, and must concern ourselves with those who share our conviction to fight for freedom. You can't sacrifice good people, Richard, and risk a just cause, for those who will not see. To do that would be a betrayal to those with brave hearts who have joined us, and to whom you are responsible."

"You're right." Richard released a pent-up sigh. He felt the same, but it was a comfort to hear it from her. "Does Anderith have a large army?"

"Well . . . yes," Kahlan said. "But the real defense for Anderith is not their army. It's a weapon called the Dominie Dirtch."

While he thought the name sounded like High D'Haran, with everything else on his mind the translation didn't immediately spring to mind.

"Is it something we can use to stop the Order?"

Staring off, deep in thought as she considered his question, Kahlan plucked the tops of the grass.

"It's an ancient weapon of magic. With the Dominie Dirtch, Anderith has always been virtually immune to attack. They are part of the Midlands because they need us as trading partners, need a market for the vast quantities of food they grow. But with the Dominie Dirtch they're nearly autonomous, almost outside the alliance of the Midlands.

"It's always been a tenuous relationship. As Mother Confessors before me, I forced them to accept my authority and abide by the rulings of the Council if they were to sell their goods. Still, the Anders are a proud people, and always thought of themselves as separate, better than others."

"That's what they may think, but not what I think—and not what Jagang will think. So what about this weapon? Could it stop the Imperial Order, do you think?"

"Well, it hasn't had to be used on a big scale for centuries." Kahlan brushed the head of a stalk of grass across her chin as she thought it over. "But I can't imagine why not. Its effectiveness discourages any attack. At least in ordinary times. Since the last large conflict, it's only been used in relatively minor troubles."

"What is this protection?" Cara asked. "How does it work?"

"The Dominie Dirtch is a string of defense not far in from their borders with the wilds. It's a line of huge bells, spaced far apart, but within sight of one another. They stand guard across the entire Anderith frontier."

"Bells," Richard said. "How do these bells protect them? You mean they're used to warn people? To call their troops?"

Kahlan waved her stalk of grass the way an instructor might wave a switch to dissuade a student from getting the wrong idea. Zedd used to wave his finger in much the same way, adding that impish smile so as not to give Richard a harsh impression as he was being corrected. Kahlan, though, was not correcting, but schooling, and as far as the Midlands were concerned, Richard was still very much a student.

The word "schooling" stuck in his head as soon as it crossed his mind.

"Not that kind of bell," Kahlan said. "They don't really look much like bells, other than their shape. They're carved from stone that over the ages has become encrusted with lichen and such. They are like ancient monuments. Terrible monuments.

"Jutting up as they do from the soil of the plains, marching off in a line to the horizon, they almost look like the vertebra of some huge, dead, endlessly long monster."

Richard scratched his jaw in wonder. "How big are they?"

"They stand up above the grass and wheat on these fat stone pedestals, maybe eight or ten feet across." She passed her hand over her head. "The pedestals are about as tall as we are. Steps going up the bell itself are cut into each base. The bells are, I don't know, eight, nine feet tall, including the carriage.

"The back of each bell, carved as part of the same stone, is round . . . like a shield. Or a little like a wall lamp might have a reflector behind it. The Anderith army mans each bell at all times. When an enemy approaches, the soldier, when given the order, stands behind the shield, and the Dominie Dirtch—these bells—are then struck with a long wooden striker.

"They emit a very deep knell. At least behind the Dominie Dirtch it's said to be a deep knell. No one attacking has ever lived to say what it sounds like from that side, from the death zone."

Richard had gone from simple wonder to astonishment. "What do the bells do to the attackers? What does this sound do?"

Kahlan rolled the heads of the grass in her fingers, crumbling them.

"It sloughs the flesh right off the bones."

Richard couldn't even imagine such a horrific thing. "Is this a legend, do you think, or do you know it to be a fact?"

"I once saw the results—some primitive people from the wilds intent on a raid as retribution for harm to one of their women by an Anderith soldier."

She shook her head despondently. "It was a grisly sight, Richard. A pile of bloody bones in the middle of a, a . . . gory heap. You could see hair in it—parts of scalp. And the clothes. I saw some fingernails, and the whorled flesh from a fingertip, but I could recognize little else. Except for those few bits, and the bones, you wouldn't even know it had been human."

"That would leave no doubt; the bells use magic," Richard said. "How far out does it kill? And how quickly?"

"As I understand it, the Dominie Dirtch kill every person in front of them for about as far as the eye can see. Once they're rung, an invader takes only a step or two before their skin undergoes catastrophic ruptures. Muscle and flesh begin coming away from bone. Their insides—heart, lungs, everything—drops from under the rib cage as their intestines all

361

give way. There is no defense. Once begun, all before the Dominie Dirtch die."

"Can an invader sneak up at night?" Richard asked.

Kahlan shook her head. "The land is flat so the defenders are able to see for miles. At night torches can be lit. Additionally, a trench extends in front of the entire line so no one can crawl up unseen through the grass or wheat. As long as the line of Dominie Dirtch is manned, there's no way to get past it. At least, it has been thousands of years since anyone has gotten past."

"Does the number of invaders matter?"

"From what I know of it, the Dominie Dirtch could kill any number gathered together and marched toward Anderith, toward those stone bells, as long as the defending soldiers kept ringing them."

"Like an army . . ." Richard whispered to himself.

"Richard, I know what you're thinking, but with the chimes loose, magic is failing. It would be a foolhardy risk to depend on the Dominie Dirtch to stop Jagang's army."

Richard watched Du Chaillu off in the grass, her head in her hands as she wept.

"But you said Anderith also has a large army."

Kahlan sighed impatiently. "Richard, you promised Zedd we would go to Aydindril."

"I did. But I didn't promise him when."

"You implied it."

He turned back to face her. "It wouldn't break the promise to go somewhere else first."

"Richard—"

"Kahlan, maybe with magic failing, Jagang sees this as his chance to successfully invade Anderith and capture its stores of food."

"That would be bad for us, but the Midlands has other sources of food."

"And what if food isn't the only reason Jagang is going to Anderith?" He cocked an eyebrow. "He has people with the gift. They would know as well as Zedd and Ann that magic was failing. What if they could figure out it was the chimes? What if Jagang saw this as his chance to take a formerly invincible land, and then, if things change, if the chimes are banished . . . ?"

"He would have no way of knowing it was the chimes, but even if he did, how could he know what to do to banish them?" ·

"He has some gifted people with him. Gifted from the Palace of the Prophets. Those men and women have studied the books in the vaults there. For hundreds of years they've studied those books. I can't imagine how much they know. Can you?"

The emerging possibilities and implications etched alarm into Kahlan's face. "You think they may have a way to banish the chimes?"

"I have no idea. But if they did—or went to Anderith and there uncovered the solution—think about what it would mean. Jagang's army, en masse, would be in the Midlands, behind the Dominie Dirtch, and there wouldn't be anything we could do to rout them.

"At their will, they could, where and when they wish, charge into the Midlands. Anderith is a big land. With the Dominie Dirtch in his control, we would be unable to scout beyond the border and so would have no idea where his troops were massing. We couldn't possibly begin to guard the entire border, yet his spies would be able to sneak out to detect where our armies waited, and then slip back in to report to Jagang.

"He could then race out through holes in a net spread too thin and drive his attack into the Midlands. If need be, they could strike a blow and then withdraw back behind the Dominie Dirtch. If he used just a little planning and patience, he could wait until he found a weak place, with our troops too distant to respond in time, and then his entire army could roar through gaps in our lines and into the Midlands. Once past our forces, they could rampage virtually unchecked, with us only able to nip at their heels as we chased after them.

"Once ensconced behind the stone curtain of the Dominie

Dirtch, time would be on his side. He could wait a week, a month, a year. He could wait ten years, until we became dull and weak from bearing the weight of constant vigilance. Then, he could suddenly burst out upon us."

"Dear spirits," Kahlan whispered. She gave him a sharp look. "This is all just speculation. What if they don't really have a way to banish the chimes?"

"I don't know, Kahlan. I'm just saying 'What if?' We have to decide what to do. If we decide wrong, we could lose it all."

Kahlan let out a breath. "You're right about that."

Richard turned and watched Du Chaillu kneel down. Her hands were folded, her head bowed, in what looked to be earnest prayer.

"Does Anderith have any books, any libraries?"

"Well, yes," Kahlan said. "They have a huge Library of Culture, as they call it."

Richard lifted an eyebrow. "If there is an answer, why does it have to be in Aydindril? In Kolo's journal? What if the answer, if there is one, is in their library?"

"If there really is an answer in some book." Wearily, Kahlan gripped a handful of her long hair hanging down over her shoulder. "Richard, I agree that all of this is worrisome, but we have a duty to others to act responsibly. Lives, nations are at stake. If it came down to a sacrifice of one land to save the rest, I would reluctantly, and with great sorrow, leave that land to their fate while I did my duty to the greater number.

"Zedd told us we had to get to Aydindril in order to reverse the problem. He may have called it by another name, but the problem is much the same. If doing as he asked will stop the chimes, then we must do it. We have a duty to act in our best judgment to the benefit of all."

"I know." The millstone of responsibility could be unnerving. They needed to go both places. "There's just something about this whole thing that's bothering me, and I can't figure it out. Worse, I fear the lives it will cost if we make the wrong choice."

Her fingers closed around his arm. "I know, Richard."

He threw up his hands and turned away. "I really need to take a look at that book, *Mountain's Twin*."

"But didn't Ann say she wrote in her journey book to Verna, and Verna said it had been destroyed?"

"Yes, so there's no way—" Richard spun back to her. "Journey book." A flash of realization ignited. "Kahlan, the journey books are how the Sisters communicate when one goes on a long journey away from the others."

"Yes, I know."

"The journey books were made for them by the wizards of old—back in the time of the great war."

Her face twisted with a puzzled frown. "And?"

Richard made himself blink. "The books are paired. You can only communicate with the *twin* of the one you have."

"Richard I don't see—"

"What if the wizards used to do the same thing? The Wizard's Keep in Aydindril was always sending wizards off on missions. What if that's how they knew what was going on everywhere? How they coordinated everything? What if they used them just like the Sisters of the Light used them? After all, wizards of that time created the spell around the Palace of the Prophets and created the journey books for the Sisters to use."

She was frowning. "I'm still not sure I understand—"

Richard gripped her shoulders. "What if the book that was destroyed, *Mountain's Twin*, is a journey book? The twin to Joseph Ander's journey book?"

CHAPTER 33

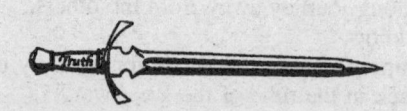

KAHLAN WAS SPEECHLESS.

Richard squeezed her shoulders. "What if the other, Joseph Ander's half of that pair, still exists?"

She wet her lips. "It's possible they might keep something like that in Anderith."

"They must. They revere him—after all, they named their land in his honor. It seems only logical that if it still existed they would keep such a book."

"It's possible. But that isn't always the way, Richard."

"What do you mean?"

"Sometimes a person isn't appreciated in his own time. Sometimes they aren't recognized as important until much later, and sometimes then only to promote the contemporary causes of those currently in power. Evidence of a person's true thoughts can be an inconvenience in such cases, and sometimes is destroyed.

"Even if that isn't the case, and they did respect his thinking, the land changed its name to Anderith since Zedd left the Midlands. Sometimes people are revered because not enough remains of their philosophy for people to find objectionable, and so the person can become valuable as a symbol. Most likely nothing of Joseph Ander's remains."

Taken aback by the logic of her words, Richard rubbed his chin as he considered.

"The other unknown," he finally said, "is that words written in journey books can be wiped away, to make room for new communications. Even if everything I'm thinking is true, and he wrote back to the Keep with the solution to the chimes, the book still exists, and it's actually in Anderith, it still might do us no good, because that passage could easily have been wiped clean to make room for a future message.

"But," he added, "it's the only solid possibility we have."

"No, it isn't," Kahlan insisted. "Another choice and the one with more weight of credibility on its side, is what we must do back at the Wizard's Keep."

Richard felt himself drawn inexorably toward Joseph Ander's legacy. If he had any proof that his attraction to it wasn't simply his imagination, he would have been convinced.

"Kahlan, I know . . ."

His voice trailed off. The hairs at the back of his neck began rising, prickling his neck like needles of ice. His golden cloak lifted lethargically in the lazy breeze. The slow wave billowing through it cracked like a whip when it reached the corner. The skin on his arms danced with gooseflesh.

Richard felt the gossamer fingers of wickedness slipping up his spine.

"What's the matter?" Kahlan asked, consternation chilling her expression.

Without answering, gripped by dread, he turned and scanned the grassland. Emptiness stared back. Verdant waves rippled before him, painted with bold strokes of sunlight. In the distance knots of dark clouds at the horizon boiled from within with flickering light. Even though he couldn't hear the thunder, every now and again he could feel the drumbeat underfoot.

"Where's Du Chaillu?"

Cara, standing a few paces away as she kept an eye on the idle men, pointed. "I saw her off that way a few minutes ago."

Richard searched but didn't see her. "Doing what?"

"She was crying. Then I think she looked like she might have been going to sit down for a rest, or maybe to pray."

That was what Richard had seen, too.

He called out Du Chaillu's name over the grasslands. In the distance, a meadowlark's crystalline song warbled across the vast silence of the plains. He cupped his hands beside his mouth and called again. The blade masters, when there was no answer the second time, sprang to action, fanning out into the grass to search.

Richard trotted off in the direction Cara had pointed, the direction he, too, remembered last seeing her. Kahlan and Cara were right on his heels as he picked up speed, cutting through the tall grass and splashing through puddles. The blade masters and hunters searched as they ran, and with no reply as all called Du Chaillu's name, their search became frantic.

The grass, a singular, undulating, sentient thing alive with mocking contempt, teased them with bowing nods to draw the eye first here, and then there, hinting but never divulging where it hid her.

Out of the side of his vision, Richard caught sight of a dark shape, distinct from the mellow green of new grass rising and falling above the washed-out tan of the lifeless stalks beneath the waves. He cut to the right, muddling leadenly through a spongy area where the mat of grass, as if it floated on a sea of mud, kept giving way beneath his feet.

The ground firmed. He spotted the out-of-place dark shape and altered his course slightly as he splashed through an expanse of standing water.

Richard came suddenly upon her. Du Chaillu reposed in the grass, looking like she might be sleeping, her dress smoothed down to the backs of her knees, her legs below it a pasty white.

She was facedown in water only inches deep.

Racing through the wet grass, Richard dove over her to avoid falling on her. He snatched the shoulders of her dress and yanked her back, rolling her onto her back on the grass beside him. The front of her sodden dress plastered itself across her pronounced pregnancy. Strings of wet hair lay across her bloodless face.

Du Chaillu stared up with dark dead eyes.

She had that same odd, lingering look of lust in her eyes Juni had had when Richard found him drowned in the shallow stream.

Richard shook her limp body. "No! Du Chaillu! No! I saw you alive only a minute ago! You can't be dead! Du Chaillu!"

Her mouth slack, her arms splayed clumsily, she exhibited no response. There was no response to show. She was gone.

When Kahlan put a comforting hand on his shoulder, he fell back with an angry cry of anguish.

"She was just alive," Cara said. "I just saw her alive only moments ago."

Richard buried his face in his hands. "I know. Dear spirits, I know. If only I'd realized what was happening."

Cara pulled his hands away from his face. "Lord Rahl, her spirit might still be with her body."

Blade masters and Mud People hunters were tumbling to their knees all around.

Richard shook his head. "I'm sorry, Cara, but she's gone." Stark, taunting memories of her alive cavorted unbidden through his mind.

"Lord Rahl—"

"She's not breathing, Cara." He reached to close her eyes. "She's dead."

Cara gave his wrist a fierce tug. "Did Denna not teach you? A Mord-Sith would teach her captive to share the breath of life!"

Richard grimaced away from Cara's blue eyes. It was a gruesome rite, the sharing of pain in that way. The memory flooded through him with horror to match that of Du Chaillu's death.

A Mord-Sith shared her victim's breath while he was on the cusp of death. It was a sacred thing to a Mord-Sith to share his pain, share his breath of life as he slipped to the brink of death, as if to view with lust the forbidden sight of what lies beyond in the next world. Sharing, when the time came to kill him, his very death by experiencing his final breath of life.

Before Richard killed his mistress in order to escape, she had asked him to share her last breath of life.

Richard had honored her last wish, and had taken into himself Denna's last breath as she died.

"Cara, I don't know what that has to do with—"

"Give it back to her!"

Richard could only stare. "What?"

Cara growled and stiff-armed him out of her way. She dropped down beside the body and put her mouth over Du Chaillu's. Richard was horrified by what Cara was doing. He thought he had managed to give the Mord-Sith more respect for life than this.

The sight staggered him with the obscene memory, seeing it new again before his eyes, seeing her crave that corrupt intimacy again. It stunned him to see Cara covet something so ghastly from her past. It angered him she had not risen above her brutal training and way of life, as he had hoped for her.

Pinching Du Chaillu's nose, Cara blew a breath into the dead woman. Richard reached for Cara's broad shoulders to rip her away from Du Chaillu. It enraged him to see it, to see a Mord-Sith do such a thing to the freshly dead.

He paused, his hands floating there above her.

Something in Cara's urgency, in her demeanor, told him all was not what it had at first seemed. With one hand under Du Chaillu's neck and the other holding her nose closed, Cara blew another breath. Du Chaillu's chest rose with it, and then slowly sank again as Cara took another for herself.

A blade master, his face red with rage, reached for Cara, since Richard seemed to have changed his mind. Richard caught the man's wrist. He met Jiaan's questioning eyes and simply shook his head. Reluctantly, Jiaan withdrew.

"Richard," Kahlan whispered, "what in the world is she doing? Why would she do such a grotesque thing? Is it some kind of D'Haran ritual for the dead?"

Cara took a deep breath and blew it into Du Chaillu.

"I don't know," Richard whispered back. "But it's not what I thought."

Kahlan looked even more bewildered. "And what could you have possibly thought?"

Unwilling to put such a thing into words, he could only stare into her green eyes. He could hear Cara blow another deep breath into Du Chaillu's lifeless corpse.

He turned away, unable to watch. He couldn't understand what good Cara thought she was doing, but he couldn't sit there while others watched.

He tried to convince himself that, as Kahlan had suggested, perhaps it was some D'Haran ritual to the departing spirit. Richard staggered to his feet. Kahlan caught his hand.

He heard a wet sputtering cough.

Richard swung back around and saw Cara hauling Du Chaillu over onto her side. Du Chaillu gasped with a choking breath. Cara slapped the woman's back as if she were burping a baby, but with more force.

Du Chaillu coughed and gasped and panted. Then she threw up. Richard fell to his knees and held her thick mass of dark hair out of her way as she vomited.

"Cara, what did you do?" Richard was dumbfounded to see a dead woman come back to life. "How did you do that?"

Cara thumped Du Chaillu's back, making her cough out more water. "Did Denna not teach you to share the breath of life?" She sounded annoyed.

"Yes, but, but it wasn't . . ."

Du Chaillu clutched at Richard's arm as she panted and spat up more water. Richard stroked her hair and back in a comforting manner to let her know they were there with her. The squeeze on his arm told him she knew.

"Cara," Kahlan asked, "what have you done? How did

you bring her back from death? Was it magic?"

"Magic!" Cara scoffed. "No, not magic. Not anything near magic. Her spirit had not yet left her body, that's all. Sometimes, if their spirit has not had time to leave their body, you still have time. But it must be done immediately. If so, you can sometimes give them back the breath of life."

The men gestured wildly as they all jibber-jabbered excitedly to one another. They had just witnessed a marvel that was sure to be the birth of a legend. Their spirit woman had traveled to the world of the dead—and returned.

Richard stared slack-jawed at Cara. "You can? You can give dead people back the breath of life?"

Kahlan whispered encouragement as she picked wet strands of hair from Du Chaillu's face. She had to stop and hold back the hair when the woman's coughing was interrupted by another bout of heaving. As grim and sick as Du Chaillu looked, she was breathing better.

Kahlan took a blanket the men handed down and wrapped it around Du Chaillu's shivering shoulders. Cara leaned close to Richard, so no one else would hear.

"How do you think Denna kept you from death for so long when she tortured you? There was no one better at it than Denna. I am Mord-Sith, I know what would have been done to you, and I knew Denna. There would have been times she had to do this to keep you from dying when she was not yet finished with you. But it would have been blood, not water."

Richard remembered that, too—coughing up frothy blood as if he were drowning in it. Denna was Darken Rahl's favorite, because she was the best; it was said she could keep her captive alive and on the cusp of death longer than any other Mord-Sith. This was part of how she did that.

"But I never thought . . ."

Cara frowned. "You never thought what?"

Richard shook his head. "I never thought such a thing was possible. Not after the person had died." After she had just done something noble, he didn't have the heart to tell

372

Cara he had thought she was sating some grisly appetite from her past. "You did a miraculous thing, Cara. I'm proud of you."

Cara scowled. "Lord Rahl, stop looking at me like I am a great spirit come to our world. I am Mord-Sith. Any Mord-Sith could have done this. We all know how."

She snatched his shirt collar and pulled him closer. "You know of it, too. Denna taught you, I know she did. You could have done this as easily as I."

"I don't know, Cara, I've only taken the breath of life. I've never given it."

She released his collar. "It is the same thing, just in the other direction."

Du Chaillu sprawled herself across Richard's lap. He smoothed her hair with gentle empathy. She clutched at his belt, his shirt, his waist, holding on for dear life, as he tried to keep her calm.

"My husband," she managed between gasping and coughing, "you saved me . . . from the kiss of death."

Kahlan was holding one of Du Chaillu's hands. Richard took the other and placed it on a leg sheathed in leather.

"Cara is the one who saved you, Du Chaillu. Cara gave you back the breath of life."

Du Chaillu's fingers kneaded at Cara's leather-clad leg, groping their way up until she found Cara's hand.

"And the *Caharin*'s baby. . . . You saved us both. . . . Thank you, Cara." She gasped another rattling breath. "Richard's child will live because of you. Thank you."

Richard didn't think it the proper time to point out paternity.

"It was nothing. Lord Rahl would have done it, but I was closer and beat him to it."

Cara briefly squeezed the hand before standing to make way for some of the grateful blade masters to get close to their spirit woman.

"Thank you, Cara," Du Chaillu repeated.

Cara's mouth twisted with the distaste of people appreciating her for having done something compassionate. "We are all glad your spirit had not yet left you, so you could stay, Du Chaillu. Lord Rahl's baby, too."

CHAPTER 34

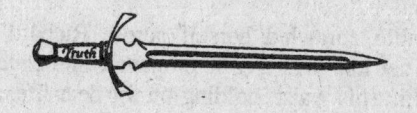

NOT FAR OFF, DU Chaillu was being tended to by the blade masters and most of the hunters. The Baka Tau Mana spirit woman had returned from the spirit world, or near to it, and Richard could see she had left behind her warmth. The blankets were insufficient, so Richard had told the men they could make a fire to help warm her if they all stayed together to reduce the chances of any surprises.

Two of the Mud People cleared grass and dug a shallow pit while the other hunters made tightly wound grass billets. Twisting wrung out most of the moisture. They coated four of the grass bundles in a resinous pitch they carried with them and then stacked them in a pyramid. With those burning, they windrowed the rest of the grass billets around the little fire to dry them out. In short order they had dry grass for firewood and a good fire going.

Du Chaillu looked like death warmed up a bit. She was still very sick. At least she was alive. Her breathing was better, if interrupted by coughing. The blade masters were seeing to it that she drank hot tea while the hunters-turned-mother-hens cooked her up some tava porridge. It appeared she would recover and remain in the world of life for the time being.

Richard found it miraculous to think a person could come alive again after dying. Had someone told him such a thing, instead of him seeing it himself, he doubted he would have believed them. In more ways than one, his beliefs had been skewed and his thinking altered.

Richard no longer had any doubt as to what they must do.

Cara, arms folded, watched the men as they took care of Du Chaillu. Kahlan, too, was watching with fascination equal to any of the rest of them—except Cara; she didn't think it was at all out of the ordinary for a dead person to breathe again. What was ordinary for a Mord-Sith seemed very different from what others thought ordinary.

Richard gently took ahold of Kahlan's arm and pulled her closer. "Before, you said no one had gotten past the Dominie Dirtch in centuries. Did someone once get past them?"

Kahlan turned her attention to him. "It's unclear and a matter of dispute, outside of Anderith, anyway."

Ever since it had first been mentioned by Du Chaillu, Richard had gotten the feeling Anderith wasn't Kahlan's favorite place.

"How so?"

"It's a story requiring some explanation."

Richard pulled three pieces of tava bread from his pack and handed one each to Cara and Kahlan. He settled his gaze on Kahlan's face.

"I'm listening."

Kahlan twisted a small chunk off her tava bread, apparently pondering how to begin.

"The land now known as Anderith was once invaded by people known as the Hakens. The people of Anderith teach that the Hakens used the Dominie Dirtch against the people who were then living there, those people now called the Anders.

"When I was young and studied at the Keep, the wizards

375

taught me differently. Either way, it was many centuries ago; history has a way of getting muddled by those controlling the teaching of it. For example, I would venture the Imperial Order will teach a very different account of Renwold than we would teach."

"I'd like to hear about Anderith history," he said as she ate the chunk of tava bread she had torn off. "About the history as the wizards taught you."

Kahlan swallowed before she began. "Well, centuries ago—maybe as long as two to three thousand years ago—the Haken people came out of the wilds and invaded Anderith. It's thought they were a remote people whose land possibly became unsuitable for some reason. Such a thing has happened in other places, for example when a river's course is changed by an earthquake or flood. Sometimes a formerly productive area will become too dry to support farming or animals. Sometimes crops fail and people will migrate.

"Anyway, according to what I was taught, the Hakens somehow made it past the Dominie Dirtch. How, no one knows. Many of them were slaughtered, but they somehow finally made it past and conquered the land now known as Anderith.

"The Anders were a mostly nomadic people, composed of tribes who fought fiercely among themselves. They were uneducated in things like written language, metalworking, construction, and such, and they had little social organization. In short, compared to the Haken invaders they were a backward people. It wasn't that they weren't smart, just that the Hakens were a people possessed of advanced learning and methods.

"Haken weapons were also superior. They had cavalry for example, and they had a better grasp of coordination and tactics on a large scale. They had a clear command structure whereas the Anders bickered endlessly over who would direct their forces. That was one reason the Hakens, once past the Dominie Dirtch, were easily able to bring the Anders to heel."

Richard handed Kahlan a waterskin. "The Hakens were a people of war and conquest, I take it. They lived by conquest?"

Kahlan wiped water that was dribbling down her chin. "No, they weren't the type to conquer simply for booty and slaves. They didn't make war for mere predation.

"They brought with them their knowledge of everything from making leather shoes to working iron. They were a literate people. They had an understanding of higher mathematics and how to apply it to endeavors such as architecture.

"Their core skill was farming on a large scale, with plows pulled by oxen and horses, rather than hand-hoed gardens like the Anders kept to supplement their hunting and gathering of things growing wild. The Hakens created irrigation systems and introduced rice in addition to other crops. They knew how to develop and select better strains of crops, such as wheat, to give them the best use of land and weather. They were experts at horse breeding. They knew how to breed better livestock and raised vast herds."

Kahlan handed back the waterskin and ate a bite of tava bread. She gestured with the half-eaten tava.

"As is the way of conquest, the Hakens ruled as victors often do. Haken ways supplanted Ander ways. Peace came to the land, albeit peace enforced by Haken overlords. They were harsh, but not brutal; rather than slaughtering the Anders as was the custom of many conquering invaders, they enfolded the Anders into Haken society, even if it was at first as cheap labor."

Richard spoke with his mouth full. "The Anders, too, benefited from the Haken ways, then?"

"Yes. Under direction of the Haken overlords, food was plentiful. Both the Haken and the Ander people prospered. The Anders had been a sparse population always on the brink of vanishing. With abundant food the population multiplied."

When Du Chaillu fell to a coughing fit, they turned to her. Richard squatted and dug through his pack until he found a cloth packet Nissel had given them. Unrolling it, he found inside some of the leaves Nissel had once given him to calm pain. Kahlan pointed out the ground herbs supposed to settle the stomach. He tied some into a cloth and handed the bag of ground herbs to Cara.

"Tell the men to put this in the tea and let it steep for a bit. It will help her stomach. Tell Chandalen that Nissel gave it to us—he can explain it to Du Chaillu's men, so they won't worry."

Cara nodded. He put the leaves in her palm. "Tell her that after she drinks the tea, she should chew one of these leaves. It will calm her pain. Later, if she is sick at her stomach again, or in pain, she can chew another."

Cara hurried to the task.

Cara would likely not admit it, but Richard knew she would appreciate the satisfaction of giving assistance to someone in need. He couldn't imagine how much greater the satisfaction would be to bring a person back to life.

"So, what happened then, with the Hakens and the Anders? Everything went well? The Anders learned from the Hakens?" He picked up his tava bread for a bite. "Brotherhood and peace?"

"For the most part. The Hakens brought with them orderly rule, where before the Anders squabbled among themselves, often leading to bloody conflicts. The invading Hakens had actually killed fewer Anders than the Anders themselves regularly killed in their own territorial wars. At least, so said the wizards who taught me.

"Though I'm not saying it was by any means entirely fair or equitable, the Hakens did have a system of justice; it was more than the simple mob rule of the Anders, or the right of the strongest. Once they had conquered the Anders and shown them their ways, they taught the Anders to read."

"The Anders, who had been a backward people, may have been ignorant, but they are a very clever people. They may not devise things on their own, but they are quick to grasp a better way and make it their own on a whole new scale. In that way, they are brilliant."

378

Richard waved his rolled up tava bread. "So, why isn't it called Hakenland, or something? I mean, you said the vast majority of people in Anderith are Haken."

"That's later. I'm coming to it." Kahlan pulled off another chunk of tava. "The way the wizards explained it to me was that the Hakens had a system of justice, which, once they settled in Anderith, and with the spreading prosperity, only became better."

"Justice, from the invaders?"

"Civilization does not unfold fully developed, Richard. It's a building process. Part of that process is the mixing of peoples, and that mixing is often via conquest, but it can often bring new and better ways. You can't impulsively judge situations by such simple criteria as invasion and conquest."

"But if one people comes in and forces another people—"

"Look at D'Hara. Because of conquest—by you—it is coming to be a place of justice, where torture and murder are no longer the way of rule."

Richard wasn't about to argue that point. "I suppose. But it just seems such a shame for a culture to be destroyed by another that invades them. It isn't fair."

She gave him one of her looks akin to looks Zedd sometimes gave him: a look that said she hoped he would see truth rather than repeat by rote a popular but misguided notion. For that reason, he listened carefully as she spoke.

"Culture carries no privilege to exist. Cultures do not have value simply because they are. Some cultures, the world is better off without." She lifted an eyebrow. "I submit, for your consideration, the Imperial Order."

Richard let out a long breath. "I see what you mean."

He took a swig of water as she ate some more tava. It still seemed somehow wrong to him for a culture, with its own history and traditions, to be wiped out, but he understood, to an extent, what she was saying.

"So the Ander way of life ceased to be. You were saying, about the Haken system of justice?"

"Despite what we may now think of how they came to

be there, the Hakens were a people who valued fairness. In fact, they considered it essential to an orderly and prosperous society.

"Thus, over time, subsequent generations of Hakens gave increasing freedoms to the Anders they had conquered, eventually coming to view them as equals. Those subsequent generations came to share sensibilities similar to ours, and also came to feel shame at what their ancestors had done to the Ander people."

Kahlan gazed out over the plains. "Of course, it's easier to feel shame if those guilty are centuries dead, especially when such discrediting, by default, confers upon yourself a higher moral standard without having to stand the test in the true environment of the time.

"Anyway, their adherence to their notion of justice turned out to be the beginning of the downfall of the Haken people. The Anders, because of their conquest, always hated the Hakens and never ceased to harbor a hunger for revenge."

One of the hunters, who had been cooking up porridge, brought over a warm piece of tava bread cupped in each hand and heaped with thick steaming porridge. Kahlan and Richard each gratefully took the hot food and she thanked him in his language.

"So how could a Haken system of justice," Richard said, after they each had eaten some of the porridge laced with sweet dried berries, "result in the Hakens now being virtual slaves because of the Anders' sense of justice? That just doesn't seem possible."

He saw that Du Chaillu, wrapped in blankets beside the fire, wasn't interested in porridge. Cara had steeped the tea with the bag of herbs, and was hunkered beside Du Chaillu, seeing to it that she at least sipped some from a small wooden cup.

"A system of justice was not the cause of the Haken downfall, Richard, merely a step along the way—one of the bare bones of history. I'm only telling you the salient points. The results. Such shifts in culture and society take place over time.

"Because of fair laws, the Anders were able to make advances that in the end resulted in them being able to seize power. Anders are no different than anyone else in their hunger for power."

"The Hakens were a ruling people. How did it get from there to the other way round?" Richard shook his head. He had a hard time believing it was as the wizards portrayed it.

"There is more in the middle." Kahlan licked porridge off a finger. "Once the Anders had access to fair laws, it became for them the sharp end of a wedge.

"Once folded into the society, Anders used their freedom to gain status. At first, it was participation in business, the labor trades which became guilds, and membership on small local councils, things like that. One step at a time.

"Make no mistake, the Anders worked hard, too. Because the laws became fair to all, they were able to gain through their own hard work the same sorts of things the Hakens had. They became successful and respected.

"Most importantly, though, they became the moneylenders.

"You see, the Anders, it turned out, had a talent for business. Over time they became the merchant class instead of simply the working class. Being the merchants enabled families, over time, to acquire fortunes.

"They eventually became moneylenders, and thus a financial power. A few large and extensive Ander families controlled much of the finances and were to a large extent the unseen power behind Haken rule. Hakens grew complacent, while the Anders remained focused.

"Anders also became teachers. Almost from the beginning, the Hakens considered teaching a simple role the Ander people should be allowed to fill, freeing Hakens for more adult matters of rule. The Anders took on all aspects of teaching—not just the teaching itself—incrementally gaining control of the instruction of fit teachers, and therefore of the curriculum."

Richard swallowed a mouthful of porridge. "I take it that was, for the Hakens, somehow a mistake?"

With her half-eaten tava-bread plate of porridge, Kahlan gestured for emphasis. "Besides reading and math, the children were taught history and culture, ostensibly so they would grow up to understand their place in their land's culture and society.

"The Hakens wanted all children to learn a better way than war and conquest. They believed the Ander teachings of brutal Haken conquest at the expense of noble Ander people would help their children to grow up to be civilized, with respect for others. Instead, the guilt it put on young minds contributed to the erosion of the cohesive nature of Haken society, and of respect for the authority of Haken rule.

"And then came a cataclysmic event—a ruinous decade-long drought. It was during this drought that the Anders finally made their move to oust Haken rule.

"The entire economy was based on the production of crops—wheat, mostly. Farms failed, and farmers were unable to deliver export crops for which the merchants had already paid them. Debts were called due as everyone tried to survive the hard times. Many without great financial resources lost their farms.

"There might have been government controls placed on the economic system, to slow the panic, but the ruling Hakens feared to displease the moneylenders who backed them.

"And then worse problems erupted.

"People began dying. There were food riots. Fairfield was burned to the ground. Haken and Ander alike rose up in violent lawless rioting. The land was in chaos. Many people left for other lands, hoping to find a new life before they starved.

"The Anders, though, used their money to buy food from abroad. Only the financial resources of the wealthy Anders could purchase food from afar, and it was that food supply that was the only hope of survival for most people. The

Anders, with this supply of food from abroad, were seen as the hand of salvation.

"The Anders bought out failed businesses and farms from people desperate for money. The Anders' money, meager as it was, and their food supply, was the only thing keeping most families from starving.

"It was then the Anders began to extract the true price, and their vengeance.

"The government, run by the Hakens, was blamed by the mobs in the streets for the starvation. Anders, with their merchant connections, fomented and spread the insurrection from place to place. Anarchy befell the land as the Haken rulers were put to death in the streets, their bodies dragged before cheering crowds.

"Haken intellectuals drew the blood lust of frightened people for somehow being responsible for the starvation. Well-educated Hakens were viewed as enemies of the people, even by the majority of Hakens who were farmers and laborers. The purge of the learned Hakens was bloody. In the rioting and lawlessness, the entire Haken ruling class was systematically murdered. Every Haken of accomplishment was suspect, and so put to death.

"The Anders swiftly ruined, by either financial means or violent mobs, any Haken business or concern left.

"In the vacuum, the Anders seized power and brought order with food for starving people, Ander and Haken alike. When the dust settled, the Anders were in control of the land, and with strong forces of mercenaries they could afford to hire, soon held the land in an iron grip."

Richard had stopped eating. He could hardly believe what he was hearing. He stared transfixed as Kahlan swept her hand expansively in telling of the downfall of reason.

"Anders changed the order of everything, making black white and white black. They declared no Haken could fairly judge an Ander, because of the ancient Haken tradition of injustice to Anders. Conversely, Anders asserted, because they had for so long been subjugated by their wicked Haken overlords, that they understood the nature of inequity, and so would be the only ones qualified to rule in matters of justice.

"Woeful tales of Haken cruelty were the currency of social acceptance. Frightened Hakens, in an attempt to prove the horrific charges untrue, and avoid being singled out by the well-armed troops, willingly submitted to Ander authority and those merciless mercenaries.

"The Anders, so long out of power, were ruthless in pressing their advantage.

"Haken people were forbidden to hold positions of power. Eventually, supposedly because the Haken overlords required Anders to address those overlords by surname, even the right to have a surname was denied the Hakens, unless they somehow proved themselves worthy and received special permission."

"But haven't they intermixed?" Richard asked. "After all that time, didn't the Haken and Ander people intermarry? Didn't they all blend together into one people?"

Kahlan shook her head. "From the beginning, the Anders, a tall dark-haired people, thought wedding the redheaded Hakens was a crime against the Creator. They believe the Creator, in His wisdom, made people distinct and different. They didn't believe people should interbreed like livestock being bred for a new quality—which was what the Hakens had done. I'm not saying it didn't occasionally happen, but to this day such a thing is rare."

Richard rolled up his last bite of tava with porridge. "So, what's it like there, now?" He popped the bite in his mouth.

"Since only the downtrodden—the Anders—can be virtuous, because they were oppressed, only they are allowed to rule. They teach that Haken oppression continues to this day. Even a look from a Haken can be interpreted as a projection of hate. Conversely, Hakens cannot be downtrodden, and thus virtuous, since by nature they are corrupt.

"It's now against the law for Hakens to learn to read, out of fear they would again seize rule and go on to brutalize and butcher the Ander people, as surely as night always extinguishes day, to put their words to it. Hakens are required to attend classes called penance assembly to keep them in line. It's all systematized and codified the way Anders now rule Hakens.

"Keep in mind, Richard, the history I told you is what was taught me by the wizards. What the Anders teach is quite different. They teach that they were an oppressed people who by their own higher nature have, after centuries of domination, once again exerted their cultural superiority. For all I know, their version could even be true."

Richard was standing, hands on hips, staring incredulously. "And the council in Aydindril allowed this? They allowed the Anders to enslave the Haken people in such a fashion?"

"The Hakens meekly submit. They believe as they were taught by Ander teachers—that this is a better way."

"But how could the Central Council allow such a perversion of justice?"

"You forget, Richard, the Midlands was an alliance of sovereign lands. The Confessors helped see to it that rule in the Midlands was, to a certain extent, fair. We did not tolerate murder of political opponents, things like that, but if a people like the Hakens willingly went along with the way their land worked, the council had little say. Brutal rule was opposed. Bizarre rule was not."

Richard threw up his hands. "But the Hakens only go along because they are taught this nonsense. They don't know how ridiculous it is. It is the equivalent of the abuse of an ignorant people."

"Abuse maybe to you, Richard. They see it differently. They see it as a way to peace in their land. That is their right."

"The fact they were deliberately taught in a way to make them ignorant is proof of the abuse."

She tilted her head toward him. "Aren't you the one who just told me the Hakens had no right to destroy the Ander culture? Now you argue the council should have done no less?"

Richard's face reflected frustration. "You were talking about the council of the Midlands?"

Kahlan took another drink and then handed him the waterskin.

"This all happened centuries ago. No one land was strong enough to enforce law on the rest of the Midlands. Together, through the council, we simply try to work together. The Confessors interceded when rulers stepped outside the bounds.

"Had we tried to dictate how each sovereign land was to be ruled, the alliance would have fallen apart and war would have replaced reason and cooperation. I'm not saying it was perfect, Richard, but it allowed most people to live in peace."

He sighed. "I suppose. I'm no expert on governing. I guess it served the people of the Midlands for thousands of years."

Kahlan picked at her tava bread. "Things like what happened in Anderith are one reason I came to understand and believe in what you are trying to accomplish, Richard. Until you came along, with D'Hara behind your word, no one land was strong enough to set down just law for all peoples. Against a foe like Jagang, the alliance of the Midlands had no chance."

Richard couldn't really imagine how it must have been for her, as Mother Confessor, to see what she had worked for her entire life fall apart. Richard's father, Darken Rahl, had set in motion events that had altered the world. Kahlan, at least, had seen the opportunity in the chaos.

Richard rubbed his brow as he considered what to do next.

"All right, so I now understand a bit about the history of Anderith. I'm sure that if I knew the history of D'Hara I'd find that far more sordid, and yet they now follow me and struggle for justice—strange as I realize that sounds. The spirits know some people have hung the crimes of D'Hara's past around my Rahl neck.

"From what you've told me of Anderith history, they

sound like a people who would never submit to the rule of the Imperial Order. Do you think we can get Anderith to join with us?"

Kahlan took a deep breath as she considered it. He had been hoping she would say yes without having to think about it.

"They are ruled by a sovereign, who is also their religious leader. That element of their society hearkens back to the religious beliefs of the Anders. The Directors of the Office of Cultural Amity hold sway over who will be named Sovereign for life. The Directors are supposed to be a moral check on the man appointed Sovereign—in a way like the First Wizard selecting the right person to be Seeker.

"The Anderith people believe that once anointed by the Directors, the man named Sovereign transcends mere matters of the flesh, and is in touch with the Creator Himself. Some fervently believe he speaks in this world for the Creator. Some view him with the reverence they would reserve for the Creator Himself."

"So, he's the one who will need to be convinced to join us?"

"In part, but the Sovereign doesn't really rule in the day-to-day sense. He's more a figurehead, loved by the people for what he represents. Nowadays Anders make up less than maybe fifteen or twenty percent of the population, but the Hakens feel much the same about their Sovereign.

"He has the power to order the rest of the government to a course, but more often he simply approves the one they select. For the large part, the ruling of Anderith is done by the Minister of Culture. The Minister sets the agenda for the land. That would be a man named Bertrand Chanboor.

"The Minister of Culture's office just outside Fairfield is the governing body that ultimately would make the decision. The representatives I met with in Aydindril will report our words to Minister Chanboor.

"No matter the dim history, the present-day fact is that Anderith is a power to be reckoned with. If the ancient Anders were a primitive people, they are no longer so. They are wealthy merchants who control vast trade and wealth. They govern with equal skill; they have a secure grip on their power and their land."

Richard scanned the empty grasslands. Ever since the chime had come to kill Du Chaillu, and he had felt the hairs at the back of his neck stand on end, he kept checking for the feeling, hoping that, if it came again, he would be aware of the sensation sooner and be able to warn everyone in time.

He glanced over to see Cara feeding Du Chaillu porridge. She needed to be back with her people, not carrying her unborn child all over the countryside.

"The Anders are not fat, soft, lazy merchants, either," Kahlan went on. "Except for the army, where a semblance of equality exists, only Anders are allowed to carry weapons, and they tend to be good with them. The Anders, despite what you may think of them, are no fools and neither are they to be easily won over."

Richard again gazed out over the grasslands as he made plans in his head.

"In Ebinissia, in Renwold," he said, "Jagang has shown what he does to people who refuse to join him. If Anderith doesn't join us, they will again fall to a foreign invasion. This time, though, the invaders will have no sense of justice."

CHAPTER 35

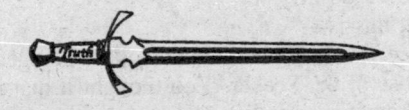

RICHARD, CONSIDERING EVERYTHING KAHLAN had told him, and what the chimes had, in their own brutal way, told him, stood staring off toward Aydindril. Learning some of the history of Anderith only made him feel more sure of his decision.

"I knew we had to be going the wrong way," he said at last.

Kahlan frowned out over the empty plains to the northeast, where he was looking. "What do you mean?"

"Zedd used to tell me that if the road is easy, you're likely going the wrong way."

"Richard, we've been all through that," Kahlan said with weary insistence as she pushed her cloak back over her shoulder. "We need to get to Aydindril. Now, more than ever, you must see that."

"The Mother Confessor is right," Cara said, returning from Du Chaillu, now that the woman was resting. Richard noticed that Cara's knuckles were white around her Agiel. "These chimes must be banished. We must help Zedd set magic right again."

"Oh, really? You don't know, Cara, how pleased I am to hear that you are now such a devotee of magic." Richard looked around, checking for their gear. "I have to go to Anderith."

"Richard, we very well could be leaving inactive in Aydindril a spell that would be the solution to the chimes."

"I'm the Seeker, remember?" Richard was thankful for Kahlan's counsel, and he highly valued it, but now that he had heard what she had to say, analyzed the options, and made his decision, his patience was at an end. It was time to act. "Let me do my job."

"Richard, this is—"

"You once swore an oath before Zedd—pledged your life in the defense of the Seeker. You thought it that important. I'm not asking for your life, only your understanding that I'm doing as I must."

Kahlan took a breath, trying to be tolerant and calm with him when he was hardly hearing her. "Zedd urged us to do this for him so he would be able to counter the ebbing of magic." She tugged his sleeve to get his attention. "We can't all go rushing off to Anderith."

"You're right."

Kahlan frowned suspiciously. "Good."

"We're not all going to Anderith." Richard found their blanket and snatched it up. "As you said, Aydindril is important, too."

Kahlan seized the front of his shirt and hauled him around to face her.

"Oh no you don't." She shook her finger in his face. "Oh no you don't, Richard.

"We're married. We've been through too much. We're not going to separate now. Not now. And certainly not just because I'm angry with you for forgetting to tell Zedd about your first wife. I'll not have it, Richard, do you hear me?"

"Kahlan, this has nothing to do—"

Her green eyes afire, she shook him by his shirt. "I'll not have it! Not after all it took for us to be together."

Richard glanced at Cara, not far away. "Only one of us needs to go to Aydindril." He took her hand from his shirt, giving it a little squeeze of reassurance before she could say anything more.

"You and I are going to Anderith."

Kahlan's brow twitched. "But if we both . . ." She suddenly looked over at Cara.

Alarm shifted to the Mord-Sith. "Why are you both looking at me like that?"

Richard put an arm around Cara's shoulders. She didn't seem to like it one bit, so he took the arm away.

"Cara, you have to go to Aydindril."

"We are all going to Aydindril."

"No, Kahlan and I must go to Anderith. They have the Dominie Dirtch. They have an army. We have to get them to join us, and then prepare them for the coming of the Order. I need to see if there's anything there that will help stop the chimes. We're a lot closer to Anderith now than I would be if I had to go there from Aydindril. I can't not look into it.

"It could be that we can stop the chimes and Anderith will surrender and we will be able to use the Dominie Dirtch to halt or even destroy Jagang's army. Too much is at stake to let such opportunity slip through our fingers. It's too important, Cara. Surely, you can see I have no choice?"

"No, you have a choice. We can all go to Aydindril. You are Lord Rahl. I am Mord-Sith. I must stay with you to protect you."

"Would you rather I sent Kahlan?"

Cara pressed her lips tight but didn't answer.

Kahlan took him by his arm. "Richard, as you said, you are the Seeker. You need your sword—without it you are vulnerable. It's in Aydindril. So is the bottle with the spell, and Kolo's journal, and libraries of other books that may hold the answer.

"We have to go to Aydindril. Had you only told Zedd, we might not be in this position, but now that we are, we must do as he asked."

Richard straightened and looked her in the eye as she

folded her arms. "Kahlan, I'm the Seeker. As the Seeker, I have an obligation to do what I think is right. I admit I made a mistake before, and I'm sorry, but I can't allow that mistake to make me flinch from my duty as I believe it to be.

"As the Seeker, I'm going to Anderith. As Mother Confessor, you must do what your heart and duty dictate. I understand that. I want you with me, but if you must take another path, I will still love you the same."

He leaned closer to her. "Choose."

Her arms still folded, Kahlan regarded him in silence. At last, her ire melted and she nodded. She glanced briefly at Cara.

Seeming to think there was one person too many for the delivery of the inevitable orders, she spoke to him in a low voice. "I'm going to see how Du Chaillu is getting on."

When Kahlan was out of earshot, Cara began to speak. "My duty is to guard and protect the Lord Rahl and I will not—"

Richard held up a hand to silence her.

"Cara, please, listen to me a minute. We've been through a lot together, the three of us. The three of us have been to the brink of death together. We each have the others to thank in more ways than one for our lives today. You are more to us than a guard and you know it.

"Kahlan is your sister of the Agiel. You are my friend. I know I mean more to you than simply being your Lord Rahl, or with the bond gone you wouldn't have to stay with me. We are all bonded in friendship."

"That is why I cannot leave you. I will not leave you, Lord Rahl. I will guard you whether or not you allow it."

"How does it feel to be without your Agiel?"

She didn't answer. It looked as if she didn't trust herself to try to speak.

"Cara, would it surprise you to learn I feel the same way about the Sword of Truth? I have been without it longer than you have been without your Agiel. It's an awful gnawing feeling in the pit of my stomach. A constant empty ache, like I need nothing so much as to feel that terrible thing in my hand. The same with you?"

She nodded.

"Cara, I hate that sword, the same as you surely, somewhere inside, must hate your Agiel. One time, you surrendered it to me. Remember? You and Berdine and Raina? I asked you to forgive me that I had to ask you to keep your weapon for now to help us in our struggle."

"I remember."

"I would like nothing more than not to need the sword. I would like the world to be at peace, and I could put that weapon in the Keep and leave it there.

"But I need it, Cara. Just as you need your Agiel, just as you feel an emptiness without it, feel vulnerable and defenseless and afraid, and ashamed to admit it, I feel the same. Just as you need your Agiel because you want nothing more than to protect us, I need my sword to protect Kahlan. If anything happened to her because I didn't have my sword . . .

"Cara, I care about you, that's why it's important for you to understand. You are no longer just Mord-Sith, just our protector. You are more than that now. It's important for you to think, and not simply to react. You must be more than Mord-Sith if you are to be of true help as our protector.

"I'm depending on you to continue to be an important person in this struggle, a person who can make a difference. Now you must go to Aydindril in my place."

"I won't follow those orders."

"I'm not ordering you, Cara. I'm asking you."

"That is not fair."

"This isn't a game, Cara. I'm asking for your help. You are the only one I can turn to."

She scowled off toward the thunderstorm on the distant horizon as she pulled her long blond braid over her shoulder. She gripped it in her fist the way she gripped her Agiel in the heat of anger. The breeze fluttered the wisps of blond hair along the side of her face.

"If you wish it, Lord Rahl, I will go."

Richard put a comforting hand on the back of her shoulder. This time she didn't tense, but welcomed the hand.

"What do you wish me to do there?"

"I want you to get there and back as soon as possible. I need my sword."

"I understand."

When Kahlan glanced their way, Cara signaled for her and Kahlan returned at a trot.

Cara stiffened her back as she addressed Kahlan. "Lord Rahl has ordered me to return to Aydindril."

"Ordered?" Kahlan asked.

Cara simply smirked. She lifted the Agiel at Kahlan's chest. "For a woods guide, he gets himself in a lot of trouble. As a sister of the Agiel, I would ask you to watch over him in my place, but I know I do not need to say the words."

"I won't let him out of my sight."

"You need to catch up with General Reibisch's army, first," Richard said. "You can get horses from him and make better time to Aydindril.

"But I also very much need him to know what we're doing. Tell him the whole story. Tell Verna and the Sisters, too. They will need to know, and they may have knowledge that would be of use."

Richard stared off toward the southwest horizon. "I also need an escort, if we are to march into Anderith and demand their surrender."

"Don't worry, Lord Rahl, I intend on ordering Reibisch to send men to guard you. They will not be as good as having a Mord-Sith near, but they will still protect you."

"I need enough for an impressive escort. When we march into Anderith, I think it would be best if we looked serious, rather than just Kahlan and me and a few guards going alone. Especially since Kahlan's power could fail at any time. I want to look to the people there like we mean business."

"Now you are beginning to make sense," Cara said.

"A thousand men should do for an impressive escort," Kahlan said. "Swordsmen, lancers, and archers—their best—

and extra horses, of course. And we'll need messengers. We have important news of the chimes and Jagang that must be sent out. We need to coordinate our forces and keep everyone informed. We have armies in various lands we may need to bring south at once."

Cara nodded. "I will personally select the soldiers to be sent for your escort. Reibisch will have elite troops."

"Fine, but I don't want his fighting ability harmed by taking key men," Richard said. "Tell the general I also want him to send detachments to watch the routes north from the Old World he had intended to watch, just in case.

"The most important thing, though, is that I want his main force to turn around and head back this way."

"Is he to be allowed to attack at will?"

"No. I don't want him risking his army against the Order out on these plains. It would be too costly. As good as his men are, they wouldn't stand a chance against a force the size of the Order's until we can get more men down here. More importantly, I don't want him attacking because his greatest value is if Jagang doesn't know Reibisch's force is there.

"I want Reibisch to come west, shadowing Jagang, but staying north and remaining well away. Tell him to use as few scouts as possible—just enough to keep track of the Order, no more. Jagang mustn't know Reibisch's force is there. Those D'Haran men will be all that stands between the Order and the Midlands if Jagang suddenly turns north. Surprise will be his only ally until we can get messengers to bring in more troops.

"I don't want to risk Reibisch's men if it isn't absolutely necessary. But I need him to be the stopgap, if things go wrong.

"If Anderith surrenders, we can combine their army with ours. If we can banish the chimes, have the Anderith army under our command, and get more of our other forces down here in time, we might even be able to trap Jagang's army with the ocean at his back. It might be possible to then use our forces to drive him into the teeth of the Dominie

Dirtch. That weapon could kill without our men losing their lives to do it."

"And in Aydindril?" Cara asked.

"You heard Zedd explain what must be done?"

"Yes. On the fifth column on the left, inside the First Wizard's enclave, sits a black bottle with a gold filigree top. It must be broken with the Sword of Truth. Berdine and I have gone with you to the First Wizard's enclave. I remember well the place."

"Good. You can use the sword to break the bottle as well as I." She nodded. "Just set the bottle on the ground, like Zedd told us, get the sword, and break the bottle."

"I can do that," Cara said.

Richard knew very well how much Cara didn't like to have anything to do with magic. He remembered well, too, how she and Berdine hadn't liked going into the First Wizard's enclave. There was also the matter of the Keep's shields of magic.

"If the magic of the Keep is really down, you won't have any trouble getting through the shields; they will be down, too."

"I remember what they feel like. I will know if they are still alive with magic, or if I can pass."

"Tell Berdine everything you know about the chimes. She may already have valuable information. If nothing else, she has Kolo's journal and with what you tell her she will know what to search for."

Richard held up a finger for emphasis. With his other hand, he gripped her shoulder.

"But before Berdine, the sword and the bottle first. Don't let either sit vincible for one moment longer than necessary.

"The chimes may try to stop you. Be aware of that. Be alert and on guard. Stay away from water and fire as best as you can. Don't take anything for granted. They may know the spell in the bottle can harm them.

"Before you leave, we will talk to Du Chaillu and see if she can shed light on how they seduce a person to their death. If she can remember, that may be valuable in warding the chimes."

Cara nodded. If she was afraid, she didn't show it.

"Once I get to General Reibisch, I will ride like the wind. I will go first to the Keep and get your sword and then break the bottle. After that, I will bring your sword, Berdine, and the book. Where will I find you?"

"In Fairfield," Kahlan said. "Most likely with our troops, not far out of the city, near the Minister of Culture's estate. If we have to depart, we will leave a message for you, or some of our men. If we can't do that, we will try to tell General Reibisch."

Richard hesitated. "Cara . . . you will need to take the sword from its scabbard to break the bottle."

"Of course."

"But be careful. It's a weapon of magic, and Zedd thinks it will still work—still have magic."

Cara sighed with unpleasant thoughts. "What will it do when I draw it?"

"I don't know for sure," Richard said. "It may react to different people in different ways, depending on what they bring to the completion of the magic. I'm still the Seeker, but it may work for anyone holding it. I just don't know how its magic will affect you.

"But it's a weapon that uses rage. Just be careful, and realize that it will want to draw you out, much as you draw it out. It will foment your emotions, especially your anger."

Cara's blue eyes gleamed. "It will not have to try hard."

Richard smiled. "Just be careful. After you break the bottle, don't take the sword from its scabbard for any reason less than a matter of life or death. If you kill with it . . ."

Her brow drew down when his voice trailed off. "If I kill with it . . . what?"

Richard had to tell her, lest she do something dangerous. "It gives pain."

"Like an Agiel?"

He nodded reluctantly. "Maybe worse." His voice lowered as the memories flooded back. "Anger is required to counter the pain. If you are filled with righteous rage, that will protect you, but dear spirits it will still hurt you."

"I am Mord-Sith. I will welcome the pain."

Richard tapped the center of his chest. "It hurts you in here, Cara. You don't want that kind of pain, believe me. Better your Agiel."

She gave him a sad smile of understanding. "You need your sword. I will bring it to you."

"Thank you, Cara."

"But I will not forgive you for making me leave you without protection."

"He will not be without protection."

They all turned. It was Du Chaillu. She was pale, her hair a mess, but wrapped in a blanket she no longer shivered. Her face was a picture of grim determination.

Richard shook his head. "You need to go back to your people."

"We go with my husband. We protect the *Caharin*."

Richard decided not to argue the husband part. "We'll have troops with us before we can get to Anderith."

"They are not blade masters. We will take Cara's place protecting you."

Cara bowed her head to Du Chaillu. "This is good. I will rest better knowing you and your blade masters do this."

Richard shot Cara an annoyed glance before turning his attention to the Baka Tau Mana spirit woman.

"Du Chaillu, now that you're safe, I'll not have you risking your lives needlessly. You've already had a brush with death. You must get back to your people. They need you."

"We are the walking dead. It does not matter."

"What are you talking about?"

Du Chaillu clasped her hands. The blade masters were spread out behind her, her royal escort. Beyond them, the Mud People hunters watched. As sick as she still looked, Du Chaillu was once again looking noble.

"Before we left," she said, "we told our people we were dead. We told them we were lost to the world of life, and we would not be returned to them unless we reached the *Caharin* to warn him and made sure he was safe. Our people wept and mourned us before we departed, because we are dead to them. Only if we do as we said will we be able to return.

"Not long ago, I heard the chimes of death. Cara, the *Caharin's* protector, pulled me back from the spirit world. The spirits, in their wisdom, allowed me to return so I might fulfill my duty. When Cara returns with your sword, and you are safe, only then can we have our lives returned to us so that we might return home. Until then, we are the walking dead.

"I am not asking if we may be allowed to travel with you. I am telling you that we *are* going to travel with you. I am the Baka Tau Mana spirit woman. I have spoken."

Clenching his teeth, Richard lifted his hand to shake an angry finger at her. Kahlan caught his wrist.

"Du Chaillu," Kahlan said, "I, too, have taken such an oath. When I went to the walled city of Ebinissia and saw the people butchered by the Imperial Order, I vowed vengeance. Chandalen and I came across a small army of young recruits who also had seen the dead of their home city. They were determined to punish the men responsible.

"I swore a covenant that I was dead, and could only be returned to life when the men who committed those crimes were punished. The men with me gave up their lives too, to live again only if we succeeded. One in five of those young men returned to the living with Chandalen and me. But before we did, every one of the men who murdered the people of Ebinissia died.

"I understand such an oath as you have given, Du Chaillu. Such a thing is sacred and not to be ignored. You and the blade masters may come with us."

Du Chaillu bowed to Kahlan. "Thank you for honoring my people's ways. You are a wise woman, and worthy of being wife to my husband, too."

Richard rolled his eyes. "Kahlan—"

"The Mud People need Chandalen and his men. Cara is

doing as you ask of her, and going to General Reibisch and then on to Aydindril. Until the general can send men to join with us, we will be alone and vulnerable. Du Chaillu and her men will be valuable and welcome protection.

"With so much at stake, Richard, our pride is the last thing we need to be considering. They are coming."

Richard took in Cara's blue eyes, icy cold with resolve. She wanted this. Du Chaillu's dark eyes were iron hard. Her mind was made up. Kahlan's green eyes . . . well, he didn't want to even think about what was in her green eyes.

"All right," he said. "Until the soldiers can reach us, you may come along."

Du Chaillu directed a puzzled look at Kahlan. "Does he always tell you, too, things you already know?"

CHAPTER 36

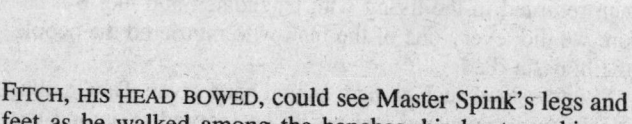

FITCH, HIS HEAD BOWED, could see Master Spink's legs and feet as he walked among the benches, his boots making a slow thunk, thunk, thunk against the plank floor. Around the room, a few people, mainly the older women, sniffled as they wept quietly to themselves.

Fitch couldn't blame them. He, too, was occasionally reduced to weeping at penance assembly. The lessons they learned were necessary if they were to fight their evil Haken ways—he understood that—but that didn't make listening any easier.

When Master Spink lectured, Fitch preferred to look at the floor rather than by chance meet the man's gaze. To meet the gaze of an Ander as he taught the horrors of what was done to his ancestors by Fitch's was shaming.

"And so it was," Master Spink went on, "that the Haken horde came by chance upon that poor farming village. The menfolk, with frantic concern for their families, had gathered together with those other simple Ander men from farms and other villages around. Together, they prayed to the Creator that their effort to repulse the bloodthirsty invaders might succeed.

"In desperation, they had already left nearly all their foodstuffs and livestock as a peaceful offering for the Hakens. They had sent messengers to explain the offerings, and that they wished no war, but none of those brave messengers ever returned.

"So it was a simple plan these men had, to go to the crest of a hill and wave their weapons overhead to make a show of strength, not to invite a fight, of course, but in an urgent effort to convince the Hakens to pass their villages by. These men were farmers, not warriors, and the weapons they waved were simple farm tools. They didn't want a fight; they wanted peace.

"So, there they were, those men I've taught you about—Shelby, Willan, Camden, Edgar, Newton, Kenway, and all the rest—all those good and kind men who you have come to know over these last few weeks as I've told you their stories, their loves, their lives, their hopes, their simple and decent dreams. There they were, up there on that hill, hoping for no more than to convince the Haken brutes to pass them by. There they were, waving their tools—their axes, their hoes, their sickles, their forks, their flails—waving them in the air, hoping to keep those wives and children you've also come to know safe from harm."

Thump, thump, thump went Master Spink's boots as he came closer to Fitch.

"The Haken army did not choose to pass those simple men by. The Hakens instead, laughing and hooting, turned their Dominie Dirtch on those gentle Ander men."

Some of the girls gasped. Others wailed aloud. Fitch himself felt a twist of fear in his gut, and a lump in his throat. He had to sniffle himself as he imagined their gruesome death. He had come to know those men on the hill. He knew their wives' names, their parents' names, and their children.

"And while those murderous Haken bastards in their fine, fancy uniforms"—Fitch could see the boots halt right beside him where he sat on the end of the bench near the center aisle—"stood laughing, stood cheering, the Dominie Dirtch rang out with its terrible violence, tearing the flesh from those men's bones."

Fitch could feel Master Spink's dark-eyed glare on the back of his neck as the women and many of the men sobbed their grief aloud.

"The wails of those poor Ander farmboys rose into the Ander sky. It was their last scream in this life, as their bodies were torn apart by the excellently dressed, laughing, jeering Haken horde with their weapon of heartless slaughter, the Dominie Dirtch."

One of the older women cried out with the horror of it. Master Spink still stood over Fitch. Right at that moment, Fitch wasn't as proud of his messenger garb as he had been earlier, when the other people had whispered to each other in astonishment as he took his seat.

"I see you have yourself a fine new uniform, Fitch," Master Spink said in a voice that made Fitch's blood go cold.

Fitch knew he was expected to say something.

"Yes, sir. Though I was a lowly Haken scullion, Master Campbell was kind enough to give me a job as a messenger. He wants me to wear this uniform so all Hakens might see that with Ander help we can do better. He also wants the messengers to reflect well on his office as we help in his work of spreading the word of the Minister of Culture's good work for our people."

Master Spink cuffed Fitch on the side of the head, knocking him from the bench. "Don't talk back to me! I'm not interested in your Haken excuses!"

"I'm sorry, sir." He knew better than to get up from his hands and knees.

"Hakens always have excuses for their crimes of hate. You're wearing a fancy uniform, just like those murderous Haken overlords enjoyed wearing, and you enjoy it the same as they, and then you try to make it seem as if you don't.

"To this day, we Anders suffer grievously under the unceasing scourge of Haken hate. Without question, every look from a Haken conveys it. We can never be free of it. There are always Hakens in uniforms they enjoy wearing to remind us of the Haken overlords.

"You prove your filthy Haken nature by trying to defend the indefensible—your self-centered arrogance, your pride in yourself, your pride in a uniform. You all hunger to be Haken overlords. Everyday, as Anders, we must suffer such Haken abuse."

"Forgive me, Master Spink. I was wrong. I wore it out of pride. I was wrong to let my sinful Haken nature rule me."

Master Spink grunted his contempt, but then went on with the lesson. Knowing he deserved more, Fitch sighed, grateful to be let off so easy.

"With the menfolk murdered, that left the women and children of the village defenseless."

The boots thunk, thunk, thunked as the man started out again, walking among the Hakens sitting on simple benches. Only after he had started away did Fitch dare to get up off his hands and knees and once more take his seat on the bench. His ear chimed something awful, like when Beata had struck him. Master Spink's words bored through that hollow ringing.

"Being Hakens, of course, they decided to go through the village and have their wicked fun."

"No!" a woman in back cried out. She fell to sobbing.

Hands clasped behind his back, Master Spink walked on, ignoring the interruption. There were frequently such interruptions.

"The Hakens, wishing a feast, went to the village. They were of a mind for some roasted meat."

People fell to their knees, trembling with fear for the people they had come to know. Benches all over the room scuffed against the floor as most of the rest of the people in the room also went down on their knees. Fitch joined them.

"But it was a small village, as you know. After the Hakens slaughtered the livestock, they realized there wasn't enough meat. Hakens, being Hakens, didn't want for a solution for long.

"The children were seized."

Fitch wished for nothing so much as he wished for the lesson to be over. He didn't know if he could bear to hear any more. Apparently, some of the women were of the same mind. They collapsed to their faces on the floor, hands clasped, as they wept and prayed to the good spirits to watch over those poor, innocent, slain Ander people.

"You all know the names of those children. We will now go around the room and you will each give me one of the names you have learned, lest we forget those young lives so painfully taken. You will each give me the name of one of the children from that village—little girls and little boys—who were roasted alive in front of their mothers."

Master Spink started at the last row. Each person in turn, as he pointed to them, spoke the name of one of those children, most beseeching after it that the good spirits watch over them. Before they were allowed to leave, Master Spink described the horror of being burned alive, the screams, the pain, and how long it took for the children to die. How long it took for their bodies to cook.

It was so grisly and sinister a deed that at one point, for just the briefest moment, Fitch considered for perhaps the first time whether the story could really be true. He had trouble imagining anyone, even the brutal Haken overlords, doing such a horrific thing.

But Master Spink was Ander. He wouldn't lie to them. Not about something as important as history.

"Since it's getting late," Master Spink said, after everyone had given a child's name, "we will leave until next assembly the story of what the Haken invaders did to those women. The children, perhaps, were lucky not to have to see their mothers used for such perversions as the Hakens did to them."

Fitch, along with the rest of the assembly behind him, burst through the doors when they were dismissed, glad to escape, for the night, the penance lesson. He had never been so glad for the cool night air. He felt hot and sick as the images of such a death as those children suffered kept going through his head. The cool air, at least, felt good on his face. He pulled the cool purging air into his lungs.

As he was leaning against a slender maple tree beside the path to the road, waiting for his legs to steady, Beata came out the door. Fitch straightened. There was enough light coming from the open door and the windows so she would have no trouble seeing him—seeing him in his new messenger's outfit. He was hoping Beata would find it more appealing than did Master Spink.

"Good evening, Beata."

She halted. She glanced down the length of him, taking in his clothes.

"Fitch."

"You look lovely this evening, Beata."

"I look the same as always." She planted her fists on her hips. "I see you've fallen in love with yourself in a fancy uniform."

Fitch suddenly lost his ability to think or speak. He had always liked the way the messengers looked in their uniforms, and had thought she would, too. He had been hoping to see her smile, or something. Instead, she glared at him. Now he wished more than anything he had just gone home straightaway.

"Master Dalton offered me a position—"

"And I suppose you'll be looking forward to next penance

405

assembly so you can hear about what those Haken beasts in their fancy uniforms did to those helpless women." She leaned toward him. "You'll like that. It will be almost as much fun for you as if you were there watching."

Fitch stood with his jaw hanging as she huffed and stormed off into the night.

Other people walking down the street saw the tongue-lashing she had given him, a filthy Haken. They smiled in satisfaction, or simply laughed at him. Fitch stuffed his hands in his pockets as he turned his back to the road and leaned a shoulder against the tree. He brooded as he waited for everyone to move along on their own business.

It was an hour's walk back to the estate. He wanted to be sure those returning there had gone on so he could walk alone and not have to talk to anyone. He considered going and buying himself some drink. He still had some money left. If not, he would go back and find Morley, and they would both get some drink. Either way, getting drunk sounded good to him.

The breeze abruptly felt cooler. It ran a shiver up his spine.

He almost leaped out of his boots when a hand settled on his shoulder. He spun and saw it was an older Ander woman. Her swept-back, nearly shoulder-length hair told him she was someone important. Streaks of gray at the temples told him she was old; there wasn't enough light to see exactly how wrinkled she was, but he could still tell she was.

Fitch bowed to the Ander woman. He feared she might want to take up where Beata had left off, and take him to task for something or other.

"Is she someone you care about?" the woman asked.

Fitch was taken off guard by the curious question. "I don't know," he stammered.

"She was pretty rough with you."

"I deserved it, ma'am."

"Why is that?"

Fitch shrugged. "I don't know."

He couldn't figure out what the woman wanted. It gave him gooseflesh the way her dark eyes studied him, like she was picking out a chicken for dinner.

She wore a simple dress that in the dim light looked like it might be a dark brown. It buttoned to her neck, unlike the more revealing fashion most Ander women wore. Her dress didn't mark her as a noble woman, but that long hair said she was someone important.

She seemed somehow different from other Ander women. There was one thing about her that Fitch did think odd: she wore a wide black band tight around her throat, up close at the top of her neck.

"Sometimes girls say mean things when they're afraid to admit they like a boy, fearing he won't like her."

"And sometimes they say mean things because they intend them."

"True enough." She smiled. "Does she live at the estate, or here in Fairfield?"

"Here in Fairfield. She works for Inger the butcher."

She seemed to think that was a little bit funny. "Perhaps she is used to more meat on the bones. Maybe when you get a little older and fill yourself in more she will find you more appealing."

Fitch stuffed his hands back in his pockets. "Maybe."

He didn't believe it. Besides, he didn't figure he would ever fill in, as she put it. He figured he was old enough that he was about how he would be.

She went back to studying his face for a time.

"Do you want her to like you?" she asked at last.

Fitch cleared his throat. "Well, sometimes, I guess. At least, I'd like her not to hate me."

The woman had one of those smiles like she was well pleased with something, but he doubted he'd ever understand it.

"It could be arranged."

"Ma'am?"

"If you like her, and would like her to like you, it could be arranged."

Fitch blinked in astonishment. "How?"

"A little something slipped into what she drinks, or eats."

Understanding came over him all at once. This was a woman of magic. At last he understood why she seemed so strange. He'd heard people with magic were strange.

"You mean you could make something up? Some spell or something?"

Her smile grew. "Or something."

"I just started working for Master Campbell. I'm sorry, ma'am, but I couldn't afford it."

"Ah, I see." Her smile shrank back down. "And if you could afford it?"

Before he could answer, she squinted up at the sky in thought. "Or perhaps it could be ready later on, when you get paid." Her voice turned to little more than a whisper, like she was talking to herself. "Might give me time to see if I couldn't figure out the problem and get it to work again."

She looked him in the eye. "How about it?"

Fitch swallowed. He surely didn't want to offend an Ander woman, and one with the gift, besides. He hesitated.

"Well, ma'am, the truth is, if a girl's ever going to like me, I'd just as soon she liked me because she liked me—no offense, ma'am. It's kind of you to offer. But I don't think I'd like it if a girl only liked me because of a spell of magic. I think that wouldn't make me feel very good about it, like only magic could make a girl like me."

The woman laughed as she patted his back. It was a soft, lilting laugh of pleasure, not a laugh like she was laughing at him. Fitch didn't think he'd ever heard an Ander who was talking to him laugh in quite that way.

"Good for you." She gestured her emphasis with a finger. "I had a wizard tell me as much once, a very long time ago."

"A wizard! That must have been frightening. To meet a wizard, I mean."

She shrugged. "Not really. He was a nice man. I was a very little girl at the time. I was born gifted, you see. He told me to always remember that magic was no substitute for people truly caring about you for who you were yourself."

"I never knew there were wizards around."

"Not here," she said. She flicked a hand out into the night. "Back in Aydindril."

His ears perked up. "Aydindril? To the northeast?"

"My, but aren't you a bright one. Yes. To the northeast. At the Wizard's Keep." She held out a hand. "I'm Franca. And you?"

Fitch took her hand and held it lightly as he dipped to a knee in a deep bow. "I'm Fitch, ma'am."

"Franca."

"Ma'am?"

"Franca. That's my name. I told you my name, Fitch, so you could call me by my name."

"Sorry, ma'am—I mean Franca."

She let out her little laugh again. "Well, Fitch, it was nice to meet you. I must be headed back to the estate. I suppose you will be off to get drunk. That seems to be what boys your age like to do."

Fitch had to admit the idea of getting drunk sounded very good to him. The possibility of hearing about the Wizard's Keep sounded intriguing, though.

"I think I'd best be getting back to the estate myself. If you wouldn't mind having a Haken walk with you, I'd be well pleased to go along. Franca," he added in afterthought.

She studied his face again in that way that made him fidget.

"I'm gifted, Fitch. That means I'm different than most people, and so most all people, Ander and Haken both, think of me the way most Ander people think of you because you're Haken."

"They do? But you're Ander."

"Being Ander is not enough to overcome the stigma of having magic. I know what it feels like to have people dislike you without them knowing anything about you.

"I'd be well pleased to have you walk along with me, Fitch."

Fitch smiled, partly in the shock of realizing he was having a conversation with an Ander woman, a real conversation, and partly in shock that Anders would dislike her—another Ander—because she had magic.

"But don't they respect you because you have magic?"

"They fear me. Fear can be good, and bad. Good, because then even though people don't like you, they at least treat you well. Bad, because people often try to strike out at what they fear."

"I never looked at it that way before."

He thought about how good it had made him feel when Claudine Winthrop called him "sir." She only did because she was afraid, he knew, but it still made him feel good. He didn't understand the other part of what Franca said, though.

"You're very wise. Does magic do that? Make a person wise?"

She let out the breathy laugh again, as if she found him as amusing as a fish with legs.

"If it did, then they would call it the Wise Man's Keep, instead of the Wizard's Keep. Some people would be wiser, perhaps, had they not been born with the buttress of magic."

He'd never met anyone who'd been to Aydindril, much less the Wizard's Keep. He could hardly believe a person with magic would talk to him. To an extent, he was worried because he didn't know anything about magic and he figured that if she got angry she might do him harm.

He thought her fascinating, though, even if she was old.

They started out down the road toward the estate in silence. Sometimes silence made him nervous. He wondered if she could tell what he thought with her magic.

Fitch looked over at her. She didn't look like she was paying any attention to his thoughts. He pointed at her throat.

"Mind if I ask what sort of thing that is, Franca? That band you wear at your throat? I've never seen anyone wear anything like it before. Is it something to do with magic?"

She laughed aloud. "Do you know, Fitch, that you are the first person in a great many years to ask me about this? Even

410

if it is because you don't know enough to fear asking a sorceress such a personal question."

"Sorry, Franca. I didn't mean to say nothing offensive."

He began to worry he had stupidly said something to make her angry. He surely didn't want an Ander woman, and one with magic besides, angry with him. She was silent for a time as they walked on down the road. Fitch stuck his sweating hands back in his pockets.

At last she spoke again. "It isn't that, Fitch. Offensive, I mean. It just brings up bad memories."

"I'm sorry, Franca. I shouldn't have said it. Sometimes I say stupid things. I'm sorry."

He was wishing he had gone to get drunk, instead.

After a few more strides, she stopped and turned to him. "No, Fitch, it wasn't stupid. Here."

She hooked the throat band and pulled it down for him to see. Even though it was dark, there was a moon and he could see a thick lumpy line, all white and waxy-looking, ringing her neck. It looked to him to be a nasty scar.

"Some people tried to kill me, once. Because I have magic." Moonlight glistened in her moist eyes. "Serin Rajak and his followers."

Fitch never heard the name. "Followers?"

She pulled the throat band back up. "Serin Rajak hates magic. He has followers who think the same as he. They get people all worked up against those with magic. Gets them in a state of wild hate and blood lust.

"There's nothing uglier than a mob of men when they have it in their heads to hurt someone. What one alone wouldn't have the nerve to do, together they can easily decide is right and then accomplish. A mob takes on a mind of its own—a life of its own. Just like a pack of dogs chasing down some lone animal.

"Rajak caught me and put a rope around my neck. They tied my hands behind my back. They found a tree, threw the other end of the rope over a limb, and hoisted me up by that rope around my neck."

411

Fitch was horrified. "Dear spirits—that must have hurt something awful."

She didn't seem to hear him as she stared off.

"They were stacking kindling under me. Going to have a big fire. Before they could get the fire lit, I managed to get away."

Fitch's fingers went to his throat, rubbing his neck as he tried to imagine hanging on a rope around his neck.

"That man—Serin Rajak. Is he a Haken?"

She shook her head as they started out again. "You don't have to be Haken to be bad, Fitch."

They walked in silence for a time. Fitch got the feeling she was off somewhere in her memories of hanging by a rope around her throat. He wondered why she didn't choke to death. Maybe the rope wasn't tight, he decided—tied with a knot so it would hold its loop. He wondered how she got away. He knew, though, that he'd asked enough about it, and dared ask no more.

He listened to the stone chips crunching under their boots. He stole careful glances, now and again. She no longer looked happy, like she had at first. He wished he'd kept his question to himself.

Finally, he thought maybe he'd ask her about something that had made her smile before. Besides, it was why he had really wanted to walk along with her in the first place.

"Franca, what was the Wizard's Keep like?"

He was right; she did smile. "Huge. You can't even imagine it, and I couldn't tell you how big it is. It stands up on a mountain overlooking Aydindril, beyond a stone bridge crossing a chasm thousands of feet deep. Part of the Keep is cut from the mountain itself. There are notched walls rising up like cliffs. Broad ramparts, wider than this road, go to various structures. Towers rise up above the Keep, here and there. It was magnificent."

"Did you ever see a Seeker of Truth? Did you ever see the Sword of Truth, when you was there?"

She frowned over at him. "You know, as a matter of fact, I did. My mother was a sorceress. She went to Aydindril to

see the First Wizard about something—what, I've no idea.
We went across one of those ramparts to the First Wizard's
enclave in the Keep. He has a separate place where he had
wonders of every sort. I remember that bright and shiny
sword."

She seemed well pleased with telling him about it, so he
asked, "What was it like? The First Wizard's enclave? And
the Sword of Truth?"

"Well, let me see. . . ." She put a finger to her chin to
think a moment before she began her story.

CHAPTER 37

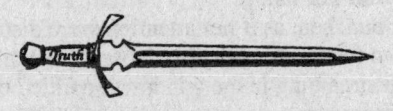
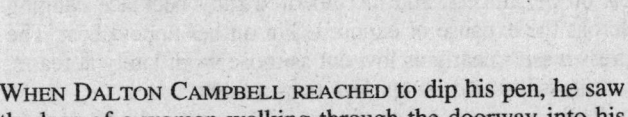

WHEN DALTON CAMPBELL REACHED to dip his pen, he saw
the legs of a woman walking through the doorway into his
office. By the thick ankles he knew before his gaze lifted
that it was Hildemara Chanboor. If there was a woman with
less appealing legs, he had yet to meet her.

He set down the pen and rose with a smile. "Lady Chanboor, please, come in."

In the outer office, the morning sunlight revealed Rowley
on duty, standing ready to summon the messengers should
Dalton have call for them. He didn't at the moment, but
with Hildemara Chanboor paying a visit, that eventuality
seemed more likely.

As she closed the door, Dalton went around his desk and

pulled out a comfortable chair in invitation. She wore a wool dress the color of straw. The color of the dress conveyed a sickly pallor to her flesh. The hem came to midcalf on her puffy, straight, pillar-like legs.

Hildemara glanced briefly at the chair, but remained standing.

"So good to see you, Lady Chanboor."

She put on a smile. "Oh, Dalton, must you always be so proper? We've known each other long enough for you to call me Hildemara." He opened his mouth to thank her, but she added, "When we're alone."

"Of course, Hildemara."

Hildemara Chanboor never made visits to inquire after anything so mundane as matters of work. She only arrived like a chill wind before a storm. Dalton decided it best to let the foul weather build on its own, without his help, like some wizard summoning it forth. He also thought it better to keep the meeting on a more formal level, despite her indulgence with her name.

Her brow bunched, as if her attention were distracted. She reached out to fuss with a possibly loose thread on his shoulder. Sunlight streaming in the windows sparkled off the jewels on her fingers, and the bloodred ruby necklace hanging across the expanse of exposed skin on her upper chest. The dress wasn't nearly as low-cut as those worn lately at feasts, yet he still found its cut less than refined.

With a woman's tidy touch, Hildemara picked and then smoothed. Dalton glanced, but didn't see anything. Seeming to have satisfied herself, her hand gently pressed out the fabric of his light coat against his shoulder.

"My, my, Dalton, but don't you have fine shoulders. So muscular and firm." She looked into his eyes. "Your wife is a lucky woman to have a man so well endowed."

"Thank you, Hildemara." His caution prevented him saying another word.

Her hand moved to his cheek, her bejeweled fingers gliding over the side of his face.

"Yes, she is a very lucky woman."

"And your husband is a lucky man."

Chortling, she withdrew her hand. "Yes, he is often lucky. But, as is said, what is commonly thought luck is often merely the result of incessant practice."

"Wise words, Hildemara."

The cynical laugh evaporated and she soon returned the hand to his collar, ordering it, as if it needed ordering. Her hand wandered to the side of his neck, a finger licking the rim of his ear.

"The word I hear is that your wife is faithful to you."

"I am a lucky man, my lady."

"And that you are equally faithful to her."

"I care for her deeply, and I also respect the vows we have taken."

"How quaint." Her smile widened. She pinched his cheek. He thought it more stern than playful in manner. "Well, someday I hope to convince you to be a little less . . . stuffy, in your attitudes, shall we say."

"If any woman could open my eyes to a broader attitude, Hildemara, it would be you."

She patted his cheek, the cynical laugh returning. "Oh, Dalton, but you are an exceptional man."

"Thank you, Hildemara. Coming from you that is quite the compliment."

She took a breath as if to change the mood. "And you did an exceptional job with Claudine Winthrop and Director Linscott. Why, I never imagined anyone could so deftly lance two boils at once."

"I do my best for the Minister and his lovely wife."

She regarded him with cold calculation. "The Minister's wife was quite humiliated by the woman's loose lips."

"I don't believe she will be any further—"

"I want her done away with."

Dalton cocked his head. "I beg your pardon?"

Hildemara Chanboor's expression soured.

"Kill her."

Dalton straightened and clasped his hands behind his back. "Might I inquire as to the reason you would request such a thing?"

"What my husband does is his business. The Creator knows he is what he is and nothing short of castration will change it. But I'll not have women humiliating me before the household by making me look a fool. Discreet indulgences are one thing; publicly airing tales to make me the butt of whispering and jokes is quite another."

"Hildemara, I don't believe Claudine's loose talk was in any way meant to place you at any disadvantage, nor should it, but rather to denounce Bertrand for inappropriate conduct. Nevertheless, I can assure you she has been silenced and has lost her position of trust among people in authority."

"My, my, Dalton, but aren't you the gallant one."

"Not at all, Hildemara. I just hope to show you——"

She took hold of his collar again, her manner no longer gentle. "She has become revered by foolish people who actually believe that load of dung about starving children and putting men to work with her law. They crowd her door seeking her favor in any number of causes.

"Such reverence by the people is dangerous, Dalton. It gives her power. Worse, though, was the nature of the charges she made. She was telling people Bertrand forced himself on her. That amounts to rape."

He knew where she was going, but he preferred she put words to it, and clear excuse to her orders. Such would later leave him with more arrows should he ever need them and her less room for denial, or for abandoning him to the wolves, if it suited her purpose or worse, her mood.

"An accusation of rape would elicit hardly more than a yawn from the people," Dalton said. "I could easily get them to see such a thing as the prerogative of a man in a position of great power who needed a simple and harmless release of tension. None would seriously begrudge him such a victimless act. I could easily prove the Minister to be above such common law."

Her fist tightened on his collar.

"But Claudine could be brought into the Office of Cultural Amity and invited to testify. The Directors fear Bertrand's power, and skill. They are jealous of me, too. Should they have a mind, they might champion the woman's cause as offensive to the Creator, even if outside commoners' law.

"Such a supposed offense against the Creator could disqualify Bertrand from consideration for Sovereign. The Directors could join forces and take a stand, leaving us suddenly helpless and at their mercy. We could all be out looking for new quarters before we knew what happened."

"Hildemara, I think—"

She pulled his face closer to her own.

"I want her killed."

Dalton had always found that a plain woman's kind and generous nature could make her tremendously alluring. The other side of that coin was Hildemara; her selfish despotism and boundless hatred of anyone who stood in the way of her ambition corrupted any appealing aspect she possessed into irredeemable ugliness.

"Of course, Hildemara. If that is your wish, then it shall be done." Dalton gently removed her hand from his collar. "Any particular instructions as to how you would like it accomplished?"

"Yes," she hissed. "No accident, this deed. This is killing and it should look like a killing. There is no value in the lesson if my husband's other bedmates fail to grasp it.

"I want it to be messy. Something that will open women's eyes. None of this dying-peacefully-in-her-sleep business."

"I see."

"Our hands must look entirely clean in this. Under no circumstances can suspicion point to the Minister's office— but I want it to be an object lesson to those who might consider wagging their tongues."

Dalton already had a plan in mind. It would fit the requirements. No one would think it an accident, it would certainly be messy, and he knew exactly where fingers would point, should he need fingers to point.

He had to admit that Hildemara had valid arguments. The

417

Directors had been shown the glint off the Minister's axe. They might decide in their own self-interest to swing an axe themselves.

Claudine could make more trouble. It was unwise to knowingly allow such a potential danger to remain at large. He regretted what had to be done, but he couldn't disagree that it needed doing.

"As you wish, Hildemara."

Her smile paid another visit to her face.

"You have been here only a short time, Dalton, but I have come to greatly respect your ability. And, too, if there is one thing I trust about Bertrand, it's his ability to find people who can accomplish the job required. He has to be good at choosing people to properly handle the work, you see, or he might have to actually take care of matters himself, and that would require him to vacate the loins of whoever fascinated him at the moment.

"I trust you didn't get to where you are by being squeamish, Dalton?"

He knew without doubt she had placed discreet inquiries as to his competence. She would already know he was up to the task. Further, she would not risk such a demand had she not been sure he would honor it. There were others to whom she could have turned.

With ever so much care, he spun a new line on his cobweb.

"You requested a favor of me, Hildemara. The favor is well within my capacity."

It was not a favor, and they both knew it; it was an order. Still, he wanted to fasten her more closely to the deed, if only in her own mind, and such a seed would set down roots.

Ordering a murder was a great deal worse than any accusation of a petty rape. He might someday have need of something within her sphere of influence.

She smiled with satisfaction as she cupped his cheek. "I knew you were the right man for the job. Thank you, Dalton."

He bowed his head.

Like the sun going behind a cloud, her expression darkened. Her hand moved down his face until a single finger lifted his chin.

"And keep in mind that while I may not have the power to castrate Bertrand, I can you, Dalton. Any time it pleases me."

Dalton smiled. "Then I shall be sure to give you no cause, my lady."

CHAPTER 38

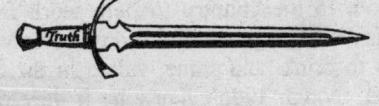

FITCH SCRATCHED HIS ARM through his crusty old scullion clothes. He'd never realized what rags they were until he'd been in his messenger uniform for a while. He relished the respect he was given as a messenger. It wasn't like he was important or anything, but most people respected messengers as someone with a responsibility; no one ever respected scullions.

He hated putting back on his old clothes. It felt like putting back on his old life, and he never wanted to go back to that. He liked working for Dalton Campbell, and would do anything to keep that job.

For this, though, his old clothes were necessary.

The sweet melody of a lute rippled in from a faraway inn. Probably the Jolly Man tavern, over on Wavern Street, he guessed. They often had a minstrel sing there.

The piercing warbles from a reed shawm intermittently cut through the night. At times the shawm went silent, and then the minstrel sang ballads whose words were unintelligible because of the distance. The tune, though, was quick and pleasant and made Fitch's heart beat faster.

He glanced back over his shoulder and in the moonlight saw the grim faces of the other messengers. They, too, were all back in the clothes of their former lives. Fitch intended to remain in his new life. He wouldn't let the other men down. No matter what, he wouldn't let them down.

They looked a scruffy bunch, they did. Dressed as they were, no one would likely recognize them. No one would be able to tell them from any of the other young redheaded Haken men in rags.

There were always young Haken men around in Fairfield, hoping for someone to hire them for any task. Often they were chased away from the streets where they gathered. Some went out to the country to help work farms, some found work in Fairfield if only for a day, some went behind the buildings to drink, and some waited in the dark to rob people. Those, though, didn't live long if they were caught by the city guards, and they usually were.

Morley's boots creaked as he shifted his weight as he crouched beside Fitch. Fitch, like the rest of the men, wore his boots for this, even though they were part of his uniform; people wouldn't be able to tell anything from boots.

Even though Morley wasn't yet a messenger, Master Campbell had asked him to join Fitch and the others who weren't off to distant places with messages. Morley had been disappointed that he didn't get to be a messenger along with Fitch. Fitch told him what Master Campbell had said about Morley being useful from time to time for various work, and how he would someday likely join the messenger service. For now, that was good enough hope for Morley.

Fitch's new friends among the messengers were nice enough, but he was glad to have Morley along. He and Morley had been kitchen scullions together for a long time.

That meant something. When you'd been getting drunk with someone for years, it was a strong bond, as Fitch figured it. Morley seemed to feel the same and was glad to be asked along so he might prove himself.

Despite his fear, Fitch, too, didn't want to let Dalton Campbell down. More than that, for this task, he and Morley both had cause. For them, unlike the other men, this was personal. Still, it had Fitch's palms sweating and he had to wipe them on his knees every few minutes.

Morley nudged Fitch. Fitch peered off to the dimly lit road outside the row of two- and three-story stone buildings. He saw Claudine Winthrop step out onto the landing attached to the front of one of them. There was a man beside her, just as Master Campbell had said there would be—a finely dressed Ander wearing a sword. By the narrow scabbard it looked a light sword. Quick, but deadly, Fitch imagined as he gave it a few parries in his mind.

Rowley, in his messenger outfit, stepped up to the tall Ander man as he came down off the landing and handed him a rolled message. Rowley and the man spoke as he broke the seal and unfurled the paper, but Fitch was too far away to hear the words.

Music rose from an inn in the distance. At the Jolly Man, the minstrel sang and played his lute and shawm. People, most wearing a light cloak or shawl, talked and laughed as they passed up and down the street. Men somewhere in a hall all laughed together now and again. Carriages with folded-down tops carried finely dressed folks. Horses and wagons went by, jangling and clopping, adding to the confusion of noise at the edge of Fairfield.

The man stuffed the paper in the pocket of his dark doublet as he turned to Claudine Winthrop, gesturing as he spoke words Fitch couldn't hear. She looked up the street into Fairfield, and then shook her head. She lifted a hand toward the estate, toward the road where Fitch and the other messengers in their old clothes waited. She was smiling and seemed in a good mood.

The man with her then took up her hand, shaking it as

he seemed to bid her a good night. She waved a farewell as he hurried off down the street and into the city.

Dalton Campbell had sent the message with Rowley. Now that the message was delivered, Rowley vanished into the streets. Rowley had instructed them as to exactly how it was to work. Rowley always instructed them. If Master Campbell wasn't around, Rowley always knew what to do.

Fitch liked Rowley. For a Haken, the young man seemed pretty confident in himself. Dalton Campbell treated him with respect, just like he treated everyone else, but maybe with a little more. If Fitch were blind he might have thought Rowley was Ander. Except he treated Fitch kindly, if in a businesslike manner.

Claudine Winthrop, alone, turned to the road back to the estate. Two of the patrolling city guard, big Ander men armed with cudgels, ambled up the street and watched her go. It wasn't a great distance. Just an hour's walk or so.

The night was pleasant, warm enough to be comfortable, and not so warm that the walk would work up a sweat. And the moon was out. A pleasant night for a brisk walk back to the estate. She snugged her cream-colored shawl around her shoulders, covering her skin, though there wasn't as much flesh showing as Fitch had seen before.

She could have sat down on a bench and waited for one of the carriages that regularly ran back and forth between the estate and the city, but she didn't. There was really no need. When a carriage caught up with her as she walked back, she could always take it then, if she tired of walking.

Rowley was off to insure that the carriage was delayed with an errand.

Fitch waited with the rest of the men, where Rowley told them to wait, and watched Claudine Winthrop walking briskly up the road. The beat of the music strummed in Fitch's head. The sound felt connected to the pounding of his heart.

He watched her coming up the road, his finger tapping against his bent knee as the shawm played a bouncy tune Fitch knew, called "Round the Well and Back," about a man chasing a woman he loved, but who always ignored him. The man finally had enough and chased her in the song until he caught her. He then held her down and asked her to wed him. She said yes. Then the man lost his nerve and she was the one who chased him round the well and back.

As Claudine strode down the road, she looked to be less comfortable with her decision to walk. She glanced at the fields of wheat to her right and the sorghum to her left. She quickened up her pace as the light of the city fell away behind her. Only moonlight accompanied her down the ribbon of road between the silent fields to each side.

Fitch, squatted down on the balls of his feet, could feel himself rocking, his heart was pounding so hard. He wished he wasn't there, going to do what he was going to do. He knew nothing would ever be the same again.

He wondered, too, if he really would be able to do as he had been told to do. He wondered if he would have the nerve. There were enough other men, after all. He wouldn't really have to do anything. They could do it.

But Dalton Campbell wanted him to do it. Wanted him to learn what was necessary when people didn't do as they promised they would do. Wanted him to be part of the team of messengers.

He had to do this to be part of the team. To really be part. They wouldn't be afraid like he was. He couldn't show his fear.

He was frozen, staring wide-eyed as she got closer, her shoes crunching against the road. He felt terror rising up inside at the whole idea. He wished she would turn around and run. She was still far enough away. It had seemed so simple when he had nodded to Dalton Campbell's instructions.

It sounded plain enough when he stood there in Dalton Campbell's office, as he explained it. In the light. It made sense in the light. Fitch had tried to help her with a warning. It wasn't his fault she went against orders.

It seemed altogether different in the dark, out in a field, as he watched her, all alone, getting closer.

He set his jaw. He couldn't let the others down. They would be proud of him for being as tough as they. He would show them he could be one of them.

This was his new life. He didn't want to go back to the kitchen. Back to Gillie twisting his ear and scolding him for his vile Haken ways. Back to being "Fetch," like he was before Dalton Campbell gave him a chance to prove himself.

Fitch nearly cried out in startled fright when Morley sprang up, lunging for the woman.

Before he had time to think, Fitch flew after his friend.

Claudine gasped. She tried to cry out, but Morley clamped a meaty hand over her mouth as he and Fitch tackled her. Fitch whacked his elbow painfully against the ground as they all crashed to the road. The impact drove a deep grunt from her as Morley landed on her with all his weight.

Her arms flailed. Her legs kicked. She tried to scream, but couldn't get much out. They were far enough out that no one was likely to hear even if she did.

She seemed all elbows and knees. She twisted and fought for her life. Fitch finally snagged one of her arms and twisted it behind her back. Morley got a good grip on her other arm and hauled her to her feet. With a cord, Fitch secured her wrists behind her back as Morley stuffed a rag in her mouth and tied a gag around her head.

Morley and Fitch each grabbed her under an arm and started dragging her down the road. She dug in her heels, twisting and pulling. The other men swarmed all around. Two of them each grappled a leg and lifted her clear of the ground. Another man took ahold of her hair.

Together, the five of them, with the others in a tight knot around them, trotted maybe another half mile down the road, farther away from the city. Claudine Winthrop, in the clutch of terror, screamed against the gag. She wrenched and squirmed violently the whole way.

She had good cause to be in such panic, after what she'd done.

When they were out of sight of the city and then some, they cut off the road to the right, through the wheat field. They wanted to be off the road in case someone came along. They didn't want to have a coach unexpectedly come upon them. They didn't want to have to drop her and run for it. Dalton Campbell would not like to hear that they messed up.

When they'd gone over a gentle swell in the land, to where they figured they were out of sight and out of earshot, they finally dumped her on the ground. She cried out with muffled screams against the gag. In the moonlight Fitch could see her wide eyes, like a hog at butcher.

Fitch panted, less from exertion than from his dread at what they were doing. His heart pounded in his ears and thumped against his chest. He could feel his knees trembling.

Morley lifted Claudine Winthrop to her feet and held her up from behind.

"I warned you," Fitch said. "Are you stupid? I warned you not to ever again tell anyone your treasonous accusations against our Minister of Culture. It's a lie that the Minister raped you, and you said you'd stop saying it, and now you've broken your word."

She was shaking her head vigorously. That she was trying to deny it only made Fitch more determined.

"I told you not to say those vile lies about our Minister of Culture! You said you wouldn't! You told me you wouldn't. Now you've gone flapping your tongue again with those same hateful lies."

"You tell her, Fitch," one of the other men said.

"That's right. Fitch is right," another said.

"You gave her a chance," still another said.

Several of the men clapped Fitch on the back. It made him feel good that they were proud of him. It made him feel important.

She shook her head. Her brow was bunched to a knot of skin in the middle.

"They're all right," Morley said as he shook her. "I was there. I heard him tell you. You should have done what you was told. Fitch gave you a chance, he did."

She frantically tried to talk against the gag. Fitch yanked it down below her chin.

"No! I never did! I swear, sir! I never said anything after you told me not to! I swear! Please! You have to believe me—I wouldn't tell anyone—not after you told me to keep quiet—I wouldn't—I didn't!"

"You did!" Fitch's fists balled into tight knots. "Master Campbell told us you did. Are you now calling Master Campbell a liar?"

She shook her head. "No! Please, sir, you must believe me!" She started to sob. "Please sir, I did as you said."

Fitch was enraged to hear her deny it. He had warned her. He had given her a chance. Master Campbell had given her a chance, and she had continued with her treason.

Even her calling him "sir" didn't bring him much delight. But the men behind urging him on did.

Fitch didn't want to hear any more of her lies. "I told you to keep your mouth shut! You didn't!"

"I did," she said as she wept, hanging in Morley's arms. "I did. Please, I told no one anything. I never told—"

Hard as he could, Fitch slammed his fist square into her face. Straight in. All his might. He felt bone snap.

The blow stung his fist, but it was only a far-off pain. Great gouts of blood bloomed across her face in lurid gushes.

"Good one, Fitch!" Morley called out, staggered a step by the blow. Other men agreed. "Give it to her again!"

Feeling pride at the praise, Fitch let the rage go wild. He cocked his arm. She was trying to harm Dalton Campbell and the Minister—the future Sovereign. He liberated his anger at this Ander woman.

His second blow to her face tumbled her out of Morley's grip. She crashed to her side on the ground. Fitch could see her jaw was unhinged. He couldn't recognize her face, what with the way her nose was flattened and with all the blood.

It was shocking, in a distant sort of way, like he was watching someone else doing it.

Like a pack of dogs, the rest of the men were on her. Morley was the strongest, and fierce. They lifted her. They all seemed to be punching her at once. Her head snapped one way and then the other. She doubled over from punches in the gut. The men walloped her in the kidneys. Blow after blow rained down, driving her from the arms that were holding her up, pummeling her to the ground.

Once she was down, they all started kicking her. Morley kicked the back of her head. Another man stomped down on the side of it. Others kicked her body so hard it lifted her from the ground, or rolled this way and that. The sounds of the blows, hollow and sharp, almost drowned out the grunts of effort.

Fitch, landing a kick in her ribs, seemed to be in some quiet place, watching the whole thing. It disgusted him, but it excited him at the same time. He was part of something important, with other good men, doing important work for Dalton Campbell and the Minister of Culture—the future Sovereign.

But a part of him was sickened by what was happening. A part of him wanted to run crying from what was happening. A part of him wished they had never found her coming out of that building.

But a part of him was wildly excited by it, excited to be part of it, excited to be one of the men.

He didn't know how long it went on. It seemed forever.

The thick smell of blood filled his nostrils and seemed to coat his tongue. Blood saturated their clothes. It gloved their fists. It was splattered across their faces.

The heady experience filled Fitch with a profound sense of camaraderie. They laughed with the exhilaration of brotherhood.

When they heard the sound of the carriage, they all froze. Sharing the same wild look in their eyes, they stood panting as they listened.

The carriage stopped.

Before they had a chance to find out why, or anyone came over the hill, they all, as one, ran for it, ran for a dunk in a distant pond to wash off the blood.

CHAPTER 39

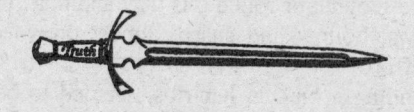

DALTON GLANCED UP FROM the report when he heard the knock.

"Yes?"

The door opened and Rowley's head of red hair poked in.

"Master Campbell, there's someone out here wants to see you. Says his name is Inger. Says he's a butcher."

Dalton was busy and wasn't in the mood to handle kitchen troubles. There were already enough troubles he needed to handle. There were any number of problems, running the gamut from the trifling to the serious, needing his attention.

The murder of Claudine Winthrop had created a sensation. She was well known and widely liked. She was important. The city was in an uproar. But, if a person knew how to properly handle such things, confusion created opportunity. Dalton was in his element.

He had made sure Stein was addressing the Directors of Cultural Amity at the time of the murder so no one would be able to raise any suspicion of him. A man with a cape of human scalps, even if they were taken in war, tended to raise suspicion.

The city guard had reported seeing Claudine Winthrop leaving Fairfield to walk back to the estate—commonly done, even at night; it was a heavily traveled road and previously believed perfectly safe. The guard reported, too, young Haken men gathered that night drinking before the murder. People naturally surmised she had been attacked by Hakens and loudly decried the incident as yet more proof of Haken hatred of Anders.

Guards now escorted people who walked at night.

There was a chorus of demands that the Minister do something. Edwin Winthrop, taken by the shock of his wife's murder, was bedridden. From his bed he, too, sent demands for justice.

Several young men had later been arrested, but were released when it was proven they had been working at a farm the night of the murder. Men in a tavern the next night, emboldened by rum, went searching for the "Haken killers." They found several Haken boys they were sure were guilty and beat them to death in front of cheering onlookers.

Dalton had written several speeches for the Minister and had issued orders in his name for a number of crisis measures. The murder gave the Minister an excuse to allude, in his fiery speeches, to those who opposed him for Sovereign as being responsible for stirring up contempt for the law and thus violence. He called for more stringent laws regulating "rancorous language." His addresses to the Office of Cultural Amity, if not the new laws, weakened the knees of Directors suspicious of the Minister.

Before the crowds who gathered to hear his words, the Minister had called for new measures—unspecified—to deal with violence. Such measures were always unspecified and only rarely was any real action taken. The mere impassioned plea was all that was required to convince the people the Minister was decisive and effective. Perception was the goal and all that really mattered. Perception was easily accomplished, required little effort, and it never had to stand the test of reality.

Of course, taxes would have to be raised in readiness to fund these measures. It was a perfect formula: opposition was seen as fostering violence and equated to the brutality of Haken overlords and murderers. The Minister and Dalton thus gained control over a larger portion of the economy. Control was power.

Bertrand relished being at the center of it all, issuing orders, denouncing evil, convening various groups of concerned citizens, reassuring people. The whole thing most likely would soon die out as people went on to other things and forgot about the murder.

Hildemara was happy; that was all that mattered to Dalton.

Rowley stood with his head in the door, waiting.

"Tell Inger to take his problem to Mr. Drummond," Dalton said as he picked up another of his messages. "Drummond is the kitchen master and is responsible for the feast. I gave him a list of instructions. The man ought to know how to order meat."

"Yes, sir."

The door closed and the room fell silent except for the gentle sound of spring rain. Gentle steady rain would be good for the crops. A good harvest would help annul grievances about the burden of new taxes. Dalton relaxed back in his chair and resumed his reading.

It seemed the person writing the message had seen healers going to the Sovereign's residence. He wasn't able to talk to the healers, but said they were in the Sovereign's residence the whole night.

It could be someone other than the Sovereign needing help. The Sovereign had a huge household, after all—nearly the size of the Minister's estate, except it was exclusively for the use of the Sovereign. Business, what there was of it for the Sovereign, was conducted in a separate building. There, too, he took audiences.

It wasn't uncommon for a healer or two to spend the night with a sick person at the Minister of Culture's estate, either, but that didn't mean the Minister himself was in need of healing. The greatest danger to the Minister was from a jealous husband, and that was highly unlikely; husbands tended to earn favor through their wives' trysts with high officials. Raising objections was unhealthy.

Once Bertrand was Sovereign, the possibility of injured feelings would no longer be a concern. It was a great honor for a woman to be with the Sovereign—it approached being a holy experience. Such divine couplings were widely believed to be blessed by the Creator Himself.

Any husband would push his wife into the Sovereign's bed, were she solicited. The prestige of this privilege conveyed along with the holiness a peripheral effect; the husband was the principal beneficiary of this collateral sanctity. Where the holy recipient of the Sovereign's carnal notice was young enough, the blessings embraced her parents.

Dalton returned to the previous message and read it again. The Sovereign's wife hadn't been seen in days. She failed to show up for an official visit to an orphanage. Perhaps she was the one who was sick.

Or, she might be at her husband's bedside.

Waiting for the old Sovereign to die was like walking a tightrope. The wait brought sweat to the brow, and quickened the pulse. The expectation was delicious, all the more so because the Sovereign's death was the one event Dalton couldn't control. The man was too heavily guarded to risk helping him to the afterlife, especially when he only hung to life by a thread anyway.

All he could do was wait. But everything had to be carefully managed in the meantime. They had to be ready when the opportunity came.

Dalton went to the next message, but it concerned nothing more than a man who had a complaint against a woman for supposedly casting spells to afflict him with gout. The man had been—publicly—trying to enlist Hildemara Chanboor's help, since she was universally recognized for her purity and good deeds, by having sex with him in order to drive out the evil spell.

Dalton let out a brief chuckle at his mental image of the coupling; the man was obviously deranged, besides having no taste in women. Dalton wrote down the man's name to give to the guards and then sighed at the nonsense that took up his time.

The knock came again. "Yes?"

Rowley again stuck in his head. "Master Campbell, I told the butcher, Inger, as you said. He says it isn't about kitchen matters." Rowley lowered his voice to a whisper. "Says it's about trouble at the estate, and he wants to talk to you about it, but if you won't see him, he says, he'll have to go to the Directors' office, instead."

Dalton opened a drawer and swept the messages into it. He turned over several reports that sat on his desk before he rose.

"Send the man in."

Inger, a muscular Ander, perhaps a decade older than Dalton, entered with a bob of his head.

"Thank you for seeing me, Master Campbell."

"Of course. Please come in."

The man dry-washed his hands as he bobbed his head again. He looked surprisingly clean, compared with what Dalton expected of a butcher. He looked more like a merchant. Dalton realized that to supply the estate the man probably had a sizable operation, and so would be more like a merchant than a laborer.

Dalton held out a hand in invitation. "Please, have a seat, Master Inger."

Inger's eyes darted about the room, taking it all in. He did everything but let out a low whistle. A small merchant, Dalton amended to himself.

"Thank you, Master Campbell." The burly man clamped a meaty hand on the chair back and flicked it closer to the desk. "Just plain Inger is fine. Used to it being Inger." His lips twitched with a smile. "Only my old teacher used to call me Master Inger, and that was just before I'd get my knuckles rapped. Usually when I neglected a reading lesson. I never got my knuckles rapped for numbers lessons. I liked numbers. Good thing, as it turns out. Numbers help with my business."

"Yes, I can see where they would," Dalton said.

Inger looked off at the battle flags and lances as he went on. "I have a good business, now. The Minister's estate is my biggest customer. Numbers are necessary for a business. Got to know numbers. I have a lot of good people working for me. I make them all learn numbers so I don't get shorted when they deliver."

"Well, the estate is quite pleased with your services, I can assure you. The feasts wouldn't be the success they are without your valuable help. Your pride in your business is obvious in your fine meats and fowl."

The man grinned as if he'd just been kissed by a pretty girl in a booth at a fair. "Thank you, Master Campbell. That's very kind of you. You're right about me taking pride in my work. Most people aren't as kind as you to notice. You are as good a man as folks say."

"I try my best to help people. I am but their humble servant." Dalton smiled agreeably. "Is there some way I can help you, Inger? Something I could smooth out at the estate to make your job easier?"

Inger scooted his chair closer. He placed an elbow on the desk and leaned in. His arm was as big as a small rum cask. His timid mannerisms seemed to evaporate as his thick brow drew down.

"The thing is, Master Campbell, I don't take any guff from the people who work for me. I spend time teaching them my ways with cutting and preparing meat, and teaching them numbers and such. I don't put up with people who don't do their work and take pride in it. Cornerstone of a successful business, I always say, is the customer being satisfied. Those who work for me who don't toe the line my way see the back of my hand or the door. Some say I'm harsh about it, but that's just the way I am. Can't change at this age."

"Sounds a fair enough attitude to me."

"But on the other hand," Inger went on, "I value those who work for me. They do good by me, and I do good by them. I know how some people treat their workers, especially their Haken workers, but I don't go in for that. People treat me right, I treat them right. It's only fair.

"That being the way things are, you come to be friends with people who live and work with you. Know what I mean? Over the years they come to be almost like family. You care about them. It's only natural—if you have any sense."

"I can see how—"

"Some of them that work for me are the children of people who went before them and helped me become the respected butcher I am." The man leaned in some more. "I got two sons and they're good enough lads, but I sometimes think I care about some of those who live and work with me more than I care about those two boys.

"One of them who works for me is a nice Haken girl named Beata."

Alarm bells started chiming in Dalton's head. He remembered the Haken girl Bertrand and Stein had summoned upstairs for their amusement.

"Beata. Can't say as the name rings a bell, Inger."

"No reason it should. Her business is with the kitchen. Among other things, she delivers for me. I trust her like she were a daughter. She's smart with numbers. She remembers what I tell her. That's important because Hakens can't read, so I can't give them a list. It's important they remember. I never have to load for her; after I tell her what's to go she gets it right. I never have to worry about her getting orders wrong or being short."

"I can see—"

"So, all of a sudden, she doesn't want to deliver to the estate."

434

Dalton watched the man's fist tighten.

"We had a load to bring over today. An important load for a feast. I told her to go get Brownie hitched to the cart because I had a load for her to take to the estate.

"She said no." Inger's fist smacked the desktop. "No!"

The butcher sat back a little and righted an unlit candle that had taken flight.

"I don't take well to people I employ telling me no. But Beata, well, she's like a daughter. So, instead of giving her the back of my hand, I thought to reason with her. I figured maybe it was some boy she didn't like anymore she didn't want to see, or something like that. I don't always understand the things a girl can get in her head to make them go all moody.

"I sat her down and asked her why she didn't want to take the load to the estate. She said she just didn't. I said that wasn't good enough. She said she'd do double loads to somewhere else. She said she'd dress fowl all night as punishment, but she wouldn't go to the estate.

"I asked her why she didn't want to go, if it was because someone there did something to her. She refused to tell me. Refused! She said she wasn't going to take any more loads there and that was all there was to it.

"I told her that unless she told me why, so I could understand it, she was going to take the load out to the estate whether she wanted to or not.

"She started to cry."

Inger was making a fist again.

"Now, I've known Beata since she was sucking her thumb. I don't think that in the last dozen years I've ever seen that girl cry but once before. I've seen her slice herself open good when she was butchering, and she never cried, even when I stitched her. Made some real faces in pain, but she didn't cry. When her mother died, she cried. But that was the only time.

"Until I told her today she had to go to the estate.

"So, I brought the load myself. Now, Master Campbell, I don't know what went on here, but I can tell you that whatever it was, it made Beata cry, and that tells me it wasn't nothing good. She always liked going before. She spoke highly of the Minister as a man she respected for all he'd done for Anderith. She was proud to deliver to the estate.

"No longer.

"Knowing Beata, I'd say someone here had their way with her. Knowing Beata, I'd say she weren't willing. Not willing at all.

"Like I said, I almost think of that girl as my daughter." Dalton didn't take his eyes off the man. "She's Haken."

"So she is." Inger didn't take his eyes off Dalton.

"Now, Master Campbell, I want the young man who hurt Beata. I intend to hang that young man up on a meat hook. From the way Beata was bawling, I have a feeling it wasn't just one young man, but maybe more. Maybe a gang of boys hurt her.

"I know you're a busy man, what with the murder of that Winthrop woman, rest her soul, but I'd appreciate it if you looked into this for me. I don't intend to let it go by."

Dalton leaned forward and folded his hands on the table.

"Inger, I can assure you I won't tolerate such a thing happening at the estate. I consider this a very serious matter. The Minister of Culture's office is here to serve the people of Anderith. It would be the worst possible result if one or more men here harmed a young woman."

"Not if," Inger said. "Did."

"Of course. You have my personal assurance that I, personally, will pursue this to resolution. I'll not stand for anyone, Ander or Haken, being in any kind of danger at the estate. Everyone must be entirely safe here. I'll not allow anyone, Ander or Haken, to escape justice.

"You must understand, however, that with the murder of an important woman, and the possible danger to the lives of other people, including Haken women, my first responsibility lies there. The city is in a tumult over it. People expect such a grievous act to be punished."

Inger bowed his head. "I understand. I will accept your

436

personal assurance that I will have the name of the young man or men responsible." The chair scraped across the floor as Inger rose. "Or the not-so-young man."

Dalton stood. "Young or old, we will put all due effort into finding the culprit. You have my word."

Inger reached out and clasped hands with Dalton. The man had a crushing grip.

"I'm pleased to know I came to the right man, Master Campbell."

"You did indeed."

"Yes?" Dalton called out at the knock on the door. He expected he knew who it was and kept writing instructions for the new guards he was ordering posted at the estate. Guards at the estate were separate from the army. They were Anders. He wouldn't trust authentic guard duty to the army.

"Master Campbell?"

He looked up. "Come in, Fitch."

The boy strode in and stood erect before the desk. He seemed to be standing taller since he had put on the uniform and even more so since the business with Claudine. Dalton was pleased with the way Fitch and his muscular friend had followed instructions. Some of the others had given Dalton a confidential report.

Dalton set down the glass dipping pen. "Fitch, do you remember the first time we talked?"

The question staggered the boy a bit. "Yes . . . uh, yes, sir," he stammered. "I remember."

"Up the hall a ways. Near the landing."

"Yes, sir, Master Campbell. I surely was grateful for you not—I mean, for the kind way you treated me."

"For me not reporting you were somewhere you didn't belong."

"Yes, sir." He licked his lips. "That was very good of you, Master Campbell."

Dalton stroked a finger along his temple. "I recall you told me that day how the Minister was a good man and you wouldn't like to hear anyone say anything against him."

"Yes, sir, that's true."

"And you proved yourself as good as your word—proved you would do whatever needed doing to protect him." Dalton smiled just a little. "Do you remember what else I told you that day on the landing?"

Fitch cleared his throat. "You mean about me someday earning my sir name?"

"That's right. So far, you are living up to what I expected. Now, do you remember what else happened that day on the landing?"

Dalton knew without a doubt the boy remembered. It wouldn't be something he would soon forget. Fitch fidgeted as he tried to think of a way to say it without saying it.

"Well, sir, I . . . I mean, there was . . ."

"Fitch, you do recall that young lady smacking you?"

Fitch cleared his throat. "Yes, sir, I remember that."

"And you know her?"

"Her name is Beata. She works for the butcher, Inger. She's in my penance assembly."

"And you must have seen what she was doing up there? The Minister saw you. Stein saw you. You must have seen them with her?"

"It wasn't the Minister's fault, sir. She was getting what she'd asked for. Nothing more. She was always fawning over him, talking about how handsome he was, talking about how wonderful he was. She was always sighing aloud whenever she mentioned his name. Knowing her, she asked for what she got. Sir."

Dalton smiled to himself. "You liked her, didn't you, Fitch?"

"Well, sir, I don't know. It's kind of hard to like a person who hates you. Kind of wears you down, after a time."

Dalton could plainly see the boy's feelings for the girl. It was written all over his face, even if he denied it.

"Well the thing is, Fitch, this girl might of a sudden be

interested in causing trouble. Sometimes girls get that way, later. You will someday come to learn that. Be careful of doing what they ask, because they will sometimes later want to make it seem they never asked at all."

The boy looked bewildered. "I never knew such a thing, sir. Thank you for the advice."

"Well, as you said, she got no more than she asked for. There was no force involved. Now, though, she might be having second thoughts, and be looking to cry rape. Much the same as Claudine Winthrop. Women who are with important men sometimes do that, later, to try to get something. They get greedy."

"Master Campbell, I'm sure she wouldn't—"

"Inger paid me a visit a little earlier."

Fitch lost a little color. "She told Inger?"

"No. She told him only that she refused to deliver here to the estate. But Inger is a smart man. He figures he knows the reason. He wants what he figures to be justice. If he forces this girl, Beata, to charge a man, the Minister could be unjustly subjected to ugly accusations."

Dalton stood. "You know this girl. It may be necessary for you to handle her in the same way you dealt with Claudine Winthrop. She knows you. She would let you get close to her."

Fitch lost the rest of his color. "Master Campbell . . . sir, I . . ."

"You what, Fitch? You have lost your interest in earning a sir name? You have lost your interest in your new work as a messenger? You have lost your interest in your new uniform?"

"No sir, it's not that."

"Then what is it, Fitch?"

"Nothing, sir. I guess . . . like I said, anything that happened is no more than what she asked for. I can see that it wouldn't be right for her to be accusing the Minister of something wrong when he didn't do nothing wrong."

"No more than it was right for Claudine to do the same."

Fitch swallowed. "No, sir. No more right than that."

Dalton returned to his chair. "I'm glad we understand each other. I'll call you if she becomes a problem. Hopefully, that won't be necessary.

"Who knows, perhaps she will think better of such hateful accusations. Perhaps someone will talk some sense into her before it becomes necessary to protect the Minister from her wrongful charges. Perhaps she will even decide that butchering work is not for her, and she will go off to work on a farm, or something."

Dalton idly sucked on the end of the pen as he watched Fitch pull the door closed behind himself. He thought it would be interesting to see how the boy handled it. If he didn't, then Rowley surely would.

But if Fitch handled it, then all the pieces would fall together into a masterful mosaic.

CHAPTER 40

MASTER SPINK'S BOOTS THUNKED on the plank floor as he strode among the benches, hands clasped behind his back. People were still sobbing about the Ander women. Sobbing about what was done to them by the Haken army. Fitch thought he'd known what the lesson was going to be, but he was wrong. It was more horrible than he could have imagined.

He could feel his face glowing as red as his hair. Master

Spink had filled in a lot of the sketchy parts of Fitch's understanding of the act of sex. It had not been the pleasurable learning experience he had always anticipated. What he had always viewed with longing was now turned to repugnance by the stories of those Ander women.

It was made all the worse by the fact that there was a woman to each side of him on the bench. Knowing what the lesson was going to be, all the women had tried to sit together to one side of the room and all the men had tried to sit on the other side. Master Spink never much cared where they sat.

But when they'd filed in, Master Spink made them sit where he told them. Man, woman, man, woman. He knew everyone in the penance assembly, and knew where they lived and worked. He made them sit all mixed up, next to people from somewhere else, so they wouldn't know the person next to them so well.

He did that to make it more embarrassing for them when he told the stories of each woman and what was done to her. He described the acts in detail. There wasn't a lot of sobbing for most of it. People were too shocked by what they heard to cry, and too embarrassed to want to call attention to themselves.

Fitch, for one, had never heard such things about a man and a woman, and he'd heard a lot of things from some of the other scullions and messengers. Of course, the men were Haken overlords, and naturally they weren't at all kind or gentle. They meant to hurt the Ander women. To humiliate them. That was how hateful the Hakens were.

"No doubt you all are thinking," Master Spink went on, " 'that was so long ago. That was ages ago. That was the Haken overlords. We are better than that, now,' you are thinking."

Master Spink's boots stopped in front of Fitch. "Is that what you are thinking, Fitch? Is that what you are thinking in your fine uniform? Are you thinking you are better than the Haken overlords? That the Hakens have learned to be better?"

"No, sir," Fitch said. "We are no better, sir."

Master Spink grunted and then moved on. "Do any of you think the Hakens nowadays are outgrowing their hateful ways? Do you think you are better people than in the past?"

Fitch stole a glance to each side. About half the people tentatively raised their hands.

Master Spink exploded in rage. "So! You think Hakens are nowadays better? You arrogant people think you are better?"

The hands all quickly dropped back into laps.

"You are no better! Your hateful ways continue to this day!"

His boots started their slow thump, thump, thump as he walked among the silent assembly.

"You are no better," he repeated, but this time in a quiet voice. "You are the same."

Fitch didn't recall the man's voice ever sounding so defeated. He sounded as if he was about to cry himself.

"Claudine Winthrop was a most respected and renowned woman. While she was alive, she worked for all people, Hakens as well as Anders. One of her last works was to help change outdated laws so starving people, mostly Hakens, were able to find work.

"Before she died, she came to know that you are no different than those Haken overlords, that you are the same."

His boots thumped on across the room.

"Claudine Winthrop shared something with those women of long ago—those women I've taught you about today. She shared the same fate."

Fitch was frowning to himself. He knew Claudine didn't share the same fate. She died quick.

"Just like those women, Claudine Winthrop was raped by a gang of Hakens."

Fitch looked up, his frown growing. As soon as he realized he was frowning, he changed the expression on his face. Fortunately, Master Spink was on the other side of the room, looking into the eyes of Haken boys over there, and didn't see Fitch's startled reaction.

"We can only guess how many hours poor Claudine Winthrop had to endure the laughing, taunting, jeering men who raped her. We can only guess at the number of cruel heartless Hakens who put her through such an ordeal out there in that field but, by the way the wheat was trampled, the authorities say it must have been between thirty and forty men."

The class gasped in horror. Fitch gasped, too. There hadn't been half that number. He wanted to stand up and say it was wrong, that they didn't do such vile things to Claudine, and that she'd deserved killing for wanting to harm the Minister and future Sovereign and that it was his duty. Fitch wanted to say they'd done a good thing for the Minister and for Anderith. Instead, he hung his head.

"But it wasn't thirty to forty men," Master Spink said. He pointed his finger out at the room, sweeping it slowly from one side to the other. "It was all of you. All you Hakens raped and murdered her. Because of the hate you still harbor in your hearts, you all took part in that rape and murder."

He turned his back to the room. "Now, get out of here. I've had all I can stand of your hate-filled Haken eyes for one day. I can endure your crimes no longer. Go. Go, until next assembly and think on how you might be better people."

Fitch bolted for the door. He didn't want to miss her. He didn't want her to get out into the street. He lost track of her in the shuffle of others hurrying to get out, but he did manage to squeeze to near the head of the line.

Once out in the cool night air, Fitch moved off to the side. He checked those who'd left before him and rushed out to the street, but he didn't see her. He waited in the shadows and watched the rest of the people coming out.

When he saw her, he called her name in a loud whisper.

Beata halted and looked over. She peered into the shadows trying to tell who it was calling her name. People pushed past to get down the path, so she stepped off it, closer to him.

She no longer wore the dusky blue dress he liked so well,

the dress she had worn that day she went up to meet the Minister. She now had a wheat-colored dress with a dark brown bodice above the long flare of skirt.

"Beata, I have to talk to you."

"Fitch?" She put her hands on her hips. "Fitch, is that you?"

"Yes," he whispered.

She turned to leave. He snatched her wrist and yanked her into the shadows. The last of the people hurried off down the path, eager to go home and not interested in two young people meeting after assembly. Beata tried to wrench her arm free, but he kept a grip on it as he dragged her farther into the black shadows of the trees and bushes to the side of the assembly hall.

"Let go! Let go, Fitch, or I'll scream."

"I have to talk to you," he whispered urgently. "Come along!"

She instead fought him. He dragged and pulled until he at last reached a place deeper in the brush where they wouldn't be seen. If they were quiet, no one would hear them, either. Moonlight fell across them in the gap of brush and trees.

"Fitch! I'll not have your filthy Haken hands on me!"

He turned to her as he let go of her wrist. Immediately, her other arm came around to strike him. He'd been expecting it and caught her wrist. She slapped him hard with her other hand.

He slapped her right back. He hadn't hit her very hard at all, but the shock of it stunned her. A Haken man striking anyone was a crime. But he hadn't hit her hard at all. It wasn't his intent to hurt her, only to surprise her and make her pay attention.

"You have to listen to me," he growled. "You're in trouble."

In the moonlight he could clearly see her glower. "You're the one in trouble. I'm going to tell Inger you dragged me in the bushes, struck me, and then—"

444

"You've already told Inger enough!"

She was silent a moment. "I don't know what are you talking about. I'm leaving. I'll not stand here and have you strike me again, now that you've proven your hateful Haken ways with women."

"You're going to listen to me if I have to throw you on the ground and sit on you."

"You just try it, you skinny little eel."

Fitch pressed his lips tight as he tried to ignore the sting of the insult.

"Beata, please? Please just listen to me? I have important things I need to tell you."

"Important? Important to you, maybe, but not important to me! I don't want to hear anything you have to say. I know what you're like. I know how you enjoy—"

"Do you want to see the people working for Inger get hurt? Do you want Inger to get hurt? This has got nothing to do with me. I don't know why you think so low of me, but I'll not try to talk you out of it. This is only about you."

Beata folded her arms with a huff. She considered for a moment. He glanced to the side and checked through a gap in the brush to make sure no one on the street was watching. Beata smoothed her hair back above an ear.

"As long as you don't try to tell me what a fine young man you are in your fancy uniform, like those overlord beasts, then talk. But be quick about it. Inger has work for me."

Fitch wet his lips. "Inger went to the estate with the load today. He went because you refused to deliver to the estate anymore—"

"How do you know that?"

"I hear things."

"And how did—"

"You going to listen? You're in a lot of trouble and a lot of danger."

She put her fists on her hips but remained silent, so he went on. "Inger figures you got taken advantage of at the estate. He came and demanded something be done. He's demanding the name of the ones responsible for hurting you."

She appraised him in the moonlight.

"How do you know this?"

"I told you, I hear things."

"I didn't tell Inger any of that."

"Don't matter. He figured it out on his own or something—I don't know—but the important thing is he cares about you and he's hot for something to be done. He's got this idea in his head that he wants justice done. He's not going to let it go. He's set on causing trouble over it."

She sighed irritably. "I should never have refused to go. I should just have done it—no matter what might have happened again to me."

"I don't blame you, Beata. If I was you, I might've of done the same."

She eyed him suspiciously. "I want to know who told you all this."

"I'm a messenger, now, and I'm around important people. Important people talk about what's going on around the estate. I hear what they say, that's all, and I heard about this. The thing is, if you were to say what happened, people would see it as you were trying to hurt the Minister."

"Oh, come on, Fitch, I'm just a Haken girl. How could I hurt the Minister?"

"You told me yourself that people are saying he'll be the Sovereign. Have you ever heard anyone say anything against the Sovereign? Well, the Minister is almost to be named Sovereign.

"How do you think people will take it if you had your say about what happened? Do you think they'd believe you're a good girl telling the truth and the Minister was lying if he denies it? Anders don't lie, that's what we're taught. If you say anything against the Minister, you'll be the one marked a liar. Worse, a liar trying to do harm to the Minister of Culture."

She seemed to consider what he said as if it were an unsolvable riddle.

"Well . . . I'm not going to, but if I did say anything, the Minister would admit what I said was the truth—because it would be. Anders don't lie. Only Hakens are corrupt of nature. If he said anything about it, he would admit the truth."

Fitch sighed in frustration. He knew Anders were better than them, and that Hakens had the taint of an evil nature, but he was beginning to believe the Anders weren't all pure and perfect.

"Look, Beata, I know what we've learned, but it isn't always exactly true. Some of the things they teach don't make sense. It isn't all true."

"It's all true," she said flatly.

"You may think so, but it isn't."

"Really? I think you just don't want to admit to yourself how disgusting Haken men are. You just wish you didn't have such a depraved soul. You wish it wasn't true what Haken men did to those women long ago, and what Haken men did to Claudine Winthrop."

Fitch swiped his hair back from his forehead. "Beata, think about it. How could Master Spink know what was done to each of those women?"

"From books, you dolt. In case you've forgotten, Anders can read. The estate is full of books that—"

"And you think those men who were raping all those women stopped to keep records? You think they asked the women their names and all and then wrote it all down just right so there would be books listing everything they did?"

"Yes. That's exactly what they did. Just like all Haken men, they liked what they did to those women. They wrote it down. It's known. It's in books."

"And what about Claudine Winthrop? You tell me where the book is what tells about her being raped by the men who killed her."

"Well, she was. It's obvious. Hakens did it, and that's what Haken men do. You ought to know what Haken men are like, you little—"

"Claudine Winthrop made an accusation against the Minister. She was always yearning over him and acting interested in him. Then, after she caught his eye and she willingly gave herself to him, she decided to change her mind. She started saying he forced himself on her against her will. Just like what really happened to you. Then, after she started telling people such vicious lies that he raped her, she ended up dead."

Beata fell silent. Fitch knew Claudine was only trying to make trouble for the Minister—Dalton Campbell told him so. What happened to Beata, on the other hand, wasn't willing, but even so, Beata wasn't trying to make trouble over it.

Crickets chirred on as she stood in the darkness staring at him. Fitch glanced around again to make sure no one was close. He could see through the brush that people were strolling along the street. No one was paying any attention to the dark bushes where the two of them were.

Finally she spoke, but her voice didn't have the heat in it anymore. "Inger doesn't know anything, and I've no intention of telling him."

"It's too late for that. He already went to the estate and got people stirred up that you was raped there. Got important people stirred up. He made demands. He wants justice. Inger is going to make you tell who hurt you."

"He can't."

"He's Ander. You're Haken. He can. Even if he changed his mind and didn't, because of the hornets' nest he swatted, the people at the estate might decide to haul you before the Magistrate and have him put an order on you to name the person."

"I'll just deny it all." She hesitated. "They couldn't make me tell."

"No? Well it would sure make you a criminal, if you refused to tell them what happened. They think it's Haken men who did it and so they want the names. Inger is an Ander and he said it happened. If you didn't tell them what they ask they'd likely put you in chains until you changed your mind. Even if they didn't, at the least, you'd lose your work. You'd be an outcast.

"You said you wanted to join the army, someday—that it's your dream. Criminals can't join the army. That dream would be gone. You'd be a beggar."

"I'd find work. I work hard."

"You're Haken. Refusing to cooperate with a Magistrate would get you named a criminal. No one would hire you. You'd end up a prostitute."

"I would not!"

"Yes you would. When you got hungry and cold enough, you would. You'd have to sell yourself to men. Old men. Master Campbell told me the prostitutes get horrible diseases and die. You'd die like that, from being with old men who—"

"I would not! Fitch, I wouldn't. I wouldn't."

"Then how you going to live? If you get named a Haken criminal for refusing to answer a magistrate's questions, how you going to live?

"And if you did tell, who would believe you? You'd be called a liar and that would make you a criminal for lying about an Ander official. That's a crime, too, you know— lying about Ander officials by making false accusations."

She searched his eyes for a moment. "But it's not false. You could vouch for the truth of what I say.

"You said you wanted to be the Seeker of Truth, remember? That's your dream. My dream is joining the army, and yours is being a Seeker of Truth. As someone who wants to be a Seeker, you'd have to stand up and say it was true."

"See? You said you'd never tell, and now you're already talking about telling."

"But you could stand up with me and tell the truth of it."

"I'm a Haken. You think they're going to believe two Hakens against the Minister of Culture himself? Are you crazy?

"Beata, no one believed Claudine Winthrop, and she was Ander and she was important besides. She made the accusation to try to hurt the Minister, and now she's dead."

"But, if it's the truth—"

"And what's the truth, Beata? That you told me about what a great man the Minister was? That you told me how handsome you thought he is? That you looked up at his window and sighed and called him Bertrand? That you was all twinkly-eyed as you was invited up to meet the Minister? That Dalton Campbell had to hold your elbow to keep you from floating away with delight at the invitation to meet the Minister just so he could tell you to relay his message that he liked Inger's meats?

"I only know you and he . . . Maybe you got demanding, after. Women sometimes later get that way, from what I hear: demanding. After they act willing, then they sometimes make accusations in order to get something for themselves. That's what people say.

"For all I know, maybe you was so thrilled to meet him you hiked up your skirts to show him you was willing, and asked him if he'd like to have you. You never said anything to me. All I got from you was a slap—maybe for seeing you was having yourself a good time with the Minister when you was supposed to be working. For as much as I know about it, that could be the truth."

Beata's chin trembled as she tried to blink the tears from her eyes. She dropped to the ground, sat back on her heels, and started crying into her hands.

Fitch stood for a minute dumbly wondering what he should do. He finally knelt down in front of her. He was frightfully worried at seeing her cry. He'd known her a long time, and he'd never even heard stories of her crying, like other girls. Now she was bawling like a baby.

Fitch reached out to put a comforting hand on her shoulder. She shrugged the hand away.

Since she wasn't interested in being comforted, he just sat there, on his own heels, and didn't say anything. He thought briefly about going off and leaving her alone to her crying, but he figured maybe he should at least be there if she wanted something.

"Fitch," she said between sobs, tears streaming down her cheeks, "what am I going to do? I'm so ashamed. I've made

450

such a mess of it. It was all my fault—I tempted a good Ander man with my vile, wanton Haken nature. I didn't mean to, I didn't think I was, but that's what I did. What he did is all my fault.

"But I can't lie and say I was willing when I wasn't—not even a little. I tried to fight them off, but they were too strong. I'm so ashamed. What am I going to do?"

Fitch swallowed at the lump in his throat. He didn't want to say it, but for her sake he had to tell her. If he didn't, she was liable to end up like Claudine Winthrop—and he might be the one who would be called on to do it. Then everything would be ruined because he knew he couldn't do that. He'd be back in the kitchen, scrubbing pots—at best. But he'd do that before he'd hurt Beata.

Fitch took her hand and gently opened it. He reached in his coat pocket. In her palm he placed the pin with a spiral end. The pin Beata used to close the collar of her dress. The pin she had lost up on the third floor that day.

"Well, as I figure it, you're in a pack of trouble, Beata. I don't see as there's any way out of it but one."

CHAPTER 41

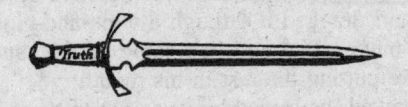

Teresa smiled. "Yes, please."

Dalton lifted two dilled veal balls from the platter held out by the squire. The Haken boy genuflected, spun with a light step, and glided past. Dalton set the meat on the charger he shared with Teresa as she nibbled on her favorite of suckling rabbit.

Dalton was tired and bored with the lengthy feast. He had work of importance that needed tending. Certainly his first responsibility was tending the Minister, but that goal would be better served handling matters behind the curtain of governance than on stage nodding and laughing at the Minister's witticisms.

Bertrand was waving a sausage as he told a joke to several wealthy merchants at the far end of the head table. By the merchants' guttural laughter, and the way Bertrand wielded the sausage, Dalton knew what sort of joke it was. Stein particularly enjoyed the bawdy story.

As soon as the laughter died down, Bertrand graciously apologized to his wife and asked that she forgive his joke. She let out a titter and dismissed it with an airy wave of a hand, adding that he was incorrigible. The merchants chuckled at her good-natured indulgence of her husband.

Teresa gently elbowed Dalton and whispered, "What was that joke the Minister told? I couldn't hear it."

"You should thank the Creator he didn't bless you with better hearing. It was one of Bertrand's jokes, if you follow."

"Well," she said with a grin, "will you tell me when we get home?"

Dalton smiled. "When we get home, Tess, I'll demonstrate it."

She let out a throaty laugh. Dalton picked up one of the veal balls and dragged it through a wine-and-ginger sauce. He let her have a bite and lick some of the sauce off his finger before putting the rest in his mouth.

As he chewed, he turned his attention to three of the Directors across the room engaged in what looked to be a serious conversation. They gestured expansively while leaning in, frowning, shaking their heads, and holding up fingers to make their point. Dalton knew what the conversation concerned. Nearly every conversation around the room involved a similar topic: the murder of Claudine Winthrop.

The Minister, wearing a purple-and-rust-striped close-fitting sleeveless jerkin over a golden-wheat-patterned sleeved doublet, draped his arm over Dalton's shoulders as he leaned close. The white ruffs at the Minister's wrist were stained with red wine, making him look as if he were bleeding from under the tight sleeve.

"Everyone is still quite upset over Claudine's murder," said Bertrand.

"And rightly so." Dalton dipped a mutton cube in mint jelly. "It was a terrible tragedy."

"Yes, it has made us all realize how frail is the grip we have on the ideals of civilized behavior we so cherish. It has shown us how much work yet lies before us in order to bring Hakens and Anders together in a peaceful society."

"With your wise leadership," Teresa said with genuine enthusiasm as Dalton ate the mutton cube, "we will succeed."

"Thank you for your support, my dear." Bertrand leaned just a little closer to Dalton, lowering his voice a bit, too. "I hear the Sovereign might be ill."

"Really?" Dalton sucked the mint jelly off his finger. "Is it serious?"

Bertrand shook his head in mock sorrow. "We've had no word."

"We will pray for him," Teresa put in as she selected a slender slice of peppered beef. "And for poor Edwin Winthrop."

Bertrand smiled. "You are a most thoughtful and kind-hearted woman, Teresa." He stared at her bodice, as if to see her kind heart beating there, behind her exposed cleavage. "If I am ever stricken ill, I could ask for no more noble a woman than you to pray to the Creator on my behalf. Surely, His own heart would melt at your tender beseeching words."

Teresa beamed. Hildemara, nibbling on a slice of pear, asked her husband a question and he turned back to her.

Stein leaned in to converse with them about something. They all pulled back when a squire brought a platter of crisped beef.

As Stein took a handful of the crisped beef, Dalton glanced again at the Directors, still engaged in their discussion. He scanned the table opposite them and caught the eye of Franca Gowenlock. The woman's face told him that she was unable to detect any of it. Dalton didn't know what was wrong with her powers, but it was becoming a serious impediment.

A squire held a silver platter toward the Minister. He took several slices of pork. Another came with lamb in lentil, which Hildemara favored. A steward poured more wine for the head table before moving on. The Minister enfolded a husband's arm around Hildemara's shoulder and spoke to her in a whisper.

A server entered carrying a large basket piled high with small loaves of brown bread. He took it to the serving board to be transferred onto silver trays. From a distance, Dalton couldn't tell if there was any problem with the bread. A large quantity of it had been declared unfit for the feast and had been consigned for donation to the poor. Leftover food from feasts, usually great quantities of it, was distributed to the poor.

Master Drummond had had some sort of trouble down in the kitchen earlier in the day with the baking of the bread. Something to do with the ovens going "crazy," as the man described it. A woman was badly burned before she could be doused. Dalton had more important things to worry about than baking bread, and hadn't inquired further.

"Dalton," the Minister said, returning his attention to his aide, "have you managed to prove out any evidence about the murder of poor Claudine Winthrop?"

On the other side of the Minister, Hildemara looked keenly interested in hearing Dalton's answer.

"I've been looking into several promising areas," Dalton said without committing himself. "I hope to soon reach a conclusion to the investigation."

As always, they had to be circumspect when they spoke at feasts, lest words they would not want repeated be carried to listening ears. Gifted listeners other than Franca might be present and having no trouble with their ability. Dalton, to say nothing of Bertrand and his wife, didn't doubt that the Directors might be using the gifted.

"Well, the thing is," Bertrand said, "Hildemara tells me some people are getting quite concerned that we aren't taking the matter seriously enough."

Dalton began to offer evidence to the contrary, when Bertrand held up a hand and went on.

"Of course this isn't true at all. I know for a fact how hard you've been working on apprehending the criminals."

"Day and night," Teresa said. "I can assure you, Minister Chanboor, Dalton is hardly getting any sleep of late, what with how hard he has been working since poor Claudine's murder."

"Oh I know," Hildemara said as she leaned past her husband to pat Dalton's wrist in a show for Teresa and any watching eyes. "I know how hard Dalton has been working. Everyone appreciates all he is doing. We know of the great number of people he has brought in to be interviewed for information.

"It's just that some people are beginning to question if all the effort is ever going to produce the guilty party. People fear the killers still among them and are eager to settle the matter."

"That's right," Bertrand said, "and we, more than anyone, want the murder solved so as to have the peace of mind that our people can rest safely again."

"Yes," Hildemara said, with a cold glint in her eye. "It must be solved."

There was no mistaking the icy command in her tone. Dalton didn't know if Hildemara had told Bertrand what she had ordered be done with Claudine, but it wouldn't really matter to him. He was finished with the woman and had moved on to others. He wouldn't mind at all if she cleaned up his mess behind him and silenced any potential trouble.

Dalton had been expecting that the Minister and his wife might grow weary of the people complaining, before the people grew weary of talking about the murder of a prominent woman from the estate. As a precaution, he already had laid plans; it looked as if he was to be forced into them.

His first choice would be to wait, for he knew the talk would soon die down and the whole matter would be forgotten, or at most people would occasionally click their tongues in passing sorrow and perhaps even titillation. But Bertrand liked to be seen as competent in his office. The toll on others was only a minor consideration to him. To Hildemara, it was irrelevant. Their impatience, however, was dangerous.

"I, as much as anyone, want the killers found," Dalton said. "However, as a man of the law, I am bound by my oath of office to be sure we find the true killers, and not simply accuse someone falsely just to see someone punished.

"I know you have sternly given me this very caution in the past," Dalton lied for any listening ears.

When he saw Hildemara about to object to any delay, Dalton added in a low, suddenly ill-humored tone, "Not only would it be wrong to be so hasty as to falsely accuse innocent men, but were we to rashly charge men with the crime, and after the sentence it turned out the Mother Confessor wished to take their confessions, and she found we had sentenced innocent men, our incompetence would be rightly denounced not only by the Mother Confessor, but the *Sovereign* and the *Directors* as well."

He wanted to make sure they fully grasped the risks involved.

"Worse, though, should we sentence men to death and carry out the executions before the Mother Confessor was allowed to review the case, she might interject herself in a way that could not only topple the government, but see top officials touched by her power as punishment."

Bertrand and Hildemara sat wide-eyed and silent after Dalton's quiet but sobering lecture.

"Of course, Dalton. Of course you're right." Bertrand's fingers fanned the air in a motion like a fish wriggling its fins to swim backward. "I didn't mean to give the impression I meant any such thing, of course.

"As Minister I cannot allow a person to be falsely accused. I wouldn't have such a thing happen. Not only would it be a terrible injustice to the ones falsely accused, but in so doing it would allow the real killers to thus escape to kill again."

"But that said"—a tone of threat returned to Hildemara's voice—"I think you must be close to naming the killers? I've heard such good things about your abilities that I suspect you are merely being thorough. Surely the Minister's chief aide will soon see justice done? The people will want to know the Minister of Culture is competent. He must be seen as effective in seeing this through to resolution."

"That's right," Bertrand said, eyeing his wife until she eased back into her seat. "We wish a just resolution."

"Added onto that," Hildemara said, "there is talk of a poor Haken girl recently being raped. Rumors are spreading rapidly about the rape. People think the two crimes are connected."

"I heard whispers of that, too," Teresa said. "It's just terrible."

Dalton might have guessed Hildemara would have found out about that and want it cleaned up, too. He had been prepared for that eventuality, as well, but hoped to skirt the issue if he could.

"A Haken girl? And who is to say she's telling the truth? Perhaps she is attempting to cover a pregnancy out of wedlock and is claiming rape so as to gain sympathy in a time of heightened passions."

Bertrand dragged a slice of pork through a small bowl of mustard. "No one has yet come forward with her name, but from what I've heard, it is believed to be genuine. People are still trying to discover her name so as to bring her before a magistrate."

Bertrand frowned with a meaningful look until he was

sure Dalton understood that they were talking about the butcher's girl. "It is feared not only to be true, but to be the same ones who attacked Claudine. People fear the same criminals have now struck twice, and fear they will be striking again."

Bertrand tilted his head back and dropped the pork in his mouth. Stein, on the other side of Hildemara, watched the conversation with growing disdain as he ate crisped beef. He, of course, would solve the matter quickly with his blade. Dalton would, too, were it that simple.

"That is why," Hildemara said as she leaned in once more, "the crime must be solved. The people must know who is responsible." Having delivered the order, she straightened in her chair.

Bertrand squeezed Dalton's shoulder. "I know you, Dalton. I know you don't want to come out and say it until you have the whole crop sheafed, because you are too modest, but I know you have the crime solved and will soon announce the killers. And before people go to the trouble of hauling a poor Haken girl before a magistrate. After she has obviously already suffered in this, it would be a shame for her to suffer further humiliation."

They wouldn't know, but Dalton had already talked to Fitch to start the rock down the hill. He could see, though, that he was going to have to give it a push himself in a new direction.

Stein, over on the other side of Hildemara, tossed his bread on the table with disgust.

"This bread is burned!"

Dalton sighed. The man enjoyed his foolish outbursts. He was treacherous to ignore, lest, like a child, he do something to get attention. They had been leaving him out of the conversation.

"We had trouble of some sort with the ovens down in the kitchen," Dalton said. "If you don't like dark bread, cut off the burned crust."

"You have trouble with witches!" Stein roared. "And you

talk about cutting off the crust? That is your solution?"

"We have trouble with ovens," Dalton said through gritted teeth as he cast a wary glance to the room to see if anyone was paying attention to the man. A few women, too far away to hear, were batting their lashes at him. "Probably a plugged flue run. We'll have it fixed tomorrow."

"Witches!" Stein repeated. "Witches have been casting spells to burn the bread here. Everyone knows that when there's a witch in the neighborhood she can't resist casting spells to burn bread."

"Dalton," Teresa whispered, "he knows about magic. Maybe he knows something we don't."

"He's a superstitious person, that's all." Dalton smiled at her. "Knowing Stein, he's playing a joke on us."

"I could help you find them." Stein tipped his chair back and began picking his nails with his knife. "I know about witches. It's probably witches that killed that woman, and raped the other. I'll find them for you, since you can't. I could use another scalp for my cape."

Dalton tossed his napkin on the table as he excused himself from Teresa. He rose, strode around the Minister and his wife, and leaned close to Stein's ear. The man stank.

"I have specific reasons for doing things the way I have them planned," Dalton whispered. "By doing it my way, we will get this horse to plow the field for us, pull our cart, and carry our water. If I simply wanted horse meat, I wouldn't need you; I'd butcher it myself.

"Since I have already warned you before to watch your words and you seem not to have understood, let me explain it again in a way you will understand."

Stein's grin showed his yellow teeth. Dalton leaned closer.

"This is a problem partly created by you and your inability to make gracious use of what is offered you freely. Instead, you saw fit to force a girl who wasn't offering or willing. I can't change what's done, but if you ever again speak out of turn in such a way as to cause a sensation, I will personally slit your throat and send you back to the emperor in a basket. I will ask him to send us someone with more brains than a rutting pig."

Dalton pressed his boot knife, hidden in the palm of his hand with only the very tip exposed, to the underside of Stein's chin.

"You are in the presence of your superiors. Now, clarify to the good people at the table that you were only making a crude joke. And Stein—it had better be convincing or I swear you will not survive the night."

Stein chuckled agreeably. "I like you, Campbell. You and I are much alike. I know we're going to be able to do business; you and the Minister are going to like the Order. Despite your fancy dancing at dinner, we are the same."

Dalton turned to Hildemara and Bertrand. "Stein has something to say. As soon as he finishes, I must go see to some new information. I think I may have uncovered the names of the killers."

CHAPTER 42

FITCH HURRIED ALONG THE dimly lit corridor. Rowley had told him it was important. Morley's bare feet thumped against the wood floor. It sounded odd to Fitch, now. Having never worn boots, it had taken Fitch time to get used to the way they sounded. Now bare feet sounded odd to him. Beyond odd, it was a sound that reminded him of being a shoeless scullion, and he didn't like to be reminded of that part of his life.

Being a messenger was like a dream come true.

Through the open windows the sounds of the music at the feast drifted in. The woman with the harp was playing and singing. Fitch loved the pure sound of her voice as she sang along with her harp.

"Got any idea what this is about?"

"No," Fitch said. "But I wouldn't think we would have messages to take this time of night. Especially when there's a feast going on."

"I hope it doesn't take long."

Fitch knew what Morley meant. They'd only just settled down to get drunk. Morley had found a nearly full bottle of rum and they were looking forward to getting drunk out of their minds. Not only that, but Morley had a washgirl he knew who said she'd like to get drunk with them. Morley told Fitch that they should let her get drunk first. Fitch was panting at the implications.

Besides that, and just plain liking to get drunk, he wanted to forget his talk with Beata.

The outer office was empty and had a hollow quiet to it. Rowley hadn't returned with them, so there was just the two of them. Dalton Campbell, pacing slowly with his hands clasped behind his back, saw them and waved them in.

"There you both are. Good."

"What can we do for you, Master Campbell?" Fitch asked.

The inner office was lit by lamps, giving it a warm feeling. The window was open and the light drapes glided to and fro in a light breeze. The battle flags rustled a little in the breeze.

Dalton Campbell let out a sigh. "We have trouble. Trouble about the murder of Claudine Winthrop."

"What sort of trouble?" Fitch asked. "Is there anything we can do to fix it?"

The Minister's aide wiped a hard across his chin.

461

"You were seen."

Fitch felt an icy wave of dread tingle up his back. "Seen? What do you mean?"

"Well, you remember you told me you heard a coach stop, and then you all ran off to that pond to dunk yourselves."

Fitch gulped air. "Yes, sir?"

Dalton Campbell sighed again. He tapped a finger against the desk as he seemed to consider how to put it into words.

"Well, the coach driver was the one who found the body. He turned back to get the city guard."

"You told us that already, Master Campbell," Morley said.

"Yes, well, I have only just learned that before he left, he had his assistant remain behind. The man followed your trail through the wheat. He followed you to the pond."

"Dear spirits," Fitch breathed. "You mean he saw all of us swimming and washing ourselves clean?"

"He saw you two. He's just now named your names. Fitch and Morley, he said—from the kitchen at the estate."

Fitch's heart was hammering out of control. He tried to think, but panic was welling up around his ears faster than he could tread it.

Good reason or not, they would still put him to death.

"But why didn't this man say something before, if he saw us?"

"What? Oh. I guess he was in shock over the sight of the body, and all, so he—" Dalton Campbell waggled a hand. "Look, there's no time to discuss what's already happened. We can't do anything about that, now."

The tall Ander pulled open a drawer. "I feel terrible about this. I know you two have done good work for me—for Anderith. But the fact remains, you were seen."

He took a heavy leather pouch from the drawer and plunked it down on the desk.

"What's going to happen to us?" Morley asked. His eyes were the size of gold sovereigns. Fitch knew how his friend felt. His own knees were trembling as he tried to imagine how they would execute him.

A new terror rose up inside his throat, almost pushing out a scream. He recalled Franca telling him how that mob put a rope around her neck and pulled her up to build a fire under her while she was strangling and her feet were kicking in the air. Except Fitch didn't have any magic to help him get away. He reached up and felt the coarse rope around his neck.

Dalton Campbell slid the leather pouch across the desk. "I want you two to take this."

Fitch had to concentrate to understand what Dalton Campbell had said. "What is it?"

"It's mostly silver. There is some gold in there, too. Like I said, I feel terrible about this. You two have been a big help and have shown me you are to be trusted. Now, though, with someone having seen you and able to identify you as being the ones . . . you would be put to death for killing Claudine Winthrop."

"But you could tell them—"

"I can tell them nothing. My first responsibility is to Bertrand Chanboor and the future of Anderith. The Sovereign is ill. Bertrand Chanboor could be called upon to become the new Sovereign any day. I can't throw the whole land into chaos over Claudine Winthrop. You two are like soldiers in war. In war, good people are lost.

"Besides, with emotions over this running so strong, no one would listen to me. An angry mob would drag you away and . . ."

Fitch thought he might faint. He was breathing so fast he was near to passing out. "You mean we're to be put to death?"

Dalton Campbell looked up from his thoughts. "What? No." He pushed at the leather pouch again. "I told you, this is a lot of money. Take it. Get away. Don't you understand? You must get away or you will be put to death before the sun sets again."

"But where will we go?" Morley asked.

Dalton Campbell waved a hand toward the window.

"Away. Far away. Far enough away that they well never find you."

"But if it could be cleared up, somehow, so that people knew we was only doing what had to be done—"

"And raping Beata? You didn't have to rape Beata."

"What?" Fitch said with a long breath. "I would never—I swear, I would never do that. Please, Master Campbell, I wouldn't."

"It doesn't matter what you would never do. As far as the people after you are concerned, you did it. They're not going to stop so that I can reason with them. They won't listen. They think the same people who raped and killed Claudine raped Beata, too. They won't believe you, not when a man can identify you as the ones who killed Claudine Winthrop. Whether you raped Beata or not doesn't matter. The man who saw you is an Ander."

"The people after us?" Morley wiped a trembling hand over his pallid face. "You mean to say there's people already after us?"

Dalton Campbell nodded. "If you stay here you will be put to death for both crimes. Your only chance is to get away—and fast.

"Because you've both been such dependable men for me, and served so well in the cause of Anderith culture, I wanted to warn you so you could have a chance to escape, at least. I'm giving you my life savings to help you escape."

"Your savings?" Fitch shook his head. "No, sir, Master Campbell, we'll not take your savings. You have a wife and—"

"I insist. If necessary, I will order it. The only way I'll be able to sleep at night is knowing I could at least help you in this small way. I do whatever I can to take care of my men. This is the least I can do for you two brave men."

He pointed at the leather pouch. "Take it. Split it between you. Use it to get far away. Start a new life."

"A new life?"

"That's right," Master Campbell said. "You could even buy yourselves swords."

Morley blinked in astonishment. "Swords?"

"Of course. There is enough there to buy you each a dozen swords. If you went to a new land, you wouldn't be thought of as Hakens, as you are here. In many places you would be free men and you could buy yourselves swords. Get yourselves a new life. New work, new everything. With money like that, you could meet nice women and court them properly."

"But we've never even been out of Fairfield," Morley said, near tears.

Dalton Campbell put his hands on his desk and leaned toward them. "If you stay here, you will be put to death. Guards have your names, and are no doubt searching for you as we speak. They are probably right on your heels. I pray to the Creator they didn't see you coming up here. If you want to live, take the money and run. Find yourselves a new life."

Fitch snatched a quick look over his shoulder. He didn't see anyone or hear anyone, but they could be on them at any moment. He didn't know what to do, but he did know they had to do as Dalton Campbell said and get away.

Fitch swept the leather pouch off the desk. "Master Campbell, you are the best man I've ever known. I wish I could have worked for you for the rest of my life. Thank you for telling us they're after us and giving us a start."

Dalton Campbell reached out with a hand. Fitch had never clasped hands with an Ander before, but it felt good. It made him feel like a man. Dalton Campbell gripped Morley's hand, too.

"Good fortune to you both. I would suggest you get some horses. Buy them—don't steal them, or that will give them your trail. I know it will be difficult, but try to act normal or you will make people suspicious.

"Take care with the money, don't waste it on prostitutes and rum or it will be gone before you know it. If that happens, you will be caught and you won't live long enough to die from the diseases the whores give you.

"If you use your heads with the money, spend it frugally,

it will keep you in good stead for a few years, give you time to establish new lives wherever you find you like it."

Fitch reached out and shook hands again. "Thank you for all the advice, Master Campbell. We'll do as you say. We'll buy horses and then get away.

"Don't you worry about us. Both Morley and I have lived on the streets before. We know how not to get caught by Anders wishing us harm."

Dalton Campbell smiled. "I suppose you do. May the Creator watch over you, then."

When Dalton returned to the feast, he found Teresa, sitting in his chair, engaged in an intense conversation with the Minister. Her lilting laugh chimed above, while Bertrand's chuckle rumbled below, the middling drone of the feast. Hildemara, Stein, and the merchants at the other end of the table were engrossed in their own whispered discussion.

Smiling, Teresa reached out and took Dalton's hand. "There you are, darling. Can you stay now, please? Bertrand, tell Dalton he works too hard. He has to eat."

"Why, yes, Dalton, you do work harder than any man I've known. Your wife is frightfully lonely without you. I've been trying to keep her entertained, but she isn't interested in my stories. She is quite polite about it, even though she only wishes to tell me what a good man you are when I already know it."

Bertrand and Teresa encouraged him to return to his seat as she moved back to hers. Dalton held a finger up to his wife, imploring patience for just a moment longer. He moved around and put one hand on the Minister's shoulder and the other on Hildemara's as he leaned down between them. They both tipped their heads in.

"I have just now received new information that confirms my suspicions. As it turns out, the first reports of the crime

466

were sensationalized. Claudine Winthrop was in reality murdered by just two men." He handed the Minister a folded piece of paper secured with a wax seal. "Here are their names."

Bertrand took the paper as a smile spread on his wife's face.

"Now, please listen carefully," Dalton added. "I was on to them, but before I was able to arrest them they stole a great deal of money from the kitchen account and escaped. An intensive search is already under way."

He lifted a questioning eyebrow as he looked to each face to make sure they understood he was fabricating a story for a reason. Their own expressions told him they grasped the unspoken meaning between his words.

"Tomorrow, when it pleases you, announce the names of the men on that piece of paper. They worked in the kitchen. They raped and killed Claudine Winthrop. They raped a Haken girl who works for the butcher, Inger. And now they have robbed the kitchen account and run."

"But won't the Haken girl have something to say?" Bertrand asked, worried she might deny they were the ones and turn the finger to him, if forced to talk.

"Unfortunately, the ordeal was too much for her, and she ran off. We don't know where she went, probably to live with distant family, but she won't be back. The city guard has her name; should she ever try to return, I will know about it first and personally see to her interrogation."

"Then she isn't here to contradict the conviction of the murderers." A scowl returned to Hildemara's face. "Why should we give them the night to escape? That's foolish. The people will want an execution. A public execution. We could give them quite the show of it. Nothing like a good public execution to satisfy people."

Dalton took a patient breath. "The people want to know who did it. Bertrand is going to give them the names. That will show everyone the Minister's office discovered the killers. That they ran before the names were even announced proves them guilty."

Dalton drew down his own brow. "Anything more than that could bring trouble in the form of the Mother Confessor. That is trouble beyond our ability to control.

"An execution would serve no purpose and bring great risk. The people will be satisfied with knowing we have solved the crime and the killers are no longer among them. To do more would risk everything as we stand in the doorway to the Sovereign's chamber."

Hildemara began to object.

"The man is right," Bertrand said with authority.

She relented. "I suppose."

"I will make an announcement tomorrow, with Edwin Winthrop at my side, if he is well enough," Bertrand said. "Very good, Dalton. Very good indeed. You've earned yourself a reward for this one."

Dalton smiled at last. "Oh, I have that all planned out, too, Minister."

Bertrand's sly chuckle returned. "No doubt, Dalton. No doubt." The laugh turned to a belly laugh that even infected his wife.

Fitch had to wipe tears from his eyes as he and Morley rushed down the halls of the estate. They went as fast as they could without running, remembering what Dalton Campbell told them about trying to act normal. When they saw guards, they quickly changed their route to avoid being seen up close. From a distance, Fitch was just a messenger and Morley an estate worker.

But if they saw any guards, and the guards tried to stop them, then they would have to bolt. Fortunately, the ruckus of the feast covered the sound of their feet on the wood floors.

Fitch had an idea that might help them escape. Without explaining, he pulled Morley's sleeve, urging him to follow.

Fitch turned them to the stairwell. They took the steps two at a time down to the lower floor.

Fitch made two turns and in short order found the room he wanted. It was deserted. Carrying a lamp, they both slipped inside and shut the door.

"Fitch, are you crazy, shutting us in here? We could be halfway to Fairfield by now."

Fitch licked his lips. "Who are they looking for, Morley?"

"Us!"

"No, I mean, from the way they're thinking, who are they looking for. A messenger, and a kitchen scullion, right?"

Morley scratched his head as he kept looking at the door. "I guess."

"Well, this is the estate supply room—where they keep some of the livery. Before a seamstress fitted me up with my uniform, I got one from down here to wear till she was done with mine."

"Well, if you got your uniform, then what are we doing—"

"Take off your clothes."

"Why?"

Fitch growled in frustration. "Morley, they're looking for a messenger and a scullion. If you put on a messenger's outfit, then we'll be two messengers."

Morley's eyebrows went up. "Oh. That's a good idea."

In a rush Morley stripped out of his filthy scullion clothes. Fitch held out the lamp as he searched the shelves for outfits of messengers for the Minister's aide. He tossed Morley some dark brown trousers.

"Do these fit?"

Morley stepped into the legs and pulled them up. "Good enough."

Fitch pulled out a white shirt with ruffled collar. "How about this?"

Fitch watched as Morley tried to button it. It was too small to fit over Morley's broad shoulders.

"Fold it back up," Fitch said as he searched for another.

Morley tossed the shirt aside. "Why bother?"

"Pick it up and fold it back up. You want us to get caught? I don't want it to look like we was down here. If they don't know someone took clothes, then we can get away better."

"Oh," Morley said. He plucked up the shirt and started folding with his big hands.

Fitch handed him another that was only just a little too big. In short order Fitch found a sleeved doublet quilted with an interlocking cornucopia design. The edges were trimmed with the distinctive brown and black braided-wheat banding of Dalton Campbell's messengers.

Morley poked his arms through the sleeves. It fit fine. "How do I look?"

Fitch held up the lamp. He let out a low whistle. His friend was built a lot stouter than Fitch. In the messenger uniform Morley looked almost noble. Fitch never thought of his friend as good-looking, but now he was a sight.

"Morley, you look better than Rowley does."

Morley grinned. "Really?" The grin vanished. "Let's get out of here."

Fitch pointed. "Boots. You need boots, or you'll look foolish. Here, put on these stockings or you'll get blisters."

Morley hauled up the stockings and then sat on the floor while he matched up boot soles with the bottom of his foot until he found a pair that fit. Fitch told him to pick up all his old clothes so no one would know they had been there and taken an outfit, if they even discovered it missing— there was a lot of livery stored in the room and it wasn't orderly enough to tell if one outfit was gone.

When they heard boots in the hall, Fitch blew out the lamp. He and Morley stood frozen in the dark. They were too terrified to breathe. The boots came closer. Fitch wanted to run, but if they did they would have to run out the door, and that was where the men were.

Men. He realized it was boots from two men. Guards. Guards making their rounds.

Once again, Fitch felt panic at the idea of being put to

death before a jeering crowd. Sweat trickled down his back.

The door opened.

Fitch could see the man, standing with his hand on the doorknob, outlined in the dim light from the hall. He could see the sword at the man's hip.

Fitch and Morley were back a ways in the room, in an aisle between shelves. The long rectangle of light from the doorway fell across the floor and came almost right up to Fitch's boots. He held his breath. He dared not move a muscle.

Maybe, he thought, the guard, his eyes accustomed to the light, didn't see the two of them standing there in the dark.

The guard closed the door and walked on with his fellow, who was opening other doors in the hall. The sound of footsteps receded into the distance.

"Fitch," Morley said in a shaky whisper, "I'd be needing to relieve myself something awful. Can we get out of here? Please?"

Fitch had to force his voice to return. "Sure."

He made for where he remembered seeing the door in the pitch blackness. The light of the empty hall was a welcoming sight. The two of them hurried on to the nearest way out, the service entrance not far from the brewer's room. Along their way they dumped Morley's old clothes in the rag bin near the service dock.

They heard the old brewer singing a drunken song. Morley wanted to stop and lift something to drink. Fitch licked his lips as he considered Morley's idea. It sounded good to him, too. He surely would like a drink right then.

"No," he finally whispered. "I'd not like to be put to death for a drink. We have plenty of money. We can buy a drink later. I don't want to be here a second longer than necessary."

Morley nodded reluctantly. They rushed out the service doors and out onto the dock. Fitch leading, they hurried on down the steps—the steps Claudine had come up the first time he and Morley had their talk with her. If only she'd listened to them, and done as Fitch warned her.

471

"Aren't we going to get any of our things?" Morley asked.

Fitch stopped and looked at his friend standing in the light coming from the estate windows.

"You got anything worth dying for?"

Morley scratched his ear. "Well, no, I guess not. Just a nice carved stick game my pa gave me. I guess I don't have much else but some of my other clothes, and they're just rags, really. This outfit is better than any of them—even my assembly clothes."

Penance assembly. Fitch realized with a sense of joy they would never have to go to penance assembly again.

"Well, I don't have anything worth taking, either. I got a few coppers left in my trunk, but that's nothing compared to what we're carrying now. I say we get to Fairfield and buy some horses."

Morley made a face. "You know how to ride a horse?"

Fitch looked around to make sure there weren't any guards about. He gave Morley a gentle shove to get them moving.

"No, but I reckon we'll learn fast enough."

"I reckon," Morley said. "But let's buy gentle horses."

As they made the road, they both looked back over their shoulders at the estate for the last time.

"I'm glad to be away from there," Morley said. "Especially after what happened in there today. I'll be glad not to have to go into that kitchen again."

Fitch frowned over at his friend, "What are you talking about?"

"You didn't hear?"

"Hear what? I was off in Fairfield delivering messages."

Morley grasped Fitch's arm and brought them to a panting halt. "About the fire? You didn't hear about the fire?"

"Fire?" Fitch was baffled. "What are you talking about?"

"Down in the kitchen. Earlier today. Something went crazy wrong with the ovens and the hearth—the whole thing."

"Wrong? Like what?"

Morley lifted his arms up as he made a roaring sound with the spit in his throat. His arms spread, apparently to imitate flames expanding outward. "It just flared up something awful. Burned the bread. Got so hot it split a cauldron."

"No," Fitch said in astonishment. "Did anyone get hurt?"

A fiendish grin spread on Morley's face. "Gillie got burned real bad." With an elbow he jabbed Fitch in the ribs. "She was making a sauce when the fire went crazy. She got her ugly prune face burned up. Her hair was afire and everything."

Morley laughed with the satisfaction of one who had waited years for recompense. "She probably won't live, they say. But at least as long as she lives, she'll be in a horrible pain."

Fitch had mixed feelings. He felt no sympathy for Gillie, but still . . .

"Morley, you shouldn't be glad an Ander got hurt. That just shows our hateful Haken ways."

Morley made a scornful face and they started out again. They ran the entire way, diving into the fields whenever a carriage came along the road. They hid in the wheat, or the sorghum, depending on which side offered the most cover. There they lay and caught their breath until the carriage passed.

In a way, Fitch found the experience of running away more a liberation than a frightful flight. Away from the estate he felt less fear of getting caught. At night, anyway.

"I think we should hide in the day," he said to Morley. "In the beginning at least. Hide in the day somewhere safe as we go along, and where we can see if anyone is coming. We can travel at night so people won't see us, or if they do, won't be able to see who we are."

"But what if someone finds us in the day when we're sleeping?"

"We'll have to stand watches. Just like soldiers do. One

473

of us stands watch while the other gets sleep."

Morley seemed to find Fitch's logic a marvelous thing. "I never thought of that."

They slowed to a walk as they neared the streets of Fairfield. There, they knew how to disappear as effectively as they did in the fields when a carriage came along the road.

"We can get some horses," Fitch said, "and still make some distance tonight."

Morley thought a minute. "How we going to get out of Anderith? Master Campbell said there are places where it don't matter that we're Haken. But how we going to get past the army at the border with the Dominie Dirtch?"

Fitch gave the shoulder of Morley's doublet a tug. "We're messengers. Remember?"

"So?"

"So, we say we have official business."

"Messengers have official business outside of Anderith?"

Fitch gave that some thought. "Well, who's to say we don't? If we say we have urgent business they can't keep us until they send word back. That would take too long."

"They might ask to see the message."

"We can't be showing secret messages to them, now can we? We'll just say it's a secret mission to another land we can't name with an important message they aren't allowed to see."

Morley grinned. "I think this is going to work. I think we're going to get away."

"You bet we are."

Morley pulled Fitch to a halt. "Fitch, where are we going to go? Do you got any idea about that part of it?"

This time it was Fitch who grinned.

CHAPTER 43

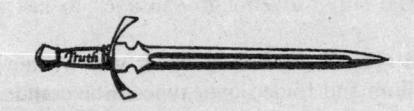

BEATA SQUINTED IN THE bright sun as she set down her bag. She wiped her windblown hair back from her eyes. Since she couldn't read she couldn't tell what the sign above the towering gate said, but there was a number before it: twenty-three. She knew numbers, so she knew she'd found the place.

She stared at the word after the number, trying to remember it so she might someday recognize it for the word it was, but trying to make sense of it was impossible. It just seemed incomprehensible marks carved in a piece of wood. Chicken scratchings made no less sense. She couldn't remember a chicken scratching; she couldn't understand how people remembered the seeming indecipherable marks that made up words, but they did.

Once again, she hoisted the cloth bag holding all her belongings. It had been an awkward load to lug along, what with it bouncing against her thigh, but it wasn't unbearably heavy and she often switched hands when her arm got tired.

She didn't really have all that much to carry with her: some clothes; her pair of cobbler-made shoes, which had belonged to her mother, and which Beata only wore for something special so she wouldn't wear them out; a comb carved out of horn; soap; some keepsakes a few friends had given her; some water; a gift of some lace; and sewing supplies.

Inger had given her a lot of food. She had a variety of sausages made from different meats, some as thick as her arm, some long and thin, some in coils. They were the heaviest things in her bag. Even though she had given several away to people she'd met who were hungry and one to a farmer and his wife who gave her a ride in their wagon for two days, she still had enough sausages to last a year, it seemed.

Inger had given her a letter, too. It was written on a fine piece of vellum and folded over twice. She couldn't read it, but he read it to her before she left so she'd know what it said.

Every time she stopped for a rest along the way, she'd taken out the letter, carefully unfolded it in her lap, and pretended to read it. She'd tried to remember just the way Inger told her the words so she could try to tell which word was which. She couldn't. Hen scratching was all it was to her.

Fitch made marks in the dust one time, and told her it meant "Truth." Fitch. She shook her head.

Inger hadn't wanted her to leave. He said he needed her. She said there were plenty of other people he could hire. He could hire a man with a back stronger than hers. He didn't need her.

Inger said she was good at the work he needed. He said he cared about her almost as if she were his daughter. He told her about when her mother and father first came to work for him, and she was still a toddler. Inger's eyes were red when he asked her to stay.

Beata almost cried again, but she held it in. She told him she loved him like a favorite uncle, and that was why she had to go—if she stayed, there would be trouble and he would only be hurt because of it. He said he could handle it. She said if she stayed she would be hurt or even killed, and she was afraid. He had no answer for that.

Inger had always made her work hard, but he was fair. He always made sure she was fed. He never beat her. Sometimes he'd backhand one of the boys if they talked back to him, but never the girls. But then, the girls didn't talk back to him in the first place.

Once or twice he'd gotten angry at her, but he never hit her. If she did something foolish enough to get him angry, he'd make her gut and debone pullets till well into the night. She didn't have to do that very often, though. She always tried her best to do right and not cause trouble.

If there was one thing Beata thought was important, it was doing as she was told and not causing trouble. She knew she'd been born with a vile Haken nature, just like all Hakens, and she wanted to try to act better than her nature.

Every once in a great while Inger would wink at her and tell her she'd done a good job. Beata would have done anything for those winks.

Before she left, he hugged her for a long time, and then sat her down while he wrote out the letter for her. When he read it to her, she thought he had tears in his eyes. It was all she could do to keep hers from erupting again.

Beata's mother and father had taught her not to cry in front of others, or they would think her weak and foolish. Beata was careful to only cry at night, when no one would hear her. She could always hold it back until night, in the dark, alone.

Inger was a good man, and she would greatly miss him—even if he did work her fingers to the bone. She wasn't afraid of work.

Beata wiped her nose and then sidestepped to make way for a wagon rolling toward the gateway. It looked a big place. At the same time, it looked lonely, all by itself out in the windswept middle of nowhere, sitting up on its own low hill. The gate through the bulwark appeared the only way in, except straight up the steep earthwork ramparts.

As soon as the wagon went by, Beata followed it through the tall gates and into the bailey. People were bustling about everywhere. It was like a town inside the gates. It surprised her to see so many buildings, with streets and alleyways between them.

A guard just inside finished talking to the wagon driver and waved him on. He turned his attention to Beata. He gave her a quick glance up and down, not showing anything of what he might be thinking.

"Good day."

He used the same tone as he used with the wagon driver—polite but businesslike. There were more wagons coming up behind her and he was busy. She returned the greeting in kind.

The dark Ander hair at his neck was damp from sweat. It was probably hot in his heavy uniform. He lifted a hand and pointed.

"Over there. Second building on the right." He gave her a wink. "Good luck."

She nodded her thanks and hurried between horses before they closed up and she'd have to go all the way around. She narrowly missed stepping in fresh manure with her bare feet. Crowds of people were going in every direction. Horses and wagons made their way up and down the streets. It smelled of sweat, horses, leather, dust, dung, and the new wheat growing all around.

Beata had never been anyplace but Fairfield before. It was intimidating, but it was also exciting.

She found the second building on the right easy enough. Inside an Ander woman was sitting behind a desk writing on a rumpled, well-used piece of paper. She had a whole stack of papers to one side of her desk, some well worn and some fresh-looking. When the woman looked up, Beata curtsied.

"Afternoon, dear." She gave Beata a look up and down, as the guard had done. "Long walk?"

"From Fairfield, ma'am."

The woman set down her dipping pen. "Fairfield! Then it was a long walk. No wonder you're covered in dust."

Beata nodded. "Six days, ma'am."

A frown crept onto the woman's face. She looked to be a woman who frowned a lot. "Why did you come here, then, if you're from Fairfield? There were any number of closer stations."

Beata knew that. She didn't want a closer station. She wanted to be far away from Fairfield. Far away from trouble. Inger had told her to come here, to the twenty-third.

"I worked for a man named Inger, ma'am. He's a butcher. When I told him what I wanted, he said he'd been here and knew there to be good people here. It was upon his counsel I came here, ma'am."

She smiled with one side of her mouth. "Don't recall a butcher named Inger, but he must have been here, because he's right about our people here."

Beata set down her bag and pulled out the letter. "Like I said, he counseled I come here, ma'am."

He counseled her to get far away from Fairfield, and this place was. She feared stepping closer to the desk, so she leaned forward and stretched to hand her precious letter to the woman.

"He sent this letter of introduction."

The woman unfolded the letter and leaned back to read it. Watching her eyes going along each line, Beata tried to remember Inger's words. She was sorry to find the exact words fading. It wouldn't be long before she recalled only the main thrust of Inger's words.

The woman set down the letter. "Well, Master Inger seems to think a great deal of you, young lady. Why would you want to leave a job where you got along so well?"

Beata hadn't been expecting to have anyone ask her why she wanted to do this. She thought briefly, and quickly decided to be honest, but not too honest.

"This has always been my dream, ma'am. I guess that a person has to try out their dream sometime. No use in living your life and never trying your dream."

"And why is it your dream?"

"Because I want to do good. And because the Mi . . . the Minister made it so women would be respected here. So they'd be equal."

"The Minister is a great man."

Beata swallowed her pride. Pride did a person no good; it only held them back.

"Yes, ma'am. He is. Everyone respects the Minister. He passed the law allowing Haken women to serve along with the Ander men and women. That law also says all must show respect to those Haken women who serve our land. Haken women owe him a great debt. Minister Chanboor is a hero to all Haken women."

The woman regarded her without emotion. "And you had man trouble. Am I right? Some man wouldn't keep his hands off you, and you finally had enough and finally got up the courage to leave."

Beata cleared her throat. "Yes, ma'am. That's true. But what I told you about this always being my dream is true, too. The man just decided it for me sooner, that's all. It's still my dream, if you'll have me."

The woman smiled. "Very good. What's your name, then?"

"Beata, ma'am."

"Very good, Beata. We try to follow Minister Chanboor's example here, and do good."

"That's why I came, ma'am; so I could do good."

"I'm Lieutenant Yarrow. You call me Lieutenant."

"Yes, ma—Lieutenant. So . . . may I join?"

Lieutenant Yarrow pointed with her pen. "Pick up that sack over there."

Beata hoisted the burlap sack. It felt like it was loosely filled with firewood. She curled a wrist under it and held it against a hip with one arm.

"Yes, Lieutenant? What would you like done with it?"

"Put it up on your shoulder."

Beata hoisted it up and curved her arm around and forward over the sack so it would bulge up the muscle and the wood wouldn't rest on her shoulder bone. She stood waiting.

"All right," Lieutenant Yarrow said. "You can put it down."

Beata set it back where it had been.

"You pass," the lieutenant said. "Congratulations. Your dream just came true. You're in the Anderith army. Hakens can never be completely cleansed of their nature, but here you will be valued and be able to do good."

Beata felt a sudden swell of pride. She couldn't help it.

"Thank you, Lieutenant."

The lieutenant waggled her pen, pointing it back over her shoulder. "Out back, down the alleyway to the end, just below the rampart, you will find a midden heap. Take your bag out there and throw it on with the rest of the offal."

Beata stood in mute shock. Her mother's shoes were in there. They were expensive. Her mother and father had saved for years to buy those shoes. There were keepsakes in her bag, given by her friends. Beata held back tears.

"Am I to throw out the food Inger sent, too, Lieutenant?"

"The food, too."

Beata knew that if an Ander woman told her to do it, then it was right and she had to do it.

"Yes, Lieutenant. May I be excused, then, to see to it?"

The woman appraised her for a moment. Her tone softened a little. "It's for your own good, Beata. Those things are from your old life. It won't do you any good to be reminded of your old life. The sooner you forget it, food included, the better."

"Yes, Lieutenant, I understand." Beata forced herself to be bold. "The letter, ma'am? May I keep the letter Inger sent with me?"

Lieutenant Yarrow looked down at the letter on her desk. She finally folded it twice and handed it back.

"Since it's a letter of recommendation and not a memento of your old life, you may keep it. You earned it with your years of service to the man."

Beata touched the pin that held closed her collar at her throat—the one with the spiral end, the one Fitch had returned to her. Her father had given it to her when she was

481

young, before he had died from a fever. She had lost it when the Minister and that beast, Stein, pulled it out and tossed it away into the hall so they could open her dress and have a look at her.

"The pin, Lieutenant Yarrow? Should I throw it away, too?"

As she had watched her father making the simple pin, he had told her it represented how everything was all connected, even if you couldn't see it from where you stood, and how if you could follow everything round and round, someday it would all come to a point. He told her to always keep her dreams, and if she did good, the dreams would come round to her, even if it was in the afterlife and it was the good spirits themselves answered the wishes. She knew it was a silly children's story, but she liked it.

The lieutenant squinted as she peered at the pin. "Yes. From now on, the people of Anderith will provide everything you require."

"Yes, Lieutenant. I look forward to serving them well to repay them for the opportunity only they could provide."

A smile softened the woman's face. "You're smarter than most who come in here, Beata. Men and women, both. You catch on quick, and you accept what's required of you. That's a good quality."

The lieutenant stood up behind her desk. "I think, with training, you could be a good leader—maybe a sergeant. It's tougher than plain soldier training, but if you can measure up, in a week or two you'll be in charge of your own squad."

"In charge of a squad? In only a week or two?"

The lieutenant shrugged. "It's not difficult, being in the army. I'm sure it's a lot less difficult than learning to butcher."

"Won't we have to learn to fight?"

"Yes, but while important at a basic level, fighting is for the most part a trivial and outmoded function of the army. The army was once a refuge for extremists. The fanaticism of warriors suffocates the society they are charged with protecting."

She smiled again. "Brains are the major requirement and women are more than equal there. With the Dominie Dirtch, brawn is unnecessary. The weapon itself is the brawn and, as such, invincible.

"Women have the natural compassion required to be officers—for instance the way I explained why you must discard your old things; men don't bother with explaining to their troops why something is necessary. Leadership is a nurturing of those under your command. Women bring wholesomeness to what used to be nothing but a savage fellowship of destruction.

"Women who defend Anderith are given the recognition to which they are entitled, the recognition they earn. We help the army contribute to our culture, instead of simply menace it, as before."

Beata glanced down at the sword at Lieutenant Yarrow's hip. "Will I get to carry a sword and everything?"

"And everything, Beata. Swords are made to wound in order to discourage an opponent, and you will be taught how. You will be a valued member of the Twenty-third Regiment. We are all proud to serve under Bertrand Chanboor, the Minister of Culture."

The Twenty-third Regiment. That was where Inger told her he thought she should go to join: the Twenty-third Regiment. That was what the sign over the gate had said.

The Twenty-third Regiment was the one that tended the Dominie Dirtch. Inger said soldiers who tend the Dominie Dirtch had the best job in the army, and were the most respected. He called them "the elite."

Beata thought back to Inger. It already seemed another life.

As she had been leaving his place, Inger gently took ahold of her arm and turned her back. He said he believed some man at the estate had hurt her and asked her to tell him if that was true. She nodded. He asked her to tell him who it was.

Beata told him the truth.

He had cleared his throat and told her he finally understood why she had to leave. Inger was probably the only Ander who would have believed her. Or cared.

Inger had wished her a good life.

"Again," the captain ordered.

Beata, being first in line, lifted the sword and ran forward. She stabbed with her weapon at the straw man swinging by a rope. This time, she ran her sword right through his leg.

"Beautiful, Beata!" Captain Tolbert said. He always praised them when he approved of what they did. Being Haken, Beata found such praise an odd experience.

She almost fell trying to pull the sword back out of the straw man's leg as she ran past. She at least managed it, if not with grace. Sometimes the others didn't.

Fortunately for Beata, she had years of experience with blades. Although the blades had been smaller, she knew something about wielding blades and stabbing them where you intended.

Despite being Haken and supposedly not allowed to use knives because they were weapons, Beata had worked for a butcher and so it was overlooked, since butchers were Ander and they kept a tight rein on their Haken workers. Butchers only let the Haken girls and women cut up meat, along with the Anders. The Haken boys and men working for them did the lifting and lugging, mostly—the things not requiring them to handle blades.

Three of the other girls, Carine, Emmeline, and Annette, were Haken, too, and had never held anything more than a dull bread knife before. The four Ander boys, Turner, Norris, Karl, and Bryce, were not from wealthy families and had never handled a sword before, either, but as boys they had played with sticks as swords.

Beata knew that Anders were better than Hakens in every

484

way, but she was having a difficult time making sure she didn't wrongly show up Turner, Norris, Karl, and Bryce. They were best suited to grinning moronically. That was about it, as far as she could tell. Most of the time they pranced around bragging about themselves to each other.

The two Ander girl recruits, Estelle Ruffin and Marie Fauvel, didn't have any experience with swords, either. They did like swinging their new swords about, though, as did the rest of them. They were better at it, too, than the four Ander boys. For that matter, even the Haken girls, Carine, Emmeline, and Annette, were better than the four boys at soldiering.

The boys could swing harder, but the girls were better at hitting the target. Captain Tolbert pointed that out so the boys would understand they weren't any better than the girls. He said to the boys that it didn't matter how hard you could swing a sword, if you couldn't hit anything.

Karl had gashed his leg the first day, and it had to be sewn closed. He hobbled around, still grinning, a soldier with a scar in the works.

Emmeline poked at the straw man's leg as she ran by. She missed the swinging leg and her sword's tip caught in the rope around the straw waist. She fell flat on her Haken face.

The four Ander boys erupted in laughter. The girls, Ander and Haken both, didn't. The boys called Emmeline a clumsy ox and a few other rude things under their breath.

Captain Tolbert growled in anger as he snatched the collar of the nearest: Bryce. "I've told you before, you may have laughed at others in your old life, but not here! You don't laugh at your fellow soldiers, even if that soldier is a Haken. Here you are all equal!"

He shoved Bryce away. "Such a violation of respect to fellow soldiers requires punishment. I want each of you to name for me what you think a fair punishment."

Captain Tolbert pointed at Annette and asked her to name a fair punishment. She thought a moment and then said she thought the boys should apologize. Carine and Emmeline, the other two Haken girls, spoke up that they agreed. He asked Estelle. She pushed back her dark Ander hair and said the boys should be kicked out of the army. Marie Fauvel agreed, but added they could be let back in the next year. The four boys, when asked their idea of fair punishment, said just to be told not to do it again.

Captain Tolbert turned to Beata. "You hope to be a sergeant. What would you say was a good punishment, if you were a sergeant?"

Beata had her answer ready. "If we're all equal, then we should all be treated equal. Since the four of them think it's so funny, the whole squad should have to dig a new latrine instead of having dinner." She folded her arms. "If any of us gets hungry as we're digging, well, we have these four boys to thank."

Captain Tolbert smiled with satisfaction. "Beata has named a fair punishment. That will be it, then. If anyone objects, they can head home for their mothers' skirts because they don't have the courage it takes to be a soldier and stick up for their fellow soldiers."

Estelle and Marie, Anders both, cast dark glares at the Ander boys. The boys hung their heads and stared at the ground. The Haken girls weren't any happier about it, but the boys were more worried about the glares from the Ander girls.

"Now," Captain Tolbert said, "let's finish the drill so you can all get to digging when the dinner bell is rung."

No one groaned. They had learned better than to complain.

Sweat ran down Beata's neck as they marched two abreast along the narrow road. It was a path, really—just two ruts from the supply wagons. Captain Tolbert led them, Beata was at the head of the five soldiers in the left rut, and Marie

486

Fauvel marched to her right, at the head of the five soldiers behind her.

Beata felt pride marching in front of her squad of soldiers. She had worked hard the two weeks of training, and had been named sergeant, just as Lieutenant Yarrow said she might. Beata had the stripes of the rank sewn on each shoulder. Marie, an Ander, was named corporal—second-in-command of the squad. The other eight had earned the rank of soldier.

Beata guessed the only real earning to it was that if you got kicked out before you finished the training, then you didn't get to be a soldier. None of them that started got kicked out, though.

The uniform was uncomfortable in the afternoon heat, although she was getting used to it. They all wore green trousers. Over that they wore long padded and quilted tan tunics cinched at the waist with a light belt. Over the tunic they wore chain mail.

Because the mail was heavy, the women had to wear only vested chain mail, without sleeves. The men had to wear mail with arms of mail, too, and it was longer. They also had to wear hoods of mail that covered their head and necks. When they were marching, they swathed it down around their necks. When they had to wear it, they wore a leather helmet over top. They all had leather helmets.

Beata was thankful the women didn't have to wear all the rest of it, though. Being the sergeant, she had to sometimes pick up the men's mail to inspect it. She couldn't imagine marching all day with that much weight. What she had was enough. The fun of marching with a heavy sword had worn off; now it was a chore.

They each had a long cloak, but with it being as warm as it was, the cloaks were only buttoned to their right shoulders, letting them hang to the side. Over the mail they wore their sword belts. Additionally, they each carried a pack and, of course, their two spears each and a knife worn opposite their sword on the same belt.

Beata thought they looked a smart squad. The pikemen she had seen back at the Twenty-third Regiment had been the best-looking soldiers. They were a sight. The men were handsome in the pikemen outfits. She had pleasant dreams about those men. The women somehow looked dull, by comparison, even though they had the same outfits.

Beata saw something dark ahead, standing up above the field of grass. As they got closer, she thought it looked to be ancient stone. Off behind it, closer to them, were three squat stone buildings. The roofs were shingled, maybe with slate.

Beata felt a twinge of dread at seeing the huge, silent, awful thing.

It was the Dominie Dirtch.

The Dominie Dirtch were the one thing of the Hakens the Anders kept to use. Beata recalled the lessons she learned about how the Hakens murdered countless Anders with these weapons. They were terrible things. It looked as old as it was, its edges softened over time by the weather, the wind, and the hands that tended it.

At least now that the Anders governed them, they were only instruments of peace.

Captain Tolbert halted them among the buildings. Beata could see soldiers up on the stone base of the enormous, bell-shaped, stone Dominie Dirtch. There were soldiers in the buildings, too. The squad there had been at station for months, and was being relieved by Beata's squad.

Captain Tolbert turned to them. "These are the barracks. One for the women and one for the men. See it stays that way, Sergeant Beata. The other buildings are used for kitchen and dining, meetings, repairs, and everything else." He pointed to the farther building. "That over there is storage."

He ordered them to follow as he marched on. They marched behind him in their two neat rows as he went past the Dominie Dirtch. It towered over them, a dark menace. The three women and one man up on the base around the bell-shaped part watched them pass.

Out in front of the Dominie Dirtch a ways, he stopped and told them to be at ease and to spread out. They formed a loose line, shoulder to shoulder.

"This is the frontier. The border of Anderith." The captain pointed out at the seemingly endless grassland. "That, out there, is the wilds. Beyond this place are the lands of other peoples. We keep those others from coming and taking our land from us."

Beata felt her chest swelling with pride. She was the one protecting the Anderith border. She was doing good.

"Over the next two days, I and the squad here will teach you what you need to know about guarding the border and about the Dominie Dirtch."

He walked down the line and halted in front of Beata, looking her in the eye. He smiled with pride.

"Then, you will be under the capable charge of Sergeant Beata. You will follow her orders without fail, and if she is unavailable, the orders of Corporal Marie Fauvel." He gestured behind them. "I will take a report from the squad I lead back to the Twenty-third Regiment, and I will treat very harshly any soldier who failed to at all times follow the orders of their sergeant."

He glared at the entire line. "Keep that in mind. Keep in mind, too, that the sergeant has a responsibility to live up to her rank. If she fails in that, I expect you to report it when I come back for you when it's your turn to be relieved.

"Supply wagons will be coming once every two weeks. Keep your supplies orderly and mind how long they must last.

"Your primary duty is to tend the Dominie Dirtch. In that, you are the defense of our beloved land of Anderith. From up on the watch station of the Dominie Dirtch, you will be able to see the next Dominie Dirtch to each side. They extend along the entire border to guard the frontier. The squads on duty are not changed at the same time, so experienced soldiers are always to each side.

"Sergeant Beata, it will be your responsibility, once your squad is trained and we depart, to see to it your soldiers are on duty at your Dominie Dirtch, and then to go meet with the squads to each side to coordinate with them all matters of defense."

Beata saluted with a hand to her brow. "Yes, Captain."

He smiled. "I'm proud of you all. You all are good Anderith soldiers, and I know you will do your duty."

Behind her towered the terrible Haken weapon of murder. Now, she was to be in charge of it in order to do good.

Beata felt a lump in her throat. For the first time in her life, she knew she was doing good. She was living her dream, and it was good.

CHAPTER 44

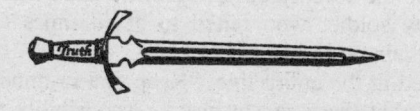

THE BURLY SOLDIER GAVE her the side of his boot on her rump. She had tried to hurry out of his way as soon as he kicked, but she wasn't fast enough. She pressed her lips tight against the sting of it.

If only the power of the gift worked, she would have done him a turn. She considered using her cane, but, keeping in mind her business, thought better of dispensing justice just then, no matter how sorely it was needed.

Rattling her three copper coins in her tin cup, Annalina Aldurren, former Prelate of the Sisters of the Light, the most powerful women in the Old World for over three-quarters of a millennium, moved on to beg from the soldiers gathered round the next fire.

Like most soldiers, the next bunch she came upon as she moved through the camp showed interest when she first approached, thinking she might be a whore, but their ardor for female companionship quickly faded when she came into the ring of firelight and gave them a big gap-toothed grin—or the illusion of one, anyway, with the aid of some greasy soot on a few selected teeth.

It was quite convincing, actually, along with the rags she had layered over her dress, the dung-soaked head wrap—lest anyone decide they could overlook the craggy smile—and the walking cane. The cane was the worst; affecting a bad back was giving her one.

Twice, soldiers got it in their heads they could disregard her shortcomings in view of the scarcity of women. While they were handsome enough, in that savage brute sort of a way, she had to politely decline their offers. Rejecting such insistent invitations had been messy. Fortunately, what with all the commotion of camp life, no one noticed a man dying of a suddenly slit throat. Such a death among men like those of the Imperial Order would not even be questioned.

Taking a life was something Ann did only with great reluctance. Given the mission of these soldiers, and the use to which they would have put her before killing her, her reluctance was surmountable.

Like the soldiers gathered around the next fire as they ate and told stories, none thought anything of her wandering among them. Most gave her a look-see, but quickly went back to their stew and coarse camp bread washed down with ale and bawdy stories. A beggar elicited little more than a grunt intended to keep them moving along.

With an army this size, there was an entire culture of camp followers. Tradesmen traveled with their own wagons, or shared one with others. They followed in the wake of the army, offering a wide variety of services not provided by the Imperial Order. Ann had even seen an artist busy at drawing portraits of proud officers on a historic campaign. Like any artist wishing to have steady employment and the use of all his fingers, he used his talents to the customers' best advantage, putting them in triumphant poses, showing them with knowing eyes and handsome smiles—or all-conquering glowers, depending on the men's preference.

Peddlers sold everything from meats and vegetables to rare fruits from back home—Ann herself hungered for such succulent reminders of the Old World. Business was brisk in amulets for good luck. If a soldier didn't like the food provided by the Imperial Order, and he had money, there were people to make him nearly anything he desired. Like a cloud of gnats, gamblers, hucksters, harlots, and beggars buzzed around the huge army.

In the guise of a beggar, Ann was easily able to negotiate the Order's camp, searching as she would. It cost her only an occasional boot to the behind. Searching an army the size of this one was quite an undertaking, though. She had been at it nearly a week. She was bone weary and growing impatient.

In that week she could have managed to live reasonably well from what she gathered under her cover of begging—as long as she didn't mind eating maggot-infested, rotting meat and moldering vegetables. She accepted such offerings graciously, and then discarded them when out of sight. It was a cruel joke by the soldiers, giving her the garbage they had intended to throw out. There were some among the beggars who would salt and pepper it through and then eat it.

Each day when it got too late to search, she returned to the camp followers and spent a little of her own money to buy humble but somewhat more wholesome food. Everyone thought she earned the meager amount begging. The truth be known, she was not very good at the business of begging, and a business it was. A few of the beggars, feeling sympathy when they saw her act, tried to help her improve her technique.

Ann endured such distractions lest it be discovered she was more than she presented herself to be. Some of the

492

beggars made a good living at it. It was a mark of their talent that they could coax a coin from men such as these.

She knew that by cruel fate people were occasionally thrust, against their wishes, into helpless begging. She also knew from hundreds of years of experience trying to give them help that most beggars clung tenaciously to the life.

Ann trusted no one in the camp, but of all the people there, she trusted beggars least. They were more dangerous than the soldiers. Soldiers were what they were and made no pretense. If they didn't want you around, they would order you away or give you the boot. Some would simply show her a blade in warning. If they intended you harm, or murder, they made their intent clear.

Beggars, on the other hand, lived lives of lies. They lied from the time they opened their eyes in the morning until they told the Creator a lie in their bedtime prayers.

Of all the Creator's miserable creations, Ann most disliked liars—and those who repeatedly placed their trust and security in the hands of such liars. Liars were Creation's jackals. Deception to a noble end, though regrettable, was sometimes necessary for a greater good. Lying for selfish reasons was the fertile dirt of immorality, from which sprouted the tendrils of evil.

Trusting men who demonstrated a proclivity to lie proved you a fool, and such fools were nothing more to the liar than the dust beneath their boots—there to be trod upon.

Ann knew liars were the Creator's children, the same as she, and that she was duty bound to view them with patience and forgiveness, but she couldn't. She simply couldn't abide liars and that was that. She was resigned to the fact that in the afterlife she would have to take her lumps for it.

Begging was proving to be time-consuming, so in order to cover as much ground as possible, Ann tried to do as little of it as possible. Every night the camp was jumbled all over again, making it impossible to rely on the merit of previous searches, so she determined to make as much of each foray as possible. Fortunately, because the army was so vast, they did tend to stay in roughly the same order—

493

much like a string of cargo wagons stopping along a road for the night.

In the mornings it was well over an hour after the leading edge started out before the tail began to move. At night the lead was cooking dinner long before the rear guard halted. They didn't cover a great deal of ground each day, but their progress was inexorable.

Beyond their purpose, Ann was disturbed by their direction of travel. The Order had been gathering for quite some time down around Grafan Harbor in the Old World. When they finally began to move, they had streamed up from those shores into the New World, but they turned with the coast, following it west, to where Ann had unexpectedly encountered them.

Ann was no military tactician, but it struck her immediately as an odd thing for them to do. She had assumed they would attack north into the New World. That they were heading in such a seemingly fruitless direction told her there must be a good reason; Jagang did nothing without reason. While he was ruthless, confident, and bold, he was not rash.

Jagang was skilled in the fine art of patience.

The people of the Old World had always been anything but a homogeneous society. Ann had, after all, been observing them for over nine centuries. She considered it charitable to merely say they were diverse, fractious, and intractable. There had been no two areas of the Old World that could agree on up from down.

In the nearly twenty years she had been watching him, Jagang had methodically consolidated the seemingly ungovernable into a cohesive society. That it was brutal, corrupt, and inequitable was another matter; he had made them one and in so doing forged a force of unprecedented might.

What the parents might have been—independent and loyal only to their small place in the world—the children were not. A large percentage of the Imperial Order troops and command had been babes or young children when the Order seized power. They had grown up under the rule of Jagang, and as children always did, believed as they were

494

taught by those who led them, adopting the same values and morals.

The Sisters of the Light, however, served a higher purpose than the affairs of governance. Ann had seen elected governments, kings, and other rulers come and go. The Palace of the Prophets and the Sisters, existing under the ancient spell that dramatically slowed their aging, always remained. While she and her Sisters did work to help bring out mankind's better nature, their calling was in areas of the gift, not rule.

But she did keep an eye to rulers, lest they interfere with the Creator's gift. Jagang, in recently committing himself to the elimination of magic, had overstepped matters of rule. His reign had become material to her. Now, he was moving into the New World, in his efforts to extinguish magic.

Ann had observed over time that whenever Jagang swallowed a new land or kingdom, he would settle in as he began to infiltrate the next, and the next after that. He would find willing ears and, with tempting promises of juicy slices of the graft to come, woo them into weakening their own defenses in the mask of virtue: peace.

Some lands' discipline and defenses were so eviscerated from within that they threw out a welcoming carpet for Jagang rather than dare defy him. The foundations of some formerly strong lands became so riddled with the termites of diminished purpose, so decayed with the decadence of smug moderation, and so emaciated with the vacillating aims of appeasers, that even when they saw the enemy coming and did resist, they were easily toppled when the Imperial Order finally pushed.

With the unexpected direction the Order was taking to the west, Ann was beginning to worry that Jagang had been doing the unimaginable: sending envoys on covert missions sailing around the great barrier—years before Richard destroyed the Towers of Perdition. Such missions would have been incredibly risky. Ann would know; she had done so herself.

It was possible Jagang had books of prophecy, or wizards

with the talent, who gave him reason to believe the barrier would come down. After all, Nathan had told Ann that very thing.

If so, Jagang was not simply marching off for the purpose of exploration, exploitation, and conquest. From her experience watching him come to dominate the entirety of the Old World, she knew Jagang rarely rolled down a road he hadn't first had widened and smoothed.

Ann paused in the darkness between groups of men. She squinted off in several directions. Hard as it was for her to believe, she hadn't even seen Jagang's tents yet. She wanted to find them because she hoped they might give her a valuable clue in finding her Sisters of the Light; he likely would keep them near.

She sighed in exasperation at not seeing anything but more fires and troops. In the darkness and confusion of the Order's camp, she knew she could be close and still not see Jagang's tents.

The worst of it, though, was not having the gift to aid her. With the gift she could easily have listened to distant conversations, cast small spells, and conjured discreet aid. Without the gift, she found the search a frustrating and fruitless experience.

She could hardly believe she could be this close to the Sisters of the Light and not find them. With the gift, she would have been able to sense them were she close enough.

Beyond the aid it would have provided, there was more to it. Being unable to use the gift was like being denied the Creator's love. Her lifetime of devotion to doing the Creator's work, coupled with the glory of touching her inner magic—her Han, the force of life—had always been supremely gratifying. Not that there hadn't been frustrations, fears, and failures, but there always was the opening of herself to her Han to make up for every trial.

For over nine centuries her Han had been her constant companion through life. Her inability to touch her gift had on more than one occasion driven her to the verge of tears.

She felt little different, for the most part—as long as she

didn't think about it. But when her thoughts turned to touching that inner light, and she couldn't, it felt like a slow suffocation of the mind.

As long as she didn't try to use her gift, it seemed it was still there, waiting, like a comforting friend seen out of the corner of her eye. But when she reached for it, put the weight of thought against it, it felt as if the ground opened and she plummeted into a terrifying black abyss.

Without her gift, and no longer living under the protection of the spell that had been around the Palace of the Prophets, Ann was no different than anyone else. She was, in reality, little more than a beggar. She was simply an old woman, aging like anyone else, with no more strength than any other old woman. The insights, knowledge, and—she hoped—wisdom of having lived as long as she had were her only advantages.

Until Zedd banished the chimes, she would be, for the most part, helpless. Until Zedd banished the chimes. If Zedd banished the chimes . . .

Ann picked the wrong route—between wagons standing close together—and came to an impasse with someone going the other way. She excused herself and started to back up out of the way. Beggars were obeisant, even though it was insincere.

"Prelate?"

Ann froze.

"Prelate, is that you?"

Ann looked up into the startled face of Sister Georgia Cifaro. They had known each other for more than five hundred years. The woman's mouth was working as she tried to find words.

Ann reached out and patted the hand holding a pail of steaming porridge. Sister Georgia flinched.

"Sister Georgia, thank the Creator I've found one of you, at last."

Sister Georgia cautiously reached out and touched Ann's face, seemingly testing if it were real.

"You're dead," Sister Georgia said. "I was at your funeral

ceremony. I saw . . . you and Nathan . . . your bodies were sent into the Light on the funeral pyre. I saw it. We prayed all night as we watched you and Nathan burn."

"Really? How sweet of you. You always were such a considerate person, Sister Georgia. That would be just like you, standing guard through the darkness, praying for me. I'm so appreciative.

"But, it wasn't me."

Sister Georgia flinched again. "But, but, Verna was named Prelate."

"Yes, I know. I wrote the orders, remember." The woman nodded. Ann went on. "I had a reason. Nonetheless, I'm quite alive, as you can well see."

At last, Sister Georgia set down the bucket and threw her arms around Ann.

"Oh, Prelate! Oh, Prelate!"

That was all Sister Georgia could get out before she started bawling like a baby. Ann managed to get her calmed down in short order with some short words. They were in no place to risk being seen in such a way. Their lives were at stake, and Ann couldn't have them lost for no more reason than a woman weeping out of control.

"Prelate, what's wrong with you? You smell like dung, and you look a mess!"

Ann chuckled. "I didn't dare allow my beauty to be witnessed by all these men, or I would have more offers of marriage than I could turn down."

Sister Georgia laughed, but it dissolved into tears again. "They're beasts. All of them."

Ann comforted her. "I know, Sister Georgia. I know." She lifted the woman's chin. "You are a Sister of the Light. Straighten yourself up, now. What is done to this body is not what matters. Our eternal souls are what concerns us. Beasts in this life can do what they will to your body, but they cannot touch your pure soul.

"Now, act what you are: a Sister of the Light."

Sister Georgia smiled through the tears. "Thank you, Prelate. I needed to hear your scolding to remember my calling. Sometimes it's all too easy to forget."

Ann went to her purpose. "Where are the others?"

Sister Georgia lifted a hand to point off to Ann's right and a little behind. "Over there."

"Are you all together?"

"No. Prelate, some of the Sisters have sworn themselves to the Nameless One." She bit her lower lip and wrung her hands. "There are Sisters of the Dark in our order."

"Yes, I know."

"You do? Well, Jagang keeps them elsewhere. The Sisters of the Light are together, but I don't know where the Sisters of the Dark are, nor do I care to."

"Praise the Creator," Ann said with a sigh. "That was what I was hoping—that there wouldn't be any of them among you."

Sister Georgia glanced over her shoulders. "Prelate, you must get out of here or you will be killed or captured." She started pushing Ann, trying to turn her around and get her to leave.

Ann seized Sister Georgia's sleeve in an attempt to get the woman to listen.

"I'm here to rescue the Sisters. Something has happened to give us the rare opportunity to help you escape."

"There is no way—"

"Silence," Ann growled in a whisper. "Listen to me. The chimes are loose."

Sister Georgia gasped. "That's not possible."

"Oh really? I'm telling you it is so. If you don't believe me, then why do you think your power is gone?"

Sister Georgia stood mute as Ann listened to the raucous laughter of men gambling not far away. The Sister's gaze kept searching the area beyond the wagons, fearing they would be caught.

"Well?" Ann asked. "What did you think was the reason for your power being gone?"

Sister Georgia's tongue darted out to wet her lips. "We

aren't allowed to open ourselves to our Han. Jagang only allows us to do so if he wants something. Otherwise, we mustn't. He's in our minds—he's a dream walker, Prelate. He can tell if we touch our Han without permission. It's something you don't dare try twice.

"He can control it. He can make you very sorry for anything you do which he doesn't like." The woman was dissolving into tears again. "Oh, Prelate . . ."

Ann pulled the woman's head down to her shoulder. "There, there. Hush now. It's all right now, Georgia. Hush now. I'm here to get you away from this madness."

Sister Georgia pulled back. "Away? You can't. The dream walker is in our minds. He could be watching us right this very minute. He can do that, you know."

Ann shook her head. "No, he can't. The chimes, remember? Your magic has failed, his magic has failed. He is no longer in your head. You are free of him."

Sister Georgia began objecting. Ann gripped her arm and started her moving.

"Take me to the other Sisters. I'll have no argument, do you hear? We must get away while we have a chance."

"But Prelate, we can't—"

Ann seized the ring through Sister Georgia's lip. "Do you want to continue to be a slave of this beast? Do you want to continue to be used by him and his men?" She gave the ring a tug. "Do you?"

Tears welled in the woman's eyes. "No, Prelate."

"Then get me to the tent with the other Sisters of the Light. I intend on getting you all away from Jagang this very night."

"But Prelate—"

"Move! Before we're caught here!"

Sister Georgia snatched up the pail of porridge and scurried off. Ann followed on her heels, with Georgia glancing back over her shoulder every few paces. The woman hurried along at a good clip, skirting every campfire and group of men by as wide a margin as she could without getting closer to men on the other side.

Even as she did, men still occasionally noticed her and reached out to snatch at her skirt. Most would laugh when she squeaked and scooted away.

When another man caught the Sister's wrist, Ann put herself between them. She smiled at the man. He was so surprised he let go of Sister Georgia. The two of them made a quick escape.

"You are going to get us killed," Sister Georgia whispered as she hustled between wagons.

"Well, I didn't think you were in the mood for what the fellow had in mind."

"If a soldier insists, we have to. If we don't . . . Jagang teaches us lessons if we don't—"

Ann shoved her onward. "I know. But I'm going to get you out of here. Hurry up. We must get the Sisters and escape while we have the chance. By morning, we'll be long gone and Jagang won't know where to look."

The woman opened her mouth to object, but Ann shoved her onward.

"As the Creator is my witness, Sister Georgia, I've seen more shilly-shallying out of you in the last ten minutes than your first five hundred years in this world. Now, get me to the other Sisters, or I'll make you wish for Jagang's clutches instead of mine."

CHAPTER 45

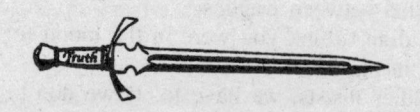

ANN TOOK A QUICK glance around as Sister Georgia lifted the tent flap. Satisfied that no one was paying any attention, Ann ducked inside.

A crowd of women huddled inside the dimly lit tent, some lying down, some sitting on the ground hugging their knees, some with arms around one another like frightened children. Not many even bothered to look up. Ann couldn't recall seeing such a cowed-looking bunch.

She reproved herself; these women had suffered unspeakable abuse.

"Shoo," Sister Rochelle, sitting near the tent opening, said, without meeting Ann's eyes. "Out with you, beggar."

"Good for you, child," Ann said. "Good for you, Sister Rochelle, for keeping beggars from your humble home."

Half the women looked up at the sound of Ann's voice. Wide eyes stared in the dim candlelight. Some of the women pushed at others who weren't paying attention, or swatted an arm, or pulled on a sleeve.

Some were dressed in outfits Ann could scarcely believe. The clothes covered them from neck to ankle, but were so sheer as to leave the women, for all practical purposes, naked. Others had on their own dresses, but they were in a state of wretched disrepair. A few had on little more than rags.

Ann smiled. "Fionola, you look well, considering your ordeal. Sister Kerena. Sister Aubrey. Sister Cherna, you look to be getting some gray hair. It happens to us all, but you wear it well."

Women all round blinked with disbelieving eyes.

"It's really her," Sister Georgia said. "She's really alive. She didn't die, like we thought. Prelate Annalina Aldurren lives."

"Well," Ann said, "Verna is the Prelate, now, but . . ."

Women were rushing to their feet. It rather reminded Ann of sheep watching a wolf coming down the hill. They all looked like they might bolt for the countryside.

Sisters of the Light were women of strength, women of fortitude, women of decisive intelligence. Ann feared to consider what it would have taken to reduce all these women to such a sorry looking state.

She ran a gentle hand down a head beside her. "Sister Lucy. You are a sight for my tired eyes." Ann smiled with genuine joy. "You all are." She felt a tear roll down her own cheek. "My dear, dear Sisters, you are all a blessed sight to my eyes. I thank the Creator He has led me to you."

And then they were all falling to knees to bow to her, to whisper their prayers to the Creator for her safety, to weep with disbelief.

"There, there. None of that," she said, wiping her fingers across the cheek of Sister Lucy, clearing away the tears. "None of that. We have important business, and we've no time for a good cry, not that I'm saying you aren't all entitled. But later would be an excellent time for it, while right now is not."

Sisters kissed the hem of her dress. More came forward on their knees to do the same. They were the lost, who were now found. It nearly broke Ann's heart.

She smiled her best Prelate smile and indulged them, touching each head, blessing each of them by name and thanking the Creator aloud for sparing each life and guarding each soul. It was an informal, formal audience with the Prelate of the Sisters of the Light.

She didn't think it the proper time to insist on reminding them she was no longer the Prelate, that she'd given the office to Verna for safekeeping. At that moment of joy, it just wasn't important.

Ann allowed the reunion to go on for only a few minutes before forcing it to an end.

"Listen now, all of you. Hush. We will have more than enough time later to share our joy at being together. Now I must tell you why I have come.

"Something terrible has happened. But as you know more than most, there must be balance in all things. The balance is that the terrible event will, in the Creator's balance, allow you to escape."

"The Prelate says the chimes are loose," Sister Georgia put in. Everyone gasped. "She believes it."

The clear implication was that Sister Georgia didn't believe it, that it was impossible, and anyone would have to be a fool to think it was so.

"Now, listen to me, all of you." Ann let her brow draw down in a look every woman in the room knew well enough to bring sweat to their brows. "You all remember Richard?" There were nods all around. "Well, it's a long story, but Jagang loosed a plague that killed thousands of people. It was a horrifying death for countless people. Untold numbers of children perished. Untold numbers of children were left orphans.

"Sister Amelia—"

"She's sworn to the Keeper!" several Sisters in the back gasped aloud.

"I know," Ann said. "She is the one who went to the underworld. She brought back the plague for Jagang. She murdered so many innocent people. . . .

"Richard was able to use his power to stop the plague."

There were astonished looks all around, accompanied by whispering. Ann imagined she was probably telling them too much all at once, but she had to explain enough so they would understand what was at stake.

"Richard contracted the plague, and in order to save his life, the Mother Confessor used magic." Ann held up a finger to silence them. "Nathan escaped." Again, gasps filled the tent. Ann hushed them lest they fall to wailing. "Nathan told the Mother Confessor the names of the chimes in order to save Richard's life. It was a terrible choice to make, but I believe he only did it to save Richard. The Mother Confessor spoke the names of those three chimes aloud to complete the spell to save Richard.

"The chimes are here. She called them into this world. I have personal knowledge of this. I have seen them, and I have seen them kill."

This time, there were no protests. Even Sister Georgia seemed convinced. Ann felt vindicated in her decision to tell them this much of it.

"As you all know, the chimes being loose has the potential to bring about an unprecedented cataclysm. It has begun. Magic is failing. All our magic is diminished to the point where it is useless. However, in the meantime Jagang's magic is useless, too.

"While this is so, we can get you all out of here."

"But what difference do the chimes make?" someone asked.

Ann drew a patient breath. "With the chimes here, magic is failing. That means Jagang's magic as a dream walker has failed just as our gift has failed. Your minds are all free of the dream walker."

Sister Georgia stared in disbelief for a moment. "But what if the chimes go back to the underworld? That could happen unexpectedly at any time. Jagang would be back in our heads. You can't tell he's there, Prelate. You can't tell.

"The chimes could already have fled back to the world of the dead. They may not have succeeded in gaining a soul. They may have fled to the protection of the Nameless One. The dream walker could be back in my head, watching me, as we speak."

Ann grasped the woman's arms. "No, he's not. Now, listen to me. My magic has failed. Yours is gone, too. All of us are without the gift. I will be able to tell when it returns—any of us can. For now, it's gone, and so is the dream walker."

"But we aren't allowed to use our gift without permission," a Sister to the right said. "We couldn't tell when our power returned to know the chimes had fled this world."

"I will know immediately," Ann said. "Jagang doesn't prevent me from touching my Han, if I can."

Sister Kerena stepped forward. "But if the chimes do go back, then His Excellency will return to—"

"No. Listen. There is a way to prevent the dream walker from ever again entering your mind."

"That's not possible." Sister Cherna's eyes darted about, as if Jagang might be hiding in the shadows, watching them. "Prelate, you must get out of here. You're going to be caught. Someone might have seen you. They could be telling Jagang as we speak."

"Please, get away," Sister Fionola said. "We are lost. Forget about us and get away. It can come to no good end, you being here."

Ann growled again. "Listen to me! It is possible to be safe from the dream walker entering your mind. We can all get away from his evil grip."

Sister Georgia was back to disbelieving. "But I don't see how—"

"How do you think he doesn't enter my mind? Don't you think he would want me? The Prelate herself? Wouldn't he get me if he could?"

They were all silent as they considered.

"Well, I guess he would." Sister Aubrey's brow drew down. "How is it he isn't able to take you, too?"

"I'm protected. That's what I'm trying to tell you. Richard is a war wizard. You all know what that means: he has both sides of the gift."

The Sisters blinked in astonishment, and then they all fell to whispering to one another.

"Furthermore," Ann went on, bringing the cramped tent full of women to silence, "he is a Rahl."

"What difference does that make?" Sister Fionola asked.

"The dream walkers are from the time of the great war. A wizard of that time, a war wizard named Rahl, an ancestor of Richard's, conjured a bond to protect his people from them. Gifted descendants of the House of Rahl are born with this bond with his people that protects them from dream walkers.

"The people of Richard's land are all bonded to him as their Lord Rahl. Because of that, and because of the magic of it passed down to him, they are all protected from the dream walker. That keeps Jagang from their minds. A dream walker can't enter the mind of anyone bonded to the Lord Rahl."

"But we are not his people," women all around were saying.

Ann held up a hand. "It doesn't matter. You only have to swear your loyalty to Richard—swear it meaningfully in your heart—and you are safe from the dream walker."

She passed a finger before their eyes. "I have long been sworn to Richard. He leads us in our fight against this monster, Jagang, who would end magic in this world. My faith in Richard, my bond to him, my being sworn to him in my heart, protects me from Jagang entering my mind."

"But if what you say about the chimes being here in this world is true," a Sister in the back said in a whine, "then the magic of the bond will fail, too, so we would have no protection."

Ann sighed and tried to remain patient with these frightened and intimidated women. She reminded herself to keep in mind these women had been in the savage hands of the enemy for a long time.

"But the two cancel each other, don't you see."

Ann turned up her palms, like scales, moving them up and down in opposition. "As long as the chimes are here, Jagang's magic doesn't work, and he can't enter your minds." She moved her hands in the opposite direction.

"When the chimes are banished, and if you are sworn to Richard, then his bond keeps Jagang from your mind. Either one or the other protects you.

"Do you all see? You must only swear to Richard, who leads the fight against Jagang, fights for our cause—the cause of the Light—and you never again need fear the dream walker being able to reach you.

"Sisters, we can get away. Tonight. Right now. Do you at last see? You can be free."

They all stared dumbly. Finally, Sister Rochelle spoke up.

"But, we aren't all here."

Ann looked around. "Where are the rest? We will collect them and leave. Where are they?"

Again, the women retreated into frightened silence. Ann snapped her fingers at Sister Rochelle for her to answer. Finally the woman spoke again.

"The tents."

Every woman in the room cast her eyes down. The gold rings through their lower lips shone in the candlelight.

"What do you mean, the tents?"

Sister Rochelle cleared her throat, trying to keep the tears struggling to break through from doing so.

"Jagang, when one of us displeases him, or he is angry with us, or he wants to punish us, or teach us a lesson, or simply wishes to be cruel, sends us to the tents. The soldiers use us. They pass us around."

Sister Cherna fell to the ground weeping. "We must be whores for his men."

Ann gathered her resolve. "Listen to me, all of you. That ends right now. Right now, you are free. You are again Sisters of the Light. Do you hear me? You are no longer his slaves!"

"But what about the others?" Sister Rochelle asked.

"Can you get them?"

Sister Georgia drew up tall and stiff. "You wait here, Prelate. Sister Rochelle, Aubrey, and Kerena will go with me to see what we can do." She gave the three a look. "Won't we? We know what we must do."

The three nodded. Sister Kerena put a hand under Ann's arm.

"You wait here. Will you? Wait here until we return."

"Yes, all right," Ann said. "But you must hurry. We need to get out of here before it gets too late in the night, or we will raise suspicions traipsing through the camp when everyone else is sleeping. We can't wait for—"

"Just wait," Sister Rochelle said in a calm voice. "We will see to it. Everything will be all right."

Sister Georgia turned to the tent full of Sisters. "See to it she waits, will you? She must wait here."

The Sisters nodded. Ann put her fists on her hips.

"If you take too long, we will have to leave without you. Do you understand? We can't—"

Sister Rochelle put a hand against Ann's shoulder. "We will be back in plenty of time. Wait."

Ann sighed. "The Creator be with you."

Ann sat among Sisters, who seemed to recede back into the prison of their private thoughts. Their joy, so evident when they had first seen her, had faded. They were once again distant and unresponsive.

They stared off without listening as Ann tried telling them some of the lighter stories of her adventures. She chuckled as she recounted incommodious moments, hoping someone would become interested and perhaps smile, at least. No one did.

None of them asked anything, or even seemed to be listening. They would no longer even meet her gaze. Like trapped animals, they wanted only to escape the terror.

Ann was growing more uncomfortable by the moment. By the moment, sitting among these women she knew so well, her hackles were beginning to rise at the thought that maybe she didn't know them as well as she had believed.

Sometimes, trapped animals didn't know enough to run for an open gate.

When the tent flap opened, they scooted away from her. Ann rose.

Four huge men, layered in leather plates, belts, straps, hides over their shoulders, and weapons jangling from their belts, ducked into the tent, followed by Sisters Georgia, Rochelle, Aubrey, and Kerena. The men's stringy, greasy hair whipped from side to side as they checked to each side. By the way they carried themselves they looked to Ann to be men of more authority than mere soldiers.

Sister Rochelle pointed. "That's her. The Prelate of the Sisters of the Light."

"Rochelle," Ann growled, "what's this about? What do you think—"

The man seeming to be in charge seized her jaw, turning her head left, then right, as he appraised her. "You sure?" His dark glower moved to Sister Rochelle. "She looks like the rest of the beggars to me."

Sister Georgia pointed at Ann. "I'm telling you, that's her." The man's eyes turned to Sister Georgia as she went on. "She's just fixed herself up like that to get in here."

The man gestured the other soldiers forward. They brought manacles and chains. Ann tried to fight them off, to twist away, but the soldier who seized her, unconcerned, gripped her fists and pulled them out for another man to clamp on the manacles.

Two of them forced her to the ground as another man set down an anvil. They held the manacles' ears on the anvil as they hammered pins through the holes and then mushroomed the heads of the pins, locking the manacles on permanently. They made them too tight, so they dug into her flesh, but the men were indifferent to her unintended cry of pain.

Ann knew better than to struggle when it could do no good, so she made herself become still. Without her Han, she was as helpless as a child against these big men. The

Sisters mostly cowered as far away as they could get. None watched.

The men hammered closed the open links at the end of the chains. Ann let out a grunt as she was slammed face down in the dirt. More manacles were affixed to her ankles. More chains were attached. Big hands lifted her. A chain around her waist webbed all the rest together.

Ann was not even going to be able to feed herself.

One of the men scratched his thick beard. "And she has no one with her?"

Sisters Georgia and Rochelle shook their heads.

He chuckled. "How'd she get to be the Prelate, if she's that dumb?"

Sister Georgia curtsied without meeting his eyes. "We don't know, sir. But she is."

He shrugged and started to leave, but then halted and cast his gaze over the shivering women on the floor. He pointed a thick finger at a Sister in one of the absurd transparent outfits.

"You."

Sister Theola flinched. She closed her eyes. Ann could see her lips moving in a futile prayer to the Creator.

"Come along," the man commanded.

Trembling, Sister Theola stood. The other three men grinned their approval of their leader's choice as they shoved her out ahead of them.

"You said you wouldn't," Sister Georgia spoke up, if meekly.

"Did I?" the man asked. He showed her a wicked grin. "Changed my mind."

"Let me go in her place," Sister Georgia called out as the man turned to leave.

He turned back. "Well, well. Aren't you the noble one." He seized Sister Georgia's wrist and pulled her after as he went out through the flap. "Since you're so eager, you can come along with her."

After the men left with the two women, the tent fell to

terrible silence. None of the Sisters would look at Ann as she sat hobbled in the chains.

"Why?" Ann had spoken the word softly, but it rang though the tent like the huge bell atop the Palace of the Prophets. Several Sisters quailed at the single word. Others wept.

"We know better than to try to escape," Sister Rochelle said at last. "We all tried at first. We truly did, Prelate. Some of us died trying. It was prolonged and horrible.

"His Excellency taught us the futility of trying to escape. Aiding anyone in an attempt to escape is a grave offense. None of us wishes that lesson visited upon us again."

"But you could have been free!"

"We know better," Sister Rochelle said. "We can't be free. We belong to His Excellency."

"As victims at first," Ann said, "but now by choice. I willingly risked my life that you might be free. You were given the option, and you chose to remain slaves rather than reach for freedom.

"Worse, though, you all lied to me. You lied in the cause of evil." The women hid their faces as Ann delivered a withering glare. "And each of you knows what I think of liars—what the Creator thinks of those who lie in the cause of opposing his work."

"But Prelate—" Sister Cherna whined.

"Silence! I've no use for your words. You no longer have any right to have me hear them.

"If I ever get out of these chains, it will be by the aid of those who sincerely serve the Light. You are no better than the Sisters of the Dark. At least they have the honesty to admit their vile master."

Ann fell silent when a man stepped through the opening into the tent.

He was average in height and powerfully built, with massive arms and chest. His fur vest was open, revealing dozens of jewel-studded gold chains hanging from his bull neck. Each thick finger held a ring worthy of a king.

His smooth shaved head reflected points of light from the

512

candles. A fine gold chain ran from a gold ring in his left nostril to another in his left ear. The long braided ends of his mustache hung past his jaw, matching the braid in the center under his lower lip.

His eyes, though, marked the nightmare of the dream walker.

They had no whites to them at all. The murky orbs were clouded over with sullen dusky shapes shifting in a field of inky obscurity, yet Ann had no doubt whatsoever that he was looking right at her.

She couldn't imagine the gaze of the Keeper himself being any worse.

"A visitor, I see." His voice matched his muscle.

"The pig can speak," Ann said. "How fascinating."

Jagang laughed. It was not an agreeable sound.

"Oh, darlin, but aren't you the brash sort. Georgia tells me you'd be the Prelate herself. That true, darlin?"

She noticed out of the corner of her eye that every woman in the tent was on her knees with her face to the dirt in a deep bow. Ann couldn't say she didn't understand their not wanting to meet the man's disturbing gaze.

She gave him a pleasant smile. "Annalina Aldurren, former Prelate of the Sisters of the light, at your service."

The cleft between his prodigious chest muscles deepened as he pressed his hands together in the pose of prayer and bowed toward her with mock respect of her rank.

"Emperor Jagang, at yours."

Ann sighed irritably. "Well, what's it to be, Jagang? Torture? Rape? Hanging, beheading, burning?"

The grisly grin visited him again. "My, my, darlin, but don't you know how to tempt a man."

He grabbed a fistful of hair and lifted Sister Cherna.

"See, the thing is, I got plenty of these regular Sisters, and I got plenty of the other kind, too, the ones sworn to the Keeper. I confess to liking them better." He arched an eyebrow over a forbidding eye. "They can still use some of their magic."

513

Sister Cherna's eyes watered in pain as he gripped her throat. "But I've only got one Prelate."

Sister Cherna's feet were clear of the ground by several inches. She couldn't breathe, but made no effort to fight. His terrible massive muscles rippled and glistened in the candlelight.

The cords in his arm strained. Cherna's eyes widened as his grip tightened. Her mouth gaped in silent fright.

"So," Jagang said to the others, "she confirmed everything about the chimes? Told you everything about them?"

"Yes!" several offered at once, clearly hoping he would release Sister Cherna.

Not everything, Ann thought. If Zedd was ever going to succeed at anything, she hoped the chimes would be it.

"Good." Jagang dropped the woman.

Sister Cherna crumpled in a heap, her hands tearing at her throat as she struggled to get air. She couldn't get her breath. Jagang had crushed her windpipe. Her fingers clawed at the air. As she lay at his feet, she began turning blue.

With desperate effort, she struggled her way into Ann's lap. Ann stroked the poor ruined woman's head with an outpouring of helpless compassion.

Ann whispered her love and forgiveness to Sister Cherna, and then silently prayed to the Creator and to the good spirits.

Sister Cherna's arms, twitching in agony, circled Ann's waist in gratitude. Ann could do nothing but pray that the Creator would forgive his child as she died a burbling death in Ann's lap. At last, she stilled with the merciful release of death.

Jagang kicked Sister Cherna aside. He seized the chain around Ann's throat and with one hand easily hauled her to her feet. Cloudy shapes in his inky eyes shifted in a way that unsettled her stomach.

"I think you may be of some use. Maybe I can pull off your arms and send them to Richard Rahl, just to give him nightmares. Maybe I can trade you for something of value.

But fear not, I will think of a use for you, Prelate. You are now my property."

"You can have my existence in this world," Ann said with grim commitment, "but you cannot touch my soul. That gift of the Creator is mine, and mine alone."

He laughed. "A fine speech." He jerked her face closer. "One I've heard before." His eyebrows arched with delight. "Why, I think every woman in this room has said the same to me. But you know what, Prelate? They put the lie to it today, didn't they?

"They all gave you over, when they could have escaped. At the least, they could have saved your life at no risk to themselves. But they chose to remain slaves when you offered them freedom.

"I'd say, Prelate, that I have their souls, too."

"Sister Cherna sought me at death, not you, Jagang. She sought goodness and love, even though she had betrayed me. That, Emperor, is the mark of a soul's true intent."

"A difference of opinion, then." He shrugged. "What say we kill the rest, one at a time, and see each vote of devotion, then tally the votes at the end? To be fair, though, we'll take turns killing them. I killed mine. Your turn."

Ann could do no more than glare at the beast.

He let out a belly laugh. "No? See, you aren't so confident in winning the votes of your Sisters' souls."

He turned to the Sisters, still on their knees. "Fortune for you today, darlins. The Prelate seems to have ceded your souls."

His dark gaze returned to Ann. "By the way, you are probably hoping the chimes will be banished. We share the hope. I have use for magic, but if I have to, I can certainly win this way, too.

"But if the chimes are banished, it will do you no good. You see, those manacles and chains are invested with a spell spun by my other Sisters. You know the ones. The Sisters of the Dark. As you know, they have use of Subtractive Magic, and that, my dear Prelate, still works.

"I just didn't want you to suffer with false hope."

"How considerate of you."

"Don't fret, though. I will think of some creative use for you."

He cocked his arm. His bare shoulders bulged from the fur vest. His biceps were bigger than the waist of many women in the room.

"For now, though, I think I'd like you unconscious."

She tried to pull power forth. Her gift did not respond.

Ann watched the fist coming, but could do nothing to stop it.

CHAPTER 46

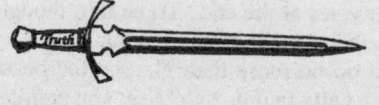

ZEDD SCRATCHED HIS CHIN as he looked around. He didn't see anyone. It was a peculiar alleyway, narrow and dark. He peered down to the little place at the end. The gloomy residence looked deserted.

That was a good sign.

Zedd stroked Spider's nose. "You wait here. Understand? Wait here for me."

The horse tossed her head and nickered agreeably. Smiling, Zedd scratched her ear. In response, she pressed her forehead against his chest, holding it there to let him know she would be well pleased if he were to want to continue scratching the ear for the rest of the afternoon.

Named after the unsettling leggy black splotch on her creamy rump, Spider had proven an excellent purchase, despite the high price. Being young, strong, and brimming with equine enthusiasm, the horse enjoyed trotting and occasional spirited runs. She had gotten him to Toscla in remarkably good time.

Since he had arrived, he had learned that Toscla was now called Anderith. In fact, he had almost been hauled off his horse by a man who accused Zedd of using the old name as an affront. Fortunately, Spider knew nothing of the peculiar human sensitivity to mere words; she was happy to leap into a gallop.

Zedd, without use of the gift and being vulnerable, besides feeling his age, had been resigned to a long and arduous journey afoot across the wilds. But by the magic of luck, on his third day out of the Mud People's village, he ran across a man who turned out to be an agent in trade agreements. Since he frequently went back and forth between clients, the man traveled with several horses. He could afford to be without his extra until he reached his destination, especially at the price Zedd offered, and so had parted with Spider.

The formidable journey Zedd anticipated ended up being remarkably short and not at all unpleasant, as long as he didn't dwell on his reasons for traveling to Anderith.

Mingling into line at the frontier, Zedd had been allowed through the checkpoint along with wagons, merchants, and traders of every sort. Dressed as he was in his fine maroon and black robes with silver brocade cuffs and gold brocade around the neck and down the front along with a gold buckle on a red satin belt, he was easily able to pass himself off as a merchant. He told the officers at the border that he had fruit orchards to the north and was on his way to Fairfield in order to negotiate trade agreements.

By the look of the soldiers he saw at the border, the people of Anderith placed too much faith in the Dominie Dirtch. It had been a long time since he had been to the land formerly called Toscla, but back then the border had been defended by as formidable and well trained an army as there was. The army had deteriorated until now it was nothing more than the hollow deterrent of ignorant confidence.

Zedd noticed Spider's ears turn toward the empty-looking home down at the end of the alleyway. Every muscle in the horse was at full attention. Zedd guessed that perhaps a horse was as good at certain things as some of his magic might have been. He found the thought disagreeable. He wanted his magic back.

After giving Spider a pat of reassurance, and once again asking her to wait there, Zedd made his way down the narrow alleyway. Tall clapboard walls to each side kept out most of the light. Nevertheless, a wide variety of herbs grew beside the narrow footpath. Many of the herbs Zedd saw growing there didn't enjoy the light at all. Some of them were exceedingly rare; they ordinarily hissed at light, but now they looked sickly.

Zedd made sure to step on each of the three steps going up to the door, rather than skip any. Such perfunctory attempts at stealth would be a mistake, if this was the place he hoped it was. Glancing in the gap of the curtains, he could see it was dark inside. He didn't see any eyes evaluating him, but he strongly suspected, if not with the aid of magic then with common sense, that they were there.

He took one last look over his shoulder at Spider standing attentively, her ears pricked toward him. She lifted her head, opened her mouth, and neighed. Zedd reached up and knocked.

The door creaked as it opened. No one was behind it.

"Enter," came a voice from the shadows beyond, "and state your request."

Zedd stepped into the gloom of the narrow room. Little light came in the gap between the heavy curtains, and the light from the door died out before daring to trespass very far. He could see no furniture, only the floorboards stretching off into the dim distance where she remained.

He turned and peered up at the top of the door. He pointed a bony finger at it.

"Nice touch, the rope used to open the door while you stay over there. Very effective."

"Who are you to tempt my anger?"

"Tempt your anger? Oh, dear no. You have it all wrong. I'm here looking for a sorceress."

"Take care, stranger, with what you wish. Wishes have an unpleasant manner of sometimes coming to be. State your name."

Zedd bowed dramatically. "Zeddicus Zu'l Zorander." He cocked his head to regard with one eye the woman in the shadows. "That would be Zeddicus Zu'l Zorander, as in, First Wizard Zeddicus Zu'l Zorander."

The woman staggered into the light, her fair features set in astonishment. "First Wizard . . ."

Zedd put on a disarming smile. "Franca Gowenlock, I'm hoping?"

Slack-jawed and wide-eyed, she seemed only able to nod.

"My, my, but haven't you grown." Zedd held his hand out below his beltline. "You couldn't have been any bigger than this when I last saw you." He smiled with sincere admiration. "You look to have grown into a very lovely woman."

She blushed as she reached up to plump her hair. "Why, I have gray hair."

"The bloom of it becomes you. It truly does."

He meant it. She really was an attractive woman. Her nearly shoulder-length hair swept back to display proud features in a most appealing manner. The kiss of gray at her temples only enhanced her mature beauty.

"And you . . ."

"Yes," he said with a sigh, "I know. I'm not exactly sure when it was that it happened, but I've grown into an old man."

A grin growing on her face, she stepped up and curtsied, holding out the skirts of her simple brown dress as she dipped.

"I am honored to have you in my humble home, First Wizard."

519

Zedd waggled a hand. "None of that, now. We're old acquaintances. Just Zedd would do fine by me."

She rose. "Zedd, then. I can hardly believe the Creator has answered my prayer in so direct a manner. Oh, but how I wish my mother were still alive to see you again."

"She, too, was a lovely woman. May the good spirits watch over her kind soul."

Beaming, Franca took his face in both hands. "And you are as handsome as I remember."

"Really?" Zedd straightened his shoulders. "Why, thank you, Franca. I try to take care of myself. Wash regularly, and such—with a few herbs and special oils I occasionally add in the water. I think that accounts for my skin still being so supple."

"Oh, Zedd, you can't imagine how happy I am to see you. Thank the Creator." She was still holding his face in her hands. Her eyes welled with tears. "I need help. Oh, First Wizard, I so desperately need your help."

He took her hands in his. "Odd you should mention that."

"Zedd, you helped my mother, once. Now you must help me. Please. My power has failed. I've tried everything I can think of. I've consulted books of charms, spells, and bewitching. None of them have been any help. I've had to tie that rope atop the door to fool people and keep them wary.

"I've been worried sick. I've hardly slept. I've tried—"

"The chimes are loose."

Her lashes fluttered as she stared dumbly at him. Her silent home seemed to stretch with her, to turn an ear toward him with her, to hold its breath with her.

"What did you say?"

"The chimes are loose."

"No," she said, appearing to be in a state of confused shock, "I don't think that's it. I think it may be a heating of my blood. Possibly caused by a hex placed on me by women of lesser talent but greater ambition. Jealousy, I believe it to be, along with a vengeful nature. I try not to step on people's toes, as it were, but there have been times—"

Zedd grasped her shoulders. "Franca, I came here because

520

I'm hoping you can help me. The Mother ... my granddaughter-in-law ... unintentionally set the chimes free while urgently summoning the aid of powerful magic in a final recourse to save the life of my grandson.

"I need your help. That's why I've come. My gift, too, has failed. All magic is failing. The world of life is in terrible danger. I don't need to explain to a woman of your talents the consequences of such an event. We need to see if there is anything we can do to banish the chimes. As First Wizard, I've come to call upon you for help."

"Your grandson? Is he ... did he survive the ordeal? Did he recover?"

"Yes. Fortunately, with the aid of the woman then to be his wife, he survived and is now well."

She put a fingernail between her teeth for a moment, her dark-eyed gaze shifting about as she considered his words. "There is that much good in it, then, that he survived. But then in return for their help, that would mean the chimes could cross the veil. . . ."

Her brow puckered. "Your grandson, you say. Has he the gift?"

A thousand things at once flashed through Zedd's mind. He answered with a simple "Yes."

Franca smiled briefly and politely, to show she was pleased for Zedd, and then moved into action. She threw back the drapes, took hold of his arm, and steered him to a table at the rear. She opened a heavy drape over a little window in the back to let light flood across the table. The dark mahogany tabletop had a Grace inlaid in silver.

Franca graciously gestured for him to sit. While he did, she retrieved two cups. After pouring tea from a pot hung over the glowing embers in the hearth, she set one before him and then sank into a chair across from him.

She dithered before saying, "I suspect there must be more to it."

Zedd sighed. "There is a great deal more, but time is running short."

"Mind hitting a few of the high spots for me?"

521

"Well, all right, then." Zedd took a sip of tea first. "Do you recall D'Hara?"

Her hand with the teacup paused on its way to her lips. "And how could one not recall D'Hara?"

"Yes, well, the thing is, my daughter was Richard's—that's my grandson, Richard—my daughter was Richard's mother. He was fathered through a cruel act of rape."

"I'm so sorry," she said with sincere sympathy. "But what does that have to do with D'Hara?"

"The man who fathered him was Darken Rahl, of D'Hara."

Her hands took on a decided tremble. She had not yet managed to get the tea to her mouth. With care, Franca set down her full cup lest she spill her tea before ever tasting it.

"Do you mean to tell me that this grandson of yours is the progeny of two lines of wizards—and is the very same Lord Rahl demanding the surrender of all lands of the Midlands?"

"Ah, well, yes, that would be him."

"And that this grandson of yours, the Lord Rahl himself, is the same one who is going to be wedded to the Mother Confessor herself?"

"It was a lovely ceremony," Zedd said. "Quite lovely. Rather exclusive, it was, but still stylish."

Franca put her forehead in her hand. "Dear spirits, that is a lump to swallow."

"Oh, yes. He's also a war wizard. I forgot—sorry. He was born with both sides of the gift."

Her head came up. "What?"

"You know, both sides. Subtractive Magic, as well as the usual Additive. Both sides."

"I know what 'both sides' means."

"Oh."

Franca swallowed. "Wait just a minute. The chimes . . . you mean it was the Mother Confessor who called them?"

"Well, she—"

The woman rose in a rush, her chair scraping against the

floor. "It's Lord Rahl who—dear spirits, the Mother Confessor herself pledged the soul of Lord Rahl—a war wizard with both sides of the gift—to the chimes?"

"It's not as bad as all that. She had no knowledge of the spell; she didn't do it intentionally. She's a good person and would never deliberately do such a thing."

"Deliberate or not, if the chimes get ahold of him—"

"I've sent them both off to a safe place—to where the chimes can't get to him. We have no need to fear that part of it."

She sighed with relief. "Thank the Creator for that much."

Zedd took another sip. "But that still leaves us without our power, and the world without magic, and possibly on the brink of ruin. Like I said, I need some help."

Franca finally sank back into her chair when Zedd nodded toward it. He smiled and told her the tea was excellent, and that she should have some herself.

"Zedd, I think you need the Creator Himself to come help you. What do you think I can possibly do? I'm just an obscure, middling, unremarkable sorceress in a far-flung land. Why would you come to me?"

Zedd squinted. He pointed. "What are you hiding with that neck band?"

Her fingers brushed her throat. "A scar. You remember the Blood of the Fold?" Zedd nodded that he did. "Well, most every place has men like that, men who hate magic, men who think those with magic are responsible for every miserable thing that happens in their lives."

"Yes, every place has its zealots."

"Here, zealotry went by the name Serin Rajak. He's the usual type: vicious and vengeful. He's talented at expressing his delusions in a way that whips up the emotions of others and pulls them into his wicked ways."

"So his idea of ridding the world of evil was killing you?"

"Me and those like me."

She briefly pulled down the neck band to reveal a scar.

"He hanged me by my neck while he and his followers started to build a fire under me. He's rather fond of burning.

Thinks it purges the world of the person's magic—keeps it from lingering after death."

Zedd sighed. "It never ends. So, apparently you convinced him to leave you be."

She smiled. "Cost him an eye, what he did to me."

"Can't say I blame you."

"It was a long time ago."

Zedd sought to change the subject. "I presume you've heard about the war with the Old World?"

"Of course. We've had representatives from the Imperial Order here to discuss the matter with our people."

Zedd sat up straighter. "What? The Order has people here?"

"That's what I'm telling you. Certain people in the government listen closely to what the Imperial Order has to say. I fear the Order is making offers to high officials. And has been doing so for quite some time."

She watched him over the rim of her cup as she took a sip. She seemed to decide to tell him more.

"Some people have been considering sending a secret message to the Mother Confessor, to ask that she come and investigate."

"With the chimes loose, she will be without her power, the same as you and I. Until the chimes are banished, she can be no help with anything like that."

Franca sighed. "Yes, I see what you mean. It would be best if we could see the chimes banished."

"In the meantime, perhaps people here should investigate the matter."

She set down her cup. "Who is going to question the Minister of Culture's office?"

"The Directors," Zedd offered.

She turned her cup around and around on the tabletop. "Maybe" was all she said.

When Zedd didn't say anything, she sought to fill the silence. "In Anderith, you do what you must to get along."

"There are always those who will." Zedd slouched back in his chair. "It will end up being irrelevant anyway. Anderith is going to have to surrender to Richard and the new D'Haran empire he is gathering to resist the invasion of the Imperial Order."

Zedd took another sip. "Did I mention he is also the Seeker of Truth?"

Franca looked up. "No, you neglected to mention it."

"Richard won't allow Anderith to carry on in the manner they seem to be doing—to have corrupt officials colluding with the Order. He and the Mother Confessor will put an end to such dangerous clandestine scheming. That's one of the reasons he's been forced to seize power. He means to consolidate rule under fair and open law."

"Fair law," she mused, as if it were a child's wish. "We are a prosperous land, Zedd. Anders have a good life. If it were the Hakens listening to the Imperial Order, I could understand it, they could be said to have cause, but Anders are the ones listening, and they are the ones already with power."

Zedd contemplated his tea. "Nothing nettles some people more than other people being free. In much the same way that Serin Rajak fellow hates those who have magic, the ruling elite—or those who would be—despise freedom. They find joy only in perpetuating misery."

Zedd sought to take the frost off the chill subject. "So, Franca, do you have a husband, or do the handsome men of the world still have a chance to court you?"

Franca smiled to herself for a time before she spoke. "My heart belongs to someone. . . ."

Zedd reached across the table and patted her hand. "Good for you."

She shook her head as her smile ghosted away. "No. He's married. I can't allow my feelings to be known. I would forever hate myself if I gave him any reason to decide to leave his beautiful bride and take up instead an aging spinster like me. I dare not let him even guess my feelings."

"I'm sorry, Franca," he said in gentle sympathy. "Life—or should I say love—sometimes seems so unfair. At least it may seem so now, but someday . . ."

Franca dismissed the matter with a gesture—more for herself than for him, he thought. She met his gaze again.

"Zedd, I'm flattered you would come to me—for that matter that you would even remember my name—but why would you think I can help you? You have more power than I. Or at least you did."

"To be quite honest, I didn't come for the purpose of seeking your help in the way you might think. I came here because as a young wizard I learned this to be the place where the chimes were entombed—in Toscla, or Anderith, as it's now called."

"Really? I never knew that. Where in Anderith are they entombed?"

Zedd spread his hands. "I was hoping you might know. You were the only name I knew from here, so I came seeking you out. I need help."

"I'm sorry, Zedd, but I had no idea the chimes were entombed here." She again took up her cup and sipped in thought. "However, if, as you say, the chimes can't get the soul of your grandson, they might eventually be pulled back into the world of the dead. We might need do nothing to bring it about. The whole problem might just vanish."

"Yes, there is that hope, but you must keep in mind the nature of the underworld."

"Meaning?"

Zedd tapped the outer circle of the Grace inlaid on the tabletop. "Here begins the underworld, where life crosses over." He glided his hand past the table's edge. "Beyond is eternity.

"Because the underworld is eternal, time has no meaning. There may be beginning when we cross over, but there is no end, so the concept of time unravels there. It is only here in the world of life where time is defined by beginning and end giving it some reference points, that it has significance.

"The chimes were conjured from that timeless place beyond, and derive their power from there, so time is meaningless to them.

"Perhaps it's true that without obtaining the soul they

crossed over to help, they will be pulled back to the underworld. However, to timeless beings, their time here may be viewed by them as but an instant as they wait to see if they will succeed, or as they enjoy a bit of frolic at bringing death and destruction, except that instant to them could be a millennium to this world. It could be ten millennia and still be but a meaningless twinkle in time to them—especially since they have no souls and can't really experience life."

She had been hanging on every word, seeming to be starved for conversation of things few but the gifted could comprehend.

"Yes, I see your point." She raised a finger. "But by the same token, they could be gone today—vanish as we speak—feeling endless frustration in a world with time, once they begin to find they must function within the alien confines of time and a schedule. The soul they seek, after all, has only so much time in this world. They must pursue and capture his soul while he lives."

"Well put and a worthy consideration, but how long shall we wait? At some point it will be too late for things of magic to recover. Some surely now lie ailing with the fading of magic. How long until they die out forever?

"I see your stargazers wilting out on the path to your home." Zedd lifted an eyebrow. "But much worse, how long until magic such as that of the gambit moth fails? What if the crops now growing are soon tainted?"

Her face, creased with concern, turned away.

Not knowing her well, Zedd didn't bring it up, but without magic, Jagang and the Imperial Order were only that much more powerful. Without magic to aid them, many more would die fighting him, and it very well could be blood spilled to no good end.

"Franca, as guardians of the veil, protectors of helpless creatures of magic, and as stewards of magic's promise to mankind, we must act with all due haste. We know not where the line lies that makes meaningful aid too late."

She nodded thoughtfully. "Yes. Yes, you are right, of course. Why do you need to know where the chimes are entombed? What will that help you accomplish?"

"Their ancient banishment, in order to nullify the original conjuring that brought them here, would have by necessity had to again breach the veil. Such a counterspell would itself have had to be balanced with an ancillary spell to allow their return to the world of life. Such a return spell could have been exceedingly narrow in terms—invocation of threes and all that—but it wouldn't matter; the mere existence of a return mechanism was all the balance the banishment spell would have required."

Zedd slowly ran his finger around the rim of his teacup. "From what I know of the matter, I believe the nature of their existence dictates that the chimes can only return to the world of life, once the narrow requirements of the balancing mechanism are met, through the gateway of their banishment. That's why I've had to come here."

She stared off in reflection. "Yes, that makes sense. The gateway, wherever it is, would be open."

"Being as you don't know where the chimes are entombed, perhaps you can be my guide."

Her gaze came back to him. "Where could we look? Do you have in mind a place to start?"

After another sip, Zedd set down his cup.

"My idea was you might be able to help me get into the library."

"The Library of Culture? At the Minister of Culture's estate?"

"That's the one. They have ancient texts there. At least they used to. Since the chimes were banished here in Anderith, the library might contain records or other information so I could find where it took place, and thus the gateway. They might even have other information of use."

"What are the names of the books you seek? Perhaps I know them."

"I don't know what books might be of help, if such books even exist, or if they do, that they are here. I will just have to start looking through those volumes in the library and see what we can find."

She leaned forward. "Zedd, there are thousands of books there."

"I know. I've seen them before."

"And if you find a book that names this place, then what?"

Zedd shrugged in a deliberately vague manner. "First step first."

If he could find no information on the mechanism of their banishment, he had an idea of what he might have to do should he be able to find the location of the entombment. Even if he did find such information and it was a simple matter, without the use of his magic he would be helpless to reverse the problem.

He might be forced to take desperate measures.

"So, what about the Library of Culture? Can I get in there?"

"I think I could help with that much of it. As an Ander, and one known at the Minister's estate, I'm trusted with access. Not everyone is. Those in authority have been altering history to such an extent that those of us who have lived a bit of it don't even recognize our own past, much less trust the rest of what we're told."

She emerged from her private thoughts and straightened with a brave smile. "When do you wish to go there?"

"The sooner the better."

"Do you think you could pretend to be a visiting scholar?"

"I think I could manage to look like I have difficulty recalling my own name."

CHAPTER 47

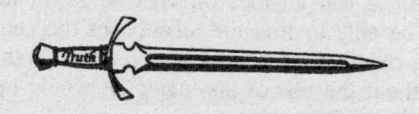

"OH, HOW KIND!" ZEDD exclaimed in mock delight as the woman set down the heavy volume in the glow from the tall lamp. "I'm sure of it now. I've no doubt. You can be nothing other than a good spirit come to assist me, Mistress Firkin."

The woman abruptly turned as shy as a teenage girl. Her cheeks reddened as she smiled.

"It's my job, Master Rybnik."

He leaned closer to her and lowered his voice to a playful whisper. "I prefer beautiful women call me Ruben."

Zedd, when circumstances required the use of an assumed name, favored the name Ruben Rybnik. He thought it a dashing name. Leading a simple life fostered the urge for occasional flamboyance. Zedd considered lighthearted diversion essential to balance. Something as simple as using the name Ruben Rybnik satisfied that need.

The woman blinked, not catching on to the flirtation— surprising, he thought, considering she was nice enough looking that she would have to have had ardent suitors throughout her long life. Zedd was forced to clarify himself.

"Therefore, Mistress Firkin, I prefer you call me Ruben."

She stared blankly, and then, as he saw in her dark brown eyes realizations making connections, a sudden giggle burst forth to echo through the long room. A few people down at other tables glanced up. He noticed the eyes of one of the guards turn their way. Mistress Firkin put the back of her hand to her grin as her face went scarlet.

"Ruben." She giggled again with the mischievousness of using his first name. She glanced around before leaning toward him. "Vedetta."

"Ah," Zedd cooed. "Vedetta. What a lovely name."

She tittered as she scurried off, her shuffling steps echoing softly through the huge room—the lower of two floors of the elegant Anderith Library. From his place at a table, Zedd had long since watched through the windows as the sun set. The array of lamps lit with a warm glow the honey-colored oak of the room and provided illumination for those still more interested in devouring words than dinner.

Zedd dragged in front of himself the heavy volume Vedetta Firkin had found. A quick glance told him it was of no value. He opened it anyway so as to appear he was reading it with earnest interest.

He was not. The book he was really reading was to the upper right, but even with his head lowered, he could still turn his eyes up to the right and read the other, and any nosy person wandering past would be fooled. There were a few such people about.

He had already created a sensation with his grand entrance when he stood at the head of the library and made sweeping proclamations of having a hypothesis of law involving the accountability of secondary suppliers of goods to the signatories in trade agreements nullified by clauses involving acts of Creation not specifically specified in the subtext but implied by common law of ancient trading principles, and he knew he would be able to prove them out with the fine examples of rational law set forth in the examples found in the history of Anderith law.

No one had been bold enough to dispute his claims. Everyone in the library was perfectly happy to let him do his research. It helped to have Franca escorting him, since she was known in the library.

It was late, and the people running the library wanted to go home, but they feared incurring the wrath of anyone having such extraordinary command of law. Because he lingered, a few others did, too. Zedd didn't know if it was to take advantage of the extra time the library was open, or to keep him under observation.

Franca sat across the table but down a ways to provide room for all the books spread out in front of the two of them. She pored through books and occasionally brought to his attention items she thought he might need to see. Franca was smart, and pointed out things few others would grasp, things that could conceivably be significant, but so far he had seen nothing of any practical use. He wasn't sure exactly what it was he was searching for, but he was sure he hadn't seen it yet.

Deep in concentration, Zedd started when someone touched his shoulder.

"Sorry," Vedetta whispered.

Zedd smiled at the shy lady. "Quite all right, my dear Vedetta." He lifted his eyebrows in question.

"Oh." She reached into the pocket of her apron. She turned red again as her hand fished around.

The hand paused. "Found it."

"Found what?" Zedd whispered.

She leaned closer, lowered her voice yet more. Zedd noticed Franca watching from across the table as her head was bowed to a book.

"We aren't supposed to let just anyone see this. It's very precious and rare." Her face flushed red again. "But you are a special man, Ruben, so brilliant and all, that I brought it out of the vault for you to see for just a minute."

"Really, Vedetta? How extraordinarily kind of you. What is it, then?"

"I don't rightly know. Exactly. But it belonged to Joseph Ander himself."

"Realllly," Zedd drawled.

She nodded in earnest. "The Mountain."

"What?"

"The Mountain. That's what some of that time called him. When I don't have anything to do, I sometimes read the ancient texts of the time—to learn more about our revered ancestor, Joseph Ander. Back then, as I gather, some called him the Mountain."

Zedd was at full attention as he watched her draw the hand from her apron. She had something small. His heart sank because he thought it too small to be a book.

But then his heart felt as if it skipped a beat when he saw it was indeed a small black book.

A journey book.

It even had the stylus still in the spine.

Zedd wet his lips as she held it out in both hands before him. Zedd put a finger to his lower lip. She had no intention of letting such a valuable piece out of her possession, even if he was a fancy scholar. Over near the vault door two armed guards scanned the patrons, but paid Zedd no particular attention.

"May I see inside, Vedetta?" he asked in a strained whisper.

"Well . . . well, I guess it can't hurt."

The woman carefully opened the cover. The journey book was in pristine condition, but then, the one Ann had carried was just as old, and in just such good condition. Journey books were things possessed of magic, so that probably explained their being nearly as good as new despite their thousands of years of use. That, and the care with which the Sisters handled the valuable books. The people here used no less care.

Zedd froze in midbreath.

Mountain.

He understood. *Mountain's Twin* was the mate to this journey book. It all fell into place in his head. *Mountain's Twin* had been destroyed, and, along with it, possibly the disposition of the chimes.

But this book, Joseph Ander's journey book, would have the same words—if they hadn't been wiped away with the stylus.

He watched, spellbound, as Vedetta Firkin turned the first blank page over. A three-thousand-year-dead wizard was about to speak to him.

Zedd stared at the words there on the next page. He stared as hard as he could. They made no sense. A spell, he feared, to keep anyone from reading it.

No, that wasn't it. Besides, magic had failed; such a spell wouldn't still work. As he studied the writing, he realized it was a language he didn't know.

Then it came to him. It was in High D'Haran.

Zedd's heart sank. Virtually no one knew High D'Haran anymore. Richard had told him he'd learned it. Zedd didn't doubt him, but Richard was off on his way to Aydindril. Zedd would never be able to find, much less catch, him.

Besides, the people in the library were not going to let him take this book, and Zedd had no magic to do anything about it.

"What a glorious thing to see," Zedd whispered as he watched the woman slowly turn the pages before his eyes.

"Yes, isn't it," she said with deep reverence. "I sometimes go in the vault and just sit and look at the things written by Joseph Ander, and imagine his fingers turning the pages. It gives me shivers," she confided.

"Me, too," Zedd said.

She seemed pleased to hear it. "It's too bad no one has ever been able to translate it. We don't even know what language it might be. Some of our scholars here suspect it to be an ancient code used by wizards.

"Joseph Ander was a wizard," she confided in a hushed tone. "Not everyone knows it, but he was. He was such a great man."

Zedd wondered how they could possibly know he was great if they had no idea what he said. But then he realized that was precisely why they thought he was so great.

"A wizard," Zedd repeated. "One would think a wizard would want his words known."

Vedetta giggled. "Oh, you don't know anything about wizards, Ruben. They're like that. Mysterious and all."

"I suppose," he said absently as he tried to pick out a word he might possibly make sense of as they flipped past his eyes.

None did.

"Except," Vedetta confided in a very low whisper as her eyes shifted to each side for a quick look, "this here." She tapped a page very near the end. "These words here I managed, by an accident of coincidence, to decipher. Just these two."

"You did?" Zedd squinted at the words. " 'Fuer Owbens.' " He looked up into her excited eyes. "Vedetta, do you really know what 'Fuer Owbens' means, or do you just think you might?"

She frowned with seriousness. "I really know. I quite by chance came across a place in another book, called *Tinder Dominion*, where it mentions the same words and uses both versions. It was about some—"

"So, you deciphered the words. What do they mean?"

She put her mouth close to his ear. "The Ovens."

Zedd turned his head and looked into her dark eyes. "The Ovens?"

She nodded. "The Ovens."

He frowned. "Any idea what that means?"

Vedetta snapped closed the little black journey book.

"Sorry, but I don't." She straightened. "It's getting late, Ruben. The guards said that after I showed you this, they want to close the library."

Zedd didn't try to hide his disappointment. "Of course. Everyone will want to go home and get some dinner and sleep."

"But you can come back tomorrow, Ruben. I'd love to help you some more tomorrow."

Zedd was stroking his lip as his mind raced, going over every scrap of information he had learned and trying to think if any of it would be of any use at all. It didn't seem so.

"What?" He looked up at her. "What was that?"

"I said I hope you will come back tomorrow. I'd love to help you again." She smiled in her shy way. "You're more

535

of a challenge than most who come in here. Few people care to research such ancient books as do you. I think that's a shame. People nowadays don't respect the knowledge of the past."

"No, they don't," he said in all seriousness. "I'd love to return tomorrow, Vedetta."

Her face went red again. "Perhaps ... if you'd like, you could come back to my apartment and I could fix you something to eat?"

Zedd smiled. "I would love that, Vedetta, and you truly are a kind lady, but it wouldn't be possible. I'm with Franca. She's my hostess, and we must get back to Fairfield and discuss all our research. My project, you know. The law."

Her wrinkles sagged. "I understand. Well, I hope to see you tomorrow."

Zedd caught her sleeve as she started to turn away. "Vedetta, perhaps tomorrow I could take you up on your offer? If it would be open for tomorrow, that is."

Her beaming smile reappeared. "Why, yes, tomorrow would be better, actually. I would have a chance to—well, tomorrow would be fine. My daughter will be gone tomorrow evening, I'm sure, and we could have a lovely dinner, just the two of us.

"My husband died six years ago," she added as she fussed with her collar. "A fine man."

"I'm sure he was." Zedd stood and bowed deeply. "Tomorrow it is, then." He held up a finger. "And thank you for showing me the special book from the vault. I was most honored."

She turned and started off, taking a big smile with her. "Good night, Ruben."

He waggled his fingers in a wave while giving her a wide grin. As soon as he saw her vanish into the vault, Zedd turned and gestured to Franca.

"Let's go."

Franca closed her books and came around the table. Zedd offered his arm as they ascended the grand staircase together. The oak railing, nearly a foot across and sculpted in an exquisite profile, reflected the points of lamplight from the lamps flanking the stairwell.

"Any luck?" she whispered when they were out of earshot of the others.

Zedd checked over his shoulder to make sure none of the people who had shown interest in the two of them were closing in behind. There were at least three people Zedd found suspicious, but they were too far back cleaning up their papers and putting away books to hear—unless they were gifted.

Since magic didn't work, he didn't need fear that. A small convenience of magic's failure.

"No," Zedd said with resignation. "I didn't see anything of any use at all."

"What was that little book she brought out of the vaults? The one she wouldn't let you hold?"

Zedd waved a hand. "Nothing of any use. It was in High D'Haran." He looked over out of the corner of his eye. "Unless you know High D'Haran?"

"No. I've only seen it a couple of times in my life."

Zedd sighed. "The woman knew the meaning of only two words out of the entire book: 'The Ovens.' "

Franca halted on the stairs. They were near the top.

"The Ovens?"

Zedd frowned. "Do you know what that means?"

Franca nodded. "It's a place. Not many people but the gifted would know it. My mother took me there once."

"What is it? What kind of place?"

Franca squinted off into her memories. "Well . . . it's an abnormally hot place. A cave. You can feel the power—the magic—in that hot cave, but there's nothing there."

"I don't understand."

Franca shrugged. "Neither do I. There's nothing there, but it's a strange place that only the gifted would appreciate. It just gives you a kind of . . . I don't know. Kind of a thrill of power running through you just to stand in there, in the Ovens. But those without the gift can't feel anything."

She checked the others, to make sure they weren't listening. "It's a place we don't tell people about. A secret place—just for the gifted. Since we don't know what's in there, we keep it secret."

"I need to go see this place. Can we go now?"

"It's way up in the mountains—several days away. If you want, we can leave in the morning."

Zedd thought it over. "No, I think I would prefer to go alone."

Franca seemed hurt, but if it was what he thought it might be, he didn't want her anywhere near it. Besides, he didn't really know this woman, and he wasn't sure he could trust her.

"Look, Franca, it could be dangerous, and I'd never forgive myself if anything happened to you. You've already given me selflessly of your time and trouble—and risked enough."

That seemed to make her feel better. "I guess someone will have to tell Vedetta you won't be able to make dinner tomorrow. She will be disappointed." Franca smiled. "I know I would be, were I her."

CHAPTER 48

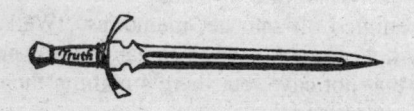

ZEDD GRUNTED WITH THE weight as he slid the saddle off Spider. He was getting too old for this sort of thing, he decided. He smiled at the irony.

He flopped the saddle down over a log to keep it off the

ground. Spider happily surrendered the rest of the tack, which Zedd laid over the top of the saddle. He covered it all with the saddle blanket.

The log with the gear lay against the trunk of an old spruce, so it was out of the weather, to an extent, anyway. He stacked pine boughs over the tack, leaning them up against the spruce's trunk, interlocking them, to keep the gear dry as best he could. The drizzle would soon turn to rain, he had no doubt.

Spider, free of duty, cropped grass nearby, but kept an eye and an ear to him. It had been a hard four-day ride across the Drun River and up into the mountains. Harder on him than on the horse; the horse wasn't old. Zedd, seeing that Spider was happily engaged, turned to his own business.

A small stand of a half-dozen spruce screened the view of his destination. He walked quickly along the quiet shore to skirt the trees. Once beyond them, he stepped onto a thumb of rock jutting out, almost as if it were set there as a podium.

Hands on hips, Zedd looked out over the lake.

It was a beguiling spot. Behind him, the thick forest stopped well short of the lake, as if afraid to approach too close, leaving the lone level and gentle access, but for the few brave spruce, empty of trees. The peninsula was covered here and there with brush but mostly it held thick tufts of grasses. Small blue and pink wildflowers cavorted among the grass.

Sheer rock walls rose up around the rest of the deep mountain lake. If the isolated and remote stretch of water had a name, he didn't know it. There was no practical way to reach it but this one shore.

Across and to the left, the jagged mountains, with a sloping field in their lap, rose up ever higher into the distance, providing little opportunity for much more than scraggly trees, here and there, to set down tenacious roots. To the right, dark stone cliffs obscured the view beyond, but he knew that past them were more mountains yet.

On the other side of the lake, a waterfall cascaded over

the edge of a prominent jutting wall of rock. Before him, the calm lake reflected the tranquil scene.

The icy waters tumbling into the lake came from the highlands, from the vast lake higher up in the bleak wasteland, where the warfer birds alone watched. These were part of the headwaters of the Dammar River, which in turn flowed into the Drun. This cold water, coming from a place of death, would meander down into the Nareef Valley below, and give life.

Behind the waterfall were the Ovens.

In the rock wall behind that tumbling water, three thousand years before, through a gateway to the underworld, the chimes had once been entombed.

And now they were free.

There they awaited their soul.

At the very thought, Zedd could feel gooseflesh, like a thousand spiders, on his legs.

He tried again, as he had countless times, to call his gift of magic. He tried his best to convince himself that this time it would come. He spread his arms, lifting them, palms up, toward the sky, as he labored to cajole forth magic.

The placid lake saw no magic from him. The mountains waited, and were silent in his failure.

Zedd, feeling very alone, very old, let out a chesty sigh. He had imagined it a thousand different ways.

But he had never imagined this would be how he died.

This was why he couldn't let Richard know it was the chimes themselves that were loose. Richard would not have accepted what Zedd intended, what Zedd knew he must do.

Turning his mind away from the smothering melancholy, he surveyed the lake. He had to keep his mind on what he was doing, or he could easily fail and his sacrifice would be for naught. If he was going to do this, he intended to do it right. There was satisfaction to be derived in a job well done, even a job such as this one.

As he studied the scene with an experienced eye, what at first looked to be peaceful waters now revealed more. The water was alive with things unseen, moving in lurking currents, seething with dark intent.

The water was alive with the chimes of death.

Zedd looked back to the waterfall. He could make out, just beyond it, the dark maw of the cave. He had to get there, across the water, across the water churning with chimes.

"Sentrosi!" Zedd opened his arms. "I have come to freely offer the soul you seek! My soul! What is mine, I surrender to you!"

Flames boiled out around the column of water, swallowing it in great gouts of fire that roared forth, rolling and tumbling out of the place called the Ovens. The fire turned the surface of the lake orange with reflections of its heat. For a moment, the waterfall was rendered steam. Inky black smoke billowed up with the white steam, tangling together in a sinister pillar that marked the maw of death.

A clear chime rang out, reverberating through the mountains.

Sentrosi had answered.

The answer was yes.

"Reechani!" he called to the water before him. "Vasi!" he called to the air about him. "Let me pass, for I have come to surrender my soul to you all."

The water swirled and turned, as if schooling fish gathered at the shore before him. More, though, the water itself seemed alive, eager, hungry. Zedd guessed it was.

The air felt thick around him, pressing in, urging him forward.

The water rose up and curled in a gesturing motion toward the Ovens. The air buzzed with chimes, countless separate bells that together created one crystalline sound. The air smelled as if it were burnt.

Since it had already started to rain, Zedd didn't see that it really mattered if he got any wetter. He stepped out into the water.

Rather than having the swim he expected, he found the

surface solid enough to hold him, almost like ice, except it moved. Ripples radiated out from his footstep, touching and retreating, as if it were no more than a mere puddle he splashed through. Each step he took found support.

It was the support of the chimes, of Reechani, bearing him to his doom, to their queen. Vasi, the chimes of the air, escorted him, a robe of death all around.

Zedd could feel the touch of the underworld in the air. He could feel the damp death at his feet. He knew each step might be his last.

He remembered Juni, the Mud People hunter, who had drowned. Zedd wondered if Juni had felt the peace he sought, the peace he had been offered, before he died.

Knowing the purpose of the chimes, Zedd strongly suspected that, after tempting with tantalizing tranquillity and before they extracted the life, they delivered their terror.

Before he reached the waterfall, something unseen pierced the watery column. Intangible hands split the waterfall in two, leaving an opening in the middle where he might pass into the cave beyond. Sentrosi, the fire, preferred him reasonably dry, he supposed.

Stepping onto the opening in the rock, before going through into the cave, he heard Spider let out a snort of censure. Zedd turned.

The horse stood at the bank, feet spread, muscles tense. Her ears were pinned back, her eyes aglare. Her tail whipped from side to side, slapping her flanks.

"It's all right, Spider," Zedd called back to the agitated animal. "I give you your freedom." Zedd smiled. "If I don't come back . . . enjoy your life, my friend. Enjoy your life."

Spider released a drawn-out angry squeal. Zedd gave her a last wave, and the squeal became a deep bellow.

Zedd turned and stepped beyond the tumbling water, into the darkness. The curtain of the waterfall closed behind him.

He didn't hesitate. He intended to give the chimes what they wanted: a soul. If he could do it in a way that would preserve his life in the process, he would, but without his magic he had little hope of accomplishing such a thing as he intended and at the same time remaining whole.

Being First Wizard, he had some knowledge of the problem at hand. The chimes needed a soul to stay in the world of life—that was the manner in which they had been conjured forth. More than that, they needed a specific soul: the one promised.

Beings from the underworld, and soulless beings at that, would have limitations to their understanding of the concept of what it would be to have a soul, or the nature of the soul they were promised. Naturally, there were certain intrinsic precepts that applied, but beyond that, the chimes were in what was to them an alien world. His only hope was that ignorance.

Since Zedd was so closely related to Richard, and Richard's life had been passed down through Zedd, their souls shared ethereal bonds and connections; just as in body, their souls were related. In much the way they shared some things, the shape of their mouth, for instance, their souls shared characteristics.

Even so, each of them was a unique individual, and therein lay the danger.

His hope was that the chimes would mistake his as the soul they needed, take his as the soul they needed, and, it ultimately being the wrong one, choke on it. So to speak.

It was Zedd's only hope. He knew no other way to stop the chimes. With each passing day the threat to the world of life grew more grave. Every day people died. Every day magic grew weaker.

As much as he wished to live, he could think of no other way but to forfeit his life to stop the chimes, now, before it was too late.

When they opened themselves to the soul they were pledged, and they were thus vulnerable, he hoped his soul would ruin the flow of the spell through which they entered this world.

Given that he was a wizard, it was no wild hope; it was, in fact, a reasoned approach. Dubious, but reasoned.

Zedd knew that at the least, such a thing as he planned

would disrupt the spell to some extent—rather like shooting an arrow at an animal, meant to kill, but if off target, wounding at least.

What he didn't know was what it would do to him. Zedd had no delusions, though. He reasonably expected that what he did, if it didn't strip his soul from him and in so doing kill him, would anger the chimes and they would extract their vengeance.

Zedd smiled. The balance to it was that he would at last again see his beloved Erilyn, in the spirit world, where he knew her soul waited for him.

Inside, the heat was oppressive.

The walls were slowly rolling, tumbling, turning, twisting, liquid fire.

He was in the beast.

In the center of the pulsing cave, Sentrosi, the queen of fire, turned her lethal gaze on him. Tongues of flame tasted the air around him. She smiled—a whorl of yellow flame.

One last time, Zedd made a futile attempt to call his magic.

Sentrosi rushed toward him with frightening speed, frightening need.

Zedd felt searing pain through every nerve as unimaginable agony seized his very soul.

The world ignited. His scream exploded as a deafening chime.

Richard cried out. The pain of the ripping, ringing chime felt as if it splintered his skull.

He was only dimly aware of things around him as he tumbled back over the flanks of his horse. The pain of crashing to the ground was a pleasant diversion from the overpowering toll overwhelming his control and driving his scream.

He held his head as he curled into a ball in the road, crying uncontrollably with the hurt.

The world was fiery agony.

All around, people leaped from horses, shrieking orders. Richard could only perceive them as blurry shapes darting about. He couldn't comprehend the words. He couldn't recognize anyone.

He couldn't understand anything but the pain.

He could do nothing more than maintain his thread of connection to consciousness, to life, as he struggled against the merciless torrent of agony.

That he had passed the test of pain, lived through it, as must all who would be wizards, was the only thing that kept him alive. Without the lessons learned, he would already be dead.

He was alone in a private inferno.

He didn't know how long he could maintain his hold on life.

Everything seemed to have gone crazy at once. Beata tore across the grassy ground, running for all she was worth. Terror rampaged through her.

Turner's scream had stopped. It had been horrifying while it lasted, but it had only lasted seconds.

"Stop!" Beata shrieked with all the power in her lungs. "Stop! Are you crazy? Stop!"

The air still reverberated with the sound of the Dominie Dirtch. The low-pitched knell lifted dust from the grass, so that it looked like the ground all around was smoking. It trembled and rolled dirt into little balls. It toppled a little lone tree the last squad had planted.

It made the whole world vibrate with a ghastly drone.

Tears streamed down Beata's cheeks as she raced across the field, shrieking for them to stop ringing the bell.

Turner had been out front, scouting on regular patrol to make sure the area before the Dominie Dirtch was clear.

His scream had ended mere seconds after the Dominie Dirtch had been rung, but its pain and horror still echoed inside her head. It was a cry she knew she would never be able to forget as long as she lived.

"Stop!" she yelled as she snatched the railing to spin herself around onto the stairs. "Stop!" she cried again as she raced up the steps.

Beata burst onto the platform, fists raised, ready to pummel the fool who'd rung the Dominie Dirtch.

Beata halted, panting madly, looking about. Emmeline stood frozen in wide-eyed shock. Bryce, too, seemed out of his senses. He just stared at her in frozen panic.

The long striker, used to ring the Dominie Dirtch, still stood in its holder. Neither of the two up on the platform was even near it. Neither had used the wooden striker to unleash the deadly weapon.

"What did you do!" she screamed at them. "What did you do to ring it! Have you gone mad!" She glanced over her shoulder to the bony pile of gore that had moments before been Turner.

Beata thrust out her arm, pointing. "You killed him! Why would you do it? What's wrong with you?"

Emmeline slowly shook her head. "I've not moved a step from this spot."

Bryce was beginning to tremble. "Me neither. Sergeant, we never rang the thing. I swear. We weren't even near it. Neither of us was near it. We didn't do it."

In the silence as she stared at them, Beata realized she heard distant screams. She looked off across the plains, to the next Dominie Dirtch. She could just make out people over there running around as if the world had gone insane.

She spun and peered in the opposite direction. It was the same: people screaming, running around. Beata shielded her eyes from the sun and squinted into the distance. There were the remains of two soldiers out in front of their weapon.

Estelle Ruffin and Corporal Marie Fauvel reached what was left of Turner. Estelle, holding fistfuls of her hair, started screaming. Marie turned and started retching.

It was the way she was trained. It was the way things were done. They said it had been done that way for millennia.

Each squad, from each Dominie Dirtch, sent a patrol out at the same time to scout the area. That way, if there was anything or anyone sneaking around out there, it couldn't simply evade one soldier and hide elsewhere.

It wasn't just hers. Every Dominie Dirtch down the line had rung, seemingly of its own accord.

Kahlan clutched at Richard's shirt. He was still out of his senses with pain. She couldn't get him out of the ball he had rolled into. She didn't know what exactly was going on, but she feared she knew.

He was obviously in mortal danger of some sort.

She'd heard him cry out. She saw him tumble off his horse and hit the ground. She just didn't know why.

Her first thought was that it was an arrow. She had been terrified it was an arrow from an assassin and it had killed him. But she could see no blood. Her emotions walled off, she had searched for blood, but on her rapid initial inspection had found none.

Kahlan glanced up as a thousand D'Haran soldiers spread out around them. The first instant, when Richard screamed and fell from his horse, without orders from her, they had gone into action. Swords cleared scabbards in a blink. Axes came off belt hangers into ready fists. Lances were leveled.

In the perimeter around them, men had flipped a leg over their horses' necks and leaped to the ground, ready to fight, weapons already to hand. Other men, closing ranks, forming the next circle of protection, turned their horses outward, ready to charge. Still more, the outer fringe of crack troops, had rushed off to find the assailants and clear the area of any enemy.

Kahlan had been around armies her entire life, and knew about fighting troops. She knew by the way they reacted that these men were as good as they came. She hadn't needed to issue any orders; they executed every defensive maneuver she would have expected, and did them faster than she could have shouted the commands.

Above her and Richard, the Baka Tau Mana blade masters formed a tight circle, swords out and at the ready. Whatever the attack was, arrow or dart or something else, Kahlan couldn't imagine the people protecting them allowing another chance at their Lord Rahl. If nothing else, there were now too many men suddenly layered around them for an arrow to make it through.

Kahlan, somewhat stunned by the sudden confusion, felt a flutter of worry that Cara would be angry they let harm come to Richard. Kahlan, after all, had promised to let no harm come to him—as if a promise to Cara were required.

Du Chaillu pushed her way between her blade masters to squat down on the other side of Richard. She had a waterskin and cloth to dress a wound.

"Have you found the injury?"

"No," Kahlan said as she picked around on him.

She pressed a hand to the side of Richard's face. It reminded her of when he'd had the plague, out of his mind with fever and not knowing where he was. He couldn't have been stricken with sickness, not the way he cried out and fell from his horse, but he did feel as if he was burning up with fever.

Du Chaillu dabbed a wet cloth against Richard's face. Kahlan saw that Du Chaillu's own face was creased in worry.

Kahlan continued her examination of Richard, trying to see if he had been hit by some sort of dart, or perhaps a bolt from a crossbow. He was trembling, almost in convulsions. She searched frantically, pulling him onto his side to check his back, trying to find what was hurting him. She concentrated on her job, and tried not to think of how worried she was, lest shock take her.

Du Chaillu stroked Richard's face when Kahlan eased him onto his back, seeming to discount the need to look for a wound. The spirit woman bent forward, cooing softly in a chant with words Kahlan didn't understand.

"I can't find anything," Kahlan said at last in exasperation.

"You won't," Du Chaillu answered, distantly.

"Why's that?"

The Baka Tau Mana spirit woman murmured fond words to Richard. Even if Kahlan couldn't understand their literal meaning, she understood the emotion behind them.

"It is not a wound of this world," Du Chaillu said.

Kahlan glanced about at the soldiers ringing them. She put her hands protectively on Richard's chest.

"What does that mean?"

Du Chaillu pushed Kahlan's hands gently away.

"It is a wound of the spirit. The soul. Let me tend to him."

Kahlan pressed her own hand tenderly to Richard's face. "How do you know that? You don't know that. How could you know?"

"I am a spirit woman. I recognize such things."

"Just because—"

"Did you find a wound?"

Kahlan remained silent for a moment, reconsidering her own feelings. "Do you know what we can do to help him?"

"This is something beyond your ability to help." Du Chaillu bowed her head of dark hair as she pressed her hands to Richard's chest.

"Leave me to it," Du Chaillu murmured, "or our husband will die."

Kahlan sat back on her heels and watched as the Baka Tau Mana spirit woman, head bowed and hands on Richard, closed her eyes as if going into a trance of some sort. Words whispered forth, meant for herself perhaps, but not for others. She trembled. Her arms shook.

Du Chaillu's face contorted in pain.

Suddenly, she fell back, breaking the connection. Kahlan caught her arm, lest she topple.

"Are you all right?"

Du Chaillu nodded. "My power. It worked. It was back."

Kahlan looked from the woman to Richard. He seemed calmer.

"What did you do? What happened?"

"Something was trying to take his spirit. I used my ability to annul such power and kept the hands of death from him."

"Your power is back?" Kahlan was dubious. "But how could that be?"

Du Chaillu shook her head. "I don't know. It returned when the *Caharin* cried out and fell from his horse. I knew because I could again feel my bond to him."

"Maybe the chimes have fled back to the underworld."

Again Du Chaillu shook her head. "Whatever it was, it is passing. My power fades again." She stared off a moment. "It is again gone. It was only there long enough to help him."

Du Chaillu issued quiet orders for her men to stand down, that it was over.

Kahlan wasn't convinced. She glanced again to Richard. It did look like he was calming. His breathing was evening out.

His eyes abruptly opened. He squinted at the light.

Du Chaillu leaned over him and pressed the wet cloth to his forehead, dabbing off the sweat.

"You are all right, now, my husband," she said.

"Du Chaillu," he muttered, "how many times do I have to tell you, I'm not your husband. You are misinterpreting old laws."

Du Chaillu smiled up at Kahlan. "See? He is better."

"Thank the good spirits you were here, Du Chaillu," Kahlan whispered.

"Tell him that when he again complains I should leave him."

Kahlan couldn't help smiling at Richard's frustration with Du Chaillu and with her blessed relief that he was indeed better. Tears now suddenly tried to burst forth, but she banished them.

"Richard, are you all right? What happened? What made you fall from your horse?"

Richard tried to sit up but Kahlan and Du Chaillu both pushed him back down.

"Both your wives say to rest for a time," Du Chaillu said.

Richard stopped trying to get up. His gray eyes turned to Kahlan. She clutched his arm, again silently thanking the good spirits.

"I'm not sure what happened," he finally said. "It was like this sound—like a deafening bell—exploded in my head. The pain was like . . ." His face lost some of its color. "I don't know how to explain it. I've never felt anything like it before."

He sat up, this time brushing their restraining hands aside. "I'm all right, now. Whatever it was, it's gone. It has passed."

"I'm not so sure," Kahlan said.

"I am," he said. He looked haunted. "It was like something tearing at my very soul."

"It didn't get it," Du Chaillu said. "It tried, but it didn't get it."

She was dead serious. Kahlan believed her.

Hide twitching, the horse stood motionless, her hooves rooted to the grassy ground. Her instinct demanded she run. Ripples of panic quivered through her flesh, but she remained unmoving.

The man was beyond the falling water, in the dark hole. She didn't like holes. No horse did.

He had screamed. The ground had shaken. That had been a long time ago. She hadn't moved since then. Now it was silent.

The horse knew, though, that her friend still lived.

She let out a long, low bellow.

He still lived, but he didn't come out.

The horse was alone.

There was no worse thing for a horse than being alone.

CHAPTER 49

ANN OPENED HER EYES. She was surprised, in the dim light, to see a face she had not seen for months, not since she was still the Prelate, back at the Palace of the Prophets in Tanimura, in the Old World.

The middle-aged Sister was watching her. Middle-aged, Ann amended, if you considered five hundred and a few years old to be middle-aged.

"Sister Alessandra."

Forming the words aloud hurt. Her lip was not healed. Her jaw still didn't work too well. Ann didn't know if it was broken. If it was, there was nothing for it. It would have to heal as it would; there was no magic to do it for her.

"Prelate," the woman greeted, in an aloof tone.

She used to have a long braid, Ann recalled. A long braid

she always looped around and pinned to the back of her head. Now her graying brown hair was chopped off and hung loose, not quite touching her shoulders. Ann thought it better balanced her somewhat prominent nose.

"I brought you something to eat, Prelate, if you feel up to it."

"Why? Why did you bring me something to eat?"

"His Excellency wanted you fed."

"Why you?"

The woman smiled just a little. "You dislike me, Prelate."

Ann did her best to glare. The way her face was swollen, she wasn't sure she was doing a good job of it.

"As a matter of fact, Sister Alessandra, I love you as I love all the Creator's children. I simply abhor your actions—that you have sworn your soul to the Nameless One."

"Keeper of the underworld." Sister Alessandra's smile grew a little wider. "So, you can still care about a woman who is a Sister of the Dark?"

Ann turned her face away, even though the steaming bowl did smell savory. She didn't want to talk to the fallen Sister.

In her chains, Ann couldn't feed herself. She unconditionally refused to accept food from the Sisters who had lied to her and betrayed her rather than have their freedom. Up until now, soldiers fed her. They disliked the duty. Their distaste for feeding an old woman had apparently resulted in Sister Alessandra's appearance.

Sister Alessandra lifted a spoonful of soup to Ann's mouth.

"Here, have some of this. I made it myself."

"Why?"

"Because I thought you might like it."

"Getting bored, Sister, pulling the legs off ants?"

"My, my, Prelate, but don't you have the memory. I haven't done that since I was a child, first come to the Palace of the Prophets. As I recall, you were the one who convinced me to stop doing that, recognizing I was unhappy to leave my home.

"Here, now, have a taste. Please?"

553

Ann was sincerely surprised to hear the woman say "please." She opened her mouth for the spoon. Eating hurt, but not eating was making her weak. She could have refused to eat, or done something else to get herself killed, she supposed, but she did have a mission, and therefore a reason to live.

"Not bad, Sister Alessandra. Not bad at all."

Sister Alessandra smiled with what looked to be pride. "I told you so. Here, have some more."

Ann ate slowly, trying to gently chew the soft vegetables so as not to further hurt her jaw. She simply swallowed the tough chunks of meat, not even bothering to mash them flat, lest she undo whatever healing her jaw was managing to do.

"Your lip looks like it's going to be scarred."

"My lovers will be disappointed my beauty is marred."

Sister Alessandra laughed. Not a harsh or cynical laugh, but a lilting laugh of true amusement.

"You always could make me laugh, Prelate."

"Yes," Ann said with venom, "that was why I for so long failed to realize you had joined the side of evil. I thought my little Alessandra, my happy little Alessandra, would not be drawn to the heart of wickedness. I so believed you loved the Light."

Sister Alessandra's smile withered. "I did, Prelate."

"Bah," Ann scoffed. "You only loved yourself."

The woman stirred the soup for a time and finally brought up another spoonful. "Perhaps you are right, Prelate. You usually were."

Ann carefully chewed the lumps in the soup as she surveyed the grimy little tent. She had caused such a ruckus being with the Sisters of the Light that Jagang apparently had ordered her to be housed in her own small tent. Each night a long steel pin was driven into the ground and she was chained to it. The tent was erected around her.

In the day, when they prepared to move out, she was thrown in a rough wooden box latched with a hasp held tight with a pin or lock of some sort. She wasn't sure, since she was always inside the box when they put it on and took it off. The box, with her in it, was then loaded on an enclosed wagon without windows or ventilation. She knew because she peeked out the crack where the lid of her box didn't fit well.

After they stopped for the night, they eventually took her out and one of the Sisters escorted her to the latrine before they staked her to the ground and put up her tent. If need took her in the day, she had little choice as to what to do about it. It was either wait, or don't.

Occasionally they didn't bother with the tent, and simply left her chained to the stake, like a dog.

Ann had come to like her little tent, and was pleased when it was erected around her. It was her private sanctuary, where she could stretch her cramped legs and arms, lie down, and pray.

Ann swallowed the mouthful of soup. "So, did Jagang say you were to do more to me than feed me? Perhaps rough me up for his amusement, or yours?"

"No." Sister Alessandra sighed. "Just feed you. From what I gather, he hasn't decided what to do with you, but in the meantime he wants you kept alive so you might be of value to him one day."

Ann watched the woman stir the bowl of soup. "He can't get in your mind, you know. Not now."

Sister Alessandra looked up. "What makes you think that?"

"The chimes are loose."

The spoon stilled. "So I've heard." The spoon again started circling. "Rumors. That's all it is."

Ann squirmed, trying to get more comfortable on the rough ground. It seemed to her that with all her natural padding she shouldn't be so troubled by lumps on the ground.

"I wish it were only rumors. Why do you think your magic doesn't work?"

"But it does."

"I mean your Additive Magic."

The woman's brown eyes turned down. "Well, I guess

I've not really tried to use it, that's all. If I were to try, it would work, I've no doubt."

"Try, then. You'll see I'm right."

She shook her head. "His Excellency does not permit it, unless he specifically requests it. It is . . . unwise to do other than His Excellency says to do."

Ann leaned toward the woman. "Alessandra, the chimes are loose. Magic has failed. For Creation's sake, why do you think I'm in this predicament? If I could use magic, don't you think I would have caused just a little trouble when I was captured?

"Use your head, Alessandra. You're not stupid, don't act it."

If there was one thing about Alessandra, she wasn't stupid. How a smart woman could fall prey to the Keeper's promises, Ann didn't know. She guessed lies could fool even smart people.

Ann avoided using the appellation "Sister" not only because it was a term of respect, but because it seemed a way of speaking more directly, more intimately, to a woman Ann had known and liked for half a millennium. Using the title "Sister" seemed only to invoke her connection to the Sisters of the Dark.

"Alessandra, Jagang can't get into your head. His power as a dream walker has failed, just the same as my power has failed."

Sister Alessandra watched without evident emotion.

"Perhaps his power works in conjunction with, or even through, ours, and he could still get into the minds of the Sisters of the Dark."

"Bah. Now you're thinking like a slave. Go away if you're going to think like a slave—like the Sisters of the Light, I'm ashamed to say."

The woman seemed reluctant either to leave or to end the discussion. "I don't believe you. Jagang is all-powerful. He must surely be watching now, through my eyes, as we speak, and I simply don't know it."

Ann was forced to take the spoonful of soup when it

556

unexpectedly swooped toward her mouth. She chewed slowly as she studied the woman's face.

"You could come back to the Light, Alessandra."

"What!" The instantaneous flash of anger in the woman's eyes melted to amusement. "Prelate, you have gone loony."

"Have I?"

Sister Alessandra pressed another spoonful to Ann's lips. "Yes. I am sworn to my master of the underworld. I serve the Keeper. Eat, now."

Before Ann could swallow, another spoonful came at her. She ate a half dozen more before she could get a word out.

"Alessandra, the Creator would forgive you. The Creator is all-loving and all-forgiving. He would take you back. You could come back to the light. Wouldn't you like to return to the Creator's loving embrace?"

Unexpectedly, Sister Alessandra backhanded her. Ann toppled to her side. The woman hovered, glowering.

"The Keeper is my master! You will not speak blasphemy! His Excellency is my master in this world. In the next, I am sworn to the Keeper. I will not listen to you profane my oath to my master. Do you hear?"

Ann feared that what healing her jaw had done had now been undone. It hurt something awful. Her eyes watered. Sister Alessandra finally seized Ann's filthy dress at the shoulder and hauled her up straight.

"I will not have you saying such things. Do you hear?"

Ann kept silent, fearing to elicit another angry outburst. Apparently, the subject was as sore as Ann's jaw.

Sister Alessandra picked up the bowl of soup. "There isn't much left, but you should finish it."

Alessandra stared down at the bowl, as if watching the spoon stirring around in it. She cleared her throat. "Sorry I hit you."

Ann nodded. "I forgive you, Alessandra." The woman's eyes, no longer filled with anger, turned up. "I do, Alessandra," Ann whispered sincerely, wondering at the terrible emotions struggling within her former disciple.

The eyes turned down again. "There is nothing to forgive.

I am what I am, and nothing will change it. You've no idea of the things I've done to become a Sister of the Dark." She looked up with a distant expression. "You've no idea of the power I was granted in return. You can't imagine, Prelate."

Ann almost asked her what good it did her, but held her tongue and finished the soup in silence. She winced in pain with every swallow. The spoon clanked when Alessandra dropped it in the empty bowl.

"It was very good, Alessandra. The best meal I've had in . . . however long I've been here. Weeks, I guess."

Sister Alessandra nodded and rose. "If I'm not busy, I will bring you some tomorrow, then."

"Alessandra." The woman turned back. Ann met her gaze. "Could you sit with me for a bit?"

"Why?"

Ann chuckled bitterly. "I'm stuffed in a box every day. I'm staked to the ground every night. It would be nice to have someone I know sit with me for a bit, that's all."

"I'm a Sister of the Dark."

Ann shrugged. "I'm a Sister of the Light. You still brought me soup."

"I was ordered to."

"Ah. More honesty than I received from the Sisters of the Light, I'm sorry to say." Ann squirmed off a loop of chain and then flopped down on her side, turning away from Sister Alessandra. "Sorry you had to be interrupted to take care of me. Jagang probably wants you to go back to whoring for his men."

Silence reigned inside the tent. Outside, soldiers laughed, drank, and gambled. Smells of meat roasting drifted in. At least Ann's stomach wasn't grumbling with hunger. The soup had been good.

Ann heard the sound of a woman's scream in the distance. The scream turned to chiming laughter. One of the camp followers, no doubt. Sometimes, the screams were sincere terror. Sometimes the sound of them made Ann sweat, thinking about what was happening to those poor women.

At last, Sister Alessandra sank back down. "I could sit with you a bit."

Ann rolled over. "I would like that, Alessandra. I really would."

Sister Alessandra helped her sit up, and then the two of them sat in awkward silence while they listened to the camp sounds.

"Jagang's tent," Ann said at last. "I heard it was something. Quite the fancy sight."

"Yes, it is. It's like a palace he sets up each night. I can't say I favor going there, though."

"No, after my encounter with the man, I imagine not. Do you know where we're going?"

The other shook her head. "Here, there, it makes no difference. We are slaves serving His Excellency."

It had the ring of hopelessness to it, and made Ann think to gently turn that feeling to hope. "You know, Alessandra, he can't get into my mind."

Sister Alessandra looked up with a frown, and Ann told her how the bond to the Lord Rahl protected anyone sworn to him. Ann was careful to frame it in terms of what it meant to her, and to the others sworn to Richard, on a personal level, rather than to make it sound like an offer. The woman listened without objection.

"Now," Ann said in conclusion, "the magic of Richard's bond as the Lord Rahl doesn't work, but then, Jagang's magic doesn't work either, so I'm still safe from the dream walker." She chuckled. "Unless he walks in the tent, that is."

Sister Alessandra laughed with her.

Ann rearranged her manacled hands in her lap, hauling the chains closer so she could have enough slack to cross her legs.

"When the chimes eventually go back to your master in the underworld, then Richard's bond will work again, and I will once again be protected from Jagang's magic, when it returns, too. In all this, that is the one comfort I have—

knowing I'm safe from Jagang's power entering my mind."

Sister Alessandra sat mute.

"Of course," Ann added, "it must be a relief for you to be without Jagang in your mind for the time being, at least."

"You don't know when he's there. You feel no different. Except . . . if he wants you to know."

She smoothed the lap of her dress when Ann didn't say anything. "But I think you don't know what you're talking about, Prelate. The dream walker is in my mind, right now, watching us."

She looked up, waiting for Ann to argue. Instead, Ann said, "You just think on it, Alessandra. You just think on it."

Sister Alessandra gathered up the bowl. "I'd best be going back."

"Thank you for coming, Alessandra. Thank you for the soup. And thank you for sitting with me. It was nice to be with you, again."

Sister Alessandra nodded and ducked out of the tent.

CHAPTER 50

ALTHOUGH IT WAS HARDLY noticeable, the grassy ground stretching to the horizon before Beata's Dominie Dirtch was slightly higher than the ground to each side of the enormous stone weapon, and so provided firmer footing, especially for horses. After the recent rains the gentle swale to the right was muddy. To the left it wasn't any better. Because of the unique lay of the land, especially after rain, people tended to approach Beata's post, her Dominie Dirtch, more often than others.

There weren't many, but those in the area traveling into Anderith from the grasslands of the wilds were inclined to come to her station first. Beata enjoyed being able to be in charge for a change, to pass judgment on people and say if they could enter. If she thought they looked like people who should not be let in, she sent them on to a border station, where they could apply for entry with the station guards.

It felt good to be the one in control of important matters, instead of being helpless. Now, she decided things.

It was exciting, too, when travelers came through—something different, a chance to talk to people from afar, or to see their strange dress. There were rarely more than two or three people traveling together. But they looked up to her; she was in charge.

This bright sunny morning, though, Beata's heart hammered against her ribs. This time, those who approached were different. This time, there were considerably more than a few. This time, it looked like a true threat.

"Carine," Beata ordered, "stand ready at the striker."

The Haken woman squinted over at her. "You sure, Sergeant?" Carine had terrible eyesight; she rarely saw anything beyond thirty paces, and these people were off at the horizon.

It was something Beata had never done before, ordering out the striker. At least, not when people approached. They practiced taking it out, of course, but she'd never ordered it out. If she wasn't there, the ones on duty were supposed to take it out if they judged a threat approached, but with Beata there, it was up to her to order it readied. She was in charge. They depended on her.

Since the terrible accident, they'd added an extra bar across the rack where the striker stood, even though they knew it wasn't the striker that had rung the weapon. No one told them to do it; Beata just felt better with another restraint on the striker. It made them feel like they were doing something about the accident, even if they weren't, really.

No one knew why all the Dominie Dirtch had rung.

Beata wiped her sweaty palms on her hips. "I'm sure. Do it."

Other times, when people approached, it was easy enough to tell they were harmless. Traders with a cart, some of the nomadic people of the wilds wanting to trade with the soldiers stationed at the border—Beata never let them through—merchants taking an unusual route for one reason or another, even some special Ander guard troops returning from far patrols.

Those Ander guard troops weren't regular army soldiers. They were special. They were men only, and they looked to Beata like they were used to dealing with trouble of one sort or another. They paid no heed to regular Anderith soldiers, like Beata.

She'd ordered them to stop, once, as they approached. Beata knew who they were, because Captain Tolbert had instructed her and her squad about the special Ander guard troops, and told them to let the men pass at will if they came by. She'd only wanted to ask them, being fellow soldiers and all, if they needed anything.

They didn't stop when she ordered it. The man leading simply smirked as he rode past with his column of big men.

These people who approached, though, were not guard troops. Beata didn't know what to make of them, except they had the look of a serious threat. She could make out hundreds of mounted soldiers in dark uniforms spreading out as they halted.

Even from a distance, it was a formidable sight.

Beata glanced to her side, and saw Carine drawing back the striker. Annette seized the shaft to help strike the Dominie Dirtch.

Beata sprang toward them and caught the shaft of the striker before they could swing it.

"No order was given! What's the matter with you? Stand down."

"But Sergeant," Annette complained, "they're soldiers—a lot of soldiers—and they aren't ours. I can tell that much."

Beata shoved the woman back. "They're giving the signal. Can't you see?"

"But, Sergeant Beata," Annette whined, "they aren't our people. They've no business—"

"You don't even know their business yet!" Beata was frightened and angry that Carine and Annette had almost rung the weapon on their own. "Are you crazy? You don't even know who they are. You could be killing innocent people.

"You're both going to stand an extra duty tonight and for the next week for not following orders. Do you understand?"

Annette hung her head. Carine saluted, not knowing how she was supposed to react to such discipline. Beata would have been angry at any of her squad trying to wrongly ring the Dominie Dirtch, but deep down inside, she was glad it was the two Haken women, and not one of the Anders.

On the horizon, a person on horseback waved a white flag on the end of a pole, or lance. Beata didn't know the distance the Dominie Dirtch could kill. Maybe if Carine and Annette had rung it, it wouldn't have harmed the people out there, but after what happened to Turner, she hoped never to see the weapon rung while people were in front of it—unless they clearly were attacking.

Beata watched as the strange troops waited where they were while only a few people approached. Those were the rules, the way Beata and her squad were taught. People had to wave a flag of some sort, and if there were many, only a few were supposed to approach to state their business and ask permission to pass.

It wasn't a risk to have a few people approach. The Dominie Dirtch could kill an enemy even if they were only one step away, out in front of it. They would still die. How close people came was really irrelevant—so was the number, for that matter.

Four people, two on foot and two on horseback, came forward, leaving the rest behind. As they got closer, she could see it was two men and two women. One man and woman rode, another pair walked. There was something about the woman on horseback . . .

When Beata realized who the woman had to be, her heart felt as if it had leaped up into her throat.

"You see?" Beata said to Carine and Annette. "Can you imagine if you'd rung that thing? Can you imagine?"

The two, jaws agape, stared out at the approaching people. Beata's knees trembled at the thought of what had almost happened.

Beata turned and shook a fist at the two. "Put that thing away. And don't you dare go near the Dominie Dirtch! Do you understand?"

Both saluted. Beata turned and raced down the steps two at a time. In her whole life, she never imagined anything like this.

She never imagined she would actually meet the Mother Confessor herself.

She gaped, along with the rest of her squad who came out to see, as the woman in the long white dress rode forward. One man rode to her right. A man and woman were on foot. The woman was pregnant. The man on foot, on the Mother Confessor's left, was dressed in loose clothes of no particular style. He had a sword, but kept it sheathed.

The man riding on the Mother Confessor's right was something else entirely. Beata had never seen such a man, all dressed in black, with a golden cape billowing out behind. The sight took her breath.

Beata wondered if it could be the man she'd heard was to marry the Mother Confessor: Lord Rahl. He certainly looked a lord. He was just about the most imposing-looking man Beata had ever seen.

Beata shouted to the two up on the platform. "Get down here!"

The two women dashed down the steps and Beata lined them up with the rest of her squad. Corporal Marie Fauvel,

Estelle Ruffin, and Emmeline stood to Beata's right. The two from up on the platform joined the three Ander men, Norris, Karl, and Bryce, on her left. They all formed up in a straight line, watching as the four people came right up to them.

As the Mother Confessor dismounted, without anyone needing to issue orders, Beata and her whole squad fell to their knees and bowed their heads. On her way to her knees, Beata had seen the Mother Confessor's beautiful white dress and long fall of gorgeous brown hair. Beata had never seen hair such as that, so long and elegant-looking. She was used to seeing dark Ander hair, or red Haken hair, so hair that shone honey brown in the sunlight was such an extraordinarily rare sight that it made the woman look almost other than human.

Beata was glad to have her head bowed, so afraid was she to meet the Mother Confessor's gaze. Only profound fear had prevented Beata from staring in awe.

All her life she had heard stories about the power of the Mother Confessor, about the feats of magic she could do, about how she could turn people to stone with a look if she didn't like them, or other things far worse.

Beata gulped air, panting, on the verge of panic. She was just a Haken girl, suddenly feeling very out of place. She never expected to find herself before the Mother Confessor.

"Rise, my children," said a voice from above.

Just the sound of it, how gentle, how clear, how seemingly kind it was, greatly eased Beata's fear. She never thought the Mother Confessor would have a voice so . . . so womanly. Beata had always thought it might be a voice like a spirit, screeching out from the world of the dead.

With the rest of her squad, Beata rose to her feet, but she kept her head bowed, still fearing to look up directly into the Mother Confessor's eyes. Beata had never been instructed how to behave when she met the Mother Confessor herself, it being an event no one ever thought could possibly happen to her, a Haken girl. But here it was, happening.

"Who is in charge here?" It was the Mother Confessor's

voice, still sounding nice enough, but it had a clear ring of authority that was unmistakable. At least she didn't sound like she intended to call lightning down on anyone.

Beata took a step forward, but kept her eyes aimed at the ground. "I am, Mother Confessor."

"And you are?"

Beata's racing heart refused to slow. She couldn't make herself stop trembling. "Your humble servant, Mother Confessor. I am Sergeant Beata."

Beata nearly jumped out of her skin when fingers lifted her chin. And then she was looking right into the green eyes of the Mother Confessor herself. It was like looking on a tall, beautiful, smiling, good spirit.

Good spirit or not, Beata stood frozen in renewed terror.

"Glad to meet you, Sergeant Beata." The Mother Confessor gestured to her left. "This is Du Chaillu, a friend, and Jiaan, another friend." She laid her hand on the shoulder of the big man beside her. "This is Lord Rahl," she said, as her smile widened, "my husband."

Beata's gaze moved at last to the Lord Rahl. He, too, smiled pleasantly. Beata had never had such important people smile at her in such a way. It was all because she had joined the Anderith army, to become an evil Haken doing good, at last.

"Mind if I go up and have a look at the Dominie Dirtch, Sergeant Beata?" Lord Rahl asked.

Beata cleared her throat. "Uh—well—no, sir. No sir. Please, I would be happy to show you the Dominie Dirtch. Honored, I mean. I mean I would be honored to show you."

"And our men," the Mother Confessor asked, bringing Beata's babbling to a merciful end, "may they approach, now, Sergeant?"

Beata bowed. "Forgive me. I'm sorry. Of course they may, Mother Confessor. Of course. I'm sorry. If you will permit me, I will see to it."

After the Mother Confessor gave a nod, Beata raced up the steps ahead of the Lord Rahl, feeling a fool for not at once telling the Mother Confessor she was welcome in Anderith. Beata snatched up the horn and blew the all-clear to the squad at the Dominie Dirtch on each side. She turned to the waiting distant soldiers and blew a long note, to let them know they were granted permission to approach the Dominie Dirtch in safety.

The Lord Rahl was coming up the stairs. Beata pulled the horn from her lips and backed against the railing. There was something about him, just his presence, that took her breath. Not even the Minister of Culture himself, before he did what he did, struck her with such a feeling of awe as did this man, the Lord Rahl.

It wasn't just his size, his broad shoulders, his penetrating gray eyes, or his black and gold outfit with the broad belt holding gold-worked leather pouches and strange symbols. It was his presence.

He didn't look proper and fancy like the Ander officials, like Dalton Campbell or the Minister of Culture, but rather, he looked noble, purposeful, and at the same time . . . dangerous.

Deadly.

He was kind enough looking, and handsome, but she just knew that if he ever turned those gray eyes on her in anger, she might be struck dead just by their intensity.

If ever there was a man who looked as if he could be the husband of the Mother Confessor, this was the man.

The pregnant woman came up the stairs, her eyes taking everything in. There was something about this dark-haired woman as well that seemed noble. She and the other man, both with dark hair, almost looked Ander. She had on the oddest dress Beata had ever seen; there were little different-colored strips of cloth tied on all up the arms and over the shoulders.

Beata held out a hand. "This, Lord Rahl, is the Dominie Dirtch." Beata wanted to say the woman's name, too, but it had flown out of her head, and she couldn't remember it.

Lord Rahl's eyes roamed over the huge bell-shaped stone weapon.

"It was created thousands of years ago by the Hakens,"

567

Beata said, "as a weapon of murder against the Anders, but it now serves instead as a means for peace."

Clasping his hands loosely behind his back, Lord Rahl surveyed the uncountable tons of stone that made up the Dominie Dirtch. His gaze glided over every nuance of it in a way she had never seen anyone else look at it. Beata almost expected him to speak to it, and the Dominie Dirtch to answer.

"And how would that be, sergeant?" he asked without looking at her.

"Sir?"

When he turned to her at last, his gray eyes arrested her breath.

"Well, the Hakens invaded Anderith, right?"

Under the scrutiny of those eyes, she had to struggle to make her voice work. "Yes, sir." It came out as little more than a squeak.

He lifted a thumb, pointing back at the stone bell. "And do you suppose the invaders rode in with these Dominie Dirtch slung over their backs, then, Sergeant?"

Beata's knees started trembling. She wished he wouldn't ask her questions. She wished he would just leave them be and go on to Fairfield and talk to the important people who knew how to answer questions.

"Sir?"

Lord Rahl turned and gestured to the stone rising up before him. "It's obvious these weapons were not brought in, Sergeant. They're too big. There are too many of them. They had to be constructed here, where they stand, with the aid of magic, no doubt."

"But the Haken murderers, when they invaded—"

"They're pointed out there, Sergeant, toward any invaders, not in, toward the people of Anderith. It's clear they were built as weapons of defense."

Beata swallowed. "But we were taught—"

"You were taught a lie." He looked decidedly unhappy about what he was seeing. "This is plainly a defensive weapon." He peered off to the Dominie Dirtch to each side,

568

surveying them with a critical eye. "They work together. They were placed here as a line of defense, they weren't the tools of invasion."

The way he said it, with almost a tone of regret, didn't seem at all to Beata like he meant any offense. He seemed to have spoken what came into his mind as he realized it himself.

"But the Hakens . . ." Beata said in hardly more than a whisper.

Lord Rahl stood politely, waiting for her to offer an argument. Her mind was spinning with confused thoughts.

"I'm not an educated person, Lord Rahl. I'm only a Haken, evil by nature. Forgive me for not being taught good enough to be able to better answer your questions."

He heaved a sigh. "It doesn't require an education, Sergeant Beata, to see what's right before your eyes. Use your head."

Beata stood mute, unable to reconcile the conversation. This was an important man. She'd heard things about the Lord Rahl, about what a powerful man he was, about how he was a magician with the power to make day into night, up into down. He wasn't a man who ruled just one land, like the Minister of Culture and the Sovereign, but a man who ruled the mysterious empire of D'Hara, and now was capturing all of the Midlands.

But he was a man, too, who was married to the Mother Confessor. Beata had seen the look in the Mother Confessor's eyes when she looked at the Lord Rahl. Beata knew from that look that the woman loved and respected this man. It was as plain as day that she did.

"You should listen to what he says," the pregnant woman said. "He is also the Seeker of Truth."

Beata's jaw dropped. She spoke before her fear could muzzle her. "You mean that's the Sword of Truth you carry, sir?"

It looked an ordinary weapon to her, little different from hers. It was just a black leather scabbard, nothing special, and a leather-wrapped handle.

569

He looked down and lifted the weapon clear of the scabbard and then let it drop back. His face lost its spirit.

"This? No . . . it's not the Sword of Truth. I don't have it with me . . . right at the moment."

Beata didn't have the nerve to ask why not. She wished she could have seen the real sword. It had magic. That would have been something—for her to see the Sword of Truth Fitch thought so much about, instead of him seeing it. Being in the army, and in charge of a Dominie Dirtch, she was doing more than he ever would.

Lord Rahl had turned to the towering weapon. He seemed to have forgotten that anyone else existed, as he focused on the lichen-covered stone before him. He stood as still as the stone. He seemed almost one with it.

His hand reached out to touch the Dominie Dirtch.

The woman snatched his wrist, holding his hand back.

"No, my husband. Do not touch this thing. It is . . ."

Lord Rahl turned to look into her eyes, finishing what she'd left unsaid. "Evil."

"You can feel it, then?"

He nodded.

Of course it was evil, Beata wanted to say; it was made by Hakens.

Beata's brow bunched in puzzlement. The woman had called him "husband," but the Mother Confessor had said the Lord Rahl was her husband.

Lord Rahl, seeing his troops drawing close, started down the stairs two at a time. The woman took in the Dominie Dirtch one last time and then moved to follow him.

"Husband?" Beata was unable to resist asking the pregnant woman.

She lifted her chin as she turned to Beata. "Yes. I am the wife of the Lord Rahl, the Seeker, the *Caharin*, Richard."

"But, but the Mother Confessor said . . ."

The woman shrugged. "Yes, we are the both of us his wives."

"Both? Two . . . ?"

The woman started down the stairs. "He is an important

man. He can have more than one wife." The woman stopped and looked back. "I once had five husbands."

Beata's eyes widened as she watched the woman disappear down the stairs. The morning air rumbled with the approach of the mounted soldiers. Beata had never even imagined such ferocious-looking men. She was glad for her training; Captain Tolbert had told her that with her training, she could defend Anderith against anyone, even men like these.

"Sergeant Beata," Lord Rahl called up to her.

Beata went to the rail in front of the bell. He had stopped on his way to his horse out front and turned back. The Mother Confessor was taking up the reins. She put a foot in a stirrup.

"Yes, sir?"

"I don't suppose you rang that thing about a week ago?"

"No, sir, we didn't."

He turned to his horse. "Thank you, Sergeant."

"But it chimed by itself back then."

The Lord Rahl stiffened in place. The pregnant woman spun back around. The Mother Confessor, halfway up onto her horse, dropped back to the ground.

Beata raced down the steps so she wouldn't have to shout the awful details down at him. The rest of her squad had pulled way back behind the Dominie Dirtch, fearing to be in the way of such important people; fearing, Beata supposed, that the Mother Confessor might set them afire with a look. Beata still feared the woman, but the edge of her fear had been dulled.

Lord Rahl whistled to the soldiers and wheeled his arm, ordering them to hurry through, past the Dominie Dirtch, out of the way of harm, should the Dominie Dirtch again ring of its own accord. As hundreds of mounted men galloped around both sides, he hurried to usher the Mother Confessor and the pregnant woman, along with the other man, around to the rear of the stone base.

Once the women were safely past, he seized the shoulder of Beata's uniform and hauled her back, protectively, away from the front of Dominie Dirtch. She stiffened to attention—mostly in fear—before him.

His brow had drawn down in a way that made Beata's knees tremble. "What happened?" he asked in a quiet voice that seemed as if it could have caused the Dominie Dirtch to ring again.

The Mother Confessor had come to stand beside him. His pregnant wife stood on his other side.

"Well, we don't know, sir." Beata licked her lips. "One of my men . . . Turner, he was . . ." She gestured out behind Lord Rahl. "He was out on patrol when the thing rang. It was an awful sound. Just awful. And Turner . . ."

Beata could feel a tear roll down her cheek. As much as she didn't want this man and the Mother Confessor to see her showing weakness, she couldn't keep that tear back.

"In the late afternoon?" Lord Rahl asked.

Beata nodded. "How did you know?"

He ignored the question. "All of them rang? Not just this one, but all of them up and down the line rang, didn't they?"

"Yes, sir. No one knows the reason. Some officers came down the line, checking them, but they couldn't tell us anything."

"Were a lot of people killed?"

Beata abandoned his gaze. "Yes, sir. One of my men, and a lot of others, from what I was told. Wagons with merchants at the border, people returning to pass through the border . . . anyone out front of the Dominie Dirtch when they rang. . . . It was just awful. To die in such a fashion . . ."

"We understand," the Mother Confessor said in a compassionate tone. "We're sorry for your loss."

"So no one has any idea why they rang?" Lord Rahl pressed.

"No, sir, at least no one told us the reason. I've talked to the squads to each side, at the next Dominie Dirtch to each side, and it was the same with them; theirs, too, chimed on their own, but no one knows why. The officers who came past must not have known the reason either, because they was asking us what happened."

Lord Rahl nodded, seeming in deep thought. The wind lifted his golden cloak. The Mother Confessor pulled some hair back from her face, as did Lord Rahl's pregnant wife.

Lord Rahl gestured off at the rest of her squad. "And these people, they are all you have here, guarding the border? Just you few . . . soldiers?"

Beata glanced up at the weapon towering over them. "Well, sir, it only takes one person to ring the Dominie Dirtch."

His gaze again appraised the rest of her squad. "I suppose. Thank you for your help, Sergeant."

He and the Mother Confessor swiftly mounted up. She and the people on foot moved out with the rest of their soldiers. Lord Rahl turned back to her.

"Tell me, Sergeant Beata, do you think I—and the Mother Confessor—are not as good as the Ander people? Do you think us evil of nature, too?"

"Oh no, sir. Only Hakens are born tainted with vile souls. We can never be as good as Anders. Our souls are corrupt and unable to be pure; their souls are pure, and unable to be corrupt. We cannot ever be completely cleansed; we can only hope to control our vile nature."

He smiled sadly down at her. His voice softened. "Beata, the Creator does not create evil. He would not create and bestow upon you souls of evil. You have as much potential for good as anyone else, and Anders have a potential for evil equal to anyone."

"That's not what we're taught, sir."

His horse tossed her head and danced sideways, eager to be off after the others. With a pat on his horse's glossy brown neck, as if speaking to her through that gentle hand, he settled her.

"As I said, you were taught wrong. You are as good as anyone else Beata—Haken, or Ander, or anyone. That's our purpose in this struggle: to make sure that all people have an equal chance.

"You be careful with that thing, Sergeant, that Dominie Dirtch."

Beata saluted with her hand to her brow. "Yes, sir, I surely intend to."

His gaze connected solidly with hers and he tapped his fist to his heart to return the salute. Then, his horse leaped into a gallop to catch the others.

As Beata watched him go, she realized that this had probably been the most exciting thing that would happen in all the rest of her entire life—speaking with the Mother Confessor and the Lord Rahl.

CHAPTER 51

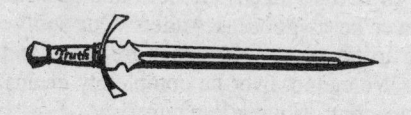

BERTRAND CHANBOOR LOOKED UP when Dalton came into the room. Bertrand's wife was there, too, standing before his ornate desk. Dalton met her eyes briefly. He was a bit surprised to see her there, but guessed this was important enough for her to meet with her husband.

"Well?" Bertrand asked.

"They confirmed what we were told," Dalton said. "They saw it with their own eyes."

"And they have soldiers?" Hildemara asked. "That part is true, also?"

"Yes. The best guess is near a thousand men."

Cursing under her breath, she tapped a finger against Bertrand's desk as she considered. "And the fools at the border just let them through without a care."

"We cultivate such an army, you will recall," Bertrand reminded her as he stood. "They also let through our 'special Ander guard troops,' after all."

"The people at the border can't be blamed," Dalton put in. "They couldn't very well refuse the Mother Confessor entry. The man could be none other than the Lord Rahl himself."

Erupting in rage, the Minister heaved his glass dipping pen. It clattered across the floor before shattering against the far wall. He went to the window and leaned against the sill as he gazed out.

"For Creation's sake, Bertrand, get a grip on yourself," Lady Chanboor growled.

He turned in red-faced anger and shook a finger at his wife.

"This could ruin everything! We've worked years at this, carefully cultivated the relationship, sown the seeds, pulled the weeds that have sprung up, and just when we're about to finally reap the harvest of our lives, she comes riding in with that—that—that D'Haran bastard Lord Rahl!"

Hildemara folded her arms. "Well that really solves the problem, throwing a fit. I swear, Bertrand, sometimes you have less sense than a drunken fisherman."

"And the sort of pompous wife who drives him to it!"

He ground his teeth and pulled aside his chair, no doubt preparing to launch into an extended tirade. Dalton could almost see her back arch, fur lift, and claws lengthen.

Dalton was usually ignored, like a piece of furniture, when they started in on each other. This time, he had better things to do than wait for it to broaden into a worse argument that would only waste valuable time. He had to issue orders, depending on what was decided. He had to get people in place.

He thought about Franca, wondering if she might have recovered her power. He hadn't seen much of her lately, and when he had, she seemed distracted. She had been spending a lot of time in the library. It would be valuable at a time like this to have Franca's assistance. Her true assistance.

"The Mother Confessor and the Lord Rahl are riding hard, and my men only just made it ahead of them," Dalton said, before Bertrand could lay into his wife, or she could throw something at him. "They should be here within the hour—two at most. We should be prepared."

Bertrand glared a moment before pulling his chair close and sitting. He folded his hands on the table. "Yes, you're right, Dalton. Quite right. First thing is to get Stein and his men out of sight. It wouldn't do to have—"

"I've already taken the liberty of seeing to it, Minister. I've sent some of them on an inspection of grain storage facilities, and others wanted to look over the strategic routes into Anderith."

Bertrand looked up. "Good."

"We've worked too many years to lose it all, now, when we're this close," Hildemara said. "However, if we just keep our heads, I don't see any reason we can't proceed with everything as planned."

Her husband nodded, having cooled considerably, as he did when he put his mind to difficult matters. He had the odd ability to be in a fit of rage one moment, and smiling the next.

"Possibly." He turned to Dalton. "How close is the Order?"

"Still quite a distance, Minister. Stein's 'special Ander guard troops' who arrived the day before yesterday told me four weeks at least. Probably a bit more."

Bertrand shrugged and arched an eyebrow, a sly smile coming to his lips. "Then we will simply have to stall the Mother Confessor and the Lord Rahl."

Hildemara put her fists on his desk and leaned toward her husband.

"The two of them, the Lord Rahl and the Mother Confessor, will be expecting our answer. They've long since explained to our representatives in Aydindril the choice we

576

have, and sent them back with the offer of joining the D'Haran Empire, or facing the probability of conquest and the resulting loss of standing in our own land."

Dalton agreed with her. "Ours would be a land they would turn their forces to if we don't agree to the terms of surrender. Were we some small, unimportant land, they would no doubt ignore us as we stall, but we will be an immediate prime target should we refuse to join them."

"And they have forces somewhere down in the South, from what I've heard," Hildemara put in. "The Lord Rahl is not a man to be denied, or played for a fool. Some of the other lands—Jara, Galea, Herjborgue, Grennidon, and Kelton, among others—have already fallen or joined willingly. Lord Rahl has considerable forces of his own from D'Hara, but with those lands his army is formidable."

"But they aren't all down here," Bertrand said, for some reason suddenly quite calm. "The Order will be able to crush them. The Dominie Dirtch can hold off any force from the D'Haran Empire."

Dalton thought the confidence unfounded. "From what my sources tell me, this Lord Rahl is a wizard of formidable talent. He is also the Seeker of Truth. I fear such a man may have ways of defeating the Dominie Dirtch."

Hildemara scowled. "Besides, the Mother Confessor, the Lord Rahl, and perhaps a thousand troops are already inside the line of Dominie Dirtch. They will demand our surrender. We would be stripped of power if that happens. The Order won't be here for weeks—by then too late."

She shook her finger at her husband. "We've worked too many years to lose it all now."

Bertrand tapped his thumbs as he smiled. "Then we will just, as I said before, have to stall them, won't we, my dear?"

The D'Haran troops were a dark ribbon on the road behind them as Richard and Kahlan led them toward the Minister of Culture's estate. A dark ribbon bristling steel. The sun was not an hour from setting behind scattered clouds, but at least they had arrived.

Richard pulled his damp D'Haran shirt away from his chest as he watched a curious raven circling overhead. With raucous calls, it let its lordly presence be known, as was the way with ravens.

It had been a warm and humid day. He and Kahlan both wore extra clothes the soldiers brought so their own would be clean and fit for the meeting they both knew would soon come.

Richard glanced back over his shoulder and received a murderous look from Du Chaillu. He had made her ride a horse so they could make the distance and not take another day. Their journey had taken far too long as it was.

The Baka Tau Mana did not like riding horses. As often as not, Du Chaillu would simply have ignored him when he told her to ride. This time, she knew if she ignored his request she would be left behind.

It had apparently taken Cara some time to locate General Reibisch's forces and send an escort of troops. Richard, Kahlan, and the Baka Tau Mana had been on foot, slogging through late-spring deluges, for far too long. They hadn't made a lot of distance on foot before the D'Haran troops finally arrived with horses.

Du Chaillu had also slowed their journey, although not purposely. She endlessly protested that riding would harm her baby before it was born—the baby Richard had suggested she bear. Because of her unborn child, Richard was reluctant to force her to ride.

He hadn't wanted her along in the first place. After the D'Haran troops had arrived with supplies and extra horses she refused to return home, as she had previously promised she would.

To her credit, she never complained about the difficulty

of the journey. But when Richard made her ride, it put her in a vile mood.

Kahlan, at first cool about having the Baka Tau Mana's spirit woman along, had warmed to the situation ever since the day Richard fell from his horse. Kahlan credited Du Chaillu with saving his life. Richard appreciated Du Chaillu's eagerness to help, but didn't believe it was her doing that kept him alive.

He wasn't at all sure what had happened. Since seeing the Dominie Dirtch, and hearing how they had chimed on their own at the same time he felt the crippling pain, he knew the whole thing had to be tied together somehow, and he didn't believe Du Chaillu held much sway over it. This was something much bigger than she realized, and more complex than Richard could understand.

Richard hadn't slowed for anything since he saw the Dominie Dirtch, even her pregnant condition. Since being close to those stone bells and feeling some of what he felt, she had been more cooperative about his hurry.

Richard lifted a hand when he spotted the rider trailing a plume of dust. He could hear orders being relayed back through the ranks in response to his signal, bringing the entire column to a jangling halt. Only when it had stopped, in the sudden silence, did he realize how much noise it made when they were on the move.

"This will be our greeting," Kahlan said.

"How far to the Minister's estate?" Richard asked.

"Not far. We're more than halfway from Fairfield. Maybe a mile."

Richard and Kahlan dismounted to meet the approaching rider. A soldier took the reins to Kahlan's horse. Richard handed his back to the man, too, and then stepped away from the others. Kahlan alone walked with him. He had to signal with a hand to keep the soldiers from forming a defensive ring around them.

The young man leaped from his horse before it had skidded to a stop. Holding the reins in one hand, he went to a knee in a bow. Kahlan greeted him in the way of the Mother Confessor and he rose. He wore livery of black boots, dark trousers, white shirt with a fancy collar and cuffs, and tan quilted doublet with black and brown braiding around the edges.

The man bowed a head of red hair to Richard. "Lord Rahl?"

"Yes, that's right."

He straightened. "I'm Rowley. The Minister of Culture sent me to greet you and extend his joy to have you and the Mother Confessor grace the people of Anderith with your presence."

"I'm sure," Richard said.

Kahlan elbowed his ribs. "Thank you, Rowley. We will need a place for our men to set up camp."

"Yes, Mother Confessor. The Minister wanted me to tell you that you're welcome to choose any ground in our land. If it would be acceptable, you may have the grounds at the estate for your use."

Richard didn't like that idea at all. He didn't want the men confined in such a way. He wanted them to be close, but able to set up a proper defensive position. Despite what anyone else thought, he had to treat this as being potentially hostile territory.

He gestured to the wheat field. "What about here? We will of course reimburse the landowner for the crops we ruin."

Rowley bowed. "If it pleases you, Lord Rahl. The Minister wished the choice to be yours. The land is Anderith common ground, and the crops excess, of no real value or concern.

"After you see to your escort, at your convenience, the Minister wishes to invite you to dinner. He asked me to relay his eagerness to meet you, and to see the Mother Confessor again."

"We don't—"

Kahlan elbowed him again. "We would be happy to join Minister Chanboor for dinner. Please ask him, though, to

580

understand that we have been riding hard, and are tired. We would appreciate it if he kept the dinner small, no more than three courses."

Rowley was clearly not prepared for this request, but promised to relay it at once.

Once the man was riding back, Du Chaillu stepped up.

"You need a bath," she announced to Richard. "Jiaan says there is a pond not far over this hill. Come, we will bathe."

Kahlan's brow tightened. Du Chaillu smiled sweetly.

"I usually must suggest it," she said. "He is shy when we bathe together. His face turns red"—she pointed at Richard's face—"just like that, when we undress to bathe. His face turns red like that whenever he tells me to take off my clothes."

Kahlan folded her arms. "Really."

Du Chaillu nodded. "Do you enjoy bathing with him, too? He seems to enjoy it—bathing with women."

Now Richard knew how displeased Du Chaillu was with her horseback ride, and how she intended to even the score.

Kahlan's green eyes turned to him. "What is it with you and women and water?"

Richard shrugged, not about to play the game. "You want to join us? It might be fun." He winked at her and then turned and seized Du Chaillu's arm. "Come along, then, *wife*. We'll go first, maybe Kahlan will join us later."

Du Chaillu yanked her arm away. The joke had gone too far for her. "No. I do not wish to go near the water."

Her eyes betrayed obvious fear. She didn't wish to give the chimes a chance to drown her again.

CHAPTER 52

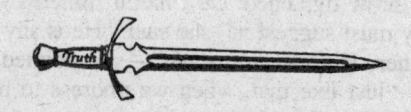

RICHARD SIGHED IMPATIENTLY AS he surveyed the people enjoying the dinner. An intimate dinner, Bertrand Chanboor had called it. Kahlan had whispered to Richard that, for Anderith, fifty or sixty people was considered an intimate dinner.

When Richard looked out at the people, many of them, especially the men, glanced away. Many of the women did not. It was fortunate, the way they were batting their lashes at him, that Kahlan was not jealous. She hadn't really been jealous of Du Chaillu; she knew the woman was simply trying to nettle him. He knew, though, he was going to have to explain how innocent his single bath with Du Chaillu had been.

It was hard explaining anything to Kahlan, what with having so many people around all the time. Even when they slept, they had blade masters, and now troops, standing over them every minute. It wasn't very intimate, much less romantic. He was beginning to forget they were married, for all the time they had alone together.

Their purpose, though, made such considerations pale into insignificance. The awareness of people dying because of the chimes being loose was not conducive to intimacy.

Sitting close to her, sharing food from the trencher, seeing the lamplight reflect in her green eyes, off her hair, seeing the way her thick tresses nestled in the curve of her neck, he was beginning to think about weeks before, in the spirit house—the last time he had made love to her . . . remembering her lush naked body. It was an impossible mental image to forget.

Kahlan cleared her throat. "He asked you a question, Richard," she whispered.

Richard blinked. "What?"

"Minister Chanboor asked you a question."

Richard turned to the other side. "I'm sorry, my mind was elsewhere. On an important action."

"Yes, of course," Minister Chanboor said, smiling. "I was just curious as to where you grew up."

A long-forgotten memory of youth surfaced in Richard's mind, a memory of wrestling with his older brother—his stepbrother, Michael. He had so enjoyed the playful tumbles they had. It had been a time of laughter.

"Oh, you know—wherever there was a good fight."

The Minister stumbled around for words. "I, I suppose you had a good teacher."

His stepbrother had later, when they were grown, betrayed him to Darken Rahl. Michael had betrayed many people. Because of Michael's betrayal, many innocent people had died.

"Yes," Richard said, the memory standing in stark relief between him and the Minister's expectant face. "I did have a good teacher. Last winter I had him beheaded."

The Minister paled.

Richard turned back to Kahlan. She hid her smile. "Good answer," she whispered to him from behind a napkin so she couldn't be heard over the music coming from the harp set before and below their table.

The Lady Chanboor, on Kahlan's other side, if she was appalled, didn't show it. Dalton Campbell, on the far side of the Minister, raised an eyebrow. Beyond him, his wife, Teresa, a nice woman, Richard thought, hadn't heard his words. When Dalton turned and whispered them to her, her

583

eyes went wide, more in titillation than horror.

Kahlan had warned him these people responded to power, and suggested he show them more intimation of force than offers of accommodation if they were to gain the Anders' cooperation.

The Minister, a piece of rolled beef dripping a red sauce in his fingers, gestured and sought to change the subject to something less bloody.

"Lord Rahl, don't you wish any meat?"

The meat course seemed to Richard to have gone on for an hour. He decided to tell the man the flat truth.

"I'm a war wizard, Minister Chanboor. Like my father, Darken Rahl, I don't eat meat." Richard paused to be certain he had the attention of everyone at the table. "Wizards, you see, must maintain balance in their lives. Not eating meat is balance for all the killing I do."

The harpist missed a note. Everyone else held their breath.

Richard filled the dragging silence. "I'm certain that by now you have heard the proposal I've made for the lands of the Midlands to join with us. The terms are fair and equitable to all. Your representatives would have brought our terms to you. If you join willingly, your people will be welcomed. If you oppose us . . . well, if you oppose us, then we will have to conquer you and the terms will be harsh."

"So I've been told," the Minister said.

Kahlan leaned in. "And you have been informed my word backs Lord Rahl's? You know my advice is for all lands to join us?"

The Minister tipped his head in a slight bow. "Yes, Mother Confessor, and please be assured we value greatly your sound advice."

"Then is it your intention to join with us, Minister, in our struggle for freedom?"

"Well . . . you see, Mother Confessor, it is not quite that simple."

"Fine," Richard said, beginning to rise. "I will see the Sovereign, then."

"You can't," Dalton Campbell said.

Richard, a scowl growing, sank back down. "And why would that be?"

The Minister licked his lips. "The Sovereign, the Creator watch over his blessed soul, is very ill. He is bedridden. Not even I have been able to see him. He is in no condition to talk, from what the healers and his wife tell me. Speaking with him would be hopeless, since he is rarely conscious."

"I'm so sorry," Kahlan said. "We had no idea."

"We would take you to see him, Mother Confessor, Lord Rahl," Dalton Campbell said in a sincere-sounding voice, "but the man is so ill he would be unable to offer his advice."

The harpist went into a louder, more complex and dramatic piece, using every string, it seemed.

"Then you will have to decide without his advice," Richard said. "The Imperial Order is already invading the New World. We need everyone we can get to resist their tyranny, lest their dark shadow cover us all."

"Well," the Minister said as he intently picked at invisible things on the tablecloth, "I want the land of Anderith to join with you and your noble cause. I really do. As do most of the people of Anderith, I'm sure—"

"Good. Then that's settled."

"Well, no, it's not." Minister Chanboor looked up. "Though I might wish it, as would my wife, and as Dalton has so forcefully advised we do, we cannot decide something this important on our own."

"The Directors?" Kahlan asked. "We will speak with them straightaway."

"They are part of it," the Minister said, "but not all. There are others who must be part of such a momentous decision."

Richard sat puzzled. "Who else is there?"

The Minister leaned back in his chair and gazed out at the room for a time before his dark eyes turned back to Richard.

"The people of Anderith."

"You are the Minister of Culture," Kahlan said heatedly as she leaned in. "You speak for them. You have but to say it will be so and it will."

The man spread his hands. "Mother Confessor, Lord Rahl, you are asking us to surrender our sovereignty. I can't callously do that on my own."

"That is why it is called 'surrender,' " Richard growled.

"But you are asking our people to cease to be who they are, and become one with you and your people. I don't think you realize what that means. You are asking us to surrender not only our sovereignty, but our very culture.

"Don't you see? We would cease to be who we are. We have a culture stretching back thousands of years. Now you come in, one man, and ask the people to throw away all that history? How can you think it so simple a matter to forget our heritage, our forebears, our culture?"

Richard drummed his fingers on the table. He gazed out at the people enjoying the dinner, who had no idea how important were the words being spoken at the head table.

"You misstate it, Minister Chanboor. We have no desire to destroy your culture"—Richard leaned toward the man—"although from what I've heard of it, there are unfair aspects of it that will not be allowed. Under our law, everyone is treated equally.

"As long as you follow the common laws, you may retain your culture."

"Yes, but—"

"In the first place, it is a matter of necessity to the very freedom of hundreds of thousands of people of the New World. We will not tolerate a risk to so many. If you don't join us, we will conquer you. When that happens, you will lose your say in the common laws we set down, and you will pay penalties that will cripple your land for a generation."

The heat in Richard's eyes moved the Minister back a few inches. "Worse, though, would be if the Imperial Order gets to you first. They will not impose financial penalties, they will crush you. They will murder and enslave you."

"The Imperial Order demanded the surrender of Ebinissia," Kahlan said in a distant voice. "I was there. I saw what the Order did to those people when they refused to surrender and become slaves. The men of Imperial Order tortured and butchered every man, woman, and child in the city. Every last one. Not one person was left alive."

"Well, any men who would—"

"Over fifty thousand men of the Order participated in slaughtering the innocent people of Ebinissia," Kahlan said in a coldly powerful voice. "I led the troops who hunted them down. We killed every last man who had been in on the butchery in Ebinissia."

Kahlan leaned toward the Minister. "Many wept for mercy. I have declared, as Mother Confessor, no mercy for the Order. That includes any who side with them. We killed every last one one of those men, Minister Chanboor. Every last one."

The frightful chill of her words stunned everyone at the table into silence. Dalton Campbell's wife, Teresa, looked as though she might run from the table.

"Your only salvation," Richard finally said, "is to join with us. Together, we are forming a formidable force capable of turning back the Imperial Order and preserving peace and freedom in the New World."

Minister Chanboor finally spoke. "As I said, if it were my choice, I would agree to join you, as would my wife, as would Dalton. The problem is, Emperor Jagang has made generous offers to people here, offers of peace and—"

Kahlan shot to her feet. "What! You have been talking to those murderers!"

Some of the people around the room paused in their conversations to glance up at the head table. Some, Richard had noticed, had never taken their eyes off the Minister and his guests.

The Minister, for the first time, seemed undaunted. "When your land is threatened with extinction by opposing forces, neither of which were invited to demand our surrender, it is our duty as leaders and advisors to listen to what each side has to say. We wish no war, but war is being thrust upon us. It is incumbent on us to hear what our choices might be. You cannot fault us for listening to our options."

"Freedom or slavery," Richard said, standing beside his wife.

The Minister stood up, too. "Listening to what people have to say is not considered an offense, here in Anderith. We don't attack people before they make threats. The Imperial Order implored us not to listen to what you have to say, but here you are. We offer people the opportunity to speak."

Richard's hand tightened on the hilt of his sword. He expected to feel the raised letters made of gold wire, the letters spelling out the word "Truth." He was momentarily surprised to find them missing.

"And what lies did the Order tell you, Minister?"

Minister Chanboor shrugged. "As I said, we like your offer better."

He held his hand out in invitation. Reluctantly, Richard and Kahlan returned to their seats.

"I must tell you right up front, Minister," Richard said, "whatever it is you want, we'll not give it to you. Don't even bother listing to us your conditions. As we've explained to your representatives back in Aydindril, we have made the same offer to all the lands. In order to be fair to all, there can be no exceptions, and no special accommodations for some."

"We ask for none," Minister Chanboor said.

When Kahlan touched Richard's back, he recognized it as a signal to take a breath and keep hold of his temper. He took the deep breath and reminded himself of their purpose. Kahlan was right. He had to think, and not just react.

"All right, Minister, what is the problem keeping you from accepting our terms of surrender?"

"Well, as I said, if it were up to me and—"

"What is the problem?" Richard's tone was deadly, deep breath or not.

He was already considering his troops, less than a mile away. The guards at the estate would present little opposition for such elite D'Haran soldiers. It was not an option he wished to fall back on, but he might be forced to it. They couldn't let the Minister—inadvertently or otherwise—interfere with stopping Jagang.

The Minister cleared his throat. Everyone else at the table was rigid, almost afraid to move, as if they could read Richard's thoughts in his eyes.

"This affects everyone in our land. You are asking us to forsake our culture, as is the Imperial Order—although with you it would be less of a change and we would be able to retain some of our ways.

"This is not something I can impose on our people. It must be up to them."

Richard's brow twitched. "What? What do you mean?"

"I can't dictate such a thing to our people. They will have to decide for themselves what to do."

Richard lifted a hand. He let it fall back to the table. "But, how can they do that?"

The Minister wet his lips. "They will all decide what shall be the fate of all by their vote."

"Their what?" Kahlan asked.

"Their vote. They must each be given the opportunity to state their wishes in this."

"No," Kahlan said flatly.

The Minister spread his hands. "But, Mother Confessor, you say this is about the freedom of our people. How can you insist I impose such a thing on them without their say?"

"No," Kahlan repeated.

Everyone else at the table seemed in shock. Lady Chanboor's eyes looked as if they might pop from her head at her husband's suggestion. Dalton Campbell sat stiffly, his mouth hanging open a bit. Teresa's brows were arched in shock. Clearly, none of them had known Minister Chanboor's intention, nor did they look to believe it wise, but they remained silent, nonetheless.

"No," Kahlan said again.

"And how can you expect our people to believe your sincerity in the cause of freedom, if you refuse to allow them to choose their own fate? If what you offer is truly freedom, then why would you fear the people exercising freedom in choosing it? If what you offer is so fair and good, and the Imperial Order so brutal and unfair, then why would you not allow our people to freely choose to join with you? Is there something in it so vile you would not allow them to see their fate and choose it willingly?"

Richard glanced back at Kahlan. "He has a point—"

"No," Kahlan snapped.

Still no one else moved, so intent were they on the future of their land, hanging in the balance.

Richard took Kahlan's arm. He turned briefly to the Minister. "If you will excuse us for a moment, there are a few matters we must discuss."

Richard pulled Kahlan away from the table, back near the curtains behind the service table. He glanced out the window to make sure no one was nearby, listening. People at the head table, rather than watching, sat back in silence and looked out at the dining room full of people eating, talking, and laughing, not realizing the drama taking place at the head table.

"Kahlan, I don't see why—"

"No. No, Richard, no. What part of 'no' don't you understand?"

"The part that has your reason in it."

She heaved an impatient sigh. "Look, Richard, I just don't think it's a good idea. No, that isn't correct. I think it's a terrible idea."

"All right. Kahlan, you know I depend on your opinion in things like this—"

"Then take it. No."

In frustration, Richard raked his fingers back through his hair. He glanced around again. They were being ignored.

"What I was about to say is, I'd like to know your reason. The man has a point. If we're offering people a chance to join us in our fight for the freedom of everyone, then why would we deny them a chance to freely choose to join our side? Freedom shouldn't be something imposed on unwilling people."

Kahlan squeezed his arm. "I can't give you a reason, Richard. Yes, it sounds right. Yes, I understand the reasoning behind it. Yes, it would only be fair."

Her hand on his arm tightened. "But my gut instinct is screaming 'no.' I must trust my instinct in this, Richard, and so must you. It's strong and it's insistent. Don't you do this."

Richard wiped a hand across his face. He tried to come up with a reason they should oppose such a thing. He was only beginning to come up with more reasons it would make sense—and for more than the simple need of Anderith siding against the Order.

"Kahlan, I trust you, I really do. You're the Mother Confessor, and have had a lifetime of learning and experience in ruling people. I'm just a woods guide. But I'd like a little more reason than, 'Your gut says "no." ' "

"I can't give you more. I know these people, and I know they are arrogant and devious. I don't believe Bertrand Chanboor cares at all about what the people want. He and his wife care only about themselves, from what I know of them. Something about this just isn't right."

Richard ran a finger down her temple. "Kahlan, I love you. I trust you. But this is these people's lives. Bertrand Chanboor will not be the one deciding—that's the whole point. If what we have to offer is right, then why shouldn't the Anderith people be able to say yes to it themselves? Don't you think they would then have more invested in the cause than if their leaders choose for them?

"Do you think it fair we demand their culture be so altered, and tell them it's the right thing to do, and yet refuse to offer them the freedom to join willingly? Why can only the leader choose for all his people? What if the Minister wished to join with Jagang? Would you not then want the people to have the chance to overthrow the leader and choose freedom instead?"

She ran her fingers back into her hair, seeming unable to express her reservations and frustrations. "Richard, you're making it sound . . . right, but I just . . . I don't know, I just feel it's a mistake. What if they cheat? What if they intimidate people—threaten them. How would we know? Who is to watch people say what they want? Who is to watch the fairness of the count?"

Richard ran a thumb along the silken sleeve of her white Mother Confessor's dress. "Well then, what if we put conditions on it? Conditions to make sure we are in control, and not they."

"Such as?"

"We have a thousand men here. We could use them to go to all the cities and towns in Anderith and watch the people vote. Everyone could put a mark on a piece of paper . . . say, either a circle to join us, or an X not to. Then our men could guard the papers and watch them counted. They would make sure it was fair."

"And how would people really know what it means, either way?"

"We would have to tell them. Anderith isn't that big. We could go to each place and explain to the people there why they must join us—why it's so important to them and how they would suffer if the Imperial Order instead takes them. If truth really is on our side, it won't be that difficult to make most people see it."

She chewed her lip as she considered. "How long? The scouts report the Order will be within striking distance in less than six weeks."

"Then we say four. Four weeks and the people vote. That would give us more than enough time to go around and talk to people, tell them how important this is. Then, after they vote to join us, we would have plenty of time to bring our army down and use the Dominie Dirtch to stop Jagang."

Kahlan pressed a hand to her stomach. "I don't like it, Richard."

He shrugged. "All right, then. General Reibisch's army is on the way. They'll be here before Jagang can reach Anderith. We told him to stay north, out of sight, but we could take our men, capture the Dominie Dirtch, and overthrow the government here.

"From what I've seen of their army, it wouldn't take long."

"I know," Kahlan said, frowning in thought. "I don't understand it. I've been here before. Their army was a formidable force. The people we've seen look little more than . . . children."

Richard gazed out the window. With all the lights coming from so many windows, the grounds were well enough lit to see how beautiful they were. It looked a peaceful place to live.

"Poorly trained children," he said. "I can't understand it, either. Except, as the soldier at the border, Beata, said: It only takes one person to ring the Dominie Dirtch.

"Maybe they have no need to expend their assets to support a big army when all they need do is have a few soldiers at the border, manning the Dominie Dirtch. After all, you would know as well as anyone the vast resources required to maintain a sizable force. Every day they must be fed. That's why Jagang is headed this way. Maybe Anderith just doesn't need to deplete their resources."

Kahlan nodded. "Maybe. I know the Minister of Culture has a long tradition of private backers—moneylenders, merchants, and such—to help champion their goals. Supporting an army is hugely expensive, even for a wealthy land. But I think there's more to it for an army to deteriorate in such a fashion."

"So, what do you think? Vote, or conquest?"

She looked into his eyes. "I still say no vote."

"You know people will be hurt. Killed. It isn't going to be bloodless. We may have to kill their soldiers—like Sergeant Beata, back at the Dominie Dirtch. They may be little more than children, but they will resist us taking them, and they will probably be killed.

"We can't let them keep control of the Dominie Dirtch. We have to seize those weapons, if we are to let our army in. We can't risk our men being slaughtered by those things."

"But the magic is failing."

"They rang just over a week ago. People out in front of them were killed. They still work. We can't count on them failing.

"It's either attack, or let them do as the Minister suggested: let the people decide their own fate. But even if something goes wrong, we could possibly still use the option of our troops. With what's at stake, I wouldn't hesitate to resort to attacking them if need be. Too many other lives are at risk."

"That's true. We always have that to fall back on."

"But there's one more thing we must consider. Perhaps the most important element."

"What's that?" she asked.

"The chimes. That's why we're here, remember? This business with letting the people decide may work to our advantage with the chimes."

She didn't look at all convinced. "How?"

"We need to search the library. If we can find what we need to know to stop the chimes—like what Joseph Ander once did—then we can do it before it's too late for magic. You haven't forgotten, have you, about the gambit moth, and all the rest?"

"No, of course not."

"And your Confessor's power, and Du Chaillu's magic, and the bond and all the rest. Jagang can easily win without magic; the danger from the Order would only grow stronger. We are just two people, like any others, without magic to protect us—to help us. There is no place so dangerous as a world without magic.

"While we stall for four weeks, we may be able to find the information we need about the chimes. And with traveling around to talk to people about voting to join us, that would be the perfect cover to keep anyone from being suspicious as to what we're doing. I think it risky to let these

594

people know magic has failed. Best to keep them on edge."

Richard leaned close. "Kahlan, the chimes may be the most important part in this. This would buy us time to search. I think we should agree to let the people of Anderith vote."

"I still say no, but if you want to try it"—she pressed finger and thumb to the bridge of her nose—"I can't believe I'm agreeing to this—then I will trust your judgment, Richard. You are, after all, the Lord Rahl."

"But I depend on you for advice."

"You are also the Seeker."

He smiled. "But I don't have my sword."

Kahlan smiled back. "You've gotten us this far. If you say we should try this, then I'll go along, but I don't like it. Still, you are right about the chimes. That's our first responsibility. This will help us search for the solution to the chimes."

Richard was relieved that she had finally agreed, but worried about her reasons for being reluctant. With her hand on his arm, they returned to the head table. The Minister, his wife, and Dalton Campbell rose.

"There are conditions," Richard said.

"Such as?" the Minister asked.

"Our men will watch everything, to insure no one cheats. Everyone will have to vote at the same time, so people can't go to more than one place and vote more than once. They will gather in cities and towns, and each will mark a piece of paper, either with a circle to join into one whole with us, or an X to leave their fate to the cruel fangs of fate. Our men will watch the counting and reporting so that we know everything has been fair."

The Minister smiled. "Excellent suggestions. I concur with every one of them."

Richard leaned toward the man. "One more thing."

"That being?"

"All the people will vote. Not just Anders, but the Hakens, too. They are part of the land, just as are the Anders.

Their fate will be altered by this, too. If there is to be a vote, all people of Anderith will vote."

Lady Chanboor and Dalton Campbell shared a look. The Minister spread his hands, his smile growing.

"But of course. All people will vote. It is settled, then."

CHAPTER 53

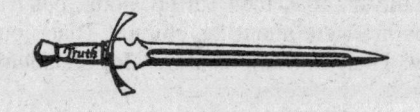

HILDEMARA WAS LIVID. "BERTRAND, you're going to be skinned alive by Jagang's men, and I will delight in watching, my only regret being that you have sealed me to a similar fate!"

Bertrand lifted a hand dismissively. "Nonsense, my dear. Rather, I've managed to stall the Mother Confessor and the Lord Rahl while Jagang draws ever closer."

Dalton, for once, tended to agree with Hildemara. Despite everything else, she was a brilliant strategist. On the face of it, it seemed that if given the choice, the people, the Hakens for sure, would go with the freedoms of Lord Rahl's empire rather than willingly submit to the tyranny of the Imperial Order.

But Dalton knew, too, that there had to be something behind Bertrand's self-satisfied smile. The man had the uncanny knack of tactical calculation coldly bereft of emotional bias toward his desired outcome, which would corrupt the validity of the equation. Bertrand only jumped if he knew he could span the chasm; he didn't leap simply because he *wished* to span it.

From his vast knowledge of law, Dalton knew there were few weapons as effective in eviscerating an adversary as the simple tactic of delay. He hoped Bertrand wasn't wielding a weapon that would gore them, instead of the enemy.

"Minister, I'm afraid this could be troublesome. To stall Lord Rahl is worthy, but not if it serves no better end than to allow him to enflame the people against the Imperial Order and drive them into the arms of his cause, instead. Were that to happen, we would be unable to fulfill our agreements. We would then be at the center of the storm of war."

"And Jagang would make an example of us, to show others what happens to those who don't deliver as promised," Hildemara added.

Bertrand took a swig from the goblet he'd brought with him to the private study. He set down the silver goblet on a small marble tabletop and savored the taste of rum before swallowing.

"My dear wife, and my trusted aide, do you both fail to see the simple brilliance in this? We are going to stall them so the Imperial Order can have time to get here. Stall them until it's too late for them to do anything effective. On top of everything else, can you imagine how grateful Jagang will be when we can hand him his greatest enemy?"

"And how would we accomplish that?" his wife asked.

"A month of this voting business will enable the Order to get the rest of their advance guard in place. They can then take the Dominie Dirtch at their discretion. Lord Rahl's forces, even if he has them close, will be precluded from coming to the rescue of the Lord Rahl and the Mother Confessor, once they lose the people's support. Jagang will be invincible.

"The emperor gets a land and the people to work it, as promised, and we are handsomely rewarded for handing it to him. We will have unquestioned authority. No more Directors to worry about—ever again. We will rule Anderith for life, the way we choose, without worry of opposition."

Life, for the people of Anderith, would go on, Dalton knew. For the most part, the lives of many would be much the same, if poorer, serving the greater good of the Order. There would be the inevitable dislocations and deaths. Some would be taken away to serve the emperor. Most would be grateful just to live.

Dalton wondered at his own fate, if he had not become the trusted chief aide to the Minister, and thus by service and by necessity brought into the arrangement. He shuddered to think what might have become of Teresa.

"If he indeed honors his agreements," Hildemara muttered.

"The emperor, his forces having a safe haven immune from attack, will be only too happy to honor our agreements," Bertrand said. "What he promised us, in return for the task of seeing to it the people of Anderith work on as they do now, is vast beyond our ability to ever spend; to him, however, it is but a pittance compared to what he will gain. We must simply see to it the Order is supplied with food while they conquer the Midlands. He will happily pay as agreed."

Lady Chanboor huffed irritably. "But it will come to no good end when Lord Rahl gets the people to vote to join with him."

Bertrand chortled. "You must be joking. That, my dear, is the simplest part of the whole thing."

She folded her arms as if to demand to know how.

Dalton, too, was worried about that much of it. "So then, you have no intention of actually allowing the vote to take place?"

Bertrand looked from one to the other.

"Don't you see? We will easily win such a vote."

"Perhaps with the Anders," she said, "but the Hakens? You have placed our fate in the hands of the Hakens? Who outnumber us many times over? They will choose freedom."

"Hardly. The Hakens are kept ignorant. They don't have the capacity to comprehend the issues. They believe the only way they can attain anything, from work to food—even to joining the army—is by our benevolent hand. They believe what freedoms they have, or hope to have, can only be granted them by Anders. With freedom comes responsibility—not the easy path they would prefer."

His wife looked unmoved. "How can you be so sure?"

"We will have speakers go before the people, wringing their hands, shedding tears, expressing deep fear for what will become of the people at the mercy of the cruel D'Haran Empire, in the uncaring hands of a Lord Rahl who doesn't know the first thing about their needs as Hakens and only cares about his own dark magic. The Haken people will be so terrified of losing what crumbs we grant them they will shrink from the loaf before them—if we simply make them believe the loaf is poison."

Dalton's mind was already spinning with thoughts of how they might accomplish the Minister's plan. The true possibilities it presented were only just dawning on him.

"We must consider how to frame it properly," Dalton said. "It would be best if we remained completely out of it."

"My thought, exactly."

"Yes . . ." Hildemara drawled as she imagined, now caught up in the scheme. "We must appear as if we're looking to the people for direction, rather than the other way around."

"Others will speak the words we craft," Bertrand said as he nodded to her. "We must at all cost remain above it—look as if our hands are bound by a noble adherence to fairness, with our fate in the hands of the wisdom of the people, as if we put that principle and their wishes above all else."

"I have men who would be good at expressing the proper tone." Dalton stroked a finger beneath his lower lip. "Wherever Lord Rahl goes, those who speak for us must go behind, and deliver the message we fashion."

"That's right," Bertrand said. "A message more powerful, more cutting, more frightening."

Deep in thought, trying to envision all requisite elements of the strategy, Dalton waggled a finger.

"Lord Rahl and the Mother Confessor will bring swift and unpleasant action, should they suspect such a thing. In fact, it would be best if they never even knew of the things the people are told—at least in the beginning. Our messages must be delivered only after they have gone on to the next place.

"Let them offer hope. We will come behind and portray the hope of freedom they offer as lies—frighten people out of such thoughts."

Dalton knew how easily the minds of the people could be manipulated with the right words, especially if people were distracted by other matters and confused with contradictions.

"If done well, the people will resoundingly approve of us as we at the same time betray them." Dalton smiled at last. "When I get through with them, they will cheer us on to the task."

Bertrand took another swig of rum. "Now you're thinking like the man I hired."

"But when the people reject his offer," Hildemara said, "Lord Rahl will no doubt react badly to losing; he will turn to force."

"Possibly." Bertrand set down the goblet. "But by then the Order will have captured the Dominie Dirtch, and it will be too late for Lord Rahl to do anything about it. He and the Mother Confessor will be isolated, without hope of reinforcements."

"Lord Rahl and the Mother Confessor will be trapped in Anderith . . ." She smiled at last, closing her clawed fingers into a fist. "And Jagang will have them."

Bertrand grinned. "And reward us." He turned to Dalton. "Where are the D'Haran troops billeted?"

"Between here and Fairfield."

"Good. Let Lord Rahl and the Mother Confessor have anything they want. Let them do whatever they wish. We must appear to be most accommodating."

Dalton nodded. "They said they wanted to see the library."

Bertrand swept up his goblet again. "Fine. Let them have the run of it—see what they wish. There is nothing in the library that could be of any help to them."

Richard turned to the ruckus.

"Shoo!" Vedetta Firkin yelled. The old woman cast her arms forward, adding physical threat to the verbal one she had already delivered. "Shoo, you thief!"

The raven out on the board attached to the windowsill leaped about, flapping its wings, loudly expressing its displeasure with her. She looked around and then snatched a stick up from where it leaned against the wall, ready to hand for propping the next window open. Wielding the stick like a sword, she leaned out the open window and swiped at the raven. Wings outstretched, neck plumage ruffed, feathers on its head lifted like horns, it hopped back and screeched at her.

Again she slashed at the big black bird. This time the raven made a strategic withdrawal to a nearby branch. From a position of safety, it delivered a boisterous lecture. She slammed the window shut.

Vedetta Firkin turned and, after setting down the stick, triumphantly brushed clean her hands. She lifted her nose as she returned to people business.

Richard and Kahlan had spoken with her when they came into the library in order to put her mind at ease. Richard wanted to insure her cooperation rather than have her perhaps get the notion that it was somehow her duty to hide books from them. She had responded brightly to their casual and friendly manner with her.

"Sorry," she whispered in low voice, as if to compensate for the yelling. She scurried closer to Richard and Kahlan.

"I tacked that board to the sill, and I put seeds on it for the birds, but those vile ravens come and steal the seeds."

"Ravens are birds, too," Richard said.

The woman straightened, a little befuddled. "Yes, but . . . they're ravens. Nuisance birds, they are. They steal all the seeds and then the lovely little songbirds don't come by. I so love the song birds."

"I see," Richard said with a smile before he turned back to his book.

"Anyway, Lord Rahl, Mother Confessor, sorry for the disturbance. I just didn't want those noisy ravens bothering you like they're apt to do. Best to just get rid of them right off. I will try to keep it quiet for you from now on."

Kahlan smiled up at the woman. "Thank you, Mistress Firkin."

She paused before turning away. "Excuse me for saying so, Lord Rahl, but you have a delightful smile. It reminds me very much of the smile of a friend of mine."

"Really? Who would that be?" Richard asked, absently.

"Ruben—" Her face reddened. "He's a gentleman friend."

Richard showed her the smile she liked. "I'm sure you give him reason to smile, Mistress Firkin."

"Ruben," Kahlan muttered as the woman started to leave. "Reminds me of Zedd. He used to sometimes use the name Ruben."

Richard sighed with longing for his missing grandfather. "I wish that old man was here, now," he whispered to Kahlan.

"If you need anything," Vedetta Firkin said over her shoulder as she shuffled away, "please don't hesitate to ask. I'm quite knowledgeable about the culture of Anderith— about our history."

"Yes, thank you," Richard called after the woman, using the opportunity while her back was turned to give Kahlan's leg an intimate squeeze under the table.

"Richard," Kahlan said in a rising tone, "keep your mind on your work."

Richard patted her thigh in acquiescence. It would be easier to keep his mind on what he was reading without the sweet warmth of her so near. He flipped the book closed and pulled another close. He opened the old book of town records and scanned for anything that looked remotely useful.

They had not found a wealth of information, but he had managed to find enough to piece together facts that might be useful. Without doubt, the library was proving worth his time, as he was beginning to get a sense of the place that had been missing before. It truly was a library of culture. Because of their attitudes and professed beliefs, Richard doubted that many people had the vaguest idea of the obscure history right under their noses, hiding in plain sight.

He was coming to the realization that much of ancient Anderith, before the Hakens, had benefited from direction that eclipsed the development of the people at the time. A benevolent hand had protected them.

By the ancient songs and prayers he had found set down, and the later accounts of the way homage was paid to this shepherding protector, Richard suspected it to be the hand of Joseph Ander. Such adoration would suit the man, as Kolo described him. Richard recognized much of the miraculous guidance as possibly being the work of a wizard. Without this figure after he was gone, the people were like orphans, lost without the succor of idols they worshiped but which no longer answered them. They were bewildered and at the mercy of forces they didn't understand.

Richard leaned back and stretched as he yawned. The old books infused the library with a musty aroma. Rather intriguing, in a long-hidden-mystery sort of way, but the smell was not altogether pleasant, either. He was beginning to long for the fresh sunny air on the other side of the windows as much as he longed for the end of the long-hidden-mystery.

Du Chaillu sat nearby, stroking a loving hand over her unborn baby as she studied a book with intricate illuminations on many of its pages. There were drawings of small animals: ferrets, weasels, voles, foxes, and such. She couldn't read, but the book full of drawings had her in a constant grin. She'd never seen anything like it. Richard had never seen her dark eyes sparkle so. She was as delighted as a child.

Jiaan lounged nearby. At least, the blade master did a good imitation of lounging. Richard knew he was simply making himself unobtrusive so he could watch everything. A half-dozen D'Haran soldiers strolled the room. There were Ander guards, too, at the doors.

Some of the other people had immediately left the library, fearing they might disturb the Mother Confessor and Lord Rahl. A few remained. Spies, Kahlan had suggested to him, sent to watch them. He had already formed that opinion.

He didn't trust the Minister any more than Kahlan did. From the first time the subject of Anderith had come up, her obvious distaste for the place had colored his view of it. The Minister of Culture had done nothing to alter his impression, and had lent weight to Kahlan's warnings about the man.

"Here," Richard said, tapping the page. "Here it is again."

Kahlan leaned close and looked. She made a sound deep in her throat at seeing the name: Westbrook.

"What this is saying here confirms what we've found before," Richard said.

"I know the place. It's a little town. Not much there, from what I recall."

Richard lifted his arm and signaled for the attention of the old woman. She came scurrying back at once.

"Yes, Lord Rahl? May I be of assistance?"

"Mistress Firkin, you said you know a lot about the history of Anderith."

"Oh, yes, I do. It's my favorite subject."

"Well, I've now found several places where it mentions a place called Westbrook. It says Joseph Ander once lived there."

"Yes, that's true. It's up in the foothills of the mountains. Up above the Nareef Valley."

Kahlan had already told him that much, but it was good

to know the woman wasn't trying to mislead them, or conceal information.

"And is there anything left there of him? Anything that belonged to him?"

She smiled her enthusiasm, pleased he wanted to know about Joseph Ander, the namesake of her land. "Why, yes, there is a small shrine to Joseph Ander there. People may go and see the chair he once used, and a few other small items.

"The house he lived in burned down just recently— terrible fire it was—but some things were saved because they had been taken away while the house was undergoing repairs. Water kept getting in, ruining things. Wind ripped up roof shingles. Tree branches—must have been—broke the windows and the wind got in there something fierce, blowing the rain in, getting everything wet. Ruined a lot of the valuable things of his. Then the fire—from lightning, people believe—burned the place to the ground.

"But some of his things were saved, like I said, because they were out of there while repairs were being made— before the fire. So, now, those things are displayed so people can see them. See the actual chair he sat in."

She leaned down. "And, most interesting to me, there are some of his writings still intact."

Richard sat up straighter. "Writing?"

She nodded her gray head of hair. "I've read them all. Nothing really important. Just his observations about the mountains around where he lived, about the town, and about some of the people he knew. Nothing important, but it is still interesting."

"I see."

"Not important, anyway, like his things we have here."

Richard was now at full attention. "What things?"

She swept a hand out. "We have some of his writings, here, in our vault. His dealings with others, letters, books on his beliefs. Things like that.

"Would you like to see them?"

Richard tried his best not to look too interested. He didn't want these people to know what he was looking for; that was why he hadn't asked for anything specific in the first place.

"Yes, that would be interesting. I've always had an interest in . . . in history. I'd like to see his writings."

He, along with Vedetta Firkin, noticed someone coming down the stairs. It was a messenger of some sort—Richard had seen a number of them, all dressed the same. The red-headed man saw Mistress Firkin talking to Richard and Kahlan, so he spread his feet and clasped his hands behind his back as he waited at a distance.

Richard didn't want to be talking about Joseph Ander's works while a messenger stood watching, so he gestured. "Why don't you see to him?"

Vedetta Firkin bowed her appreciation of his indulgence. "Excuse me for just a moment, then."

Kahlan shut her book and set it atop the others she had already been through. "Richard, we need to get going. We have meetings with the Directors and a few other people. We can come back."

"Right." He let out a sigh. "At least we don't have to meet with the Minister again. I couldn't take another of those feasts."

"I'm sure he will be just as glad we declined his invitation. I don't know why, but the two of us always seem to somehow spoil festive gatherings."

Richard agreed and went to collect Du Chaillu. Mistress Firkin returned as Du Chaillu was getting up.

"I would be happy to locate the books and bring them out of the vault for you, Lord Rahl, but I have a quick errand to run first, if you could wait for just a short time. I won't be long. I'm sure you will find the writings of Joseph Ander a delight. Not many people get the chance to see them, but for someone as important as yourself and the Mother Confessor, I would—"

"To tell you the truth, Mistress Firkin, I would love to see the books. Right now, though, we must go speak with the Directors, but I could return afterward, later this afternoon, or this evening?"

"That would be perfect," she said, grinning and drywashing her hands. "It will give me time to locate them all and pull them out. I will have them ready for you when you return."

"Thank you so much. The Mother Confessor and I can't wait to see such rare books."

Richard paused and turned back to her. "And Mistress Firkin, I'd suggest you give that raven some seeds. The poor thing looks frantic."

She waggled her fingers in a wave. "If you say so, Lord Rahl."

He stood when the old woman came into the room on the arm of one of his messengers.

"Mistress Firkin, thank you for coming."

"Well, my, my, Master Campbell, but don't you have a fine office." She peered around as if she was interested in purchasing the place. "Yes, very fine indeed."

"Thank you, Mistress Firkin."

He tilted his head, ordering the messenger out. The man shut the door behind himself.

"Oh, and look," she said, pressing her hands prayerfully together under her chin. "Look at all the fine books. Why, I never knew there were so many fine volumes up here."

"Law books, mostly. My interest is in the law."

She turned her attention his way. "A fine calling, Master Campbell. A fine calling. Good for you. You keep at it, now."

"Yes, I intend as much. Mistress Firkin, speaking of the law, that brings me to the subject of my calling you up here."

She gave a sidelong glance to the chair. He deliberately didn't offer it, but instead kept her standing.

"I had a report of a man visiting the library who was also interested in the law. It seems he made a big to-do." Dalton put his fists on the leather pad inlaid into his desk and leaned forward on them, fixing her with a glare. "It was reported that you took a restricted book out of the vault, without authorization, and showed it to him."

As quick as that, she went from a chatty old woman to a terrified old woman.

While what she'd done wasn't altogether uncommon, it was a violation of the rules, and thus the law. Most such laws were only selectively enforced, with violations only mildly punished, if at all. But occasionally people did get into trouble over violating such laws. As a man of the law, Dalton understood the value of laws widely ignored; they ensnared nearly everyone, thus giving you power over people. Hers was a serious offense, just one step below theft of cultural treasures, if he chose to pursue it.

She fumbled with a button at her throat. "But I never let him touch it, Master Campbell. I swear. I kept it in my hand every moment. I even turned the pages. I was only letting him look at the writing of our glorious founding father. I didn't intend—"

"Nonetheless, it is not permitted, and it was reported, therefore I must take action."

"Yes, sir."

Dalton straightened. "Bring me the book." He tapped his desk. "Bring me the book at once. At once, do you understand?"

"Yes, sir. At once."

"You bring it up here and put it on my desk so I can look it over. If there is no valuable information that might have been betrayed to a spy, I will not recommend any disciplinary action—this time. But you had better not be caught breaking the rules again, Mistress Firkin. Do you understand?"

"Yes, sir. Thank you, sir." She was nearly in tears. "Master Campbell, the Mother Confessor and the Lord Rahl have been down in the library."

"Yes, I know."

"Lord Rahl asked to see Joseph Ander's books and writings. What should I do?"

Dalton could hardly believe the man was wasting his time looking over such useless books. He almost felt sorry for the Lord Rahl in his ignorance. Almost.

"The Mother Confessor and Lord Rahl are honored guests as well as being important people. They may see any book in our library. There are to be no restrictions on them. None. You hereby have authorization to show them anything we have."

He tapped his desk again. "But that book you showed to that other man, that Ruben fellow, I want that book on my desk, and I want it now."

The woman was fidgeting like she was about to wet herself.

"Yes, sir. Right away, Master Campbell." She scurried from the room, her entire life now focused on retrieving the book.

Dalton didn't really care about the book—whatever it was. He simply didn't want the people in the library to get sloppy and start violating the rules. He couldn't have people he didn't trust in charge of valuable things.

His cobweb was humming with matters more important than some useless, dusty old book by Joseph Ander, but he had to mind everything, regardless of how minor. He would take a look at the book, but just her bringing it was what mattered to him.

Every once in a while it was necessary to throw a bit of fright into people to remind them who was in charge and who held sway over their life. Word of this would spread to others in the household. The fear from this one incident would straighten everyone's back. If it didn't, the next time he would put the violator out of the household in order to make an impression.

Dalton sank back into his seat and returned to his stack of messages. Most disturbing of them was the one saying the Sovereign was improving. He was reported to be eating again. Not a good sign, but the man couldn't last forever. Sooner or later, Bertrand Chanboor would be Sovereign.

There were a number of messages and reports about other people dying, though. People out in the country were frightened by strange occurrences—deaths out of the ordinary. Fires, drownings, falls. Country people, terrified of things in the night, were coming into the city, seeking safety.

People in the city, too, were reported to be dying from similar events, and were similarly frightened. Seeking safety, they were fleeing the city and going into the countryside.

Dalton shook his head at the foolishness of people's fears. He gathered the reports into a stack. Just before he put them to the candle flame, a thought struck him. His hand paused. He pulled the sheaf of messages back from the flame.

Something Franca once said had given him an idea.

They might be of use. He stuffed the reports into a drawer.

"Sweetheart, are you still working?"

Dalton looked up at the sound of the familiar voice. Teresa, wearing an alluring rose-colored dress he didn't recall seeing before, was sweeping into the room.

He smiled. "Tess, darling. What brings you up here?"

"I came to catch you with a mistress."

"What?"

She went past his desk to pause and gaze out the window. A green velvet sash gathered the waist of the dress, accentuating her curves. He envisioned his hands where the sash embraced her.

"I was pretty lonely last night," she said as she watched people out on the lawns.

"I know. I'm sorry, but there were messages I had to—"

"I thought you were with another woman."

"What? Tess, I sent you a message, explaining that I had to work."

She turned to him. "When you sent word you would be working late, I didn't think much of it. You've been working late every night. But when I woke up and it was almost dawn, and you weren't there beside me . . . well, I thought sure you were in the bed of another woman."

"Tess, I wouldn't—"

"I thought of going and throwing myself at Lord Rahl, just to get even, but he has the Mother Confessor and she's more beautiful than me, so I knew he would just laugh and turn me away.

"So, I got dressed and came up here, just to be able to say I knew you weren't really working, when you later lied and told me you were. Instead of an empty office, I saw all your messengers scurrying around like they were preparing to go off to war. I saw you in here handing out papers, issuing orders. You really were working. I watched for a while."

"Why didn't you come in?"

She finally glided over to him and settled herself into his lap. She put her arms around his neck as she gazed into his eyes.

"I didn't want to bother you when you were busy."

"But you aren't a bother, Tess. You're the only thing in my life that isn't a bother."

She shrugged. "I was ashamed to have you know I thought you were cheating on me."

"Then why now confess it?"

She kissed him, with a kiss only Tess could give, breathless, hot, wet. She pulled back to smile as she watched him look down her cleavage.

"Because," she whispered, "I love you, and I miss you. I just got my new dress. I thought it might tempt you to my bed."

"I think you more beautiful than the Mother Confessor."

She grinned and gave him a peck on the forehead. "How about coming home for just a while?"

He patted her bottom as she stood. "I'll be along shortly."

Ann peeked and saw Alessandra watching her pray. Ann had asked the woman if it would bother her were Ann to pray before the meal.

Alessandra, at first taken by surprise, had said, "No, why should it?"

Sitting on the bare ground inside her grimy tent, Ann, in earnest, devoted herself to the prayer. She let herself fill with the joy of the Creator, in much the same way she opened herself to her Han. She let the Light fill her with joy. She let her heart feel the peace of the Creator in her, let herself be thankful for all she had, when others were so much worse off.

She prayed that Alessandra would feel just a ray of warm Light, and open her heart to it.

When she finished, she reached as far as the chains would allow and kissed toward her ring finger in fidelity to the Creator, to whom she was symbolically wedded.

She knew Alessandra would recall the indescribable satisfaction of praying to the Creator, of opening your heart in thanks to the one who had given you your soul. There were times in the life of every Sister when she had quietly, privately, piously wept with the joy of it.

Ann saw the twitch of longing as Alessandra almost reflexively brought her own finger to her lips.

As a Sister of the Dark, such an act would be a betrayal of the Keeper.

Alessandra had pledged that soul, given by the Creator, to the Keeper of the underworld—to evil. Ann couldn't imagine there was anything the Keeper could give in return that could match the simple joy of a prayer expressing thanks to the One from which all things emanated.

"Thank you, Alessandra. That was kind of you to let me say my prayer before I eat."

"Nothing kind to it," the woman said. "Simply gets the food down easier so I can get on with my other business."

Ann nodded, glad she had felt the Creator in her heart.

CHAPTER 54

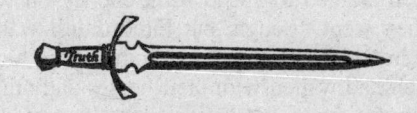

"WHAT ARE WE GOING to do?" Morley whispered.

Fitch scratched his ear. "Hush, I'm planning it out."

Fitch had no idea what to do, but he didn't want Morley to know that. Morley was impressed that Fitch had found the place. He had come to depend on Fitch knowing what to do.

Not that there was that much to know. Mostly they rode hard. They had all that money Dalton Campbell had given them, so they didn't have to know much. They could buy food; they didn't have to hunt it, or gather it. They could buy any gear they needed; they didn't have to fashion it themselves.

Fitch had learned that money went a long way toward making up for what a person didn't know. Having grown up on the streets of Fairfield, he did know how to guard his money, and how to keep from being cheated, robbed, or tricked out of it. He was careful with the money, never using it to buy flashy clothes or anything that would make it look like they were worth knocking over the head, or worse.

The one surprise was that no one much cared that they were Hakens, or even seemed to know. They were treated decent by most folks, who thought them polite young men.

Fitch didn't let Morley talk him into buying drinks at inns; he knew that would be a sure way to let unsavory people know they had money, and being drunk only made it easier to forget to be careful. Instead they bought a bottle, and only when they'd set up a camp for the night, somewhere people weren't likely to come across them, did he and Morley get drunk. They did that a lot at first. It helped Fitch forget that people thought he had raped Beata.

Morley had wanted to spend some money on whores at one town they went through, but Fitch didn't want to. He finally gave in and let Morley do it, being as the money was his, too. Fitch had waited with their horses and other things outside town. He knew what sometimes happened to travelers coming into Fairfield to visit prostitutes.

Afterward, a grinning Morley said he'd watch over their things while Fitch went back and had his turn at visiting a woman. Fitch had been tempted, but the idea made him all jittery. Just when he thought he'd worked up the nerve, he'd imagine the woman laughing at him, and then his knees would get to shaking and his palms to sweating something fierce. He just knew she'd laugh.

Morley, he was big and strong, and manly. Women wouldn't laugh at Morley. Beata used to always laugh at Fitch. He didn't want to have some woman he didn't even know start laughing at his skinny frame as soon as he got his clothes off.

He finally decided he didn't want to risk his purpose, or waste any of their money on it. He didn't know how much it would cost to get to where they were going and feared running out too soon. Morley called him a fool, and said it was more than worth it. It was all he talked about for the week after. Fitch had gotten to wishing he'd done it just to shut Morley up.

As it turned out, he needn't have worried about money. They hadn't spent much at all—not compared with what they had. The money had helped make it a swift journey. With money, they could trade for fresh horses and keep going without having to care for the animals by slowing their pace.

Morley shook his head. "All this way, and here we are stuck this close."

"I said hush. You want to get us caught?"

Morley fell silent, except for scratching his stubble. Fitch wished he had more than a few hairs on his chin. Morley had a beard coming in. Fitch sometimes felt like a kid next to Morley, with his broad shoulders and stubble all over his face.

Fitch watched as the distant guards patrolled back and forth. There was no way in except the bridge. Franca had told him that much, and now that he was here he could see it plain for himself. They had to get across that bridge, or it was over.

Fitch felt a strange whispering wind caress the back of his neck. He shivered after it moved on.

"What do you suppose he's doing?" Morley whispered.

Fitch squinted, trying to see better into the distance. It looked like one of the guards was climbing up onto the stone side of the bridge.

Fitch's jaw dropped. "Dear spirits! Did you see that!"

Morley gasped. "What did he do that for?"

Even at the distance, Fitch could hear the men yelling, running to the edge, looking over.

"I can't believe it," Morley breathed. "Why would he jump?"

Fitch shook his head. He was about to speak when he saw a man on the other side of the bridge climb up on the stone edge.

Fitch thrust out his arm. "Look! There goes another one!"

The man reached out with his arms, embracing the air, as he leaped off the bridge, out into the chasm.

Then, as the soldiers ran to that side, a third leaped to his death. It was crazy. Fitch lay there on his belly, dumb-founded.

In the distance, the sounds of men screaming as yet more

jumped off the bridge were like chimes ringing. They drew weapons, only to drop them and climb up on the stone walls themselves.

Something felt like it pushed at Fitch's back, like his own imagination urging him to take his chance while he had it. The sensation tickled at the back of his neck. He scrambled to his feet.

"Come on, Morley. Let's go."

Morley followed as Fitch ran back down to the horses, hidden in the trees. Fitch stuffed his foot in the stirrup and sprang up into the saddle. Morley was right behind him as Fitch gave his horse his heels, urging her into a gallop up the road.

It was a climb, up the switchbacks, and he couldn't see through the trees if the soldiers were getting themselves collected. He didn't know if they would be in such a state of shock and confusion that the two of them could get through. Fitch didn't see that they had any other chance but this one. He didn't know what was happening, but it wasn't likely that guards jumped off the bridge every day. It was now or never.

As they came around the last bend, they were racing like the wind. He thought that with the havoc, he and Morley could charge past the last of the guards and get over the bridge.

The bridge was empty. There were no soldiers anywhere. Fitch let their horses slow to a walk. It ran chills up his spine remembering all the men he had seen only moments before. Now only the wind guarded the bridge.

"Fitch, are you sure you want to go up there?"

His friend's voice had a tremble to it. Fitch followed Morley's gaze then, and saw it, too. It stuck out of the stone of the mountain, like it was made of the mountain, like it was part of the mountain. It was dark, and evil-looking. It was just about the wickedest place he had ever seen, or could imagine. There were ramparts, and towers, and walls rising up beyond the monumental crenellated outer wall.

He was glad to be sitting in a saddle; he didn't know if

his legs would have held him at the sight of the place. He had never seen anything as big or as sinister-looking as the Wizard's Keep.

"Come on," Fitch said. "Before they find out what happened and send more guards."

Morley looked around at the empty bridge. "And what happened?"

"It's a place with magic. Anything could have happened."

Fitch scooted his bottom forward in the saddle, urging his horse ahead. The horse didn't like the bridge and was only too happy to run. They didn't stop running as they barreled through the opening in the outer wall, under the spiked portcullis.

There was a fenced yard for the horses inside. Before they turned the horses loose, Fitch told Morley to leave the saddles on them so they could make a quick departure. Morley wasn't any more interested in lingering than was Fitch. Together, they raced up the dozen wide granite steps worn smooth and swayback over the centuries, surely by the feet of countless wizards.

Inside, it was just like Franca had told him, only her words of how big it was couldn't match the truth of the sight. A hundred feet overhead a glassed roof let in the sunlight. In the center of the tiled floor stood a clover-leaf-shaped fountain. Water shot fifteen feet into the air above the top bowl, flowing over each bigger one underneath until it ran into a pool at the bottom surrounded by a white marble wall that could be a bench.

Red marble columns were as big as Franca said. They held up arches below a balcony that ran all the way around the oval-shaped room. Morley whistled. It echoed back from the distance.

"Come on," Fitch said, shaking himself out of his awe.

They ran through the hall Franca had told him about and burst through a door at the top of several flights of stairs. They followed a walkway round square buildings without windows and then climbed stairs that followed halfway around a tower, to a walkway tunneling under what looked to be a road overhead, before they crossed a stone bridge over a small, green courtyard far below.

At last, they came to a massive rampart as broad as a road. Fitch looked out over the right side, between the gaps in the crenellation big enough for a man to stand in. He could see the city of Aydindril spread out below. For a boy who grew up in the flat land of Anderith, it was a dizzying sight. Fitch had been impressed by a lot of things he'd seen along the way, but nothing came close to this place.

At the other end of the rampart, a dozen immense columns of variegated red stone held up a protruding entablature of dark stone. Six of the columns stood to each side of a gold-clad door. Above were more layers of fancy stonework, some of it decorated with brass plaques and round metal disks, all of them covered with strange symbols.

As they crossed the long rampart, Fitch realized the door had to be at least ten or twelve feet tall, and a good four feet wide. The gold-clad door was marked with some of the same symbols as on the plaques and disks.

When Fitch pushed on the door, it silently swung inward.

"In here," Fitch whispered. He didn't know why he was whispering, except that maybe he feared to wake the spirits of the wizards who haunted the place.

He didn't want the spirits to make him jump from the rampart like the soldiers had done from the bridge; it looked like the edge dropped off down the mountain for thousands of feet.

"You sure?" Morley asked.

"I'm going in. You can wait here or go with me. It's up to you."

Morley's eyes were looking all around, not seeming able to decide on where to settle. "I guess I'll go with you."

Inside, to each side, glass spheres, about as big as a head, sat on green marble pedestals, like armless statues waiting to greet visitors to the huge room of ornate stonework. In the middle, four columns of polished black marble, at least as big around as a horse was long, from head to tail, formed a square that supported arches at the outer edges of a central dome.

There were wrought-iron sconces holding candles all around the room, but up in the dome a ring of windows let light flood in, so they didn't need to light the candles. Fitch felt like he was in a place the Creator Himself might have. He felt like he should drop to his knees and pray in such a place.

A red carpet led down the wing they were in. In a row down each side of the carpet were six-foot-tall white marble pedestals. Each had to be bigger around than Master Drummond's belly. Up on top of each pedestal were different objects. There were pretty bowls, fancy gold chains, an inky black bottle, and other objects, carved from burled wood. Some of the things Fitch couldn't make sense of.

He didn't pay much attention to the things on the columns; he looked instead across the huge room, to the other side of the central dome. There, he saw a table piled with a clutter of things, and there, leaning against the table, looked to be the thing he'd come for.

Between each pair of the black columns topped in gold, a wing ran off from the vast central chamber. To the left it looked like a disorderly library, with books stacked all over the floor in tall columns. The wing to the right was dark.

Fitch trotted down the red carpet. At the end, broad steps, near to a dozen, went down into the sunken floor of cream-colored marble at the center of the First Wizard's enclave below the dome. He took the steps two at a time up the other side, up toward the table before a towering round-topped window straight ahead.

A confusion of things were piled all over the table: bowls, candles, scrolls, books, jars, spheres, metal squares and triangles—there was even a skull. Other bigger objects sat cluttered around on the floor.

Morley reached for the skull. Fitch slapped his hand away.

"Don't touch nothing." Fitch pointed at the skull staring

up at them. "That could be a wizard's skull, and if you touch it, it might come back to life. Wizards can do that, you know."

Morley yanked back his hand.

Fingers trembling, Fitch finally reached down and picked up the thing he'd come for. It looked just like he'd imagined it must look. The gold and silver work was as beautiful as anything Fitch had ever seen, and he'd seen a lot of fine gold and silver work at the Minister's estate. No Ander had anything to approach the beauty of this.

"That it?" Morley asked.

Fitch ran his fingers over the raised letters in the hilt. It was the one word he could read.

"This is it. The Sword of Truth."

Fitch felt rooted to that spot as he held the magnificent weapon, letting his fingers glide over the wire-wound hilt, the downswept cross guard, the finely wrought gold and silver scabbard. Even the leather baldric was beautifully made, feeling buttery soft between his finger and thumb.

"Well, if you're taking that," Morley said, "what do you think I can take?"

"Nothing," came a voice from behind them.

They both flinched and cried out as one. Together, they spun around.

They both blinked at what they saw, hardly believing their eyes. It was a gorgeous blue-eyed blond woman in a red leather outfit that clung like a second skin. It showed her womanly shape to an extent Fitch had never seen. The low-cut dresses the Ander women wore showed the tops of their breasts, but this outfit, even though it covered everything, somehow seemed to show more. He could see her lean, well-defined muscles flexing as she strode toward them.

"That's not yours," the woman said. "Give it here before you boys get hurt."

Morley didn't like being called a boy anymore, at least not by some lone woman. Fitch could see his powerful muscles tense.

The woman put her fists on her hips. For a woman by

herself with the two of them more than her match, she had a lot of nerve. Fitch didn't think he'd seen many women who could scowl as good as she could, but he wasn't really afraid. He was a man on his own, now, and he didn't have to answer to no one.

Fitch remembered how helpless Claudine Winthrop had been. He remembered how easy it was to hold her helpless. This was a woman, just like Claudine, no more.

"What are you two doing in here?" she asked.

"I guess we could ask you the same," Morley said.

She glared at him and then held her hand out to Fitch. "That doesn't belong to you." She waggled her fingers. "Hand it over before I lose my temper and I end up hurting you."

At the same instant, Fitch and Morley bolted in opposite directions. The woman went for Fitch. Fitch tossed the sword to Morley. Morley, laughing, caught the sword, waving it at the woman, teasing her with it.

Fitch cut around her back and headed toward the door. She lunged for Morley. He tossed the sword over her head and outstretched arms.

The three of them raced across the sunken floor in the center of the room. She dove for Fitch and caught his leg, tripping him. As he went down, he heaved the sword to Morley.

She was up and running before Fitch could roll to his feet. Morley shouldered one of the white marble columns, toppling it across the red carpet before her. The bowl atop the column crashed to the floor, shattering into a thousand shards that skittered across the marble and carpet with a soft chiming, almost musical, tinkling sound.

"You two don't have any idea what you're doing!" she yelled. "Stop it at once! That isn't yours! This is no child's game! You've no right to touch anything in this place! You could be causing great harm! Stop it! Lives are at stake!"

She and Morley danced around the opposite sides of another column. When she lunged for him, he shoved the column toward her. She cried out when the heavy gold vase atop the column tumbled and hit her shoulder. Fitch didn't know if it was pain or rage that caused her to shout.

The three of them serpentined around the columns on both sides of the red carpet, heading ever closer to the door. Fitch and Morley tossed the sword back and forth between them, keeping her off guard. Fitch pushed over one of the columns to slow her and was shocked at how heavy it was. The way Morley shoved them over Fitch had thought they would be easy to topple; they weren't, so he didn't try another.

She was yelling at them to stop destroying the priceless things of magic, but when Morley toppled the one with the inky black bottle atop it, she screamed. The column crashed down. The bottle tumbled through the air.

She dove across the floor, her long blond braid flying out behind as she hit and slid. The bottle bounced through her hands, flipping up, then hit the carpet and rolled, but it didn't break.

By the look on her face, Fitch would have thought it was her own life that was just spared by the bottle not breaking.

She scrambled to her feet and charged for them as they went through the door. Outside, Morley, chuckling, tossed the sword to Fitch as they ran along the edge of the rampart.

"You boys have no idea what is at stake. I need that sword. This is important. It doesn't belong to you. Give it to me, please, and I will let you go."

Morley had that look in his eye, the look like he wanted to hurt her. Hurt her bad. He'd had that look with Claudine Winthrop.

Fitch just wanted the sword, but he could see they were going to have to do something serious to stop her, else she was going to cause them no end of trouble. He wasn't about to give up the sword. Not now, not after everything they'd been through.

"Hey, Fitch," Morley called, "I think it's time you had your turn at a woman. This one's even free. What say I hold her down for you?"

Fitch surely thought she was a good enough looking

woman. And she was the one causing them trouble. It would be her own fault. She wouldn't let them be. She wouldn't mind her own business. She had it coming.

Fitch knew that since he was doing it for the right reasons, for good reasons, he deserved to be the Seeker of Truth. This woman had no right to interfere with that.

Out in the bright sun, her red leather seemed an angrier color. Her face surely was. She looked like someone had lifted her up by her long blond braid, and dunked her in blood.

"I try to do it his way," she muttered to herself. "I try to please him." Fitch thought she might be crazy, standing there, hands on hips, talking to the sky. "And what does it get me? This. Enough. I've had enough of this."

She forced out an angry breath, then pulled free red leather gloves she had tucked over her double strap belt cinching the top of her outfit tight at the waist. The way she drew on the gloves, wiggling her fingers into them, had a frightening finality to it.

"I'm not warning you boys again," she said, this time in a growl that lifted the hair at the back of Fitch's neck. "Give it over, and give it over now."

While she was glaring grimly at Fitch, Morley moved on her. He swung his big fist to punch the side of her head. As hard as he swung, Fitch thought he was going to kill her with the first blow.

The woman didn't even look Morley's way. She caught his fist in the flat of her hand, yanked it around, and in a blink spun under it, twisting his arm around behind him. Her teeth clenched, and she drove his arm up. Fitch was shocked to hear Morley's shoulder let out a sickening pop. Morley cried out. The pain dropped him to his knees.

This woman was like no woman Fitch had ever seen before. Now, she was coming for him. She wasn't running, but striding with a determination that caught Fitch's breath short.

He stood frozen, not knowing what to do. He didn't want to abandon his friend, but his feet wanted to run. He didn't want to give up the sword, either. He blindly groped the crenellated wall behind him as he started backing along it.

Morley was up. He rushed the woman. She just kept coming for Fitch—for the sword. Fitch decided he might have to take the sword out and stab her—in the leg, or something, he speculated. He could wound her.

But then it didn't look like he was going to have to; Morley was closing on her, an enraged bull at full charge. There would be no stopping the big man this time.

Without even turning to the onrushing Morley, she smoothly sidestepped—never taking her glare from Fitch—and brought her arm up, ramming her elbow squarely into Morley's face.

His head snapped back. Blood sprayed out.

Not even breathing hard, she turned and seized Morley's good left hand. With her fingers in his palm and her thumb on the back of his hand, she bent it down at the wrist until Morley's knees were buckling as she backed him toward the wall.

Morley was whimpering like a child, begging her to stop. His other arm was useless. His nose had been flattened horribly. Blood gushed from his face. It had to be all over her, too, but with her red leather, Fitch couldn't tell.

She backed Morley steadily, mercilessly, to the wall. Without a word, she seized him by the throat with her other hand, and, calmly, indifferently, shoved him backward through the notch of a crenellation, out into thin air.

Fitch's jaw dropped. He never expected her to do that—for it to go that far.

Morley screamed his lungs out as he dropped backward down the side of the mountain. Fitch stood frozen, listening to his friend from the flat place of Anderith plummet down the side of a mountain. Morley's scream abruptly ended.

The woman wasn't talking anymore, making any more demands. She was simply coming for Fitch, now. Her blue eyes fixed on him. He knew without doubt that if she caught him, she'd kill him, too.

This was no Claudine Winthrop. This was no woman who was going to call him "sir."

Fitch's feet finally got their way.

If there was one thing about Fitch that was better than Morley and all his muscles, it was that Fitch could run like the wind. Now, he ran like a gale.

A quick glance back shocked him; the woman could run faster. She was tall, and had longer legs. She was going to catch him. If she did, she'd smash his face, just as easily as she smashed Morley's. She'd throw him to his death, too. Or take the sword from him and cut out his heart.

Fitch could feel tears streaming down his cheeks. He'd never run so fast. She was running faster.

He flew down steps, falling more than running. He dove over the side of the landing and down the next flight. Everything was a blur. Stone walls, windows, railings, steps—all flashed by in a smear of light and dark.

Fitch, clutching the Sword of Truth to his chest, sailed through a doorway, caught the edge of the thick door with his free hand, and slammed it shut. As the door was still banging closed in its frame, he toppled a big stone pedestal across the floor behind the door. It was heavier than the white marble columns, but his terror gave him strength.

Just as the granite pedestal hit the floor, she crashed into the heavy oak door. The impact drove the door open a few inches. Dust billowed up. Everything was still for a moment; then the woman let out a dazed groan and Fitch knew she'd been hurt.

Not wasting the chance, he ran on through the Wizard's Keep, closing doors, pushing things over behind them if there was anything handy. He didn't even know if he was going the right way. His lungs burned as he ran, crying for his friend. Fitch could hardly believe it had happened, that Morley was dead. He kept seeing the image over and over in his mind. He almost expected the big dumb fool to catch up and grin and say it was a joke.

The sword in Fitch's arms had cost Morley his life. Fitch

had to wipe at his eyes so he could see. A look over his shoulder showed a long, twisting, empty hallway.

But he could hear doors crashing open. She was coming.

She wasn't going to quit for nothing. She was an avenging spirit come to take his life in return for him removing the Sword of Truth from its place in the Wizard's Keep. He ran on, faster.

Fitch burst out into the sunlight, disoriented for a moment. He twisted around and saw the horses. Three. His and Morley's, and the woman's. Saddlebags with her things hung on the fence.

In order to free his hands, Fitch ducked his head under the sword's baldric, setting the leather strap over his right shoulder and diagonally across his chest to let the weapon hang at his left hip as it was designed. He caught up the reins of all three horses. He seized the saddle of the one closest and sprang up.

With a cry to urge them on, he gave his horse his heels. It was her horse; the stirrups were adjusted too long and his feet wouldn't reach them, so he hugged his legs to the horse's belly and hung on for his life as the big animal galloped through the paddock gate with the other two horses being pulled along behind.

As the horses hit the road at full speed, the woman in red stumbled out of the Keep, blood all over the side of her face. She clutched a black bottle in one hand. It was the bottle from back in the Keep, the bottle that had fallen but not broken.

He bent forward over the horse's neck as it raced down the road. Fitch glimpsed back over his shoulder. The woman was running down the road after them. He had her horse. She was on foot, a long way from another horse.

Fitch tried to push thoughts of Morley from his mind. He had the Sword of Truth. Now he could go home and use it to help him prove he didn't rape Beata, and that he did what he did to Claudine Winthrop to protect the Minister from her ruinous lies.

Fitch looked over his shoulder again. She was a lot farther

back, but still running. He knew he dare not stop for anything. She was coming. She was coming after him and she wasn't going to stop for anything or anyone.

She wasn't going to give up. She wasn't going to rest. She wasn't going to stop. If she caught him, she'd tear his heart out.

Fitch thumped his heels against the horse, urging her to run faster.

CHAPTER 55

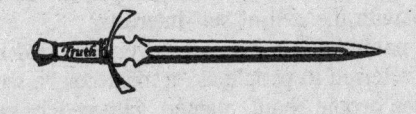

KAHLAN BENT OVER RICHARD'S shoulder and rubbed his back as he sat at the little table.

"Anything?" she asked.

He swiped his hair back from his forehead. "I'm not sure, yet." He tapped the vellum scroll. "But there's something about this. . . . It has more specific information than most of Ander's writings back at the library at the Minister's estate."

Kahlan smiled. "I hope so. I'm going to stretch my legs, check on the others."

A sound of assent eased from deep in his throat as he studied the scroll.

They had spent two days at the library in the estate, going over everything there about or from Joseph Ander. It was mostly his writings about himself, and what he believed to be previously undiscovered insights into human behavior.

He went on at great length about how his observations were more relevant to the course of human events than were those of anyone who had come before him.

A lot of the reading was accompanied by raised eyebrows. It was almost like listening to an adolescent who thought he knew everything, and failed to see how genuinely ignorant he was. One was left to silently read his words, helpless to correct some of the more grandiose declarations that any adult should have long before outgrown.

Joseph Ander believed he had the perfect place where he could shepherd people in the ideal life, without any exterior forces being able to upset his "balanced community," as he called it. He explained that he realized he no longer needed the support or advice of others—meaning the wizards at the Keep in Aydindril, Richard believed—and that he had even come to realize such outside contamination was profoundly harmful because it corrupted the people in his collective community with the evil of self-interest.

Not one name but his own was ever recorded by Joseph Ander. He referred to people as "a man," or "a woman," or said that "the people" built, planted, gathered, or worshiped.

Joseph Ander seemed to have found the perfect place for himself: a land where his powers exceeded anyone else's, and where the people all adored him. Richard believed Joseph Ander was misinterpreting fear as adoration. In any event, the situation allowed the man to establish himself as an esteemed and celebrated leader—a virtual king—with unquestioned authority over a society where no one else was allowed to display individualism or exert superiority.

Joseph Ander believed he had established a blissful land where suffering, greed, and envy had been eliminated— where cooperation replaced avarice. Purification of the culture—public executions—brought this harmonious state of the collective community into balance. He called it "burning away the chaff."

Joseph Ander had come to be a tyrant. People professed their belief in him and lived by his ways, or they died.

Richard squeezed Kahlan's hand before she turned to go.

The little building wasn't big enough for the others to fit inside. It was only big enough for the little table and Joseph Ander's chair, which, to the horror of the old man whose duty it was to watch over the priceless artifacts, Richard was occupying. The old man didn't have the courage to refuse Richard's request.

Richard wanted to sit in Joseph Ander's chair to get a feel for the man. Kahlan had enough of a feel for the totalitarian despot.

Down the path a ways, people from the town of Westbrook were gathered. They stared in awe as Kahlan lifted her hand in a wave of acknowledgment. Many went to a knee simply because she had looked their way.

Soldiers had already brought word of the approaching vote, as they had carried word to many a place. With Richard and Kahlan here, the people hoped to hear them speak on the subject of joining with the D'Haran Empire as most of the rest of the Midlands was. To these people, the Midlands, even though they were part of it, seemed a strange and distant land. They lived their lives in this one small place, most hearing little word, other than rumor, of the outside world.

D'Haran guards gently kept the crowd at a distance while Richard viewed the artifacts of their luminary founder and namesake to their land. Baka Tau Mana blade masters backed the guards. Richard had told the soldiers to act friendly and "be nice."

Walking down the path, Kahlan spotted Du Chaillu alone, off the path, resting on a bench made of a split log and set in the shade beneath a spreading cedar. Kahlan had come to respect the spirit woman's firm resolution. She seemed to have righteously insisted on coming for no reason other than her determination to help Richard—her "husband," the *Caharin* to her people. Kahlan, after Du Chaillu had helped him that day he fell from his horse, was less dismayed to have her along.

While Du Chaillu had several times reminded Richard that as his wife she would be available should he desire her, she never made any advances on behalf of herself. In a bizarre way, it seemed nothing more than her being polite. It appeared that while Du Chaillu would be perfectly happy to serve and submit in any and every capacity as his wife, she offered services more out of duty and respect for her people's laws than from personal desires.

Du Chaillu worshiped what Richard represented. She did not worship Richard, as such. While Richard found little comfort in that, Kahlan did.

As long as it stayed that way, Du Chaillu and Kahlan observed an uneasy truce. Kahlan still didn't entirely trust the woman, not when Richard was the object of her attention—duty or otherwise.

For her part, Du Chaillu viewed Kahlan, in her role as leader of her people, in her magic, and as wife to Richard, not as a superior, but simply as an equal. Kahlan was ashamed to admit to herself that in all of it, she was irritated by that more than anything.

"Mind if I sit with you?"

Du Chaillu leaned back, stretching herself, to rest her shoulders against the tree. She held a hand toward the empty spot beside her, granting the request. Kahlan smoothed her white Mother Confessor's dress behind her knees and sat down.

Tucked in between trees in a little side area of the path, they were invisible to passersby. It was an intimate spot, more appropriate for two lovers than for the two wives of the same man.

"Are you all right, Du Chaillu? You look a bit . . . frazzled."

Du Chaillu puzzled at Kahlan's expression of concern. At last she smiled as she understood its meaning. She took Kahlan's hand and put it against her firm, round belly, pressing the hand flat and holding it tight with both of hers. The woman was getting quite large.

Kahlan felt the life move in Du Chaillu. Felt the child move.

Du Chaillu smiled proudly. Kahlan withdrew the hand.

Kahlan nested her hands in her lap. She stared off at the gathering clouds. This was not the way it was to be. She always thought it would be joyous.

"It displeases you?"

"What? No . . . not at all. It's a marvelous thing."

Du Chaillu's fingers hooked Kahlan's chin, pulling her face back around.

"Kahlan, you have tears?"

"No. It's nothing."

"You are unhappy, because I have a child?"

"No, Du Chaillu, no, I'm not unhappy—"

"You are unhappy because I have a child, and you do not?"

Kahlan held her tongue, lest she lose control of herself.

"You should not be unhappy, Kahlan. You will have a child. Someday. It will happen."

"Du Chaillu . . . I'm pregnant."

Du Chaillu put a hand against the small of her back and stretched. "Really? I am surprised. Jiaan has not told me that you and our husband have been together in that way."

Kahlan was shocked to know that Du Chaillu would be getting such reports. In a way, she was relieved that there had been nothing to report, and in a way she wished there had been, just to vex her competition as a wife.

"Our husband must be very happy. He seems to like little ones. He will be a good—"

"Richard doesn't know. You must promise me, Du Chaillu, that you will not tell him."

The woman frowned. "Why would I make you such a promise?"

Kahlan leaned a little closer. "Because I'm the one who made Richard let you come with us. Because I'm the one who said you could stay with us even after our men came. You had promised Richard you would leave when our men came, but then you wanted to stay with us, and I made him let you. Remember?"

Du Chaillu shrugged. "If you wish it, then I will not tell him. Anyway, you should keep the secret and surprise him in your own time." She gave Kahlan a smile. "The *Caharin*'s wives must stick together."

"Thank you," Kahlan whispered.

"But when . . . ?"

"On our wedding night. When we were with the Mud People, just before you came along."

"Ah. That would be why I did not hear of it."

Kahlan let it pass.

"But why do you not wish to have Richard know? He would be happy."

Kahlan shook her head. "No, he wouldn't. It is going to be big trouble." Kahlan lifted the necklace with the small stone. "This was given to us by a witch woman, to keep us from conceiving a child for now. It's a long story, but for now, we must not have one or we will have trouble."

"So then why are you with child?"

"Because of the chimes. Magic has failed. But before we knew it . . . Well, we didn't know the necklace wouldn't work on the night we were married. The magic was supposed to keep us from conceiving a child, but its magic had failed. This wasn't supposed to happen."

Kahlan had to bite the inside of her cheek to help keep the tears back.

"Richard would still be happy," Du Chaillu offered in a consoling whisper.

Kahlan shook her head. "You don't understand everything involved. His life would be in great danger if people found out. The witch woman has vowed to kill this child, but more, I know her; she will decide that to prevent future trouble she will have to kill me or Richard."

Du Chaillu thought it over. "Well, soon will be this foolish vote, where people tell him what he should already know, that he is the *Caharin*. After that, everything will be all right. Then you could go into hiding to have the baby." The spirit woman put a hand on Kahlan's shoulder. "You will come with me, back to the Baka Tau Mana. We will protect you until you have the *Caharin*'s child. We will protect you and your child."

Kahlan drew a steady breath to prevent a sob. "Thank you, Du Chaillu. You are a kind person. But that wouldn't help. I must do something to get rid of it. Find an herb woman, or a midwife. I need to shed this child before it's too late."

Du Chaillu reached out and took Kahlan's hand again and put it back over the baby. Kahlan squeezed shut her eyes as she felt the child moving.

"You cannot do that to the life in you, Kahlan. Not to the life come of your love. You must not. It would be worse."

Richard came out of the little building, holding the scroll. "Kahlan?" he called. She could see him through a gap in the trees, but he didn't see her on the bench.

Kahlan turned to Du Chaillu. "You gave your word you will keep this secret."

Du Chaillu smiled and touched Kahlan's cheek the way a grandmother might compassionately touch a grandchild. Kahlan knew she had just been touched not by Du Chaillu, Richard's first wife, but by Du Chaillu, spirit woman to the Baka Tau Mana.

Kahlan rose, at the same time putting on her Confessor's face. Richard spotted her and hurried over.

He looked back and forth between her and Du Chaillu. Finally, he disregarded his puzzlement and showed her the scroll.

"I knew it had something to do with the word 'school.' "

"What?" Kahlan asked.

"The Dominie Dirtch. Look here." He tapped the scroll. "It says he didn't fear intervention from jealous colleagues since he was"—Richard ran a finger under the words as he read aloud—" 'protected by the demons.' "

Kahlan didn't have the slightest idea what he was talking about. "And this is important, because . . . ?"

Richard was reading the scroll again. "What? Oh, yes. Well, when you first told me the name, Dominie Dirtch, I thought it was High D'Haran, but I couldn't figure out its meaning. It's one of those tricky multidimensional phrases I've told you about.

"Anyway, 'Dominie' is a word having to do with schooling, as in teaching, or training, or, more important, controlling. Now that I've seen this other part, it's jogged my mind to the translation of the thing.

" 'Dominie Dirtch' means 'Schooling the Demons.' "

Kahlan could only stare for a moment. "But . . . what does that mean?"

Richard threw up his arms. "I don't know, but it's all coming together, I'm sure."

"Well, all right," Kahlan said.

He frowned at her. "What's wrong? Your face is, I don't know . . . funny-looking."

"Well, thank you."

He turned red. "I didn't mean it looks bad."

Kahlan waved a hand before herself. "No, it's nothing. I'm just tired. We've been doing so much hard traveling and endless talking to people."

"Do you know a place called the Ovens?"

"Ovens." Kahlan frowned in thought. "Yes, I remember the place. It's not far from here, in fact. Up a little higher above the Nareef Valley."

"How far?"

Kahlan shrugged one shoulder. "We could be there in a couple of hours, by midafternoon, if it's important for some reason."

"Ander talks about it in these scrolls. He obliquely mentions it in conjunction with the demons—the Dominie Dirtch. That was the passage where I put the two together."

Richard looked down the path to the group of people gathered, waiting patiently. "After we talk to these people, I would like to go up there and have a look around."

Kahlan took his arm. "It's a pretty place. I wouldn't mind seeing it again. Now, let's go tell these people why we need them to mark their circle to join us."

The expectant faces were mostly Haken. Most worked on farms around the small town of Westbrook. Like all the people come to see them as they had traveled around Anderith, these people were concerned and worried. They knew change was in the wind. To most people, change was dangerous.

Rather than addressing them coldly, Richard walked among them, asking their names, smiling at their children, trailing a hand or a thumb along the cheek of the young ones. Because this was really the way Richard was, because it was sincere and not an act, within a matter of minutes he had a gaggle of children around him. Mothers smiled as he touched young heads, dark-haired and redheaded alike. The worried creases in the foreheads of fathers, too, loosened.

"Good people of Anderith," Richard began as he stood among them, "the Mother Confessor and I have come to talk with you, not as rulers, but as your humble champions. We do not come to dictate, but to help you understand the choices ahead of us all, and the chance you have to decide for yourselves what your future will be."

He beckoned with an arm, and Kahlan gently worked her way through the throng of smiling children to join him at his side. She had thought they might fear a big man like Richard, dressed as he was in a black and gold outfit that made him look all the more imposing, but many pressed up against him as if he was a favorite uncle.

It was the white dress of the Mother Confessor they feared, warned as most in the Midlands were from birth of the Mother Confessor and her power. They made way for her, doing their best not to come in contact with her white dress as they tried to remain close to Richard. Kahlan ached to have them crowd around her the way they crowded around Richard, but she understood. She had a lifetime of understanding.

"The Mother Confessor and I were married because we love each other. We also love the people of the Midlands and D'Hara. Just as we wanted to be joined in marriage so that we could look forward to life together, we want the people of Anderith to be joined with us and the other people of the Midlands, to go with us into a strong and secure future, one which provides you and your children hope for a better life.

"Tyranny is marching up from the Old World. The Imperial Order would enslave you. They offer you no choice but to submit or to die. Only if you join with us will you have a chance to be safe.

"The Mother Confessor and I believe that if we join the people of the Midlands and D'Hara together, all standing together as one to uphold our freedom, we can repel this threat to our homes and security . . . and to our children's future.

"If we timidly submit to tyranny, we will never have the chance to test our wings. Never again will our spirits lift proudly on the winds of hope. No one will have the chance to raise a family in peace, or be able to dream their children will do better, or achieve more.

"If we do not stand against the Imperial Order, we will live under the shadow of slavery. Once that happens, we will descend forever into the darkness of oppression.

"This is why we have come to speak with you. We need you to stand with us, to stand with peace-loving people, with those who know the future can be bright and filled with hope.

"We need you to join with us and mark a circle to complete our alliance for freedom."

Kahlan listened, as she had for weeks, as Richard spoke from his heart about what it would mean to join with them in the cause of freedom.

At first, the people were tense and cautious. Before long, Richard's nature had won most over. He had them laughing, and then brought them to the verge of tears as he pulled forth their yearning for the freedom to chance greatness by showing them the simple power they could have if they and their children were permitted to learn, to read.

At first, this made people nervous, until Richard put it in terms they could understand: a letter written to a parent living elsewhere, or to a child gone in search of a better life. He made them understand the value of knowledge and how it could make their life better in ways that had meaning to

636

them with opportunities for better work, or accomplishing more in the work they had.

"But the Imperial Order will not allow you to learn, because knowledge is dangerous to oppressors. To those who would dominate you, knowledge must be crushed, because people who understand are people who will stand against the unfairness of the elite.

"I would have everyone learn, so they can decide for themselves what they want. That is the difference: I trust you to learn, to do better, to strive for your goals, simple and great. The Imperial Order trusts not, but will dictate everything.

"Together, we will have one land, with one set of laws that make it safe for all people, where no one man—be he magistrate or Minister or emperor—is above the law. Only when all must bow to the same law is every person free.

"I came into this not to rule, but to uphold the principle of freedom. My own father, Darken Rahl, was a dictator who ruled through intimidation, torture, and murder. Not even he was above the law I hope us all to live by. I took over his rule so that he could no longer abuse his people. I lead free people—I do not rule subjects.

"I don't wish to tell you how to live, I instead wish to have all of you live in peace and safety the lives you choose for yourselves. I would like nothing more for myself and the Mother Confessor—my wife—than to raise a family together in peace and security with little need to devote myself to matters of ruling.

"I would ask you to mark a circle, and join with us, for your own sake, for the sake of those to come."

Dalton leaned a shoulder against the corner of the building and folded his arms as he listened. Director Prevot, from the Office of Cultural Amity, spoke from a balcony above a large crowd in one of the city squares. He had been going on for quite a while.

The crowd, mostly Haken, had gathered to hear of the coming events. Rumors were coursing through the city. People were frightened. They had come, mostly, not to see how they might avoid a calamity, but to see if they need bother to worry about the rumors.

Dalton viewed the situation with concern.

"Shall you suffer while the special few are rewarded?" Director Prevot called out to the crowd. They answered with a collective "No."

"Shall you be worked to death while the chosen ones from D'Hara only grow richer?"

Again the crowd shouted, "No!"

"Shall we let our good works of helping all Hakens rise above their nature be cast aside by this one man? Shall we allow our people to again be led astray by the cruel deception of education?"

The crowd shouted their agreement with Director Prevot, some waving their hats, as Dalton had instructed them to do. There were perhaps fifty of his Haken messengers in the crowd, dressed in their old clothes, doing their best to pump emotion into the responses to Director Prevot's speech.

There were people caught up in the passion of the words, no doubt, but for the most part the crowd silently watched, judging if their own lives would be altered by what they heard. Most people weighed matters on a scale, with their life on one side, and the events before them on the other side. Most people were satisfied with the way things were, so only if the events on the other side of the scale threatened to outweigh or change their lives did they become concerned.

Dalton was not pleased. These people, while agreeing, did not see the events on the other side of the scales as much affecting their life.

Dalton knew they had a problem.

The message was getting out, but it was falling on little more than indifferent ears.

"He is making a lot of good points," Teresa said.

Dalton hugged her shoulders. "Yes, he is."

"I think the man is right. The poor Hakens will only be hurt if we don't continue to see to their well-being. They aren't prepared to handle the cruelty of life on their own."

Dalton's gaze moved among the people standing like statues as they watched the Director pour out his passion.

"Yes, darling, you're right. We must do more to help the people."

Dalton realized, then, what was missing, and what he must do.

CHAPTER 56

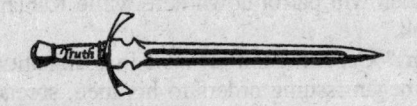

"No," RICHARD SAID TO Du Chaillu.

She folded her arms in smoldering anger. The way her big round belly stuck out made her pose look almost humorous.

Richard leaned toward her and lowered his voice. "Du Chaillu, can't you understand I would like to be alone with my—with Kahlan, for just a little while? Please?"

Du Chaillu's anger faltered. Her frown melted.

"Oh, I see. You want to be intimate with your other wife. This is good. It has been a long time."

"That's not—" Richard put his fists on his hips. "And just how would you know, anyway?"

She didn't answer his question, but smiled. "Well, all right then. If you promise not to take too long."

He wanted to say it would take as long as it took, but he feared what her answer might be. Richard straightened and said simply, "We promise."

Captain Meiffert, a big, blond-headed D'Haran officer in charge of the troops sent to escort Richard and Kahlan to Anderith, didn't like the idea of them being alone any more than did Du Chaillu, but he was more circumspect in expressing his objections. General Reibisch had apparently told the man he could speak his mind to the Lord Rahl, if it was an important matter, without fear of punishment.

"Lord Rahl, we would be too far away to respond should you need us. . . . To help protect the Mother Confessor," he added as an afterthought, thinking it might sway Richard's decision.

"Thank you, Captain. There is only this one trail up there. Since no one knew where we were headed, no one could be lying in wait. It isn't far and we won't be gone long. You and your men will patrol down here while Kahlan and I go have a look."

"Yes, sir," Captain Meiffert said in resignation. He immediately began issuing orders to his men, spreading them out at stations and sending some on scout.

Richard turned to the two messengers who had come from General Reibisch. "Tell the general I'm pleased with the speed he's making, and I'm pleased to know he believes he can make it before Jagang's forces arrive. Tell him the same orders he already has are still in effect; I want him to stand off."

Nearly every day messengers came and went, entering past different Dominie Dirtch at the border so as to be less noticed. Richard had given General Reibisch orders to stay well to the north, well beyond Jagang's screen of scouts, sentries, and spies. If it came to a fight, surprise was one of the most valuable elements the D'Haran army could possess. The general agreed with that much of it, but was loath to leave Richard with only a thousand men in potentially hostile territory.

Richard had explained, in the letters he'd written the man,

that while he understood the general's concern, they needed to keep his force hidden until and unless they were called. Richard had explained in gruesome detail the horrific and futile death awaiting them at the border if the army tried to breach the Dominie Dirtch. Until they won the agreement of the Anderith people, they dared not approach their border in force.

Moreover, Richard didn't trust Minister Chanboor. The man's tongue was too smooth. Truth didn't wear a tongue smooth; lies did.

The Dominie Dirtch were a spider's web waiting to claim the careless. The look of easy conquest could be a trap to lure the D'Haran force to their death. More than anything, Richard feared all those brave young men being slaughtered before the Dominie Dirtch. Especially when he knew such sacrifice could accomplish nothing. They would die and the Dominie Dirtch would still stand untouched.

General Reibisch had written back, promising Richard that, once they were in place to the north, they would charge south without pause should Richard call upon them, but he promised to stay put until called.

"Yes, Lord Rahl," the taller messenger said as he clapped a fist to his heart, "I will tell the general your words." They both wheeled their horses and trotted off down the road.

Richard checked that his bow and quiver were secure before he climbed into his saddle. Kahlan flashed him her special smile as they turned their horses up the trail. She, too, Richard knew, was relieved to be alone at last, if for only a brief ride up a side trail.

It was wearing to have people constantly around them. When they held hands, eyes took it in. If they did so in front of people while speaking to them, Richard could tell by the looks that it was news that would visit a thousand ears before a few days passed. He knew by the unblinking stares that it would be spoken of for years to come. At least it was a favorable thing for people to gossip about. Better they should talk about the married Lord Rahl and Mother Confessor holding hands than something awful.

Richard watched Kahlan sway in the saddle, spellbound by the taper of her body down to her waist, the flare of her hips. He thought she had just about the most alluring shape he had ever seen. He sometimes found it remarkable to think a woman like that would love him, a man who had grown up in a little place in Hartland.

Richard missed his home. He guessed those feelings had surfaced because the forest trail up the mountain reminded him so much of places he knew. There were hills and mountains to the west of where he grew up, remote places, that were much like the forests and mountains in which they found themselves.

He wished they could return to visit his home in Hartland. He had seen remarkable things since leaving the autumn before, but he guessed none held your heart like the place you grew up.

When the trail passed near a steep decline affording a view, Richard looked off to the northwest, through gaps in the peaks. They were probably closer to where he had grown up than they had been since he left. They had come across those same mountains into the Midlands, through the boundary while it had still been up, at a place called Kings' Port. It wasn't very far to the northwest.

Despite how close it might be, because of the weight of his responsibilities, home in Hartland was now a very distant place.

Besides the responsibility of being Lord Rahl and having everyone depending on him, there was Jagang, who, given half a chance, would enslave the New World as he had the Old. People depended on Richard for everything from the bond that protected them from the dream walker, to pulling everyone together into one force to stand against Jagang's huge armies.

Sometimes, when he thought about it, it seemed he was living someone else's life. Sometimes he felt like a fraud, as if people were one day going to wake up and say, "Now, wait a minute, this Lord Rahl fellow is just a woods guide named Richard. And we're listening to him? We're following him into war?"

And then there were the chimes. Richard and Kahlan were inextricably involved with the chimes. They were responsible for the chimes being in the world of life. Even though it was unintentional, they had brought forth the chimes of death.

In their travels around Anderith to talk to people, they had heard stories of the strange deaths. The chimes were greatly enjoying their visit to the world of life. They were having a marvelous time killing people.

In response to the danger, people had fallen back to old superstitions. In some places people gathered together to pay homage to the evil spirits loosed upon the world. Gifts of food and wine were left in clearings in the woods, or in fallow fields. Some folks thought mankind had violated moral bounds, had become too corrupt, and the avenging spirits had been sent by the Creator to punish the world.

Some people left gifts of stones in the center of roads, and piled yet more rocks at crossroads. No one could explain to Richard exactly why, and were annoyed that he would question the old ways. Some put dead flowers out in front of their door at midnight. Good-luck charms were in great demand.

The chimes killed anyway.

The one thing that made the weight of it all tolerable was Kahlan. She made the effort of the struggle bearable. For her, he would endure anything.

Kahlan raised an arm. "Just up there."

Richard dismounted with her. Most of the trees were spruce or pine. Richard cast about until he found a young silver-leafed maple and tied the reins of their horses to a low branch. Tying reins to pine or spruce, or worse, a balsam, resulted often as not in sticky reins.

Richard looked up when he heard a snort. Not far off, a horse, its ears perked forward, watched them. Grass hung from each side of its mouth, but it had stopped chewing.

"Well, hello girl," Richard called.

Wary, the horse tossed its head and backed a few steps to add to its distance. When Richard tried to get closer, it backed away more yet, so he halted. A creamy chestnut color, the horse had an odd leggy splotch of black on its rump. When Richard called to it again, trying to coax it closer, it turned and ran.

"I wonder what that's about," he said to Kahlan.

Kahlan held out her hand in invitation. Richard took it.

"I don't know. Maybe someone's horse has gotten away. It seems to be uninterested in having anything to do with us, though."

"I suppose," Richard said as he let her lead him by the hand.

"This is the only way in," she told him as they walked along the lake shore, around a small clump of spruce.

The clouds had been building all day, threatening thunderstorms. Now, as they walked out onto a nub of rock sticking up at the end of the flat spit of land, the sun emerged between the towering, billowing clouds.

It was a beautiful sight, a shaft of warm sunlight breaking through amber clouds, slanting down between the mountains to touch the still lake. Across the way, water tumbled over a prominence of rock, sending up into the warm air a drifting mist that sparkled in the sunlight above the golden water. Richard took a deep breath, savoring the sweet aroma of woods and lake. It was almost like home.

"This is the place." She gestured. "Up there, higher up, is the desolate place where the paka plant grows, and the gambit moth lives. These pure waters come from that poisoned area."

The air shimmered in the afternoon light. "It's beautiful. I could stay here forever. I almost feel like I should be scouting new trails."

They stood for a while, hand in hand, savoring the view.

"Richard, I just wanted to tell you that the last couple of weeks as we've talked to people . . . I've really been proud of you. Proud of the way you've shown people hope for the future.

"Whatever happens, I just want you to know that. That I'm proud of the way you've handled it."

He frowned. "You sound like you don't think we'll win."

She shrugged. "It doesn't matter. What will be will be. People don't always do what's right. Sometimes they don't recognize evil. Sometimes people choose evil because it suits them or because they're afraid, or because they think they will get something for themselves out of it.

"The most important thing is that we've done our best, and you've shown people the truth. You put their well-being, their safety, before all else, so if we do triumph, it will be for the right reasons. You've given them the chance to prove their heart."

"We'll win." Richard gazed out over the still water. "People will see the truth in it."

"I hope so."

He put his arm around her neck and kissed the top of her head. He sighed with the pleasure of the mountain lake, the quiet.

"There are places deep in the mountains to the west of where I grew up that I don't think anyone but me has ever visited. Places where the water falls from the rocks high overhead, higher than here, and makes rainbows in the afternoon air. And after you swim in the clear pools, you can curl up on the rocks behind the waterfall and watch the world through the falling water.

"I've often dreamed of taking you there."

Kahlan slipped her arm around his waist. "Someday, Richard, we'll visit your special places."

As they stood close, watching the waterfall, Richard was reluctant to break the spell of the dream, especially to talk about their purpose, but at last he did.

"So, why is it called the Ovens?"

Kahlan lifted her chin to point. "Behind the waterfall is a cave that's warm. Sometimes hot, I'm told."

"I wonder why Joseph Ander mentioned the place?"

Kahlan rested a hand on his shoulder. "Maybe even Joseph Ander appreciated a beautiful place."

"Maybe," he mumbled as he searched the scene for a sign of why the wizard would have been interested in this spot. Richard didn't think much of Joseph Ander's sensibilities or that he had a keen appreciation of such natural beauty. While the man spoke at length about the beauty of nature, it was always in regard to the orderly makeup of a society.

Richard noted that all the rock of the mountains around them was a peculiar greenish gray, except the rock of the cliff across the lake, where the waterfall was. That rock was darker. Not a lot, but it was definitely different. It had more gray than green in it, probably because the grain of the granite had black flecks, although from the distance, it was hard to tell.

Richard raised his arm, pointing across the lake to the wall from which the water cascaded in a majestic downward arc.

"Look at that rock, and tell me what you think of it."

Kahlan, her white Mother Confessor's dress glowing in the sunlight, almost looked like Richard's dream-image of a good spirit. She blinked at him.

"What do you mean? It's a rock."

"I know, but look at it. Tell me what strikes you about it."

She looked at the cliff and back at him. "It's a big rock."

"No, come on, be serious."

Kahlan sighed and studied the cliff for a time. She looked around at the mountains, especially the nearest to the left a little, the one rising up so prominently from the water's edge.

"Well," she said at last, "it's darker than the rock of the mountains around here."

"Good. What else strikes you about it?"

She studied the wall a while longer. "It's an unusual color. I've seen it before."

She suddenly looked up at him. "The Dominie Dirtch."

646

Richard smiled. "That's what I think, too. The Dominie Dirtch have that same shade of color as that rock over there, but none of the mountains around have it."

Her face screwed up in an incredulous frown. "Are you saying that the Dominie Dirtch were cut from this stone—way up here in the mountains—and hauled all the way down to where they are today?"

Richard shrugged. "Could be, I guess, although I don't know much about moving stonework on such a large scale. I studied the Dominie Dirtch; they looked to be carved of one piece of rock. They weren't assembled. At least the one we saw."

"Then . . . what?"

"Joseph Ander was a wizard, and the wizards of his time were able to do things even Zedd would find astounding. Perhaps Joseph simply used this rock as a starting place."

"What do you mean? How?"

"I don't know. I don't know as much about magic as you—maybe you could tell me. But what if he simply took a small rock from here for each Dominie Dirtch and then when he got to where they are today, made them big."

"Made them big?"

Richard opened his hands in a helpless gesture. "I don't know. Used magic to make the rock grow, or even used the structure of the grain in the rock as a sort of guide to reproduce it with Additive Magic into the Dominie Dirtch."

"I was thinking you were going to come up with something silly," Kahlan said. "That actually makes sense, as far as I know about magic."

Richard was relieved not to have embarrassed himself. "I think I'll take a swim over to the cave, and see what's there."

"Nothing, from what I learned. Just a hot cave. It doesn't go in far—maybe twenty feet."

"Well, I don't particularly like caves, but I guess it can't hurt to go have a look."

Richard pulled off his shirt. He turned to the water.

"Aren't you going to take off your pants?"

Richard glanced back to see her sly grin.

"I thought I'd wash the smell of horse off them."

"Oh," Kahlan said in exaggerated disappointment.

Smiling, Richard turned back to the water to jump in. Just before he could, a raven came screeching down at him. Richard had to leap back lest the big black bird hit him.

Arm extended behind him, Richard backed Kahlan off the rock.

The bird cawed. The loud cry echoed off the mountains. The raven swooped down before them again, narrowly missing Richard's head. Gaining height, the bird circled. The air whistled through its feathers as it dove at them, driving them back from the water.

"Is that bird crazy?" Kahlan asked. "Maybe it's protecting a nest? Or do all ravens behave like that?"

Richard had a grip on her arm, ushering her back to the trees. "Ravens are intelligent birds, and they will protect their nest, but they can be odd, too. I fear this one is more than a raven."

"More? What do you mean?"

The bird settled on a branch and ruffled its glossy black feathers, looking pleased with itself, as ravens were wont to do.

Richard took his shirt when she held it out. "I'd say it's a chime."

Even at the distance, the bird seemed to hear him. It flapped its wings, hopping back and forth on the branch, looking quite agitated.

"Remember at the library? The raven outside the window, making such a fuss?"

"Dear spirits," she breathed in worry. "Do you think this could be the same one? You think it followed us all this way?"

Richard glanced back at her. "What if it's a chime, and heard us, and came up here to wait for us?"

Kahlan now looked genuinely frightened. "What should we do?"

They reached their horses. Richard yanked his bow off

the saddle. He pulled a steel-tipped arrow from the quiver.

"I think I should kill it."

The instant Richard came out from behind the horse, the bird spotted the bow and leaped—almost flinched—into the air with a loud squawk, as if it hadn't expected him to resort to a weapon.

When Richard nocked the arrow, the bird took wing, fleeing with frantic calls and screeches.

"Well," Richard murmured, "wasn't that weird."

"At least we now know it was a chime. The one you shot back at the Mud People's village—the chicken that wasn't a chicken—must have let the other chimes know."

Perplexed, Richard shook his head. "I guess."

"Richard, I don't want you swimming that lake. There could be chimes waiting in it. It would be foolish to swim when the chimes are loose."

"But they seem afraid of me."

She put her hand on the side of his neck to keep his gaze.

"What if they're just lulling you into overconfidence, and want to get you out into the middle of deep water? Can you imagine? Zedd told us to stay away from water."

She rubbed her arms, looking suddenly chilled.

"Richard, please, let's get out of here? There's something about this place . . ."

Richard threw on his shirt and then drew her close.

"I think you're right. There's no need to push our luck, not after a run-in with that raven-that-isn't-a-raven. Besides, Du Chaillu would be so angry we got killed she'd have her baby before it was time."

Kahlan clutched his shirt in her fists. She had a suddenly stricken look. "Richard . . . do you think we could . . ."

"Could what?"

She released his shirt and patted his chest. "Could get out of here."

"I think we should."

They rushed back, both now eager to be away from the lake. He helped her up onto her horse. "I think we found what we came for, anyway—the rock the Domine Dirtch was made from. I think that we need to change our plans."

"What do you mean?"

"I think we better get back to Fairfield and look through all those books again, in the light of what we now know."

"But what about the vote? The places we've yet to visit?"

"We were going to have to divide up the men anyway and send them out to watch over the voting and counting and then return the results to Fairfield. We can send them now and have the men speak to the people in each place first. There are men among them I would trust to speak for us. They've heard what we've had to say enough times.

"We might as well divide them up here and get them on their way while we get back to the estate. Besides, we wouldn't do wrong to see to making sure we convince all the people in Fairfield to vote to join us."

Kahlan nodded. "Our first responsibility is the chimes. It won't do us any good to win the vote if the chimes kill everyone."

Richard's eye was caught by something. He swung down from his saddle and tossed Kahlan the reins to his horse. He crossed the grass back to the clump of spruce.

"What is it?" Kahlan called, eager to be off.

Richard lifted a drying bough. "A saddle. Someone's left their things here, and covered them to keep them dry."

"Probably from that horse we saw," she said.

"Maybe it belongs to a trapper, or something," Richard said. "But it looks to have been here for a while."

"Well, unless you plan on stealing somebody's things, Richard, let's get out of here."

When the raven let out a call, Richard hurried back to his horse. "Just seems strange, that's all."

As they started down the trail, Richard looked over his shoulder. He saw several ravens circling far up in the sky. He didn't know which one was the raven-that-wasn't-a-raven. Maybe they all were.

He took his bow from its place on the saddle and hooked it over his shoulder instead.

CHAPTER 57

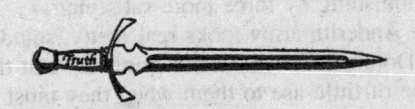

DALTON GAZED OUT THE window of his office as he listened to Stein reporting the number and location of Imperial Order soldiers now stationed as special Anderith guard troops inside Anderith. The Dominie Dirtch were as good as in Jagang's hands. Should Lord Rahl bring his forces—if he even had any close enough—toward Anderith, he would quickly be a leader without an army to lead.

"The emperor also sent word that he wishes me to personally express, on his behalf, his appreciation for the efficient cooperation he has been receiving. From my men's reports, the Minister looks to have done a remarkable job of taking the teeth out of the Anderith army. They will present even less of an obstacle than we thought."

Dalton looked back over his shoulder, but saw no smirk on the man's face. He put his boots up on Dalton's desk and leaned back in his chair to clean his fingernails with a dagger. Stein looked contented.

Dalton reached over and picked up the useless but valuable little book the woman had brought up from the library, the book once belonging to Joseph Ander. He set it on the other side of his desk so Stein's boots wouldn't damage it.

From what Teresa reported to him, Dalton thought Stein

should have every reason to be contented, what with the number of women living their daydreams by tattling to eager ears the raw excitement they had found in the bed of the foreign savage. The more outrageously he treated them, the more delighted they were to gossip about it.

With the number of women offering themselves willingly, Dalton found it remarkable the man would so frequently still turn his lust on the unwilling. He guessed Stein found the thrill of vanquishing by force more satisfying.

"Yes, the Anderith army looks real pretty, standing there behind the Dominie Dirtch." Stein grinned. "But their false pride will be of little use to them when they must meet the true face of war."

"We have kept our part of the bargain."

"Believe me, Campbell, I know the worth of you and the Minister. Farming may be less glamorous than conquest, but without food, an army grinds to a halt. None of us wishes to take up the pastime of tending the land, but we wish to continue eating. We understand your worth in knowing how to keep the system going. You will be a valuable asset to our cause.

"And Emperor Jagang wishes me to assure you he looks forward to rewarding such good works, once he arrives."

Dalton kept the problems to himself. "When might we expect his arrival?"

"Soon," Stein said, dismissing further detail with a shrug. "But he is concerned about the situation with Lord Rahl. He is leery as to why you would seem to put faith in an outcome so fickle as the voice of the common people."

"I must admit, I share his concern." Dalton heaved a sigh. He still wished Bertrand had chosen a less risky road, but as Dalton had come to learn, Bertrand Chanboor relished the risky route, much as Stein preferred unwilling partners.

"But, as I've explained," Dalton went on, "by such tactics we will be able to trap Lord Rahl and the Mother Confessor. Without them to lead the enemy forces, the war will quickly fall into a rout, leaving the Midlands a plum for Jagang's picking."

"And so the emperor is content to let you play this out."

"But, there are risks involved."

"Risks? Anything I can do to help?"

Dalton took his seat, scooting his chair close to his desk. "I believe we must do more to discredit the cause of Lord Rahl, but in that, there is danger. Mother Confessors, after all, have ruled the Midlands for thousands of years. They have not held sway because they have nice smiles. They are women with formidable teeth, as it were.

"The Lord Rahl, too, is said to be a wizard. We must tread with care, lest we force them into abandoning this vote in favor of action. If that were to happen, it could ruin the plans in which we all have so much invested."

"I told you, we have troops in place. Even if they have an army anywhere close, they can't get it into Anderith, not past the Dominie Dirtch." Stein chuckled without humor. "But I would be happy to have them try."

"As would I. The point is, the Lord Rahl and the Mother Confessor are here, and they are trouble enough."

"I've told you before, Campbell, you shouldn't worry about magic. The emperor has clipped the claws of magic."

Dalton carefully folded his fingers together before himself on the desk. "You say that often enough, Stein, and as much as I wish to, I find little comfort in mere words. I, too, could promise things, but you expect results that can be seen."

Stein waved his knife. "I've told you before, the emperor intends to end magic so men of vision can lead the world into a new era. You will be part of that. Magic's time has passed. It is dying."

"So is the Sovereign, but he's not yet dead."

Stein went back to cleaning his nails, paying exaggerated attention to them. He seemed undaunted by Dalton's doubts and went on to try to dispel them.

"You will be pleased to know, then, that unlike your beloved Sovereign, the bear of magic no longer has fangs—it is toothless. It is no longer a weapon to be feared."

Stein lifted the corner of his cape made of human scalps. "Those of magic's talents will contribute to my collection.

I take the scalps while they are still alive, you know. I enjoy their screams while I'm cutting it off them."

Dalton was unimpressed by the man's boasting and his attempts to shock, but wished he knew what Stein was talking about when he alluded to the end of magic. He knew from Franca's inability to use her gift that something was going on, but he didn't know what or, more important, the extent to which it was impaired. He didn't know if Stein was telling the simple truth, or an ignorant version of wishful thinking layered over some Old World superstition.

Either way, the time had come to act. They could ill afford to let it go on as it was. The measure of how far they dared go in showing their opposition to joining Lord Rahl was the problem Dalton faced. It was necessary to take a stand in order to fire people into saying no to Lord Rahl, but a weak stand was as good as no stand. On the other hand, it was far too dangerous to reach through the bars and twist the nose of the bear if it still had its teeth and claws.

Dalton wondered if he might be able to press Stein into being more forthcoming. "It sounds then as if we have a serious problem."

Stein looked up. "How so?"

Dalton opened his hands in a gesture of befuddlement. "If magic is no longer a weapon, then the Dominie Dirtch, in which we all have invested so much faith, is of no use, and all our plans will fail. I would call that a serious problem."

Stein took his feet from Dalton's desk and slid the knife back into its sheath. Putting an elbow on the desk, he leaned forward.

"Not to worry. You see, the thing is, the emperor still has control of his Sisters of the Dark; their magic works for him. From what they've told us, something has happened, though. From what I gather, something of magic has gone awry and caused the power of those on Lord Rahl's side to fail.

"Jagang has learned that Lord Rahl no longer has magic

backing him. His magic is going to fail. The man is, or soon will be, naked to our blades."

Dalton was now at full attention. If it was true, that would change everything. It would mean he could implement the full extent of his plans at once. It would mean he could take the necessary action and not have to worry over the repercussions or even reprisals from Lord Rahl.

Better yet, Lord Rahl and the Mother Confessor would have to place even more of their hope in the vote, while at the same time Dalton, without fear of their actions, insured their loss.

If, that was, it was true about magic failing.

Dalton knew one way he might find out.

But first, the time had come for Dalton to pay a visit to the ailing Sovereign. The time had come to act. He would do it that very night, before the feast planned for the next day.

As hungry as she was, Ann was not looking forward to being fed.

She had long since been staked to the ground and the grimy tent erected around her, so she knew it was getting to be about that time. An any moment she expected a burly Imperial Order soldier to storm in with her bread and water. She didn't know what had happened to Sister Alessandra; Ann hadn't seen the woman in well over a week.

The soldiers disliked the duty of feeding an old woman. She suspected their comrades made sport of their domestic duty. They would come in, grab her hair in their fist, and push the bread in her mouth, packing it in with stubby filthy fingers, as if they were stuffing a goose for roasting. As Ann tried to swallow the dry mass before she choked, they would start pouring water down her throat to wash down the bread.

It was an unpleasant experience, one over which Ann had

no control. As much as she enjoyed food, she was coming to fear it would be the end of her.

Once, the soldier who came to feed her had simply thrown the bread on the ground and set a wooden bowl of water beside it, as if she were a dog. He seemed proud of himself in that he had shown her disrespect and saved himself considerable trouble all at the same time.

He didn't realize it, but Ann much preferred that method. After he had his laugh and left, she could flop on her side, squirm close, and eat the bread at her own pace, even if she didn't have the luxury of wiping off the dirt.

The tent flap opened. A dark shape stepping in blocked out the campfires beyond. Ann wondered what it would be: stuffed goose, or dog-eating-off-the-ground. To her surprise, it was Sister Alessandra, bringing a bowl giving off the aroma of sausage soup. She even had a candle with her.

Sister Alessandra pressed the candle into the dirt to the side. The woman was not smiling. She said nothing. She didn't meet Ann's gaze.

In the dim candlelight, Ann could see that Alessandra's face was bruised and scraped. She had a nasty cut on the cheekbone below her left eye, but it looked to be on the mend. The relatively minor wounds seemed to be a variety of ages, from old and near healed to freshly inflicted.

Ann didn't have to ask how the woman came to be in such a condition. Her cheeks and both sides of her jaw were red and raw from the stubble of countless unshaven faces.

"Alessandra, I'm relieved to see you . . . alive. I feared greatly for you."

Alessandra raised one shoulder in a gesture of feigned indifference. She wasted no time in bringing a steaming spoonful of sausage soup to Ann's mouth.

Ann swallowed before she had time to savor the taste, such was her hunger. But just the warm feel of it in her stomach was solace.

"I feared greatly for myself, too," Ann said. "I dreaded those men were as likely to kill me as get the food stuffed in me."

"I know the feeling," Alessandra said under her breath.

"Alessandra, are you . . . are you all right?"

"Fine." She seemed to have retreated to an emotionless place.

"You're not badly injured, then?"

"I'm better off than some of the others. If we . . . if we get hurt, a bone broken, or something like that, Jagang allows us to use our magic to heal one another."

"But healing is Additive Magic."

Sister Alessandra brought the spoon to Ann's mouth. "That is why I'm lucky; I've no broken bones, like some of the others. We've tried to help them, to heal them, but we were unable to, and so they must suffer." She met Ann's gaze. "A world without magic is a dangerous place."

Ann wanted to remind the woman that she had told her as much, that the chimes were loose, and magic—Additive Magic anyway—wouldn't work.

As Alessandra fed Ann another spoonful, she said, "But I guess you tried to tell me that, Prelate."

Ann gave a shrug of her own. "When people tried to convince me the chimes were loose, I at first wouldn't believe them, either. We have that in common. I would say that as exceptionally stubborn as you are, Sister Alessandra, there is hope you could one day be Prelate."

Alessandra, seemingly against her will, smiled with Ann.

Ann watched the spoon, with a chunk of sausage, linger in the bowl. "Prelate, did you fully expect the Sisters of the Light would believe you that magic had failed and that they would willingly try to escape with you?"

Ann looked up into Alessandra's eyes. "Not fully, no. Although I hoped they would trust my word, having always known me as a woman who values truth, I knew the possibility existed, so great was their fear, that—whether they believed me or not—they would refuse to leave.

"Slaves, slaves to anything or anyone, despite how much they abhor it, will often cling to that slavery out of fear the alternative would be insufferable. Look at a drunk, a slave

657

to liquor, who thinks us cruel for trying to get him to abandon his slavery."

"And what were you planning in the event the Sisters of the Light refused to abandon their slavery?"

"Jagang uses them, uses their magic, the same as he uses yours. When the chimes are banished magic will return and the Sisters will have their power back. Many people will die at their hands, no matter how unwilling are those hands. If they refused to cast off their slavery and leave with me, they were to be killed."

Sister Alessandra lifted an eyebrow. "My, my, Prelate. We are not so different after all. That would have been the reasoning of a Sister of the Dark as well."

"Just common sense. The lives of a lot of people are at risk." Ann was famished, and eyed with longing the spoon holding the sausage as it hovered above the nearly full bowl.

"So, why were you caught, then?"

Ann sighed. "Because I didn't think they would lie to me, not about something so important. Though it would be no reason to execute them, it will make the onerous but necessary task a little easier."

Alessandra finally fed Ann the spoonful of sausage. This time, Ann made herself chew it slowly so as to enjoy its flavor.

"You could still escape with me, Alessandra," Ann said in a quiet tone after she had finally swallowed.

Alessandra picked something from the bowl and cast it aside. She stirred the soup again.

"I told you before, that would not be possible."

"Why? Because Jagang told you so? Told you he is still in your mind?"

"That's one reason."

"Alessandra, Jagang promised you that if you took care of me, he wouldn't send you out to the tents to whore for his men. You told me that was what he said."

The woman paused with the spoon, her eyes brimming with tears. "We belong to His Excellency." With her other hand, she touched the gold ring through her bottom lip—

the mark of Jagang's slaves. "He can do with us as he wishes."

"Alessandra, he lied to you. He said he wouldn't do that if you took care of me. He lied. You can't trust a liar. Not with your future or your life. That was my mistake, but I wouldn't give a liar a second chance at harming me. If he lied about that much of it, how much else is he lying about?"

"What do you mean?"

"About how you can never escape because he is still in your mind. He is not, Alessandra. Just as he can't get into my mind, he can't get into yours for now. Once the chimes are banished, yes, but not now.

"If you swear loyalty to Richard, then you will be protected even after the chimes are banished. You can get away, Alessandra. We could do our grisly duty with the Sisters who lied and chose to stay with another liar, and then escape."

Sister Alessandra's voice was as emotionless as her face. "Prelate, you forget, I am a Sister of the Dark, sworn to the Keeper."

"In return for what, Alessandra? What has the Keeper of the underworld offered you? What has he offered that could be better than eternity in the Light?"

"Immortality."

Ann sat watching the woman's unflinching gaze. Outside, men, some of whom had abused this helpless five-hundred-year-old Sister of the Dark, laughed and carried on their nightly amusements. Smells, both fair and foul, drifted in and out of the tent: sizzling garlic, dung, roasting meat, burning fur, the sweet smell of a birch log in a nearby fire, stale sweat.

Ann, too, did not flinch from the gaze.

"Alessandra, the Keeper is lying to you."

Emotion returned to the Sister's eyes.

She stood and poured the nearly full bowl of soup on the ground outside the tent.

Sister Alessandra, one foot outside, one inside, turned back.

"You can starve for all I care, old woman. I would rather go back to the tents than listen to your blasphemy."

In her forlorn solitary silence, in her pain of body and soul, Ann prayed to the Creator, asking that He give Sister Alessandra a chance to return to the Light. She prayed, too, for the Sisters of the Light, as lost now as were the Sisters of the Dark.

From her place sitting chained in the dark and lonely tent, it seemed the world had gone mad.

"Dear Creator, what have you wrought?" Ann wept. "Is it all lies, too?"

CHAPTER 58

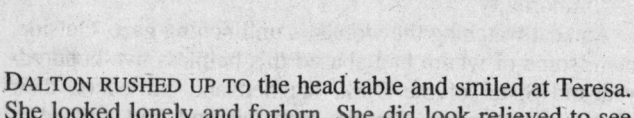

DALTON RUSHED UP TO the head table and smiled at Teresa. She looked lonely and forlorn. She did look relieved to see him, though, even though he was late. He saw too little of her lately. There was no helping it. She understood.

Dalton kissed her cheek before taking his seat.

The Minister only acknowledged him with a brief glance. He was busy sharing a lusty look with a woman at a table to the right of the dining hall. It looked as if she could be making suggestive gestures with a piece of rolled beef. The Minister was smiling.

Rather than being repelled by Bertrand's sexual indulgences, many more women were actually attracted to him because of it, even if they had no intention of acting on that attraction. It seemed to be a quirk of the female mind that some women were irresistibly drawn to tangible evidence of sexual virility, regardless of its impropriety. It was a visceral whiff of danger, something tantalizing but forbidden. The more some men behaved the rogue, the heavier many women panted.

"I hope you've not been too bored," Dalton whispered to Teresa, pausing momentarily to appreciate the glow of her faithful affection.

Other than his brief smile to Teresa, he was doing his best to maintain his customary placid face with the fruition of all his work close at hand. He took a long drink of wine, not tasting it, but impatient for its effects to settle in.

"I've missed you, that's all. Bertrand has been telling jokes." Teresa blushed. "But I can't repeat them. Not here, anyway." Her smile, her mischievous smile, stole onto her face. "Maybe when we get home, I'll tell you."

He mimed a smiled, his mind already racing forward to weighty matters. "If I get in early enough. I have to get a new batch of messages out yet tonight. Something"—he forced himself to stop drumming his fingers on the table—"something important, momentous, has happened."

Tantalized, Teresa leaned forward. "What?"

"Your hair is growing out well, Tess." It was as long as her present station allowed it. He couldn't keep himself from hinting. "But I do believe it may have considerably longer to grow."

"Dalton . . ." Her eyes were widening as she considered what he could possibly mean, but confusion visited her face, too, for she was unable to imagine how the fulfillment of his long-held ambition was possible, given present circumstances. "Dalton, has this anything to do with . . . with what you have always told me . . ."

His sober expression took the rest of her words. "I'm sorry, darling, I shouldn't get ahead of myself. I may be reading too much into it, anyway. Be patient, you will hear in a few minutes. Best if news such as this come from the Minister."

Lady Chanboor glanced briefly to the woman with the rolled meat. The woman, as if doing nothing more than minding her table companions, pulled her curls across her face as she returned her gaze to them. Hildemara gave Bertrand a brief, private, murderous glare before leaning past him toward Dalton.

"What have you heard?"

Dalton dabbed wine from his lips and returned the napkin to his lap. He thought it best to get the perfunctory information out of the way, first. Besides, it would help put into perspective the importance of what had to be done.

"Lord Rahl and the Mother Confessor are working from sunup until sundown, visiting as many places as they can. They are speaking to crowds eager to hear them.

"The Mother Confessor draws crowds agog to see her, if nothing else. I'm afraid the people are responding to her with more warmth than we would wish. That she recently married has won the hearts and love of many. People cheer the happy, newly wedded couple wherever they go. Country people come from miles around to the towns where she and Lord Rahl speak."

Folding her arms, Lady Chanboor muttered a curse to the newlyweds, expressing it in remarkably vulgar profanity, even for her. Dalton idly wondered at what obscene attributes she ascribed to him, when he had unknowingly displeased her and wasn't about. He knew some of the colorful invectives she used about her husband.

Although some of the staff knew all too well the petulant side of her, the people at large believed her so pure that vituperation could not possibly cross her lips. Hildemara well understood the value of having the support of the people. When she, as Lady Chanboor, loving wife of the Minister of Culture, champion of wives and mothers everywhere, toured the countryside to promote her husband's good works, to say nothing of cultivating their relationship with wealthy backers, she received fawning receptions not unlike the ones the Mother Confessor was receiving.

Now, more than ever, she would need to play that part well, were they to succeed.

Dalton took another drink of wine before going on. "The Mother Confessor and the Lord Rahl met with the Directors several times, and I hear the Directors have expressed to them their pleasure with the fair terms of Lord Rahl's offer, and with his reasoning, in addition to his stated purpose."

Bertrand's fist tightened. His jaw muscles flexed.

"At least," Dalton added, "in the company of the Lord Rahl they express pleasure. Once Lord Rahl left to tour the countryside, the Directors, after more reasoned thought, had a change of heart."

Dalton met the gaze of both the Minister and his wife to check he had their attention before he went on.

"This is very fortunate, with what has just happened."

The Minister studied Dalton's face before letting his gaze wander back to explore the young lady. "And what just happened?"

Dalton took Teresa's hand under the table.

"Minister Chanboor, Lady Chanboor, I regret to inform you the Sovereign has died."

Recoiling with the shock of the news, Teresa gasped, before putting her napkin to her face so people wouldn't see her sudden tears of grief. Teresa was loath to let people see her cry.

Bertrand's intent gaze locked on Dalton's. "I thought he was getting better."

It was a statement of suspicion—not that he would be at all against the Sovereign's death. Suspicion because he was unsure Dalton would have the wherewithal to accomplish such a thing, and more than that, as to why Dalton would take such a bold step, if indeed he had.

Although the Minister without doubt privately would be delighted that the old Sovereign had vacated his position in such a timely fashion, any hint of his demise being by other than natural causes could compromise everything they had worked for just as they stood at the threshold of victory.

Dalton leaned toward the Minister, not shying from the innuendo. "We have trouble. Too many people are willing to mark a circle to have us all joined with Lord Rahl. We need to make this a personal choice, between our loving benevolent Sovereign and a man who may have evil in his heart for our people.

"As we have previously discussed, we need to be able to deliver to . . . our backer, on commitments already made. We can no longer afford the risk this vote presents. We must now take a more forceful stand against joining with Lord Rahl, despite the risk that course holds."

Dalton lowered his voice even more. "We need you to take such a stand with the weight of the words of the Sovereign. You must be the Sovereign, and put voice to those words."

A satisfied smile spread on Bertrand's face. "Dalton, my loyal and resourceful aide, you have just earned yourself a very important appointment to the soon-to-be vacant office of Minister of Culture."

Everything, at long last, was clicking into place.

Hildemara's expression was stunned—but pleased—disbelief. She knew the layers of protection around the Sovereign; she knew because she had tried but failed to penetrate them.

By the look on her face, she was no doubt envisioning herself as wife to the Sovereign, worshiped as near to a good spirit in the world of life as a person could get, her words profoundly more weighty than those of the mere wife to the Minister, a station that only moments before had been lofty, but now seemed paltry and unworthy of her.

Hildemara leaned past her husband to gently seize Dalton's wrist. "Dalton, my boy, you are better than I thought you were—and I thought very much of you. I never would have guessed it possible . . ." She left the deed unspoken.

"I do my duty, Lady Chanboor, no matter the difficulty. I know results are all that matter."

She gave his wrist another squeeze before releasing him. He had never seen her so genuinely appreciative of anything he accomplished. Claudine Winthrop's end had not even brought him a nod of approval.

Dalton turned to his wife. He had been careful; she hadn't heard his whispered words. In her grief, she wasn't even paying attention. He put a consoling arm around her shoulders.

"Tess, are you all right?"

"Oh, Dalton, the poor man," she sobbed. "Our poor Sovereign. May the Creator keep his soul safe in the exalted place he has earned in the afterlife."

Bertrand leaned around behind Dalton to compassionately touch Teresa's arm. "Well put, my dear. Well put. You have expressed perfectly the loving sentiments of everyone."

Bertrand affected his most somber expression as he rose from his chair. Rather than lifting a hand as he usually did, he stood in silence, head bowed, hands clasped before him. Hildemara lifted her finger and the harp fell silent. Laughter and talking trailed off as people realized something out of the ordinary was taking place.

"My good people of Anderith, I have just received the most sorrowful news. As of tonight, we are a people lost and without a Sovereign."

The room, rather than breaking into whispering, as Dalton expected, fell into a stunned, dead silence. Dalton then realized, for the first time, really, that he had been born and lived his entire life under the reign of the old Sovereign. An era had ended. Many in the room had to be thinking the same thing.

Bertrand, every eye on him, blinked as if to hold back tears. His voice, as he went on, was mournful and quiet.

"Let us all now bow our heads and pray the Creator takes the soul of our beloved Sovereign to the place of honor he has earned with his good works. And then I must leave you to your dinner as I forgo mine to immediately call the Directors to their duty.

"Considering the urgency of the situation with both Lord

Rahl and Emperor Jagang vying for our allegiance, and with the dark cloud of war hanging over us, I will petition, on the behalf of the people of Anderith, that the Directors name a new Sovereign this very night, and, whoever he might be, urge that on the morrow that mere man be consecrated as our new Sovereign, linking our people directly once more to the Creator Himself so that we can at last have the direction our old and faithful Sovereign, because of his age and ill health, was unable to provide."

Teresa clutched his sleeve. "Dalton," she whispered as she stared at Bertrand Chanboor in wide-eyed reverence, "Dalton, do you realize he could very well be our next Sovereign."

Dalton, not wanting to spoil the sincerity of her epiphany, laid a hand gently on her back. "We can hope, Tess."

"We can pray, too," she whispered, her eyes glistening with tears.

Bertrand spread his hands before the wet eyes of the frightened crowd.

"Please, good people, bow your heads with me in prayer."

Dalton, pacing near the door, took Franca's arm as soon as she stepped into the room. He shut the door.

"My dear Franca, so good to see you. And to get a chance to talk with you. It has been a while. Thank you for coming."

"You said it was important."

"Yes, it is." Dalton held out a hand in invitation. "Please, have a seat."

Franca smoothed her dress under her as she sat in a padded chair before his desk. Dalton leaned back against the desk, wanting to be closer to her, to appear less formal than sitting behind his desk.

He felt something under his backside. He saw what it was

and pushed the little book of Joseph Ander's back on his desk, out of his way.

Franca fanned her face. "Could you open a window, please, Dalton? It's frightfully stuffy in here."

Though it was just dawn, the sun yet to break the horizon, she was right; it was already hot and promised to be a stifling day. Smiling, Dalton went behind his desk and lifted the window all the way. He glanced over his shoulder, and at her gestured insistence, opened two more windows.

"Thank you, Dalton. You are kind to indulge me. Now, what's so important?"

He came back round the desk to once more lean back against it as he gazed down at her. "Were you able to hear anything at the feast last night? It was an important evening, what with the tragic announcement. It would be helpful if you were able to report on what you heard."

Franca, looking distressed, opened a little purse hung round her waist, hidden under a layer of brown wool. She withdrew four gold coins and held them out.

"Here. This is what you've paid me since I've . . . since I've had the difficulty with my gift. I've not earned it. I've no right to keep your money. I'm sorry you had to call me all the way in here because I didn't return your payment sooner."

Dalton knew how much she needed the money. With her gift not working, neither did she. Franca was going broke. With no man in her life, she had to earn a living or starve. For her to return the money he'd paid her was a serious statement.

Dalton pushed her hand away. "No, no, Franca, I don't want your money—"

"Not my money. I've done nothing to earn it. I've no right to it."

She offered the coins again. Dalton took her hand in both his and held it tenderly.

"Franca, we're old and dear friends. I'll tell you what. If you don't think you've earned the money, then I will give you the opportunity to earn it right now."

"I told you, I can't—"

"It doesn't involve using your gift. It involves something else you have to offer."

She drew back with a gasp. "Dalton! You've a wife! A beautiful young bride—"

"No, no," Dalton said, caught off guard. "No, Franca. I'm sorry if I ever led you to believe I would . . . I'm sorry if I wasn't clear."

Dalton found Franca an intriguing, attractive woman, even if she was a little older, and quite odd. Though it hadn't been in his mind, and even though he would not entertain such an offer, he was nevertheless disappointed to find she thought the idea repulsive.

She eased back into her seat. "Then what is it you want?"

"The truth."

"Ah. Well, Dalton, there's truth, and then there's truth. Some more trouble than others."

"Wise words."

"Which truth is it you seek?"

"What's wrong with your magic?"

"It doesn't work."

"I know that. I want to know why."

"Thinking of going into the wizard business, Dalton?"

He took a breath and clasped his hands. "Franca, it's important. I need to know why your magic doesn't work."

"Why?"

"Because I need to know if it's just you, or if there is something wrong with magic in general. Magic is an important element to the life of many in Anderith. If it doesn't work I need to know about it so this office can be prepared."

Her scowl eased. "Oh."

"So, what's wrong with magic, and how universal is the difficulty?"

She retreated into a gloom. "Can't say."

"Franca, I really need to know. Please?"

She peered up at him. "Dalton, don't ask me—"

"I'm asking."

She sat for a time, staring off at the floor. At last she took one of his hands and pressed the four gold coins into it. She stood to look him in the eye.

"I will tell you, but I won't take money for it. This is the kind of thing I won't take money for. I will only tell you because I . . . because you are a friend."

Dalton thought she looked as if he had just sentenced her to death. He motioned to the chair and she sank back into it.

"I appreciate it, Franca. I really do."

She nodded without looking up.

"There's something wrong with magic. Since you don't know about magic, I'll not confuse you with the details. The important thing for you to know is that magic is dying. Just as my magic is gone, so is all magic. Dead and gone."

"But why? Is there nothing that can be done?"

She thought it over awhile. "No. I don't think so. I can't be sure, but I can tell you that I'm pretty sure the First Wizard himself died trying to fix the problem."

Dalton was stunned by such a thing. It was unthinkable. Though it was true he didn't know anything about magic, he knew of many of its benefits to people, such as Franca's healing—not only the body, but the comfort she brought to troubled souls.

He found this more momentous than the mere death of a man who was Sovereign. This was the death of much more.

"But will it come back? Will something happen to, to, I don't know . . . heal the problem?"

"I don't know. Like I said, a man far more knowledgeable about it than I wasn't able to reverse the difficulty, so I tend to think it irreversible. It's possible it could come back, but I fear it is already too late for that to happen."

"And what do you believe the consequences of an event of this nature will be?"

Franca, losing her color, said only, "I can't even guess."

"Have you looked into this? I mean, really looked into it?"

"I've been secluded, studying everything I could, trying everything I could. Last night was the first night I've even been out in public for weeks." She looked up with a frown. "When the Minister announced the death of the Sovereign, he said something about the Lord Rahl. What was that about?"

Dalton realized the woman was so out of touch with the day-to-day business of life in Anderith that she didn't even know about Lord Rahl and the vote. With this news, he now had urgent matters he had to attend to.

"Oh, you know, there are always parties contending for the goods Anderith produces." He took her hand and helped her up. "Franca, thank you for coming and for confiding in me with this news. You have been more help than you could know."

She seemed flustered to find herself being rushed out, but he couldn't help it. He had to get to work.

She paused, her face inches from his, and looked him in the eye. It was an arresting gaze—power or no power. "Promise me, Dalton, that I won't come to regret telling you the truth."

"Franca, you can count—"

Dalton spun at a sudden racket behind him. Startled, he drew Franca back. A huge black bird had come in the open window. A raven, he believed it to be, although he had never seen one this close.

The thing sprawled across his desk, its wing tips nearly reaching each end of it. It used its wide-spread wings and its beak to try to help get its footing on the flat, smooth leather covering. It let out a squawk of angry frustration or perhaps surprise at its smooth and awkward roost.

Dalton rushed around the side of the desk, to the silver scroll stand, and drew his sword.

Franca tried to stay his arm. "Dalton, don't! It's bad luck to kill a raven!"

Her intervention, and the bird unexpectedly ducking, caused him to miss an easy kill.

The raven let out a racket of squawking and screeching as it scrambled to the side of his desk. Dalton gently, but forcefully, pushed Franca aside and drew back his sword.

The raven, seeing with its big eye what was coming, snatched up the little book in its beak. Holding tight the book once belonging to Joseph Ander, it sprang to wing inside the room.

Dalton slammed shut the window behind his desk, the one the bird had come in through. The bird came for him. Claws raked his scalp as he slammed shut the second window, and then the third.

Dalton took a swing at the fury of flapping feathers, just barely contacting something with his sword. The bird, cawing loud enough to hurt his ears, shot toward the window.

Dalton and Franca both covered their faces with an arm as the window shattered, sending shards of glass and bits of window mullion everywhere.

When he looked, he saw the bird glide to the branch of a nearby tree. It grasped the branch, stumbled, and grasped again, finally getting its footing. It looked to be injured.

Dalton tossed his sword on the desk and seized a lance from the display with the Ander battle flags. With a grunt of effort, he launched the lance through the broken window at the bird.

The raven, seeing what he was about, took to wing with the book. The lance just missed it. The bird vanished into the early-morning sky.

"Good, you didn't kill it," Franca said. "That would have been bad luck."

Dalton, red-faced, pointed at the desk. "It stole the book!"

Franca shrugged. "Ravens are curious birds. They often steal things to take to a mate. They mate for life, ravens."

Dalton tugged at his clothes, straightening them. "Is that so."

"But the female will cheat on the male. Sometimes, while he is out collecting twigs for their nest, she will let another male take her."

"Is that so?" he said, miffed. "And why should I care?"

Franca shrugged. "Just thought it an interesting fact you would like to know." She stepped closer, surveying the damage to the window. "Was the book valuable?"

Dalton carefully brushed bits of glass from his shoulders. "No. Fortunately it was just a useless old book, written in a long-dead language no one nowadays understands."

"Ah," she said. "Well, there is that much good in it. Be thankful it was not valuable."

Dalton put his hands on his hips. "Look at this mess. Just look at it." He picked up a few black feathers and tossed them out the broken window. He saw there was a crimson drop on his desk. "At least it paid with its blood for its treasure."

CHAPTER 59

"THE TIME HAS COME," Bertrand Chanboor, newly installed and consecrated Sovereign of Anderith, called to the immense crowd spread out below the balcony, overflowing the square into surrounding streets, "to take a stand against hatred!"

Since he knew the cheering would go on for a time, Dalton took the opportunity to glance down at Teresa. She smiled bravely up at him as she dabbed her eyes. She had been up most of the night, praying for the soul of the dead Sovereign, and for strength to the new one.

Dalton had been up most of the night strategizing with Bertrand and Hildemara, planning what they would say.

Bertrand was in his element. Hildemara was in her glory. Dalton had the reins.

The offensive had begun.

"As your Sovereign, I cannot allow this cruel injustice to be thrust upon the people of Anderith! The Lord Rahl is from D'Hara. What does he know of our people's needs? How can he come here, for the first time, and expect we would turn our lives over to his mercy?"

The crowd booed and hissed. Bertrand let it go on for a time.

"What do you think will happen to all you fine Haken people if Lord Rahl has his way? Do you think he would give a moment's care to you? Do you think he would bother to wonder if you have clothes, or food, or work? We have labored to see to it you can find work, with laws like the Winthrop Fair Employment Law designed to bring the bounty of Anderith to all people."

He paused to let the people cheer him on.

"We have been working against hatred. We have struggled against people who don't care if children starve. We have worked to make life for all the people of Anderith better. What has Lord Rahl done? Nothing! Where was he when our children were starving? Where was he when men could not find work?

"Do we really want all our hard work and advancements to be suddenly wiped away by this heartless man and his privileged wife, the Mother Confessor? Just when we are reaching the most critical point in our reforms? When we have so much work yet to do for the people of Anderith? What does the Mother Confessor know about starving children? Has she ever cared for a child? No!"

When he started in again, he pounded his fist against the balcony railing to make each point. "The plain truth is that Lord Rahl cares only for his magic! His own greed is the reason he has come here! He has come to use our land for his own greed!

"He would poison our waters with his vile conjuring! No

673

more could we fish, because his magic would make our lakes, our rivers, and our ocean into dead waters while his poisonous magic works its way for him to create his gruesome weapons of war!"

People were shocked and angered to learn such things. Dalton gauged the reaction to each word so that he might hone them for the speeches to come, and for the messages he would send out to blanket the land.

"He creates evil creatures so that he may press his unjustified war. Perhaps you have heard of people dying strange, unexplained deaths. Do you think it some random event? No! It is the magic of Lord Rahl! He creates these vile creatures of magic and then turns them loose to see how well they kill! These deadly creatures burn to death or drown innocent people. Others are dragged helpless by these marauders of the night up to rooftops and thrown to their deaths."

Spellbound, people gasped.

"He uses our people to hone his dark craft for war!

"His dark sorcery would fill the air with a vile haze that would seep into every home! Do you want your children breathing Lord Rahl's magic? Who knows the agonizing deaths of innocent children, breathing in his careless incantations? Who knows the deformities they will suffer should they swim in a pond he has used to steep a spell.

"This is what we invite should we fail to stand against this rape of our land! He would let us die a choking death so that he can bring in his powerful friends to steal our wealth. That is the true reason he comes to us!"

People were now properly alarmed.

Dalton leaned toward Bertrand and whispered out of the side of his mouth. "The air and the water frightened them the most. Reinforce it."

Bertrand gave him an almost imperceptible nod.

"This is what it means, my friends, to let this dictator loose among us. The very air we struggle to breathe will be tainted with his sinister magic, the water befouled with his witchcraft. While he and his cohorts laugh at the suffering of honest, hardworking people, Ander and Haken alike, they grow rich at our expense. He will use our pure air and clean water to grow his foul things of magic to press a war no one wants!"

People were shouting in anger, shaking their fists, to hear their Sovereign reveal these ugly truths. There was horror, fear, and revulsion, but mostly there was anger. For some, to their disillusionment with Lord Rahl and the Mother Confessor was added the indignation of having been taken for fools, while for others their suspicions about such heartless, powerful people were merely confirmed.

Bertrand held up a hand. "The Imperial Order has offered to purchase our goods at prices far above those we now receive." They applauded and whistled.

"Lord Rahl would steal it from you! That is your choice, good people, to listen to the lies of this vile magician from the distant D'Hara who would trick you into giving away your rights, who would use our land to propagate his things of vile magic to press on with a needless war, who would let your children starve or die from the harmful effects of his mad spells, or to sell what you grow and produce to the Imperial Order and enrich your families as never before."

Now the crowd was truly worked up. People, with fresh goodwill toward their new Sovereign, were for the first time hearing solid reasons to reject Lord Rahl. More than that, solid reason to fear him. But best of all, solid reasons to hate him.

Dalton was crossing some items from the list in his hand when he saw they weren't as effective, and circling others that received the biggest reactions. As he and Bertrand knew it would, the word "children" provoked the biggest reaction, inciting a near riot at the terrible things about to happen to them. The mere mention of the word "children" caused reason to evaporate from people's heads.

War, too, had the effect they had expected. People were terrified to learn it was Lord Rahl pressing the war, and that there was no need for it. People would want peace at any cost. When they discovered the cost, they would pay. It would be too late for them to do otherwise.

"We must get past this, my people, put it in the past, and get on with the business of Anderith. We have much work to do. Now is not the time to give up all we have accomplished to become a slave state to this magician from afar, a man obsessed with wealth and power, a man who only wants to drag us all into his foolish war. There could be peace, if he would only give peace a chance—but he won't.

"I know such a man would cast aside our traditions and religion, leaving you without a Sovereign, but I fear for you, not myself. I have so much yet to do. I have so much love to give to the people of Anderith. I have been blessed, and I have so much to give back to the community.

"I beg of you, I beg of you as proud people of Anderith all, to show your contempt for this sly demon from D'Hara, show him you see his wicked ways.

"The Creator Himself, through me, demands you stand up to Lord Rahl when you vote your conscience by putting an X through his evil! Ex through his tricks! Ex through his lies! Ex through his tyranny! Ex through him and the Mother Confessor, too!"

The square roared. The buildings around shook with it as it went on and on. Bertrand held his arms up in front of himself, crossing them to make a big X everyone could see as they cheered him.

Hildemara, at his side, applauded as she fixed him with her customary public adoring gaze.

When the crowd finally quieted as he raised a silencing hand, Bertrand held the hand out to his wife, introducing her to the people. They cheered for her almost as long as for him.

Hildemara, pleased beyond measure with her new role, spread her hands for quiet. She got it almost instantly.

"Good people of Anderith, I cannot tell you how proud I am to be the wife of this great man—"

She was drowned out by the roaring cheer. Her out-stretched arms finally succeeded in again bringing silence.

"I cannot tell you how I've watched as my husband has worked his heart out for the people of Anderith. Caring not for recognition, unnoticed, he has labored tirelessly for the people, without regard even to his own rest or nourishment.

"When I would ask him to rest, he would say to me, 'Hildemara, as long as there are hungry children, I cannot rest.' "

As the crowd again went wild, Dalton had to turn away to take a sip of wine. Teresa clutched his arm.

"Dalton," she whispered, "the Creator has answered our prayers to deliver us Bertrand Chanboor to be Sovereign."

He almost laughed, but saw the awe in her eyes as she looked at the man. Dalton sighed to himself. It was not the Creator who delivered them Bertrand, but Dalton himself.

"Tess, wipe your eyes. The best is yet to come."

Hildemara went on. "And for the sake of those children, I ask that every one of you reject the hate and division Lord Rahl would peddle to our people!

"Reject the Mother Confessor, too, for what does she know of common people? She is a woman born into advantage, born into wealth. What does she know of hard work? Show her that her birthright of dominance is at an end! Show her we will not willingly submit to her hateful treatment of poor working people! Show her we reject her privileged life! Ex through the Mother Confessor and her pompous demands of people she doesn't even know!

"I say the Lord Rahl and the Mother Confessor have enough wealth! Don't give them yours, too! They've no right to it!"

Dalton yawned and rubbed his eyes as the cheering turned to chanting of the name Chanboor. He couldn't remember sleeping. He'd had to twist the arm of one of the Directors to make it unanimous. Such unanimity inferred divine intervention on behalf of the chosen Sovereign, and served to strengthen his mandate.

When at last Bertrand again stepped up and addressed the crowd, Dalton was only half listening until he heard his name mentioned.

"This is why, among other reasons too numerous to mention, I have personally involved myself in the selection process. It is with special pride I introduce to you the new Minister of Culture, a man who will protect and serve as well as any who have gone before him"—Bertrand held out his hand—"Dalton Campbell."

Beside him, Teresa fell to her knees, bowing her head to Bertrand.

"Oh, Sovereign, Your Greatness, thank you for recognizing my husband. Bless you for what you have done for him."

Rather than feeling proud of the appointment, Dalton felt a bit let down. Teresa knew the work he put in to getting where he had gotten, but now she ascribed it all to the greatness of Bertrand Chanboor.

Such was the power of the Sovereign's word. As he looked out over the crowd of cheering people, and thought about the words he would say to back Bertrand and Hildemara, he guessed it was just as well, for the people, too, would be just as swayed by the Sovereign's stand on the coming vote.

But there was yet more to come. Dalton had yet to unleash the final element.

The smell, like a prisoner rushing to escape, hit him full-on as the door was dragged open. It was too dark to see. Dalton snapped his fingers, and the big Ander guards yanked the torches from the rusty brackets and brought them along.

"Are you sure he's still alive?" Dalton asked. "Do you ever check?"

"He's alive, Minister."

Dalton was momentarily confused, and then staggered by

the title. Whenever someone addressed him by the title it took a split second to realize they meant him. Just the sound of it, Minister of Culture, Dalton Campbell, left him reeling.

The guard held out the torch. "Over here, Minister Campbell."

Dalton stepped over men so filthy they looked nearly invisible against the greasy-black floor. Fetid water ran through a depression in the center of the blackened brick. Where it came into the room it provided drinking water, such as it was. Where it went out it was a latrine. The walls, the floor, the men, were alive with vermin.

At the far side of the room, across the foul water, a small barred window, about head height and too small for a man to crawl through, opened onto an alley. If family or friends cared if the prisoners lived, they could come to the alley and feed them.

Because the men's arms and feet were secured in wooden blocks to restrain them, they couldn't fight one another for food. They could do little more than lie on the floor. They couldn't walk because of the blocks; at best they could hop a short distance. If they could straighten enough, they could put their mouth up near the window and receive food. If no one fed them, they died.

All the prisoners were naked. The torchlight reflected off greasy-black bodies, and he saw that one of the prisoners was a skinny old woman without teeth. Dalton wasn't even sure some of the men were alive. They showed no reaction to the men stepping over them.

"I'm surprised he's alive," Dalton said to the guard.

"He has those who believe in him, still. They come every day and feed him. He speaks to them, through the window, after they feed him. They sit and listen to him ramble on, as if what he had to say were important."

Dalton had no idea the man still had his followers; it was a bonus. With ready followers, it would take little time to have the movement under way.

A guard dipped a torch to point. "There he is, Minister Campbell. That's the fellow."

The guard kicked the man lying on his side. The head turned their way. Not fast, not slow, but deliberate. Rather than the cowed look Dalton expected, one fiery eye glared up.

"Serin Rajak?"

"That's right," the man growled. "What do you want?"

Dalton squatted down beside the man. He had to make a second attempt at drawing a breath. The stench was overpowering.

"I've just been appointed Minister of Culture, Master Rajak. Only today. As my first act, I've come to right the injustice done you."

Dalton saw then that the man was missing an eye. He had a badly healed sunken scar where it had once been.

"Injustice. The world is full of injustice. Magic is loose to harm people. Magic has put me here. But I've not given in to it. No sir, I've not. I'll never give in to the evil of magic.

"I gladly gave an eye in the cause. Lost it to a witch. If you expect me to renounce my holy war against the vile purveyors of magic, you can just leave me here. Leave me, do you hear? Leave me! I'll never give in to them!"

Dalton backed away a little as the man floundered wildly on the floor, yanking at restraints that even someone who was only half crazy could see would never surrender their grip to his trying. He thrashed until fresh blood colored his wrists.

"I'll not renounce the struggle against magic! Do you hear? I'll not give in to those who inflict magic on those of us who worship the Creator!"

Dalton put a restraining hand on the man's greasy shoulder.

"You misunderstand, sir. Magic is doing great damage to our land. People are dying from fires and drowning. People, for no reason, are leaping off buildings and bridges—"

"Witches!"

"That is what we fear—"

"Witches cursing people! If you fools would only listen, I tried to warn you! I tried to help! I tried to rid the land of them!"

"That's why I'm here, Serin. I believe you. We need your help. I've come to release you, and beg you help us."

The white of the man's one eye as he stared up was a beacon in the inky night of filth.

"Praise the Creator," he whispered. "At last. At last I've been called to do His work."

CHAPTER 60

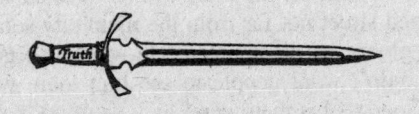

RICHARD WAS STUNNED BY the sight. The wide thoroughfare was packed with people, nearly all carrying candles, a glowing flood of faces washing up Fairfield's broad main avenue. They flowed around the trees and benches in the center between the two sides of the road, making them look like treed islands.

It was just turning dark. The afterglow at the horizon in the western sky, behind the peaks of distant mountains showing through a thin gap in the gathering clouds, was a deep purple with a pink blush. Overhead, leaden clouds had been gathering all afternoon. The deep rumble of sporadic thunder could be heard in the distance. The humid air smelled damp while at the same time dust churned up by the hooves of the horses rose to choke the air. Occasionally, there fell an errant drop of rain, fat and ripe with the promise of more to follow.

D'Haran soldiers surrounded Richard, Kahlan, and Du Chaillu in a ring of steel. The mounted men all around them reminded Richard of a boat, floating in the sea of faces. The soldiers skillfully refused to give way without looking like they were forcing people aside. The people ignored them; their attention seemed to be on getting where they were going, or maybe it was just too dark for the people to recognize them, thinking they were part of the Anderith army.

The Baka Tau Mana blade masters had vanished. They did that, sometimes. Richard knew they were simply taking up strategic positions in case of trouble. Du Chaillu yawned. It was the end of a long day of traveling that saw them finally returning to Fairfield.

Richard didn't like the looks of what he saw, and led everyone with him off the main avenue packed with people to a deserted street not far from the main city square. In the gathering gloom he dismounted. He wanted to get a closer look, but didn't want people to see him there with all the soldiers. Good as his men were, they were no match for the tens of thousands of people in the streets. A colony of tiny ants, after all, could overpower a lone insect many times their size.

Richard left most of the men behind to wait and watch the horses while he took Kahlan and a few men with him to see what was happening. Du Chaillu didn't ask if she could come along, she simply did. Jiaan, having scouted the area to his satisfaction and found it reasonably safe, joined them. In the shadows of two-story buildings to either side of a north-south street opening onto the square, they watched unnoticed.

A masonry platform with a squat stone railing across the front sat at the head of the square. From it, public announcements were made. Before they went away, Richard had spoken there to interested, earnest people. Richard and Kahlan had come into Fairfield on their way back, intending to speak again at the square before they went on to the estate. It was urgent to start the tedious task of combing through all the books either by or about Joseph Ander, searching for a key to stopping the chimes, but Richard had wanted to reinforce the positive things he had told these people before.

In the last few days the chimes had grown worse. They seemed to be everywhere. Richard and Kahlan had been able to stop some of their own men, overcome with the irresistible call of death, just before they leaped into fire, or slipped into water. They hadn't been in time for others. None of them had been getting much sleep.

The gathered multitude started chanting.

"No more war. No more war. No more war." It was a dull drone, deep and insistent, like the quaking of the distant thunder.

Richard thought it a good sentiment, one he wholeheartedly embraced, but he was disturbed by the anger in people's eyes, and the tone in their voices as they chanted it. It went on for a time, like thunder booming in from the plains, building, growing.

A man near the platform held up his young girl on his shoulders for the people to see. "She has something to say! Let her speak! Please! Hear my child!"

The crowd called out encouragement. The girl, ten or twelve years old, climbed the steps at the side and, looking determined, marched across the platform to stand at the rail. The crowd quieted to hear her.

"Please, dear Creator, hear our prayers. Keep Lord Rahl from making war," she said in a voice powered by simplistic adolescent zeal. She looked to her father. He nodded and she went on. "We don't want his war. Please, dear Creator, make Lord Rahl give peace a chance."

Richard felt as if an arrow of ice had pierced his heart. He wanted to explain to the child, explain a thousand things, but he knew she would not understand a one of them. Kahlan's hand on his back was cold comfort.

Another girl, maybe a year or two younger, climbed the

steps to join the first. "Please, dear Creator, make Lord Rahl give peace a chance."

A line was forming, parents bearing children of all ages to the steps. They all had similar messages. Most stepped forward and simply said, "Give peace a chance," some not seeming to even comprehend the words they spoke before they returned to proud parents.

It was plain to Richard that the children had been practicing the words all day. The words were not the language of children. That hardly softened the hurt, knowing they believed it.

Some of the children were reluctant, some were nervous, but most seemed proud and happy to be part of the great event. By the passion in their voices, he could tell the older ones believed they were speaking profound words that had a chance to alter history, and avert what was, to them, a pointless loss of life, a disaster for nothing of any good.

A young boy asked, "Dear Creator, why does Lord Rahl want to hurt children? Make him give peace a chance."

The crowd went wild cheering him. At seeing the reaction, he repeated it, and again it was cheered. Many in the crowd were weeping.

Richard and Kahlan shared a look beyond words. It was obvious to them both that this was no spontaneous outpouring of sentiment; this was a groomed and rehearsed message. They had been getting reports of this sort of thing, but to see it made his blood run cold.

A man Richard recognized as a Director named Prevot finally stepped up onto the platform.

"Lord Rahl, Mother Confessor," the man shouted out over the crowd, "if you could hear me now, I would ask, why would you bring your vile magic to our peace-loving people? Why would you try to drag us into your war, a war we don't want?

"Listen to the children, for theirs are the words of wisdom!

"There is no reason to resort to conflict before dialogue. If you cared about the lives of innocent children, you would sit down with the Imperial Order and resolve your differences. The Order is willing, why are you not? Could it be you want this war so you might conquer what isn't yours? So you may enslave those who reject you?

"Listen to the wise words of all these children and please, in the name of all that is good, give peace a chance!"

The crowd took up the chant, "Give peace a chance. Give peace a chance. Give peace a chance." The man let it go on for a time, and then started in again.

"Our new Sovereign has much work to do for us! We desperately need his guiding hand. Why must Lord Rahl insist on distracting our Sovereign from the work of the people? Why would Lord Rahl put our children at such great peril?

"For his greed!" the man shouted in answer to his own questions. "For his greed!"

Kahlan put a comforting hand on Richard's shoulder. He felt little comfort. He was watching all his work being consumed by the heat from the flame of lies.

"Dear Creator," Director Prevot called out, lifting his clasped hands to the sky, "we give thanks for our new Sovereign. A man of peerless talent and unrivaled devotion, the most ethical Sovereign ever to reign over us. Please, dear Creator, give him strength against the wicked ways of Lord Rahl."

Director Prevot spread his arms. "I ask you, good people, to consider this man from afar. A man who took the Mother Confessor of all the Midlands to be his wife."

The crowd grumbled in growing displeasure—the Mother Confessor, after all, was their Mother Confessor.

"Yet this man, this man who shouts for all to hear of his moral leadership, of his desire for what is right, already has another wife! Wherever he goes, he takes her, too, fat with his child! Yet as this other wife still carries his unborn child, he marries the Mother Confessor, and drags her with him, too, as his concubine! How many more women will this sinful man take to sire his wicked offspring? How many bastard children has he created here, in Anderith? How

685

many of our women have fallen to his boundless lust?"

The crowd was genuinely shocked. Besides the moral implications, this was a disgrace to the Mother Confessor.

"This other woman proudly admits being Lord Rahl's wife, and further confirms it to be his child! What kind of man is this?

"Lady Chanboor was so shocked by this uncivilized conduct she took to her bed, weeping, to recover her senses! The Sovereign is beside himself with the scandal of such behavior being brought into Anderith. They both ask that you reject this rutting pig from D'Hara!"

Du Chaillu pulled on Richard's sleeve. "This is not true. I will go explain it to them, so they may see it is not evil, as this man says. I will explain it."

Richard put a restraining hand on her. "You're doing no such thing. These people wouldn't listen."

Jiaan spoke in heated words. "Our spirit woman is not a woman who would be immoral. She must explain that she has acted by the law."

"Jiaan," Kahlan said, "Richard and I know the truth. You and Du Chaillu and the others with you, you all know the truth. That is what matters. These people have no ears for the truth.

"This is how tyrants win the will of the people: with lies."

Having seen enough, Richard was about to turn to go when a bright orange whoosh of fire erupted out in the crowd. A candle, presumably, ignited a girl's dress. She let out a piercing scream. Her hair caught fire.

By the speed of the fire, Richard realized it was no accident.

The chimes were among them.

Not far away, a man's clothes caught flame. The crowd went into a terrible fright, screaming in fear that Lord Rahl was using magic against them.

It was a frightening, sickening sight, seeing the girl and the man flailing as crackling flames raced up their clothes, the sizzling fire catching as if they had been dunked in pitch, as if the fire were a thing alive.

The crowd scattered in panic, knocking both old and young sprawling. Parents tried to cover the burning girl with a shirt to put out the fire, but it, too, ignited, adding fuel to the conflagration. The burning man crumbled to the ground. He was little more than a dark stick figure in the center of an intense yellow-orange blaze.

As if the good spirits themselves could no longer stand it, the skies opened up in a downpour. The roar of the rain drumming the dry ground covered the roar of the fire and the shouts and cries of the people. Darkness descended as the candles were extinguished by the rain. In the square, two fires continued to burn: the girl and the man. The chimes danced over their flesh in liquid light. There was nothing to be done for the two souls lost.

If Richard didn't do something, there would be nothing to be done for anyone; the chimes would consume the world of life.

Kahlan pulled Richard away. It required little effort. They ran back through the darkness and rain and gathered up their horses and the rest of the men. Richard, leading his horse by the reins, guided them to a side route through Fairfield.

"The reports were accurate," Richard said as he leaned toward Kahlan. "It's clear these people have been turned against us."

"Fortunately the vote is only a few days off," Kahlan answered back through the din of rain. "We may lose some people here, but at least we have a chance with the rest of Anderith."

As they walked their horses through the rain, Richard moved the reins to his other hand and put an arm around Kahlan's shoulders. "Truth will win out."

Kahlan didn't answer.

"The important thing is the chimes," Du Chaillu said. She looked both saddened and frightened. "Whatever else happens, the chimes must be stopped. I do not want to die again by them. I do not want our child to die by them.

"Whatever happens here, this is only one place. The chimes, though, are everywhere. I do not want to bring my baby into a world with the chimes. There will be no safe place if they are not stopped. That is your true job, *Caharin*."

Richard put his arm around her shoulders. "I know. I know. Maybe I can find the thing I need in the library at the estate."

"The Minister and Sovereign have taken the other side," Kahlan said. "They may not be interested in allowing us to use the library any longer."

"We're using it," Richard said, "one way, or another."

He guided them down a street that paralleled the main avenue, a street that once out of the city would turn to join into the main road toward the Minister's estate. It was on that road, closer to the estate, that their troops were stationed.

Richard noticed Kahlan staring off at something. He followed her gaze in the rain and darkness to a small sign visible in the lamplight coming from a window beneath it.

The sign offered herbs for sale and the services of a midwife.

Du Chaillu was huge. Richard supposed that she must be near to having her baby—whether she wanted it to be born into such a world or not.

CHAPTER 61

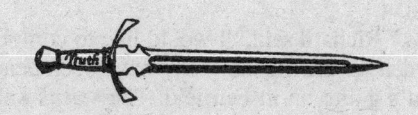

IT HAD BEEN A long day, the last hour of it spent slogging through the drenching downpour to where the remainder of their troops were stationed. Well over half of them had been sent off around Anderith to oversee the upcoming vote. Feeling ill, Du Chaillu was in no condition to ride; it was a miserable walk and exhaustion finally claimed her—not something she would have admitted lightly. Richard and Jiaan took turns carrying her the remaining distance.

Richard was thankful for the rain for one reason, though. It had cooled the tempers of the throng in Fairfield and sent them home.

Ordinarily Richard would have insisted that Du Chaillu go straight off to her own tent, but after the events in Fairfield, he understood her gloomy mood and realized she needed their company more than she needed rest. Kahlan must have understood, too, for rather than chasing the spirit woman from their tent, as she had had to do on more than one occasion, she gave her a dried tava biscuit to suck on, saying it would settle her stomach. Kahlan sat Du Chaillu down on the padded blanket that was the bed and with a towel dried her face and hair while Jiaan went to get her some dry clothes.

Richard sat at the small folding table he used to write

messages, orders, and letters, mostly to General Reibisch. After having been to the city, he desperately wanted to write the general and order him into Anderith.

From outside the tent, a muffled voice asked permission to enter. When Richard granted it, Captain Meiffert lifted back the heavy flap, propping it up with a pole to act as a little roof to keep the rain from their doorway. He shook himself, as best he could, under the small roof before stepping inside.

"Captain," Richard said, "I would like to compliment you and your men on the reports. They have been dead accurate about what's going on in Fairfield. The spirits know I wish I could yell at you and dismiss the messengers for getting it wrong, or embellishing the facts, but I can't. They were only too right."

Captain Meiffert didn't look pleased to have gotten it right. The situation was nothing to be pleased about. With a finger, he wiped his wet blond hair across his forehead.

"Lord Rahl, I believe we should now bring General Reibisch's army south, into Anderith. The situation is growing more tenuous by the day. I have a fistful of reports about special Ander guard troops. They are reported to be not at all like the regular Anderith army we have seen."

"I agree with the captain," Kahlan said from the ground beside Du Chaillu. "We need to be in the library, trying to find something of use against the chimes. We don't have time to counter the things being said to sway people to reject us."

"That's just here," Richard said.

"Are you so sure? What if it's not? Besides, as I said, we don't have the luxury of time to devote to it. We have more important things to worry about."

"The Mother Confessor is right," Captain Meiffert insisted.

"I have to believe truth will win out. Otherwise, what is there left to do? Lie to people to get them to join our side?"

"It seems to be working for those who oppose us," Kahlan pointed out.

Richard wiped his wet hair back from his forehead. "Look, there's nothing I would like better than to simply call General Reibisch down here. Really, there isn't. But we can't."

Captain Meiffert wiped water from his chin. The man seemed to have anticipated the reason for Richard's reluctance and was ready with a reply.

"Lord Rahl, we have enough men here. We can send word to the general, and before he comes into sight, we can take the Dominie Dirtch from the Anderith army and safely let our men through."

"I've run that very thought through my mind a thousand times," Richard said. "One thing keeps ringing a warning in my head."

"What's that?" Kahlan asked.

Richard turned sideways on his small folding stool so he might speak to her as well as the captain.

"We don't know for sure how the Dominie Dirtch work."

"So, we ask someone here," Kahlan said.

"It's not a weapon they use. We can't count on their expertise. Yes, they know that if they're being attacked they ring the things and the enemy will be killed."

"Lord Rahl, we have a thousand men, once they all return from watching the vote. We can take the Dominie Dirtch in a wide swath and General Reibisch will be able to safely bring his army through. Then we can use his men to take the rest, all along the frontier, and the Imperial Order will not be able to get through. Perhaps they will even approach, thinking they will be able to pass, and then we will have the opportunity to use the Dominie Dirtch against them."

Richard turned the candle on the table round and round in his fingers as he listened, and then in the silence that followed.

"There's one problem with that," he said at last, "and that is what I've already said: we aren't sure how they work."

"We know the basics of the things," Kahlan said, her frustration growing.

"But the problem is," Richard said, "that we don't know

enough. First of all, we can't take all the Dominie Dirtch all along the frontier. There are too many—they run along the entire border. We could only take some, like you suggested, Captain.

"Therein lies the problem. Remember when we came through? How those people were killed when the Dominie Dirtch rang?"

"Yes, but we don't know why they rang," Kahlan said. "Besides, what difference does that make?"

"What if we capture a stretch of the Dominie Dirtch," Richard said, looking back and forth between Kahlan and Captain Meiffert, "and then tell General Reibisch it's safe to bring his army in. What if, when all those men are just about there, Anderith soldiers somewhere else, ones still in control of the Dominie Dirtch, ring theirs?"

"So what?" Kahlan asked. "They will be too far away."

"Are you sure?" Richard leaned toward her for emphasis. "What if that rings them all? What if they know how to ring the entire line?

"Remember when we came in, how they said they all rang, and everyone out in front of the Dominie Dirtch was killed? They all rang together, as one."

"But they didn't know why they all rang," Kahlan said. "The soldiers didn't ring them."

"How do you know that one person somewhere along that entire line didn't ring their Dominie Dirtch, and caused them all to ring? Maybe accidentally, and they're too afraid to admit it for fear of their punishment, or perhaps one of those young people stationed there, out of boredom, just wanted to try it?

"What if the same thing happens while our army is out there before those murderous things? Can you imagine? General Reibisch has near to a hundred thousand men—maybe more by now. Can you imagine his entire force killed in one instant?"

Richard looked from Kahlan's calm face to the captain's alarmed expression. "Our entire army down here in the South, at once, dead. Imagine it."

"But I don't think—" Kahlan began.

"And are you willing to risk the lives of all those young men on what you think? Are you so sure? I don't know that the Dominie Dirtch work together like that, but what if they do? Maybe one rung in anger rings them all. Can you say it won't?

"I'm not willing to put the innocent lives of those brave men to such a deadly gamble. Are you?" Richard looked back to Captain Meiffert. "Are you? Are you a gambler, Captain? Could you so easily wager the lives of all those men?"

He shook his head. "If it was my own life, Lord Rahl, I would willingly risk it, but not for all those lives."

The roar eased up as the rain slowed a little. Men went by outside the opening of the tent, taking feed to the horses. For the most part, the camp sat in pitch blackness; fires were forbidden except where essential.

"I can't disagree with that." Kahlan lifted her hands and then in frustration let them drop back into her lap. "But Jagang is coming. If we don't win the people to our cause so they will stand against him he will take Anderith. He will be invincible behind the Dominie Dirtch and be able to stab into the Midlands at will and bleed us to death."

Richard listened to the rain drumming on the tent roof and splashing outside the open doorway. It sounded like the kind of steady rain that was going to be with them for the night.

Richard spoke softly. "As I see it, we have only one option. We must go back to the library at the estate and see if we can find anything useful."

"We haven't yet," Kahlan said.

"And with the people in charge now taking a stand against us," Captain Meiffert said, "they might resist that."

Richard made a fist on the table as he met the man's blue-eyed gaze. Richard once again wished he had the Sword of Truth with him.

"If they resist, Captain, then you and your men will be called upon to do what you constantly train for. If they resist, and if we have to, we'll cut down anyone who lifts a finger to oppose us and then we'll level the place. We just need to get the books out of there first."

Relief eased the expression on the man's face. The D'Harans seemed to harbor a fear that Richard might be unwilling to act; Captain Meiffert looked assuaged to hear otherwise.

"Yes, Lord Rahl. The men will be ready in the morning, when you are."

Kahlan's point about there possibly being nothing of value at the estate was worrisome. Richard remembered the books in the library. While he couldn't recall the details of the information, he remembered the subjects well enough to know that finding the answer was a long shot. Still, it was the only shot they had.

"Before I go"—Captain Meiffert pulled a paper from his pocket—"I thought you should know a number of people have requested an audience when you have time, Lord Rahl. Most of them were merchants wanting information."

"Thank you, Captain, but I don't have time now."

"I understand, Lord Rahl. I took the liberty of telling them as much." He shuffled his little notes. "There was one woman." He squinted in the dim candlelight to make out the name. "Franca Gowenlock. She said it was extremely urgent, but would give no information. She was here most of the day. She finally said she had to return to her home, but she would be back tomorrow."

"If it's important, she'll be back and I'll talk to her."

Richard looked down at Du Chaillu, to see how she was feeling. She looked comforted by Kahlan's care.

Behind him rose a sudden commotion. The captain pitched backward with a cry as if felled by magic. The candle flame fluttered wildly at the intrusion of a wind, but stayed lit.

Richard spun to the sound of a dull thump. The candle wobbled across the top of the shuddering table, right up to the edge.

A huge raven had crashed sprawling onto the tabletop.

Richard scooted back in surprise, drawing his sword as he stood, wishing again that it were the Sword of Truth with its attendant magic. Kahlan and Du Chaillu shot to their feet.

The raven had something black in its big beak. With all the confusion—the wind, the candle nearly toppling, the flame fluttering, the table teetering, and the tent sides flapping—he didn't immediately recognize the object in the raven's beak.

The raven set it on the table.

The inky black bird, water beaded on glossy feathers like the night itself come into their tent, looked exhausted. The way it lay sprawled on the table with its wings open, Richard didn't think it was well, or possibly it was injured.

Richard didn't know if a thing possessed of the chimes could really be injured. He recalled the chicken-that-wasn't-a-chicken bleeding. He saw a smear of blood on the tabletop.

Whenever that chime-in-a-chicken had been around, even if he couldn't see it, the hairs at the back of Richard's neck had stood up, yet, with this raven-that-wasn't-a-raven right before him on the table, he hadn't reacted that way.

The raven cocked its head, looking Richard in the eye. It was as deliberate a look as he'd ever gotten. With its beak, the bird tapped the center of the thing it had laid on the table.

Captain Meiffert sprang up then and swung his sword. At the same time, Richard flung up his arms, shouting "No!"

The raven, as the sword came down, hurled itself off the table onto the ground and ran between the captain's legs. Once past the man, it took wing and was gone.

"Sorry," the captain said. "I thought . . . I thought it was attacking you with magic, Lord Rahl. I thought it was a thing of dark magic, come to attack you."

Richard let out a deep breath as he gestured forgiveness to the man. The man was only trying to protect him.

"It was not evil," Du Chaillu said in a soft voice as she and Kahlan came closer.

Richard sank back down on his stool. "No, it wasn't."

Kahlan and Du Chaillu stood over his shoulder, looking.

"What omen did the messenger from the spirits bring you?" the spirit woman asked.

"I don't think it was from the spirit world," Richard said.

He picked up the small, flat object. In the dim light, he suddenly realized what it was. He stared incredulously.

It was just like the one Sister Verna used to carry. He had seen her use it countless times.

"It's a journey book."

He opened the cover.

"That has to be High D'Haran," Kahlan said of the strange script.

"Dear spirits," Richard breathed, as he read the only two words on the first page.

"What?" Kahlan asked. "What is it? What does it say?"

"*Fuer Berglendursch.* You're right. It's High D'Haran."

"Do you know the meaning?"

"It says, 'The Mountain.' " Richard turned and peered up at her in the flickering candlelight. "That was Joseph Ander's cognomen. This is Joseph Ander's journey book. The other, the one that was destroyed, its twin, was called *Mountain's Twin.*"

CHAPTER 62

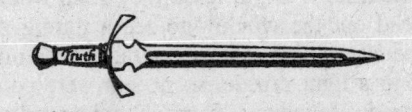

DALTON SMILED AS HE stood at an octagonal table of rare black walnut in the reliquary in the Office of Cultural Amity, where displayed on the walls around the room were objects belonging to past Directors: robes; small tools; implements of their profession, such as pens and beautifully carved blotters; and writings. Dalton was looking over more modern writings: reports he had requested from the Directors.

Any ambivalence the Directors might feel, they kept to themselves. Publicly, they now threw themselves into the task of supporting the new Sovereign. It had been made plain to them that their very existence now depended not only upon their fealty, but upon their enthusiasm in that devotion.

As he read the script of addresses they were to deliver, Dalton was annoyed by shouts coming in through an open window overlooking the city square. It sounded like an angry mob of people. Judging by the boisterous encouragement from the crowd, he assumed it was someone delivering a diatribe against Lord Rahl and the Mother Confessor.

Following the lead of noted people such as the Directors, ordinary people had now taken to loudly voicing the tailored notions they had been fed. Even though Dalton had expected it, he never failed to find it remarkable the way he had but to say a thing enough times, through enough people, and it became the popular truth, its provenance lost as it was mimicked by ordinary people who came to believe that it was their own idea—as if original thought routinely came forth from their witless minds of clay.

Dalton let out a bitter snort of contempt. They were asses and deserved the fate they embraced. They belonged to the Imperial Order, now. Or, at least, they soon would.

He glanced out the window to see a throng making its way into the city square. The heavy rain of the night before had turned to a light drizzle, so people were coming back out. The steady downpour overnight failed to wash away the blackened places on the cobble paving in the square where the two people had burned to death.

The crowd, of course, blamed the tragedy on the magic of Lord Rahl, venting his wrath against them. Dalton had instructed his people to bitterly make the accusation, knowing the seriousness of the charge would outweigh the lack of evidence, much less the truth.

What had really happened, Dalton didn't know. He did know this was far from the first such incident. Whatever it was, it was an appalling misfortune, but if misfortune was to happen, it could have hardly picked a better time. It had punctuated Director Prevot's speech perfectly.

Dalton wondered if the fires had anything to do with what Franca had told him about magic failing. He didn't see how, but he didn't think she had told him everything, either. The woman had been behaving quite oddly of late.

At the knock, Dalton turned to the door. Rowley bowed.

"What is it?"

"Minister," Rowley said, "the . . . woman is here, the one Emperor Jagang sent."

"Where is she?"

"Down the hall. She is having tea."

Dalton shifted his scabbard at his hip. This was not a woman to trifle with; she was said to have more power than any ordinary such woman. More power even than Franca. Jagang had assured him, though, that unlike Franca, this woman still had firm control of her power.

"Take her to the estate. Give her one of our finest rooms. If she gives you any—" Dalton recalled Franca's talent for overhearing things. "If she gives you any complaints, see to resolving them to her satisfaction. She is a most important guest, and is to be treated as such."

Rowley bowed. "Yes, Minister."

Dalton saw Rowley smile with one side of his mouth. He, too, knew why the woman was there. Rowley was looking forward to it.

Dalton just wanted it done with. It would require care. They had to wait and pick their own time. They couldn't force it, or the whole thing could come undone. If they handled it right, though, it would be a great accomplishment. Jagang would be more than grateful.

"I appreciate your generosity."

Dalton turned at the sound of a woman's voice. She had stepped into the doorway. Rowley backed out of her way.

She looked middle-aged, with gray hair mixing in with the black. Her simple, dowdy, dark blue dress ran from her neck, over her rather thick-boned shape, and all the way to the floor.

Her presence was dominated by a smile that only vaguely touched her lips, but was ever so evident in her brown eyes. It was as nasty a simper as Dalton had ever seen. It unashamedly proclaimed a mien of superiority. Because of the lines at the corners of her mouth and eyes, the self-satisfied smirk seemed enduringly etched on her face.

A gold ring pierced her lower lip.

"And you would be?" He asked.

"Sister Penthea. Here to wield my talent in service to His Excellency, Emperor Jagang."

Her smooth flow of words was laced with crystalline frost.

Dalton bowed his head. "Minister of Culture, Dalton

Campbell. Thank you for coming, Sister Penthea. We are most appreciative of your courtesy in lending your unique assistance."

She had been sent to wield her talent in service to Dalton Campbell, but he thought better of putting too fine a point on it. Dalton didn't need to remind her she was the one with a ring through her lip; it was obvious to them both.

At the sound of screams, Dalton again glanced across the room, out the window, thinking it was the parents or family returned to see the sight of the grisly deaths the night before. People had been coming by all morning, leaving flowers or other offerings at the site of the deaths until they looked like a grotesque garden midden. Frequent wails of anguish rose up into the gray day.

Sister Penthea turned his attention to business. "I need to see the ones chosen for the deed."

Dalton motioned with a hand. "Rowley, there, he will be one of them."

Without word or warning, she slapped the palm of her hand to Rowley's forehead, her fingers splayed into his red hair, grasping his head as if she might pluck it like a ripe pear. Rowley's eyes rolled back in his head. His entire body began to tremble.

The Sister murmured thick words that had no meaning to Dalton. Each, as it oozed forth, seemed to take root in Rowley. The young man's arms flinched when she stressed particular words.

With a last phrase, raising in intonation, she gave Rowley's head a sharp shove. Letting out a small cry, Rowley crumpled as if his bones had dissolved.

In a moment, he sat up and shook his head. A smile told Dalton he was fine. He brushed clean his dark brown trousers as he stood, looking no different, despite his added lethality.

"The others?" she asked.

Dalton gestured dismissively. "Rowley can take you to them."

She bowed slightly. "Good day, then, Minister. I will see

to it immediately. The emperor also wished me to express his pleasure at being able to be of assistance. Either way, muscle or magic, the Mother Confessor's fate is now sealed."

She wheeled around and stormed away, Rowley following in her wake. Dalton couldn't say he was sorry to see her go.

Before he could return to reading his reports in earnest, he again heard the cheering. The sight when he lifted his head to look out the window was unexpected. Someone was being dragged into the square, a mob of people following behind as the people already in the square parted to make way, cheering on those entering, some of whom carried scraps of crates, tree branches, and sheafs of straw.

Dalton went to the window and leaned on the sill with both hands as he peered down at the sight. It was Serin Rajak, at the head of a few hundred of his followers all dressed in white robes.

When he saw who they had, who they were dragging into the square, who was screaming, Dalton gasped aloud.

His heart pounding with dread, he stared out the window, wondering what he could do. He had guards with him, real guards, not Anderith army soldiers, but two dozen men. He realized it was a futile thought even as he had it; armed though they were, they stood no chance against the thousands in the square. Dalton knew better than to stand before a crowd intent on violence—that was only a good way to have the violence turned your way.

Despite his feelings, Dalton dared not side against the people in this.

Among the men with Serin Rajak, in among the man's followers, Dalton saw one in a dark uniform: Stein.

With icy dread, Dalton realized the reason Stein was there, and what he wanted.

Dalton backed away from the window. He was no stranger to violence, but this was an atrocity.

At last, he ran back into the corridor that echoed his footfalls, descended the steps, and raced down the hall. He didn't know what to do, but if there was anything . . .

He reached the entry set behind fluted stone columns out-side the building, at the top of the cascade of steps. He halted well back in the shadows of the interior, assessing the situation.

Outside, on the landing partway down the steps, guards patrolled to keep people from thoughts of coming up into the Office of Cultural Amity. It was a symbolic gesture. This many people would easily sweep aside the guards. Dalton dared not give people in such a foul mood a reason to turn their anger to him.

A woman, holding the hand of a young boy, pulled him along as she pushed her way to the front of the crowd. "I am Nora," she proclaimed to the people. "This is my son, Bruce. He's all I got left, because of witches! My husband, Julian, was drowned because of a dark curse from a witch! My beautiful daughter Bethany was burned up alive by a witch's spell!"

The boy, Bruce, wept, mumbling it was true, wept for his father and sister. Serin Rajak held up the woman's arm.

"Here is a victim of the Keeper's witchcraft!" He pointed to a wailing woman near the front. "There is another! Many of you here have been harmed by curses and hexes from witches! Witches using evil from the Keeper of the Dead!"

With a crowd in this ugly a mood, Dalton knew this could come to no good end, but he could think of nothing to do to stop it.

It was, after all, the reason he had released Serin Rajak: to rouse anger against magic. He needed people to be stirred up against those with magic, to see them as evil. Who better than a zealot to foment such hatred?

"And here is the witch!" Serin Rajak thrust his arm out to point at the woman whose hands were bound behind her, the woman Stein held by the hair. "She is the Keeper's vile tool! She casts evil spells to harm you all!"

The mob was yelling and screaming for vengeance.

"What should we do with this witch?" Rajak shrieked.

"Burn her! Burn her! Burn her!" came the chant.

Serin Rajak flung his arms toward the sky. "Dear Creator, we commend this woman to your care in the flames! If she be innocent, spare her harm! If she be guilty of the crime of witchcraft, burn her!"

As men threw up a pole, Stein bore his captive facedown to the ground. He pulled her head up by her hair. With his other hand, he brought up his knife.

Dalton, his eyes wide, was unable to blink, to breathe, as he watched Stein slice from one ear to the other, across the top of Franca's forehead. Her scream ripped Dalton's insides, as Stein ripped back her scalp.

Tears ran down Dalton's cheeks as blood ran down Franca's face. Shrieking in pain and immeasurable terror, she was lifted and bound to the pole. The whites of her eyes stood out from a mask of blood.

Franca didn't argue for her innocence or beg for her life. She just screamed in paralyzed horror.

Straw and wood were thrown up around her. The mob pressed in, wanting to be close, to see it all. Some reached out and stole a swipe at the blood coursing down her face, eager for a memento of witch's blood on their fingertips, to prove their power, before they sent her to the Keeper.

Horror dragging him by his throat, Dalton staggered partway down the steps.

Men with torches pushed through to the front of the roaring mob. Serin Rajak, wild with rage, climbed the clutter of wood and straw at her feet to shout in Franca's face, to call her every sort of vile name, and accuse her of every sort of evil crime.

Dalton, standing helpless on the steps, knew all the words to be false. Franca was not one of those things.

Just then, a most extraordinary thing happened. A raven swooped down from the gray sky, fixing its angry claws in Serin Rajak's hair.

Serin screamed that it was the witch's familiar, come to protect its mistress. The crowd responded by throwing things at the bird while at the same time Serin tried to fight it off. The bird flapped and squawked, but held on to the man's hair.

With such frightening determination that Dalton began to think that the charges it was the witch's familiar seemed true, the huge inky black bird used its beak to stab out Serin's good eye.

The man screamed in pain and rage as he fell from the tinder around Franca. As he did, the mob heaved on the torches.

A wail such as Dalton had never heard rose from poor Franca as the flames exploded through the dry straw and up the length of her. Even from where he stood, Dalton could smell the burning flesh.

And then, in her terror, in her pain, in her burning death, Franca turned her head, and saw Dalton standing there on the steps.

She screamed his name. Over the roar of the crowd, he couldn't hear it, but he could read it on her lips.

She screamed it again, and screamed she loved him.

When Dalton read those words on her lips, they crushed his heart.

The flames blistered her flesh, till the scream pushed from her lungs sounded like the shriek of the lost souls in the world of the dead.

Dalton stood numb, watching it, realizing only then that his hands were holding his head, and he was screaming too.

The crowd surged forward, eager to smell the roasting flesh, to see the witch's skin burn. They were wild with excitement, their eyes mad with it. As the mob pressed in, the ones in front were pushed so close it singed off their eyebrows, and this, too, they relished, as the witch screamed and burned.

On the ground, the raven was pecking wildly at the blinded, almost forgotten, Serin Rajak. He swung his arms, unseeing, trying to get the vengeful bird away. Darting in between his flailing arms, the raven's big beak snatched, twisted, and tore chunks of flesh from his face.

704

The crowd began pelting the bird anew with anything handy. The bird, finally looking as if it was losing strength, flapped helplessly as everything from shoes to flaming branches arced through the air toward it.

For reasons he didn't understand, Dalton, weeping, found himself cheering the bird against all odds, knowing it, too, was about to die.

Just as it looked as if the end was near for the valiant, avenging raven, a riderless horse charged into the square. Blocked by the mob, it reared wildly, knocking people aside. It spun and kicked, injuring people, snapping bones, breaking heads. People fell back as the golden chestnut-colored horse, ears pinned back, snorting with an angry scream, charged into the center of the crowd. Frightened people, trying to fall back, were unable to make way for the press of other people behind them.

The horse, seeming to have gone insane with anger, trampled anyone in its way to get to the center of the square. Dalton had never heard of a horse running toward a fire.

As it reached the middle of the melee, the raven, with a last desperate effort, flapped its great black wings and made it up onto the horse's back. When the horse wheeled, Dalton thought for a moment that it had another bird on it, as if there were two black ravens, but then he realized the second was just a splotch of black color on the horse's rump.

With the raven's claws clutching the horse's mane just above the withers, the horse reared up one last time before coming down and charging off in a dead run. The people who could, leaped out of the way. Those unable to do so were trampled by the enraged beast.

Alone on the steps, Franca's screams thankfully ended, Dalton saluted the golden chestnut mare and avenging raven as they fled at a full gallop from the city center.

CHAPTER 63

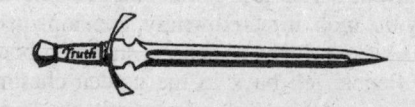

BEATA SQUINTED OUT OVER the plains in the dawn light. It was good to see that the sun was going to shine, once it reached the horizon. The rain of the last few days had been wearing. Now there were only a few dark purple clouds, like a child's charcoal scribbles, across the golden eastern sky. From up on the stone base of the Dominie Dirtch, beneath that immense sweep of sky overhead, she could see forever, it seemed, out onto the vast plains of the wilds.

Beata saw that Estelle Ruffin was right in calling her up top. In the distance a rider was coming. He was taking the dry ground, right toward them. The rider was still a goodly distance, but by the way he was running his horse, he didn't look like he intended to stop. Beata waited until he was a little closer, and then cupped her hands around her mouth and yelled.

"Halt! Halt where you are!"

Still he came on. He was probably still too far away to hear her. The plains were deceptive; sometimes it took a rider much longer to reach them than it seemed it should.

"What should we do?" Estelle asked, having never had a rider approach so fast before, looking like he didn't intend to stop.

Beata was finally used to Anders relying on her and asking her for instructions. She was not only getting used to her authority, she had come to delight in it.

It was ironic. Bertrand Chanboor had made the laws that enabled Beata to join the army and command Anders, and Bertrand Chanboor had caused her to avail herself of the laws. She hated him, and at the same time he was her unwitting benefactor. Now that he was Sovereign, she tried, as was her duty and hard as it was, to feel only love for him.

Just the night before, Captain Tolbert had come by with some D'Haran soldiers. They were riding down the line of Dominie Dirtch to take the votes of the squads stationed at each weapon. They'd all talked about it, and though Beata didn't see their votes, she knew her squad all marked an X.

Beata had a strong feeling about Lord Rahl, having met and talked to him, that he was a good man. The Mother Confessor, too, seemed much kinder than Beata had expected. Still, Beata and her squad were proud to be in the Anderith army, the best army in the world, Captain Tolbert told them, an army undefeated since the creation of the land, and invincible now.

Beata had responsibility. She was a soldier who commanded respect, now, just as Bertrand Chanboor's law said. She didn't want anything to change.

Even though it was for Bertrand Chanboor, their new Sovereign, and against Lord Rahl, Beata had proudly marked an X.

Emmeline had her hand on the striker, and Karl stood close to it, too, anticipating Beata ordering it out. Beata, instead, motioned the two away from the thing.

"There's only one rider," Beata said in a calm voice of authority, settling their nerves.

Estelle heaved a sigh in frustration. "But Sergeant—"

"We are trained soldiers. One man is no threat. We know how to fight. We've been trained in combat."

Karl shifted his sword on his weapons belt, eager for the responsibility of doing some real soldiering. Beata snapped her fingers, pointing to the steps.

"Go, Karl. Get Norris and Annette. The three of you meet me down at the front line. Emmeline, you stay up here with Estelle, but I want both of you to stand away from the striker. I'll not have you ringing this weapon for no more threat than a lone rider. We'll handle it. Just stay at your post and keep watch."

Both women saluted with a hand to their brow. Karl did a quick version before he raced down the steps, breathless with the possibility of real action. Beata straightened her sword at her hip and went down the steps in a dignified manner more befitting her rank.

Beata stood beside the huge stone weapon at the line, as they called it; beyond, the Dominie Dirtch would kill. She clasped her hands behind her back as Karl raced up with Norris and Annette. Annette was still putting on her chain mail.

Beata finally understood the shouts coming from the rider racing toward them. He was screaming for them not to ring the Dominie Dirtch.

Beata thought she recognized the voice.

Karl had his hand on the hilt of his sword. "Sergeant?"

She nodded and the two men and one woman drew steel. It was the first time they'd done so for a potential threat. They were all three beaming with the thrill of it.

Beata cupped her hands around her mouth again. "Halt!"

This time the rider heard her. He hauled back on the reins and drew his lathered horse to a stumbling, clumsy halt a little distance out.

Beata's jaw dropped.

"Fitch!"

He grinned. "Beata! Is that you?"

He dismounted and walked his horse toward her. The horse looked in sorry shape. Fitch didn't look much better, but he still managed to swagger.

"Fitch," Beata growled, "get over here."

Disappointed that Beata knew the man and there didn't look like there wasn't going to be any swordplay, Karl, Norris, and Annette returned their weapons to their scabbards.

708

They all stared openly, though, at the weapon Fitch was wearing.

It was held on with a baldric running over the right shoulder opposite the sword and scabbard at his left hip, thereby helping balance the weight. The leather of the baldric was finely tooled and looked old; Beata knew leatherwork, and hadn't seen anything that fine. The scabbard was embellished with simply peerless silver and gold work.

The sword itself was remarkable, what she could see, anyway. It had a downswept, brightwork cross guard. The hilt looked wound in silver wire, with a bit of gold, too, glinting in the early light.

Fitch, chest puffed up, smiled at her. "Good to see you, Beata. I'm glad to see you got the job you were after. I guess both of us got our dream after all."

Beata knew she had earned her dream. Having known Fitch a good long time, she doubted the same of him.

"Fitch, what are you doing here, and what are you doing with that weapon?"

His chin lifted. "It's mine. I told you that someday I'd be Seeker, and now I am. This here is the Sword of Truth."

Beata stared down at it. Fitch turned the weapon out a little so she could see the hilt with writing in gold wire. It was the word Fitch had drawn in the dust that one day at the Minister's estate. She remembered it: TRUTH.

"The wizards gave you that?" Beata pointed, incredulous. "The wizards named you Seeker of Truth?"

"Well . . ." Fitch glanced back over his shoulder, out to the wilds. "It's a long story, Beata."

"Sergeant Beata," she said, not about to be outdone by the likes of Fitch.

He shrugged. "Sergeant. That's great, Beata." He glanced over his shoulder again. "Um, can I talk to you?" He cast a wary eye to those watching their every word. "Alone?"

"Fitch, I don't—"

"Please?"

He looked worried, like she'd never seen him before. Behind the cocky attitude he was distraught.

709

Beata took hold of his filthy messenger's jacket at the collar and pulled him along, away from the others. All their eyes followed. Beata guessed she didn't blame them; it was the most interesting thing that had happened since the day the Mother Confessor and Lord Rahl came through.

"What are you doing with that sword? It isn't yours."

Fitch's face took on the familiar pleading expression she knew so well. "Beata, I had to take it. I had to—"

"You stole it? You stole the Sword of Truth?"

"I had to. You don't—"

"Fitch, you are a thief. I should arrest you and—"

"Well, that would be fine by me. Then I could prove the charges are false."

She frowned. "What charges?"

"That I raped you."

Beata was thunderstruck. She couldn't even say anything.

"I got accused of what the Minister and Stein did to you. I need this Sword of Truth to help me prove the truth—that I didn't do it, that the Minister is the one who did it and—"

"He's the Sovereign now."

Fitch sagged. "Then not even this sword will help me. The Sovereign. Boy, this is a real mess."

"You've got that right."

He seemed to get life back in him. He seized her by her shoulders. "Beata, you got to help me. There's a crazy woman after me. Use the Dominie Dirtch. Stop her. You can't let her through."

"Why? She the one you stole the sword from?"

"Beata, you don't understand—"

"You stole that sword, but it's me that don't understand? I understand you're a liar."

Fitch sagged. "Beata, she murdered Morley."

Beata's eyes widened. She knew how big Morley was. "You mean, she has magic, or something?"

Fitch looked up. "Magic. Yes. That must be it. She has magic. Beata, she's crazy. She killed Morley—"

"Imagine that, someone kills a thief and that makes her a crazy murderer. You are a worthless Haken, Fitch. That's all you are—a worthless Haken who stole a sword that doesn't belong to them and they never could earn."

"Beata, please, she's going to kill me. Please don't let her through."

"Riders coming," Estelle called out.

Fitch nearly jumped out of his skin. Beata looked up at Estelle, but saw she was pointing to the rear, not out to the wilds. Beata relaxed a bit.

"Who are they?" she called up at Estelle.

"Can't tell, yet, Sergeant."

"Fitch, you got to give that thing back. When this woman comes, you have to—"

"Rider coming, Sergeant," Emmeline called, pointing out to the wilds.

"What's she look like?" Fitch called up, frantic as a cat with its tail afire.

Emmeline looked out to the plains for a minute. "I don't know. She's too far away."

"Red." Fitch called. "Does it look like she's in red?"

Emmeline peered off another minute. "Blond hair, wearing red."

"Let her pass!" Beata ordered.

"Yes, Sergeant."

Fitch threw up his arms, looking suddenly terrified. "Beata, what are you doing? You want to get me killed? She's crazy! The woman is a monster, she's—"

"We'll have a talk with her. Don't worry, we'll not let the little boy get drubbed. We'll find out what she wants and take care of it."

Fitch looked hurt. That did not displease Beata, not after all the trouble he was causing, after he stole something as valuable as the Sword of Truth. A valuable thing of magic. Now the fool boy had gone and got his friend Morley involved in thieving and got him killed for it.

And to think, she once thought she could fall in love with Fitch.

He hung his head. "Beata, I'm sorry. I just wanted to make you proud—"

"Thieving is not something to be proud of, Fitch."

"You just don't understand," he muttered, on the verge of tears. "You just don't understand."

Beata heard an odd ruckus from the next Dominie Dirtch. Shouts and such, but no alarm. As she turned to look, she saw the three special Anderith guards, the ones Estelle had spotted, trotting in on their horses. She wondered what they would want.

She turned to the sound of the galloping horse coming in. Beata jabbed a finger against Fitch's chest.

"Now, you just keep quiet and let me do the talking."

Rather than answer, he stared at the ground. Beata turned and saw the horse race past the stone base. The woman was indeed wearing red. Beata had never seen anything like it, a red leather outfit from head to toe. Her long blond braid was flying out behind.

Beata's guard went up. She had never seen a look of determination such as was on this woman's face.

She didn't even bother to halt her horse. She simply dove off it at Fitch. Beata shoved Fitch out of the way. The woman rolled twice and came up on her feet.

"Hold on!" Beata cried. "I told him we'd settle this with you, and he'd give you back what's yours!"

Beata was baffled to see that the woman held a black bottle by its neck. To dive off a horse with a bottle . . . maybe Fitch was right; maybe she was crazy.

She didn't look crazy. But she did look resolved to carry this matter into the next world if she had to.

The woman, her sky-blue eyes fixed on Fitch, ignored Beata. "Give it over now, and I'll not kill you. I'll only make you regret being born."

Fitch, instead of giving up, drew the sword.

It made a ring of steel such as Beata, used to the sound of blades, had never heard.

Fitch got a strange look on his face. His eyes were going wide, like he might faint, or something. His eyes had a decidedly strange look in them, a shimmering light that gave

Beata gooseflesh. It was a look of some kind of awesome inner vision.

The woman held the bottle out in one hand, like it was a weapon. With her other hand, she waggled her fingers, taunting Fitch to come closer, to attack her.

Beata stepped in to restrain the woman until they could talk it over.

Beata next realized she was sitting on the ground. Her face stung something fierce.

"Stay out of it," the woman said in a voice like ice. "There is no need for you to be hurt. Do yourself a favor and stay down."

Her blue eyes turned to Fitch. "Come on, boy. Either give it up, or do something about it."

Fitch did something about it. He swung the sword. Beata could hear the tip whistle going through the air.

The woman danced back a step and at the same time thrust with the black bottle. The sword shattered it into a thousand pieces that filled the air like a storm cloud.

"HA!" the woman cried in triumph.

She grinned wickedly.

"Now I'll take the sword."

She flicked her wrist. When she did, a red leather rod hanging on a gold chain at her wrist spun up into her hand. At first she looked expectantly overjoyed, but the look turned to confusion, and then to bafflement as she stared at the thing in her hand.

"It should work," she mumbled to herself. "It should work."

When she looked up she saw something that brought her back to her senses. Beata glanced over, but didn't see anything odd.

The woman seized Beata's outfit at the shoulder and hauled her to her feet. "Get your people out of here. Get them out now!"

"What? Fitch is right. You are—"

She thrust her arm out, pointing. "Look, you fool!"

The special Anderith guards were coming toward them, chatting among themselves. "Those are our men. They're nothing to worry—"

"Get your people out of here right now, or you will all die."

Beata huffed at being ordered about by some crazy woman treating her like a child. She called over to Corporal Marie Fauvel, not twenty feet away as she was walking out to see what the commotion was all about.

"Corporal Fauvel," Beata called out.

"Yes, Sergeant?" the Ander woman asked.

"Have those men wait there until we get this settled." Beata put her fists on her hips as she turned to the woman in red.

"Satisfied?"

The woman ground her teeth and grabbed Beata's shoulder again. "You little fool! Get you and your other children moving right now or you will all die!"

Beata was getting angry. "I'm an officer in the Anderith army, and those men . . ." Beata turned to point.

Marie Fauvel stepped in front of the men, held up a hand, and told them they would have to wait.

One of the three unceremoniously drew his sword and swung it with casual, but frightening, power. Accompanied by the sickening thwack of blade hitting bone, it cut Marie clean in half.

Beata stood stupefied, not really believing what she was seeing.

Working for a butcher, she'd seen so much slaughtering it hardly ever warranted a second look. She'd cleaned the guts from so many different animals that seeing guts seemed to her just a natural thing. Guts didn't appall Beata in the least.

Seeing Marie there on the ground, with her guts spilling out of her top half, in one way seemed only a curiosity, a human animal's guts so similar to other animals', but human.

Marie Fauvel, separated from her hips and legs, gasped,

clutching at the grass, her eyes wide as her brain tried to comprehend the shock of what had just happened to her body.

It was so dauntingly horrifying Beata couldn't move.

Marie pulled at the grass, trying to drag herself away from the men, toward Beata. Her lips moved, but no words came out, just low, hoarse grunts. Her fingers lost their power. She slumped, twitching like a freshly butchered sheep.

Up on the Dominie Dirtch, both Estelle and Emmeline screamed.

Beata pulled free her sword, holding it aloft for all to see. "Soldiers! Attack!"

Beata checked the men. They were still coming.

They were grinning.

And then the world turned truly mad.

CHAPTER 64

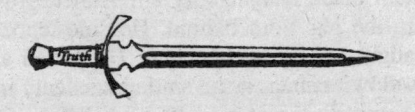

NORRIS RUSHED FORWARD, LIKE they'd been trained, going for the legs of one man. The man kicked Norris in the face. Norris fell back, holding his face, blood running out through his fingers. The man picked up Norris's fallen sword and plunged it through his gut, pinning Norris to the ground, leaving him to squirm in screaming agony, to shred his fingers on the sharp blade.

Karl and Bryce were rushing in with weapons drawn. Carine charged out of the barracks with a spear. Annette was right behind her with another.

Beata felt a surge of conviction. The men were going to be surrounded. Her soldiers were trained for combat. They could handle three men.

"Sergeant!" the woman in red called. "Get back!"

Beata was terrified, but she still felt annoyed by the woman, who obviously didn't know the first thing about soldiering. Beata was also ashamed for the woman's cowardice. Beata and her soldiers would stand and fight—they would protect the worthless woman in red, who feared to stand up to a mere three of the enemy.

Fitch, too, Beata was proud to note, rushed forward with his prize sword, ready to fight.

As they all rushed in, only the man who had cut down Marie even had his sword out. The other two still had their weapons sheathed. She was furious that they would take Beata's squad so lightly.

Beata, better accustomed to stabbing meat with a blade than were the rest of her squad, confidently went for a man. She didn't see how, but he effortlessly dodged her.

Startled, she realized that this was not at all like stabbing straw men, or carcasses hanging from a hook.

As Beata's blade caught only air, Annette rushed up to stab him in the leg from behind. He sidestepped Annette, too, but caught her by her red hair. He pulled a knife and in an easy, slow manner, as he smiled wickedly into Beata's eyes, slit Annette's throat as if he were butchering a hog.

Another man caught Carine's spear, snapped it in half with one hand, and rammed the barbed point in her gut.

Karl swung his sword low at the man Beata missed, trying to hamstring him, and got his face kicked, instead. The man swung his sword down at Karl. Beata sprang forward and blocked his strike.

The power of the ringing blow of steel against steel hammered her weapon from her hand. Her hands stung so much she couldn't flex her unfeeling fingers. She realized she was on her knees.

The man swung down on Karl. Karl held his hands up protectively before his face. The sword severed his hands at midpalm before it split his face to his chin.

The man turned back to Beata. His blood-slicked sword was coming for her face, next. Seeing it coming, Beata could do nothing but scream.

A hand snatched her hair and violently yanked her back. The sword tip whistled right past her face, hitting the ground between her legs. It was the woman in red who had just saved Beata's life.

The man's attention was caught by something else. He turned to look. Beata looked, too, and saw riders coming. Maybe as many as a hundred. More special Anderith guards, just like these three.

The woman in red pulled Bryce back just before he was killed. As soon as she turned to something else, he rushed back at the enemy despite her orders to stay back. Beata saw a sword, the blade red, erupt from the middle of Bryce's back, lifting him from his feet.

The big man who had hacked Karl now turned his attention back to Beata. She tried to scurry back, but his long stride was faster. In her panic, she couldn't get her feet. Beata knew she was going to die.

As the sword swung down on her, she couldn't think what to do. She began a prayer she knew she wouldn't get a chance to finish.

Fitch leaped in front of her, his sword blocking the killing blow. The enemy's blade shattered on Fitch's weapon. Beata blinked in surprise. She was still alive.

Fitch took a fierce swing at the man. He sidestepped, Fitch's blade just missing his middle as he arched his back.

With icy efficiency as the blade was going by him, the man casually unhooked a spiked mace from a hanger on his weapons belt. As Fitch was still whipping around with the momentum, the man took a swift, powerful, backhanded swing.

The blow tore off the top of Fitch's skull. Pink chunks

717

of his brains splattered up Beata's tunic. Fitch crumbled to the ground.

Beata sat frozen in shock. She could hear her own cries, like a panicked child. She couldn't make herself stop. It was like she was watching someone else.

Instead of killing her, the man turned his consideration to Fitch, or rather, Fitch's sword. He pulled the gleaming weapon from Fitch's limp hand, and then yanked the baldric and scabbard free of the dead weight of the body.

More mounted men were just arriving as the man slid the Sword of Truth back into the scabbard.

He smiled and winked at Beata. "I think Commander Stein would like to have this. What do you think?"

Beata sat stunned, Fitch's body right in front of her, his brains all over her, his blood emptying out on the ground.

"Why?" was all Beata could say.

The man was still grinning. "Now that you all had your chance to vote, Emperor Jagang is casting the deciding ballot."

"What you got, here?" another man called as he dismounted.

"Some decent-looking girls."

"Well, don't kill 'em all," the man complained goodnaturedly. "I like mine warm and still moving."

The men all laughed. Beata whimpered as she pushed with her heels, scooting away from the men.

"This sword is something I've heard of. I'm taking it to Commander Stein. He'll be pleased no end to be able to present it to the emperor."

Over her shoulder, she saw another man up on the Dominie Dirtch casually disarm Estelle and Emmeline as they tried to defend their post. Emmeline leaped from the Dominie Dirtch to escape. The fall broke her leg. A man on the ground grabbed her red hair in his fist and started dragging her toward the barracks as if he had caught a chicken.

Estelle was getting kissed by the man up on the Dominie Dirtch as she beat her fists against him. The men thought her battling comical. Men in dark leather plates and belts

718

and straps covered with spikes and chain mail and fur, and with massive swords, flails, and axes, were dismounting everywhere. Others, still on their horses, were racing around and around the Dominie Dirtch, cheering.

When the men all turned to Emmeline's renewed screams of pain and terror, and to her captor's laughing, a hand snatched Beata's collar and dragged her back on her bottom.

The woman in red leather behind her growled under her breath, "Move! While you still can!"

Beata, powered by panic, scrambled up and ran with the woman while the men weren't looking. The two of them dove into a dip in the ground hidden by the tall grass.

"Stop that crying!" the woman ordered. "Stop it or you'll get us caught."

Beata forced herself to stop making noise, but she couldn't stop the tears. Her whole squad had just been killed, except Estelle and Emmeline, and they were captured.

Fitch, that fool Fitch, had just gotten himself killed saving her life.

"If you don't hush, I'll slit your throat myself."

Beata bit her lip. She had always been able to keep herself from crying. It had never been this hard.

"I'm sorry," Beata whispered in a whine.

"I just saved your fat from the fire. In return you can at least not get us caught."

The woman watched as the man with the Sword of Truth galloped away, back toward Fairfield. She cursed under her breath.

"Why'd you just drag me away?" Beata asked in bitter anger. "Why didn't you at least try to get some of them?"

The woman flicked out a hand. "Who do you think did that? Who do you think was protecting your back? One of your children soldiers?"

Beata looked then and saw what she hadn't seen before. Dead enemy soldiers sprawled here and there. She looked back to the woman's blue eyes.

"Idiot," the woman muttered.

"You act like this is my fault, like you hate me."

"Because you are a fool." She pointed angrily out at the carnage. "Three men just wiped out your post and they aren't even breathing hard."

"But—they surprised us."

"You think this some game? You're not even smart enough to realize you're nothing more than a dupe. Those in charge puffed you up with false courage and sent you out to fail. It's plain as day and you can't even see it. A hundred of you girls and boys couldn't knock down one of those men. Those are Imperial Order troops."

"But if they just—"

"You think the enemy is going to play by your rules? Real life just got those other young people killed, and the dead girls are going to be better off than the ones still alive, I can promise you that."

Beata was so horrified she couldn't speak. The woman's heated voice softened a little.

"Well, it's not all your fault. I guess you aren't old enough to know better, to know some of life's realities. You can't be expected to see what's true and not. You only think you can."

"Why do you want that sword so bad?"

"Because it belongs to Lord Rahl. He sent me to get it."

"Why'd you save me?"

The woman stared back at her. Behind those cold, calculating blue eyes, there didn't seem to be any fear.

"I guess because I, too, was once a foolish young girl captured by bad men."

"What did they do to you?"

The woman smiled a grim smile. "They made me into what I am: Mord-Sith. You wouldn't be that lucky; these men aren't anywhere near as good at what they do."

Beata had never heard of a Mord-Sith before. Their attention was drawn to Estelle's cries from up on the Dominie Dirtch.

"I need to go after the sword. I suggest you run."

"Take me with you."

"No. You cannot be of any use and will only hold me back."

Beata knew the awful truth of that. "What am I to do?"

"You get your behind out of here before those men get ahold of it or you'll be very much more than sorry."

"Please," Beata said, tears welling up again, "help me save Estelle and Emmeline?"

The woman pressed her lips tight as she considered a moment.

"That one," the woman finally said, with cold reckoning pointing at Estelle. "As I'm leaving, I'll help you get that one. Then it's up to you two to get away."

Beata saw the man laughing, groping Estelle's breasts as she tried to fight him. Beata knew what that was like.

"But we have to get Emmeline, too." She gestured off toward the barracks where they'd dragged her.

"That one has a broken leg. You can't take her; she'll get you caught."

"But she's—"

"Forget her. What are you going to do? Carry her? Stop being a fool child. Think. Do you want to try to get away with that one, or do you want to get yourself captured for sure going after both? I'm in a hurry. Decide."

Beata struggled to breathe, wishing she couldn't hear the screams coming from the barracks. She didn't want to find herself in there with those men. She already had a taste of one of them.

"The one, then. Let's go," Beata said with finality.

"Good for you, child."

The woman was deliberately calling her that, Beata knew, to put her in her place, hoping it would keep her in line and save her life.

"Now, listen and do exactly what I say. I'm not sure you'll make it, but it's your only chance."

Desperate to escape the nightmare, Beata nodded.

"I'm going to go up there and take out that man. I'll see to it you have at least two horses. I'll send the girl down while you grab the horses. Get her up on a horse with you and then head out there and don't stop for anything."

The woman was pointing out past the Dominie Dirtch, out to the wilds. "You just keep going, away from Anderith, to some other place in the Midlands."

"How are you going to keep them from getting us?"

"Who said I was? You just get the horses and then you two run for your lives. All I can do is try to give you a lead." The woman held a finger before Beata's face. "If for any reason she doesn't make it down the steps, or get on the horse, you leave her and run."

Beata, numb from terror, nodded. She just wanted to get away. She didn't care about anything else anymore. She just wanted to escape with her life.

Beata clutched the red leather sleeve. "I'm Beata."

"Good for you. Let's go."

The woman sprang up, running in a crouch. Beata followed after her, imitating her low run. The woman came up behind a soldier standing in their way and knocked his feet out from behind. As soon as he crashed to his back, before he could call out, she dropped on him, crushing his windpipe with a blow from her elbow. Two more quick blows silenced him.

"How did you do that?" Beata asked, dumbfounded.

She pushed Beata down in a thick clump of grass by the man. "Years of training in how to kill. It's my profession." She checked the Dominie Dirtch again. "Wait here until the count of ten, then follow. Don't count fast."

Without waiting for Beata's answer, she sprang into a dead run. Some men watched, confused by what was going on since she wasn't trying to escape, but heading right for the center of all the men. The woman dodged between all the horses racing around the Dominie Dirtch, their riders hooting and hollering.

The man next to Beata was burbling blood from his crushed nose, maybe drowning in it as he lay there on his back.

The man holding Estelle turned. The woman in red yanked the striker from the holder, tearing it away from the restraints. The restraints added momentum as they broke. When the striker clouted the man in the head, Beata could hear it crack his skull from where she stood, as she finally reached the count of ten. He toppled backward over the rail and fell beneath the hooves of running horses.

In the grip of terror, Beata jumped up and started running.

The woman, with a mighty swing, brought the striker around, slamming the Dominie Dirtch.

The world shook with the dull drone of the weapon going off. The sound was overpowering, like it might shimmy her teeth out of their sockets and vibrate Beata's skull apart.

The men on horseback out front screamed. Their horses screamed. The cries ended abruptly as man and beast alike came apart in a bloody blast. Men still running round the Dominie Dirtch couldn't stop in time. They skidded or tumbled past the line to their death.

Beata ran for all she was worth even as she felt her joints might come apart from the terrible chime of the Dominie Dirtch.

Wielding the striker, the woman whacked men off their horses. She seized Estelle by her arm and practically threw her down the steps as Beata gathered the reins to two frightened animals.

The men were in a state of confused panic. They didn't know what would happen with the weapon, if it would chime again and in turn kill them, too. Beata snatched a confused, terrified Estelle by the arm.

The woman in red leaped from the railing onto the back of a man still mounted. The woman still had the broken neck of the black bottle. She gripped the man around the middle and ground the broken bottle into his eyes. He fell screaming from his horse.

She scooted forward into the saddle and snatched up the reins. She reached the tired animal she had arrived on, grabbed her saddlebags, and with a cry of fury urged her horse into a dead run toward Fairfield.

"Up!" Beata screamed to a dazed and bewildered Estelle.

Thankfully, the Ander woman understood her chance to

escape and seized it as Beata, too, scrambled atop a horse. Both animals wheeled all about in the confusion.

Men went charging off after the woman in red leather. Beata was no horsewoman, but she knew what she must do. She thumped her heels against the animal's ribs. Estelle did the same.

The two of them, one Haken, one Ander, ran for their lives.

"Where are we going, Sergeant?" Estelle cried out.

Beata didn't even know what direction she was running, she was just running.

She wanted the uniform off. It was just another cruel joke played on her by Bertrand Chanboor.

"I'm not a sergeant!" Beata yelled back, tears streaming down her face. "I'm just Beata, a fool, same as you, Estelle."

She wished she had thanked the woman in red for saving their lives.

CHAPTER 65

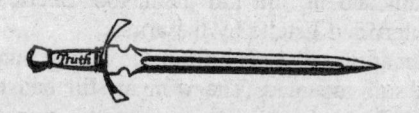

DALTON GLANCED UP TO see Hildemara gliding into his new office. She was wearing a revealing dress of a gold-colored satin with white trim, as if anyone would be interested in what she had to reveal.

He rose behind his new, expansive desk, the like of which he had never imagined would be his.

"Hildemara. What a pleasure to have you stop in for a visit."

She smiled as she peered at him like a hound eyeing a meal. She ambled around his desk to stand close beside him, leaning her bottom against the desk's edge so she could face him intimately.

"Dalton, you look marvelous in that outfit. New? Must be," she said, running a finger down the embroidered sleeve. "You look good in this office, too. Better than my worthless husband ever looked. You bring it some . . . class."

"Thank you, Hildemara. I must say, you look ravishing yourself."

Her smile widened—with true pleasure or in mockery, he wasn't sure. She had not been shy about expressing her admiration for him since the old Sovereign unexpectedly passed on. On the other hand, he knew her well enough not to be lulled into turning his back on her, in a manner of speaking. He wasn't able to decide if she was being warm and friendly, or if she hid an executioner's axe behind her back. Either way, he was on guard.

"The vote is counted from the city, and beginning to come in from the returning soldiers."

Now he thought he knew the reason for her smile, and the results of the people's say. Still, one could never be certain of such things.

"And how are the good people of Anderith responding to Lord Rahl's invitation to join with him?"

"I'm afraid Lord Rahl is no match for you, Dalton."

A tentative smile began to work its way up onto his face. "Really? How convincing is it? If it isn't a resounding rejection, Lord Rahl may feel he has cause to press his case."

She shrugged in a teasing manner. "The people of the city, of course, are reluctant to believe Lord Rahl. Seven of ten gave him an X."

Dalton tipped his head up, closed his eyes, and let out a sigh of relief.

"Thank you Hildemara," he said with a grin. "And the rest?"

"Just starting to come in. It will take the soldiers a time to ride back—"

"But so far. How goes it so far?"

She dragged a finger around on the desktop. "Surprising."

That confused him. "Surprising. How so?"

She turned a beaming smile up at him. "The worst for us is only three in four votes our way. Some places have had as many as eight and nine in ten giving Lord Rahl an X."

Dalton put a hand to his chest as he let out another sigh of relief. "I thought as much, but one can never know for sure in such things."

"Simply amazing, Dalton. You are a wonder." She turned her palms up. "And you didn't even have to cheat. Imagine that."

Dalton made two fists of excitement. "Thank you, Hildemara. Thank you for bringing me the news. If you'll excuse me, I must go straightaway and tell Teresa. I've been so busy, I've hardly seen her for weeks. She'll be so glad to hear the news."

He started to move, but Hildemara put a restraining finger to his chest. Her smile had that deadly edge to it again.

"Teresa already knows, I'm sure."

Dalton frowned. "Who would have told her before I was told?"

"Bertrand told her, I'm sure."

"Bertrand? What would he be doing telling Teresa news like this?"

Hildemara made a little simper. "Oh, you know how Bertrand talks when he's between the legs of a woman he finds thrilling."

Dalton froze. Alarm bells chimed in his head as he began recalling all the times he had been absent from Teresa since Bertrand had been named Sovereign, recalling how taken Teresa was with the figure of Sovereign. He recalled how she had spent the night up in prayer after meeting the old Sovereign. He recalled her awe at Bertrand becoming Sovereign.

He made himself stop speculating in such a fashion. Such

speculation was an insidious enemy that could eat you away from inside. Hildemara, knowing how busy he had been, was probably just hoping to give him a fright, or cause trouble. That would be like her.

"That isn't the least bit amusing, Hildemara."

Propping one hand on the desk, she leaned toward him and ran a finger of the other hand down his jaw. "Not meant to be."

Dalton stood silent, carefully trying to keep from making the wrong move before he knew what was really going on. This could still be a foolish trick of hers, just to make him angry at Tess, thinking it would somehow drive him into her own arms, or it could be nothing more than news she misunderstood. He knew, though, that Hildemara was not likely to get news like this wrong. She had her own sources and they were as reliable as Dalton's.

"Hildemara, I don't think you should be repeating slanderous rumors."

"Not a rumor, my dear Dalton. A fact. I've seen your good wife coming from his room."

"You know Teresa, she likes to pray—"

"I've overheard Bertrand brag to Stein about having her."

Dalton nearly staggered back. "What?"

The smirk spread in deadly perfection.

"Apparently, from what Bertrand tells Stein, she is quite the unrestrained courtesan, and enjoys being a very bad little girl in his bed."

Dalton felt the blood go to his face in a hot rush. He considered killing Hildemara where she stood. As his finger touched the hilt of his sword, he considered it very seriously. Finally, instead, he kept himself under control, although he could feel his knees trembling.

"I just thought you should know, Dalton," she added. "I found it quite sad: my husband is humping your wife and you don't know anything about it. It could be . . . awkward. You could inadvertently embarrass yourself, not knowing."

"Why, Hildemara?" he managed to ask in a whisper. "Why would you get so much satisfaction from this?"

At last her smile bloomed into true pleasure. "Because I always hated your smug superiority about your vows of fidelity—the way you looked down your nose, believing yourself and your wife better than all the rest of us."

By sheer force of will, Dalton restrained himself. In times of trial or exigency, he was always able to become analytical in order to apply the best solution to the situation that confronted him.

With ruthless resolve, he did that now.

"Thank you for the information, Hildemara. It could indeed have been embarrassing."

"Do me a favor and don't go all gloomy about it, Dalton. You have reason to be enormously pleased. This is the Sovereign we're talking about. It is, after all, an honor for any man to provide his wife for as revered and sublime a figure as the Sovereign of Anderith. You will be loved and respected all the more because your wife is giving the Sovereign release from the stresses of his high calling.

"You should know that, Dalton. After all, you made the man who he is: the Creator's advisor in this world. Your wife is simply being a loyal subject." She chuckled. "Very loyal, from what I've overheard. My, but it would take quite the woman to match her."

She leaned close and kissed his ear. "But I'd like to try, Dalton, dear." She looked him in the eye as she straightened. "I've always been fascinated by you. You are the most devious, dangerous man I've ever met, and I've met some real pieces of work."

She turned back from the doorway. "After you come to accept it, you will find it of no importance, Dalton. You'll see.

"And then, as you suggested to me before, once your vow was broken, I will be the first you come to? Don't forget, you promised."

Dalton stood alone in his office, his mind racing, thinking on what he should do.

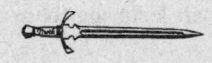

Kahlan laid her arms on his shoulders and leaned over, putting her cheek against his ear. It felt warm and comforting, despite the unneeded distraction. She kissed his temple.

"How is it going?"

Richard stretched with a yawn. Where did one begin?

"This man was bent seriously out of straight."

"What do you mean?"

"I still have a lot to translate, but I'm beginning to get a picture of what happened." Richard rubbed his eyes. "The man is sent here to banish the chimes. He at once scrutinizes the problem, and sees a simple solution. The wizards at the Keep thought it was inspired genius, and told him so."

"He must have been proud," she said, clearly meaning the opposite.

He understood her sardonic tone, and shared the sentiment. "You're right, not Joseph Ander. He doesn't say it here, but from what we've read before, I know the way he thinks. Joseph Ander would have felt not pride in himself for understanding it, but contempt for those who had failed to."

"So," she said, "he had the solution. Then what?"

"They told him to see to it at once. Apparently they were having problems similar to ours with the chimes, and wanted the threat ended immediately. He complained that if they had the good sense to send him to see to it, then they should stop telling him what to do."

"Not a good way to treat his superiors at the Keep."

"They implored him to stop the chimes because of the people dying. Apparently, they knew him well enough to realize they had better not threaten the man, at least not with the rest of the war to worry about. So, they told him to use his best judgment, but to please hurry with a solution so people would be safe from the threat.

"He was much more pleased to get such a message, but used it as a club to start lecturing the wizards at the Keep."

"About what?"

Richard ran his fingers back into his hair. It was frustrating to try to put into words what Joseph Ander was about.

"There's a lot left in here to translate. It's slow going. But I don't think this book is going to tell us how to banish the chimes. Joseph Ander just doesn't think that way—to write it down."

Kahlan straightened and turned around with her back to the table so she could stand facing him.

She folded her arms. "All right, Richard. I know you better than that. What aren't you telling me?"

Richard stood and turned his back to her as he pressed his fingers to his temple.

"Richard, don't you trust me?"

He turned to her. He took up her hand. "No, no, it isn't that. It's just . . . just that some of the things he says, I don't know where truth leaves off and Joseph Ander's madness begins. This goes beyond anything I've ever heard about, been taught, or believed about magic."

Now she did look concerned. He guessed, in one way, he was raising her fears wrongly. On the other hand, he couldn't begin to raise them to the levels of his own fears.

"Joseph Ander," he began, "thought he was just *better* than the other wizards."

"We already knew that."

"Yes, but he may have been right."

"What?"

"Sometimes, in madness resides genius. Kahlan, I don't know where to draw the line. In one way not knowing about magic is a liability, but in another it means I'm not burdened by preconceived notions, the way the wizards at the Keep were, so I might recognize the truth in his words where they did not.

"You see, Joseph Ander viewed magic not so much as a set of requirements—you know, a pinch of this, this word three times while turning round on your left foot, and all that kind of thing.

"He saw magic as an art form—a means of expression."

Kahlan was frowning. "I don't follow. Either you cast a spell properly to invoke it, or it doesn't work. Like I call my power with a touch. Like the way we called the chimes by fulfilling specific requirements of the magic, thereby releasing it."

He knew that with her magical ability, her background, and her learning about magic, she would have the same problem the other wizards did. Richard felt just a trace of the frustration Joseph Ander must have felt. In that, too, he understood the man that much better—understood a tiny bit of the frustration of having people tell you the hard facts of something when you knew better, yet couldn't get them to see the abstract concept of the greater whole right before them.

As did Joseph Ander, Richard thought to try again.

"Yes, I know, and I'm not saying that doesn't work, but he believed there was more. That magic could be taken to a higher level—to a plane beyond that which most people with the gift used."

Now she really was frowning. "Richard, that's madness."

"No, I don't think so." He picked up the journey book.

"This is in answer to something unrelated they asked—but you have to hear this to understand the way Joseph Ander thinks."

He read to her the crux of the translation.

" 'A wizard who cannot truly destroy cannot truly create.' " Richard tapped the book. "He was talking about a wizard like the gifted now, a wizard with only the Additive—like Zedd. Ander didn't even consider a man to have the gift, if he didn't have both sides. He thought of such a man as simply an aberration, and hopelessly disadvantaged."

Richard went back to the journey book and read on.

" 'A wizard must know himself or he risks working ill magic that harms his own free will.' That's him talking

731

about the creative aspects of magic beyond the structure of it. 'Magic intensifies and concentrates passions, strengthening not only such things as joy, but ruinous passions, too, and in this way they may become obsessions, and unbearable unless released.' "

"Sounds like he's trying to justify being destructive," she said.

"I don't think so. I think he's on to something important, a higher balance, as it were."

Kahlan shook her head, clearly not catching what he saw, but he could think of no way to get it across to her, so he read on.

"This is important. 'Imagination is what makes a great wizard, for with it, he is able to transcend the limitations of tradition and go beyond the structure of what now exists into the higher realm of creating the very fabric of magic.' "

"That's what you were talking about? About him thinking of it as an . . . an art form? A means of expression? Like he's the Creator Himself—weaving a cloth of magic out of nothing?"

"Exactly. But listen to this. This, I believe, may be the most important thing Joseph Ander has to say. When the chimes ceased being a problem, the other wizards cautiously asked what he did. You can almost read the anxiety in their words. This is his terse reply to their question of what he had done to the chimes.

" 'A Grace might rise in obedience to an inventive spell.' "

Kahlan rubbed her arms, clearly disturbed by the answer. "Dear spirits, what does that mean?"

Richard leaned close to her, "I think it means he dreamed up something—a new magic, outside the parameters of the original conjuring that brought the chimes into this world. Magic to suit the situation, and himself.

"In other words, Joseph Ander got creative."

Kahlan's green eyes cast about. He knew she was considering the depths of aberration with which they were dealing. This was the madman who had finally inflicted the chimes on them.

"The world is coming apart," she whispered to herself, "and you're talking about Joseph Ander using magic as an art form?"

"I'm just telling you what the man said." Richard turned to the last page. "I skipped ahead. I wanted to see the last thing he wrote the wizards."

Richard studied the High D'Haran words again to be certain of the translation, and then read Joseph Ander's words.

" 'In the end, I have concluded I must reject the Creator and the Keeper both. I instead create my own solution, my own rebirth and death, and in so doing will always protect my people. And so farewell, for I shall lay my soul on troubled waters, and thus watch over for all time that which I have so carefully wrought, and which is now safeguarded and inviolate.' "

Richard looked up. "See? Do you understand?" He saw she didn't. "Kahlan, I don't think he banished the chimes as he was supposed to. I think he instead used them for his own purposes."

Her nose wrinkled. "Used them? What can you use the chimes for?"

"The Dominie Dirtch."

"What!" She squeezed the bridge of her nose between her finger and thumb. "But then how was it possible for us to follow such a well-defined, prescribed, strict outline and inadvertently call them forth? That sort of structure is exactly what you are telling me Joseph Ander thought he was beyond."

Richard had been waiting for that exact argument. "That's the balance. Don't you see? Magic must be balanced. In order to do something creative, he had to balance it with something not creative, a very strict formula. That it is so strict in its requirements to free the chimes is in itself proof of the creativity of what he did."

He knew her well enough to tell she didn't agree, but

wasn't in the mood to argue. She said simply, "So how do we then banish the chimes?"

Richard shook his head with defeat in that much of it.

"I don't know. I fear there is no answer to that question. The wizards of Joseph Ander's time were equally frustrated by the man. In the end, they simply considered this place lost to them. I'm beginning to believe Joseph Ander created an unbreakable magic inside a puzzle without a solution."

Kahlan took the book from his hands, closed it, and placed it back on the little table.

"Richard, I think you're getting a little crazy yourself, reading the rantings of a lunatic. That's not the way magic works."

That's what the wizards at the Keep had told Ander—that he couldn't convert and control an element that was innately uncontrollable. Richard didn't tell Kahlan that, though. She wasn't prepared to think of magic in these terms.

Neither were the other wizards.

Joseph Ander had not been at all pleased to have his ideas so summarily dismissed, thus his final farewell.

Kahlan put her arms around his neck. "I'm sorry. I know you're trying your best. I'm just getting nervous. The vote should be coming back soon."

Richard put his hands on her waist. "Kahlan, people will see the truth. They have to."

She gazed off. "Richard," she whispered, "make love to me?"

"What?"

She looked up into his eyes. "It's been so long. Make love to me."

"Here? Now?"

"We can tie the tent shut. No one comes in without asking

permission anyway." She smiled. "I promise to be quiet, and not to embarrass you." With a finger, she lifted his chin. "I promise I won't even tell your other wife."

That brought a brief smile, but Richard wasn't able to keep hold of it.

"Kahlan, we can't."

"Well, I think I could. I bet I could change your mind, too."

Richard lifted the small dark stone on her necklace. "Kahlan, magic has failed. This won't work."

"I know. That's why I want to." She clutched at his shirt. "Richard, I don't care. What if we make a baby? So what?"

"You know 'so what.' "

"Richard, would it be so bad? Really?" Her green eyes were filling with tears. "Would it be so bad if we made a child together?"

"No, no, of course not. It isn't that. You know I want to. But we can't right now. We can't afford to see Shota in every shadow, waiting to do as she promised. We can't afford the distraction from our duty."

"Our duty. What about us. What about what we want?"

Richard turned away. "Kahlan, do you really want to bring a child into this world? Do you want to bring a child into the madness of this world? The madness of the chimes and a horrific war looming before us?"

"What if I said yes?"

He turned back to her and smiled. He could see he was only upsetting her. Du Chaillu being pregnant was probably making Kahlan think of having her own child.

"Kahlan, I want to, if you do. All right? Whenever you want, we will, and I'll deal with Shota. But in the meantime could we wait until we see if there is even going to be a world of life—or even a world with freedom—into which we can bring our child?"

She finally smiled. "Of course. You're right, Richard. I guess I was just getting . . . carried away. We have the chimes to deal with, and the Imperial Order . . ."

Richard took her in his arms to comfort her, when Captain Meiffert called from outside the tent. "See?" he whispered to her. She smiled.

"Yes, Captain, come on in."

The man stepped inside reluctantly. He wouldn't meet Richard's gaze.

"What is it, Captain?"

"Ah, Lord Rahl, Mother Confessor . . . the vote in Fairfield is counted. Some of our men have returned with numbers. But not all of them," he was quick to add. "There are more yet to come back. It will take a few days yet before they all travel back."

"So, Captain, what are the results?"

The man handed over a slip of paper. Richard read it, but it took a moment for it to sink in.

"Seven in ten against us," he whispered.

Kahlan gently lifted the paper from his fingers and looked at it. Without a word, she set it on the table.

"All right," he said, "we know they were telling all those lies in the city. We just have to realize it will be different out around the land."

"Richard," Kahlan whispered, "they will spread the same lies around the land."

"But we talked to those people. We spent time with them." Richard turned to Captain Meiffert. "What about the outlying places?"

"Well—"

"What about, about, that place—" Richard snapped his fingers. "Westbrook. Where we spent time looking at Joseph Ander's things. What about Westbrook? Is the vote back from there?"

The man had backed away a step. "Yes, Lord Rahl."

"And what is it, then?"

Kahlan put a hand on his arm. "Richard," she whispered, "the captain is on our side."

Richard pressed his fingers to his temples as he took a breath. "What is the vote from Westbrook, Captain?"

The man, having lost much of his color, cleared his throat.

736

"Nine of ten marked an X against us, Lord Rahl."

Richard stood stunned. He had talked to those people. He remembered some of their names, their beautiful children.

Richard felt as if the ground had disappeared from beneath his feet, and he was falling through insanity. He had been up day and night, trying to help these people have their own way over their lives, have freedom, and they rejected it.

"Richard," Kahlan said in soft sympathy, "it was nothing you did. They told those people lies. They frightened the people."

Richard lifted a hand in a vague manner. "But . . . I talked to them, explained to them that this was for them, for their future, for the freedom of their children. . . ."

"I know, Richard."

Captain Meiffert stood awkwardly. Kahlan signaled with a hand, dismissing him. He bowed and quietly backed out of the tent.

"I'm going for a walk," Richard whispered. "I need to be by myself." He waved toward the blankets. "Just go on to bed without me."

Richard walked alone into the darkness.

CHAPTER 66

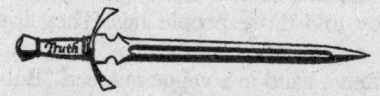

HE QUIETLY DISMISSED FOR the evening the woman dusting all the elaborate woodwork and, after closing the door behind her, went to the bedroom. Teresa turned when she heard him come in.

"Dalton." She smiled. "There you are, sweetheart."

"Tess."

He had run the entire state of affairs through his mind a thousand times and had finally come to the place where he could face Tess and know he would be able to control his response.

He had to control himself.

He had retreated into his most trusted method of handling things. Only there could he be sure of his control. He was going to handle this, just as he handled so many other things.

"I didn't expect to see you in so early."

"Tess, I heard something."

She sat at the mirror, brushing her beautiful hair.

"Really? Some interesting news?"

"A bit. I heard you have been occupying the bed of the Sovereign. Is this true?"

He knew now it was. He had pulled every thread of his cobweb.

She stopped brushing and looked at him in the mirror, her face a mix of emotions. Defiance predominated them.

"Dalton, it's not like he's another man. It's the Sovereign." She stood and turned to him, unsure how he was going to react. "He is next to the Creator."

"May I ask how this came about?"

"Bertrand said the Creator spoke to him." She stared off to a distant place. "The Creator told Bertrand that because I had been faithful to you, and had never been with another man, and because you had been faithful to me, the Creator had chosen me to be the one to release Bertrand's worldly tensions."

Her eyes focused on him again.

"So, you see, it's a reward for you, too, Dalton. For your faithfulness to me."

Dalton made himself answer. "Yes, I can see that."

"Bertrand says it is my holy duty."

"Holy duty."

"When I'm with him, it's like . . . I don't know. It's so special. To help the Sovereign in this world is an honor as well as a duty. To think, I help relieve him of the awful tension that builds up in him from being Sovereign.

"It's an awesome responsibility, Dalton, being Sovereign."

Dalton nodded. "You're right."

Seeing that he wasn't going to get angry and harm her, she stepped closer.

"Dalton, I still love you just the same."

"I'm glad to hear it, Tess. That was what I'm most worried about. I fear I've lost your love."

She grasped his shoulders. "No, silly. Never. I still love you the same. But the Sovereign has called upon me. You have to understand that. He needs me."

Dalton swallowed. "Of course, darling. But we can . . . we can still be . . . we can still be together in bed?"

"Oh, Dalton, of course we can. Is that what you were worried about? That I'd not have time for you, too? Dalton, I love you, and will always want you."

"Good." He nodded. "That's good."

"Come to bed, sweetheart, and I'll show you. You might even find me more exciting, now.

"And Dalton, it's a high honor to be with the Sovereign. Everyone will only think more of you."

"I'm sure you're right."

"Come to bed, then." She kissed his cheek. "Let me show you how happy I can make you?"

Dalton scratched his forehead. "Ah, I would love nothing better, really I would, but I have a whole pile of urgent work. The vote just came in. . . ."

"I know. Bertrand told me."

"Bertrand."

She nodded. "The Sovereign, silly. He told me. I'm so proud of you, Dalton. I know you had a part in it. It wasn't all just Bertrand's work. I know you had a hand in helping him win."

"A part. It's kind of the Sovereign to take note of my contribution."

"He speaks very highly of you, Dalton."

"I'm pleased to hear that." Dalton cleared his throat. "Ah, look, Tess, I've got to get to . . . get to my, my work. I have urgent matters."

"Should I wait up?"

Dalton waved a hand. "No. No, darling, I have to make a trip into Fairfield to see to some matters."

"Tonight? Yet tonight?"

"Yes."

"Dalton, you mustn't work so hard. Promise me you will take some time for yourself. Promise me? I worry for you."

"You shouldn't. I'm fine."

She smiled her most intimate smile. "Promise me you will make time to make love to me?"

Dalton smiled. "Of course. I promise." He kissed her cheek. "Good night, darling."

The woman holding out the vial frowned. "Do I know you?"

"No," Kahlan said, turning her face down so it would be shadowed by the lamplight. "I don't see how. I'm from far away. I only came into Fairfield for this."

Kahlan wore common clothes she used for traveling, and a head wrap made of a scarf so her long hair would be hidden. She put on the head wrap after she was away from their camp. With Richard off somewhere, the soldiers insisted on escorting her on her walk to get "some air." She had gruffly ordered them to leave her alone and go back to their posts.

Such orders would never have worked with Cara. Cara would have ignored them. The soldiers were not as fearless, or as reckless, or as smart, as Cara.

The woman sighed. "Well, I understand, my dear. A number of women have made a journey for such as this."

She held out the stoppered vial, clearly expecting payment first. Kahlan passed her a gold sovereign.

"Keep it all. I expect your silence in return."

The woman bowed her head. "I quite understand. Thank you, my dear. Very generous of you. Thank you."

Kahlan took the vial, holding it nestled in her palm, staring through its clouded glass at the clear liquid inside. She realized her other hand was on her belly. She let the arm drop to her side.

"Now," the woman said, pointing at the poorly made glass vial, "it will remain good for the night, since I just mixed it for you. You can take it whenever you please, but if you wait until morning it will likely not still be potent enough. I'd suggest you do it tonight, before you go to bed."

"Will it hurt?"

The woman's face frowned with concern. "Likely not more than a regular cycle, my dear. Not with it being this early. There will just be the bleeding, so be prepared for that."

Kahlan had meant would it hurt the baby. She couldn't bring herself to repeat the question.

"Just drink it all down," the woman went on. "It isn't so bad to taste, but you might want some tea with it."

"Thank you."

Kahlan turned to the door.

"Wait," said the woman. She came up close and took Kahlan's hand. "I'm sorry, my dear. You're plenty young, you can have another."

A thought struck her. "This won't impair my ability—"

"No, no, dear. Not at all. You'll be fine."

"Thank you," Kahlan said as she stepped toward the door, suddenly eager to be out of the little home, out into the darkness, and alone, in case she had to cry.

The woman snatched Kahlan's arm and turned her around. "I don't usually lecture young women, because by the time they come to me the time for lecturing is long past, but I hope you get yourself married, dear. I help when I'm needed, but I'd rather help you deliver your baby than shed it, I really would."

Kahlan nodded. "I feel the same. Thank you."

The streets of Fairfield were dark, but there were still people going about their business. Kahlan knew that when the Imperial Order came, the business of their lives would be soon turned inside out.

At that moment, though, she had trouble caring.

She decided she would do it before she got back. She feared Richard finding the vial, and having to explain it to him. Richard would never let her do this, but since he didn't know about her condition, she had been able to get his true feelings and wishes.

He was right. They had the rest of the people to worry about. They couldn't let their personal problem bring harm to everyone. Shota would keep her word about such a thing, and then they wouldn't be able to see to their duty. This would be best.

On the way out of the city, she saw Dalton Campbell coming up the street on horseback, so she turned down a dark street. He always seemed to be a man of careful thought. As he rode by, Kahlan thought he looked as if he was in another world. She wondered what he was doing in a part of the city that had a reputation for ill repute.

She waited until he passed before she went on her way.

As she reached the road back to the Minister's estate, where their men were camped, she saw the glint of moonlight off the top rail of a carriage in the far distance. It would be some time before the plodding carriage reached her, but she turned off the road just the same. She didn't want to meet anyone along the road, especially someone who might recognize her.

The lump in her throat was near to choking her as she walked into the field of wheat. Silent tears streamed down her cheeks. Off the road a ways, she finally sank to her knees, giving in to the tears.

As she stared at the vial resting in her palm, moonlight reflecting off the wavy glass, she couldn't recall ever feeling much lower in her life. She sobbed back a cry, stifling her weeping, reminding herself this was for the good of everyone. It was. She was sure of it.

She pulled the stopper, letting it fall from her fingers. She held the vial up, trying to see it in the watery moonlight. She pressed her other hand over their child: her child; Richard's child.

Swallowing back the tears, she put the vial to her lips. She paused, waiting until she could get control of her breathing. She didn't want to empty it into her mouth, and then not be able to swallow.

Kahlan pulled it away from her lips. She stared at it in the moonlight, again, and thought of everything this meant.

And then she turned it over, emptying the liquid out on the ground.

Immediately, she felt a wave of relief, as if her life had been spared and hope had returned to the world.

When she stood the tears were a distant memory, already drying on her cheeks. Kahlan smiled with relief, with joy. Their child was safe.

She threw the empty vial out into the field. When she did so, Kahlan saw a man standing out in the wheat, watching her. She froze.

He started toward her, purposefully, quickly. Kahlan looked to the side and saw other men coming. Behind, yet more were closing on her. Young men, she saw, all with red hair.

Not waiting an instant for the situation to get any worse, she reacted instinctively and broke into a dead run toward their camp.

Rather than trying to go between the men, she headed directly toward one. He hunkered down, feet spread, arms out, waiting.

Kahlan raced up to him and seized his arm. She looked into his eyes, recognizing him as a messenger named Rowley. Without effort of thought, and in that instant, she released her power into him, bracing for the jolt that would take him.

The same instant nothing happened, she realized it was because the chimes had caused her magic to fail. She thought she felt it within her as always, but it was gone.

In that same instant of realization, recognition, and failure, she suddenly did feel magic. Kahlan knew the tingling invasion of magic, overpowering in its onrushing surge, snaking into her like a viper down a hole, and just as deadly.

She jerked her arm back, but too late, she knew. Men closed in from both sides, less concerned now that they had her. Men behind were still running toward them.

Only an instant had passed since she first grabbed Rowley and let him go. In that time she made the only decision she could. She had only one chance: fight or die.

Kahlan kicked the man to her right in the sternum. She felt the bone snap under her boot heel. He went down with an indrawn gasp. She kneed Rowley in the groin. She gouged at the eyes of the man on her left.

It bought her an opening. She raced for it, only to be brought up short when a man behind got her by the hair, jerking her violently back. She spun, kicking him in the side, using her elbows as men closed in.

It was the last strike she landed. They caught her arms. A heavy blow slammed into her middle. She instantly knew it had done something terrible to her. Another to her face, and then another, took her senses. She couldn't get her wind. She didn't know up from down. She couldn't breathe. She tried to cover her face, but they had her arms. She gasped as more fists hammered her middle. More snapped her head this way and that. She tried to swallow the blood in her mouth before it choked her. She heard the men growl, like a pack of dogs, and grunt with the effort of hitting her as hard as they could. The fierce panic of helplessness seized her.

The blows rained down. She hung helpless. The pain was stunning. They pounded her toward the ground.

Blackness, like death itself, swallowed her.

And then the pain ebbed away into nothingness, and the merciful peace of the Light enveloped her.

In a daze, Richard walked through the field of moonlit wheat. Everything was such a mess. He felt as if so much was piled on top of him he couldn't breathe. He didn't know what to do. The chimes, the Imperial Order, none of it was going right.

Yet everyone depended on him, whether or not they knew it. The people of the Midlands counted on him to repel the Imperial Order. The D'Harans depended on him for leadership. Everyone was in danger from the chimes, and they were growing stronger by the day.

On top of that, to have worked and sacrificed so much for these people of Anderith, only to have them turn away from him, was crushing.

The worst of it, though, was that he and Kahlan had to

put it all before a child. Richard was willing to risk Shota, if Kahlan was. He knew the danger a child could pose, but he was willing to fight for their right to their own future. But how could they worry about a child now, with the chimes and the Order both ruthlessly bearing down on the world? Adding Shota into the mix would be beyond reason. Kahlan saw that, too, but he knew it was hard for her, putting duty first her whole life.

But if they didn't do their part, their duty, the world would fall to Jagang's tyranny, into slavery. If the chimes didn't kill them all first. Before any of the rest of it, they had to stop the chimes. The chimes were nobody's fault but his. He was responsible for banishing them.

Still, even if he could figure out what Joseph Ander had done, they had Jagang to deal with before they could think about having a child. Kahlan understood that. He thanked the good spirits for that one thing good in his life: Kahlan.

He realized he must be close to Fairfield. He should turn back. Kahlan would be worried. He had been gone a long time. He didn't want to worry her. She had enough worries. He hoped she wouldn't be too distraught about not having a child right now.

As he turned, he thought he heard something. He straightened and listened. He didn't know how long the noise had gone on because he hadn't been paying much attention to anything but trying to think of solutions to their problems. Now he cocked his head to hear. It sounded oddly like muffled thuds.

Without stopping to think it over, Richard started running toward the sound. As he got closer, he realized he heard men grunting in effort, panting, exerting themselves.

Richard burst upon them, a gang of men, beating someone on the ground. He seized the hair of one and yanked him back. Under the man, he saw a bloody body.

They were beating the poor soul to death.

Richard recognized the man he had. It was one of the messengers. Rowley, he thought the man's name was. He had a wild, savage look in his eyes.

Rowley, seeing that it was Richard, immediately went for his throat, crying. "Get him!"

Richard whipped his other arm around Rowley's neck, seized his chin, bent him over, and yanked back, snapping his neck. Rowley went down in a limp heap.

Another man sprang forward. His onrushing momentum was his worst mistake. Richard rammed the heel of his hand square into the man's face.

He was still falling across Rowley as Richard snatched the red hair of another, pulled him forward, and drove his knee up into the man's jaw. His jaw broken, he staggered back.

The men were all up, now, and Richard realized he might soon be joining the body on the ground. His advantage was that they were already tired from their exertion. His disadvantage was that they greatly outnumbered him, and they were mad with blood lust.

Just as they were about to dive onto Richard, they saw something and scattered. Richard spun around and saw the Baka Tau Mana blade masters sweeping in out of the night, their swords whistling through the night air.

Richard realized they must have been shadowing him as he went for his walk to be alone. He hadn't even known they were there. As they went after the mob, Richard knelt down beside the body in the trampled wheat.

Whoever it was, they were dead.

Richard stood with a sorrowful sigh. He stared down at the broken form that had once been a person, probably only a short time before. It looked like it must have been a terrible end.

If only he had been closer, sooner, he might have been able to stop it. Suddenly not having the stomach to look at the bloody body, or others nearby, Richard walked away.

He hadn't gone more than a few paces when a thought brought him to a halt. He turned around and looked. He winced at the notion, but then thought: What if it had been someone he cared about? Wouldn't he want somebody who was there to do whatever they could? He was the only one around to help, if he even could. He guessed it was worth a try—the person was already dead, there was nothing to lose.

He ran back and knelt beside the body. He couldn't even tell if it was a man or a woman, except that there were pants, so he assumed it to be a man. He put a hand under the neck and wiped some of the mask of blood from the swollen, cut lips and then put his over them.

He remembered what Denna had done to him, when he was near death. He recalled Cara doing it to Du Chaillu.

He blew a breath of life into the lifeless corpse. He lifted his mouth and listened to the breath wheeze from the body. He blew another breath, and then another, and then another.

He knelt by the body for what seemed like ages but he knew could be only minutes, blowing in the breath of life, hoping against hope that the poor unfortunate soul would still be with them. He prayed to the good spirits for help.

He wanted so much for something good to come of his experience at the hands of Denna, the Mord-Sith. He knew Denna would want life to be her legacy. Cara had already brought Du Chaillu back, proving that Mord-Sith could do more than take life.

He again prayed fervently to the good spirits to help him, to keep this soul here with this person, rather than take it now.

With a gasp, life returned.

Someone was coming. Richard looked up and saw two of the blade masters trotting back. Richard didn't need to ask if they were successful. That gang of young men would murder no more people in the night.

Someone else was coming, too. It was an older gentleman in dark clothes. He rushed up with frightened urgency.

The man was staggered by the sight. "Oh, dear Creator, not another one."

"Another one?" Richard asked.

The man fell to his knees, seeming not to hear Richard. He took up a bloody hand, pressing it to his cheek.

"Thank the Creator," he whispered. He looked up at Richard. "I have a carriage." He pointed. "Just there, on the road.

Help me, get this poor wretch to my carriage and we can take him to my home."

"Where?" Richard asked.

"Fairfield," the man said, watching the blade masters carefully, tenderly, lift the unconscious but breathing person.

"Well," Richard said, wiping the blood from his mouth. "I guess it's a lot closer than the camp with my soldiers."

Richard thought he might have to help the man, but the man refused the offer of a helping arm.

"Are you Lord Rahl, then?"

Richard nodded. The man stopped then, pulling Richard's hand up to shake it.

"Lord Rahl, I'm honored to meet you, though not under such circumstances. My name is Edwin Winthrop."

Richard pumped the man's hand. "Master Winthrop."

"Edwin, please." Edwin grasped Richard's shoulders. "Lord Rahl, this is just terrible. My beloved wife, Claudine—"

Edwin fell into tears. Richard gently took hold of his arms to be sure the man wouldn't collapse.

"My beloved wife Claudine was murdered in just this fashion. Beaten to death out on this road."

"I'm so sorry," Richard said, now understanding Edwin's reaction.

"Let me help this poor wretch. No one was there to help my Claudine as you've helped this person. Please, Lord Rahl, let me help."

"It's Richard, Edwin. I would like nothing better than for you to help."

Richard watched as Jiaan and his blade masters helped to carefully load the person into the carriage.

"I'd like three of you to go with Edwin. We can't tell if whoever is responsible for this will try again."

"There will be no one to report their failure," Jiaan said.

"They will realize it sooner or later." Richard turned to Edwin. "You must not tell anyone of this, or you will be in danger. They might come to finish the job."

Edwin was nodding as he climbed into his carriage. "I have a healer, a lifelong friend, I can trust."

Richard and two of the blade masters walked the lonely road back to camp in silence. They had previously expressed their absolute faith that he would banish the chimes that had tried to kill their spirit woman. Richard didn't have the heart to tell them he was no closer to doing so than he was back then.

When he got back, most of the camp was asleep. Richard wasn't in the mood to talk with the officers or sentries. He was thinking about Joseph Ander and the chimes.

Kahlan wasn't in their tent. She had probably gone to be with Du Chaillu. Du Chaillu had come to value Kahlan's presence—the comfort of another woman. It was close to time for the baby to be born.

Richard took Joseph Ander's journey book and a lamp and went to another tent used by officers for planning. He wanted to work on translating more of the journey book, but didn't want to keep Kahlan from sleeping when she got back. Richard knew that if he worked in their tent, she would want to sit up with him. There was no need for that.

CHAPTER 67

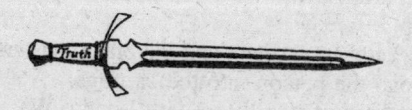

RICHARD WAS PUZZLING OVER an involved and confusing translation, trying to work through the maze of possible meanings, when Jiaan slipped into the tent. The soldiers would have asked permission to enter; the blade masters just assumed they had permission to go wherever they wanted. After the constant formality with the soldiers, Richard found it refreshing.

"*Caharin*, you must come with me. Du Chaillu has sent me."

Richard shot to his feet. "The baby? The baby is coming? I'll get Kahlan. Let's go."

"No." Jiaan put a restraining hand against Richard's shoulder. "Not your child. She sent me to get you, and she said to come alone."

"She doesn't want me to get Kahlan?"

"No, *Caharin*. Please, you must do as our spirit woman, your wife, asks."

Richard had never seen such a look of concern in Jiaan's dark eyes. The man was always stone with a sword. Richard held out a hand, inviting Jiaan to lead the way.

To his surprise, it was near dawn. Richard had been working the entire night. He hoped Kahlan was asleep; if she wasn't, she would scold him for not getting any rest.

Jiaan had two horses saddled and waiting. Richard was startled. The man would run rather than ride unless Du Chaillu told him to ride, and that was just about never.

"What's going on?" Richard gestured off toward Du Chaillu's tent. "I thought Du Chaillu wanted me."

Jiaan swung into his saddle. "She is in the city."

"What is she doing in Fairfield? I'm not sure it's safe there for her, not after they've been turning everyone against us."

"Please, *Caharin*. I beg you, come with me, and hurry."

Richard sprang up onto his horse. "Of course. I'm sorry, Jiaan. Let's go."

Richard was beginning to worry that Du Chaillu had already come to trouble from people in Fairfield. They knew she was with Richard and Kahlan. For that matter, they knew she was Richard's wife.

He urged his horse into a run. Anxiety twisted in his gut.

The door to a house set back among trees opened. Edwin peered out. Richard, by now in a state of deep concern, relaxed a bit. The person they saved was probably not making it, and they wanted him to see them before death came, since he had breathed the breath of life back into them.

Richard didn't understand what Du Chaillu was doing there, but he surmised that she had a common bond with the person, having been brought back to life in the same way herself.

Edwin, looking concerned and frightened, led them back through hallways and through well-kept rooms in the large house. It had an empty, quiet, sad feel to it. With Edwin's wife murdered, Richard thought it was to be expected.

They reached a room at the end of a short, dimly lit hall. The door was closed. Jiaan knocked softly, and then escorted the despondent Edwin away.

Edwin caught Richard's sleeve. "Anything you need, Richard, I'm here."

Richard nodded and Edwin let Jiaan take him away. The door eased open. Du Chaillu peered out. When she saw it was Richard, she came out, putting a hand to his chest, backing him away. She pulled the door closed behind herself.

She kept the restraining hand on his chest. "Richard, you must listen to me. You must listen very carefully, and not become crazy."

"Crazy? Crazy about what?"

"Richard, please, this is important. You must listen, and do as I say. Promise me."

Richard could feel the blood draining out of his face. He nodded. "I promise, Du Chaillu. What is it?"

She stepped closer. Keeping the hand on his chest, she added the other to his arm.

"Richard, the person you found . . . it was Kahlan."

"That's not possible. I'd know Kahlan."

Du Chaillu's eyes were brimming with tears. "Richard, please, I don't know if she will live. You brought her back, but I don't know if . . . I wanted you to come."

He was having trouble getting his breath. "But . . ." He couldn't think. "But, I would have known. Du Chaillu, you must be wrong. I would have known if it was Kahlan."

Du Chaillu squeezed his arm. "I did not know myself until we cleaned some . . ."

Richard made for the door. Du Chaillu pushed him back. "You promised. You promised to listen."

Richard was hardly hearing her. He couldn't think. He could only see that bloody broken body lying there in the field. He couldn't make himself believe it was Kahlan.

Richard pushed his fingers back into his hair. He struggled to find his voice. "Du Chaillu, please, don't do this to me. Please don't you do this to me."

She shook the arm. "You must have strength, or she has no chance. Please, do not go crazy on me."

"What do you need? Name it. Name it, Du Chaillu." Tears were running down his face. "Please, tell me what you need."

"I need you to listen to me. Are you listening?"

Richard nodded. He wasn't sure what she was asking, but he nodded as his mind was racing. He could cure her. He had magic.

Healing was Additive.

The chimes took all the Additive Magic.

She shook him again. "Richard."

"I'm sorry. What. I'm listening."

Du Chaillu finally could no longer hold his gaze. "She lost her child."

Richard blinked. "Then you are wrong. It can't be Kahlan."

Du Chaillu stared at the floor and took a deep breath.

"Kahlan was pregnant. She told me when we were at the place where you read the things of the Ander man."

"Westbrook?"

Du Chaillu nodded. "There, before you went with her riding alone up to the mountain lake, she told me. She made me promise not to tell you. She said only it was a long story. I think now you have the right to my broken promise.

"She has lost her child."

Richard sank to the floor. Du Chaillu hugged him as he wept uncontrollably.

"Richard, I understand your pain, but this will not help her."

Richard, somehow, forced himself to stop. He leaned back against the wall, numb and dazed, waiting for Du Chaillu to tell him what he could do.

"You must stop the chimes."

He rushed to his feet. "What?"

"You could heal her if you had your magic."

It all fell into place. He had to stop the chimes. That was all. Just stop the chimes, and then heal Kahlan.

"Richard, when we were at that place where Kahlan told me she was with child . . ." The words "with child" jolted him anew, as he realized that Kahlan was going to have a child, and he never knew, and now it had already died. ". . . Westbrook . . . Richard, listen to me. When we were there, the people said there was terrible wind, and rain, and fire that destroyed almost everything of that man."

"Yes, I believe it was the chimes."

"They hated him. You must have that same hate in your heart for the chimes so that you may vanquish them. Then you can have your magic back and heal Kahlan."

Richard's mind was racing. The chimes hated Joseph Ander. Why? Not because the man had sent them back—he didn't do that. He had instead enslaved the chimes to serve him. The Dominie Dirtch were somehow connected to what he did.

When Richard and Kahlan freed the chimes, they took their vengeance on certain of his possessions. But why the things at Westbrook, and not those in the library at the Minister's estate?

Joseph Ander's words rang in his head.

In the end, I have concluded I must reject the Creator and the Keeper both. I instead create my own solution, my own rebirth and death, and in so doing will always protect my people. And so farewell, for I shall lay my soul on troubled waters, and thus watch over for all time that which I have so carefully wrought, and which is now safeguarded and inviolate.

Troubled waters.

Richard finally understood what Joseph Ander had done.

"I have to go. Du Chaillu, I have to go." Richard seized her by the shoulders. "Please, keep her alive until I get back. You must!"

"Richard, we will do our best. You have my word as your wife."

"Edwin!"

The man came shuffling down the hall. "Yes, Richard. What can I do? Name it."

"Can you hide these people here? My wife—" Richard had to swallow to keep control. "Can you keep Kahlan here? And Du Chaillu, and her five men?"

Edwin swept his arm in a wide arc, indicating his home. "It's a big house. A lot of room. No one will know who is here. I keep few friends, and the ones I have I would trust with my life."

Richard shook the man's hand. "Thank you, Edwin. In return, I would ask you to leave your home when I come back."

"What? Why?"

"The Imperial Order is coming."

"But aren't you going to stop them?"

Richard threw up his hands. "How? More to the point, why? These people have rejected the chance I've given them. Edwin, they murdered your wife just as they tried to murder mine. And you would have me risk the lives of good people to preserve their well-being?"

Edwin sagged. "No, I suppose not. There are some of us who were on your side, Richard. Some of us tried."

"I know. That is why I'm giving you warning. Tell your

friends to get out while they can. I'm sending my men out today. The Imperial Order will be here within two weeks."

"How long will you be gone?"

"Maybe eight days—at the most. I have to get up to the wasteland above the Nareef Valley."

"Nasty place."

Richard nodded. "You've no idea."

"We will care for the Mother Confessor as well as anyone can."

"Do you have barrels, Edwin?"

The man frowned. "Yes, down in the cellar."

"Fill them with water. Collect food now. In a few days the water and anything growing may not be safe."

"Why would that be?"

Richard ground his teeth. "Jagang is coming here for food. I'm going to give him a bellyache, at least."

"Richard," Du Chaillu said in a soft voice, meeting his gaze. "I'm not sure . . . do you want to see her before you go?"

Richard steeled himself. "Yes. Please."

Richard galloped his horse the whole way back to the encampment. He could get a fresh horse there, so he didn't spare the poor animal. It looked to him as he rode in that Captain Meiffert had the troops at a high state of alert. Sentries were doubled, and posted farther out than usual. They had no doubt heard from the Baka Tau Mana that there had been trouble.

Richard hoped the man wouldn't ask about Kahlan. He didn't think he could hold himself together if he had to tell him about her, if he had to describe the sight of her in that bed.

Even knowing it was her, Richard had hardly recognized her.

It was a sight beyond horror. It broke his heart. He had never felt so alone in the world, nor known such anguish.

Instead of falling to pieces, Richard struggled to put his mind to the task at hand. He had to put Kahlan out of his mind, if he was to help her. He knew that was impossible, but he tried to keep his thoughts on Joseph Ander and what must be done.

He needed to be able to heal her. He would do anything to remedy her suffering. Thankfully, she wasn't conscious.

Richard thought he knew what Joseph Ander had done, but he didn't have the slightest idea of what he might do to counter it. He figured he had several days until he got there to think about it.

Richard still had the Subtractive side of his power. He had used that before and understood a little about it. Nathan, a prophet and Richard's ancestor, had once told him that his gift was different from that of other wizards because he was a war wizard. Richard's power worked through need. And, it was invoked by anger.

Richard had a powerful need, now.

He had enough anger for ten wizards.

The thought hit him—that was part of the way Joseph Ander described what he did. He created what he needed. Richard wished he knew how this insight might help him.

Captain Meiffert clapped a hand to the leather over his heart as Richard leaped off his horse.

"Captain, I need a fresh horse. In fact, I had better have three. I have to go." Richard pressed his fingers to his forehead, trying to think. "I want you to get these men packed up, and as soon as all the rest come in from watching the vote, I want you out of here."

"Where are we going, Lord Rahl, if I might ask?"

"You and your men are going back to General Reibisch. I won't be going with you."

The captain followed Richard as he went to gather up his and Kahlan's things. As Captain Meiffert followed, he issued orders to several of his men, calling for fresh horses for Lord Rahl, along with supplies. Richard told one of the soldiers he wanted their best mounts for a long hard ride. The man ran off to see to the task.

The captain waited outside as Richard went into the tent to pack. He began gathering their things. When he picked up Kahlan's white Mother Confessor dress, his hands began trembling, and he fell to his knees, overcome with grief.

Alone in the tent, he prayed, begging the good spirits as never before to help him. He promised them anything they wanted in return. Recalling that the only thing he knew he could do was to banish the chimes so he might heal Kahlan, he set about finishing as quickly as he could.

Outside, the horses were waiting. It was just getting light.

"Captain, I want you and your men to get back to General Reibisch as soon as you can."

"And the Dominie Dirtch? With the reports of the special Ander guard units, I think we may have trouble. Will we be safe going past the Dominie Dirtch?"

"No. From the reports, I would suspect the guard troops to be Imperial Order men. I would also expect them to take the Dominie Dirtch in order to keep Reibisch at bay.

"From this moment on, you are to consider yourself in enemy territory. Your orders are to escape. If anyone tries to stop you, kill them and keep going.

"If the Order, as I suspect, takes the Dominie Dirtch, we can use the one weakness they will have—they will be spread too thin to resist you in force.

"Assume Imperial Order troops will be manning the Dominie Dirtch. Concentrate your force into a cavalry charge and punch through their line. Because they have control of the Dominie Dirtch, they probably won't offer much resistance, thinking they can kill you once you go past."

The man was looking worried. "Then . . . you think you will have the stone weapons down by then, Lord Rahl? You will counter their magic?"

"I hope to. But I may not. Just in case, I want you and all your men to plug your ears and your horses' ears with wax and cotton, or cloth. Plug them tight so you can't hear until you're over the horizon."

"You mean that will protect us?"

"Yes."

Richard thought he understood the way the Dominie Dirtch worked. Du Chaillu had told them that when she drowned, she heard the chimes of death. Joseph Ander would have needed a way to control and focus the killing power of the chimes. He gave them the answer in what he had created.

"The Dominie Dirtch are bells. They would be bells for a reason: to be heard. If you can't hear them, then you won't be harmed."

The captain cleared his throat. "Lord Rahl, I don't mean to question your knowledge of things of magic, but can a weapon of that much destructive power be defeated so easily?"

"It was done before, I believe. I think the Haken people who once invaded must have figured it out, too, and in so doing were able to get past."

"But, Lord Rahl—"

"Captain, I'm the magic against magic. Trust me. It will work. I trust you to be the steel, trust me with the magic."

"Yes, Lord Rahl."

"Once past, head for General Reibisch. This is important. Tell him I want him to pull back."

"What? Now that you have the way past the Dominie Dirtch, you don't want him to use it?"

"The Dominie Dirtch are going to be destroyed. I can't leave them for Jagang to hide behind, but I don't want our forces to come down here. Jagang is also coming here for food for his army. I hope to spoil some of that food.

"Tell the general my orders are for him to protect the routes up into the Midlands. Out here on the plains he doesn't stand a chance against the Order's numbers. He will have a better chance keeping Jagang from advancing into the rest of the Midlands if our forces fight our way, not Jagang's."

"Yes, sir. Wise advice."

"It should be, it's General Reibisch's advice. I hope, too, to reduce the Order's numbers. Tell him to use his discretion."

"What about you, Lord Rahl? Where is he to find you?"

"You tell him to worry about his men, not me. I'm . . . not sure where I'll be. Reibisch knows what to do. That's why they made him a general. He would know better than I what to do about soldiering."

"Yes, sir. The general is a good man."

Richard held up a finger for emphasis. "This is important. I want you to follow this order, and I want Reibisch to follow it.

"The people of Anderith have made their choice. I don't want a single one of our men lifting a weapon to help them. I don't want any of our men to have to shed blood for these people. Understand? Not one!"

The color left the captain's face. He backed away a half step.

"Not. One. Drop. Of. Our. Blood," Richard said.

"Yes, sir. I will tell the general your exact words."

"My orders." Richard climbed up into the saddle. "And I mean that. You're all good men, Captain Meiffert. Someday, I want you going home to your families—not dying for nothing."

The captain saluted with a fist to his heart. "Our sincere hope, too, Lord Rahl."

Richard returned the salute, and then trotted his horse out of camp for the last time, on his way to perform his final duty.

CHAPTER 68

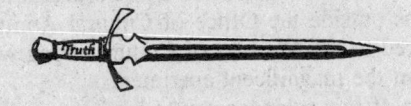

"DARLING, I'M HOME," DALTON called toward the bedroom.

He had sent up a bottle of wine, along with a plate of Teresa's favorite dish, suckling rabbits roasted in a red wine sauce. Mr. Drummond was most pleased to be able to keep his job by complying with the unusual request.

Perfumed candles were lit around the rooms, the drapes were drawn, and the servants all sent away.

The master and the mistress wanted to be alone.

Teresa met him at the bedroom door with a glass of wine and a smile. "Oh, sweetheart, I'm so glad you were able to come in early tonight. I've so looked forward to it all day."

"As have I," he said with his best smile.

She gave him a mischievous look. "I'm so looking forward to proving to you how much I love you, and to thank you for being so understanding about my duty to the Sovereign."

Dalton slipped the silk robe from her shoulders, kissing her bare flesh. She giggled as he worked his kisses up her neck. She made a feeble effort to slow his advances.

She hunched her head against his face. "Dalton, don't you want some wine?"

"I want you," he said, in an intimate growl. "It's been too long."

"Oh, Dalton, I know. I've ached for you."

"Then prove it," he teased.

She giggled again against his continued kisses.

"My, but what's gotten into you, Dalton?" She moaned. "Whatever it is, I like it."

"Tess, I've taken the day off tomorrow, too. I want to make love to you tonight, and all day tomorrow."

She responded to his intimacies as he guided her toward their big bed with the hammered-iron posts that looked like the columns outside the Office of Cultural Amity, the bed that belonged to the Minister of Culture, along with everything else in the magnificent apartments.

Once, all of this splendor would have brought him great pleasure. Pleasure in what he had accomplished, in what he had attained, in how far he had come.

"Dalton, please don't be disappointed, but Bertrand is expecting me tomorrow afternoon."

Dalton shrugged as he gently placed her on the bed. "Well, we have tonight, and in the morning again. Right?"

She beamed. "Of course, sweetheart. Tonight, and for the morning. Oh, Dalton, I'm so happy you understand about the Sovereign needing me."

"But I do, darling. You may think this sounds strange, but, in a way, I find it . . . exciting."

"You do?" She grinned her wicked grin. "I like the idea of that. You being excited, I mean."

She watched as he opened her robe and kissed her breasts. He came up for breath.

"To know the Sovereign himself chooses my wife, my beautiful Tess, and by the direct word of the Creator at that, is the best compliment a loyal Ander man could ever have."

"Dalton," she said, breathless from his kisses and caresses. "I've never seen you like this." She drew him closer. "I like it. I like it a lot. Come here, let me show you how much."

Before she began, she pulled back.

"Dalton, Bertrand was pleased, too. He said he liked your attitude. He said he found it exciting, too."

"We all need our Sovereign to guide us into the future and bring us the Creator's words. I'm so glad you can help relieve the Sovereign's stress in this life."

She was panting now. "Yes, Dalton, I do. I really do. It's so . . . I don't know, so wonderful to have such a high calling."

"Why don't you tell me all about it, darling, as we make love. I'd like to hear it all."

"Oh, Dalton, I'm so glad."

Dalton allowed himself a couple of days to recover after being with Tess. It had been an experience he once would have found the height of his existence. It once would have been a source of joy.

After the experience, though, he needed to deprive himself of Tess for several days in order to be in a state of heightened need for a task such as he must now perform.

The hallway was deserted outside her quarters and offices. Bertrand was in the opposite wing, with Teresa, having the stresses of his high office relieved. Dalton had made sure it was a time when Teresa was with Bertrand. The thought of it would help him to focus on the work at hand.

Bertrand and his wife made sure they rarely encountered one another. Having their quarters in opposite wings helped.

She did sometimes visit him, though. Their screaming battles were legendary among the staff. Bertrand one day sported a cut over his eye. He was usually able to duck the objects she hurled at him, but on that occasion she had caught him off guard.

Partly because of Hildemara's popularity, but mostly because of her dangerous connections, Bertrand dared not confront, cross, or do away with his wife. She had warned him he had better hope she didn't die a sudden death of natural causes—or any other causes—lest his own health suddenly fail, too.

It was a threat Bertrand did not take lightly. For the most part, he simply avoided her. There were times, though, when his penchant for risk caused him to make foolish comments or in some other way embarrass her, and then she went looking for him. It mattered not where he was, either—in his bed, his privy, or a meeting with wealthy backers. Bertrand generally avoided troubles with her by trying to take care, but there were times when he provoked her ire.

It was a relationship that had worked on this estranged level for years, and had borne them a daughter neither cared for. Dalton had only seen her recently when they brought her back from boarding school in order to stand with them at public addresses decrying the horrors of an uncaring Lord Rahl and the Mother Confessor.

Now the Lord Rahl had been rejected by the people. Now the Mother Confessor was . . . well, he wasn't sure what had become of her, but he was reasonably sure she was dead. It had cost Dalton some good men, but in war there were always losses. He would replace them if need be.

Serin Rajak had died, too—a terrible infection that turned his blind face to a festering mass—but Dalton couldn't say he was at all unhappy about that. His grieving followers reported it a lingering and painful death. No, Dalton was not at all unhappy about that.

Hildemara opened the door herself. A good sign, he thought. She was wearing a dress more revealing than usual. Another good sign, he hoped, since she had known he was coming.

"Dalton, how kind of you to ask to pay me a visit. I've wondered how you've been getting along and thought a talk long overdue. So, how have you been, since your wife has been serving the needs of our Sovereign?"

He shrugged. "I've come to my way of dealing with it."

Hildemara smiled, a cat seeing a mouse. "Ah . . . and so the lovely gifts?"

"To thank you. For—Might I come in?"

She opened the door wider. He stepped inside, looking around at the unrestrained opulence. He had never been in the private quarters of the Sovereign and his wife.

Of course, his own wife was quite familiar with them, and had described them—Bertrand's, anyway—in great detail.

"You were saying? About thanking me?"

Dalton clasped his hands behind his back. "For opening my eyes." He gestured behind himself and smiled. "And your door, I might add."

She chuckled politely. "I sometimes open my door to handsome men. I find it a . . . sometimes rewarding experience."

He closed the distance and took up her hand, kissing the back of it while looking her in the eye. He thought it a pathetically contrived act, but she responded as if she believed it sincere, and as if she were well pleased by the token of respect.

Dalton had researched her private activities. It had taken every favor owed him, as well as some direct threats, and even an appointment of standing. He now knew what she liked, and what she didn't. He knew she didn't like aggressive lovers. She liked them on the young side, and attentive. She liked to be treated with the utmost reverence.

She like to be fawned over.

He approached this visit like an elaborate feast, with each course in order, and building to the main attractions. In this way, with a plan, he found it easier to proceed.

"My lady, I fear to be so forward with a woman of your station, but I must be honest."

She went to a table of inlaid silver and gold. From a silver tray, she picked a cut-glass bottle and poured herself a glass of rum. She also poured one for him, without asking, and handed it to him with a smile.

"Please, Dalton. We have a long history. I would like nothing better than your honesty. After all, I was honest with you about your wife."

"Yes," he said, "you were, weren't you."

She took a sip and then laid a wrist over his shoulder.

"And are you still languishing about that? Or have you come to face the realities of life?"

"I must admit, Hildemara, that I have been . . . lonely,

what with my wife so often . . . occupied. I never expected to find myself with a wife so often unavailable."

She clucked sympathetically. "You poor dear. I know just how you feel. My husband is so often occupied himself."

Dalton turned away, as if embarrassed. "Since my wife is no longer bound by our vows, I find I have . . . desires she is unable to satisfy. I'm ashamed to admit it, but I'm not experienced in this sort of thing. Most men, I guess, would find this sort of endeavor comes naturally to them. I don't."

She came close up behind him, putting her mouth next to his ear. "Do go on, Dalton. I'm listening. Don't be shy—we're old friends."

He turned to come face-to-face with her, giving her the chance to display her cleavage—something she believed was greatly appreciated.

"Since my wife no longer is bound by her vows, being called upon by the Sovereign, I don't see why I should be bound by mine. Especially when I have . . . longings."

"Well, of course not."

"And you once told me that I should come to you first, if anything changed with the status of my vows. Well, if you're still interested, things have changed."

Her answer was to kiss him. He found it less repulsive than he feared. By closing his eyes he was able to actually enjoy it, after a fashion.

He was surprised, though, when she shifted immediately to the more advanced matters of the encounter. It would make little difference in the end result. If she wanted to go straight to it, that was fine by him.

CHAPTER 69

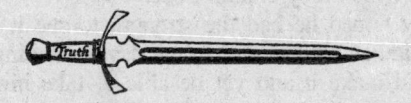

IT WAS AS FORBIDDING a place as Richard had heard, the highlands above the Nareef Valley: a bleak wasteland. The wind howled in dirty gusts.

He would expect Joseph Ander to pick such a place.

The mountains surrounding the dead lake were just as dead. They were rocky, brown, and barren of life, their peaks all crowned with snow. The thousands of runnels coming down the slopes sparkled in the sunlight, like fangs.

Juxtaposed with the bleak wasteland was the green of the paka plants, which looked almost like water lilies in the vast waters stretching across the wide lap of the surrounding mountains.

Richard had left the horses down lower and climbed the narrow foot trail he found that led up to the lake. He had tied the horses on loose tethers and removed their tack, so that if he failed to return, they could eventually escape.

Only one thing drove him on, and that was his love for Kahlan. He had to banish the chimes so that he could heal her. It was his sole purpose in life. He stood now on the sterile soil beside the poison waters, knowing what he had to do.

He had to outthink, outcreate Joseph Ander.

There was no key to the riddle of the chimes; there was

no answer. There was no solution waiting to be found. Joseph Ander left no seam in his tapestry of magic.

His only chance was to do what Joseph Ander never would have expected. Richard had studied the man enough to understand the way he thought. He knew what Ander believed, and what he expected people would try. Richard could do none of those things and expect to succeed. Richard would do that which Joseph Ander chided the wizards to do, but which they couldn't see.

He only hoped he had the strength to see it through to the end. He had ridden hard in the day, switching horses so they would make it and yet be able to take him back. At night he had walked them until he could walk no more.

He was exhausted, and hoped only that he could hold out long enough. Long enough for Kahlan.

From the gold-worked leather pouch on his belt he pulled white sorcerer's sand. With the sand, Richard carefully began drawing a Grace. Starting with the rays representing the gift, he drew it exactly opposite from the way Zedd told him it must be drawn. He stood in the center, laying the lines of the gift inward, toward himself.

He drew the star, representing the Creator, next, and then the circle of life, and the square for the veil, and lastly, the outer circle for the beginning of the underworld.

Imagination, Joseph Ander had said, was what made a great wizard, for only a wizard with imagination was able to transcend the limitations of tradition.

A Grace might rise in obedience to an inventive spell.

Richard intended to raise more than that.

From his place inside the Grace, Richard lifted his fists to the sky.

"Reechani! Sentrosi! Vasi! I call you forth!"

He knew what they needed. Joseph Ander had told him.

"Reechani! Sentrosi! Vasi! I call you forth and offer you my soul!"

The water rippled as the wind rose. The water moved with deliberate intent. The wind coming across the water ignited into roiling flame.

They were coming.

Richard, charged with need and with anger, lowered his arms, pointing his fists off toward the edge of the lake, where it flowed at last over the rocky lip and on down into the Nareef Valley. His entire being focused there.

Through his need and his anger, he called the Subtractive side of his power, the side from the darkest things, the side from the underworld, from the shadows in the dark forever of the netherworld.

Black lightning exploded, the bolts from his fists twisting together in a rope of howling annihilation focused by his need, powered by his wrath.

The edge of the mountain lake erupted in violence. The rock beyond disintegrated in a shower of steam and rubble from the touch of the black lightning. In an instant, the lower lake shore at the edge was no more. The destructive force of the Subtractive Magic vaporized it out of existence.

With a thundering roar, the lake began to empty.

The water churned as it pulled itself over the side. The edge foamed and frothed. The paka plants swirled with the water, tearing from the lake bottom. The vast lake of poisonous water plummeted over the brink.

The fire coming across the lake, the wind on the water, and the churning water itself slowed as they approached. These were the essence of the chimes, the distillation that spoke for them.

"Come to me," Richard commanded. "I offer you my soul."

As the chimes began to circle ever closer, Richard drew something else from the pouch at his belt.

And then, out in the lake, as it emptied, leaving a muddy bottom where poisonous water receded, there came a shimmering to the air just above the falling water. Something began to coalesce. To take form in the world of life.

Wavering in the air above the surface of the water, a figure began to appear. A robed figure. An old man made of smoke and glimmering light. A figure in pain.

Richard threw his fists up again. "Reechani! Sentrosi! Vasi! Come to me!"

And they did. Around him swept the substance of death. It was almost more than Richard could take, standing there in the center of a maelstrom of death. It was as abhorrent a feeling as he had ever felt.

The chimes called to him with seductive sounds from another world. Richard let them. He smiled at their summons.

He let them come, these thieves of souls.

And then he lifted his arm to point.

"Your master."

The chimes howled around him with rage. They recognized the one rising up before them.

"There he is, slaves. Your master."

"Who calls me!" came a cry from across the water.

"Richard Rahl, descendant of Alric. I am the one who has come to be your master, Joseph Ander."

"You have found me in my sanctuary. You are the first. I commend you."

"And I condemn you, Joseph Ander, to your place in the afterlife, where all must go when their time here is done."

Chimes of laughter rang out over the lake.

"Finding me is one thing, disturbing me another. But to dictate to me is altogether different. You have not the power to begin to do such a thing. You cannot even envision what I can create."

"Ah, but I have," Richard called out over the falling water. "Water, hear me. Air, see what I show you. Fire, feel the truth of it."

Around him, the three chimes turned and spun, wary of what he had to offer them.

Again, Richard thrust out his hand. "This is your master, the one who appropriated you to his bidding, instead of yours. There is his soul, stripped bare for you."

Concern darkened the face of Joseph Ander's form. "What are you doing? What do you think you can accomplish with this?"

"Truth, Joseph Ander. I strip you of the lie of your existence."

Richard lifted a hand, opening it toward Joseph Ander, opening the hand that held the balance—the black sorcerer's sand. Richard let a trickle of black lightning crackle between him and the spirit of Joseph Ander.

"There he is, Reechani. Hear him. There he is, Vasi. See him. There he is, Sentrosi, feel him through my touch."

Joseph Ander tried to throw back magic of his own, but he had consigned himself to another world, one of his own making. He could not bridge that void. But Richard had called him, and could reach through.

"Now, my chimes, this is your choice. My soul, or his. The man who would not surrender his soul to the afterlife. The man who would not go to your master in the underworld, but became your master in this world, where he enslaved you for all this time.

"Or my soul, standing here, in the center of this Grace, where I will pull you to me, and you will serve me in this world as you have served him.

"Choose, then: taking vengeance; or going back to slavery."

"He lies!" Ander's spirit cried out.

The storm of chimes around Richard made their choice. They saw the truth Richard had presented them. They crackled across the bridge Richard had created, the void in the world of life.

The world shook with the ferocity of it.

Across that bridge, with a howl of rage that could come only from the world of the dead, they seized Joseph Ander's soul and took him with them back to that world, whence they had come. They took him home.

In an instant that stretched for an eternity, the veil between those worlds was open. In that instant, death and life touched.

In the sudden silence that followed, Richard held his hands out in front of himself. He seemed to be whole. He found that remarkable.

The realization of what he had just done came over him. He had created magic. He had righted what Joseph Ander had wrongly corrupted.

Now he had to get back to Kahlan, if she was still alive. He made himself banish that thought. She had to be alive.

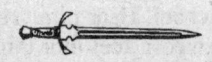

With a gasp, Zedd opened his eyes. It was dark. He groped and found walls of rock. He stumbled forward, toward light. Toward sound.

He realized he was back in his body. He was no longer in the raven. He didn't understand how that could be. It was real, though. He looked at his hands. Not feathers, hands.

He had his soul back.

He fell to his knees, weeping with relief. To lose his soul was beyond what he expected. And he had expected the worst.

Without his soul, he had been able to inhabit the raven. He brightened a bit. That was an experience he had never had. No wizard had ever succeeded in projecting himself into an animal. And to think, it had only required surrendering his soul.

He decided that once was enough.

He walked on toward the light, toward the roar of water. He remembered where he was. Reaching the edge, he dove into the lake and swam to the far shore.

Zedd dragged himself out on the far bank. Without thinking, he swept a hand down his robes to dry himself.

And then he realized his power was back. His strength, his gift was back.

At a sound he looked up. Spider nuzzled him.

Grinning, Zedd rubbed the friendly, soft nose. "Spider, girl. Good to see you, my friend. Good to see you."

Spider snorted her pleasure, too.

Zedd found the saddle and the rest of the tack where he

had left it. Just for the delight of it, he floated the blanket and saddle onto Spider's back. Spider thought it interesting. Spider was a good sport, and a good horse.

Zedd turned at a sound from above. Something was coming down the mountain. Water. The lake, for some reason, had given way. It was all coming down.

Zedd sprang up onto Spider. "Time to get out of here, girl."

Spider obliged him.

Dalton had just come back into his office when he heard someone come in behind him. It was Stein. When the man turned to close the door, Dalton glanced to the bottom of Stein's cape, and saw the scalp he had added.

Dalton went to the side table and poured himself a glass of water. He was feeling warm and a little dizzy.

Well, that was to be expected.

"What do you want, Stein?"

"Just a social visit."

"Ah," Dalton said. He took a drink.

"Nice new office you got yourself."

It was nice. Everything was the best. The only thing from his old office was the silver-scroll stand beside the desk. He liked the sword stand, and brought it along. As if reminded, he fingered the hilt of his sword in the stand.

"Well," Stein added, "you've earned it. No doubt about that. You've done good for yourself, though. Good for yourself and your wife."

Dalton gestured. "New sword, Stein? A little too fancy for your taste, I would think."

The man seemed pleased that Dalton had noticed the weapon.

"This here," he said, lifting it with a thumb by the down swept cross guard a few inches out of its scabbard, "is the

Sword of Truth. The real sword carried by the Seeker."

Dalton found it unsettling that a man like Stein would have it. "And what are you doing with it?"

"One of my men brought it to me. Quite a lot of trouble, too."

"Really?" Dalton asked, feigning interest.

"They captured a Mord-Sith in the process of bringing it to me. The real Sword of Truth, and a real Mord-Sith. Imagine that."

"Quite the achievement. The emperor will be pleased."

"He will be when I present him with the sword. He is pleased with the news you sent, too. To have defeated Lord Rahl so resoundingly is an achievement. It won't be long until our forces are here, and we catch him. And the Mother Confessor, have you found her, yet?"

"No." Dalton took another drink of water. "But with the spell Sister Penthea contributed, I don't see how she has a chance. From the look of the knuckles of my men, they did their job." He paused, looked down. "Up until they got caught and killed, anyway.

"No, this is one encounter the Mother Confessor is not going to live through. If she is still alive, I will hear about it soon enough. If she is dead,"—he shrugged—"then we may never find her body."

Dalton leaned against his desk. "When will Jagang be here?"

"Not long. Week, maybe. The advance guard maybe sooner. He is looking forward to setting up residence in your fine city."

Dalton scratched his forehead. He had things to do. Not that any of it really mattered.

"Well, I'll be around, if you need me," Stein said.

He turned back from the door. "Oh, and Dalton, Bertrand told me that you were more than understanding about your wife and him."

Dalton shrugged. "Why not? She is just a woman. I can snap my fingers and have a dozen. Hardly anything to get possessive about."

Stein seemed genuinely pleased. "I'm glad to see you've come around. The Order will suit you. We don't hold to notions of possessive attitudes toward women."

Dalton was trying to think of places the Mother Confessor could have gone to ground.

"Well, I'll love the Order, then. I don't hold with those notions myself."

Stein scratched his stubble. "I'm happy to know you feel that way, Dalton. Since you do, I'd like to compliment you on your choice of a whore for a wife."

Dalton, turning to look over papers, stiffened. "I'm sorry, what was that?"

"Oh, Bertrand, he loans her to me now and then. He was bragging on her, and wanted me to have some myself. He told her the Creator wanted her to please me. I just had to tell you, she's quite the hot one."

Stein turned toward the door.

"There's one more thing," Dalton said.

"What's that?" he asked, turning back.

Dalton brought the tip of his sword whistling around and sliced Stein's belly open just below his weapons belt. He made the cut shallow, so as not to slice through everything, just deep enough so that the man's bowels would spill out at his feet in front of him.

Stein gasped in shock, his jaw dropping, his eyes showing the whites all around as he stared down. He looked up at Dalton as he was falling to his knees. The gasp turned to panting grunts.

"You know," Dalton said, "as it turns out, I really am the possessive type. Thank the good spirits your end was quick."

Stein collapsed on his side. Dalton stepped over him, around behind him.

"But just because it's quick, I don't want you to feel you're missing out on anything, or that I'm neglecting what you have coming."

Dalton grabbed Stein's greasy hair in a fist. He sliced his

sword around the top of Stein's forehead, put a boot to the man's back, and ripped his scalp off.

He came around and showed it to the shrieking man. "That was for Franca, by the way. Just so you know."

As Stein lay on the floor, his viscera spilled out, his head bleeding profusely, Dalton casually walked to the door and opened it, pleased the new man hadn't opened the door without permission despite all the screaming.

"Phil, you and Gregory get in here."

"Yes, Minister Campbell?"

"Phil, Stein here is making a mess in my office. Please help him out."

"Yes, Minister Campbell."

"And I don't want him ruining the carpets." Dalton, as he picked up some papers from his desk, glanced down at the screaming man. "Take him over there and throw him out the window."

CHAPTER 70

RICHARD CRASHED THROUGH THE front door. He saw people there, but he headed straight for Kahlan.

Jiaan seized his arm. "Richard, wait."

"What? What is it? How is she?"

"She is still alive. She has made it past a critical time."

Richard nearly collapsed with relief. He felt tears course

down his face, but he kept himself together. He was so tired he had trouble doing the simplest things. He hadn't been able to turn the knob to open the door, and had not been able to stop, either.

"I can heal her now. My power is back."

Richard turned to the hall. Jiaan seized his arm again.

"I know. Du Chaillu has her power back, too. You must see her first."

"I'll see her later. I have to heal Kahlan before anything else."

"No!" Jiaan shouted in Richard's face.

It surprised him so that he halted. "Why? What's wrong?"

"Du Chaillu said she knows now why she came to you. Du Chaillu said we must not let you touch Kahlan until you see her first. She made me swear I would draw my sword on you before I let you near Kahlan.

"Please, *Caharin*, do not make me do that. I beg you."

Richard took a breath and tried to calm himself. "All right. If it's that important, then where is Du Chaillu?"

Jiaan lead Richard into the hall and to a door next to the room where Kahlan was. Richard took a long look at the door to Kahlan, but then followed Jiaan's urging and went in the other door.

Du Chaillu was sitting in a chair holding a baby. She beamed up at Richard. He knelt before her and looked at the sleeping bundle in her arms.

"Du Chaillu," he said in a whisper, "it's beautiful."

"You have a daughter, husband."

With all the things in Richard's head, arguing with Du Chaillu about the child's parentage was the last of them.

"I have named her Cara, in honor of the one who saved our life."

Richard nodded. "Cara will be pleased, I'm sure."

Du Chaillu put a hand on his shoulder. "Richard, are you all right? You look like you have been to the land of the dead."

He smiled a little. "In a way, I have. Jiaan said your gift is back."

She nodded. "Yes. And you must believe in it. My gift is to feel a spell and silence it."

"Du Chaillu, I need to heal Kahlan."

"No, you must not."

Richard raked his fingers back through his hair. "Du Chaillu, I know you want to help, but that is crazy."

She gripped his shirt in her fist. "Listen to me, Richard. I came to you for a reason. This is the reason, I know now. I came to save you the pain of losing Kahlan.

"She has magic in her that is a trap. If you touch her with your magic, to heal her, it will spring the magic and kill her. It was a way of making sure they killed her."

Richard, trying to remain calm, licked his lips. "But you have the power to annul spells. When we first met, Sister Verna told me so. Du Chaillu, you can annul this spell and then I can heal her."

Du Chaillu held his gaze in the grip of hers. "No. Listen to me. You are not listening to what is. You are hearing only what you wish to be. Listen to what is.

"This spell is the kind of magic I cannot touch with mine. I cannot make it fade away, like other magic. It is in her like a barb on a fishhook. Your magic that heals will trigger it, and you will kill her. Do you hear me, Richard? If you touch her with your magic you will kill her."

Richard pressed a hand to his forehead. "Then what are we to do?"

"She is still alive. If she lived this long, she has a good chance. You must care for her. She must recover without magic. Once she is better, the spell will fade away, just like a hook in a fish dissolves. Before she is well, it will be gone, but she will be well enough by then so that your magic will not be needed."

Richard nodded. "All right. Thank you, Du Chaillu. I mean that. Thank you for . . . for everything."

She hugged him even with the baby between them.

"But we have to get out of here. The Order is going to be here any time. We have to get out of Anderith."

"The man, Edwin, he is a good man. He has fixed a wagon for you to take Kahlan away."

"How is she? Is she awake?"

"In and out. We feed her a little, let her drink, give her what herbs and cures we can. Richard, she is very badly hurt, but she is alive. I think she will be well again, though. I really believe that."

Du Chaillu got up, taking her new baby with her, and led Richard to the next room. Richard was exhausted, but his heart was hammering so hard he felt wide awake again. He felt so helpless, though, that he let Du Chaillu lead him.

The curtains were drawn, and the room was dimly lit. Kahlan was lying on her back, covered most of the way with blankets.

Richard looked down at the face he knew so well but didn't recognize. The sight took his breath. He had to struggle to stay on his feet. He struggled, too, to hold back his tears.

She was unconscious. He gently took her limp hand in his, but there was no response.

Du Chaillu went around to the other side of the bed.

Richard gestured. Du Chaillu understood, and smiled at the idea. She gently laid little baby Cara in the crook of Kahlan's arm. The baby, still asleep, nuzzled in Kahlan's arm.

Kahlan stirred. Her hand partly curled around the baby, and a small smile came to her lips.

The smile was the first thing Richard recognized as Kahlan.

Outside, once they gently got Kahlan situated in the special carriage Edwin had converted, they brought it out of the carriage house, into the early-morning light. A man named Linscott, once a Director and still a friend of Edwin's, had helped make the cover for the carriage, and alter the suspension so it would ride more gently. Linscott and Edwin were part of a group that had been resisting the corrupt rule in Anderith. Unsuccessfully, it turned out. Now, at Richard's urging, they were going to leave. There weren't many, but some people were going to escape.

At the side of the house, in the shade of a cherry tree, Dalton Campbell was waiting for them.

Richard instantly tensed, prepared for a battle. Dalton Campbell, though, didn't look to have any fight in him.

"Lord Rahl, I came to see you and the Mother Confessor off."

Richard glanced over at the baffled faces of some of the others. They seemed as surprised as Richard.

"And how did you know we were here?"

The man smiled. "It's what I do, Lord Rahl. It's my job to know things. At least, it was."

Linscott was looking like he was about to go for the man's throat. Edwin, too, looked ready for blood.

Dalton didn't seem to care. Richard signaled with a tilt of his head, and Jiaan and Du Chaillu ushered everyone else back. With the rest of the blade masters nearby, none of them seemed too concerned about this one man.

"May I say, Lord Rahl, that in another time, another place, I think we could have been friends."

"I don't," Richard said.

The man shrugged. "Maybe not." He pulled a folded blanket from under his arm. "I brought this, in case you need another to keep your wife warm."

Richard was confused by the man, and by what he wanted. Dalton placed the blanket off to the side in the carriage. Richard figured that Dalton could have caused a lot of trouble if he intended it, so that wasn't what he was about.

"I just wanted to wish you good luck. I hope the Mother Confessor will be well, soon. The Midlands needs her. She is a fine woman. I'm sorry I tried to have her killed."

"What did you say?"

He looked up into Richard's eyes. "I'm the one who sent those men. If you get your magic back, Lord Rahl, please don't try to heal her with it. A Sister of the Dark provided a spell to kill her with the dark side of the magic, if healing is tried on what was done to her. You must let her get better on her own."

Richard thought he should be killing the man, but for some reason, he was just standing there, staring at him as he confessed.

"If you wish to kill me, please feel free. I don't really care."

"What do you mean?"

"You have a wife who loves you. Cherish her."

"And your wife?"

Dalton shrugged. "Ah well, I'm afraid she isn't going to make it."

Richard frowned. "What are you talking about?"

"There is a nasty illness going around among the prostitutes in Fairfield. Somehow, my wife, the Sovereign, his wife, and I have acquired it. We are already coming ill. Very unfortunate. It's an unpleasant death, I'm told.

"The poor Sovereign is weeping and inconsolable. Considering it was the one thing he feared above all else, one would think he would have been more careful in choosing his partners.

"The Dominie Dirtch, too, I've heard, have crumbled to dust. All our work seems to be coming undone. I expect that Emperor Jagang, when he arrives, is going to be quite displeased."

"We can hope," Richard said.

Dalton smiled. "Well, I've things to do, unless, of course, you wish to kill me."

Richard smiled at the man.

"A wise woman told me that the people are the willing accomplices of tyranny. They make those like you possible.

"I'm going to do the worst possible thing I could do to

you and your people—what my grandfather would have done to you.

"I'm going to leave you all to suffer the consequences of your own actions."

Ann was so cramped she feared she would be crippled for life, never to walk again. The box she was in was bouncing around in the wagon something awful as it rattled over cobblestones, adding to her misery. She felt as if someone had beaten her with a club.

If she wasn't let out soon, she was sure she would go mad.

As if in answer to the prayer, the wagon finally slowed, and then stopped. Ann sagged with blessed relief. She was near tears from the pain of hitting the sides and bottom, being unable to use her hands and feet to brace herself.

She heard the hasp being worked, and then the top opened, letting cool night air in. Ann took a thankful lungful, savoring it like a sweet perfume.

The front of the box dropped onto the bed of the wagon. Sister Alessandra was standing there, looking in. Ann peered around, but didn't see anyone else. They were in a narrow side street that looked deserted, for the most part. One old woman walked past, but didn't even glance their way.

Ann frowned. "Alessandra, what's going on?"

Sister Alessandra folded her hands in a prayerful pose. "Prelate, please, I want to return to the Light."

Ann blinked. "Where are we?"

"The city the emperor has been traveling to. It's called Fairfield. I encouraged your driver to let me drive the wagon."

"Encouraged him? How?"

"With a club."

Ann's eyebrows rose. "I see."

"And then, I'm so bad with directions, we became sepa-

782

rated from the rest of the line, and well, I guess now we're lost."

"How unfortunate for us."

"I guess that leaves looking for some of Jagang's troops and surrendering, or else returning to the Light."

"Alessandra, are you serious?"

The woman looked ready to burst into tears. The banter was over. "Please, Prelate, help me?"

"Alessandra, you don't need me. The path to the Light is through your own heart."

Sister Alessandra knelt down behind the wagon as Ann still sat in her box, her hands and feet in chains.

"Please, dear Creator," Alessandra began.

Ann listened as the woman poured her heart out. At the end, she kissed her ring finger. Ann held her breath, waiting for a bolt of lightning to strike Alessandra dead for betraying the Keeper of the underworld.

Nothing happened. Alessandra smiled up at Ann.

"Prelate, I can feel it. I can—"

Her words were cut off with a choking sound. Her eyes bulged.

Ann scooted toward her. "Alessandra! Is it Jagang? Is it Jagang in you mind?"

Alessandra nodded as best she could.

"Swear loyalty to Richard! Swear it in your heart! It's the only thing to keep the dream walker from your mind!"

Falling to the ground, Sister Alessandra twitched in convulsions of pain, at the same time mumbling words Ann couldn't understand.

At last, the woman went slack, panting in relief. She sat up and peered up into the wagon.

"It worked! Prelate, it worked." She put her hands to her head. "Jagang is gone from my mind. Oh, praise the Creator. Praise the Creator."

"How about getting these things off me, and doing your praying later?"

Sister Alessandra scurried to help. Before long, Ann had her shackles off, and she had been healed. For the first time in what seemed ages, she could again touch her own gift.

The two of them unhitched the horses and saddled them with tack from the wagon. Ann hadn't felt so joyous in years. They both wanted to get far away from the Imperial Order army.

As they made their way through the city, heading north, they came across a square filling with thousands of people all carrying candles.

Ann bent over on her horse to ask one of the young women what was going on.

"It's a candlelight vigil for peace," the woman said.

Ann was dumbfounded. "A what?"

"A candlelight vigil for peace. We are all gathering to show the soldiers coming into the city a better way, to show them the people are going to insist on peace."

Ann scowled. "If I were you, I'd be heading for a hole, because these men don't believe in peace."

The woman smiled in a long-suffering manner. "When they see us all gathered for peace, they will see that we are a force too powerful to overcome with anger and hatred."

As the young woman marched on into the square, Ann seized Sister Alessandra's sleeve. "Let's get out of here. This is going to be a killing field."

"But Prelate, these people are in danger. You know what the soldiers of the Order will do. The women . . . you know what they will do to the women. And any men who resist will be slaughtered."

Ann nodded. "I expect so. But there is nothing we can do about it. They will have peace. The dead will have peace. The living will have peace, too—as slaves."

They made it past the square just in time. When the soldiers arrived, it was worse even than Ann had envisioned. Screams of panic, then terror, and then pain rose from the trapped throng. The cries of the men and the children would end relatively quickly. The screams of the older girls and women had only just begun.

When at last they reached the countryside, Ann asked, "I told you we had to eliminate the Sisters of the Light who wouldn't escape. Did you do as you knew I wished, before you escaped with me, Sister?"

Sister Alessandra stared ahead as she rode. "No, Prelate."

"Alessandra, you knew it had to be done."

"I want to come back to the Creator's Light. I couldn't destroy the life he created."

"And by not killing those few, many more could die. A Sister of the Dark would want that. How can I trust you are telling me the truth?"

"Because I didn't kill the Sisters. If I were still a Sister of the Dark I would have. I'm telling the truth."

It would be wonderful if Alessandra had returned to the Light. That had never happened before. Alessandra could be an invaluable source of information.

"Or it shows you are lying, and are still sworn to the Keeper."

"Prelate, I helped you escape. Why won't you believe me?"

Ann looked over at the woman as they rode out toward the wilds, toward the unknown. "I can never fully believe or trust you, Alessandra, not after the lies you have told. That is the curse of lying, Sister. Once you place that crown of the liar upon your head, you can take it off again, but it leaves a stain for all time."

Richard turned when he heard the horse approaching from behind. He checked Kahlan, who lay inside the carriage, as he walked beside it. She was asleep, or possibly unconscious. At least he could now recognize a little of her face.

Richard looked again when the horse was closer, and saw a rider in red. Cara trotted her horse up close and then dismounted. She took the reins and walked up beside him. She had a limp.

"Lord Rahl, it took me a long time to catch you. Where are you going?"

"Home."

"Home?"

"That's right, home."

Cara looked up the road. "Where is home?"

"Hartland. Maybe to the west—in the mountains. There are some nice places there, places I've always wanted to take Kahlan."

She seemed to accept this and walked silently beside him for a time, leading her horse along behind.

"Lord Rahl, what about everything else? D'Hara. The Midlands. All the people."

"What about them?"

"Well, they will be waiting for you."

"They don't need me. I quit."

"Lord Rahl, how can you say such a thing?"

"I have violated every wizard's rule I know. I've . . ."

He let it go. He didn't care.

"Where is Du Chaillu?" Cara asked.

"I sent her home to her people. Her task with us was done." Richard glanced over. "She had her baby. A beautiful little girl. She named it Cara, after you."

Cara beamed. "Then I am glad it was not ugly. Some babies are ugly, you know."

"Well, this one was beautiful."

"Did it look like you, Lord Rahl?"

Richard scowled at her. "No."

Cara peered into the carriage. Her blond braid slipped forward over her shoulder.

"What happened to the Mother Confessor?"

"I just about got her killed."

Cara didn't say anything.

"I heard you were captured. Are you all right?" he asked.

Cara pushed her braid back over her shoulder. "They were fools. They didn't take my Agiel. When you fixed the magic, I made them all curse their mothers for ever meeting their fathers."

Richard smiled. That was the Cara he knew.

"And then I killed them," she added.

She held out the broken top of a black bottle. It still had the gold filigree stopper. "Lord Rahl, I failed. I didn't bring you your sword. But . . . but I managed to break the black bottle from the Wizard's Keep with the sword, at least." She stopped, her blue eyes brimming with tears. "Lord Rahl, I'm sorry. I failed. I tried my best, I swear, but I failed."

Richard stopped then. He put his arms around her. "No, you didn't fail, Cara. Because you broke that bottle with the sword, we were able to get magic back to right."

"Really?"

He nodded as he looked her in the eye. "Really. You did right, Cara. I'm proud of you."

They started walking again.

"So, Lord Rahl, how far to home?"

He thought it over a few minutes. "I guess Kahlan is my family, so that makes it home wherever we are. As long as I'm with Kahlan, I'm home.

"Cara, it's over. You can go home now. I release you."

She stopped. Richard walked on.

"But I don't have a family. They are all dead."

He looked back at her, standing in the road, looking as forlorn as anything he had ever seen.

Richard went back, put an arm around her shoulders, and started walking with her.

"We're your family, Cara, Kahlan and me. We love you. So I guess you should come home with us."

That seemed to suit her.

"Will there be people at this home place who need killing?"

Richard smiled. "I don't think so."

"Then why would we want to go there?"

When he only smiled, she said, "I thought you wanted to take over the world. I was looking forward to you being a tyrant. I say you should do it. The Mother Confessor would agree with me. That makes it two against one. We win."

"The world didn't want me. They took a vote and said no."

"A vote! There was your problem."

"I won't do it again."

Cara limped along beside him for a time and then said, "They will all find you, you know. The D'Harans are bonded to you. You are the Lord Rahl. Everyone will find you."

"Maybe. Maybe not."

"Richard?" came a soft voice.

He pulled the team up and went to the side of the carriage. Kahlan was awake. He took her hand.

"Who's that?" she asked.

Cara leaned in. "Just me. I had to come back. You see what kind of trouble you get into when I'm not watching over you?"

Kahlan smiled a little smile. She released Richard's hand and took Cara's.

"Glad you're home," Kahlan whispered.

"Lord Rahl said I saved the magic. Can you imagine? What was I thinking? I had the chance to rid myself of magic, and instead I saved it."

Kahlan smiled again.

"How are you feeling?" Richard asked.

"Terrible."

"You don't look so bad," Cara told her. "I've been much worse."

Richard gently stroked Kahlan's hand. "You'll get better. I promise. And wizards always keep their promises."

"Cold," she said. Her teeth were beginning to chatter.

Richard spotted the blanket Dalton Campbell had put on the side and pulled it closer.

The Sword of Truth fell out. He stood staring at it.

"The sword has come home, too, I guess," Cara said.

"I guess it has."